ASK NO QUARTER

ASK NO QUARTER

George Marsh

WILDSIDE PRESS

TO

HOWARD M. CHAPIN, F.R.H.S.,

LATE LIBRARIAN OF THE RHODE ISLAND HISTORICAL SOCIETY.

Originally published in 1945.
Published by Wildside Press LLC.
wildsidpress.com

1. The Great Swamp Fight

§1

"THAT'S ENOUGH till we reach home," Henry Jocelyn said to his horse, patting the sweating neck with his broad hand. "Do not crave the bellyache, do you?" And he backed the animal from the brook.

Lying flat on his chest, Jocelyn sucked up a few swift swallows of the cooling water. Rising, he drew the aromatic forest air deep into his lungs and expelled it slowly through his teeth, his head tilted to one side. It was the act of a man who was listening for some faint, far-off sound, and whose mind was troubled. As he stood motionless beside his horse, a red squirrel nervously burst into a chatter from a near-by tree, while a black-capped chickadee inspected him curiously from a seedling pine.

The serenity of early summer lay like a veil on the ancient lands of the Wampanoags. The leaves of oak and maple, of birch and beech and chestnut, were still fresh from recent rains. Thick stands of pine and cedar which splashed the lighter foliage of the hardwood hills, like shadows cast by clouds, sweetened the heavy air.

Over a narrow path through the forest, beaten for years by the hoofs of packhorses carrying corn, rye, and barley to the gristmill at the little settlement of Taunton, in Plymouth Colony, the young man had ridden on his gray horse. His tawny hair, cropped below his ears, framed a face shaped on bold lines, from which looked smoke-gray eyes, the restless eyes of a hunter rather than those of a tiller of the soil. A brain-tanned deerskin shirt, open at the neck, bared his corded throat. Buckskin breeches and leggings covered his legs. In place of the coarse, untanned leather shoes of the colonists, he wore Indian moccasins. From his belt hung a hunting ax, called on the frontiers a war hatchet. In front of his knees, as he rode, were slung two bags of corn meal, and across his saddle-bow rested a flintlock musket.

At a spring brook crossing the trail through the forest, young Jocelyn had swung from his horse, heavily built like himself, and led the animal down to drink below the rough bridge of logs.

Now, as he rubbed the velvet nose that nuzzled his shoulder, he kept thinking of the talk he had heard, at Taunton and Rehoboth, of the report that the Wampanoags had driven off cattle and burned a house down in Swansea.

"I like it not," he muttered. "Swansea is too near us. If the news be true, it means the war that's been brewing for years. Then God help us all!"

Jocelyn mounted and pushed on through the forest silence, his face taut with the thoughts that harassed him. He passed a farm already deserted by its people for the safety of the garrison houses at Taunton. A sow and her litter rooting at the edge of the woods and hens scratching near the barn were all of life that remained about the deserted buildings. He skirted a green pasture and fields of young corn and rye, and sadly shook his head as he rode on. For months the Wampanoags, whose lands lay to the west and south, reaching to Narragansett Bay and the sea, had been restless. Vague rumors had drifted up and down the frontiers. The authorities of Plymouth had overreached themselves in their dealings with the sons of the dead Massasoit who had befriended the colony since its settlement. Wamsutta, the elder, had died suspiciously on his return from a forced journey to Plymouth to deliver up his guns. And Metacomet, called Philip by the English, who had succeeded his brother as chief sachem, was said to be bitter over the treatment accorded his people. There was even talk that he plotted a union of the New England tribes. But the authorities of Plymouth and Massachusetts Bay had characteristically ignored the warnings which the settlers in touch with the Indians had sent them.

"If they've burned a house in Swansea, it means but one thing," muttered Jocelyn, slapping his horse's flank to quicken his pace. "They'll soon be here. Tonight Judith and the boy ride Dapple into Taunton behind the cow and heifers. I durst not linger at the farm. If they come by this path from the west, ours will be the first they reach. Those I count as friends may not be with them."

Suddenly he reined in his horse and listened. He could plainly hear sounds of snapping twigs and movement in the brush ahead of him. He backed the animal off the path into the scrub, snapped back the frizzan on his musket, looked to his priming, reclosed the pan cover, loosened the ax on his belt and, with cocked gun, waited. The sounds came nearer. Then he heard an English voice urging on cattle. Shortly, two cows with their calves appeared on the path, and behind them a woman astride a horse, a small child in each arm. A nameless fear looked from her eyes as she hailed Jocelyn.

"Judith and the child!" she cried. "You must get them and bring them in tonight! There's no time to lose!"

Following the woman were a man and a boy, prodding two stolid oxen with goads. "You'd best be getting your wife into Taunton," warned Slocum, the farmer, as he passed. "There's bad news from

Swansea!"

Yes, he'd best be getting Judith and the boy to safety. Why had he not listened to the warnings? Judith and the boy! All that life held for him—helpless, waiting for his homecoming that day at the last farm in the little valley. Judith, waiting, not knowing her danger. A wave of remorse twisted Jocelyn's bold features. Why had he not brought his family with him when he went to Taunton that morning? But there had been so many alarms before that had come to nought. And many of the Wampanoags were his friends. They would not harm the people who had befriended them. They would not—

What was that? Jocelyn pulled his horse back on its haunches and stiffened in the saddle, chin up, ears straining. With cocked gun thrust before him, he leaned over his horse's neck. A blue jay screeched its raucous warning. Something was moving in the brush ahead which the jay was watching. There it was again! Dry twigs snapped under the pressure of hidden feet. Again the jay screamed. The sounds were nearer. Jocelyn slowly raised his musket and jammed the butt against his shoulder. Then a loud "Whoof!" from the scrub in front of him broke the stillness, and with a shake of his white tail, a buck, reddish brown in his summer coat, leaped away through the underbrush.

Lowering his gun, Jocelyn laughed. "No sneaking Wampanoag, that one, Dapple! Had I needed meat it was ours. But we must hurry."

With a slap on the flank, he urged the horse over the path. As they left the timber and passed through an old clearing, a hen partridge and her young family flashed ahead on whirring wings.

"Judith and the boy must be put safe with Mother, at Taunton. Then the trainband will be mustered, and I with it. The pity of it," he reflected, "with the corn fair leaping from the earth and the rye never so good as this spring!"

Jocelyn gazed across the fields of a long-abandoned farm, stippled with oak seedlings and olive clumps of young cedar and juniper, and searched for signs of smoke on the western horizon. His own clearing lay three miles farther on, on the path which led to Narragansett Bay below Providence Plantations. He shaded his eyes with a thick, brown hand and looked long at a distant hill. The blood slowly drained from his face. "Smoke!" Sweat burst from his forehead and his lip twitched. Then, "Thank God!" he said, expelling a deep breath. "'Tis nought but heat haze."

He started his horse briskly forward through the hot silence of the forest. As he rode, he sought to comfort himself with the thought that there would be time, ample time, that day to bring the girl and child to the safety of the settlement. After all, there had been nothing but rumors carried by frightened farmers. No one yet knew if the Wampanoags had been shaving their heads and holding the war dance.

As he hurried over the trail, Jocelyn pictured the girl who was waiting with the boy for his return. He saw the caught masses of her golden hair touched by the sun into flame as she knitted on the bench outside the door; hair which, when loosed, rippled to her knees. Always she waited for him on the bench, and when he rode out of the forest on the rise above the clearing waved her white apron as his great dog ran barking to meet him. "God grant that Hugh grows up with her wise head and the sweet heart of her," he murmured as he pushed on.

With a prayer on his lips he urged the sweating horse over the forest path. On his arrival he would clap Judith and Hugh on Dapple's back and, with ropes on the cow and heifers, start at once. The pigs and sheep he'd drive into the forest to fend for themselves. The Indians might not find them all.

He started up the last hill, from which, shortly, he would gaze down into the valley on his home, the snug little house surrounded by Judith's flowers and herb garden, the barn, corncrib and smokehouse, the well sweep, the fields of corn and rye and oats, and the cattle and sheep in the pasture.

"Come on, Dapple!" he urged the big horse, whose neck and flanks were a lather in the heat of the windless woods. "There are oats and hay in the barn, lad. Pick up your big feet!"

The horse reached the hilltop. As Jocelyn straightened in his saddle and looked down, his face went gray. He shook like a man with fever. Numb with shock, he stared on what had been his home. In place of his house and a girl and child waiting by the door, stood a stone chimney black with char, surrounded by smoking ruins.

"The Wampanoags!" he groaned. "Judith! Name o' God! Judith!"

Tossing away the bags of meal, Jocelyn savagely pounded the horse's flanks as he galloped down off the hill and into the cleared land. The crazed man flung himself from his winded animal and searched among the charred timbers of his house for the bodies of his wife and child. They were not there. He ran to the ruin of the barn, but found no trace of those he sought. Stuck on posts, grotesquely wound about with entrails, the bloody heads of pigs grimaced, grim symbols of Wampanoag humor. Singed feathers, heads, feet, and entrails lay scattered about where the savages had made a hasty meal by roasting chickens and geese over the hot coals. All about him was desolation—the ruins of his home since boyhood!

The half-demented man ran through the trampled flower garden and followed a trail of moccasined feet through a field of young corn. "There was scarce more than six or eight!" he groaned. "They drove off the cattle and sheep. But where are Judith and the boy? Have they taken them away? There are no marks of her shoes here."

He thought of the horror of captivity for the golden-haired girl as he searched with blurred eyes for traces of her heelprints. His twitching lips tasted the salt of his tears as he choked back his grief. Then he returned to the burned house, where his horse was cropping the grass. "She may be hiding in the forest—too frightened to come out! Judith! Judith!" he shouted, his voice cracking in a sob. But the neighboring oaks and maples gave no answer.

Jocelyn ran into the woods calling: "Judith! Come out! 'Tis Henry!" He started over the path leading to the spring and stopped, staring at something that barred his way. Sprawled across the path lay the butchered body of his dog. Clamped in the bared fangs from which the crimsoned flews were lifted, stiff in death, was a blood-smeared strip of deerskin and a shred of brown flesh.

Jocelyn bent and tenderly stroked the bludgeoned head of his dog as he looked into the glazed eyes. "Shot and tomahawked you, old friend, but you died fighting! One of them will remember you."

The stricken man turned from the bloody carcass and shouted again. He thought he heard a faint cry deep in the forest, and plunged on toward the spring. Then he suddenly stopped and swayed giddily in his tracks. A wave of nausea gripped him. A low sound left his throat—a groan that voiced his agony. There, in the path before him, lay a huddled shape. A lance of sunlight thrusting through the thick foliage overhead touched a cloud of golden hair veiling the dead face of Judith Jocelyn.

His agony too deep for outward sign, Jocelyn knelt beside the body of his young wife. With shaking hands he put back the masses of gold from her gray face. The back of her head, from which the hair had been torn, was a crimson smear.

"They tomahawked and scalped her!" A shiver shook his massive shoulders. "Some beast carries it now, on his belt! Some Wampanoag beast! Her—hair!" The crazed man knelt and kissed the dead brow and lips and closed the staring blue eyes. Then with his face on her breast, he cried like a child.

After a space he rose and cast a dazed look about him. "The boy?" he groaned. "Is he dead? Or did they carry him off? Where's Hugh?"

Jocelyn took the dead girl in his arms and started back over the path. He had walked a little way when suddenly he stiffened in his tracks. "What was that? 'Twas no bird or beast!"

Again from deep in the forest came a cry. Hurrying with his burden to the cleared land, Jocelyn laid her gently on the warm earth and plunged back.

"Hugh!" he called. "Hugh, is it you, lad? 'Tis Father calling! Hugh, where are you?"

As the distracted father followed the path to the spring, deep in the forest rose the shrill whimper of a child.

"Name of God, he's alive!" Jocelyn broke into a run in the direction of the wail. "Hugh, tell me where you are!"

His son still lived, was hidden there, somewhere in the brush. He reached the spring and called, was answered from the forest beyond and, plunging into a thicket of young cedar, caught up the terrified child in his arms.

"My boy! My boy! You have no hurt? Father will let no harm come to you!" Jocelyn held the yellow-haired child of three to his heart.

"Manna! Where's my manna?" sobbed the frightened boy, as Jocelyn carried him back over the trail.

"Did Mother hide you when the Injuns came?" demanded the man.

"Yes, she hided Hugh and runned away. Where is she?"

Jocelyn's tears fell on the upturned face of his son. Her sole thought had been for the safety of the boy. She had hidden him and left the spot, that he might not be found. He covered the child's eyes with a hand when he came to the dead girl on the path, and carried him down near the ruins of the barn, placing him where he could not see what his father was doing. Here Jocelyn hitched the boy to a post with a thong. Then, finding a shovel, he started to dig a shallow grave among the wild roses Judith Jocelyn had planted with her own hands. Long since, her liverwort and violets and columbine had bloomed, but along the stone wall he had built to protect the garden from the hens and geese, hollyhocks lifted their green spears and sweetbrier ran.

After a space Jocelyn stopped digging, and his blurred eyes wandered over the trampled garden of the girl who lay dead at the edge of the clearing. His thoughts turned back to the day four years before, when they had brought the English sweetbrier from a neighboring farm, and wood lilies from the edge of the forest, and honeysuckle. And they had planted gillyflowers, honesty, and feverfew, together with lavender cotton and patience carried from Taunton. His eyes moved on to the herbs, ground under the moccasins of the Wampanoags, to the tansy, St.-John's-wort, comfrey, hyssop, and pimpernel. It was all a part of her, this garden she had loved and cared for, and now—she should sleep in it.

He carried her from where he had left her on the path and placed her beside the grave, then knelt and took a cold, brown hand in his. Slowly the blurred eyes in his stricken face moved from the upland meadow down over his ruined home. The boy called, but Jocelyn did not hear, for his thoughts were of that day in Taunton, five years before, when the trainband had met and the people of the town had made holiday on the common.

After the wrestling and shooting, Jocelyn was asked to give an exhibition of hatchet throwing, for the skill of the young giant in the deerskin shirt, who had thrown the few who had ventured a fall with him, was well known. Standing in the circle the crowd made for him, three times, at twenty paces, his belt ax spun through the air and buried its thin blade in the trunk of a young maple, while murmurs of applause arose from the watching men and girls.

As he wrenched the ax-head from the tree after his last throw, and the people sought the cider and ale and the roast pig and sheep at the slab tables set near the roasting fire, Henry Jocelyn had found himself staring into the face of a girl who had not moved away with the rest but stood watching him. Her humble walk in life was attested by her simple philomot frock with its white neckband in place of a whisk, and the coarse leather shoes with wooden heels. The eyes that met young Jocelyn's were an intense blue, and the cloud of hair that framed her face was like burnished gold.

The two had gazed into each other's eyes, the tawny-haired frontiersman and the strange girl, all unconscious of their surroundings. Then a flood of color stained her face and, embarrassed, she turned away, while he followed her with his eyes. The following spring they were married.

The thoughts of the youth who knelt beside the dead girl lingered over the happiness of their five years together, the birth of their boy and their plans for the future. He pictured her again holding the child high in her strong arms and laughing up at him as she said: "'Tis but the first of your sons, Henry Jocelyn! Some day we shall have many stout lads wherewith to clear that hundred acres of woodland beyond, and then we'll be rich!"

Now it was over—their dream! She was gone—out of his life—forever! He stared into her dead face as if he expected her to open her eyes and speak to him.

Again the fretting boy called to his father. Jocelyn straightened on his knees, while his eyes swept his fields. Were the Wampanoags returning? For himself he did not care, but the tiny lad there had his right to life. He rose and looked again, but saw nothing. Then he placed her in the warm earth and arranged the masses of golden hair above her brow, that the child might not see her mutilated head. Bringing her son to the shallow grave, Jocelyn knelt beside it, with the boy in his arms.

At the sight of the still, gray face the child burst into sobs, while Jocelyn's lips moved in prayer.

"Why is she down there, asleep?" cried the terrified boy. "Manna, open your eyes."

Jocelyn held the weeping child close to his mother and said, "Kiss her."

The boy reached and touched the cold face, but in sudden fright drew away.

"Kiss her and say good-by." Jocelyn's fingers closed on the boy's arms. "Have you fear—fear of Judith? Shame that a son of mine should fear to kiss his mother! Kiss her and say good-by."

With a stiffening of his sturdy body, the boy looked up into Jocelyn's tortured face, then turned, opened his arms to the mother who had cherished him, and kissed her on each cheek. "Manna! My manna!" he sobbed. "Goo-by, Judy!"

"Done like a man, Hugh Jocelyn."

Leaving the child at the ruined house, Jocelyn filled his arms with wood lilies and wild roses and returned to the grave.

"Farewell, Judith," he faltered, as he knelt beside her. "All joy and love and life I bury here. Farewell, Judith."

Leaning into the shallow grave he kissed the marble features, then looked long at the loved face framed in its halo of gold. He rose and covered her with the flowers she had loved, and slowly filled the grave with warm earth.

For a space Jocelyn stood beside the grave, gazing at the ruin of his home. Four years of happiness they had had there, and now she had been torn from him and her son. Judith was gone! Judith was gone! Henry Jocelyn had done with life.

Then the face of the youth hardened. A fury of hate burned in the gray eyes. He sucked in a deep breath, drew his short-handled belt ax and shook it savagely toward the west. "Wampanoags!" he muttered. "You were my father's friends and mine! Now it's war!"

§2

A COPPER smudge against a dun sky, the December sun rode the low ridges to the southwest. Lines of flickering supper fires lit the skeleton oaks, maples, and chestnuts of the forest flanking the clearing at Smith's Landing on the gray inlet where stood Richard Smith's blockhouse on the ancient Pequot Path through the Narragansett country. In the great room of the oak-timbered building General Josiah Winslow, Governor of Plymouth, in command of the troops of the United Colonies, stood with his back to the huge fireplace filled with blazing logs. From the ax-bitten summer beam and joists above his head hung flitches of bacon, hams, smoked haunches and shoulders of venison, dried pompions and herbs, strings of onions and dried apples, and hands of seed corn. Seated on the hand-hewn stools and benches, a group of square-jawed men, whose hair was cropped at the nape of their necks, listened while Winslow talked. Their faces were burned by sun and wind, and drawn lean by months of bush fighting; and the eyes of these men were grave. For they had come on a desperate mission—the destruction of the powerful Narragansetts who were about to join Philip, the Wampanoag, in his war of extermination against the New England colonies.

These gaunt and somber-eyed men were the officers of the Massachusetts Bay, Plymouth, and Connecticut troops camped in the forest outside. In the group, his black eyes as bright as a mink's and as restless, stood a small, compactly built man, wearing Indian moccasins and brain-tanned buckskin leggings and shirt. A bluish-white scar seared his face from left cheekbone to ear. On a sling at his belt hung a short-handled war hatchet. His name was Benjamin Church. Behind him stood Major Treat of Connecticut, second in command, tall and raw-boned, with the eyes and beak of a hawk, and a face tanned by sun and wind to the color of old leather.

General Winslow, a large man, his face pitted by smallpox, was saying: "Peter Freeman, the renegade Narragansett, places this Indian fort in a great swamp, fifteen miles to the southwest of us. 'Tis strong, with a blockhouse, flankers, and bastions. Now what is your counsel, gentlemen, as to method of attack?"

A bedlam of voices filled the room. "Name of God, what plans need we?" demanded Captain Moseley, a blustering former privateersman, who had many members of his old crews in his company. "Once these Narragansett dogs see with what force we have come, they'll run like rabbits."

But, warning against overconfidence, Treat and Church disagreed with the Bay man, and the argument grew bitter. Treat flung in Moseley's face his defeat at Bloody Brook, when the Connecticut man and his Mohicans had rescued Moseley's horse. Major Appleton and the Bay officers sided with Moseley. At length Winslow commanded silence.

"Until we see what we have to attack, a plan would be profitless. We will start under the stars in the morning, if there be any. Now look to your men."

The bitter December night dropped like a blanket on the camp of eleven hundred men who had come to break the power of the feared Narragansetts. From the Piscataqua to the Connecticut, and from the White Hills to the sea, Philip, the Wampanoag, had raised the Indians for a war to the death with the white men who were slowly occupying their land. Through the summer and autumn the Connecticut River settlements of Northfield, Deerfield, and Hadley had been attacked and harassed. For months the war whoop had been sounding in the night along the frontiers of the Bay Colony and Plymouth, and houses and barns left in ashes. Men had been butchered, women scalped, and children tomahawked before their mothers' eyes or carried into captivity. Horses, cattle, and sheep had been slaughtered or driven off, and the toil of years blotted out by the red raiders of the forest. The Nipmucks, Tarrantines, Quabaugs, and the upper Connecticut River tribes had joined the Wampanoags. If the powerful Narragansetts, who for generations had been the overlords of the southern New England Indians, threw their strength into this war of extermination, no farms would survive in the outlying towns of the Bay Colony and Plymouth, nor would the Connecticut settlements be safe.

Therefore, before it was too late, the leaders of the United Colonies had sent an expedition into the heart of the Narragansett country, of Rhode Island, to bring the savages to their knees. But the sure and certain doom which, because of this act, awaited the little towns of Warwick and Providence, had not given the Council of the United Colonies the slightest pause.

Over the old Providence Path from the rendezvous at Dedham, Winslow had led the Massachusetts men to Providence. There, joined by Bradford and the Plymouth troops, with Rhode Island guides, he had marched south along the west shore of the bay to the Narragansett country.

Little Rhode Island was not a member of the United Colonies, and the decision to ignore her and attack the Narragansetts on her soil had sickened the heart of the aged founder of Providence Plantations. For forty years, through fair dealing and an understanding of Indian character, Roger Williams had kept the peace between his people and their red neighbors. But his old friend, Chief Canonicus, was dead and the new chief sachem of the tribe, Canonchet, grand-nephew of Canonicus, was suspected by Massachusetts and Connecticut of plotting to join King Philip in the war. So, in defense of their own frontiers, and ignoring the protests of Williams and the terms of his charter from the crown, the troops of the United Colonies had marched into Rhode Island, leaving Providence and Warwick to their fate.

Meanwhile, safe on their island, with callous indifference, Newport and Portsmouth, under the Quaker Governor Coddington, refused to send troops to the aid of the little settlements of Upper Narragansett Bay.

Skirmishing with Narragansett scouting parties as he marched, Winslow had joined Moseley and Church, who had already defeated scattered bodies of savages and taken many prisoners. And while they waited, at Smith's blockhouse, for the arrival of the Connecticut troops, the stone garrison house of Jirah Bull, the sole white habitation remaining in the Narragansett country, had been surprised and fifteen people massacred.

So it was, on this bitter December night in the year 1675, that eleven hundred men, camped at Richard Smith's blockhouse at Cocumcussoc, on Narragansett Bay, waited for what for many would be their last dawn.

Deep in the forest, where the fires of the Plymouth troops lit the laced branches of oak and maple, three men surrounded the blazing logs in front of a low brush lean-to, wind-proofed with snow. One busied himself with the bubbling iron kettle filled with turnips, carrots, onions, and chunks of pork and beef. Two, wearing oiled leather breeches and lined leather doublets with thick duffel sleeves, squatted near the fire, warming their hands. A fourth, a massively built youth of twenty-four, dressed in deerskin and moccasins, with a bear robe wrapped about his shoulders, paced restlessly to-and-fro on the trodden snow at the rim of the circle of light thrown by the fire, the gray eyes beneath his fox-skin cap staring bleakly into the blackness.

"He will not put her from his mind," whispered Niles, a lank, hatchet-faced farmer from Taunton, who was squatted at the fire. "Last night he muttered and groaned in his sleep beside me till I was fair put to it to wake him. It was always his young wife the Wampanoags killed he was calling."

Dunbar, a raw-boned pioneer from Somerset, sadly wagged his head. "The sight of her dead, with a scalp of her long hair torn from her head, has driven him fair mad," he said, in an undertone. "He told me once it was the color of ripened wheat and her eyes blue as cornflowers. 'And now,' he said, 'some heathen savage carries it at his belt.' At that I thought the lad's veins would burst in his forehead, so filled was his face with blood and his eyes so wild."

Niles nodded. "The night Captain Prentice and his horse fetched the news of the massacre at Bull's garrison house, he whetted his knife and war hatchet to a razor's edge. Now, in close, at arm's length, I put my faith in this sword my father carried at Marston Moor with Oliver Cromwell. But, besides his musket, the lad will have nought but his knife and ax. At twenty paces he can bury the hatchet's head in a tree like an Injun."

"He little knows his strength," said Dunbar in a low tone. "When Freeman, the renegade, told us that there had been Narragansetts with the Wampanoags at the massacres at Swansea and Rehoboth, he thrust out his big hands and gripped the savage's arms until he bellowed with pain, so frenzied was the lad at the news. Two days back when he and I were out with Major Appleton's men an Indian shot at him from behind a tree, and when Jocelyn shot back and missed, the Narragansett ran at him with his tomahawk. With a yell like a heathen Injun, Jocelyn leaped to meet the savage, parried the blow aimed at him, and split the Injun's skull fair to the eyes. He's a savage man in a fight, and knows no fear."

"Ay, there's no stouter one in the colony, and he thinks only of revenge for his wife's death."

"Tch-tch! 'Tis sad to die so young!"

"Ay, 'tis so!"

At length the stew was done, and the four soldiers of Plymouth Colony squatted on their heels at the fire, to gulp greedily from their wooden bowls.

"Sergeant Wetherell says we start under the stars," said Almy, the cook, spearing with his knife a huge chunk of pork from the kettle, for they had no forks or spoons.

The tall youth across the fire raised his hawk-like eyes. "'Tis well," he said. "Many will die tomorrow at the fort. But I pray my Maker that lead will spare me while I get my fill of Narragansett blood!"

"You have good reason," returned Almy, "but remember the boy. Have a care not to waste yourself on the savages. He will need a father, now."

The face of the younger man went bitter. "'Twill be a poor father he'll have. All joy is gone from me."

The four sharers of the brush lean-to wolfed down the last of the stew, licked their fingers, wiped their mouths on the backs of their hands, slipped on their fur mittens, and rose to heap logs on the fire. Then they sat and smoked in the comforting heat. On all sides, like glowworms, the fires of the men who had kept the rendezvous at Smith's blockhouse stippled the murk of the December night. Shortly a sergeant appeared to detail a man as one of the guard and, wrapped in their robes, the remaining three lay down in the lean-to before the roaring fire.

From the clearing, yellow smudges burned through the blackness, marking the windows of the blockhouse. Seated on a settle beside the great chimneyplace, Major Treat and Church smoked long-stemmed clay pipes and talked in low tones. By the flickering light of smoky candlewood torches set in candle beams hung from the floor joists and summer beam, the other officers were finishing their supper.

"I have talked again with the Narragansett renegade," said Church in a low tone. "He warns that there are many fighting men in the fort, with much powder and shot. The strength of the tribe is there. If we try to force our way through that breach in the palisades he speaks of, he thinks we will be mowed down like grass before a scythe, and so do I."

Treat nodded. "Those are wise words. We must engage them with heavy musket fire from the front, and when they are occupied with the expected assault through the breach, surprise them by scaling the rear wall. This will divide and confuse them. Then Winslow may successfully storm through the breach with the main body."

"True," assented Church. "From the blockhouse and the bastions they are said to have flanking this opening in the wall, they will pour a murderous fire on a frontal attack, alone. General Winslow is stubborn and may not listen to us. He is greatly respected in Plymouth and the Bay, but his experience is little. I fear he will try to take the fort by storm from the front alone. If he does, few of us will return from that swamp."

Treat's lean face pictured his disgust. "The Bay people have shown little judgment in fighting the Indians. As I said to Dudley, tonight, the clergy at Boston sit on their war council and advise, as if their long noses had ever smelled powder in a fight. The clergy rule them in the Bay. At Weminisset, Hutchinson rode into an ambush with his eyes open. He had no scouts out. Up at Deerfield, Lathrop was guarding that corn to Hadley, how? Name of God! with his men's muskets on the ox carts while they picked grapes along the way. Lambs for the slaughter! It was cruel—such carelessness! I reached them with my men and the Mohicans barely in time to save Moseley, who had gone to Lathrop's aid."

Church slowly wagged his black head: "It is beyond belief. They never seem to learn. Why will they not use scouts?"

"That night," went on Treat, expelling a cloud of tobacco smoke from his mouth, "there were seventy-one new widows in the Bay Colony, and all because of stupidity. Pah! Some day Moseley, with his privateersman's insolence and his English armor, will learn to use scouts. But he'll pay a bloody price for the knowledge."

Gnawing at his upper lip, elbows on knees and chin cupped in hands, Church stared into the fire. "A few days back," he said, "Moseley's sailors charged a party of savages as they would lay aboard a ship, with much hullabaloo, shouting and swearing, thrashing through the brush, and a brave display of cutlasses."

Treat laughed. "They sought to frighten them, no doubt, with their bellowing like bulls, as one frightens children."

"Ay, and they had two great dogs with them, but the Narragansetts chopped the brutes to ribbons."

"There is but one way to fight the savage in his own forest," went on Church. "It is in his own fashion. These men from the Bay trust not their Indians and treat them like dogs. Yet the Indians could give them great aid, as do your Mohicans and Pequots. The Bay men put overmuch faith in the sword. Some of Appleton's people even carry English pikes, and I saw two espantoons. Well enough for the sergeants on parade, but in the forest they seldom reach the savage, who is like a shadow among the trees for use of sword or pike. They must learn to take cover and wait till a target offers for their muskets. You are sure of your Mohicans and Pequots?"

"They have always played me fair, and back at Hartford we have many of their women and children as hostages. I trust them. They hate the Narragansetts."

Church rose and stretched. "I'm with the General's escort tomorrow. He wished it so. But I plan to get leave to join your scouts. I have great desire to view that palisade before the council of war. There may be ways to take it without the loss of so many men."

"I, too," yawned Treat, "will circle the fort with Dennison, Avery, and our Indians before I join the council. We must not suffer those hotheads to lead the General to our ruin. The colonies will be in sad straits if we fail."

"If we fail," said Church, his face taut with worry, "God have mercy on us all!"

"Ay, if we fail there'll be a bloody counterstroke by the savages along the whole frontier. But I fear, either way, Providence and Warwick are doomed. The Newport Quakers refuse to send men to their aid."

"Yes, if the Narragansetts beat us off tomorrow, the French Indians, and some say even the Mohawks, will join Philip and the Narragansetts. That would drive us all back to the seaports for a fight to the finish. They'd swarm over the inland towns like locusts. God forbid!"

Treat's gray eyes were shot with fire as he muttered through his teeth, "It shall not happen!"

§3

Hours before the gray December dawn, breakfast fires flickered through the skeleton trees smothered in murk. Eleven hundred men, whose thoughts were focused on what that day would bring, ate from wooden bowls and trenchers in silence. Later, in line before the fires, they shivered, stamped their numb feet, and beat mittened hands against their shoulders, while company officers, with the sergeants carrying pikes as symbols of their authority, made their inspection of arms and ammunition. Then, led by Dennison and Avery, and as silent as wolves stalking deer, one hundred and fifty painted wraiths faded past into the gloom to comb the forest in front and on the flanks for an ambush. Each face was daubed with black, white, and ocher, and the head of each Mohican and Pequot was shaved, except for the waxed cockscomb carrying an eagle's feather.

Behind these scouts rode Prentice's iron-helmeted troopers, in single file, saddle leather creaking, swords rattling against stirrups and spurs, the horses' hoofs crunching the hard snow as they moved into the shadows. A few of these troopers in their youth had charged with Cromwell at Naseby, Marston Moor, and Worcester. Following them marched Moseley's privateersmen from Boston, wearing iron hats and English back and breast plates, some carrying pikes, as if they hoped to take the Indian fort as men board a ship. With them marched the pirate Cornelius, the Dutchman, and his men, recently captured off the Maine coast, who had gained their freedom by enlisting. Bringing up the rear were six savage wolfhounds wearing collars with long brass spikes, each led on a leash by one of Moseley's sailors.

Next, Oliver's company filed past, and Davenport's troops from Boston and Cambridge. Then came Appleton's men from Ipswich; Johnson, with groups from Roxbury and Weymouth; and Gardner's troops from Salem and the Essex towns. And in coon and fox-skin caps and leather doublets lined with fur, levies from the harassed frontiers of Marlboro, Lancaster, Groton, Chelmsford, and Sudbury crunched over the snow. Behind them were Plymouth men, under Bradford of Marshfield, some more familiar with the sting of salt spray and the rolling deck of a sloop than with the forest paths. Led by Lieutenant Barker, of Duxbury, and Captain Gorham, of Barnstable, farmers from Taunton and Rehoboth, from Somerset, Swansea, and the Cape.

Three hundred and fifty raw-boned, long-haired pioneers from Connecticut brought up the rear; men with craggy, wind-bitten faces, who had hacked their hill farms out of oak and maple forests. Many aped their leader, Treat, of Fairfield, in wearing deerskin and carrying war hatchets in their belts, hung beside their knives and powder horns. Over the leather doublets of others were slung baldric and sword. The companies of Marshall, Watts, and Seeley, from little Hartford, Windsor, and Stratford, passed by; and Gallup's men from Stonington and Mason's from Norwich, close to the Narragansett frontiers, whose fathers, forty years before, had broken the power of the Pequots. All these, like ghosts, moved past General Winslow and were swallowed in the murk.

The frost bit deep into faces and hands as the groping column floundered through gloom like that of a cedar swamp. Unseen windfalls sent men sprawling, with low curses, to their hands and knees, their muskets slithering off into the snow. Frozen brush and bull briers tripped and entangled them. Stumbling and slipping, they reeled into each other with the clatter of steel on steel. Before the start, orders had been issued against talking in the ranks, but as well command the insensate timber to cease snapping under the contraction of the frost as to hope to silence men thrashing blindly through the tangle of a New

England forest on a black December night.

The four comrades from Plymouth marched together, following the file of slow-moving troops. Their rabbit-skin mittens served them well, for in the withering cold the metal action and barrels of their flintlocks sucked and held the flesh of naked fingers. In front and to the rear, the creaking of stiff boots and moccasins on trampled snow fused with the execrations of men pitching headlong over down timber, rocks, and brush buried in drift.

As the coming dawn softened the lead-hued sky over the bay to purple, and the snow now lay, a gray blur, beneath their slow-moving feet, word was passed down the column to halt. Tripping on his dangling sword in a tangle of bull briers, Niles sprawled flat on his belly. Young Jocelyn turned and laughed.

"Carry your pig-sticker if you will," he called to the prostrate man. "You'll never use it but to stumble over."

With a grunt, Niles got to his feet. "It may be, before this day ends," he sputtered, "this pig-sticker, as you name it, will make full amends for this fall."

"May it bite deep into many a Narragansett skull, friend Niles," laughed Jocelyn.

"It is said to be twelve or fifteen miles, and already we have come but three or four," sighed Almy, squatting in the snow and blowing on his stiff fingers.

"With the light we will move faster," muttered Dunbar, nursing a foot in his mittened hands. "In these moccasins my feet have taken sore punishment from the rocks, for the foot-cloths over my poor socks are thin."

"Better your moose-hide shoes than my stiff boots that slip and slide till I scarce can keep moving," lamented Niles.

Jocelyn gave a laugh without mirth as he looked at his friends. "'Tis little sorrow our feet will give us if we fail today against the Narragansetts."

"We will not fail, God willing!" said Niles, dropping his mittens, which hung from his shoulders by thongs, and thrusting his cold hands under his sheepskin coat into his doublet beneath his armpits. "General Winslow will not fail."

Again Jocelyn laughed bitterly. "The savages are mad with their success this autumn. It will go hard with the colonies if we humble them not well today."

"Unto the last squaw and child!" cried Almy, fiercely.

"Unto the last squaw!" rasped Jocelyn. "They showed no mercy to my wife."

"Nor to my brother's at Swansea," added Almy.

The other two were silent, for they knew what bitterness and desolation lay in the young man's heart.

Suddenly the whinnying of the horses of Prentice's troop in the van, followed by a bedlam of noise from Moseley's wolfhounds, waked the black forest.

"Name of God! 'Tis an ambush," cried Niles, snapping back the frizzan on his flintlock and with shaking hands repriming from his horn. Almy and Dunbar eased their swords in their scabbards. Then, stiff as the oaks around them, the four friends listened to the neighing of the excited horses and the uproar of the dogs. At length Jocelyn broke the tension with a laugh.

"Content yourself, friend Niles," he said. "'Tis likely they've winded wolves that are curious of us. The bears are denned up. Horses always take on when they smell wolves."

"My hair rose stiff on my head," muttered Almy, "when the horses screamed."

The fretting of the horses ceased, and the long column resumed its march. Shortly, through the branches of the skeleton oaks and maples, groped the gray fingers of the dawn. The stars overhead dimmed, and splashes of light now streaked the east. At length, in a bank of amber haze, the sun lifted above the sullen bay in their rear, to tint the naked hills, while the column moved on over the snow.

To lessen the chances of an ambush, the guides were following an old Indian path over the high country to the east of a wide valley, with a screen of Mohicans in front and on the flanks. Noon came and Treat's scouts brought back word that the wide, flat lands, studded with ponds, where a river, called the Usquepaugh, ran through a great swamp, lay but a short march to the southwest. Major Bradford and Captain Gorham came down the column and ordered the men to eat the cold meat and journey cake in their haversacks and look to the priming of their guns.

Through the halted troops ran the thrill of suppressed excitement. Men spoke in clipped sentences, their voices thin with the pull of taut nerves. They heard each other draw in deep breaths, which they expelled in a cloud of frost as they felt the staccato beat of their hearts against their ribs. The bitter air snapped with tension. Eyes glittered savagely from beneath fur caps and iron helmets, as swords were nervously eased in scabbards and muskets reprimed. The battle that would decide the fate of the Massachusetts and Connecticut frontier towns was close at hand. The goal of their long march was near. And for many, death waited.

Finishing his food, Jocelyn rose from the fallen tree where the four sat, dropped his fur mitten on its thong, and, drawing his belt ax, tested the edge with a calloused thumb. Then he drew back his long arm and with a grunt hurled the war hatchet at a large beech twenty-five paces off. The ax spun end over end through the air and buried its thin blade in the tree, while its maple helve quivered like the shaft of an arrow.

A look of surprise and admiration lay on Almy's frost-bitten face. "How did you learn such skill?" he gasped, while the others smiled and nodded. They had seen Jocelyn hurl his hatchet before.

"I grew up with the Wampanoags. They were friends of my father. Often they ate at our house, and I hunted and fished with their children. Once I slept beneath the same robe with them. But now show me a Wampanoag and I'll show you a dead man." So bitter was the tone of Jocelyn's reply that for a time his friends were silenced.

As the powerful youth tore the ax from the tree, Almy warned: "Have a care, lad, when we reach this fort! Let's not drift apart, but hold together, that we may aid each other when in need."

Jocelyn threw a look of veiled contempt at the speaker as he drew the keen air into his lungs and pushed the ax helve through his belt. "If we storm that stockade, someone needs must be rash!"

Almy shook his head helplessly at the other two.

The march was resumed along the shoulder of the ridge flanking the flatlands on the east. Out to the west, studding the timbered plain like white disks, lay the shells of frozen ponds. Beyond the flatlands a series of long ridges cut the dun sky. Under frosted brows, the eyes of the moving men restlessly roved the naked forest on either flank, their ears taut for the sound of shots in the distance. Muscles tense as strung wire, many, as they walked, lifted and placed their feet as if fearing to make a sound. Some moved bent over their muskets like hunters stalking game; others walked erect, their features stiff as if carved from wood. All talking had ceased and the tension of troops moving up to the firing line gripped the column like a vise.

At length the long line of men wound down off the ridge into the timbered plain, their frozen breaths trailing above them like ribbons of smoke. They had traveled an hour when word was passed down from General Winslow, who was with Prentice and Appleton, that the great swamp of the Narragansetts lay hardly a mile to the southwest.

The column reached the icy shell of a brook, and Niles said:

"Freeman, the renegade, places this brook not far from the river we follow into the swamp. Shickasheen, he names it. It joins the river below the fort."

At holes broken through the ice by Prentice's troop to water their horses and slake their thirst, the Plymouth men filled their horn cups and drank. Then shots sounded to the south of them.

"Hear that?" cried Jocelyn, his eyes glittering with anticipation. "The Mohicans have found them! It won't be long, now." His frost-burned face glowed with a wild joy as he shook his flintlock in the direction of the firing.

The stinging air was electric with suspense. The order was passed down the column to halt. Their frosted breaths lifting above them in clouds, men stood frozen into strange attitudes, listening. Dunbar towered, straight as a spruce, as if on parade on training day, his hooked nose sniffing the air like a hound testing the wind. Niles nervously fingered the hilt of his sword with his left hand, his long face twisted with tension as his chin jutted like that of a runner on a mark. The stocky Almy hunched over his musket, his eyes on his feet. Like a statue, Jocelyn stood smiling into the distance, his shoulders squared, the thumb of his right mitten thrust into his belt beside his ax.

Presently a rangy figure in deerskin, wearing knife, pistol, and belt ax, but no sword, crunched past over the snow. In the agate-gray eyes of the lean face was the look of a leader of men. With him were a Connecticut captain and an ensign, leather baldrics slung over their right shoulders, carrying swords, pistols stuck through belts. Close on their heels silently moved two Mohicans, their heads freshly shaven except for the waxed war lock, and their faces daubed with white, black, and ocher paint.

"Major Treat," said Almy. "Always he wears deerskin and never a sword."

"He saved Captain Moseley and fifty men at Deerfield," added Dunbar. "He's a man to my liking."

"He goes to join the General," said Niles. "The Mohicans and Pequots are driving in the Narragansett scouts."

Jocelyn watched curiously the back of the Connecticut leader. "He carries a pistol today," he said. "But his men say he puts his faith in his ax, as do I. They are sweet tools for close work; they never miss fire."

Again there was a burst of firing in the forest, to the southwest, and men tested the action and looked to the priming of their guns as they waited with tightened muscles for the order to move.

"We are close to the big swamp now," said Almy, and his voice was thin and dry, "but it is frozen hard and will give us no trouble."

"'Tis well," replied Jocelyn, lightly, drawing his ax and tossing it into the air to snatch it by its helve on its return. "I have my fill of walking. The sight of the painted face and tufted head of a Narragansett would be welcome."

"But the sight of too many might mean our sorrow," soberly added Niles. "They have many fighting men—thousands, 'tis said—and will shoot from behind good oak timber."

Jocelyn's gray eyes squinted at the speaker. "You seem to have little stomach for what is ahead of us."

The lanky Niles met the youth's look with level, kindly eyes. "I have never shirked my duty, lad," he said quietly, "and I will do my part today. But there are five waiting back at Taunton with the wife for my homecoming. Please God they wait not in vain."

"Amen!" approved Almy and Dunbar.

The blood pushed up into Jocelyn's bronzed face. "'Tis sorry I am that I spoke lightly to my better," he said gently. "I have lost all and forget what others may have to lose."

"You forget the boy," said Niles. "He'll need you. Have a care to-day."

"The boy will forget us both," Jocelyn answered bitterly.

For a time the four comrades stood in silence. Then firing again broke out to the south, and Sergeant Wetherell's voice lifted in front of them: "March!"

At last the Plymouth men reached the small river leading into the swamp, beside which Prentice's fretting horses waited. Surrounded by a group of officers, General Winslow stood in heated argument with Treat.

"I've circled the stockade with my scouts, General," Treat was saying. "'Tis a high wall of pointed oak timber faced with an abatis of bull briers, sharpened roots, and stakes."

"'Twould be mad, then, to attempt to scale the wall in the rear," said Winslow. "We'll attack through the breach."

"But this breach has flankers and a blockhouse guarding it. A mass assault here, which the savages clearly hope for, will mean a needless slaughter. We must attack in the rear as well as in the front!"

"I favor a mass attack through the breach," snapped Major Appleton.

"And thus play into the Indians' hands," stormed Treat. "This breach was left open as bait for us. If they had time to build the blockhouse and flankers, they had time to close the breach. Are we to walk into this Narragansett bear trap like children?"

Winslow scowled. "Your plan may fail and lose us a third of our men. A mass attack driven home will carry the fort."

Appleton and Prentice vigorously nodded agreement. But Treat's eyes glittered under his fox-skin cap as his wide mouth tightened. He glanced at the approving faces of the Connecticut captains and continued: "General Winslow, they'll mow us down from that blockhouse. If they beat us off, we'll be attacked on our retreat in the night."

"We shall not be defeated, God willing!" returned Winslow.

"Do I hear Major Treat talking of defeat before we have attacked?" sneered Moseley.

Treat ignored the thrust of the man whose life he had saved at Bloody Brook, and insisted: "Sir, draw their fire and attention with a feint at the breach while I storm the rear wall with Connecticut and the

Mohicans."

"But if you are beaten off, we are in worse case than before," protested Winslow.

"I shall not be beaten off. I shall carry that wall."

The confident answer drew audible grunts of disbelief from the Bay officers. Treat's eyes glittered like sun on young ice as they swept the hostile faces surrounding him.

"This rear attack will surprise and greatly confuse them," he went on. "When surprised, savages easily lose heart. Panic will spread among them. When we've scaled the wall and have them in the rear, our bugle will signal you for the mass attack through the breach. Then it will succeed."

Winslow glanced doubtfully at Church, who stood at Treat's side, vigorously nodding his scarred head.

"Sir," the Sakonnet man insisted, "the attack on the rear wall will defeat the Narragansetts."

Winslow thoughtfully studied the hostile faces and shaking heads of the officers standing in the snow around him. He was a man of no military experience and the logic of Treat's plan, backed by Church, made him hesitate. Thus far in the war Treat and Church had been successful leaders. In fact, the only successful ones. The Governor of Plymouth rubbed his stubbled chin with his mitten.

"Have you absolute confidence that you can scale the wall?" Winslow asked at length.

Church's elbow dug into Treat's back. They were making headway.

"Yes," said Treat. "My Mohicans climb like monkeys and are hungry for the loot of the Narragansett wigwams. Furthermore, they bear the Narragansetts a bitter hatred of long standing. Some are even now cutting saplings to make bridges over the abatis before the wall. If you'll hold the attention of the savages by a movement toward the breach and engage them with heavy fire, my Connecticut men and Indians will scale the rear wall."

The General was palpably wavering. He alternately scowled and smiled, slowly nodding his head as he visibly wrestled with his problem. Then his pock-marked face set, and he turned to Appleton and Bradford. "Major Treat's plan has much merit. There is great advantage in surprise."

There were loud murmurs of dissent from the Bay officers, and Moseley elbowed his bulky frame past Appleton to reach Winslow's side. With his iron helmet, breast and back plates, his heavy naval cutlass and pistols, the former privateersman resembled one of Cromwell's Ironsides. His mouth twisted in a sneer.

"'Tis a pretty plan, no doubt—if it succeeds!" he exploded, glaring into Treat's cold eyes. "But if it fails, Massachusetts and Plymouth will have no reserves. Major Treat will never scale that wall with his chicken-livered Mohicans!"

"Major Treat *will* scale that wall!" Treat flung back, icily.

"There will be no troops except the horse held in reserve, Captain Moseley!" broke in Winslow. "I shall throw our full strength at the fort. We cannot delay! It must be taken before dark or we will never see Smith's blockhouse on this bitter night!"

Moseley's face was so swollen with his anger that it seemed about to burst. "Sir," he shouted, "is the advice of the Bay officers to be ignored? Are we children to be so flouted?"

Appleton and Oliver seized the raging privateersman by the arms and drew him away from the irate Winslow, whose homely face was red with wrath as he roared: "Sir, you have been guilty of unmeet conduct before. The Council of the United Colonies have put me in command here. Curb your unbridled tongue and respect your superior officer or—"

"General Winslow," the wiry Church pushed forward, "I've circled this stockade and the Bay officers have not." Church's eyes bored defiantly into the black looks shot at him. "There are a thousand fighting men in there and more. Major Treat's plan is our only hope to escape a bloody slaughter of brave men."

"That's my opinion, General," spoke up Bradford, ignoring the protests of the Bay officers.

Winslow nodded. His heavy jaw clamped as he surveyed the black faces of Appleton, Moseley, and the others. "I'm convinced," he said with finality. "That will be our plan of attack, Major Appleton. You will move three companies up in front of the breach as if to attack, and maintain a steady fire. But do not go in until ordered. Your remaining companies with Plymouth will move up close to support them."

As Moseley turned away with the others to join their commands, he snarled: "God help us! We're all dead men!"

Shortly the Plymouth men were moving into the thick growth of the swamp behind the Massachusetts companies. Led by Treat, the Connecticut men passed them, with a body of excited Mohicans and Pequots in full war paint, and circled back into the east.

"Where is Treat bound?" asked Jocelyn of Sergeant Wetherell, who marched beside him. "I thought Connecticut was to support the attack."

Wetherell smiled at the chafing youth whose eyes glittered with eagerness for the coming fight.

"Captain Gorham tells me that Treat makes a surprise attack on the rear wall of the stockade with his Mohicans. It was objection to that from Major Appleton and Moseley that lent such heat to their talk.

We heard them from across the river. But Church and Major Bradford were with Treat, and their counsel prevailed."

"Oh," cried Jocelyn, "so Treat attacks from the rear? 'Tis good news! Trust Treat and Church to find a way into that fort. They are the two wiliest Injun fighters in the colonies."

"Ay, lad, I believe they are. They are never ambushed."

As Plymouth advanced behind the Bay men, heavy firing broke out in front.

"There goes Massachusetts!" cried Jocelyn, repriming his gun from a small horn of priming powder slung over his shoulder. "We'll be in there soon!" He took three bullets from his pouch and jammed them between the fingers of his left hand near the knuckles to save time when he reloaded.

The Plymouth men halted and took cover.

"Can you see the stockade?" asked Almy, peering through the thick underbrush.

"No, but that windfall up there is yellow with smoke," said Niles. "See it? It must be from Bay muskets."

Again the Plymouth men moved forward through cedar and alders, swamp oak and frozen briers, with the companies now deployed. In front of them rose the intermittent firing of muskets. The light breeze drove the acrid odor of burned sulphur and saltpeter to their nostrils. Between the shots lifted the shrill whooping of the Narragansetts and the caterwauling of squaws and children as they kindled a fighting fury in the warriors. At intervals, above the mad cacophony of voices, swelled the rhythmic chant of the Narragansett battle cry, "Ju-het-tek-ee! Ju-het-tek-ee! (Fight! Fight!)" as the waiting savages whipped themselves into a frenzy. But the straining ears of the men lying in the snow caught no answering challenge from the Mohicans.

"Name of God! hear that screeching," Almy's thin voice quavered.

"There are thousands in there," muttered Niles, his long face twitching with nervous strain.

"There it is!" called Jocelyn, from the low branches of an oak where he had climbed to obtain a better view. "I see the break in the wall and the tree across it! The Bay men are moving in! They're chipping splinters off that stockade! See'm fly! Our time is near."

Again the voice of Sergeant Wetherell urged them forward through the frozen brush, on the heels of the Massachusetts men. They were still out of the short range of a flintlock but the instinct for self-preservation drove each man to seek the cover of a tree as he crept forward through the snow, doubled over his musket. At last they lay close behind the main body of the Bay men, with a view through the tangle of scrub of the Narragansett fort.

Built on higher land than the surrounding swamp, where the river forked, rose the ten-foot oak walls of the square stockade behind a cheval-de-frise of roots, pointed stakes, and masses of bull briers. The loopholes of the palisade, the flankers, and the blockhouse covering the breach in the wall spat flame and smoke at the waiting troops in the brush. Off the left flank of the Bay men, facing one of the corner bastions where he commanded a view of two walls of the stockade, lay Church with two companions. Suddenly, from in front, three Indians rose from the bushes, fired on the Bay men, ran for the stockade, crossed the river on a log frozen in the ice, and disappeared through a narrow opening in the wall.

With a shout, a group of Bay men rose from where they lay and started to follow. Church's high-pitched voice shrilled in warning: "Keep back, men! 'Tis a trap!"

The Bay men flattened on their faces as slugs from the stockade kicked up the snow and chipped the bark off trees around them. Over in front of the break in the wall, orange smoke from the coarse, black powder hung in clouds where the advance companies were pouring a heavy fire at the loopholes of the palisade. Inside, the howling of warriors and the screaming of women and children filled the sunless day with pandemonium. Intermittently the Narragansett war cry—"Ju-het-tek-ee! Ju-het-tek-ee!"—swelled above the uproar. Crouched on the firing step, young braves, daring the bullets of the colonists, bobbed tufted skulls above the pointed logs, to hurl obscene epithets and challenge their white foes to attack them. In reply, volleys from the Bay men sent the splinters spinning where the grimacing, white-daubed faces had shown themselves. Again and again the battle cry of the savages shrilled above the bedlam: "Ju-het-tek-ee! Ju-het-tek-ee!"

"All the devils in hell are in there," gasped Niles, with a sinking of the stomach. "Hear that heathenish war cry! It fair sickens me!"

"They'll sing no devil's song when we reach them with the steel," laughed Jocelyn, his eyes glittering. "'Tis time for the false attack. Why do they wait?" His voice rang with the fever that heated his blood. He filled his big chest with the keen air and blew it out between his teeth as he chafed, like a race horse, with the urge for action.

"Treat's men are cutting saplings to bridge the hedge. Give them time," replied Sergeant Wetherell, who moved coolly among his men, soothing their jumping nerves.

For a space the wild firing continued. Then the voices of the Bay officers filtered through the rattle of musketry. In front, groups of men rose to their knees.

"They're going in!" cried Jocelyn. "The Bay men are going in! God speed them!"

"No, the attack is but to hold the savages to this wall and draw their fire," insisted the Sergeant. "They'll not go in until Treat's bugle sounds."

The oak wall of the stockade belched a sheet of flame as the Bay men started on a run for the breach.

"God's name! you're right. General Winslow's sending them in," gasped Wetherell. "But why? There's been no signal from the bugle. Why go they now?"

"'Tis cruel—cruel!" groaned Niles. "They'll be cut down like corn!"

There was a burst of fire from the Bay support companies as their comrades made for the opening in the stockade.

Dunbar ground his teeth. "There's some mischance here. 'Tis too early! They'll be slaughtered!"

The fox- and coon-skin caps of the mass of running men jammed before the breach in the wall. On their way some stumbled and sprawled on their faces, not to rise. But, led by the fearless Johnson, the Bay men broke through the tree across the breach and plunged inside, to be met by a withering fire from blockhouse and flankers. Captain Johnson stopped, spun like a top, and reeled forward on his face. Davenport, in his brave buff doublet a marked man for Narragansett muskets, riddled by slugs, crumpled and died. Gardner, and Moseley with his yelling privateersmen, fought their way in and joined the others as they ran for the cover of the nearest wigwams or flattened for protection against the walls of the flankers. Shot repeatedly through the body, the gallant Gardner slumped in the snow.

At last, waving his cutlass, Moseley bellowed: "Back, men! Back through the breach!"

Firing a last volley at the loopholes of flankers and blockhouse, the men retreated, leaving behind a trail of wounded and dead.

"They're coming back," groaned Jocelyn, as the Bay men ran for the cover of the forest and fell flat on their chests. "They're beaten off! Where's Treat?"

"Treat could not scale the wall," groaned Wetherell. "Christ's blood—they sent the Bay men in too soon—too soon. There was no blast of the bugle. Treat and his dirty Injuns are beaten. God help us now! God help the colonies!"

Niles' blue lips quivered, his long face gray with horror as he muttered, "But few who went in that breach have returned."

"Now, where's your great Major Treat?" snarled Dunbar, dropping his mitten and jamming between the knuckles of his left hand three bullets from his pouch.

In his anxiety, Jocelyn savagely pounded the snow with his fist. "In God's name, why did they move before the bugle? They charged too soon—too soon. But Treat may win yet. Give him time! Treat may win yet!"

"No, he's failed," groaned Wetherell. "He's beaten off. I can hear the firing back there now. They've driven Treat off. We're lost. God pity us! We're dead men!"

"The Lord has forsaken us!" Almy gnawed his cracked lips and shivered where he lay on the snow, but not from cold. "'Tis a cruel day for the colonies. God have mercy on our souls!"

Crouched in the cover of a thicket behind the Bay supports, who were firing as fast as they could load, prime, and aim their muskets at the stockade, from which lifted a bedlam of triumphant howling, Winslow glared savagely into Church's scarred face. "Are you convinced, now?" he flung at the Sakonnet Indian fighter. "Treat's failed. They've beaten him off with his miserable Mohicans or the bugle would have sounded. Our last hope, now, is to attack with all our strength through that breach. Treat's advice and yours, Captain Church," he finished bitterly, "have brought our ruin."

Church's black eyes snapped as he doggedly shook his head. "Not yet, General Winslow." The blue-white scar on his lined face swelled with his anger. Every nerve in his body was taut as his ears strained for the sound he hoped to hear. "You were hasty, sir. You ordered the attack before the bugle sounded, contrary to the agreement with Major Treat." The ice in Church's eyes cooled Winslow's wrath. "But we're not beaten yet."

The two men lay watching the puffs of orange smoke from the loopholes of the stockade and the firing of the Bay men from the forest. Then the despairing Winslow sent a messenger to Appleton. Shortly Appleton joined them where they lay in the cedar scrub.

"'Tis all over," groaned Winslow, his heavy face sick with apprehension. His lip twitched as he faltered: "Treat's been driven off. He's failed. We must attack and—God help us!"

Appleton glared at Church, who was on his knees, head thrust forward, like a dog scenting game, as he listened to the uproar. "Damn you, your advice has lost us the Connecticut troops. Treat's beaten," he snarled at the man who ignored him as he knelt, with head tilted to one side. "On your head and Treat's, Captain Church, rests the blame for this and the blood of brave men. We'll never take that fort."

Suddenly Church's face lit with joy. "There's the bugle, General!" he cried. "I hear the Mohican war whoop! Treat's inside! He's over the wall! He's got 'em in the rear! Treat's won! In God's name, order the attack!"

Hope flamed in Winslow's pock-marked face. "You're right Church! Praise God, you're right! I hear it! It's the bugle—Treat's bugle! He's scaled the wall! He's inside, I tell you! Quick!" he shouted. "Order the attack!"

Sometime previous, when the attacking Bay companies were being driven from the stockade, the Narragansett guards at the loopholes in the rear wall had suddenly stiffened with alarm as groups of Mohicans, Pequots, and white men burst from the forest carrying backloads of trimmed saplings. Covered by the fire of their comrades directed at the loopholes, they ran boldly up to the abatis and at different points hurled their loads on the hedge of roots and briers guarding the wall. Shot from the loopholes, men reeled with their burdens and fell, but others leaped forward to finish their work. Slowly the scattered heaps of saplings grew. Men died, but dying left a pathway for their comrades. At last the hedge was bridged in many places, and with a wild cheer, four hundred Connecticut men, Mohicans, and Pequots burst from cover and charged the wall.

Occupied, as Treat had anticipated, with the fight at the breach, the Narragansetts had left the rear wall lightly defended. Before warning could be sent and aid arrive, Treat's men were swarming over the palisade like the tide over a reef. For an instant a tall figure in buckskin, grasping musket and belt-ax, his bugler beside him, was silhouetted against the gray sky. With them were Dennison, Avery, and Owaneco, the son of Uncas, the Mohican chief. Then Treat leaped to the firing step and the ground as his men drove the Narragansetts from the wall and poured a volley into the surprised savages running to defend the rear of the fort.

Jubilant over the defeat of the Bay men, howling derision at Winslow's troops outside in the brush, the Narragansetts suddenly found themselves attacked from the cover of long lines of wigwams by Connecticut men and Mohicans, who drove old men, shrieking squaws, and children before them. It was then that the bugle notes for which Church's hungry ears had been straining lifted high above the firing.

General Winslow was a changed man as he watched the Bay companies, followed by the men of Plymouth, run for the breach. "I owe you amends, Captain Church!"

Church's face was inscrutable as he nodded.

As the Plymouth men followed the Bay companies, Jocelyn saw a trimmed oak timber, pointed at one end, lying in the snow. "Sergeant Wetherell," he called, "this stick they cut for the stockade will do to batter an entrance into one of the flankers."

"Ay, just the thing. Can you fetch it? Dunbar, give him a hand. Niles, you and Almy lug their muskets."

With a laugh, Jocelyn swung the heavy oak stick to his shoulder as if it were a bag of corn and hurried on after the others. Covered by the fire of the Plymouth men, the cheering Bay companies broke through the breach. Close on their heels came Plymouth. Stumbling over dead and wounded sprawled on the snow, Jocelyn plunged on with his burden while the fire from blockhouse and flankers beat upon the assaulting column like hail, and the air was thick with smoke and the fumes of sulphur. With the timber across his shoulder, he crawled on his knees under the tree trunk and followed his comrades.

Inside the stockade, Jocelyn wheeled and crashed his battering-ram into the slab door of the left flanker as flame leaped from the loop-holes. But he hugged the oak walls and was not hit. Then, covered by the fire of his comrades, he again lunged the ram into the oak door and it shook with the blow. Once more he drew back and, with a short run, drove the log into the heavy oak. The planks split and the bars inside gave way. A bullet chipped a splinter from the ram to scratch his face and smear it with blood. Another slug scraped his shoulder. Again he drew back and made a last desperate lunge against the shattered door. With a crash the door collapsed, fell inside, and, swords in hand, a group of Plymouth men jammed through into the flanker.

Scrambling to his feet, Jocelyn drew his knife and belt ax and sprang inside the roofless bastion. There a battle without quarter was on. Their muskets useless, milling Indians and whites fought with knife, sword, and tomahawk, and even with teeth and nails, over the firing platform and on the ground below. Reaching a hand above his head, Jocelyn seized the leg of a Narragansett locked with a Plymouth man on the fire step and pulled him down on his upthrust knife. Then, knife in teeth and ax in belt, he climbed to the platform with Dunbar. There Niles and a huge savage writhed and twisted in each other's arms, powerless to use their weapons. Jocelyn's arching belt ax split the Narragansett's skull as a knife blade slices an eggshell, and he hurled the body on the struggling men below. Like madmen, shoulder to shoulder, he and Dunbar hacked and stabbed their way along the platform. Tomahawks struck at them and knives thrust, but belt ax and sword of the Plymouth men at last cleared the platform. Raging like one obsessed, the youth struck the last savage to his knees and, seizing the falling Indian, lifted him high above his head and hurled him over the pointed logs to the snow below. The flanker was won, and now, from its loopholes, the Plymouth men poured a steady fire on the blockhouse.

Shortly the voice of Sergeant Wetherell lifted above the firing.

"We must get that blockhouse, men!"

"I'll smash that door," cried Jocelyn. "Cover me with your fire."

Dunbar seized his friend. "For love o' God, lad, don't try it again," he pleaded. "You'll be slaughtered from the overhang. 'Tis loop-holed."

But the frenzied Jocelyn tore himself loose and, covered by fire from the flanker at the loopholes of the blockhouse, ran outside, lifted the oak ram lying in the snow, and charged the blockhouse door. The timber crashed against the heavy slabs like the explosion of a gun. Muskets spat fire at him from the loopholed overhang built to guard the entrance. A slug spun his fox-skin cap from his head. Another ripped his doublet. Wiping from his eyes the blood from the scratch on his forehead, he again drew back and drove the heavy ram with all his force at the weakening door, while his comrades in the flanker and from the cover of neighboring wigwams fired into the loopholes. Then, with a run, Jocelyn lunged the ram against the splintered oak and the barred door crashed. With a cheer, the Plymouth men fought their way into the blockhouse. Again Narragansett and white man, in a melee of writhing bodies, battled without quarter. Sword and knife and hatchet thrust and chopped. But the blood-mad Plymouth farmers, remembering their murdered neighbors, would not be denied. Shortly, no Narragansett remained alive inside the oak walls.

Bursting from the blockhouse, where Almy was left, wounded in the arm, Jocelyn, Dunbar, and Niles, faces and doublets smeared with powder stains and blood, joined the battle among the wigwams. Firing from the cover of tubs and baskets of corn and beans, stored in the bark houses, the Narragansetts fought with the desperation of doomed men. From the rear the shrieks of squaws, children, and old men swept before them by the battle-mad Connecticut men and the Mohicans as they fought their way through the wigwams to join the Bay companies, fused with the din of musket fire and the yells of the warriors to make the day hideous with noise. With the memories of slaughtered women and children etched on their brains, the blood-drunk colonists gave no quarter. The old, the women, and the children alike died on that bitter day. In their raids on the settlements the savages had shown no mercy. Now they received none. The troops had sworn that the Narragansetts should remember that fight in the frozen swamp.

Mad for loot, the howling Mohicans were taking grim toll of their hereditary enemies. The battle in the stockade soon resembled the sack of a medieval town. The place became a shambles. Everywhere the bodies of scalped warriors, squaws, and children sprawled on the blood-stained snow in the grotesque postures of violent death. And over it all, in the freezing air, powder smoke hung like a yellow pall.

As Jocelyn and his friends reached the wigwams, an Indian child fled screaming from a bark house, followed by one of Moseley's wolfhounds. With a leap the dog reached, pulled down its helpless prey, and slashed with its long fangs. At the same instant something spun end over end through the air and sank deep in the hairy neck of the dog behind his spiked collar. The hound rose from the child, yelped, and fell dead on the snow.

Jocelyn regained his belt ax and gazed down at the dead child.

"Why, 'tis a mere babe!" he cried to Dunbar. "We came not here to slaughter babes. The pity of it!"

Sickened with the sight, the three men turned away to meet a helmeted figure running toward them with a pike. "You killed my dog!" he roared at Jocelyn. "You killed him with your hatchet, you damned Plymouth swine! Rot my bones! but I'll—"

Moseley's sailor made a savage lunge with his pike, but the shaft was caught by a quick twist of the belt ax and deflected. With a bound, Jocelyn was on his man. Tearing the pike from the sailor's hands, he shattered the staff over his iron hat, threw it aside, and his fist crashed into the other's face. The sailor reeled away, struggling to draw his cutlass. But with a wild laugh, the Plymouth man reached him, and with the smash of a battering-ram his right fist bludgeoned the sailor senseless to the snow.

"Well, sailor," snarled Dunbar, standing over the crumpled shape, "it seems Plymouth swine have long tusks."

"Ay," said Niles, his smudged face aglow with admiration. "Name of God! that blow would have felled an ox."

As the three men hurried to join the fighting at the wigwams, groups of warriors, driven at last from cover, began to run for the wall. Jocelyn's eyes suddenly focused with horror on a huge savage who had stopped with four others to empty their muskets.

"Look, Dunbar!" he choked, pointing with his gun. "Look at his belt! The Lord has been good to me today," he cried. "It is hers! It is hers!"

The startled eyes of Niles and Dunbar followed the pointing gun. From the Indian's belt hung a scalp of long, golden hair.

"See it, Dunbar?" Jocelyn's voice was thin and shrill. "It is hers! There's none like it in all the colonies!" With the cry of a wounded beast, the frenzied man bounded toward the savages, followed by his friends. Seeing them, the Indians who had just fired back at the wigwams, started desperately to ram charges into their flintlocks, but suddenly dropped their guns, turned, and made for the wall. Niles stopped, took careful aim, and fired. A running Indian stumbled and slid on his face. Dunbar missed, while Jocelyn, dropping his empty musket, bounded ahead. Finding but a single white man close on their heels, the four Narragansetts wheeled on their pursuer. There was the clash of steel on steel as they chopped savagely at Jocelyn, who fought like a cornered wolf against the overwhelming odds. But before a tomahawk could split his head from behind, Niles and Dunbar reached him. The swords of his comrades broke the circle of savages hemming him in, and Jocelyn's belt ax flashed. His skull crushed, a Narragansett sprawled on the snow. Another dropped like a log, half beheaded by the slash of Dunbar's saber. Again Jocelyn's ax drove home on a shaved head, and the giant savage now stood alone. Turning, he leaped for the stockade wall. As Jocelyn followed close on his heels, he stopped, pivoted, and with a grunt, hurled his tomahawk. Like the dive of an otter, Jocelyn flattened under the spinning ax, bounded to his feet, and reached the running Indian as he leaped for the fire step. The Narragansett turned. His knife, lunged in a swift arc, was caught by the blade of Jocelyn's ax, and the knife hand was snatched by the wrist as the two catapulted headlong into the snow in each other's arms.

Desperately the savage strained to free his wrist from the vise of Jocelyn's grip, but powerful as he was, he had met his master. Inexorably, the Plymouth man forced him flat on his back and pinioned the knife hand to the snow. Then, with his great strength, Jocelyn straightened the Indian's arm and twisted the wrist until the bones snapped at the elbow. The knife slipped from limp fingers. Grimacing with pain, the Narragansett bit savagely at Jocelyn's neck. With a hunching blow of his fist the white man snapped back the shaved head with its tuft of hair.

"So I've found you, Narragansett!" Like the jaws of a bear trap, Jocelyn's fingers clamped on the brown throat of the savage beneath him. In a frenzied effort to free himself, the Indian writhed in his captor's arms as Jocelyn laughed mirthlessly down into the hideous face daubed across with black, white, and ocher paint.

"At last, Narragansett, I've found you!" Jocelyn repeated, his eyes black with hate. "It was you and not a Wampanoag who killed her!" Then his big frame shook with a convulsive sob. The sharp agony of the day when he had found Judith's broken body in the forest again lanced through him. His voice sank into a low murmur: "It's hers—that hair! There was none so golden in all Plymouth!"

His eyes again blazed with savagery. "You're going to pay for that hair of gold on your belt, Narragansett! You're going to die hard and slow—here in my hands, you butcher of women!"

With the snarl of a beast over his kill, the frenzied Jocelyn's fingers clamped on the Indian's throat until the bloodshot eyes bulged and the tongue protruded from the painted face. Then the circling fingers eased their grip and the savage gasped for breath. Again, like steel hooks, the fingers shut, again eased while the strangling Narragansett fought for air. As a fox tortures a wood mouse, the embittered youth slowly snuffed out the Indian's life. At last, with a shiver, the body relaxed and lay still.

"Judith! Judith!" All the bitterness of his desolate heart was in the cry. He crushed the silken strands to his lips, then thrust them to his breast beneath his leather doublet. Rising, he turned to Niles and Dunbar.

"Come on," he cried. "There's more work to do this day."

"Look!" said Niles. "They're burning the wigwams! The Mohicans are driving them out with fire."

At the far end of the stockade red flames were beginning to lick the lines of bark houses where the corn was burning like tinder. The shrieks of women and children and the whoops of the Mohicans mingled with the racket of musketry. The pungent fumes of burnt powder tainted the air. Hunted like beasts from their hiding places, old and young were followed and hacked down by Mohican tomahawk and white man's saber, their scalped bodies left to stain the snow. At length, driven from their last stand in their wigwams, the survivors of the Narragansett warriors fled in groups over the wall of the stockade, leaving their wounded and dead to the scalping knives of the blood-drunk Mohicans.

The most important battle to be fought in New England before the Revolution had been won.

As the flames roared up the lines of bark houses, to leap to the bitter sky and flood the shadow-packed stockade with light, General Winslow called a council of war. In a circle, the taut-faced survivors of his officers stood around him, their stained coats and doublets whitening with the snow which had started to fall as the wind rose.

"Major Treat, your plan saved us," Winslow said, his voice strained with meaning. "We have fought a desperate fight, and the Narragansetts are broken." He paused as his glance rested on Treat's bandaged right hand. "But the night will be bitter and the snowfall deep, so we must come to a quick decision. Major Appleton, how many captains and men have we lost?"

"There are six captains dead and many men, sir. The sergeants are calling the company rolls now. In the blockhouse and flankers in care of the surgeons and chaplains are a hundred and fifty wounded."

"I, myself, have lost three captains," announced Treat sadly, "Gallup, Marshall, and Seeley; and Mason is sorely wounded. It cost us dear to scale that wall."

"'Tis a great pity," said Winslow. "But they have gone to the reward of brave men. Now 'tis our duty to care for the wounded and the living. Major Treat and Captain Church urge that we camp here, eat, and obtain some rest while our wounded are cared for. There is great store of dried fish, corn, and beans in the wigwams, still unburned. They advise that we put off our return until daylight."

There was fierce objection from the Massachusetts officers. "Why, we would be mad to stay here!" blurted Moseley.

"Tonight, broken as they are, the savages will not rally to attack us on our march back," insisted Appleton. "But tomorrow they will gather their reserves, of which we hear there are thousands, and fall on us. I say return tonight while we may."

Over Treat's drawn face passed the ghost of a smile. "What have nine hundred able-bodied men, with the Mohicans and Pequots as well, to fear from the Narragansetts after today?"

Bradford nodded his head in agreement. "Major Treat is right," he said.

"But our guides claim the Narragansetts can raise two thousand warriors by tomorrow," protested Appleton.

Treat vigorously shook his head. "Through our spies, we of Connecticut have long known that they could put into the field little more than twelve hundred fighting men. Half of these are already roasted in those wigwams, dead on the snow, here, or have fled with their wounds to the forest. Your fears are ungrounded, Major Appleton, for they never attack superior numbers. To march back now, General Winslow, would mean the death of many wounded men."

But the Bay officers were inflexible. To a man they insisted on immediate retreat. "Our ammunition and supplies are at Smith's Landing. The savages might capture them," protested Appleton. "To stay here is madness. Better hazard the march back than to be caught without powder."

A black scowl distorted Church's scarred face. "Return over that blind trail tonight, when we have a place to sleep and care for our wounded? The plunging of the horses will kill half the men they carry. I say rest here and eat."

"I say to stay is monstrous folly," stormed Moseley, his feral eyes blazing beneath his helmet. "Our ammunition is too low to risk a fight. If we wait, they're certain to attack us on our return."

"How can they ambush us with our Mohicans in front and on our flanks and rear, Captain Moseley?" objected Treat. "You seem to forget that Connecticut troops have never been ambushed."

"But our ammunition is too low to risk a fight, Major Treat," demurred Winslow. "And this fire will soon consume the corn in the wigwams."

"The fire can be cut off if we move at once. The blockhouse and flankers are still untouched. As to powder and shot, the savages must be in the same straits as we are. I have many sorely wounded men who will die if we move tonight. In God's name, sir, think of the helpless men!"

Winslow seemed to hesitate. He scowled down at the snow at his feet, struggling with his problem, while the Bay officers, talking angrily in low tones, waited for his decision. At last he raised his face, grave with apprehension. "I wish to speak with Captain Prentice and learn the condition of his horses," he said. "I shall return at once and give you my decision. In the meantime, look to our wounded."

There were loud murmurs of protest, but Winslow left the stockade on horseback, with a guard of Plymouth men, for the brook where Prentice's troop were waiting in the forest.

Shortly Winslow returned through the scrub on horseback and approached the opening in the palisade, now cleared of the tree. Before he could enter he was stopped by the Bay officers, who had been joined by their chief surgeon, Daniel Weld. Moseley stepped forward.

"God's blood! General Winslow," he shouted, "if you are set to hold us here overnight in this death trap, I'll shoot your horse from under you before I let you enter!"

"The wounds of our men will stiffen overnight, here," protested Weld, "and tomorrow we may not move them! In God's name, let us return to Cocumcussoc!"

Winslow's uplifted hand checked further protests from the men filling the breach in the stockade. His face was crimson with rage as he cried: "Captain Moseley, your wild threats only make your case the worse. You'll hear from me later. Gentlemen, my mind is fixed. We start back tonight."

The announcement was greeted with cheers while, with a shrug, Treat scowled at the incensed Church and nodded to his superior officer on the horse. "So be it," he muttered.

The sniping at the stockade by groups of savages lurking in the swamp was increasing. It was clear that they would have to be driven off before the march back could start, or the colonists would have a pack of snapping wolves in their rear.

"General Winslow," said Church, "I ask leave to call for volunteers to clear the forest of those skulkers. We must not have them on our heels when we start."

Winslow agreed. With a hundred men and a body of Mohicans, Church left the stockade. At his side walked Dunbar and Jocelyn. The Mohican scouts disappeared in the shadows ahead and were soon firing at groups of retreating snipers.

"Keep a sharp watch," warned Church. "In this half-light some may let us pass them and fire into our backs."

The firing increased as the scouts and volunteers discovered and drove scattered groups of Narragansetts deeper into the swamp. At length the three men reached a thick stand of cedar packed with shadow.

"Have a care," warned Church, gripping his belt ax. "This is a snug place for a Narragansett ambush. We'll go right into it and drive them out if any are there."

The three men started into the cedar thicket, when two muskets flashed in their faces. Church's belt ax slipped from his hand. The flintlocks of Dunbar and Jocelyn roared blindly into the murk. Then, from a distance, a Narragansett's mocking jeer was flung back at them. Dunbar knelt to examine Church's wounds.

"He's hit in the hip," he said to Jocelyn.

There was no answer. The kneeling Dunbar turned, to find himself alone with the muttering Church. "Lad," he called, "where are you? Are you hurt?"

From the shadows came a deep sigh. Dunbar rose from the wounded Church, his heart cold with fear. "Where are you, Jocelyn?" He groped a few paces, and the toe of his moccasin collided with a body on the snow. He bent over it. "Can you speak? Where are you hit?"

"In—the chest," came the slow answer. "I am—little hurt—but—my legs—gave way. My strength—oozed from me."

"Do you bleed?"

"No, give me—your hand," Jocelyn muttered. "Once—on my feet—I may walk."

Dunbar lifted the heavy Jocelyn to his feet and groped for the wound. A slug had pierced the leather doublet beneath the collar bone. Then he called loudly. English voices answered, and aid arrived.

Back in the blockhouse, lit by torches of pitch-pine, the wound in Church's hip was dressed. Then, supported by Niles and Dunbar, his face gray under its tan, Jocelyn clamped his teeth as they removed his doublet and shirt and a surgeon examined him.

"These are but scratches on his head and shoulder, and he has bled but little," said the latter, "though it appears the bullet in his back passed desperately close to his lung. But with his youth and great strength he will soon be as sound as ever if you can get him back to Smith's Landing. God be good to us, we'll lose many on the way tonight!"

"We shall get him back," muttered Dunbar.

"Ay, we'll lose many on the way," added Niles, "but not this lad. We will care for him."

When Jocelyn's wound had been dressed and bandaged, Dunbar replaced the lock of golden hair on the boy's breast and laced up his doublet. A faint smile crossed Jocelyn's gray face as he murmured:

"I knew it was hers, Dunbar! I knew it was hers! It will leave me no more. It will always stay here—safe."

§4

SPARKS from lines of burning wigwams filled with dried corn set fire to a flanker. A sheet of flame already leaped along one wall of the stockade. Shortly, as the rising wind slanted a barrage of snow on living and dead, the fort became a roaring funeral pyre. Leaving the blazing stronghold of the Narragansetts, the column of men and horses, with a screen of Mohicans in front, on the flanks, and in the rear, began its march through the numbing cold into the needle-pointed drive of the blizzard. Behind them the sky flamed with fire-glow and the naked forest was garish with dancing light. Ahead, blackness barred their way like a wall. Men turned to fling back a last look, then, with lowered heads, plunged into the murk.

Led by troopers on foot, each carrying its burden of wounded lashed to the saddles and supported by their comrades, Prentice's horses started over the fifteen miles of drifted trail. Travois, made by lashing the ends of two poles to a horse's sides while the opposite ends trailed on the snow, carried most of the dead. Jumper sleds of birch, hastily fashioned by skilled axmen, drew wounded too weak to sit a horse. As the white slant which beat upon the floundering men thickened and the frost increased, the column moved through the drifting flatlands to the high country. When it stopped to rest, many spent from hauling sleds and supporting the wounded on horses, sagged to the snow, to fall instantly asleep, until their comrades lifted them to their feet and drove them on. Reaching the high country, the long line of snow-crusted wraiths, with their wounded and dead, halted.

"How goes it, lad?" demanded Dunbar, who with Niles had marched on either side of the horse supporting the slouched body of Henry Jocelyn.

The whitened figure lurched forward. "I'll walk now," Jocelyn muttered. "There are some worse hit—who need to ride."

"You'll stay where you are!"

"I can—walk."

"Learn if his wound bleeds," whispered Niles.

Dunbar reached under the bear robe lashed around Jocelyn's shoulders to protect him from the cold and snow, and groped with his bare hands.

"I feel no blood on his doublet nor the bandage. Tie his mittens to his wrists and pull his cap over his face, that it may not freeze," ordered Dunbar. "This wind is cruel."

As the Plymouth men stood beside their friend, a snow-crusted figure, his right arm carried in a sling, burst from the blackness.

"Are you Plymouth men?"

"Ay, sir," answered Niles.

"I hear that the Plymouth youth who smashed the doors of the flanker and blockhouse with an oak ram today was shot with Captain Church. 'Twas a gallant deed. It saved many men. Where is he? I have that in this leathern jack that will hearten him."

"He sits here, on this horse," said Niles, licking his frost-cracked and bleeding lips at the thought of blood-warming rum.

Treat peered at the slumped figure on the horse.

"Here, give him a throat-full of this rum." He handed the jack to Dunbar, who placed it to Jocelyn's lips. The half-conscious man sucked up a mouthful.

Then, to the delight of Dunbar, Niles, and the trooper who led the horse, Treat handed them the jack. Each gulped eagerly and signified his satisfaction by a loud "Ah!" and the smacking of frozen lips. Taking the leather jug, Treat placed his hand on Jocelyn's leg. "Take good care of him," he said. "We'll need him before the war ends." And he was gone.

The column again took up its slow march along the ridge where the white drive beat as pitilessly as a sand blast, on living and dead. Exhausted men with frost-bitten hands and feet sagged to the snow, to be lifted and driven on. Horses screamed and whinnied as they floundered and plunged over rocks and down timber with their helpless burdens. In their agony, wounded men prayed to their Maker or cursed him. Some begged their comrades who limped beside them to end their misery. The strong who supported them reviled the officers who had driven them to this Calvary in the snow. But the stiff shapes lashed to the poles behind the horses were silent. Their torture was over.

The troops had stopped to rest and ease the wounded. Slipping off one of Jocelyn's mittens, Dunbar squeezed the big hand. "The blood still flows in his hand," he said to Niles. "Look to his face."

Niles pushed back the fox-skin cap crusted with snow and laid his hand on Jocelyn's cold features. "'Tis not frozen," he said. "Are you in pain, lad?"

Jocelyn mumbled incoherently as he swayed in the saddle. Dunbar reached under the bear-skin robe. "He seems all right," he said, "but the plunging of the horse has hurt him sorely. I can feel him wince as I walk holding him. But he will not cry out. He's made of iron."

Shortly the news drifted down the column, passed from company to company: "General Winslow and forty men are lost. They've left the path and wandered off into the forest."

"Name of God! if the savages are on our heels they'll be slaughtered to a man," gasped Niles.

With a snort of disgust, Dunbar growled, "General Winslow has killed many a stout lad this night by listening to those Bay officers and ordering us back through this storm. He may repent it now."

"Amen!" grunted Niles, through cracked lips.

The column resumed its slow march. The shrieking of the wind through the naked forest which creaked and snapped above them fused with the groans of the wounded and the curses of exhausted men with frozen hands and feet and frost-blackened faces, shuffling knee-deep through the snow. The searing cold bit to the bone, as with lowered heads they struggled on. At the next halt those supporting their comrades found that some horses carried men no longer wounded. The lashed burdens on their backs were stiff in death. Not idle had been the warnings of Treat and Church that the march back that night would take a heavy toll.

Hours of torture followed for the men who had started that morning for the Great Swamp to save the frontier towns of the Bay colony and Plymouth. Shorter and shorter grew the intervals between the halts as numbed men, floundering through drift and brush, tripped and lay where they fell, refusing to rise, and begged to be left to the mercy of a quick death. Horses plunging in the deep snow broke their legs on down timber and rocks and were shot. And as the cold increased, ever down on the creeping column whipped the white barrage of the snow.

Slower and slower moved the crusted shapes through the moaning forest. Somewhere, over miles of torture, lay the sanctuary of Cocumcussoc. But in the hearts of those still strong, as they propped the wounded on the horses or dragged their comrades to their feet and drove them on, there was little hope of reaching Smith's blockhouse that night. Then, in a lull in the shrieking wind, a wail of despair drifted down the floundering column: "We're lost! We've left the path! God help us, we're lost!"

"Do you hear, Dunbar?" whimpered the exhausted Niles. "They say we're lost."

With arms propping Jocelyn in the saddle, the weary Dunbar leaned against the horse. "Ay, I heard." He knew that if it were true, it was but a matter of time when the weaker men like Niles and the trooper who led the horse would refuse to move and would welcome the creeping stupor of the white death as surcease from their agony. "Would you see your wives and little ones again?" he stormed. "Then stand up like men. You'll soon freeze lying there."

But the advance Plymouth company had already halted and, ignoring their cursing officers, lay slumped on the snow, oblivious of the cold which bit to their bones. Beside the snow-crusted horse where Dunbar supported the half-conscious Jocelyn, the trooper and Niles remained sprawled, refusing to rise. For a space the desperate Dunbar leaned his weight on the horse to ease his stiff legs, while the blizzard rocked the oaks above him. If Henry Jocelyn were to live, they must reach the camp soon. Then he suddenly straightened. "What's that?" he cried to the fast-drowsing men at his feet.

With groans of protest the two sat up and the three listened. Above the whining of the wind lifted far-off voices. "It sounds like the whooping of the Mohicans," said Dunbar.

" 'Tis only the wind," muttered Niles.

"It may be an ambush. Get up, damn you! and start your blood in your hands so you can handle your muskets! Get up or, God help me! I'll beat you with my sword."

The two men rose stiffly to their feet and fumblingly wiped the snow from the action of their guns. Then hoarse cheers drifted down the column of hopeless men. "'Tis the Mohicans!" rose shouts from the Plymouth company in advance. "The Mohicans see the lights of the blockhouse. We're back! We're back at the camp!"

Men crazed with joy sank to their knees and prayed. Others raved and cursed their leader, Winslow, as they reeled ahead on frozen legs and feet they could not feel. Wounded men with bloody bandages stiff with frost straightened in the saddles and forgot their agony. They were back at Smith's Landing, where fire and food and sleep—sleep after twenty hours of marching, fighting, and numbing cold—awaited them. Sleep, after exhaustion, despair, and pain. At last! Sleep!

"Thank God—we soon—may rest," blubbered Niles, as the aroused column of white wraiths again shuffled forward through the snow.

"A fire—at his feet—and a fresh dressing of the wound—will comfort him," returned Dunbar through chattering teeth as he supported the swaying figure in the saddle.

As Dunbar spoke, Jocelyn suddenly lurched forward over the horse's neck, shaken by a paroxysm of coughing. Dunbar stopped the horse, caught the sagging body in his arms, and eased Jocelyn to the snow.

They pushed back the snow-crusted cap from his face. "It's wet, Dunbar!" gasped Niles, feeling with bared hand. "That's blood on his mouth. He's coughing blood from his lungs, Dunbar. The bullet reached his lungs."

A great fear lanced through Dunbar as he groped with shaking hands beneath the bear-skin robe. The doublet was frozen stiff. It was blood—frozen blood—his fingers touched. "He's been bleeding through the bandage," he gasped. "I had not thought he was losing that blood. He never told us."

Again Jocelyn was racked by coughing. In the blackness Dunbar touched the wounded man's lips with his fingers. They came away wet.

"The plunging of the horse, Niles. The plunging of the horse was too much." Dunbar's voice was thick with grief. "But never a groan from the lad while he slowly bled to death—never a groan."

"Can we do nothing? Surgeon Fuller, of Barnstable, is with Lieutenant Barker's company. I'll fetch him, Dunbar. He may help. I'll fetch him, Dunbar."

From Dunbar's deep chest came a groan of despair. "It's too late,

Niles—too late. His doublet's stiff with frozen blood."

"Make him speak— Speak to us, man! Won't he speak to us?"

Dunbar placed his lips close to the ear of the man coughing in his arms. "Can you hear me, lad? In heaven's name, speak, lad—speak to me."

Blood oozed from Jocelyn's mouth. Dunbar wiped the quivering lips with snow. "He's going," he whispered.

With a choking sound the kneeling Niles turned away his head.

"Speak, lad! It's Dunbar, Giles Dunbar, your mate," begged the man who held the limp head of his friend on his shoulder.

Suddenly Jocelyn stiffened. His right hand clutched at his chest. "'Tis here, Judith," he muttered. "In my doublet—'tis here—safe on my heart. You can—sleep—now."

Lashed to the horse, Dunbar and Niles brought their dead back to the camp ground at Smith's blockhouse.

The following morning the lost General Winslow and his party found their way into the camp at Cocumcussoc, where a log fire burned near the blockhouse, to drive the frost from the earth that forty men might find a grave.

A sloop from Boston with supplies and ammunition reached Smith's Landing, and the men who had marched fifteen miles through the snow to battle their way into the Narragansett fort and return through the bitter night nursed their wounds and rested. In all, seven captains and seventy-odd men had died, and one hundred and fifty had been wounded. Church, Bradford, Mason, and the wounded who could be moved were sent to Newport, while Winslow waited for reinforcements from Boston.

Through the winter, the war dragged on. Shattered though they had been by the Great Swamp Fight, Canonchet rallied the survivors of the Narragansetts and joined Philip in the death struggle between Indian and white man. In the spring a single stone house at Warwick was the sole white dwelling left standing between Providence and the Narragansett shore.

In Providence, Captain Arthur Fenner and the seventy-seven-year-old Roger Williams commanded the thirty men holding the garrison houses, who, in Williams' words, were "those who stayed not away." The remaining men of the settlement, with the women and children, had taken refuge in Newport and Portsmouth.

One morning late in March, the men in the two garrison houses, aroused by the barking of dogs, looked out across the Moshassuck to see Indians in the distance. Against the objections of his friends, Roger Williams crossed the river and found there Canonchet, the Narragansett sachem.

"The men of Providence," Williams said to the Chief, "had no part in the fight in the Great Swamp. Why do you come here to attack them?"

"Brother Williams, you are a good man," replied the Narragansett in his native tongue. "For years you have been our friend. Not a hair of your head shall be touched."

"Massachusetts," warned Williams, "can send thousands of men against you, and if you kill them, the King of England will send more to take their place."

"Let them come," answered Canonchet; "we are ready. But you must return to your fort and stay there, for my young men are thirsty for blood and will burn the other houses."

The Narragansetts burned a large part of the little settlement, but the garrison houses held out and their thirty defenders escaped.

Up and down the upper Connecticut River settlements and the Massachusetts and Plymouth frontiers the allied tribes brought death and the torch. Smug in their belief in their heaven-sent wisdom of refusing to use their praying Indians as scouts, the Bay colony leaders watched their gallant but misguided officers fall into ambush. But late in the spring, reason and the example of Connecticut prevailed, and the friendly Indians were enlisted as scouts and proved their worth. Massachusetts had learned its lesson.

The hostile Indians were gradually overcome and hunted down. Canonchet was captured by Connecticut troops and executed. Later, Major Talcott, from the same colony, destroyed the fleeing remnants of the Narragansetts. And Philip, driven by Church into the swamps of his homeland, was eventually shot.

This ended the war in southern New England. The war whoop ceased to blanch the faces of women and children on lonely farms. The flames of pillaged villages no longer lit the skies. And the survivors of the red owners of the land either became the slaves of their white conquerors or, as fugitives, sought sanctuary in the northern forests.

2. The Son of Henry Jocelyn

§5

FOUR YEARS after the peace, on a day in June, a small fishing sloop with a short-gaffed, loose-footed mainsail, and the name *Sea Gull* painted on her square stern, dropped anchor in the Taunton River off the Somerset shore. A squat sailor, with enormous shoulders and a disfiguring scar across nose and cheek bone, brought alongside the sloop a skiff they had been towing. His left foot was gone, and in its place a maple peg was strapped to the stump below the knee. The sailor held the skiff while the master of the sloop, a man of medium height, with a pair of honest gray eyes, helped his wife into the boat, shipped the oars, and seated himself.

"Bring us back the making of a stout sailor man," said the peg-legged tar, with a grin that twisted his face into a grotesque mask, as the skiff moved away.

"That I hope to, Israel," answered the man rowing; "but we know not what he will favor. I trust he has much of his father in him. In that case we shall soon have a stout extra hand on the sloop."

"It may be they will be loath to part with the lad," said the woman, as the man rowed toward the wooded shore. "We have little enough to share with him." Her plain, kindly face, framed by brown hair caught under a sad-colored hood, looked older than her thirty-five years.

"They have six, so the letter read," replied the man. "Every mouth to feed, however small, means work for someone. He lost all from the Wampanoags, his house and barn and stock. It likely has been a cruel struggle to start anew."

The fisherman rowed on, while the pale blue eyes of the woman watched the shore. "It was kindly of him to take in the boy, not his own," she said.

"As the letter was read me by the Magistrate," replied the man, "the father of the lad died in Dunbar's arms after the fight at the Narragansett fort. And when he heard that the grandmother was dead at Taunton and the boy had no home, he straightway rode there and fetched him back. He put great store in Henry Jocelyn, he said in the letter."

The oarsman ran the skiff up on the shingle beach and helped his wife out. At a farmhouse near the shore they made inquiries and were told to follow the rough cart path inland through the forest. At length they reached a clearing. At the far end of a field of young corn stood a small frame house with a mud-plastered stone chimney at one end, and a barn, built of slabs set upright, around which chickens scratched. Near it stood a slab smokehouse, and the stone coping of a well, with a watering trough made from a hollowed log. Above the well hung a great sweep. In a meadow, sheep and cattle and a horse grazed together. At the approach of the strangers a large man in leather breeches and locram shirt, who had been holding an ax while a boy turned a grindstone, stopped his work. From the door of the house a woman, with two children at her homespun skirt, curiously watched.

"Good-day!" greeted the farmer.

"Good-day to you, Goodman Dunbar," returned the fisherman. "I am Thomas Stanton, fisherman, of Newport, and this is my second, Content. We are come for the boy."

The eyes of Giles Dunbar clouded as he turned to his wife, who had joined them and was furtively eying the worn but clean frock of linsey-woolsey and the coarse, untanned leather shoes, with wooden heels, of the strange woman.

Their mutual scrutiny over, Dunbar said, "I put great store by the lad, Goodman Stanton. Already he has the big bone and the proud eye of his father, though the color is blue like the mother's. There's sense in that yellow head of his far beyond his years."

"We shall sorely miss him, Goodwife Stanton," sighed Dunbar's wife, a woman with the soft eyes of a deer and a body overthin from the toil of a pioneer life. "He has a stout heart, and, oh, such a merry one, though so easily hurt. But we have six mouths to feed, and the Wampanoags left us with nought but our land. We had a neat, large house with clapboards and glass windows with leaded panes, but time we had not nor money for aught but a small house when we builded anew. Someday we hope for a better one."

"Even so, were you not kin," said Dunbar, "I would keep him. There's the making of a stout fellow and a wise one in that small body of his. But it takes a gentle hand on the halter to lead him."

"Where is he?" asked Stanton.

"Yonder in the forest with two of our younger ones. They went to seek our sow who is rooting for ground nuts with her litter. We durst not leave her out at night lest she meet a bear or a stray wolf."

" 'Twas a year before we learned that Jocelyn had died in the Great Swamp Fight," explained Stanton. "Then we had a letter writ to his mother, in Taunton; but she was dead and there came no answer. Only by good fortune we got word this spring you had taken the boy. It was a kindly act, friend Dunbar."

"No," said the big man, his eyes suddenly misty with memory. "His father died in my arms. Never have I seen his like. But his heart was broken. He treasured not his life."

"Judith was but my distant kin," spoke up Content Stanton, "but we had lost our only two and were lonely. When at last we got word you had the boy, we had the letter wrote you."

Shortly, childish shouts and laughter, and the barking of a dog, drifted up from the woods.

"They are coming," said Dunbar.

Three barelegged boys appeared, driving a sow with her squealing progeny up the path. The eyes of Tom and Content Stanton brightened with anticipation.

"He's the youngest of the three," said Dunbar, "yet he tops my two by half a head, and he but eight. He rides the bull calf like a horse, so stout and nimble is he. You never saw his father?"

Stanton shook his head.

"He was a man to fill the eye. For strength and fire there lived not his equal in all Plymouth Colony."

"What is the lad called?" asked Content.

"Hugh," answered Goodwife Dunbar.

The three boys came shouting up the lane, following the pig. Two were dark, like Dunbar, but the tumbled hair of the third caught and held the sun like burnished gold, and as they joined the waiting group at the cabin, Tom Stanton thought that the boy's eyes were a deeper blue than the sea off Block Island on a clear October day. Suddenly abashed at the presence of strangers, the boys scurried into the barn.

Stanton smiled at his wife. "Think you, you could mother that lad?"

The homely face of Content Stanton lit with pleasure. Her faded blue eyes sparkled. "'Twould be an easy task to love him, he seems that winsome!"

Dunbar's face sobered as he met his wife's doubtful look.

"Goodman Stanton," he said, "there's one promise I ask before you take the boy. You'll share with him fairly as you prosper and treat him like one of your own?"

Tom Stanton eased Dunbar's mind as to what manner of man was taking away Henry Jocelyn's son when he said: "I'm a humble man that lives by the sea. The sloop back in the river is mine, with nets and fishing gear, as is the little house we live in on the harbor shore. So long as fish swim in the sea the lad will never lack for food as, God help me! he'll not want for kindness from us two. Our own are gone. He'll be as our own."

Dunbar scowled as he stared down at his boots. Then he glanced up quickly at his wife, coughed, and rubbed his stubbled chin with a bony hand, as if laboring with a problem and the difficulty of stating it. He cleared his throat and began, "'Tis necessary and right that you know what I'm about to discover to you." As she watched her husband, a pained expression spread over the thin features of Prudence Dunbar. "In the last year or two," he continued, "the lad has given us much cause for uneasiness and doubt."

Tom Stanton and Content exchanged startled glances.

"Yes," said Dunbar, "much as we treasure him, he has given us no little concern."

"What mean you?" demanded Content.

"Why, the lad has a queer streak in him. He's fair touchy when chided for a fault. Now my lads forget a cuff or a sharp word in the next breath, but not so Hugh. He'll brood over it for days. His spirit is set so high."

"How have you managed, then?" demanded Content, her eyes serious with misgiving.

"By gentling him as you would a half-wild colt whose spirit you'd not break. I early learned he'd not be driven. Why, two summers past when I laid a light hand on him for something he'd done, his eyes filled with tears and he looked at me, his mouth all a-tremble, then took to his heels and made for the forest, where he stayed hid for two days, till I found him."

Stanton's jaw sagged as he stared doubtfully at his wife. Had they made a mistake? Would they regret this move?

But Content was smiling. "Goodwife Dunbar and I understand," she said with confidence. "The lad is more easily hurt than most. I doubt not that love will lead him where a harsh word only stiffens his strong will."

Prudence Dunbar's brown eyes softened as she nodded at the other woman. "Moody though he is at times and hard to understand, we have treasured him. For a big heart and a stout one beats in that round chest of his."

They passed the wash bench by the door, on which stood buckets and a keeler, and went inside the house into the fire room, lighted by windows of oiled paper, at one end of which was a stone and mud-plastered chimney. In the room were a table of planks hewn by hand, stools, a settle, a spinning wheel, tubs of salt beef, and a churn. Against the wall was a dresser, on which stood wooden trenchers and bowls. Some crude, homemade toys lay in a corner, and the dents on table, stools, and settle were eloquent of a household of children.

From the summer beam and floor joists, overhead, hung strings of dried apples, pompions, hands of seed corn, onions, and dried herbs. And beside a ham and a flitch of bacon were suspended the smoked haunches and tenderloin of a deer. On trammels hung from the lug-pole stretching from ledge to ledge of the chimney iron kettles simmered over a low fire. They sat down, and Prudence Dunbar brought pewter cups of hard cider, a poplar trencher heaped with smoked venison, rye-'n'-Injun bread, and a cake stuffed with wild strawberries.

But it was not without much coaxing that young Hugh Jocelyn was led by the hand from the barn by Dunbar and persuaded to face the strangers. Suspicion and covert hostility looked from his blue eyes as they stared in turn at Stanton and the smiling Content. Finally, standing at Dunbar's knee, his mouth smeared with maple sugar from a slice of bread he clutched in a brown fist, his shyness faded as Tom Stanton talked.

"What a time we'll have on the sloop, lad, you and Israel and me," Stanton said. "We'll work down at dawn past Brenton's Neck and the Dumplin's, round Brenton's Point, and bear away for the Sakonnet shore to the east'ard where the gulls are divin', with the wind in our eyes and the salt spray on our faces. Then we heave over the lines with the big hooks with the white eel-skin pulled over 'em for the fish to mark, and we sail by-and-yon through the slick where the blues chase the herrin' to the surface and the gulls dip."

The eyes of the boy deepened with interest as Stanton went on. "Of a sudden a yell from you as a big one strikes your hook, and it's fast work I make to seize you by the foot before he hauls you from the sloop and away."

The sugar-smeared mouth of the boy gaped and his eyes blinked in wonder. He had forgotten the bread in his hand. "What do we then?" he asked.

"Why, then we haul him in, and hand over hand, a ten-pound blue, snappin' and thrashin', with teeth that would take your finger off, and eyes like unto a wolf's."

The lad sat breathless. Seizing his opportunity, Tom Stanton continued: "Then we'll go a-lobsterin'. Great black ones with claws bigger'n my hand! What a pinch they can give with them claws! But the meat in 'em! Ay, that's the sweet morsel to lay on a lad's tongue! Hast ever eat lobster?"

The boy shook his yellow head. "How do we kitch 'em?" he demanded.

Dunbar smiled at his wife.

"In sunk pots of wood, lashed to a buoy," said Stanton. "Lobsters follow the bottom. Then there's big, hungry tautog that feed along the weed on the rocks and ledges. And juicy they are to eat. And there's silver-bellied squeteague and sea bass—big striped ones, and mackerel and cod and halibut in season out on the shoals. And when the sturgeon run up the rivers to spawn, we'll spear 'em by the light of a candlewood torch. In the spring there'll be shad in our net in the Sakonnet, sweet but bony, with the eggs a fit dish for a king. By the look of those stout arms, 'twill not be long e'er you toss the lance, lad. Then, someday, we'll catch a lazy old swordfish a-dozin' off Noman's Land when the sea runs oily and the sun is fair drowned in haze."

"Swordfish!" gasped the entranced boy. "They do have swords like that big one of Father Giles over the hearth with the gun?"

"Ay, lad! Their snouts grow out into a long bill like a sword, that'll split a skiff as 'twere an eggshell. And they be big fish and strong—long as a horse. When we have the iron fair in one, why, we toss over the empty rum keg lashed by a long line to the lance head, and away he goes, towing the keg. 'Tis often a pretty chase but at last he tires, and we pick up the keg and haul him aboard. On the wharf at Newport the flesh of a big one brings many a shilling from the housewives."

The dark brows of Hugh Jocelyn met as he looked doubtfully up into the face of Prudence Dunbar. With a shake of the head he tossed his yellow hair from his eyes, now almost black from the thrill Tom Stanton's words had shot through him.

"I wants to see the fish with the sword! I never seed the ocean water—only the river."

"That you shall, now!" exclaimed Stanton. "And someday we'll sight a school of whale a-spoutin' and a-rollin' off Martin's Vineyard."

"What do they spout?" demanded the entranced boy.

"Why, they spout water high in the air! They be big beasts, as big as my sloop, and a blow of their tails would fair crush her."

"Then you'll go with Goodwife Stanton—to Newport, child?" asked Prudence Dunbar.

The boy's brown face flushed as he nodded his yellow head and, reaching, had his arms about the neck of the woman, who held him close. "I loves you," he whispered, hiding his face on her breast. "I loves you and Father, and Giles and Henry and Tom and Bess, but I wants to see the fishes that are blue and them with swords, and the lop-lopsteers who has claws; and the whales that blows water. Then I'll come back."

Tom Stanton had won. With a few colorful strokes he had stirred the boy's fancy with the magic of the sea, an enchantment that would never lose its power.

It was a new and strange world into which Hugh Jocelyn entered that afternoon when he reached the river with Tom and Content Stanton and was rowed out in the skiff to the anchored *Sea Gull*. As the skiff came alongside, two hairy paws reached down and swung the excited boy over the low rail, and he stared into a grinning mask, the like of which he had never seen. The bronzed features of the broad face were crossed by a bluish-white cicatrix reaching from flattened nose to jawbone, lending to Israel's grimace a touch of the sardonic. The startled boy stared with open mouth at the scarred face of the old tar.

"Welcome to ye, lad," chuckled Brandy. "Now lay off the twistin' and wrigglin' like a wench abroad in her Sabbath finery and give old Israel a squint at ye. Look your fill at this maple leg. 'Twas lost in a good cause the very year I took this kiss from a Spanish cutlass off Hispaniola."

"This is Israel, Hugh," said Content, laying a hand on the shoulder of the awed boy as he raised his curious eyes from Brandy's wooden leg to his scarred face. "Speak to him and be not afraid."

At the words, Hugh Jocelyn straightened, and his sea-blue eyes boldly met the twinkling gaze of the leather-faced sailor. "I be not afraid," he blurted, and reached and placed his hand in Israel's gnarled fist.

"Well spoken, lad, and good mates we'll soon be. Sout-timbered ye are, of a surety, with a chest like the bow of a king's ship," chuckled Israel, his squinting eyes measuring the small boy as he would judge the lines of a newly launched brig. "An able little craft," Brandy observed to Tom Stanton, "with the blue eye of a gunner. Over big he is for his age and over big he'll be when we've put ten year of the schoolin' of the sea into him. And burn me! one the wenches' heads will turn after," he chuckled.

A frown darkened Content Stanton's face. "Sweet words for a child to hear! You sailors!" With a sniff she turned from the two men and the boy.

In all his life at the Dunbar farm Hugh had been but seldom to the shore of the river. Only at a distance had he seen sailing craft, and now, as the sloop got underway, his eyes were big from staring. Israel Brandy named the ropes, spars, and gear of the sloop to the wondering boy as they bucked the flood tide in Mount Hope Bay on their way to the narrows. It was early summer and the shoulders of

Mount Hope, near which Philip, the Wampanoag, had met his death, were green with the fresh foliage of oak and maple splashing the olive background of cedar and pine. Across the bay to the south lay Common Fence Point, beyond which the growing fields of Portsmouth lay drowsing in the afternoon sun.

Sitting on the hatch combing with Brandy, the boy watched the swelling jib and close-hauled mainsail as the sloop beat down the bay, passed through the narrows, and, leaving Hog Island to starboard, headed for the Prudence shore. With a stubby forefinger the sailor pointed out the landmarks to Hugh's roving eyes.

Aft, at the tiller, Tom Stanton said to his wife, busy with her knitting: "Israel's eyes fair sparkled at the sight of the lad. I doubt not there's the making of a smart sailor in him. His fancy was soon caught by the bluefish and the swordfish and the spouting whales."

"Ay," sighed the woman, "you two will make a rough sailor of him, no doubt."

Stanton scowled as he leaned against his tiller and slanted an eye at the bulging leach of the mainsail. "I like not what Dunbar told us about his uncertain temper and sulkin' and runnin' away when cuffed. 'Tis well enough to talk of gentlin' him with soft words. But there's no nursin' a seaman in a blow when work's to be done. I doubt not a rope's end is what the lad needs for his sulks."

"Shame on you!" spat out Content. "You talk of rope's ends and the lad not yet nine. He shall not be spirit broke! Goodwife Dunbar told me he was handier and more willin' around the farm than any of hers. But while they had to be driven, only gentlin' brought out the best in him."

"I like not a sulker," returned Stanton. "'Tis my purpose to make a stout fisherman of him. If he broods and shows peppery in the temper, so much the worse for him."

"And I doubt not when we've grown to lean on him in our old age he'll be off with some privateersman who'll turn his young head with tales of gold on the Spanish Main. Then we'll lose him or he'll return, as Israel did, lacking a leg or arm and his talk rolling with great oaths."

"I hope not to see that day," said Stanton, a scowl settling on his bronzed face. "Too many of our lads have shipped on these strange craft that come nosing into Narragansett Bay to refit; pirates, I doubt not. Some never return. Others come back to scatter Arabian gold and Spanish doubloons among the light women and to fill the ears of honest men with wild tales of the Indy Sea and the Spanish Islands."

"I noted a strange brig in the harbor when we started for Somerset," Content said.

"Ay, the crew were making merry in the Blue Porpoise when I stopped for a jack of rum. French and English and mustees, some with rings in their ears, and one, a Dutchman, lacking half a nose from the slash of a cutlass. I doubt she's an honest trader to Barbadoes and Surinam, here for pipe staves, salt fish, beef and horses, though the landlord says that is her business."

"I mean to mother him for no such end," said Content, with decision, her kindly eyes on the lad, forward, listening to Israel's steady patter.

The sloop reached the Prudence shore and started a straight reach home with the westerly breeze. To the little boy whose eyes, never before, had seen wide water nor a sloop, except at a distance, the voyage was one of pure enchantment. Standing forward at the weather rail with Israel, gripping a stay in a stout hand, his yellow hair fluttering in the wind like ripe wheat, the eyes of the wondering boy drank in the picture of sky and islands and foam-flecked bay. As the heeling *Sea Gull* buried her nose, the sting of flung spray on the boy's eager face sent him into shouts of delight. Occasionally Israel Brandy turned to the man at the tiller with a wink and a nod of approval toward the lad who, for the first time, was filling his round chest with sea air and feeling the flick of salt on his cheeks. Strange though it all was, and exciting, Israel Brandy could mark no sign of fear in the roving blue eyes of the little boy who stood beside him. Here, indeed, was the making of a rare sailor.

Familiar only with the forest and meadows of Giles Dunbar's Somerset farm, young Hugh Jocelyn gaped in amazement at the view which met his staring eyes as the sloop passed between Gould Island and Coddington Point, left Coaster's Harbor Island on the larboard, and slipping in between Goat Island and Easton's Point, entered Newport harbor. The brigs, ketches, pinks, and sloops at anchor, the wharves, with their storehouses, which reached into the fairway, and the scattered buildings of the town, which followed Thames Street along the shore and extended, in places, back into the green upland, past the sails of Benedict Arnold's windmill, held the small boy fascinated. Never had he seen a village, much less a city, such as Newport, a seaport of four hundred houses.

"What think you of Newport, lad?" asked Stanton, his twinkling eyes watching the gaping boy when the little sloop came about and dropped her anchor at her berth inside Gravelly Point. But Hugh Jocelyn was too dazed to answer.

While in the moving sloop, the little boy had been amazed and fascinated by the ever-changing panorama of water and island. That and his interest in the sloop's gear and in the handling of the big mainsail, accompanied by Israel Brandy's running comment, had, for the time being, banished thought of the Dunbars and the home he had left. For a small lad reared on a farm surrounded by forest, it was high adventure, and the thrill of it had driven all else from his mind. But when they went ashore in the skiff and stood on the gravelly beach of the Cove, the glamour of the voyage died. A sudden sense of loneliness and loss left him cold. He looked with doubtful eyes on these three strangers with whom he had cast his lot, and a swift homesickness and longing for the comfort of Prudence Dunbar's motherly arms gripped him. His small fists clenched and he swallowed hard, that they might not see the shame of his tears, but he yearned to be back at the farm with Giles and Henry and Tom and Bess. He saw again the mist in the eyes of Prudence Dunbar as she handed him the small bundle that contained his sole pair of shoes and some clothes, and caught him to her heart in a swift hug at parting.

Hugh Jocelyn stood on the beach staring at his bare feet and manfully battled with his rising emotions. It would not do to let these people see how he felt. He was ashamed of the great lump in his throat and the tears he knew were in his eyes. He was ashamed of the loneliness that almost made him shiver, so cold it made the pit of his stomach. He dug the bare toes of one foot into the gravel, with head lowered, that they might not see his face. Then a hand rested on his yellow hair, and he looked up into Content Stanton's homely features, and the mother in her shone from her kindly eyes as she smiled down at him and found his hand.

For an instant the lonely little boy gazed up at her questioningly. Then, in delight, he exclaimed: "Why, you look like Mother Prudence. She smiles that way."

Content bent down to the boy, and her arms circled him in a warm hug as she kissed his yellow head. Of a sudden, the cold and the loneliness in his heart faded and he felt warm and happy and safe.

§7

SIX years later, on a windless day in the spring of 1686, a slouchy, angular figure of a man sat dangling his thin, stockinged shanks and square-toed shoes with tarnished pinchbeck buckles, from the stringpiece of Coddington's Wharf, which reached into the Cove formed by Gravelly Point in the little harbor of Newport. Beneath his long, untidy hair, the wide brow, high-bridged nose, and sensitive mouth bore the stamp of the aristocrat, but his dark eyes were red and circled, his face pale, and his shirt rumpled and stained.

"The Honorable Richard Trelawney," he muttered, as he blinked at the sloops, shallops, and brigs anchored in the harbor. "Younger brother of Lord John Trelawney, of The Towers, Sussex, Master of Arts of Trinity Hall, Cambridge, Devotee of Bacchus and Minion of his Satanic Majesty, why hast thou not the manhood to end it all in this kindly anodyne, here, which laps the timbers at thy feet?"

The man on the wharf ran his thin fingers through the long hair which fell to his rumpled neckband. "No! No!" he exclaimed. "I'll be burned, if I send such overwelcome news to my dear brother! There is much in this little port that amuses me. It may yet furnish me ample food and housing, not to mention Canary and Madeira. And life is still sweet, though it be monstrous dull this far from London."

The speaker paused, to rest his eyes on the roofs and chimneys of the little port, and on the slowly turning sails of the stone windmill on the hill beyond. "Of a surety, I'll gather the young about me and cram their tousled heads with knowledge of which their illiterate sires are guiltless. For, clearly, of education, here, there seems little, although 'tis said there was a school, now closed for lack of a master, and money to pay him."

The Englishman burst into laughter as he slapped his lean thigh. "Dick Trelawney, of Trinity Hall, turned schoolmaster in the colonies for his bread and—ah—rum! But, Grace of God! what do I see approaching?"

The startled eyes of the younger brother of Lord John Trelawney squinted hard at a skiff moving rapidly over the water from a small sloop. "Yes, 'tis the face of a mere boy—sixteen or seventeen mayhap," he muttered. "Name of God! is this Rhode Island or the Isle of Rhodes? Newport or Hermopolis on Syros? For the muscles of a galley slave ripple over that brown back as water is rippled by wind. And the hair! Yellow as ripened Sussex corn!"

Stripped to the waist and brown as a young Indian, with a heave of his oars the boy sent the little skiff sliding up to the wharf near the curious Trelawney. Making his craft fast, he reached above his head and with no effort drew himself up to the stringpiece. Then he pulled over his head a tattered locram shirt he carried tied to his waist.

"The get of a viking!" murmured the interested Trelawney. "Or, perchance, a young Danish sea robber landing at East Anglia to harry the coast."

For a space the boy stood, hands on hips, his blue eyes doubtfully studying the man watching him. Then he slowly smiled, as he asked: "You wish to go aboard your craft? I will carry you."

The infectious smile warmed Trelawney's lonely heart as sunshine warms sand. "No," he answered. "I came here to consider the matter of a quick oblivion, my lad." The Englishman returned the smile, and there was that in it that eased the boy's embarrassment. "But my mind has changed. Come, sit here beside me! I would have talk with you.

How old are you and what is your name?"

The lad dropped beside the lanky Englishman and clasped a knee in his brown hands. "I'm fourteen years—soon fifteen. My name is Hugh Jocelyn."

Trelawney's lean jaw dropped as he stared in unbelief. "Fourteen years? Why, you have the growth of a lad years older, and a stout one!"

Young Jocelyn's eyes fell as he wiggled his toes and reddened with pleasure at the remark. "You are but lately come to Newport?" he asked shyly.

"I came but lately in the sloop *Sea Bird* from Boston Town," Trelawney chuckled. "'Tis a rare place, filled with sermons, sanctity, and sin, and the mad scratching for money." He spoke as if to himself, while the bewildered boy listened. "And no man may draw a long breath without leave of the smug clergy, but with money in his purse he may draw many a drunken breath to the profit of some Puritan churchman." With a wry smile the Englishman dismissed the subject and pointed. "You belong to that sloop out there?"

"Ay, we are fishermen, my father, Israel Brandy, and me," said the lad, proudly. "'Twas but three days agone that I fastened the lance to the father of all swordfish, the biggest fetched in for years."

"You—you hurled the lance?"

"Me? Why not?" Red blood drove into the round face. The blue eyes darkened with anger as young Jocelyn faced his doubtful questioner. "You have doubt of me? Feel that arm." He brushed back the ragged sleeve and flexed the brown biceps of his right arm, while Trelawney reached and gravely tested it.

"Slay me! but 'tis harder than so much rock, and big," admired the Englishman. "You are stout, far beyond your years, lad. Now tell me, has this fishing left you time to learn your letters? Do you read and write?"

Again the boy reddened. His eyes fell to his bare feet. "We are humble folk," he said. "Father Tom and Content may not learn me. They read not nor write themselves."

"Tch-tch!" The red-rimmed eyes of Dick Trelawney soberly contemplated the anchored craft in the harbor. His lean hand rubbed his unshaven chin as he squinted, deep in thought. After a space he asked, "Will there be no school here in winter?"

"There was a school. But there is none now for the poor. 'Tis said a schoolmaster learns the children of the gentry. The poor may not go, for they have not time or money."

"The gentry hire a tutor, eh, for their children? Well, what have the poor to do with learning?" Trelawney muttered as if unmindful of the presence of the puzzled lad. "When the poor are cozened into a bad bargain, the rightful reading of which they trust to some clerk, they bind themselves with their mark. 'Tis enough that the poor make only their mark—enough for the rich merchants, eh?"

The perplexed eyes of Hugh Jocelyn studied the face of the stranger as he rambled on. "Do you read words and set them down with a goose quill touched with ink?" asked the lad.

Ignoring the question, Trelawney abruptly demanded, "Do you and your father fish through the cold weather when the ice comes?"

"No, we hunt goose and swan till they leave the coast. And we make trips to the Sow and Pigs Reef and the shoals off Martin's Vineyard around Noman's Land for late cod, haddock, and mackerel. But while the ice lasts there is little fishing. We run home often with our shrouds and deck white with ice and snow. The Cove, here, is sometimes frozen over."

"Would you learn to read and write and the setting down of figures and their uses?"

The eager face at Trelawney's side suddenly glowed. "We have a Bible," the boy exclaimed, "but none of us may read from it. If I learned my letters I could read to Mother Content. She is not my true mother. My true mother, Judith, was killed by the Indians."

"Tch-tch! 'Tis a pity! And your father, lad?"

"He died as well, after the great fight in the swamp. Tom Stanton is my foster father. This spring we fetched a load of sturgeon to Updike Newtown and I saw at Cocumcussoc my true father's grave. A great rock marks it." The boy's voice was low with awe. "'Tis said that forty soldiers lie buried there."

"Orphan, eh?" mused Trelawney. "Stout and nimble of mind far beyond his years, with the head of a son of Thor!" He broke from his reverie to squint at the boy who watched him. "So 'tis a tutor for the spawn of the gentry but no free school for the poor for lack of taxes to pay a master? What say you, young Jocelyn, that this winter we launch a school for the sons of the humble people of Newport? Already am I pledged to a group of mincing dames to conduct a course in the manners and deportment at the court of our late King Charles, with instruction in the use of the quill and in the reading of simple English." He gave way to his laughter. "My faith! Dick Trelawney, of Trinity Hall, turned pedagogue, ladies' maid, and dancing master!"

Trelawney's self-mockery left the boy dazed. He stared at the Englishman as if he doubted his sanity. At last he said, "You lie at the King's Head?"

"No, at the Blue Porpoise, and with the bedlam of the sailors, white, black, and brown, over their blackstrap and rumbullion, 'tis small rest I lay my bones to in that ordinary." Trelawney's red eyes shifted sadly from Hugh's face to the water at their feet as he finished.

"Yet they seldom do outsit me, for my loneliness is deep and my thoughts but poor company."

The face of the boy wore a bewildered look. "The King's Head will have no brawling or late drinking," he said, after an interval. "'Tis there in the great room that the Governor and Council sit and take their comfort."

"I know. 'Tis the meeting place of the Magistrates and the rich merchants, where the latest news from overseas and the colonies is washed down with many a cup of Madeira and metheglin. The so-called gentry and the Magistrates!" With a chuckle Trelawney slapped his thigh. "Why, some of them may scarce write their names—these smug merchants who ship their pipe staves, salt fish, and beef to Jamaica and Barbadoes and bring back molasses and sugar at a pretty profit, to be turned into rum. These great men of the town, who work their slaves and their white and Indian bond servants till they drop!"

Never before had Hugh heard the merchants of Newport made so light of. Prisoners of the late war and bound out to service, Indians worked on the island farms or as extra hands on the ships, and black slaves were common. What was there strange in that?

"True, lad," continued Trelawney, "the lesser folk and the seamen seek the Blue Porpoise, the Butterfly, and other taverns where the fare is cheaper and the rum and spirits rougher to the throat and more fiery when downed. I lie at the Porpoise through no choice of my own but from the necessity of a lean purse."

The boy suddenly stood up and pointed to a small house on the shore of the Cove. "There flies the signal of Mother Content. She waves her white apron. There's no dallying when she waves. I will tell her of what you promise—that I will learn to read letters. It will hearten her."

"That you shall, lad, and write and cipher. And later, if they do not harry me from Newport as they did from Boston for scoffing at the bigotry and the iron rule of their clergy and their pretense of a university out at Cambridgetown, I promise you in time a taste of the classics and history, and more than a mouthful of good Will Shakespeare and the rest of the Elizabethans of whom they are as ignorant, in Boston, as newborn babes. For the so-called learned men among them read little but theology and that the quibbling of crackpots, and some Latin."

The boy's dark brows pulled together in his perplexity as he stared into Trelawney's smiling face. Then, with a shake of the head as he turned on the stringpiece to drop into the skiff, he laughed: "You talk like a sermon on the Sabbath. I make small sense to it. But you will hold to your promise and learn me to read?"

Trelawney roared at the boy's retort. "Name of God, well spoken! So their windy mouthings make small sense to you, eh? Nor to me, lad. Of a surety my promise holds good. You shall learn to read—and soon, if I know a quick mind when I meet one."

As the boy was about to start away in the skiff, Trelawney said, "Have a care not to drown yourself before I may put that into your yellow head which will bring you dreams—dreams strange and wonderful."

"You will come to us some night and talk to Father Tom?" pleaded Hugh.

"That I will," replied Trelawney, waving his hand as the skiff sped for the stony beach. "I shall come soon, never fear." He rose and ruefully surveyed his clothes and smoothed his long, black hair. "Name of God! the lad has shamed me," he said. "He has that about him that draws one as the sun draws water."

§8

THE excited Hugh ran his skiff up on the gravel beach of the Cove, where lay a small anchor, lobster pots, and a gill net drying on a frame in the sun beside some fish flakes, and hurried to Tom Stanton's house, set in a garden a short distance from the shore. He found Content waiting at the door.

"That strange Englishman who has lately come here from Boston, what wanted he of you that kept you with him so long on Coddington's Wharf?" she asked.

"Did you have fear he would eat me?" laughed the boy. "Oh, Mother Content, what think you he will do? He promises to learn me to make letters and read them. Then I may read to you from your Bible, so long unopened."

A smile slowly shaped itself on Content Stanton's homely face, but swiftly gave way to a look of doubt. "But we have no money wherewith to pay him. There is rumor that he is to learn letters and deportment to some dames of Newport who are not Quakers, and learn the children of some of the merchants as well."

"He said that on the wharf," replied the boy.

"He has been overlong at the Blue Porpoise for his own good," sniffed Content. "There is much drinking and carousing there by sailors and shameless women. And he is reputed to talk uncivil of the clergy. I like him not."

"He spoke not to me of money," protested the boy. "He doubted my age and felt my arm, then said he would learn me my letters and put that in my head that would learn me to dream. What meant he by that?"

Content doubtfully shook her head. "I know not, my son. But this Englishman has been much in his cups of late, learned though he may be. I doubt that we will wish him to learn you, for he will have money for it. We are too poor."

They entered the small frame house, with its diamond-shaped windowpanes set in lead, where, in the fireplace at the end of the main room, the supper was cooking in an iron kettle hung by trammels from the lug-pole. Inside the large hearth stood other kettles, a frying pan, and a trivet on which rested a pewter pot. Beside the hearth was a wash bench, with a keeler and bucket. A slab table, three stools, a settle, and a little dresser, on which stood poplar-wood trenchers, bowls, and pewter mugs, together with a spinning wheel, completed the furniture of the room. Above the stone fireplace hung two flintlock muskets, powder horns, and pouches for fine shot and bullets.

"He's coming here to talk with Father Tom," said the boy, stubbornly. "In the winter, when the fishing falls off and I am much ashore, he plans to learn me my letters. He spoke not of money. He knows we are poor."

Content Stanton frowned as she bent and stirred with a wooden spoon the fish and vegetable stew cooking in the kettle. She had heard much gossip of this Englishman who had lately been expelled from Boston and lay at the Blue Porpoise. The yellow-haired boy who watched her grave face had become, in the six years since the day the sloop had sailed to Somerset and brought him from the Dunbar farm, the very center and focus of her existence. Headstrong and difficult he had been to manage, with a tendency to moodiness, which baffled and worried his simple foster parents. And having grown, like a shoot of Portsmouth corn under the sun and sea mists, until his candid eyes now looked level with hers as they talked, her mother's heart encompassed the boy with a wall of affection to shut off a world that she, nevertheless, knew would someday burst through and take him from her.

"When Tom returns from Portsmouth with the firewood they are drawing, we will speak with him of this Englishman. But my mind is set against him. Now fill your trencher and eat, for it will be late before Goodman Dexter's lazy oxen bring the wood and your father returns."

As the hungry boy sat on the oak stool at the table and, with the freshly baked rye-'n'-Injun bread Content lifted from the oven in the chimney with a wooden peel, ate two heaped trenchers of red sturgeon and vegetable stew, his thoughts were of the lanky stranger he had met on the wharf and his strange talk. No one, before, had ever talked with him like this Englishman. Now, as he ate, he smiled with pleasure as he recalled what the stranger had said about his muscles. It was good to be praised, and by a stranger who had never seen him bury a lance head in a swordfish or bring down a gray goose or a whistling swan over the Sakonnet marshes with Tom's musket loaded with coarse shot. He liked this tall Englishman with the unkempt hair hanging to his neckband, who had talked so wildly but in such a friendly manner. Most of the Newport men who were not fishermen never so much as looked at a boy except to scold him. But this stranger had not only gossiped and laughed with him as an equal but had promised to learn him his letters. The thought sent a thrill pulsing through him to his bare toes. To be able to read! None of the boys alongshore could read. They had had no time to go to a school even when there was one.

Hardly hearing the occasional remarks of Content, who watched him closely as she knitted on a woolen stocking, Hugh wondered, as he ate, what Trelawney could have meant when he spoke of giving him a mouthful of "good old Will"—something about a "spear." Clearly 'twas a man he spoke of—but a "mouthful" of him? What did he mean by that? And who might be this "good old Will"? The Englishman was just making fun—laughing at him, no doubt. But Hugh had not cared, for had not Trelawney promised to learn him to read letters? Neither Tom nor Content, none of the fishermen and sailors he knew, and but few of the shopkeepers and artisans could read. Only the clergy, the rich merchants and magistrates, and the masters of the deep-sea ships trading to Barbadoes and Jamaica could read and figure, so Tom had told him.

How the stranger had laughed to be told that he talked like a sermon on the Sabbath! And what a pleasant laugh he had, despite his red eyes and white face that looked as if he had never seen the sun! Now what did he mean when he called, "I'll put that in your yellow head that will bring you dreams"? Dreams? What manner of dreams would the stranger put in his head?

"You say this Englishman is coming here some night to talk with Father Tom?" Content asked.

"He did say so, and I hope 'tis true."

"Well, here's Tom, now, with the oxen and wood. I hear them shouting at the beasts. We will take counsel with him when he has supped."

That night, as Tom Stanton was finishing his supper, the crunch of a peg leg on the gravel walk leading to the door announced the approach of Israel Brandy, who lived with a sister a stone's throw from Stanton's house.

"What think you, Israel, of this Englishman lately come to the Blue Porpoise learning Hugh his letters this winter?" asked Tom, as the old privateersman filled his pipe, lighted it with a red ember from the fire, and seated himself on a stool.

Israel removed his pipe, spat into the dying coals of the cooking fire, and scratched his square chin. His small eyes beneath the bristling brows closed in thought, while his mouth worked rapidly up and down in seeming unison with the laboring of his brain. Then he opened his eyes and prepared to deliver the fruit of his cogitation.

"Drop down to the shore, Hugh, and learn if the skiff lies well above the tide; 'tis overhigh tonight," ordered Tom. "We wish to talk alone."

The boy left the house, and Israel, clearing his throat, began in his husky bass voice: "Firstly, with all his faults, his broodin' and his flashin' in the pan when hard-spoken to, the lad has that in him, if suffered to grow, that'll make him a mate, and later, a master. Do you dispute me there?"

Brandy thrust forward his heavy chin, his great shoulders hunched, as he held Tom Stanton's eye. "Burn me, no! 'Tis beyond dispute," he continued, not waiting for the slow-thinking Tom to answer. "Already not yet fifteen, the lad's a seaman and handy fisherman. In a boat he's happy, and he swims like a porpoise. I say the sea's his fortune. Now—" Israel puffed hard on his pipe, blew a cloud of smoke into the air, and jabbed a huge forefinger at Stanton, "to rise above bo's'n or gunner the lad needs must learn to read and set down figgers. Sink me! 'twas lack o' that held me and you to the foc's'le in our youth, Tom Stanton. In '69, when the *Lady Belle* lost captain and mate in our fight with the pirate sloop off Tortuga, the crew voted me that was bo's'n to be captain. That was fit and proper, but narveegation I knew not nor how to cipher, and we sighted Boston, me on the poop, her sailin' master, but with a slip of a lad who had learnin' chartin' our course. No!" thundered the aroused Israel, rising and punctuating his remarks with vicious thrusts of his pipe in the air. "We'll never hold the lad to longshore fishin' when he's older. He'll go deep-sea in two year, mark my words! He's got a pair o' them sea-blue gunner's eyes. 'Fore we knows it there'll be another war and he'll ship on a privateer."

"Ay," agreed Stanton, "'tis gospel truth. The lad is bound to go deep-sea when grown."

"Then 'tis high time he knew the use of goose quill and the settin' down o' figgers. Slay me! I look to the day when I touch my forelock to Captain Hugh Jocelyn!"

As she listened to the old salt, Content Stanton's eyes flashed in anger as her woman's heart beat with dread of what the future would bring to the boy who had left the room. "He's but a child, as yet, Israel Brandy," she burst forth. "And he stays here with me, his mother! He needs not learning to sail the sloop and lead a fisherman's life off Newport. 'Twas good enough for Tom Stanton and 'twill be good enough for his foster son. I like not your wild tales of the deep sea. Look at yourself! What has privateerin' made of you?"

Israel's sole reply to the thrust was the rapid action of his expansive mouth.

Swallowing hard on an over-large mouthful of rye-'n'-Injun bread, Tom Stanton looked sharply at Content as she turned from the two men. He nodded significantly at Israel, who puffed stoically on his pipe. Then he flung at his wife, "You'd not have the boy rise in the world, eh? You'd keep him a poor fisherman like myself? He'll go far, that lad, give him the chance. But you'd keep him lashed fast to your apron strings, like a calf to a tree." There was a bitterness of middle age in Stanton's voice—the bitterness of the realization of lost opportunity and vanished hope.

Content girded herself for the struggle and boldly stood over the two men hunched on their stools. "'Tis well enough to dream of what might be," she cried, "but I've loved him from the day he came to us, a little lad. He filled the aching place in my heart left empty by those I lost. True, he's touchy and overproud, and often beyond my understanding. But for years he's been a joy and comfort, and now you'd tear him from me—take away my only child!"

Tom glanced at Israel's scowling mask and hopelessly shook his head, while Content stopped to dab at her eyes. "You'd give him learnin' and send him deep-sea to make a master of him—a great man Israel can touch his cap to," she struggled on. "But half the families on this island mourn for someone lost at sea, and someday we'd mourn for him."

Stanton's patience was near the breaking point. He rose and paced the floor while she passionately continued.

"Oh, I doubt not he'd become a master on the ship of one of our fat merchants, who'd smirk and pat his back when he come in safe with a rich cargo from Barbadoes." Stanton scowled and raised his hand in protest, but she would not be denied. "Then some year, murdered by pirates or lost in a storm, he'd not return, and I'd grieve through my old age for the lad I once held close to my heart. That's what your learnin'll do for him, Tom Stanton!" Content's voice went shrill with the violence of her emotion. "Let him abide with us—a longshore fisherman, I say—and save me a lonely old age."

The distressed woman flung herself from the room and went out to seek solace from the stars and the soft moonlight that drew a silver trail across the surface of the placid harbor.

Tom nodded at the stolid features of the puffing Israel. "To her mother's heart," he said gently, "he'll never be a man—always the little lad she took to her arms from the Dunbar's."

"Ay, 'tis so," muttered the old sailor through his pipestem, with a shake of his shaggy head. "The sea is a cruel, hard mistress; but once the call of her creeps into your blood, the tears and wailin' of all the mothers in the colonies'll scarce hold a lad to shore."

Stanton nodded. "There be few sailors in Newport that read and know figgers. If this Englishman'll learn the lad to read without payment of money 'twill be a sin to refuse him."

"Ay, a monstrous sin! But, burn me! Tom, sometimes I fear for the lad's touchiness and fancies and whims when he once leaves home and ships deep-sea."

"Yes, 'twill go hard with him at first."

"Unless he puts a brail on that sudden temper of his, he's set for trouble. With us who knows him and treasures him, 'tis understood, though sometimes hard to stand."

Tom sighed. "Among strangers he'll come upon trouble a-plenty."

"Rot my bones, he will! But if he keeps growin', there'll be few strangers who'll lightly cross him when a man. I hope by then he'll have a hawser on his temper and be done with his dreamin' and hurt feelin's."

"Amen!" muttered Tom.

§9

SHORTLY HUGH appeared at the open door with Content. "Come with me in the skiff, Israel," he said. " 'Tis the brightest night of the spring. The harbor lies flat as the floor. Those foreign sailors are singing on that brig. Let's row out and listen."

Israel wished to learn more of this stranger, Trelawney, and readily consented. It was a soft night in May and the lifting moon-bathed town and harbor in its silver magic. As the flat surface gurgled behind Hugh's dripping blades, the skiff slid toward the anchored brig lately in from Madeira and the Wine Islands, and the voices of sailors singing in a foreign tongue drifted over the water. On the shore and wharves the lighted windows of the King's Head, the Blue Porpoise, and other taverns twinkled. Here and there one of the larger dwelling houses of the wealthy merchants was lit, but for the most part the thrifty people of the little port sat outside their darkened houses in the mild spring evening and saved their tallow dips and candlewood for the long nights of winter.

Rowing close to the brig, Hugh rested on his oars. "What is it they sing, Israel?" he asked, as a languorous Latin love song, carried by a clear tenor voice, drifted to their ears. "Our people never sing that pretty."

Israel chuckled. "Nay, we English slant to sailin' and tradin' and fightin'—not to singin'. They be a mixed lot on that brig, Portygee and Spanish and mustees from the Barbary and what-not. Ripe villains, I'd name 'em, from a look at 'em I had today. There be three this night in the Porpoise, with their scuppers awash when I stopped for a taste o' rum. I like not the breed. Knife men they are, and tricky. When rolled on their beam-ends by an honest fist, they reach for a knife strapped to a leg or hid in their shirts. We English carries our knives in our belts, open to the eye of all, and in a friendly dispute delights in our fists."

"But they do sing pretty. Listen to that!" said the boy.

"Ay," sniffed the old salt, "they do sing, I allow; but once lay a Newport privateer on their beam and board 'em with some seasoned lads I've sailed with, cutlasses in their hands and hell in their hearts, and these Portygee and Spanish do sing another tune. Burn me! how they do squeal when they see the cold steel and a boardin' party of stout Newport and Portsmouth lads behind it."

Israel laughed and slapped his good leg as if the memory of a forgotten fight on a Spaniard's deck had suddenly flashed through his mind. For a long time Hugh allowed the boat to drift around the windless harbor, talking as only a boy talks when alone with the man he loves. The scattering lights in the houses disappeared, for people went early to bed and rose at daylight. Only the windows of the taverns glowed from the shore and wharves when Hugh rowed the skiff slowly homeward. They were close inshore when Israel suddenly asked:

"What goes on there? Hear you that bawling? It appears from the Blue Porpoise!"

Hugh rested on his oars. From the shore a volley of shouts and curses broke upon the tranquil night. "You be right!" cried the boy. "There's trouble stirring at the Blue Porpoise!"

"It's them Portygee I saw there this night, rolling their beams' ends under in rum which they may not carry, bein' customed to wine," said Israel, as Hugh rowed rapidly toward the glowing windows of the tavern on Thames Street. "Now keep clear of the door, lad, while I find me a club and lend Landlord Prey a hand. I want no knife stuck into your young ribs. It sounds like a brawl in the public room, and these foreign snakes carry knives and use 'em!"

The skiff slid up on the pebble beach and with much grunting Brandy began groping for a club. Not waiting for the slow Israel with his peg leg, Hugh ran up the lane to Thames Street, to the open door of the Blue Porpoise, through which issued an uproar of shouts and oaths in a foreign tongue, the sound of crashing wood and scuffling feet, and the excited voices of Landlord Prey and his servant, John.

As Hugh reached the door, a man staggered from the public room, lurched into the surprised boy in the dark outside, and stumbled on, to slump to the ground in the black shadows beside the tavern. The boy regained his balance and looked into the room. It was in a wild disorder of overturned tables, stools, and scattered pewter and wooden mugs dripping their contents on the sanded floor. Beside an upset table sprawled a swarthy sailor on his back, the blood oozing from an ugly cut on his head. Behind another table, in a corner, two others stood at bay, gripping sheath knives and snarling curses at the landlord and his stout servant, who threatened them from across the table with clubs.

Hugh's heart beat hard against his ribs. A fight! There had been many at the inns, among the sailors, but this was the first he had ever seen. A thrill shot through him as he stared at the two swart, ringed-eared foreigners who cursed so savagely as they flourished their knives from behind the tables, where they were cut off from retreat through the door by the menacing clubs of the Inn people. Who was the man who had lurched into him and fallen outside in the bushes? Another sailor? And where was Israel?

At that instant, with a spring, one of the Portuguese cleared the overturned table, dodged a savage blow from the landlord's club, and started for the door. Already inside, Hugh leaped away from the knife thrust aimed at him by the escaping sailor and fell headlong over a stool. Then the room was filled with a bull-like bellow, as the square frame of Israel Brandy suddenly blocked the open door, a heavy club in his hand. The surprised sailor stopped suddenly in a crouch, his knife poised to strike.

"Ha!" roared the old privateersman, his scarred face flaming with the joy of a fight, as he glared at his enemy. "Knife man, are yeh? Lay on, lads," he roared. "Over their rail and give 'em the steel!"

With a yell, the Portuguese leaped at the one-legged man with the scarred face who barred his way. His knife flashed in a vicious thrust, but down on the reaching forearm crashed Israel's short oak stick, and the knife slithered over the floor. A quick shift of the peg leg, and Brandy's huge left fist drove into the sailor's jaw as he stumbled past. As the Portuguese reeled sideways from the blow, an oak stool in the hands of a boy with blazing blue eyes and yellow hair bludgeoned him senseless to the floor. Hands high in air, the third sailor begged for quarter from the storming Brandy, Hugh, and the Inn people who rushed him.

"Truss him up, Landlord Prey," cried the panting Brandy, still hot with battle fever. "Clew 'em up like a brailed sail! We'll have a pretty show of these three at the whippin' post in the Parade when the Magistrates have viewed their villainous faces." Israel turned and patted

Hugh on the shoulder. "A sound blow, lad, and swung proper. There's nought like a stool to bring 'em down. He scratched you not with that knife?"

"I dodged him," said the excited Hugh.

"Well dodged, too, lad."

"But I feared for you when he thrust, Israel."

"Huh! Israel Brandy's not weathered a hundred boardin' parties to be split down the middle like a cod by a mustee like this one," he said contemptuously, poking the unconscious sailor with his peg leg. "Now, John, that you have 'em safely stowed, go call a constable and the watch, who no doubt dozes somewhere in a snug berth in some man's hay."

The two unconscious sailors were laid, bound like bags of meal, side by side, awaiting the watch, and John hurried out to rouse a constable from his bed. Then Israel said, with a grimace, as Landlord Prey wrung his hand in thanks for his aid:

"Landlord, this boardin' party, bein' Hugh and myself, will be grateful if this ship's stores, bein' retaken from the mutineers, so to speak, would supply a drop of that which would relieve the dryness in my throat."

"Well spoken, friend Israel," laughed Prey, a large, full-fleshed man, with a red face and small, pig-like eyes, and he brought two pewter mugs of rum, and one of cider for Hugh, which they clicked together in honor of their victory over the Portuguese navy.

Israel took a deep draught, cleared his throat, and turned to Hugh. "Whilst I was sailin' free for the door, lad, my leg tripped me. I saw him leap for you and my heart fair stopped. I luffed a bit when he thrust at me, and by the look of him I'll say, between you and me, he went down with all hands on board. What with the liquor and the clubbin', these two'll sleep sound." Brandy inspected his left fist. "I near stove this fluke on this one's jaw."

Landlord Prey suddenly turned to Israel. "But the Englishman? Where went he?"

"The Englishman? I saw no such," replied Brandy.

Hugh's heart suddenly faltered. "Was it him, the English stranger, who fell against me when I ran to the door?" he cried.

"Of a truth," answered the landlord. "It was him the sailors started trouble with. They were deep in their cups. He sat with them, talkin' in Portygee lingo, I take it was. Of a sudden some word was passed, and Trelawney struck a sailor with a mug. Their knives were out, and John and me run for our clubs. We come back and beat the sailor who was after him to the floor, but the Englishman staggered outside."

Hugh felt a sickness in his middle. Trelawney! He must not be hurt! Not the pleasant stranger who was to learn him to read! Not the merry Trelawney!

The three hurried outside the Inn and began a search in the shrubbery, dark with shadows. Shortly Landlord Prey called:

"He's here! Give me a hand, Hugh; you stout. We'll carry him inside, where there's light."

Hugh ran to where Prey knelt beside a crumpled shape. The worried boy touched the cold face. He spoke. But there was no reply. They carried Trelawney into the tavern and laid his limp body on a long table. A lump on the pale forehead was smeared with blood.

"Ah! Here's what doused his lights," muttered Israel. "A stool over his bow, eh?"

"But see," cried Hugh, pointing to a small slit in Trelawney's worn coat, high on the shoulder where the neckband had partly concealed it. "They reached him here, with a knife! There's blood there."

" 'Pon my soul, they did!" muttered Brandy. "But it bleeds little. A small blade it was. Steeleetto they calls 'em, scarce bigger'n a picktooth, these furriners often carry in their sleeve. Small harm it likely did him, but we'll unhook his coat and bind up the cut. It hardly reached the lung."

While they washed and bandaged the slit in his shoulder, Hugh bathed the pale face of the unconscious man. Then Landlord Prey held a sneak cup of brandy to the half-parted lips. Trelawney swallowed, choked, and opened his eyes, to meet Hugh's anxious face close to his. They held him in a sitting position and Prey poured the remainder of the brandy in the small wooden cup down the wounded man's throat.

The dazed Englishman coughed, then muttered, "What happened?"

"You're all right," soothed Hugh. "Not hurt much. You feel better?"

Trelawney's deeply circled eyes blinked at the yellow head and tanned, round face close to his. His bloodless lips slowly shaped a smile. " 'Tis you—the young viking!" he muttered, staring into the boy's solicitous face. "I called to you—in the melee—when the press was thick around me: 'A moi! A moi, Jocelyn!' And you hacked—your way—to my side. Semper fidelis! I knew. I knew."

"He's fair frenzical," muttered Israel.

Trelawney's gaze was glassy and fixed as he gripped Hugh's hand in his long fingers, while the boy wondered at his strange words. Shortly the wounded man relaxed and closed his eyes. Then the room was filled with chattering townspeople, aroused from their beds by John, the servant, who had brought the watch and a constable.

When the three Portuguese had been taken away to be locked up, and the last excited neighbor had left, Landlord Prey said to Brandy: "This Englishman, here, I doubt my wife nor the maid have time or wish to nurse him while he gains his strength. 'Tis fever from the wound, he has, for his head is become hot."

"But he would pay," said Hugh, cold with a sudden fear.

"Nay," Prey's shrewd eyes hardened. "He has little left with which to pay. Today I peered into the purse he left on his bed when he went out. 'Tis near empty. I found, also, a letter which the sloop, *Fair Maid*, just in from Boston, fetched him. I got it read by Mr. Sheldon, the Town Councilman. It said the Lord Trelawney, his brother, was pressed for funds and was sending no money. I doubt I can keep him."

Israel raised his square chin and vigorously worked his expansive mouth as he scowled at the oak timbers of the ceiling. Hugh Jocelyn's anxious eyes sought the white-faced figure on the table. Deserted by his brother. No money to pay for his keep. Sick and without friends. The merry Trelawney who, that day, had promised to learn him his letters. No, it could not happen—not to him. He should not be cast out, wounded. Fear stood in the boy's fast-winking eyes.

"'Tis cruel hard to turn a sick man out on the world," growled Brandy. The thrust of his stare drove down the small eyes of Landlord Prey.

"I keep no ordinary for those who cannot pay," muttered the latter.

Hugh's fingers closed on Israel's thick arm. "We will take him," he said. "Content shall nurse him back to health."

Israel's bushy brows lifted. "Content?" he rasped. "Lad, are you mad? Content will not take him in."

Hugh's answer was to take Trelawney's limp shape in his arms and start for the door. "I'll carry him to the skiff," he said. "Come on!"

"Well, rot my bones, but the lad's in earnest!" gasped Brandy as he stumped out of the room and followed Hugh with his burden to the shore.

Amazement and disapproval were written large on the candle-lit faces of Tom and Content Stanton as they stared at the unconscious guest Hugh had brought unannounced to their house.

"He's sick and helpless," insisted the boy; "there was nought else to do when that pinchpenny of a Landlord Prey would no longer keep him."

"But where shall he lie if we take him in? There's no bed save ours and your pallet in the loft," objected Content, when she had heard from Israel the story of the fight at the inn. Her dazed husband meanwhile paced the room doubtfully, shaking his head over the responsibility Hugh had so suddenly thrust upon them.

"He shall lie on my pallet, fetched from the loft and stowed in the corner there beside your wheel," answered the insistent boy. "Ashore, I'll tend him. When we're away on the sloop, you'll look to him, Mother Content."

She gasped, glanced at Tom, then back to the blue eyes that pleaded the cause of the unconscious Dick Trelawney. "I—I—durst not—"

"Yes, you will, Mother Content, for your heart is too kind to refuse a roof to a sick man." Hugh took the woman who adored him by the shoulders and looked into her doubtful face. "What does the minister tell us about the good Samaritan? You'll be the good Samaritan. Yes, you will!"

"I know; I know. Poor creature!" murmured Content, glancing at Trelawney's white face. "But we are—"

"Yes, we're poor," interrupted Hugh. "But 'tis summer and there be plenty of fish and clams to share with a helpless man. There's nought like clam broth for the sick. And there's tanzy, comfrey, and St.-John's-wort in the garden for his wound. Besides, do not forget, 'twill be from him that I learn to read your Bible."

Tom Stanton and Israel nodded significantly to each other as Hugh gradually overcame Content's scruples.

"Sink me!" chuckled Brandy to Stanton, "but the lad could talk a head wind into shifting to a fair one, such a way he has with him."

Tom sighed. "'Twill be hard on her to harbor a stranger, but once them blue eyes of his looks into hers and his mouth sets, it's shorten sail and run for it with poor Content—she dotes on every yellow hair in his head."

"'Twould a warmed your blood, Tom, tonight, to see him bring down that Portygee with the stool. A proper blow, I'll swear!"

§10

ON the morning following the affair at the Blue Porpoise, the bay beyond Goat Island was running white with a fresh sou'wester, and at daylight the sloop did not move from her anchorage in the Cove for the fishing grounds. So Hugh left his patient, moaning in delirium, to the kindly offices of Content, who was a competent nurse. Also, she grew in her garden many of the homely remedies of the times for fever and wounds. Launching the dory, Hugh rowed past the wharves dotted with storehouses which contained molasses and sugar from Barbadoes and Jamaica, and cod, pipe staves, lumber, and salt beef, bound for the Sugar Islands. At length he landed behind the Blue Porpoise tavern.

That morning Tom and Israel had attempted to dissuade the boy from going to the ordinary. They had warned him that under the law Landlord Prey could hold Trelawney's chest and clothes as security for the back payment of his board. But the impulsive Hugh would not be persuaded, and eventually he obtained Tom's assent. Had not he and Israel arrived in the nick of time to bring about the capture of the two sailors? the boy argued. He had to go and speak for his friend who lay helpless with fever. The landlord had already gone through the Englishman's purse and read his letters; what else might "Pinch-penny" Prey do? There might still be that in his chest which might be useful to the sick man. If Landlord Prey refused to let him bring back the chest and clothes, he could ask to be allowed to lash the chest and have it placed where it would not be robbed. That, at least, Hugh had insisted he could do for the wounded man.

As he rowed, the more Hugh thought of the callous treatment of Trelawney by Prey, the hotter his blood pulsed through his veins. He was but a boy, to be sure, but, he reasoned, as his oar blades made the water boil, already the size of many men, and old Prey should listen to him. But why should he? Prey was close-fisted and mean—had seldom spoken civilly to Hugh in his life until the night previous. He might not even listen when Hugh asked for Trelawney's chest and clothes. What could a boy do then? Hugh did not know. But he continued to drive the skiff into the wind, past the ends of the wharves, with vicious strokes of his stout arms and back.

He landed on the stony beach, went up the lane to Thames Street, and entered the public room of the Blue Porpoise, with its freshly sanded floor and great fireplace at the end. The tables and joynt-stools had been cleaned and set in order. From the great summer beam and the joists hung bunches of dried vegetables, but the casks of salt beef and fish of the thrifty Prey were kept, together with the beer, cider, and rum, in a room behind the public room, beyond reach of his none-too-scrupulous patrons.

At the side of the wide opening of the great fireplace stood a roasting-jack on which a whole pig or sheep might be browned. Near the entrance to the room, on a board against the wall, hung a sheaf of papers on which, written in uncertain longhand, was news of the shipping, legal notices, and some misspelled and worse-drawn acts of the Governor and Council, requests for the return of lost animals and runaway bond servants and slaves, and the latest news from Boston brought by sea or over the horse path.

The long room was empty, for it was early for patrons, and Hugh called, "Landlord Prey!"

A girl's voice answered from the kitchen, and presently there appeared in the doorway a comely young woman wearing a short dimity frock covered by a white apron. With sleeves rolled to her round elbows, she stood, hands on hips, and with a sidewise tilt of her dark head, smiling in the doorway. Above the shining pewter buckles of her square-toed shoes, crimson stockings made conspicuous a pair of shapely legs. Patently aware of the picture she made, she flashed her white teeth at the embarrassed boy.

"Well, Hugh Jocelyn," she greeted; "I did hear that you beat the Portygee with the knife to the floor last night with a mighty blow of a stool. 'Twill not be long before the maids of Newport are losing their hearts to that yellow head of yours and those blue eyes!"

Blood stained Hugh's brown face. He felt strangely uneasy with this young wife of Prey's. Standing barefooted in his scanty canvas breeches and coarse shirt open at the neck, baring the brown arch of his chest, he suddenly felt ashamed, almost naked, before the girl's saucy black eyes.

She was the third wife that Landlord Prey had taken to his expansive bosom in the few short years he had lived in Newport. And the gossip along that end of Thames Street was to the effect that, at last, Jonathan Prey had met his match in the spunky, black-haired wife he had brought back from Duxbury ostensibly to cook, scrub, and slave in his tavern as had her meek and dutiful predecessors. According to the wagging tongues, the first and second Goodwives Prey had worked their lean fingers to the bone with scant appreciation of their drudgery from their lord and master; and then had quietly laid themselves down and died. But the new wife was proving to be a goose of another feather. Already, in a short three months, she had wheedled the niggardly landlord into signing a bond for a female servant to aid her in the kitchen. And it was clear even to those of poor sight, that she had wheedled more clothes and whimsies from her close-fisted husband in three short months than his former "seconds" had meekly received in ten years.

Hugh Jocelyn became painfully self-conscious as the amused girl watched the effect of her words on the shy boy.

" 'Twas little I did, Goodwife Prey," he answered.

No woman had ever spoken to him like that—suggested that maids might be losing of their hearts to his yellow head. What, he wondered, was the meaning of her boldness? Was it that she knew the reason for his coming to the inn and wished to block him in his purpose?

" 'Twas Israel that did for the Portygee who was headed for the door; not I," Hugh insisted. "I only finished him. I trust they will be well whipped on the Parade for what they did to Mr. Trelawney, last night."

The dancing lights left the girl's long-lashed eyes. She seemed annoyed at the mention of Trelawney's name. "Constable Olney," she replied, "says that Magistrate Lawton will judge them tomorrow. Today they are sick from the clubbing they had. And they will be well whipped, for a certainty, for the breakage and damage in this room."

The lights returned to her eyes as she deliberately allowed them to wander from Hugh's muscular legs to his thatch of yellow hair.

"Yes, but they used a knife on Mr. Trelawney," cried the boy. "He is now frenzical with fever from the wound."

The girl frowned. "You took him home with you?"

"Yes. Landlord Prey refused to keep him. He said you would not nurse a sick man that had no money wherewith to pay."

"No more would I, Hugh," she laughed, with a toss of her black head. "Trelawney is already in our debt, and his brother, the lord, sends no money. That's the end of it. Think you I would minister to that ne'er-do-well?" The eyes of the girl lingered caressingly on the disturbed boy.

Hugh boiled inwardly at her indifference to the fate of the man who lay wounded and penniless in Tom Stanton's house. But he had come for a purpose, and he realized that a display of anger would defeat it. Landlord Prey seemed to be away. Possibly his wife would let him take away Trelawney's chest. At any rate he would ask her.

"Landlord Prey is busy?" he ventured.

The girl laughed. "He waits on the Magistrate over this matter of the Portygee. What was your business with him, Hugh? I may speak for him."

The boy smiled into her quizzical face. "I came to ask for Mr. Trelawney's chest and clothes. They are of little value, and we need the chest for him." Hugh's heart beat hard as he waited for her reply. She might let him have the chest where Prey likely would have refused. His eyes hung on hers as she seemed to consider the request; then, as he waited in doubt for her answer, he smiled. Her face lit as she watched him with puckered brows. Lights danced in her eyes as she tilted her head with a glance through black lashes that drove his own eyes in quick flight to his bare feet.

"The chest—Trelawney's chest, and his worn clothes!" She spoke as if her thoughts were far from Trelawney's effects. "They'd hardly bring five shillings, so hard are they worn. Come, I will let you see them."

Hugh's heart beat high as, with a swish of skirts and a vivid display of red-stockinged legs, she turned to the kitchen door.

"Martha!" she called to the bond servant. "Sweep out the coals, set the rye-'n'-Injun dough in the oven. 'Twill be hot enough for baking now. Start the roast, and watch that the onions and carrots in the brass kettle are not boiled to death. They've come for Mr. Trelawney's chest." Turning from the kitchen door, Candace Prey led the way to the stairway flanking the chimney.

Hugh was both elated and disturbed. It looked as if Goodwife Prey was willing to have him take Trelawney's chest and clothes away with him, but as he followed the red stockings and shining pewter buckles on the square-toed shoes up the stairway, he was strangely uneasy. Why had she looked at him that way through half-shut eyes when he talked with her? He had never had a woman look at him with eyes like that. What meant she? Was she making sport of him—of his worn clothes and bare feet?

Candace Prey led Hugh to Trelawney's small room, which held little except a bed and a chest. On the bed lay an empty wallet, with some papers beside it, a coat and breeches of worn broadcloth, and a faded camlet cloak. In the chest Hugh opened were some books, an old velvet coat and breeches, a fustian waistcoat, a few soiled neckbands and cravats, stockings, and ragged linen. A leather doublet and a pair of untanned leather shoes with tarnished pewter buckles lay on the floor.

Hugh put the papers into the empty wallet and placed it, with the clothes and shoes, in the chest, while the girl watched from the doorway. Prey had taken Trelawney's last shilling on account of the debt for board. When Hugh had closed the chest, he turned to the girl, watching him where he knelt, and said, " 'Tis strange he has no sword—a gentleman."

She smiled down at the kneeling boy. "Oh, that went long ago," she said, "with much else that filled his chest. He sat long at his cups—your sour Englishman."

"Sour?" Hugh turned where he knelt to look protestingly into the face of the girl who now stood close at his side. He felt her knee press against his shoulder.

"Sour, I said," she whispered, suddenly bending and smoothing his yellow hair with a hand. "Not young and strong like you, Hugh." With a swift movement she took the upturned face of the surprised boy between her hands and kissed him full on the mouth.

Hugh rose, freeing himself from her circling arms. Crimson with embarrassment and shaken by conflicting emotions, he stared at the smiling temptress.

"Did I give fright to the big boy who felled the Portygee with the joynt-stool?" she teased. "You little know how you tempted me. Why have you fear of me, Hugh?"

"But—but you are a woman wedded," gasped the bewildered boy, trembling unconsciously with the first gusts of adolescent ardor. "Landlord Prey! He would—"

Her dark face hardened. "Hush! Not so loud! Dost want Martha in the kitchen to hear? As for Jonathan Prey, he wed me for a cook and serving maid. Pah! He has the heart of a fish." Then the warmth swiftly returned to her face. "You are young, Hugh—how old?"

"Not yet fifteen, but soon," answered the boy, whose eyes were wide with confusion as he doubtfully watched her.

"What a great lad you are for your age! But, oh, what a shyness! I am sorry. I was fair mad, with you so young and so shy. But 'twill not be long before you learn to value the sweetness of a pair of red lips and the beat of a loving heart."

Hugh's own heart was galloping madly against his ribs, his brown face flaming. "'Tis nought to hold sorrow for," he stammered thickly, avoiding her amused eyes. "I've forgotten it and will never tell."

With a sigh and a shrug of her plump shoulders, Candace Prey turned to the door. "I've been fair frenzical over you since I saw you, the youngest of them all, win that swimming race from the young men of Newport and the sailors," she said softly. "After the race, when you stood there talking and laughing with the people on Sanford's wharf, with the sun on your wet hair and the brown muscles of your back, I fair lost my heart. But, Hugh, I believed you not so young. You look full eighteen."

"Then I may take his chest?" asked the boy, abruptly, seemingly oblivious of the caressing eyes in the doorway and her honeyed words, but, in reality, sinking his nails into his calloused palms in a heroic effort at indifference.

"Yes, take the stuff and good riddance to him!" As Hugh lifted the chest of his friend to his shoulders, she thrust forward her black head and whispered: "I can wait, Hugh! I can wait till you learn more of lovin'. But mark you! Speak to no one of this. It might bring trouble on you and me, even the whipping post and disgrace."

Balancing the chest on his shoulders, Hugh demurred: "But there's nought been done. I'll speak to no one, Goodwife Prey. Yet I fear your husband will have the chest back."

"That," she answered with a wink, "I will attend to, if you keep a silent tongue. Now just one kiss."

As he stood in the hallway with the chest on his shoulders, she kissed him again. Then, with a fling of her skirts, she ran down the stairs ahead of the boy, and he left the tavern and brought Trelawney's poor possessions home in the skiff. But on the way, his oars tore savagely at the foaming harbor water as, over and over again, his bewildered thoughts played with the memory of the red lips of Candace Prey warm upon his own, the round arms that, for an instant, had circled his neck, and the sudden fire which had leaped through him in swift response, followed by the surge of shame and embarrassment and doubt which later had engulfed him.

DAYS later, when Dick Trelawney opened his sunken eyes and blinked in a daze at the woman who stood beside his pallet, Content bent, placed a toil-roughened hand on his forehead, and smiled.

"'Tis a cool head you have this morning, Mr. Trelawney," she said. "Tansy tea and St.-John's-wort from our yard and Chirurgeon Vigneron have worked wonders on the wound and the fever; and the clam broth has heartened you."

The sick man squinted quizzically into her kindly eyes. "This is not the Blue Porpoise," he protested weakly.

"Nay, 'tis the humble house of Tom Stanton, fisherman. You were hurt—stabbed by the Portygee sailors. My son Hugh brought you here."

"Your son? The lad with the yellow hair?" Trelawney's black brows pulled together as he fought through the mists that veiled his memory.

"Yes. He brought you here from the skiff on his back the night you were hurt at the Blue Porpoise. He has tended you like a woman while the three-day storm held and the sloop sawed at her anchor. But today he is off to our broken nets and lobster pots in Sakonnet River with his father and Israel Brandy."

Trelawney smiled weakly as he repeated, "Israel—Brandy?" Then he went on: "Ah, yes! I remember. There was trouble at the Inn. And your lad succoured me. The Portuguese—they cursed all the English. But why am I here, in your house?"

Color rose in Content's plain face. "Landlord Prey—he—he said he would not keep you without pay. He said—"

The sick man on the pallet groaned and turned away his white face. "I know—I know! He cast me out and your son brought me here." Trelawney closed his eyes as if to banish the stark reality of his poverty and helplessness. "And now I am deep in your debt."

"Speak not of it. 'Twas Hugh. He would have it so. You were sick and needed nursing. He says you are to learn him his letters. It is enough return."

Tears of sudden weakness and emotion blurred Trelawney's eyes. "I shall teach him his letters and—more; oh, so much more!" he murmured. "Give me but the chance—the chance."

Content fed the invalid hot clam broth from a wooden bowl, and then, insisting that he needed sleep, went outside with her knitting. It had, indeed, been a strain, having a sick stranger lying in the room in which they lived. But during the first days of his delirium, while the May storm whipped the bay to foam, Hugh had insisted on taking complete care of Trelawney.

One warm night after the fever had turned and the patient was better, leaving Hugh with his Englishman, Content sat with Tom and Israel in the garden while the three marveled at the devotion of the boy to the man he had met but once before the fight at the Blue Porpoise.

"It must be his wish to learn to read that makes him so, as well as the kind heart of him," observed the woman.

"'Tis more nor that," Israel replied, after a long pull on his clay pipe. "Somethin' happened betwixt them two that day on Coddington's Wharf. 'Tis not uncommon for a man and a wench to take a sudden fancy and ride at the same anchor the first time they hails each other, but for a boy and a man— Burn my bones! but 'tis some magic passed betwixt 'em."

"Ay, Israel, 'tis strange," agreed Stanton.

"They set store, each on each, at sight. Now, for me," said Israel, spitting wide and far and replacing his pipe, "there's nought in that brother of a milord that wins me. I favor not these lean and hungry gentry that seek a port in the colonies from some hurricane at home. What drove this Englishman, with his masts shot away and his top hamper overboard, on these shores? But, I allow," he admitted, blowing a cloud of smoke from his expansive mouth, "when he raves, he does show great store of learnin' and carries a pretty ear for a round oath."

Content frowned. "The language! 'Twas a fright—the oaths and foul speech he made use of in his fever. And Hugh so young to hear it. But his head is now cool. The tanzy tea and comfrey did for the fever."

Stanton and Israel grinned into each other's faces. "Think you," said her husband to the solicitous Content, "that the boy hears no such talk among the sailors and along the wharves? His young ears are well tuned to it. The Englishman but raved like any sick man. There was nought of meaning in what he said."

"Ay, and mark you," added Brandy, "this nursing of him means that Hugh may learn his letters and without pay. The Englishman has so promised."

"Yes, he so promised," repeated Content, with a sigh of resignation.

Then, one afternoon, as he grew stronger and was taking the sun from a stool in the garden where he could watch the shipping, Trelawney told Content he wished to talk with her.

"I have been a great burden upon you, Goodwife Stanton," he began. "You took me in penniless and a stranger. I shall not forget it."

"It was Hugh," she replied.

With a thin hand Trelawney pushed the long hair from his thoughtful face. He was yet weak, and sweat stood on his white forehead. His long legs were pipestems, and his clothes hung on him in folds. "Goodwife Stanton," he said, "my heart is overfull and words escape me. Already I have thirty wives and maids pledged to my exercises in manners and deportment, as well as reading and writing; and yesterday Magistrate Lawton was here, as you know, to arrange for a school for the children in the autumn. There will then be wherewith to make you whole for your loss and labor in keeping me."

Content raised her hand in protest. "Say no more, Mr. Trelawney. It is Hugh you owe for it all. And you are to learn him to read and write, and lesson him in figgers. That is enough return."

"Yes, it is Hugh, I make no doubt." The dead, black eyes of the man lighted. "Do you know that that boy might go far if well directed?"

"Ay, I know." Content's plain face shone as she smiled and nodded. Then her eyes suddenly clouded. "He's a good lad and an able one. But he's given us much cause for worry and doubt."

"Worry? How mean you?"

"He has some queer streaks in him, Mr. Trelawney. His temper is that hot and contrary, sometimes, it fair drives us frenzical. He loves his father and Israel, yet I've seen him so shaken by some word of reproof that I feared he'd strike them. Then, though happy and cheery for the most part, there be times when he broods—broods over his dead father and mother. He's that easy hurt and headstrong, it frightens me for his future."

"Ah!" Trelawney nursed his chin in a bony hand as his eyes half closed in thought. "What you say interests me, Goodwife Stanton. It may well be that the traits you mention may be the making of the lad—his high spirit and pride; but, on the other hand, they may cause his undoing. I like not what you say of his brooding. It leads to no good."

"He took quick to the ways of the sea when he came to us and was strong and plucky for his age. But Tom was slow in gettin' to know him. Once, when scarce more than ten, when Tom cuffed him for some small fault, he dived off the *Sea Gull* and started to swim ashore at Noman's Land. At last Tom learned that the lad would give his all for kindness, but harsh words put the devil in him."

"Ah!" The Englishman's dark eyes lit with interest. "The lad has variety and a will of his own, and seems very human."

"He's all in all to me," sighed Content. "I've dwelt on his faults, but virtues he has many. He's brave and affectionate and of such a quick mind." Her eyes saddened. "I fear me that I shall soon lose him, what with this learning that you promise and his growing to a great lad. Soon he'll be away to sea and gone from my life."

"But if he goes with what I teach him, he'll soon be mate and master, and not a foremast hand. You would have that for him?"

"Oh, yes," Content replied, giving in to her pride in the lad.

Trelawney's eyes followed the course of a shallop leaving the harbor; then he said to her: "He's at the learning age. I believe there is in him what with guidance might make him a marked man."

"Let us talk no more," said Content with resignation. "You and Tom and Israel will have your way with him."

The talk was interrupted by the appearance of Jerusa Sugars, the carpenter, a squat little man with a taste for gossip. "Hast heard the news, Goodwife Stanton?"

"What news?"

"Rumor has it that horse messenger is in from Boston. 'Tis said at the King's Head that King's Province has been taken from us by order of President Dudley of the New England Council, and there's to be a royal government in Narragansett."

Trelawney smiled at the tense faces of the other two. Colonial politics interested him little.

"Shall we lose our charter and have a royal governor placed over us, think you?" demanded Content. "Since the new King James there is much talk of it."

Sugars slowly wagged his shaggy head as he left the yard. "Who knows? There are those in Newport who talk for it. They say they tire of Quaker rule here. The Governor and Council meet in a few days. Then much will be heard."

§12

THE great public room of the King's Head, the rendezvous of the officials and the men of substance of Newport, and often the meeting place of the Governor and Council, was buzzing with excitement. At tables waited on by swiftly moving black boys, men sat over their Canary and malmsey, sillabub and metheglin, smoking long-stemmed pipes and talking excitedly. Bronzed masters of ships drank with importers whose warehouses dotted the shores and neighboring wharves. Merchants, magistrates, and landowners conversed heatedly over the recently arrived news from Boston. A group crowded around a board hanging on the painted wall near the door of the inn, on which hung the proclamation of Joseph Dudley, new President of the Council for

New England, announcing the establishment of a royal government in Narragansett and prohibiting Rhode Island from further jurisdiction, to which instrument was affixed Dudley's wax seal, the size of a man's hand.

Some in the anxious group around the board were Quaker merchants, dressed in somber suits of philomot broadcloth and wool stockings of the same color. Others were gay in velvet and silk, with scarlet and yellow waistcoats and shining silver buckles at their knees and on their square-toed shoes. The hair of the Quakers was chopped off at the nape of their necks, but the others wore either their own hair curled to their shoulders or periwigs of the latest London fashion.

"It is coming," sighed an old Quaker, with a shake of his gray head. "Our freedom is over. Soon they will seize our charter. The new King James is willed to join all New England and New York into one royal colony."

"And how those plotters over there at the table in the corner are mouthing it," sneered a tall young man, in curled periwig, blue velvet coat and breeches, silk stockings, and a fustian waistcoat. His dark face was flushed with drink, and he teetered uncertainly back and forth on his heels.

"You mean Mr. Brinley, Richard Smith, Peleg Sanford, and the rest?"

"Ay, I mean so. For years they've been filling the ears of the Board of Trade in London with their pretty tales. They say we're ruled by illiterates and artisans, and they sicken of Quaker rule."

The Quakers in the group turned angrily on the younger man, whose name was Joseph Brenton, but his smile was so disarming that their stern faces relaxed.

"You joke of serious matters, Mr. Brenton," reproved an old Quaker.

"'Tis no joke, I agree. There are many in this colony who rejoice that our charter is to be taken from us, and who will fawn on the new governor, seated in Boston, and named by the king. And there sit five of them!" Young Brenton pointed with his ebony cane toward the table where Richard Smith, of Cocumcussoc, and Francis Brinley, great landholders, talked, heads together, with three others.

"But Peleg Sanford, our late governor, was your aunt's husband," maliciously suggested another Quaker.

A sour look spread over Brenton's face, while the glitter in his dark eyes drove the smirk from the other's features. "Blame me not for that. 'Twas not my doing. I was not forced to bed with that sack of bones. He is for a royal governor, thinking he may add to his money bags. That's sufficient. He and Brinley and Smith plot to steal much rich Narragansett land when the King's Province is divorced from us.

They've plotted with Connecticut to take King's Province; now they plot with Dudley to seize it."

"'Tis rumored that Randolph and Dudley are coming from Boston next month with the King's writ of *quo warranto*," said another. "Alas! our charter will be lost to us and all freedom of life."

Brenton smiled. "They've not got our charter yet, my friends," he said. "Until then, hearten yourselves with hope. Good-day to you!"

At a table in a corner of the public room Francis Brinley, ardent royalist and enemy of the Rhode Island charter, talked in an undertone with Richard Smith, of the Narragansett country, and Peleg Sanford, merchant and late governor.

"They take it sore," chuckled Brinley, a man of high-bred face and distinguished bearing, who, from his clothes and manner of speech, might have been mistaken for an Englishman visiting the colonies. He wore a periwig and white-lawn cravat, and his suit of blue broadcloth with silver buttons, and buckles at knees and on shoes, set off his well-made figure. "Watch the Quakers choke as they read the proclamation. When Sir Edmund Andros arrives, we'll be rid of this government of crackpots and illiterate artisans, at last."

"Sir Edmund will soon have that silly charter which John Clark and Roger Williams won by deceit from King Charles," said Sanford. "Then we shall have law and order in Newport—and on the Main."

At a near-by table sat the former governor, old Henry Bull, with the new governor, Walter Clarke, young Benedict Arnold, and Nathaniel Coddington. They were all Quakers except Arnold, but their clothes were far from somber, and Coddington followed his handsome Quaker father, now dead, in wearing a periwig and affecting gay colors.

"I have called on the freemen to join us and take counsel at the June session. 'Tis the time that Randolph has summoned us to meet," said Clarke.

"But shall we meekly submit to the loss of our charter?" demanded Arnold.

"What can we do?" asked old Henry Bull with a sad shake of his grizzled head. "We should be mad to stand suit with the crown on the *quo warranto*. When Andros arrives and demands the charter, we can do nought else but give it him."

There was the ghost of a smile on little Governor Clarke's canny Quaker face. "It may be that when Sir Edmund Andros demands our charter we shall be hard put to discover it!"

The others at the table stared at the speaker blankly, but later they had cause to recall the remark.

At this moment there was the sound of horses' hoofs and loud talk outside the inn. His face inflamed with drink, young Joseph Brenton came into the room again, with two new companions.

"There they still sit," said Brenton, "plotting how they may steal the best grass lands in King's Province!" His voice broke above the talk in the room as he flung himself on a stool at a table and pointed to the corner table where Brinley and the others lingered. He called for Madeira with a dash of brandy, and when his pewter cup was filled, rose unsteadily and, lifting the cup, proposed a toast. The room became suddenly silent as men watched curiously the grandson of the dead William Brenton, great landowner and one of the founders of the seaport.

"Gentlemen," Brenton bellowed, "I give you a toast! May the bones of those who have plotted to ruin us and deprive us of our charter rot in hell!"

For an instant heavy silence fell on the public room of the tavern, then there lifted a bedlam of voices. Some stood at their tables and drank to the toast. Brinley and his friends rose angrily to their feet, but the eyes they met were mostly hostile. Shouts of "Well spoken, young Brenton!" mingled with demands for order and cries for the ejection of the intoxicated youth. His friends took him by the arms, but he angrily threw them off as Peleg Sanford approached him, while the landlord, Timothy Whiting, impotently wrung his hands, for Joseph Brenton and his friends were among his best customers.

When the furious Sanford reached Brenton, the latter roared with laughter as he surveyed the other's spindle shanks, lanky frame, and long-nosed face. "So you would not drink to my toast, my dear kinsman?" Brenton derided.

"Have you no regard for your family that you conduct yourself so shamelessly in public?" stormed Sanford. "You're foxed, and bed is the place for you before you say more you may regret."

"Foxed, am I?" sneered the drunken youth, with a mocking bow. "My revered in-law and former governor of this fair colony, Leftenant-Colonel Sanford, whose long nose has never smelled powder, I confess I'm foxed, but 'tis from gazing into your foxy face. Pray, what office are they giving you in the new government of King's Province for your foxiness?"

Sanford's narrow face went crimson. He choked in his anger, while laughter rose from many of the tables as he returned to his seat. The friends of young Brenton gathered around him and forced him, protesting, from the room. Again the King's Head enjoyed its usual decorum.

Young Benedict Arnold and Coddington grinned into each other's faces. "Joseph is overfond of his wine," said Arnold, "but what he said sprang from no fuddled brain."

Old Henry Bull's Quaker face grimaced as he buried his nose in a beaker of sillabub, made of cider, sugar, nutmeg, and cream. "Surely in wine there lies truth," he mumbled.

" 'Twill be some time e'er Peleg Sanford again offers young Brenton advice in public," Governor Clarke commented drily. "But I fear for our future. A royal governor in Boston where they hate us! Alas! we are become a mere county, and one soon overlooked."

Men sat long that day over their wine and rum, for the charter, which was the first that granted to men the right to worship according to the dictates of their own consciences, was doomed. King James had appointed Sir Edmund Andros, late governor of New York, to be governor of all New England. The independent colony of Rhode Island and Providence Plantations would shortly be no more. The right of self-government under their own elected officials, for which the dead Roger Williams had given a lifetime of toil, was lost. The old controversy with Connecticut concerning the land west of Narragansett Bay was forgotten. It mattered little, now, whether the "Narragansett River," named in the Connecticut charter, referred to the Bay as the eastern boundary of that colony, or, as Rhode Island claimed, meant the Pawcatuck River, for both colonies were to lose their charters and be absorbed into the new colony of New England under a royal governor.

§13

FOR days after his meeting with Candace Prey at the Blue Porpoise, Hugh had expected a stern summons from the landlord to return Trelawney's effects, but no word came, and at last he decided that Prey's wife had found ways to appease her husband's greed. But as Hugh, Tom, and Israel tended the gill nets and lobster pots in the Sakonnet River, or trolled for the first run of bluefish off the shoals of the Sow and Pigs, off Cuttyhunk, and around the Devil's Bridge and Noman's Land, the boy's thoughts often reverted to that day in Trelawney's room at the Blue Porpoise and what Candace Prey had said about waiting until he learned more of loving. Certainly of loving he knew little and had thought less. Sex had not yet vexed him, for the long days of rowing and hauling on the nets had left the growing boy dead tired and ready for his pallet in the loft when his stomach was full of Content's dinner. But now, often, as he stood on the bowsprit, with the lance poised while Tom eased the sloop up to a basking swordfish, or as he lifted the silver-bellied squeteague into the dory from the gill nets, Hugh found his thoughts far adrift, playing with a pair of snapping black eyes, eyes that beckoned and were unashamed. A woman wed, she was, but yet too young for the meaty-faced Prey with his eyes of a pig. And she had said that some day Hugh would value red lips and a loving heart. What meant she to do when he grew older? His heart always beat hard in his chest at the thought, and one day when Tom had worked the sloop up where the boy could lance a loafing swordfish on the surface, Hugh's spear missed the fish so widely that Israel growled with disgust.

"What has come over you, lad? Your eye was far from the mark. You be not mooning over some maid at your tender age?"

Crestfallen and ashamed for days, Hugh had banished the black eyes and red lips of Candace Prey from his thoughts. But she soon returned to harass and plague him, yet he found himself carefully avoiding passing the Blue Porpoise.

In the meantime Trelawney was making swift progress toward health. Before he could leave and find lodgings of his own, he had completed arrangements for his class of thirty women and girls. Two of the town council, together with Magistrate Lawton, had also talked with him and committed the little seaport to a public school in the autumn. So Trelawney's hopes were high.

The Englishman sat in the garden one afternoon watching the shipping when, breaking from the south end of Goat Island, the familiar jib and bellying loose-footed mainsail of the sloop hove into view, and the little craft headed for a wharf where Tom disposed of his fish, then moved on and dropped anchor in the Cove. Hugh stripped, waved his shirt at Trelawney, and wearing his short canvas breeches, dived into the Cove for a clean-up and a swim. Time and again he circled the anchored craft with powerful overhand strokes while the Englishman watched.

"And he did all of this when he scarce knew me," muttered the man in the garden. "Brought me here on his back and found me sanctuary. Cozened Tom and Content to house me. Nursed me with his own hands. And now I am well and—I hope—a changed man." There was mist in the dark eyes of Dick Trelawney as he watched Hugh reach and draw himself up over the low rail of the sloop by a man rope. The boy shook the water from his long hair and rubbed dry his arms and shoulders.

The Englishman drew in a deep breath and expelled it, and his eyes were luminous. "Dick Trelawney," he mused, "there stands honest work for your worthless brain, here in this money-grubbing Newport. Clay for the hand of a skilled potter. What a man may be shaped from it! And if wine and lechery and wasted days have left ought of skill or wisdom in your addled pate, with God's help the lad shall be molded. Name of God, he shall be my monument!"

June came, and while Governor Clarke with the assistants and deputies of the colonial assembly sat discussing their fate, Randolph arrived in Rhode Island with the King's writ of *quo warranto*, delivered the writ, and went to Narragansett, where Joseph Dudley was organizing King's Province and appointing a court, of which Francis Brinley was made president, and on which sat the arch conspirators, Peleg Sanford and Richard Smith. The name of Kingston was changed to Rochester; of Westerley, to Haversham; and of Greenwich, to Dedford. King's Province had been lost to Rhode Island.

But the events which so stirred the colony meant little to the growing Hugh Jocelyn, absorbed in the mysteries of the written and printed word. Also, familiar with the political intrigues of the English court and Parliament, the crude picture of colonial politics played by men, many of whom were illiterates, left Trelawney cold. At odd moments through the summer and autumn, when storms held the sloop at her anchor, he pursued his labor of love with the boy who longed to read and write.

One night in November, when Tom, Israel, and Hugh had returned from a day with the geese and swan on the Sakonnet marshes, Hugh proudly took Content's Bible and, squatting near the fire, to her amazement and delight, slowly and with many pauses and repetitions, as a forefinger followed the printed words, read aloud the Twenty-third Psalm.

"Why, Hugh, you told me not you could yet read from the Bible," cried his delighted foster mother, her eyes moist with tears.

The boy gave her a rare smile. "It was a secret Mr. Trelawney and me hatched for to please you, Mother Content."

"What think you of that, Israel?" asked Tom Stanton, proudly. "The lad has already gone far."

Brandy beamed down on the smiling boy at the hearth. "Ay, he learns fast, Trelawney tells me. And by spring will be far in his figgers. In the summer the Englishman is to borrow the new rig of sightin' the sun for what they calls lateetude from a ship captain and lesson Hugh in its use."

One morning in December the people of Newport were brought from their houses and shops by the beating of a drum at the great cannon on the Parade. When the citizens had gathered about Town Sergeant Benoni Tosh and two constables, the former, a great red-faced hulk of a man, announced in a voice of thunder:

"Freemen of Newport! Give ear! By horse messenger this day come over the Boston Path 'tis reported Sir Edmund Andros, Royal Governor for New England, is landed at Boston from His Majesty's *Rose* frigate, with two companies of foot. Mr. Joseph Dudley is appointed Chief Justice for New England. God save the King!"

"Ay, and God save Rhode Island," answered a voice from the

crowd.

Men looked into each other's grave faces. Liberty in Rhode Island was at an end. The little colony of the dead Roger Williams had been absorbed into the royal colony of New England.

But life for Hugh Jocelyn went on as usual. Through midwinter, when ice blocked the harbor and the fishing ceased, the active brain of the boy was busy. Spurred by Trelawney, in his spare time from the school and the classes of women, who listened in open-mouthed delight to his tales of the court of King Charles as he taught them deportment and their letters, Hugh labored at his reading, writing, and arithmetic.

But the baffling moods which at times obsessed the boy tried the Englishman's patience and understanding, and put to the test his affection for the lad who had so stoutly championed him when he was ill and friendless. There were times when, at night, in Trelawney's lodging, squatting at the latter's knee in the candlelight, Hugh would suddenly turn from his hornbook and demand:

"What's the use of all this? I'm a fisherman's foster son and sniggered at in church by the sons of the quality for my worn kersey coat and leather breeches. A fisherman I'll always be."

"Don't be silly, Hugh."

"I tell you I will! No matter if I have learning while they scarcely may write their names, I'll always sit with Content on the long benches for the poor in the rear. And the lads in broadcloth and velvet and the maids in silk and lustring will smirk at me from their pews."

Then the patient Trelawney would shake his head and insist: "But with the knowledge I give you, you'll not always be a fisherman. You'll soon be mate and then captain in the deep-sea trade."

"But mates and captains are mostly poor men who toil for the shipowners they make rich."

"With an education and that stout heart and ambition of yours, you'll be a shipowner some day."

"You think so?"

"I know it."

Then with a smile, a shake of the yellow head, and a clamped jaw, Hugh would again turn to his hornbook, while the Englishman wondered what the future had in store for the combination of fiery temper and capacity for affection, steadfast loyalty, sensitiveness, and unreasonable pride that squatted at his feet.

14

THAT summer Hugh became sixteen. Already he topped Tom Stanton by half a head. In August came the annual swimming race fostered by the merchants of the port, who contributed a pound as a prize to the winner. The half-mile race was swum from an anchored sloop off Cannon Street to Easton's Wharf in the Cove, and Hugh had twice won it from the boys alongshore and the sailors from craft lying in the harbor. But this summer, a few days before the race a rumor ran through the taverns of the little port that a Lascar sailor of the foreign brig from the Wine Islands would compete. And gossip had it that the former pearl diver in the Indy sea had been watched at practice and his brown body had cut the water like a blue fish after herring.

That noon at a table in the King's Head, young Joseph Brenton sat with his friend, the blond, thickset John Arnold, grandson of the late governor, and big, red-cheeked Kit Sheffield, a member of the large Block Island and Newport family of merchants and landowners.

"That fisherman's son, Hugh Jocelyn, who won last year," said Brenton, "is a likely lad and a strong one. I'm not so certain the Lascar can beat him."

Arnold drained his cup of Madeira and replied with a laugh: "The lad is hardly seventeen. True, he's good in the water, but this year he has against him a mustee who 'tis said has dived for pearls in the East Indy Sea. The boy cannot win. I've already laid five pound on the Lascar."

Brenton shook his head. "It may be young Jocelyn's met his match, but I favor him. I saw him but yesterday at practice, and he made the water boil."

"I'll lay you a pound on the Lascar," said Arnold.

"Done!" laughed Brenton. "You favor the Lascar, Kit? I'll lay you another pound on our fisher boy against the Malay."

Sheffield nodded his dark head. "My hope is with our boy, but I doubt he can best a human fish; so I take you."

"You know Dick Trelawney fair dotes on this young Jocelyn," said Brenton, filling his pewter cup from a tankard of wine on the table. "And a rare companion is this younger brother of Lord John Trelawney, who's strangely turned schoolmaster in Newport."

"You've spent much time with Trelawney of late," commented Arnold.

"That I have. Since he became tutor to my aunt's children I've come to know him well. And a rare wit he has, and learning that dwarfs anything in Newport. It seems that his brother, the lord, has cut off his support, and the poor devil is forced to turn pedagogue. I often wonder what strange pass brought him to these shores, but he is silent about it."

"What of him and young Jocelyn?" asked Arnold.

"Why, he's lessoning him, and he tells me the lad has promise."

"But that will not win him this race with the Lascar," said Sheffield drily, and the three young men left the tavern for Easton's Wharf.

The anchored shipping and the wharves of Newport were crowded with spectators. Even the Quaker merchants and shipowners had left their shops and warehouses to watch the contest between the Newport lad and the sailor from the Indy sea, for the other entries in the race had been beaten by Hugh the summer before. Groups of young women and girls of the wealthy families, their silk and tiffany hoods of yellow, blue, and scarlet dropped back to their shoulders because of the heat, gossiped with their escorts on the wharves. Many of them, though Quakers, were gay with puffed virago sleeves caught with colored ribbons, and beneath their flowered silk, satin, and dimity petticoats appeared green and red stockings and red- and white-heeled shoes. Rich merchants in velvet and silk, serge and broadcloth, stood with artisans and workers in the shipyards, wearing leather breeches and loose frocks, waiting for the start of the race.

On an anchored sloop off the foot of Cannon Street the swimmers waited, stripped to their short canvas drawers. Apart from the rest, Hugh sat with Israel on a coil of rope.

"There be none to watch, lad, save this mustee," whispered the old sailor. "Keep hard by him."

Hugh laughed. He was nervous, more nervous than he had ever been before. In the last two years he had been confident he could win and had given little thought to the race. But this year the rumors of the Lascar's speed in the water had worried him. He had not seen the little brown man, squatting near, talking to another brown-skinned sailor, perform in the water. But the gossip which had reached the boy's ears had likened his opponent to a fish rather than a man. It would cut him to the bone to be beaten before all Newport by a stranger. And Hugh had promised himself that before that should happen, he would swim as tinker mackerel swim before a pursuing porpoise. So, as he talked to Israel with a brave show of confidence, he was, in reality, jumping with nerves.

As Hugh jokingly replied to a remark of one of the entries, Israel glanced at him sharply. The laugh had sounded flat and hollow. The lad was on edge, thought the sailor, but he would soon work that off in the water. Hugh, his boy, could not lose.

At the order of the starter, the swimmers lined up on the rail of the sloop. Down the half-mile course Hugh could see the gaily dressed people on the wharves and in boats, waiting. As he stood beside the Lascar he could feel his heart beat in his throat. It would be hard to lose to this little brown man whose head barely reached his shoulder.

Israel watched his protégé's poised body with satisfaction. Plenty of strength and endurance there!

The starter raised his arm, called "Ready!" and his flintlock pistol exploded. Hugh cut the harbor water beside his opponent and a roar went up from the excited spectators.

"Save your strength for the finish, lad!" bellowed Israel.

Before they had gone a hundred yards, the Lascar, moving like an eel, with a strange undulating stroke which carried him, alternately, under water and out, was far in front. Swimming hard but well within his strength, Hugh doggedly followed in his wake. But it looked as if the reports were true. The Lascar was a human fish. Another hundred yards and the sailor and the bronzed boy with the yellow hair had shaken off the field of struggling swimmers and were alone. In spite of Hugh's increasing efforts, the Lascar was slowly gaining. Was he to be disgraced, Hugh wondered, as he beat the water into foam, by a little man he could break in his two hands? Then the son of Henry Jocelyn began to swim as he had never swum before. His brown arms tore through and flung the water behind him, while his legs thrashed. He looked and saw that he was passing the halfway point at Sanford's Wharf. A roar of cheers from the people on the wharf beat in his ears.

"Swim, Jocelyn!" they called. "Speed you, lad! The Lascar tires! You gain, Hugh! You gain!"

But the foreign sailor still kept his lead, moving with the same snake-like motion, now under, now out. A stern chase is ever a long one, and Hugh was now swimming to the limit of his power, his open mouth sucking in the air in deep gasps. They were in the last quarter mile and it would soon be over. He saw Gravelly Point on his left and knew but a few hundred yards remained. Somewhere Trelawney waited with Content and Tom to see him beaten home. Content, with tears in her brave eyes! And Tom and Israel, how they would feel it! And how some of those he had beaten before would rejoice! Then, of a sudden, something surged through his tiring body like a flame—the dogged refusal to accept defeat. The Lascar should not win—not—if— Hugh suddenly saw red, and his arms churned the water in a last desperate effort to reach the man ahead of him. To his ears came the cries of those on Easton's Wharf: "Come on, Jocelyn! The Lascar tires! You gain, Jocelyn! You gain!"

The faraway voices which broke through the thundering in his ears were like the lash of a goad to a spent horse. He made the water boil in a final mad drive for the wharf. The bobbing body of the Lascar was now close. Hugh saw the whites of his eyes as he flung back an anxious look. "The Lascar's done! The Lascar's done!" hammered in his bursting brain.

They were close on Easton's Wharf, and the frantic people were urging the lad with the yellow hair to come on and win. The laboring of his tortured lungs drummed in his ears as he drove his numb arms and legs. Inch by inch he cut down the Lascar's lead, while the crowd roared. The fast-tiring Malay now swam on the surface, his mouth gaping for air, eyes bulging. Hard on his heels, like a wolf on his kill, thrashed the exhausted boy, slowly bridging the gap which separated them. Then, with a lunge, the Lascar shot forward and touched a bollard of the wharf a bare length in front of Hugh.

For a moment a deep hush gripped the crowd as they realized that Hugh had lost. Following, came a roar of applause from Easton's Wharf, and friendly hands lifted the half-conscious lad to the cap log.

"Well swum, Hugh Jocelyn! Well done, lad!" The shouts rang in the heartbroken Hugh's ears as he lay gasping for breath, while men rubbed his stiff arms and legs. But through the boy's blurred senses ran the realization that he had lost—lost to the little brown man before the people of Newport. Hugh Jocelyn was forever disgraced. He had lost. Poor Israel and Tom and Content. Their boy had failed them. He had lost!

Then a young man wearing a beaver hat, periwig, blue coat, and breeches elbowed his way through the chattering crowd surrounding Hugh. "Drink this, young Jocelyn," ordered Brenton, holding a sneak cup of brandy to Hugh's colorless lips, "and honor me with your hand. Name of God! that was a gallant effort. How you tired him out and came from the rear almost to beat him, I know not. For he's fish, not man."

"'Tis kind of you—to say so—sir," Hugh panted. "But he beat me—and I brought—shame to Newport."

"Nonsense, lad. Newport's proud of you."

Shortly Hugh was on his feet, and men and boys pressed around him to slap his broad back and shake his hand, praising his game but losing battle. Then he was aware of a pair of snapping black eyes devouring him from a distance as he stood stripped to the waist receiving the sympathy of the crowd. He became suddenly conscious of his naked brown torso as Candace Prey smiled and waved. With yellow hood flung back from her flushed face, she elbowed her way through the chattering men about him and caught his hand.

"I'm fair in tears, Hugh. But you swum nobly," she cried. "A few feet more and the race was yours." Her black eyes lingered on the brown symmetry of his shoulders and chest as he stood, embarrassed and confused, while the men around him gaped at the boldness of the young wife of Jonathan Prey to stand unabashed and talk to a lad near naked.

She swept him with a smile and turned away. And the caress of the girl's lingering eyes flicked the boy's senses like the sting of blown salt spray on naked flesh.

Then Tom and Trelawney came pushing through the crowd and gripped his hand. Aware of Hugh's humiliation and disappointment, Stanton said little, but Trelawney gave full vent to his emotion. "Hugh, I'm proud of you today. Though far in the rear, you never faltered or weakened, only swam the harder till you were close to winning. That's the spirit, lad. There was a flame in you at the finish, fighting till the last foot, that heartens me more than if you'd won easily."

"I lost," muttered Hugh. "Lost before all Newport!"

"May you always face life that way, refusing to admit defeat," said the Englishman, his arm tightening around the boy's bare shoulders.

Tom gave Hugh a locram shirt he carried and they walked ashore and found Content in her garden. In silence she went to him and kissed him on a brown cheek.

On the morning following, at daylight, Stanton called Hugh for an early start for the Sakonnet nets. But there was no reply from the pallet in the loft. Tom mounted the ladder and found that Hugh's blankets had not been touched. He descended and met Content's worried look with a shake of the head. "Hugh was not here last night."

"But where would he go—and why?" cried the frightened woman. "He was sore hurt losing the race, but he wouldn't leave us without a word."

"He has left us without a word," said Stanton, bitterly. "Name of God! where's he gone?"

The *Sea Gull* left for the Sakonnet nets without Hugh. No one had seen him. The boy had simply walked out of their lives. Through the day the dazed Tom and Israel talked little. They knew what a blow the loss of the race before all Newport had been to the pride of the sensitive boy, but they little realized the depth of that pride. And they could not understand why he had left them without a word.

That evening as the *Gull* made her mooring in the Cove, they saw Trelawney waiting on the gravel beach. As the skiff slid ashore, the Englishman's grave face whipped them with sudden fear. Had something happened to Hugh?

Brandy's set mouth and rough demand failed to mask the panic in his eyes. "Well, schoolmaster, be there news from that whelp of yours?"

"Yes, there's news. Hugh was seen to sail out of the Cove in a shallop last night, and head up the bay."

"Up the bay?" repeated Stanton. "Now where could he be headin' up the bay? What's got into him?"

"Ah!" Brandy expelled a deep breath of relief.

"What's got into him, you ask? God's breath! don't you know?" demanded the irritated Trelawney. "'Tis his pride. You know how proud and sensitive he is! Think you he brushed off losing that race, yesterday, as one whisks off a fly? He hid it from you last night but it seared him like a hot iron."

"Stab my vitals!" sputtered Brandy.

Stanton's jaw sagged as he gaped at the Englishman.

"You little sense a nature like Hugh's," went on the latter. "'Tis foolish, to be sure. But he feels disgraced and will face no one till the mood has passed."

"But where was he bound—to Providence?" muttered Stanton. "He knows no one there."

"Providence or hell," rasped Brandy, "I'm after him to bring him back by the ears and cuff some sense into his yeller head."

Trelawney smiled indulgently, for the anxiety behind Israel's harsh words was only too patent. "Scolding or cuffing is no proper medicine for that lad, Israel, and you well know it. He'd only return as good as he got. What he needs is understanding."

"Then you think he'll return when cooled off and not stay away or ship on some sloop?" demanded the dejected Stanton.

"He'll fight it out alone and when the hurt eases, he'll come home."

However, that night the *Sea Gull*, with two grim-faced men for crew, sailed for Providence in search of the shallop and the missing boy, and returned the following day with no news. In the little house on the Cove the heartsick Content went about her work with a prayer on her lips while she waited for the return of the men.

On the evening of the third day, as Trelawney sat with the silent Tom and Israel watching the harbor, the sail of a small shallop appeared behind Gravelly Point.

"Burn me! but it looks like it," broke out Israel, rising.

"'Tis Easton's missin' boat!" Stanton watched the upper half of the leg-of-mutton sail moving along the far shore of the point.

"As I told you," said Trelawney, "he had to fight it out alone. Now that the sting is less sharp, he's come home."

"Rot my bones!" exploded Israel, "but he's took years off my life. Big as he is, he needs a rope's end!"

Again Trelawney smiled. "No, Israel; what he needs is patience and understanding. Do you want to lose him?"

"Lose him? I'd liefer lose my good leg!"

"I know it. So have done with talk of rope's ends."

As Hugh ran the shallop up on the gravel beach and leaped out, a woman ran into his open arms. "Hugh! Why did you leave us, lad?" sobbed Content. "Where have you been so long?"

The three men silently took Hugh's hand in turn. "I'm glad to be home," the boy said quietly, looking at Stanton. "Do you want me back after leaving you without a word?"

"Where went you, Hugh?" asked Tom, unable to control the tremor in his voice.

"I went to Somerset to see Prudence and Giles and the children. I—I could not stay in Newport—after that day. You see they didn't know—Prudence and Giles—hadn't seen me beaten before all Newport. And they were so glad to see me."

Trelawney's warning eyes caught those of Tom and Israel and the three men fell behind while Hugh walked to the house with Content. "Don't question or scold him," cautioned the Englishman. "Leave him alone for a while with Content. He's all right, now. The wound is healing. But leave him with Content."

"So, in his hurt he turned to the Dunbars," said Tom, bitterly.

"You don't understand. He'd give his life for you all, but he turned to the Dunbars because they had not seen his shame—did not know, as you did, his humiliation. He wants no sympathy. It comforted him to be with them."

"Stab my vitals!" sputtered Israel, "what manner of fish have we ketched, to be so coaxed and petted?"

A warmth suffused Trelawney's black eyes. "We've caught a fish, Israel, who'll repay us many fold if we but give him line and handle him with wisdom."

"Ay," agreed Stanton, "a queer fish he is, but one to be sadly missed if lost."

A few days later, after much talk with Trelawney, Israel Brandy became philosopher and friend as he worked with Hugh in the skiff, picking up lobster pots off Sakonnet Point. "Lad," began the sailor, shipping his oars, filling his pipe from a pouch, and striking steel on flint from his tinder bag, to ignite the dry moss held in his thickly calloused palm, "'tis the part of a man to meet what blows come in life with a grin and ask for more."

Hugh's eyes twinkled while he watched the sober-faced Brandy puff industriously as he labored with his thoughts. "Ay, and to return them in full measure, Israel, has ever been your motto," Hugh laughed.

"Life clouts us many a blow which may not be returned, but must be borne with," insisted Brandy. "And how a man stands up under these is true test of the bowels in his belly."

Hugh's eyes clouded. "What you're trying to say is I acted not the part of a man in sailing away for Somerset?"

"Stab me, no!" sputtered the embarrassed Israel. "You proved your guts by fightin' the Lascar to the last stroke, and that day, when but a lad of ten off Noman's, you dove in and headed for the shore! What I'm beatin' up to 'gainst a stiff head wind is this: you're too touchy, lad—quicker'n primin' powder in the vent of a culverin; too easy hurt!" The sailor expelled a cloud of smoke and finished, "And worst of all, you're prouder'n a bull porpoise tryin' to butt the figgerhead off a brig!"

Hugh's eyes fell to his bare feet as his face reddened. "I'm sorry, Israel," he answered softly, "that I left you that night. But the disgrace—the taunts of the lads alongshore I've beaten—'twas hard!"

Brandy struck the gunwale a blow like the clap of a loose jib in the wind. "Slit my throat, but that's my point! You near beat the Lascar, provin' your guts beyond the doubt of any man, but might not look defeat in the face for fear of taunts and the smirks of your enemies, so run away and hid in Somerset."

Again blood colored Hugh's bronzed face. "I—I sailed to Somerset for no such reason! 'Twas that I'd shamed myself and Newport—not done my best!"

"Belay, lad! I'm fair proud of what you did that day! A boat's length more and you'd have won. Now put it from your mind and listen to Dick Trelawney. He talks rare sense. There'll be many blows from life you needs must take with a grin and not brood over."

"I know, I know," said Hugh. "But it hurt, Israel."

Brandy laughed. "Picture me comin' home from the warm seas, a lad in the twenties, shy a foot and with this face. You say losin' that race hurt? Burn me! You fancy it didn't hurt Israel Brandy when the children stared at this chopped-up bow and the maids looked and turned away? Think you the stoutest lad in Newport wasn't cut to the bone by losin' a leg?" Brandy stopped to gaze seaward. His scarred mouth worked hard, and mist hung in his bleak eyes. Then, with a grimace, he turned to Hugh. "Well, rot my bones! I was still the best gunner and cutlass man in the port and I give 'em look for look, and so with my battered top hamper I've stumped on through life."

The boy impulsively reached and had Israel's big hand in his. "You've shamed me, Israel. What you've faced with a grin makes me seem small. I promise—I promise to forget it!"

15

ONE SEPTEMBER day a shallop from Updike Newtown, across the bay, in Narragansett, sailed into Newport harbor with news. With the beating of the drum on the Parade, the deep voice of Sergeant Benoni Tosh announced that word had come that Sir Edmund Andros, the new Royal Governor for the New England Colonies, had appeared at Hartford and seized the charter of Connecticut.

The great public room of the King's Head was buzzing with excitement. Francis Brinley, Chief Justice of the new court, sat with friends, drinking the health of the Royal Governor and toasting his early arrival in Newport, when the seizure of the Rhode Island charter would spell the end of the dead Roger Williams' dream of freedom.

At the Blue Porpoise Landlord Prey and his servant, John, were busy with the arguing crowd which sat at his tables. Workers from the shipyards, still in their loose frocks, which hung to their knees, shipmasters, sailors, and artisans waited while Prey took the red-hot flipdog from the oak coals in his fireplace, blew off the ashes, and plunged it into beakers of beer laced with rum, to make the beverage foam and give it its burnt flavor. Some ordered creamy sillabub, or "kill-devil," a fiery rum, while others favored rum and hard cider, called "stonewall," and others, rum and molasses, known as "blackstrap." The room was soon noisy with heated voices. At a table sat Tom and Israel, with Hugh, for that day the sloop had not left the Cove. With them were little Jerusa Sugars, the garrulous carpenter, and the huge sergeant, Benoni Tosh, who in payment for the distinction of his presence at their table would guzzle as many drinks as they would buy him.

"Alas, we are come upon sad days," groaned Sugars, as his mournful face disappeared in a mug of flip.

Tosh eyed the speaker over the finely veined bulges of his ruddy cheeks. "No man knows what may fall out in this luckless colony, Jerusa. Mr. Brinley and his friends are in high feather and prepare to greet Sir Edmund Andros in November on his return from Connecticut when he is to seize our charter. After that, no man knows." The speaker emptied a cup of flip in one gulp, then nodded sagely at the men at the table as if he had delivered himself of a profundity.

Israel Brandy slapped down his pewter mug and roared: "Burn my bones! but all this is the work of this plottin' Francis Brinley, Sanford, and the rest. These land grabbers of Newport and Narragansett have brought this trouble upon us. The poor will now eat less and the rich grow broader of beam."

Brandy whirled about as a hand fell on his shoulder, and he glared into the scowling face of Magistrate Tripp, the cooper, who stood at his back.

"What language is this, Israel Brandy? And in the presence of the Sergeant! Keep a civil tongue in your head for your betters. You speak of a late governor of this colony and the chief justice."

With a shrug, Israel shook Tripp's hand from his heavy shoulder. "Ay, Magistrate, I speak of a late governor of this colony. But may I rot if I speak not the truth!"

Ichabod Tripp's fat face was mottled with his anger as he glared into the mutilated features of the old salt. "Have a care, Israel Brandy," he warned, "or your words may return to mock you. There is still law in this town, and magistrates and judges to see it respected."

The round face of Cooper Tripp made so silly a picture as he glowered at Brandy that Hugh smothered a broad grin in his mug of cider.

"How, now, young Jocelyn," rasped the cooper, "do you snigger at your elders and the law? You may have cause to repent it and that, soon. Why is this lad here in a tavern at his age, Tom Stanton?" he demanded. "He will come to no good end!" And the indignant minion of the law, Ichabod Tripp, Magistrate, who could barely read and write, political toady and prosperous maker of rum and sugar barrels, left them.

Sergeant Tosh's ruddy features were grave. "You had best hold your tongue, Israel, or Tripp will have you before him on charges. Know you not that he fawns on Justice Brinley and Peleg Sanford? They are in the saddle now, so keep a close tongue in your head."

"Ay, Benoni speaks wisely, Israel," cautioned Stanton.

And so, through the taverns of the little port, men sat and talked of the sinister news from Hartford and the coming of Governor Andros to seize the charter of the colony.

One November day the drum rolled its warning from the Parade, and the news spread through Newport that the sloops conveying Sir Edmund Andros and his escort of sixty British regulars were anchored in the harbor. At the peak of the largest sloop fluttered a white flag blazoned with a crimson cross on which were the letters J. R., the new standard of the troops of His Majesty, King James. The free colony of Rhode Island was no more.

After lingering in Connecticut until November, Andros had come. But the news that he had failed to take the charter at Hartford had preceded him. It had, somehow, been spirited away, but he had seized the colonial records and at the end of them had written "Finis."

In the modest house of Governor Walter Clarke, on Thames Street, two men conversed in low tones.

"It lies in my desk, take it," said the elder of the two, a small man, whose iron-gray hair fell to his neckband, and who wore the sad-colored garb of a Quaker. "Here is the key, nephew. Discover not to me what you do with it or where it lies."

The younger man took the key and left the room. Donning his beaver hat, Governor Clarke met the Deputy Governor, John Coggeshall, and a party of leading citizens, and walked to Sanford's Wharf, where he found the new Royal Governor with his staff and escort, their horses already unloaded, conversing with Francis Brinley, Peleg Sanford, and other royalists. The uniforms of Andros and his staff, scarlet faced with blue, frogged with gold braid, and ornamented with shining silver buttons, their white breeches, glittering scabbards, and polished boots, made the blue velvet suit and yellow brocaded vest of Francis Brinley seem somber in comparison. A gaping crowd of people lined the shore and wharves, watching the spectacle. Escorted by his troop of sixty horses, Andros rode through Thames Street to the house of the governor between rows of curious citizens who had never before seen British regulars and, staring with open mouths, refused to cheer. On his way, women and children leaned from opened, diamond-paned windows to marvel at the scarlet-and-blue uniforms, the beaver hats cocked on one side and caught back by gilt rosettes, and the shining scabbards clanking against the spurs of the troopers. Except from a small group of royalists, there were few cheers, for gloom hung heavily in the hearts of the people of little Newport. The freedom of Rhode Island as an independent colony was dead. Andros had come to take their precious charter.

The street outside the house of Governor Clarke was packed with a jostling crowd inspecting the gaudy uniforms and shining equipment of the regulars. Inside, before a blazing fire of oak logs in the great room, while servants brought Canary and malmsey, Brinley talked in low tones with Andros, a choleric, former army officer, wearing a black wig over a face purple from overmuch wine. Finishing his glass, the Royal Governor of the New England Colonies addressed the waiting Clarke, while Coggeshall and the Newport Assistants, who were present, stood stiffly behind him with tense faces. "Sir," began Andros, "you have had friendly notice from me of my intentions in coming to Newport after visiting Connecticut."

Governor Clarke bowed. "You were so gracious as to so inform us, Your Excellency."

"I am here, as I writ you, to obey the pleasure of His Majesty, King James, recover the charter, and destroy the seal of this Colony."

Again Governor Clarke bent his short back. "Yes, Your Excellency," he meekly replied, his keen face betraying no hint of his thoughts.

"The Colony of Rhode Island and Providence Plantations did vote not to stand suit on the writ of *quo warranto*, as you know, and has sent its agent, Major John Green, for England, with our pleas for the mercy of His Majesty, King James."

At the speech, Brinley's handsome, dark face shaped a sour smile as he whispered to the long-nosed Sanford.

"Then I herewith demand from you, late Governor of this Colony and to whose safekeeping it was delivered, the royal charter of Rhode Island," Andros snapped, and his mouth stiffened into a straight line. Clarke bowed and left the room.

Shortly he returned, consternation and perplexity written large upon his plain features, while beads of sweat burst from his forehead. "I am at a loss to discover the strangeness of what has fallen out," he stammered to the waiting Andros, who sat scowling under his black periwig, as he stroked his chin.

"What mean you?" demanded the latter.

"Your Excellency, my desk in which the charter was locked for safekeeping holds it not! It is empty!"

"Name of God! Empty?" Andros stormed, as he and Brinley sprang to their feet. "Empty? The charter lost? What means this nonsense?" He glared at the embarrassed Clarke, who sadly shook his gray head.

"Sir, I repeat, the locked drawer that did hold it is empty," insisted the penitent Quaker.

"Make search of the house, then, till you come on it," stormed Andros, his red eyes fixing the astonished Newporters.

"They are searching," replied Clarke. "I have put all my people to hunting for it."

The furious Brinley shook a finger in Clarke's guileless face and demanded, "Will you swear, Walter Clarke, that you know not where that charter lies?"

"I may not swear," meekly replied the Quaker. "As you know, Justice Brinley, 'tis contrary to my faith. But I affirm that I know not where the charter is."

"And you, John Coggeshall?" demanded Peleg Sanford, turning upon the dumfounded Deputy Governor.

Coggeshall choked with rage. "'Tis a silly question, Peleg Sanford," he exploded, "but not more so than many I've heard you put. You know I had not the charter in my keeping."

Shortly, from a door of the great room, a servant announced to Clarke: "'Tis not to be found in any chest or drawer, sir. We've made search of every room, high and low. It seems not in the house."

"Mr. Clarke," roared Andros, "it appears you take little pains for the security of that intrusted you for safekeeping. If I smelled trickery,

I would call my troopers and search the house."

A dazed look wrinkled Clarke's face. His trembling hand wiped the moisture from his forehead with a handkerchief. "It has been stolen," he sighed, with a slow shake of the head. "If you doubt me, have search made."

The narrowed eyes of the Royal Governor explored the wizened features of the little Quaker and found no guile in the candid gaze that met his. "I lie tonight at the house of Justice Brinley," he growled, "and tomorrow am for Boston. Forthwith, today, when 'tis found, bring the charter there. Now where is the seal of the colony?"

John Coggeshall left the room and returned with the great metal seal of Rhode Island.

"Take it to the street where it may be destroyed," snapped Andros, and with a stiff nod to Clarke and the Assistants, he left the house with the Newport royalists and his staff.

Outside, on Thames Street, while the crowd of onlookers murmured its hostility, a trooper broke the seal into small pieces with a hammer from the cooperage of Magistrate Tripp.

In the morning Sir Edmund Andros and his British regulars were escorted by Clarke, his Assistants, and prominent citizens, together with the local troop of horse, over the Portsmouth Road to the ferry. To the chagrin and wrath of Brinley and Sanford, the soft-voiced former Governor had reported that, to his sorrow and dismay, the charter was still missing. The all-night search had failed. With the stoicism for which his sect was famous, the little man meekly bore the threats and abuse of Andros and the royalist judges.

On his return to Newport, Clarke left Coggeshall and the escort and returned to his house on Thames Street, but his eyes were strangely bright as his horse picked its way around playing groups of children, wrangling dogs, swine, and scratching poultry. He entered the house and went to the bedroom where stood his escritoire. A key rested in the lock of the large drawer. He opened the drawer and stood for a space nodding his gray head. Before him lay a roll of parchment. A cryptic smile spread slowly over Walter Clarke's face. The fierce light of victory flamed in his eyes as he murmured, "God finds mysterious ways His wonders to perform!"

§16

THAT winter, when the ice closed the harbor, Tom, Israel, and Hugh found work in the Wanton shipyard, where ketches, sloops, and brigs were building for the growing traffic with the Sugar and Wine Islands and the southern colonies. The business of the little port was growing fast, and its shipowners and merchants were reaching farther and farther for the profitable carrying trade which had already made Boston rich. Busy with Trelawney and his studies most of the time, Hugh had caught merely fleeting glimpses of Candace Prey since the day she had so boldly come to him on Easton's Wharf after the swimming race. But the memory of her warm lips and the round arms that, for an instant, had circled his neck, often returned to vex and plague him. But any spare time he had in the evenings was pledged to Trelawney, and the Englishman's hold was strong.

As for Dick Trelawney, he had prospered. Tutor to the Brenton and Brinley children, the Coddingtons, Eastons, Arnolds, and others, and mentor in social graces to a group of housewives of prosperous but less important families, and master of a school, for which, because of lack of funds, the Council was forced to charge tuition, the Englishman was making a modest living. But at night through the winter he toiled at his labor of love—the education of Hugh Jocelyn. And Hugh, much as his wild spirits and superb health clamored for outlet and relaxation with the youth of his age, faithfully applied himself to the tasks Trelawney set for him, for the adroit Englishman had planted in the boy the seeds of ambition. Often he dreamed of some day sailing into Newport captain of his own ship.

Before the spring fishing claimed all of Hugh's time, Trelawney had given the boy the taste of "good old Will Shakespeare" he had promised that day two years before on the wharf. From a dog-eared volume Trelawney had brought from England, they read "Romeo and Juliet," and the wondering Hugh was transported to a land of poetry and high romance. It was not without much questioning and many explanations that the curious Hugh was given a picture of life in the ancient Italian city. "Theirs was a deep love, for a certainty," he had said as they finished the tragedy. "Think you any love that deep today?"

Trelawney smiled as he looked into the boy's serious face. "I believe you will love that deep, Hugh, some day. You have steadfastness and capacity for feeling in you far deeper than the ordinary."

The boy reddened as he thought of Candace. "But surely, here in Newport, no one loves as deep as those two in Verona."

"True, in the colonies," laughed Trelawney, "it often seems a man or a woman is no sooner buried than the widower or widow seeks a new mate. And little do such as these know of the meaning of love of the spirit."

"Did you ever love?"

A shadow crossed Trelawney's dark face. Then, with a shrug, he said: "I did once, truly. I was fair as mad as this young Romeo, and wrote sonnets on the curve of her lips and the arch of her brows. But she proved but a shadow—a dream."

His eyes were suddenly filled with pain, and Hugh reached and laid a hand on his shoulder. "I am sorry," said the boy. "It gives you pain to remember."

"Not to remember my love," said Trelawney, "for it was all of me; but to remember what I made of her making so light of it. Seeking to forget, I became a wastrel. That is why I am here in the colonies, to-day."

"She did not truly love you, then?"

"Nay, she knew not the meaning of the word." Trelawney drew his hand across his lean face and closed and opened his eyes as if to clear his brain of a bitter memory. "Enough of me," he said; "I wish to talk of you. You have all life before you to shape it as you will. Keep your heart free, lad, I beg of you, for women will only drag you down. You shall go far if you listen to Dick Trelawney."

Again the beckoning face of Candace returned to Hugh's thoughts. "But how is one to give them sea room?" demanded the boy. "Maids are thick as herring in this port. Would you have me a hater of women and the jest of my friends?"

Trelawney smiled. "Nay; I only beg you not to give your affections, lad. Let no maid trap that big heart of yours in the meshes of her worthless hair. Then, some day, when you have won to the top and have acquired knowledge of them through experience, you will meet the true love your heart has yearned for."

In the spring the cod reached the coast early, herring choked the streams, and sturgeon seeking spawning beds were speared by hundreds in the river narrows. Day after day the gill nets in the Sakonnet were filled with silver-bellied shad, and fat tautog and striped bass swarmed into the bay. Prices for fish soon dropped so low on the Newport wharves that Tom Stanton was making but little from his toil. Off Martin's Vineyard and Block Island the sloop often met schools of spouting bowhead whale and blowing blackfish, but the days of the sperm whale fishery and spermaceti candles and whale-oil lamps were yet to come. In one day, off the Devil's Bridge ledge, which thrusts out from Gay Head, Hugh lanced enough swordfish to load the sloop, and Tom started at once for Updike Newtown, in King's Province, on the west shore of the bay, where the farmers were always glad to barter corn and rye, dried pompions, and apples for a taste of fresh swordfish.

Reaching the little harbor the following day, Tom and Israel at once started in search of customers. Landing Hugh on the point jutting from the north shore of the bay, which was within a mile's walk of Cocumcussoc, Brandy and Stanton left the lad to make the pilgrimage to his father's grave while they sold their fish. Not since he had been taken there by Tom when a small boy of nine, had Hugh stood at the great rock marking the long grave of the forty men who were buried near the site of Richard Smith's blockhouse. Partially burned by the Indians in the war, on its ruins a new house had been built by Smith's son-in-law, Lodovic Updike.

As Hugh stood at the great boulder, barefooted, clad in tattered shirt and canvas drawers, his chest arched proudly and his chin lifted at the thought of the young father who had died that night, thirteen years before, after the fight at the Narragansett fort. Men had not yet forgotten that bitter day. Only the summer previous, when the sloop sailed up to Somerset, Giles Dunbar had told the boy that throughout the Plymouth Colony the men who had fought at the Great Swamp cherished the name of Henry Jocelyn.

He lies here, thought Hugh, somewhere, under this mound, with a lock of golden hair on his breast. Twenty and twenty-four! They were so young to die! Through the dim haze of memory the boy faintly re-called the girl who, back in the happy days, had tossed him high in her strong young arms and laughed up at him, and the big father who had carried him on his shoulder. A sudden flood of tears blurred his eyes. The dire need of that dead father and mother gripped him as he stood in reverence beside the Great Grave. Why had they left him to face the world alone? Then a wave of shame swept him as he thought of Content and Tom, of Israel and Trelawney. They loved him.

"Trelawney says I needs must keep to my books that some day Henry Jocelyn and Judith may be proud of their son, for he says they pray for me and will know."

The boy turned from the Great Grave and started back for the har-bor. As he walked he kept saying to himself, "Some day they shall be proud of their son—proud of their son."

He reached the point and looked across the water where the *Sea Gull* pulled at her anchor. There was no sign of Tom and Israel in the skiff and, wading in, Hugh started the half-mile swim to the sloop. Reaching the *Gull*, he drew himself hand-over-hand up the knotted man rope hanging over the rail, scrambled aboard, hung his shirt on a stay, and lay on the bow to dry out in the sun. He soon fell asleep and dreamed that he was back in Trelawney's room in the Blue Porpoise, on his knees before the chest, when a pair of round arms circled his neck and warm lips sought his own. He did not free himself but drew her to him until he felt her firm breasts and the beat of her heart against his. With a low laugh of victory she flung back her head and her black eyes smoldered into his. It was no embarrassed boy who now held her in his strong arms. Their lips clung, while flame searched his body as he held her, limp, alluring. Then he looked up, and from the doorway the pig-like eyes of Jonathan Prey glared evilly at his young wife in the arms of Hugh Jocelyn. With a start, Hugh waked, to find himself on the deck of the sloop.

"'Burn my bones!' as Israel says," he laughed, tingling to the marrow with his dream, "that was heading full for the shoals! But she was that sweet in the dream I could scarce have changed my course even though she be wedded woman. I wonder what thinks she of my sheering off from the Blue Porpoise this year. No doubt she thinks me afraid. Were she not wed, 'twould have been hard to so treat her even with those old watch-dogs, Israel and Trelawney, at my heels. They would keep me still a child, with half the lads and maids of Newport meeting on the wharves every fair night."

Hugh lazily stretched his brown arms, yawned, and lay on his back, watching fluffs of snowy cloud pass overhead, as he gave himself up to his daydream.

He wondered what this love could be that Shakespeare wrote of. Trelawney seemed to have only bitter memories, so warned him of all love; yet he read with him this story of Romeo and Juliet. He said 'twas a great and deathless love between the two. Could men and maids love that deep here in the colonies?

Then Hugh reflected: "They tell me my father did not wish to live after he found my mother, Judith, dead. Giles Dunbar, but last year, when we saw him, spoke of how my father seemed to have no joy in life but thought only of Judith. He lived but to find the Indian who bore the lock of yellow hair they took from her. Giles said he was fair frenzical at the Great Swamp Fight, and when he had found the Narragansett, forgot all else. Of a certainty that was a love to match with this Romeo's."

Then Hugh's thoughts returned to Candace. Could Candace love as did Juliet? He shook his head with a smile that dented his brown cheek. Could she love like Juliet, she could never have wed the meaty Jonathan Prey. To think of Candace bedding with that carcass! No, Candace wished to have her cake and eat it, as Content would say. And that was fraught with danger. If Prey complained, they might whip her on the Parade before the wives of Newport. Yet in Newport there were many wives of men at sea who lacked not for company for their loneliness, and yet were not charged with it. Why, then, did they whip that young widow, Hannah Clarke of Jamestown?

Hugh pictured in his mind that raw December day when the cowering girl had been stripped to the waist at the whipping post on the Parade, where the great gun stood by the stocks and pillory, and given ten lashes by the constable at the order of the court. It had made him wince to see her tender flesh quiver under the whip and the red welts rise on her white back. They had whipped her because of her child, whose father she would not name. But in Newport there were women who made free with the sailors off the ships at the Widow Moon's ordinary and the Break of Day House, and no one minded them. And Mary Cory had been fined but twenty shillings for her bastard child and she told not the father. Where was the justice in these courts? Why, 'twas well known that Magistrate Tripp himself went often to a certain widow's house. Yet that poor girl, Hannah Clarke, must needs be whipped on the Parade while the boys and girls made holiday of her shame. Hugh smiled as he recalled cuffing two big boys who had made sport of the girl's agony and humiliation; how the father of one had tried to strike him but he had caught his hand, laughed in his face, and thrown him to the ground. Then Israel had led him away.

Then the daydreaming boy pictured himself a Newport Romeo, climbing to Candace's rose-bowered balcony. But Candace had no roses and no balcony; and for nurse, the jealous Prey. Hugh laughed aloud at the fancy. Poor girl, she had paid dear for the whimsies and the clothes the pinchpurse Prey bought her. But there were maids in Newport who were fair, he mused, and free. Old Tripp's red-headed Anstis was fair and warm and reckless. 'Twould repay Ichabod Tripp if his daughter one day stood with an ill-'gotten babe in her arms. But no one would wish that ill fortune to the light-hearted minx. Then there was Seeth Carr, the green-eyed daughter of a prosperous cooper, whose tawny hair forever strayed from her hood, to be ruffled by the breeze. Seeth, tall and strong, already with the shape of a grown woman, who had asked him to teach her to swim. And when he had laughingly asked where, and what garb she would wear, fire had shot from her green eyes as she said, "Anywhere and in anything, or nothing, Hugh, so long as 'tis you who learns me."

He had gasped at the reply, but her green eyes had not wavered as he searched them. He was sitting with her and others on Easton's Wharf, and when the dusk fell had kissed her, to be startled by her swift response, for he had seen little of the girl. But Trelawney had come seeking him for his lesson, and she had moodily left without a word. He had hardly seen her since because of the long spring days on the sloop and the weariness that drove him to his pallet on reaching the Cove in the dusk. Seeth Carr was fair and with a strange wildness in her, and Hugh had remembered Trelawney's warning, "Flee the maids as you would the plague if you would go where I am pointing you, lad."

But in the end Hugh's thoughts returned to Candace and the first thrill a woman had given his awaking adolescence, three years before.

He had fallen asleep again in the sun, when something waked him and he sat up and looked around. Through the water toward a sloop anchored near the *Sea Gull* moved a black head pushing a ripple before it. Hugh's brows pulled together as the head turned with the stroke and he saw the swart face of an Indian.

The swimmer reached the bow of the small sloop, lifted himself from the water by the bowsprit stay, and drew himself up. For a space he lay over the bowsprit regaining his wind, exposing a lean, bare back crossed by welts caked with blood.

Hugh drew in his breath. "He's been recently whipped, and cruel! He's a Narragansett bond servant, running away from a hard master."

The Indian hunched to the bow of the craft, for an instant turned the desperate eyes of a hunted animal to the boy watching him, then threw a swift look at the shore and suddenly disappeared down the forehatch.

On the beach, at Poplar Point, stood a big man shaking his fist at the anchored sloops. Shortly he started for a skiff lying on the shore.

"There's his master, hunting him," thought Hugh. "He's a Narragansett and I should hate him. But he had no part in killing my father and mother. He was a little boy then, and in no wise to blame. And his people have paid a bitter price. Why should I hold his dark skin against him?"

The hunter of the Narragansett was already in the skiff. Hugh, lounging at the rail in his bare feet, tattered locram shirt, and canvas drawers, watched the farmer splash his way clumsily toward the *Gull.* When he neared the craft, the oarsman called, "My Injun swimmed out here. I seed him from below."

"He thinks he's on this sloop," Hugh laughed to himself.

The skiff reached the *Gull* and Hugh grinned down on the sweating oarsman. He was large-framed and heavy, with great gnarled hands. "If he swam not better than you row he could scarce help but drown," Hugh laughed.

The face of the farmer was craggy and hard, with an undershot jaw, and the small eyes were set close together. Hugh did not like it.

"You be a whelp and I like not your talk," the man in the skiff snarled. "Wurs the master to this ship?"

"True," teased Hugh, highly enjoying the baiting of the stranger, "I'm only a whelp of seventeen—but, my friend, with two good hands. Also, to right your farmer's ignorance of the sea, this is a sloop, not a ship."

The stranger's face purpled with blood. "Ho, there! Aboard the ship!" he bellowed. But there came no reply, and he turned in disgust to the grinning Hugh. "And ye were mine, I'd learn ye manners, ye whelp. My Injun boy swimmed here. Wurs he hid?"

"Oh, so you're squaw-man and wed to Narragansett wife? Or were the bans not published?"

Shaken with rage the farmer stood in the skiff, his hands gripping the rail of the sloop. At Hugh's studied insult he suddenly raised himself, scrambled aboard, and sprawled on his hands and knees on the deck while the skiff moved away with the ebb tide. Rising he shook a big-knuckled fist in Hugh's face. "I be Shadrack Fry, freeman of King's Province, and owner of one hundred acres of tilled, grass and wood land. Show me my Injun and that quickly or I fetch the constable!" he roared. "Had I ye on land I'd lesson ye fer the loose tongue in yer head!"

The stranger was inches taller than Hugh and heavier and his gnarled hands opened and shut menacingly as his close-set eyes glittered. Then he started for the open hatch. Hugh was close on his heels, and as the farmer reached the hatch, the boy gripped him by the arm. "Look! Your skiff is gone. How will you fetch the constable, now?"

The other glanced at the drifting skiff, then turned on Hugh. "My Injun's down there!" His shaking finger pointed at the hatch. "Will ye fetch him or me?"

The quick Jocelyn temper was rising. The smile faded from Hugh's brown face. Lights danced in his blue eyes as he sneered at the man who glowered at him. This stranger was big and powerful but, big as he was, he was not going into that hatch, for he would then learn that the runaway was on the other sloop. "Not I or you will fetch him!" the aroused boy bit off savagely. "You'll wait for my father's return! Then he'll give you his answer!"

With a snort of contempt the farmer again started for the hatch but Hugh jerked him back on his heels. "Keep out of that hatch!"

"Why, you unlicked cub, you—" choked the angered Fry, his craggy face purple with wrath. With a quick movement he stamped on Hugh's bare left foot with his heavy boot and struck the boy fair in the face knocking him backward to the deck.

Maddened by the pain and the sudden assault Hugh saw red. Getting to his feet Hugh dove headlong at the farmer's legs, throwing him heavily to the deck where he lay dazed and grunting.

"Get up, farmer!" The panting boy watched the other slowly regain his feet. Big as this Fry was he'd get as good as he gave. 'Twould be no half-starved Injun this time!

Then, head lowered in a bull-like rush and arms thrashing, Fry charged the waiting Hugh to be met by a smashing blow in the jaw which spun him around. From rail to rail, back and forth across the deck under the high boom of the brailed mainsail they fought. Tough as the oaks of his King's Province hills the hulking farmer swung savagely but blindly with fists like pine knots straining to batter the boy into a quick submission. But while the clumsy Fry struck wildly and often missed, the blows of the son of Henry Jocelyn, schooled by Israel Brandy, repeatedly crashed home on the other's face, smearing it with blood. Yet the farmer was stronger and much heavier than the growing boy. His jaw seemed made of iron and he took all that the desperate lad gave him. At last, sensing that he might soon be worn down by sheer bulk, Hugh put all his weight behind a blow and knocked Fry reeling back against the low rail. Then, with a lunge he carried him over the rail and the two splashed into the water.

The floundering farmer rose with a choked call for help and again went under. It was clear he could not swim and would drown. Hugh reached him to be gripped by two circling arms. Filling his lungs Hugh sank. Panic loosed the farmer's desperate hold and the boy thrust him away with a foot. They rose, and Hugh's fist clubbed the other's jaw again and again. At last the drowning man went limp, and Hugh towed him by his long hair to the anchor line.

As he held the face of the unconscious farmer above the water and clung to the hawser, a voice called, "Stab my vitals, but what goes on there?"

Hugh turned to see Tom and Israel approaching in the skiff, loaded deep with bags of grain and dried pompions. "'Tis a farmer of King's Province, Shadrack Fry by name, owner of one hundred acres, grass and tilled, come to pay his respects to his betters from Newport," laughed the boy. "Lend me a hand with his carcass. I'm fair sick of holding his ugly snout above water."

"What brought him to this, Hugh?" demanded Tom, reaching from the boat and grasping the farmer. "He is close to drowned and his face battered."

"Ay," returned the boy in the water. "He fell in a frenzy on the deck and struck his ugly face on a cleat. A mug of rum will hearten him."

Passing a line under the farmer's limp arms, they hoisted him over the rail. Then Hugh carried the bags of grain and the dried pompions and apples to the hold, while Tom and Israel made haste to revive the half-drowned man. When the rum Stanton poured down Shadrack Fry's throat had rid his stomach of the water he had swallowed, and a second noggin from the leather jack started his blood, the farmer coughed and blinked at the three bending over him. Shortly they had him sitting with back to the mast. But it required a third cup to loose his tongue.

"Ye'll pay fer this," he sputtered, glaring at the blond-haired boy squatted on the deck, rubbing his bruised foot with bear's grease. "Ye'll pay—all of ye! Wurs me Injun? I be Shadrack Fry—free-man—King's Province. Set me—shore with me Injun—or ye'll pay!"

Tom and Israel stared suspiciously at Hugh, then at the man on the deck, whose eyes were bloodshot from the effects of water and rum and whose face was cut and swelled. "What means he, Hugh?" demanded Tom.

Hugh had been thinking hard and fast. He pitied the hunted boy hiding in the forehold of the neighboring sloop, for he had seen the slavery to which many a bond servant was subjected. And he remembered the desperation in the Indian's drawn face. Then, in a flash, Hugh saw a way out. Rum and plenty of it!

"The man's fair frenzical," laughed the boy, nursing his bruised foot. "He rowed out in the skiff and called for an Indian. 'What Indian?' I asked. Then he come aboard and hit me and stomped his boot on my foot. Ugh! 'Tis near broke! But he was close to drowned, Father Tom," Hugh went on. "He needs heartening." Rising, he filled the wooden cup from the jack and held it to the farmer's blue and in no wise reluctant lips.

Brandy's expansive mouth began to twitch and the scar on his face swelled with blood as he glared at the man smacking his lips on the deck. "Hit you, did he? Burn my bones! Stomped on your bare foot, did he? Well," roared Israel, "what return had you for that?" Brandy's eyes twinkled as he marked the farmer's bruised jaw and swollen eye.

"Why, I—a—well, you know, Israel, that quick step to one side you learned me, with a heavy swing from the heel with all your weight behind it? I doubt not that is what did happen."

Israel grinned and nodded. "Of a surety, lad, it was." Then to Hugh's secret delight Israel filled the cup from the jack and said, "Have another noggin, friend," and held the cup to the farmer's slobbering mouth. The latter gulped down the rum and attempted to rise, but slumped back on the deck, his head wagging from side to side as he muttered, "Wurs me Injun? Set me—shore. Magistrate. Law on ye. Law on ye."

The worried Tom turned to the boy. "What chanced here, Hugh?"

But Hugh had no idea of betraying the cowering boy in the forehold of the sloop close by until the farmer was out of the way. "I needs had to toss him overboard, Father Tom, he was that saucy. I thought him fair loony. Let us land him and up anchor. He may stir trouble for us."

From under the matted bristles of his brows Israel's quizzical eyes explored Hugh's battered face. Then his wide mouth broke from ear to ear in the smile that transformed him into a grinning gargoyle. "Ay, Hugh and me'll put this carcass ashore, Tom," he said, "while you start easing the anchor from the mud. We sail before we have these King's Province constables on our backs."

Tom Stanton scratched his graying head as he studied the inert heap sprawled on the deck in a pool of water which had oozed from his wet clothes and soggy boots. Israel's last noggin had drowned the protests of Shadrack Fry and he lay snoring, his undershot jaw sagging on his chest.

"I see not the need for this haste, Israel," said Stanton. "But put him ashore. He came here and fought Hugh without cause. There be no Injun here. I think him doubtless frenzical."

So, with the help of Israel, the secretly relieved Hugh bundled the fluttering farmer into the skiff and left him on the beach. On the way back to the sloop Israel suddenly rested on his oars and said to the boy in the stern: "Now, lad, out with the truth of it. You left your mark on his ugly face as I lessoned you when dealin' with tall men and strong, and he hammered you as well. And this after a quarrel. That much I know. And the quarrel was over this Injun he hunted? Did'st see him and where went he?"

"Will you promise not to tell Tom till we clear the harbor?"

"Of a certainty. Between you and me there be no secrets. But a secret I marked in your face, so I filled the fool with rum to put a reef in his babbling tongue and ease Tom of his doubt. Where be this Injun?"

"The young Narragansett swum out here and lies stowed in the forehold of that sloop, there."

Brandy doubtfully shook his shaggy head and attempted a frown which culminated in a broad grin. "Batten my hatch, but you're mad as a bull whale. 'Twas the Narragansetts who killed your father."

"He was a child, then, as was I. He had nought to do with the war."

Israel filled his barrel-like chest, then blew the air through his thick lips in a heavy sigh. "That soft heart of yours, lad, will lead you I know not where. But that farmer was a big man and stout, far heftier than you. Was you long in putting him in the water?"

Hugh chuckled at the sudden shift in Brandy's thoughts. How Israel loved a fight! "Had he not shut his eyes when he swung at me I doubt I could have stood him off, so heavy and tough he was. At last I dove at him and put him over the rail."

Israel swayed on his seat, roaring with laughter. "Rot my bones! Well fought, lad! Once in the water and you had him. With Israel to lesson you, what a bucko you be growin'!"

"'Tis agreed, then, you're not to discover this to Father Tom?"

"Bound I be, till we leave Francis Brinley's stolen King's Province far astern."

§17

THE *Sea Gull* had cleared the harbor of Updike Newtown and was well on her way to Conanicut Point when Israel began, his small eyes twinkling under their mats of brows: "Tom, 'tis cruel hard, the life of some of these poor Injuns bound out to service since the war. When I see the evil face of that Fry, more like to a dogfish nor a man, with the hateful red eye of him, I was fair sunk with pity for the young Injun he hunted. Small doubt he'd work him to the bone and feed him but sufficient to keep him alive."

Hugh turned to the rail to conceal his face. Good old Israel!

"Yes, the farmer had the look of a hard master," said Tom.

"None but a rascal would stomp on Hugh's bare foot," exploded Brandy, with a brave show of indignation. "'Twas the nasty trick of a rumpuncheon of a farmer. He might a broke bones and crippled the lad for life. I itched to hammer his ugly snout myself."

"Ay, 'tis true. But where went the Injun?" demanded Stanton. "Hugh was asleep, but the farmer thought the Narragansett on the *Sea Gull*, for he boarded her. Think you the young Injun stowed away on the sloop we left at anchor?"

Israel gravely nodded. "That might be it."

Hugh laughed outright. "Father Tom, I saw him board her, but he had the look of a she deer run down by dogs I once saw at Giles Dunbar's, and I had not the heart to give him up. And when the farmer stomped on my foot and cuffed me in the face, I had liefer died than give him over."

Tom Stanton's eyes twinkled. "I thought you and Israel up to something."

The sloop had reached down the Conanicut shore and, passing Gould Island, had stood over for Newport harbor, when Hugh suddenly exclaimed: "What brig is that, lying in the cove on Conanicut? Something shines on her deck, like brass. Is it cannon?"

"Those be nine-pound demiculverins, Hugh," said Israel. "That's Peterson's brig of ten carriage guns and seventy men, and a trim sailor she looks. He refits for a cruise to the West Indy, but there is no war with the French and Spanish and he can get no papers."

"He already has some lads from the island baited with big tales of prize money, yet he may not sail as a privateer," Tom added. "I doubt not he'll slip out some night with the red flag in his chest and will fly it once he clears the Horse Latitudes."

A thrill shot through Hugh as he gazed at the rakish brig with her tall masts and long bowsprit and jib boom. A pirate! He had heard many a tale of them from Israel, but here might be an actual one.

"The talk is," said Israel, "that Justice Brinley soon calls a grand jury to hear witnesses against Peterson. But there he rides, with his ten carriage guns at his ports, and murderers and half-pound swivels on his rails, and no one says him nay while our merchants fill his hold with stores for which he pays in Spanish doubloons and Arabian sequins. 'Tis Hispaniola and the Spanish Islands he heads for of a certainty. Pirate he is or Israel Brandy's never sighted a nine-pounder."

"'Tis not the first pirate has fitted in this bay," said Tom, "and filled the moneybags of our merchants and the pockets of the light women. The naval office doubts him but does nothing."

The *Sea Gull* slipped between Goat Island and Easton's Point and anchored in the Cove. That night, as Hugh stretched on his pallet in the loft, he wondered what had become of the runaway Narragansett with the blood-caked welts striping his lean back.

Later, one evening, Trelawney dropped in at the Stantons', to find Tom and Content alone. With the sudden shift in his fortunes, the Englishman had become a changed man. He spent little time at the inns and drank sparingly. His company was much in demand, but he had forgone many a lively evening in order to work with Hugh at his books. His clothes were quiet in color but modish in cut, and pinchbeck buckles shone at his knees and on his shoes. His black periwig, left side shorter than the right, was of London make, and his white-lawn cravat immaculate. He lodged on Coddington Street, not far from Stanton's house, where, through the winter evenings, after the cod fishing off Martin's Vineyard ceased, and in his spare time in summer, Hugh read and studied. To the lonely Englishman the development of the boy's mind, his wonder at and quick appreciation of the riches of the Elizabethans set before him in the dog-eared volumes Trelawney owned and those he had recently got from England, were fit recompense for the merry evenings he missed with young Joseph Brenton and his friends at the King's Head.

"How is the lad faring with his books, Mr. Trelawney?" asked Content.

"We're going fast, and his quick young mind devours that which I offer as a puppy does meat." Trelawney's long fingers stroked his lean jaw as his eyes lingered on the embers of the supper fire. "Goodwife Stanton, you well know how the lad has endeared himself to me. Without him now, Newport for me would be empty. But he takes careful handling. At times he raves so against the gentry and the rich that I fear for him." Turning to Tom Stanton, Trelawney added, "Some day he may do something wild with that temper."

"I know; I know," said Stanton. "He's overproud for his own good and carries too high a spirit for a fisherman's son. 'Tis his poverty that gnaws at his bowels."

Content's eyes met Trelawney's. "He dreams only of the day when he sails deep-sea," she said, "and later, master of his own craft."

"But there lies his fortune," said the Englishman. "He's bound to rise if he will but curb his wild temper and discontent and take the world as he finds it."

Stanton nodded. "Ay, I fear for him. But his heart is stout and 'twill take much battering to bring him to his knees."

"Let us hope," said Trelawney, on leaving, "that he learns as he grows older. 'Twould be such a pity to have so much of heart and brain and promise wrecked on the reefs of his pride and violent prejudices. For the world will not change for Hugh Jocelyn, battle it as he may."

"'Tis true, he cannot change it," sighed Tom, nodding his grizzled head. "But that is fair hard for his young eyes to see."

It was June, and the Stantons' firewood was running low. One morning, when a half gale held the *Sea Gull* in the cove, Hugh started for the Dexters' farm to order a load. Wearing no coat—for he had none except his sea doublets—and dressed in a locram shirt, freshly laundered by Content's toil-worn hands, his only pair of leather breeches, and a stout pair of shoes with wooden heels, Hugh started, hatless, for the Portsmouth Road. His route lay down Thames Street and over the grassy Parade, with its great gun, stocks, whipping post, and cage.

"Good-morrow, Hugh Jocelyn," came a low, throaty voice from somewhere over his head as he passed a neat house with its yard of flowers and herbs, and its vegetable garden in the rear.

Hugh glanced up to an opened window, where the green eyes of Seeth Carr, chin on round arms, oval face framed by a cloud of tawny hair, looked down on him. He lifted a brown arm and called, "Good-morrow, Seeth," remembering with a sudden tingling of his blood the evening they had sat so close on the wharf. Until he passed from sight, the girl sat motionless, watching him.

He turned and walked up the Queen's Street side of the Parade, where swine, escaped from the hog-reeve, rooted, chickens scratched, and dogs quarreled. He stopped where the square-timbered pillory, the stocks, and the cage stood beside a rusty cannon. In the cage, doing penance for her unbridled tongue, cackled an old woman, in an endless stream of invective.

"Heh, heh! Hughie Jocelyn!" called Mercy Jiggles, the town scold. "Now what brings you here when you should be hawlin' fish nets? Runnin' away fer a lark in the country? I'll discover it to Content, you lazy cod's head!"

Hugh grinned. "Benoni got you again, did he?"

"Heh, heh!" The hag bared her toothless gums as she grinned through the bars of the cage. "But I told off his fat carcass afore he left!"

Past Bridge Street, Bull Gap, and Tew Lane he followed Broad Street into the Portsmouth Road, where the town ceased and the farms began, passing Tonomy Hill, which lifted to the west. Beside the low, clapboarded houses with their stone chimneys, surrounded by barns, well sweeps, and flower gardens, green parrots, brought from the West Indies by seafaring sons, scolded and laughed from stumbleberry hedges and stone walls. In grape arbors and shade trees long-tailed macaws from Martinique and Guadeloupe sat pluming their gaudy red and blue, yellow and green feathers. Wooden cages with canaries, parakeets, and other tropical birds hung in the dooryards. At one farm a pet monkey in the top of an apple tree defied a circle of teasing boys below. In many of the fields black slaves and swarthy Wampanoag and Narragansett bond servants worked side by side with white men.

Hugh turned into a winding lane which led west through the woodland. A mile beyond lay the Dexter farm. At a point where the lane made a sharp turn, Hugh knelt in the middle of the road to tighten a loose thong on his shoe. Suddenly, from beyond the bend, came the beat of horses' hoofs. Hugh looked up to stare into the flushed faces of a youth and a girl, whose mounts nervously danced and pivoted as their riders reined them in. A riding hood lined with crimson silk tilted back from the girl's flushed face and chestnut hair shot with gold. She wore a habit of Kendall-green broadcloth and a safeguard skirt for protection from brush in the narrow Portsmouth lanes. The youth, older than Hugh, was gay in beaver hat, cocked on one side, blue Watchet coat, and waistcoat of embroidered yellow satin. To guard his legs from dust and whipping bushes, stirrup hose were pulled over his boots above his knees. His face was crimson with anger as he glared at Hugh, who had not moved from the middle of the lane.

"Out of our way, sailor," he cried, "or we'll ride you down!"

Hugh coolly finished knotting the thong of his shoe, then rose and stood with hands on hips calmly surveying the two on their fidgeting horses. There was a glitter in his eyes as he said, "Ride me down, gentry, and you dare!"

The exasperated horseman rose in his stirrups and raised his whip. "Damme! you scum of a sailor," he cried. "Out of the way of your betters before my horse tramples you!"

The words drove Hugh into a cold fury. "Lay that goad on me," he said, "and I'll lesson you, whoever you are and whatever you own! Were you grown man, I'd pull you from your horse and bloody your pretty face!"

"Lash him with your whip, Richard," screamed the excited girl, her nervous horse circling the two. "Do you fear him? Lash the impudent sailor!" She urged her mount at Hugh as her brother drew back his arm.

The goad whipped across Hugh's shoulders and, with a leap, he pulled the struggling youth from his horse. The boy struck and fought desperately to free himself from the sailor's grip, but Hugh was too strong. With a laugh, he wrenched away the whip, threw it into the brush, then lifted the struggling youth and jammed him into his saddle. With a mock bow Jocelyn handed him his hat. The horse of the enraged boy pivoted and disappeared around the turn, but the girl, her face flaming with anger as she passed, leaned from her saddle and slashed the lash of her goad across Hugh's face. Galloping away, with loosed hair flying, she reached the bend in the lane, turned, and flung a swift look at the boy who stood, fists clenched with pain, his yellow head tossed back in a derisive laugh at the disappearing spitfire.

A purple welt lifted across Hugh's mouth and cheeks as he stood gazing. She was fair handsome in her rage. Who could she be?

Then the blood pushed up over his brown neck to his lacerated cheeks.

"Gentry!" he said aloud, bitterly. "Impudent sailor, am I? When we meet we needs must give them sea room or they run us down and lash us like slaves! Son and daughter of some rich merchant and land grabber, doubtless, who's wheedled and bubbled the Injuns out of their land with rum and laced coats, and who smuggles his cargoes in by night up the bay to cheat the colony and the naval office!"

Hugh reached a little spring beside the road and pressed a handful of mud against his cheek. The wet earth drove the blood from the swollen welt and felt comforting. Then he dropped to his knees, stretched forward on his hands, and drank deeply of the cold water. He rose and, glancing down at his feet, laughed. "White man's foot!" he said, as he inspected a mass of lowly plantains. "The Injuns say they were not here until the white men came and so named them. Huh! There were many things not here before the white man came, young sprigs of the rich who ride the roads lashing at any who stand in their way. I wonder who she is? What a temper she has—and snapping eyes!"

At the farm Hugh's story was listened to by Goodman Dexter with grave eyes and a wagging head. "I doubt not you hear more of this," he said. "'Twas a cruel clout she dealt you, lad. They be Brentons or Brinleys or Arnolds or some other of the great landholders' children, who gallop our roads and worry our sheep and cattle when they chance to meet them. Were they Brinleys, their father, the Chief Justice, who they say has the ear of Governor Andros since our charter is dead, will deal roughly with you."

§18

THAT evening Israel Brandy, Tom, and Content sat with Hugh, discussing his adventure. Stanton's long face and sober eyes reflected his anxiety. Puffing furiously on his pipe, Israel sat, his great paw of a hand nervously nursing his crag-like chin. Content knitted on a stocking, raising worried eyes to the two men as they talked. His face smeared with a salve of grease mixed and boiled with St.-John's-wort from the herb yard, Hugh listened.

"If the twain Hugh met today were Brinleys, 'twill go hard with us," muttered Israel, removing his pipe, that his twitching lips might work with greater freedom. "Justice Brinley walks with a high head since Governor Andros was here."

"Ay, 'twill go hard with us," sighed Stanton. "And harder still if that farmer Shadrack Fry some day sails into the harbor from Updike Newtown and charges Hugh with assault. Brinley owns much land in King's Province and will favor him."

"But 'twas Shadrack Fry assaulted me, Father Tom," objected Hugh.

"Ay, I know," sighed Stanton, the lines in his lean face deepening. "But we shall soon hear from this matter, today."

There was the crunch of gravel on the walk, and Trelawney stood in the open door.

"Here's our man," cried Hugh. "He will know."

"Know what?" demanded the Englishman, greeting the company. Then he stared in amazement at Hugh's swollen mouth and the purple welt crossing his face. "What happened you, lad? 'Twas a goad! Someone lashed you with a horse goad!"

"Ay, burn my bones!" growled Brandy, his small eyes glittering. "Some sprig of our rich land sharks, with his sister, laid a goad on my lad today. But 'twas well he was not grown man or he'd nurse bruises a-plenty tonight."

Trelawney's dark face grew serious as Hugh described the episode and the appearance and dress of the youth and girl.

"By my soul, 'twas that young jackanapes, Dick Brinley, and his mad sister, Lettice, no less! How my hands have itched to lesson them! They've fair driven me wild, for they will not learn. They can barely read and write. Oh, 'tis a shame, Hugh, that it had to be those two scamps—handsome, vain as peacocks, hotheaded, and spoiled by the doting Francis Brinley and their mother."

Brandy and Stanton stared into each other's startled faces.

"Francis Brinley!" gasped Israel. "He'll follow this up as a blue-fish follows herrin'!"

"They'll never forgive it," groaned Trelawney. "They'll make trouble!"

Dropping her knitting, Content went to the boy and, with arms around him, leaned her head on his shoulder. "Hugh! Hugh! Why did you touch him?"

Hugh affectionately patted Content's back and she returned to her stool.

Elbows on knees, chin cupped in hands, Trelawney let his active brain wrestle with the problem. Then he rose and said: "They set store by my labors with their whelps, do the Brinleys. I go there now, before 'tis too late. That hoyden, Lettice, is more willful than the boy, but has more heart. There may be ways to reach the Brinleys yet. Goodnight!"

Trelawney had not been gone long when the doorway was darkened by a hulk of a man. Hugh looked up. The Town Sergeant. So it had come.

"The Brinleys have laid charges of assault against Hugh with the Magistrates," announced Benoni Tosh, seating himself and reaching an eager hand for the cup of rum Tom offered him.

"Charges?" indignantly protested the boy. "I did but stop him striking me with his goad. He started it. Strike him I did not—just held him. Look where the girl lashed me."

"Ay, I doubt not your story, Hugh," said Tosh, glancing at the boy's face as he finished the rum. "An ugly welt, that. But they claim you've mishandled the son of the Chief Justice. 'Tis enough. Brinley rules here, now, and Ichabod Tripp and two of the other four Councilmen lick his hand like dogs."

"I did but defend myself," demurred Hugh.

"They've issued the warrant for Hugh?" asked Tom Stanton, as Content's anxious eyes winked back the tears.

"Ay, Magistrate Tripp summoned me. Already he and Town Clerk Clark had issued the warrant for Hugh's arrest and for him to be fetched before the Magistrates tonight to be freed on bond or thrown into that sty of a jail."

Israel Brandy rose and glared fiercely into Tosh's eyes. "Damn them all!" he exploded. "With Brinley on the poop of this ship, we be no longer free men!"

Tosh raised a restraining hand. "Shush, Israel! They'll have you in the stocks yet for your tongue." He turned to Stanton. "Tomorrow, Tom, the Magistrates sit without jury to consider whether the lad be bound over for the grand jury or tried by themselves for petty assault, and sentenced."

"Sentenced?" Hugh turned cold at the ugly word. What had he done to be sentenced? Shaken a sprig of the rich who would have lashed him for standing on his rights!

"They will take me and Jerusa Sugars as bond? We be both landowners and freemen," demanded Stanton, his seamed face gray with anxiety.

"To be sure, Tom. Come with me now, with Hugh. We'll stop for Jerusa on the way." Benoni poured a second cup of rum down his perpetually parched throat, smacked his lips with a loud "Ah!" and rose. Followed by Hugh, Tom, and Israel, he went out and, picking up the carpenter, Sugars, proceeded down Thames Street to the house of Ichabod Tripp. There Tom and his friend Jerusa signed the bail bond for Hugh's appearance in the morning.

As they parted, Benoni said, "You stand pledged, Tom, under your bond, that the boy will not run, else you forfeit to the Town the sum sworn."

"The boy will be there, Benoni," said Stanton. "He will not run from man or law."

Later, Trelawney returned to the Stanton house from his mission to Justice Brinley. From the gravity of his friend's face Hugh knew that the tutor of the Brinley children had failed.

"Well, Mr. Trelawney," demanded Brandy, his wide mouth twitching in his nervousness, "what word from the great man who is our lord and master since the colony is no more and James is king?"

Trelawney did not answer. He sat with brows pulled together and brooding eyes on the floor, while Stanton mixed sugar and dried pompion in a cup of home-brewed beer, gave it a dash of rum, then plunged the hot loggerhead taken from the red coals of the cooking fire into the cup. The beer foamed and became bitter, and Tom handed the cup to the Englishman.

"I begged him to consider carefully before he allowed Hugh punished for defending himself," said Trelawney, after drinking the flip, "for there are many brawls in the taverns and, I insisted, except in case of serious injury or death, few assault charges brought before that illiterate cooper, Tripp, and the Magistrates of the Town Council."

"You spoke fair and open to the great man," said Stanton.

"I did. He treats me as an Englishman, not a colonial, and gives much weight to my birth and my brother's station in England, so I may speak with him as no one else, here, dares."

"Cast off, cast off, Mr. Trelawney," said Israel, impatiently. "I'm in a fever to sail."

Trelawney smiled at the anxious Brandy, whose mouth was working furiously in his worry for Hugh's safety. "I explained to him," went on Trelawney, "for he has no learning in law though he be judge, that at English common law the shoe would be on the other foot, that that son of his was first at fault for striking Hugh, and that Hugh but acted in self-defense. And that madcap of a Lettice would, in England, pay in pretty damages for lashing Hugh over the face if he brought charges, which he would not."

"Ay, what said he to that, schoolmaster?" rasped Brandy, stumping back and forth on his peg leg.

"Name of God! he went fair mad with rage and roared that the bastard of some fisherman had laid hands on the son of Chief Justice Brinley, and by all the powers he should sweat for it, law or no law."

"The bastard of some fisherman!" Hugh's eyes glittered as he rose. "That's what I'm named, is it? That's what Justice Brinley calls the son of Henry Jocelyn, who battered in the blockhouse door at the Great Swamp Fight while he lay safe at Newport!" The welt searing the boy's face filled with blood as he glared at the silent people in the room. "The bastard of some fisherman!"

"Cease you, Hugh!" ordered Stanton. "He was in a rage. 'Tis well known who you are."

"Name of God!" cried the aroused boy. "That's what they sneer at me! A fisherman and—a bastard! I hate them all—these gentry, with their fine clothes and houses and money! I wish, now, I'd battered the face of that Brinley pup when he struck me with his goad."

"Hugh! Hugh! Be calm!" The Englishman affectionately circled the shoulders of the outraged boy with an arm. "In his heat he knew not what he said."

But the aroused lad impatiently flung off the arm of his friend. His blood was up, and he paced the room, opening and closing his hands as if gripping a Brinley throat. "Name of God! I'll show these fine gentry! Someday I'll show them!"

"Belay, lad," soothed Israel. "Brinley sits in the saddle. 'Tis for us to jump or be trampled on."

"Trampled on! That's what I was today. But if I live, I'll trample on those proud Brinleys!"

"Hush you!" Brandy had his great arms about Hugh and was patting his back. "Your time will come. Lead on, schoolmaster."

"Well," continued Trelawney, "he said he'd show these carrion along the wharves and the Quaker hypocrites who had long ruled the colony to its ruin, who was master in Rhode Island today. James was King; Andros, Governor; and, by the grace of God, Francis Brinley, Chief Justice!"

"And what said you of our boy?" demanded Brandy.

"I said 'twas a case of simple assault, either by his children or Hugh, and would come before the Town Magistrates, without jury, for it was not indictable."

"What said he then?" asked Stanton.

"He said that Magistrate Tripp, the spokesman, would see that Hugh was fed his medicine, and the more bitter it was, the better 'twould be to his liking."

"No Newport jury would hold Hugh guilty," said Stanton.

"But an appeal to a jury trial means the Court of Quarter Sessions, with Francis Brinley presiding. No, we must not put Hugh in that danger. We must abide by the action of the Town Magistrates."

"Rot me, but three of them be Brinley's men," stormed Brandy.

"Even so, we may free him," said Trelawney. "The English law is with us, if they will but follow it and not Francis Brinley's desire."

Though his heart sickened at the thought of what Trelawney's words meant, a grin spread over Hugh's disfigured face. "So, like old Shylock, Justice Brinley cries for his pound of flesh, does he? Well, I can stand in the pillory with good grace. 'Twould be cheap price to pay for the joy of ruffling the fine clothes of his coxcomb son."

Trelawney sadly shook his head. "Ay, lad, it may be worse than that if Brinley has his way."

"Worse?" Hugh exploded. "You mean the whipping post?"

"Yes. Justice Brinley said that the Town Councils of the colony had been authorized by the Court of Quarter Sessions to punish with the lash all who breached peace."

The Englishman could not meet the blazing eyes of the surprised Hugh. Israel Brandy whirled from his ceaseless parade of the room. "Burn my bones, Mr. Trelawney," he roared, "if the lad goes to the post, I seek out and cuff that spawn of Francis Brinley and go with him!"

The whipping post! The sudden realization of what that meant cut Hugh Jocelyn to the marrow. Stripped to the waist, with hands lashed above his head, and surrounded by a curious gaping crowd. The taunts and catcalls of boys who envied and hated him! The nervous giggling of women and girls, and their shrieks when the lash fell on his naked back! He recalled that December day when the whip of the constable seared the white flesh on the naked back of Hannah Clarke with crimson welts; how she moaned in her agony as the snake-like tails of the whiplash wound about her bare torso, lacerating her breasts. He saw the torture in her eyes as she shrank from the blows, quivering like a blade of grass in the wind. He remembered the crimson trickle of blood which followed the crease down her spine between the muscles of her back to the clothes about her hips. Then, able to endure no more, she had fainted, and the law had been satisfied. She had paid the price for her fault and the stubborn refusal to name the father of her child.

But there was no fear of the lash in Hugh's heart—only stung pride and humiliation at the thought of being made the laughingstock of the lads and maids of Newport. Hugh Jocelyn making a holiday for the gabbling crowd! He rose from his stool, and the muscles of his thick forearms bulged as his fingers bit into the palms of his hands.

"So it's the whipping post, is it?" said Hugh, at length. "Well, if Hannah Clarke could face it, so can I! But mark you all—" Hugh's eyes glittered above his lacerated cheeks, and the veins swelled in his temples and the brown column of his neck—"Justice Brinley will live to rue the day when he put the lash to Hugh Jocelyn!"

"There, there, lad! Take it not so hard," protested Trelawney. "'Tis not yet done, and I may find a way to the heart and sense of Francis Brinley. I am to see him in the morning after he has slept on the matter. He has given me leave to appear with you before that fat-headed cooper, Tripp, and the others. These Magistrates are as innocent of law as a shark of good will, and why the people voted Tripp a Magistrate is one of the mysteries of this New World. But I hope to confound his dull mind, if need be, with 'English law' which, I confess, never saw the light save in the brain of Dick Trelawney."

"But the three who will sit tomorrow—Tripp, Peleg Sheldon, and Joshua Heath—will do the will of Francis Brinley," demurred Stanton. "John Mumford, who is honest and fearless, is sick, and Oliver Sailes left today on his ketch for Providence. So they will all be against us."

"Yes, it will be Brinley's tools we shall have to face," admitted Trelawney. "And they will do the will of the Chief Justice—if they dare. But Brinley already sees the weakness in the case against Hugh. Yet I fear what his pride and anger will drive him to."

"You have hope, then, to turn Brinley from his purpose to send Hugh to the whipping post?" asked Tom.

"Hope, that is all. His court has given the Magistrates power to whip for breach of the peace. It all depends on his orders and whether they dare obey them in face of the evidence and the feeling of the people."

Trelawney rose and paced the floor, while the fuming Brandy resumed his seat, his large mouth working nervously in his wrath.

"Why," snorted the Englishman in disgust, "in all Newport there lives no man whose nose has ever poked into Coke on Littleton, or other book of English law. Judges and Magistrates alike are all ignorant of any law. The former governors and their assistants and deputies knew none. Mark you the wording of the old acts of the governors and council now superseded by the Royal Governor and Council for New England at Boston. Pah! Misspelled, and framed in such obscure and limping English that they, later, knew not what they meant when they passed them. I tell you 'twas a government of unlettered men; men of ability in their own business, doubtless, and of force and common sense, but lacking all training in public affairs. Now 'tis a government of Sir Edmund Andros, acting through Francis Brinley, an able man, but headstrong, and no lawyer."

Stanton and Brandy gaped at the tirade of the Englishman. Never before had they heard their great men and leaders so ridiculed and held up to scorn. And, being common men, they were first inclined to protest, but ended by grinning with pleasure.

Then, with an attempt at a smile, Hugh said, "I took one lash of the Brinley whip; I can take more."

"Oh, my Hugh!" Content rose, and hastily left the room.

Trelawney took Tom and Israel outside, leaving Hugh staring into the fire. "If Hugh is whipped, he'll never forget or forgive it, with his sensitive make-up," said the Englishman. "He'll brood over it till he's not responsible for what he does. I believe he'd be capable of killing Tripp or Brinley if they whip him."

"Ay," muttered Israel, "I believe he would; and, burn me! if they do, so will I!"

"Nonsense, Israel Brandy! Are you crazed?" Stanton protested.

"If they whip that lad," Brandy rasped, "somebody pays! Mark the word of Israel Brandy."

"And swing for it, you fool," replied Tom.

"Ay, and swing for it. I've took the risk of swinging in more than one venture with Tom Paine in the old days," Brandy muttered.

Stanton looked at him sharply in the dusk. "I'd like to know more about them days with Captain Paine—your lootin' St. Augustine and the Spanish towns in Florida!"

Trelawney impatiently broke in, " 'Tis of Hugh we have to think now, and not of how those two old buccaneers, Tom Paine and Israel Brandy, cheated the rope."

"Buccaneers? Stab me! You're free with your tongue, schoolmaster!"

"Hush, Israel! 'Tis of Hugh we have to take counsel. He must not ruin himself with any thought of revenge. We must cool him."

"Ay, we must," assented Brandy. "Hugh and I can wait."

§19

THE following morning, sweating under an iron hat and rusty breast and back plates worn over a military doublet, his long sword slung on a broad leather baldric, Constable Shubael Painter stood leaning on his espantoon before the house of Magistrate Tripp, the cooper. For it was there that the three available members of the Town Council were to meet to try Hugh Jocelyn. Around the Constable, standing with his halberd, the insignia of his office, gathered a curious crowd of chattering citizens and their wives. For the news of Hugh's trouble had traveled rapidly from the taverns to the homes of the people. And in that group stood two sober-faced men, Tom Stanton and Israel Brandy, whose eyes lit with anger as they talked together in low tones or answered questions of sympathetic neighbors.

Inside the house, Trelawney and Hugh stood in a corner of the great room waiting the arrival of the plaintiffs. Behind a table on which lay papers, goose-quill pen, inkhorn, and sand box, sat three members of the Town Council with John Clark, the Town Clerk, acting as a trial court for petty offenses or for the purpose of hearing testimony and binding over cases for the action of the grand jury. Framing his fat face with hanging curls, a black periwig of faded color and doubtful antecedents covered the bald pate of Magistrate Tripp, spokesman. His bulky body was clothed in his best suit of blue broadcloth, gay with silver buttons but spotted with the souvenirs of recent gastronomic and bibulous feats. On either side of him sat Joshua Heath and Peleg Sheldon, lean, long-haired Quakers, garbed in philomot-hued clothes, their shrewd eyes and thin-lipped mouths bearing eloquent witness to a political philosophy which maintained that since Brinley ruled in Rhode Island there were more flies in the shape of pine-tree shillings and Spanish doubloons to be caught by sugaring the great man than by opposing him with vinegar. Towering behind the four seated men stood the massive Benoni Tosh, holding a huge halberd. For Magistrate Tripp and his confreres strove to invest the deliberations of the Town Council with a dignity their pronouncements often belied.

There was a clatter of horses' hoofs on the street outside, and shortly, Richard Brinley entered with his sister and a young man some years his senior. Trelawney inspected Brinley's companion with interest. He wore a brown wig and was well made and dressed in the fashion of the time. His face carried a sneer as his keen gray eyes coolly surveyed Trelawney and Hugh. With an obsequious smirk, Tripp rose with the solemn Sheldon, Heath, and Clark, bowed and motioned the arrivals to joynt-stools set before the table. With a flirt of her small head, Lettice Brinley tipped back the green silk hood from her chestnut hair, plucked at the tiffany puffs of her virago sleeves, and, sweeping her silk petticoat around her, sat down, exposing white-heeled shoes and a pair of shapely ankles clad in green silk stockings. As the curious Hugh watched her with mingled feelings of admiration and hatred, she coolly swept the room with insolent, long-lashed eyes until they met his and stopped—suddenly widening, as if in surprise at the appearance of his mutilated face. Her dark brows, like brush strokes on her transparent skin, drew together, and a swift wave of color pushed up from the black lace whisk at her throat, as she looked away.

Never before had Hugh been near such beauty. He had had little time to look at her the day before when she had lashed him across the face and galloped away. But now, where she sat, he could mark every russet tendril that curled around her small ears, the creamy whiteness of her skin, and the modeling of her short nose, her chin, and full-lipped mouth. And shortly, he thought, the story of this spoiled spitfire would condemn him to the humiliation of the whip. A flame of hate for these pampered children of the rich suddenly burned through him. Impudent sailor, was he? Fit only to be run down by the galloping feet of her horse? Then he heard the pompous voice of Magistrate Tripp.

"You, Hugh Jocelyn, stand charged with mishandling the person of Mr. Richard Brinley, on Dexter's Lane, Town of Newport," he began. "What answer make you to the charge, guilty or not guilty?"

Trelawney stepped forward. "May it please your Honors, with the leave of Chief Justice Brinley, I am counseling the defendant and he pleads 'Not Guilty'!"

Pounding his thick fist on the table, Tripp scowled at the Englishman.

"Charged persons need no defenders in this court," he roared. "The truth will out and justice prevail while we sit as Magistrates. 'Tis a new fashion you would set, schoolmaster."

The cool thrust of Trelawney's dark eyes brought the blood into Tripp's face. "'Tis the law of England, please the Court," he announced, "and that law, by recent proclamation of Governor Andros, extends to her colonies, that a charged man may have counsel in court."

The Magistrate coughed and his face again purpled. "Oh, 'tis the law," he muttered. "Of a surety, 'tis the law. But you are no lawyer, schoolmaster. Governor Andros spoke of men learned in law."

"But there are no lawyers in Newport or this colony to defend the rights of accused men," Trelawney countered. "I am versed in English law and practice and, by your leave, will speak for the accused."

Tripp turned and pulled at Benoni Tosh's sleeve. The Sergeant bent and whispered with the three Magistrates and the Clerk, vigorously nodding his shaggy head. The spokesman made a brave show of giving the question his profound consideration as he consulted with his colleagues. His bushy brows drew together and he closed his eyes, drew down the corners of his mouth, and bowed his periwigged head in a Herculean effort to simulate thought. Then, apparently confounded by the intricacies of the problem, Ichabod Tripp proceeded to avoid its solution by abruptly announcing, "Mr. Carr Newbury will be sworn."

Trelawney whispered in Hugh's ear, "Did you see Newbury, yesterday, after you left Dexter's Lane?"

"No. I never saw him before. Who is he?"

"The son of Newbury, the shipowner. I've met him at the Brinleys'. There's some trickery here. 'Twill doubtless be perjury."

"Mr. Newbury," said Tripp, when the former was sworn, "did you meet Mr. Brinley and his sister a day back?"

"I did," said Newbury, "on the Portsmouth Road."

Hugh watched Lettice Brinley's dark brows draw together as she leaned toward the witness.

"How did you find them?" continued Tripp.

Newbury laughed. "Much the worse from the handling they'd taken from that sailor, there." He leered at the taut-faced Hugh.

"The handling they'd taken!" shouted Tripp. "How mean you? Were they hurt and beaten?"

"They were dusty and their clothes torn, your Honor. 'Twas a shame how pitiful they looked! There was dirt and a bruise on Richard's face as if from a blow."

Hugh could hear his heart hammering as his fingers bit into the palms of his hands. He glanced at Lettice Brinley, who sat with lips parted, staring at the speaker.

Trelawney stepped forward. "Do you see a bruise on Mr. Brinley's face, now?" he demanded.

"I dare say 'tis healed," sneered Newbury.

"A quick cure, your Honors!" returned Trelawney, drily.

Magistrate Tripp scowled at the Englishman, cleared his throat, and said: "Mr. Richard Brinley!"

Young Brinley, wearing his own hair curled like a periwig and dressed in plum-colored velvet with embroidered waistcoat and cravat, silver buckles shining at his knees and on his shoes, looked like a London dandy. He threw a quick glance around him and his upper lip curled as he saw Hugh's marked face. He was of good height and closely resembled his sister, but his eyes were furtive and his mouth weak. He told how his horse had collided with Hugh and how Hugh, without provocation, pulled him from his saddle and struck him in the face. "He struck me many times," shouted the angry boy. "And he beat me, for what I know not, save to make a show of his sailor's strength."

Rage at Brinley's calculated falsehood beat like waves through Hugh's tense body. The boy was taking a sweet revenge. Hugh glanced at the girl's face while her brother continued. He watched her body slowly stiffen, saw her hazel eyes, wide with surprise, grow dark as she stared at the witness. Her small hands opened and shut in her silken mitts and a slow fury seemed to flow through her body. Fascinated, Hugh wondered what thoughts were in that willful chestnut head.

"My sister," finished young Brinley, "only struck the sailor with her whip when he would seize her bridle and lay hands on her as well as me."

Brinley sat down. His dark face taut with anger, Trelawney moved forward to question the witness. But before he could speak, Lettice Brinley was on her feet, her face crimson with passion as she stamped her foot and cried: "'Tis a pack of lies they both tell! There's nought of truth in it! We did not meet Carr Newbury! He lies!"

The eyes of the Magistrates and Sergeant Tosh bulged at the girl who faced them. Hugh's jaw dropped in his amazement. What was this? There was something strange here! The girl he thought had come to send him to the whipping post had gone fair frenzical.

Flinging off her brother's restraining hand, while Trelawney listened with twinkling eyes, Lettice Brinley stormed on: "My brother made to ride him down and Hugh Jocelyn did but grasp the reins to save himself. He pulled Richard not from his horse. The horse threw him, and the sailor seated Richard again in the saddle. But I was angry and cut him with my whip—for which—I am—sorry!" She turned to the stunned Hugh and her flaming eyes caught and held his. Then she wheeled and spat savagely at her brother and the astonished Newbury, "You liars!" and ran to the door. Whirling about, her lovely, flushed face framed in a mass of wayward hair, she flung back, "Hugh Jocelyn, I'm sorry!" and disappeared.

His wig askew, the dumfounded Tripp sat staring at the door through which Lettice Brinley had fled. He shifted his amazed eyes in turn to the startled faces of his colleagues. Benoni Tosh cast a significant look at Trelawney's twitching features and nodded.

"Your Honors," said the Englishman, barely able to control the mirth in his voice, "the witnesses for the prosecution hopelessly disagree. There has been no case of assault proved against this defendant. There is now no need of his testimony. I move, your Honors, he be discharged."

Recovered from his surprise, Tripp glared at Trelawney. "Discharged?" he fumed. "Must we believe this chit of a girl against Mr. Newbury and her brother? He swears he was struck and mishandled. She says no. What does the defendant, Hugh Jocelyn, say?"

"Under English law," insisted Trelawney, "a case must be made out first before the accused is put to his defense. No case has been proved here. I move the defendant be discharged."

"We be the Magistrates here, schoolmaster!" roared Tripp. "English law for England. And Newport law for Newport. That is our motto. Now let Jocelyn tell his story."

The two wooden-faced Quakers and the clerk nodded in agreement.

With a sigh and shrug of his shoulders Trelawney motioned to Hugh to stand before the judges. Hugh stepped forward. He wore no coat, and his brown neck was bared by the open collar of his locram shirt. The sea-blue eyes above the welt which crossed his face coolly met Tripp's scowl.

"Did you lay hands on Richard Brinley?" demanded the cooper.

"He struck me with his goad. And I pulled him from his saddle and sat him back in it."

"Ah, there lies the truth, schoolmaster, that you would hide from us; but 'tis now discovered!" Tripp jeered, grinning into the cryptic faces of Sheldon and Heath. "What say you, now? The prisoner admits his guilt!"

There was nothing to say. In his pride and stubbornness Hugh had refused to take advantage of Lettice Brinley's testimony. He was beyond aid. But the Englishman pleaded: "It was in self-defense by Mistress Brinley's own words."

Tripp leaned across the table and shook a stubby finger in Hugh's face. "Did you fear attack from Richard Brinley?" he shouted.

Hugh turned slowly and his eyes drifted from the silver-buckled shoes of the embarrassed young dandy to his curled hair. He smiled as he slowly shook his head. "Fear attack from him?" he laughed. "Why should I fear attack from that coxcomb?"

Richard Brinley reddened to the ears. His angry eyes wavered before the thrust of Hugh's contemptuous stare. Tripp plumped back on his stool with a loud "Ah!" of satisfaction.

It had been hard for Hugh to deny the strange story of Lettice Brinley. She had shown him the way of escape. Trelawney's eyes had pleaded with him to save himself the shame of the whipping post. But the son of Henry Jocelyn could not hide behind a woman's skirts. He had shaken the popinjay and was glad of it. Now he was ready to pay.

"'Tis reported you carry matters with a high hand among the youth along the wharves because of your size and strength," bawled Tripp. "'Tis high time you were lessoned. I'll learn you to lay hands on your betters, and one the daughter of Chief Justice Brinley. I'll—"

Hugh steeled himself for the words which meant torture and humiliation. But Benoni Tosh bent his bulk and whispered in Tripp's ear. Then, for a space, the three Magistrates, the Clerk, and the Sergeant heatedly argued. The spokesman grunted, shook his head as if in doubt, hesitated, and again whispered with Tosh and his colleagues. At last he launched forth in a tirade at Hugh, who listened with clamped jaw and eyes which refused to waver.

"The whipping post is proper physic for such whelps as you," stormed the fat satellite of Francis Brinley. "Twenty lashes is small pay for your insolence in laying hands on your betters. 'Twould serve as meet example, for there's overmuch brawling in this port. But—but you did confess your crime when you might—" Tripp hesitated and whispered in Tosh's ear. The heads of the Magistrates again drew together as they consulted. "And, of a certainty," Tripp continued, coached by Benoni, "you have taken hurt while your accusers suffered none. That, to be sure, must be given weight—yes, it seems must be given weight. Mayhap ten lashes would be—" Tripp paused, grinned widely at the others, and cleared his throat.

Ten lashes! A chill like cold sea water moving over one's body crept up Hugh's spine. Ten lashes! Then it was the whip, after all! He saw the crowd on the Parade gathered to view his punishment and shame. He heard jeers and women's shrieks as the lash fell, raising bloody welts on his brown back. A fighting rage stormed through him. He was mad, mad with the desire to fight, to kill. These three smug Quakers and this fat carcass of a Tripp; he could strangle them now in his bare hands. Suddenly Hugh thought of Content and Tom, of Trelawney and Israel, and his anger cooled. He would take this injustice with a smile—for them.

Tripp was still clearing his throat as Hugh glanced at the bleak-faced Trelawney and wondered what caused the Magistrate to hesitate. Again Tripp, seemingly in a mental fog, consulted with the others. Finally, in a loud voice he announced their decision:

"'Twould be fit were this prisoner bound over to the Grand Jury for indictment for felony and trial before the Court of Quarter Sessions. But there appears doubt of it. It may not fall within the law. It seems simple assault and may be judged by the Town Council. Therefore the will and pleasure of this court is that Hugh Jocelyn—" Tripp paused and glared at the waiting Hugh as a cat plays with a squirrel, then went on—"guilty out of his own mouth of mishandling Richard Brinley and his sister—" Again Tripp stopped, looked around, and scowled, seemingly enjoying the intense silence of the room and the suspense of his auditors—"shall stand in the pillory on the Parade this day, from noon till sunset."

Hugh filled his lungs with a deep breath. So it was not the whipping post! But it was humiliation and shame. Poor Content! She would take it hard. He would make holiday, after all, for the gaping people of Newport. The women and maids would come to gossip and giggle, and the children to make faces and throw dirt while he stood with pinioned arms and head. But woe to any boy or man who dared laugh in his face at his plight. They should pay to Hugh Jocelyn, every one, pay with faces battered by his fists. What drove that madcap girl to his defense when she had lashed him so savagely but the day before? She was fair beautiful when she said he had not touched her brother—that the horse threw young Brinley and he had only seated him back in the saddle. He had come near to laughing at the strange conceit. But why, when she had hated him, did she now lie for him? Why had she looked so hard with those snapping eyes of hers when she turned in the door and flung back, "I'm sorry, Hugh Jocelyn!" Maids were indeed strange creatures, not to be fathomed. Then Benoni Tosh waked him from his reverie as they left the house.

"Go home, lad, and eat," he said. "I will come for you before midday. It will soon be over. And you are lucky. You would have had twenty lashes but I scared them off with talk of what the people were saying and that no grand jury would ever indict you. Yes, you are doubly in luck today, Hugh. Name of God! you shoot high. And she a Brinley! You are fair lucky, boy." And the big thumb of Benoni Tosh poked Hugh's ribs as his huge body shook with his chuckle.

The crowd in the street shouted their good wishes and clapped Hugh on the back as he joined the silent Tom Stanton and the enraged Brandy and started up Thames Street.

§20

At the house Tom offered vain comfort to Content, while Israel raged like a caged bear. The stricken woman flung her arms about the boy's neck and sobbed: "Hugh! Hugh! My own lad, they will mock and twit you, who, but a year agone, they cheered from the wharves! Oh, 'tis a cruel shame that you should stand in the pillory while the scum jeer and snigger!"

"'Tis always the way with the jealous ones," sighed Stanton.

"There, there, Mother Content," Hugh soothed. "'Tis better than the whip, and 'twill be over by sunset. Sergeant Tosh and Mr. Trelawney turned Tripp and the others from their purpose of having me whipped. And the girl—she strangely lied for me! What think you of that? The vixen who lashed me gave the lie to her brother and Newbury before them all."

"Ay, Trelawney gave me the news," said Brandy. "The maid came about with a swinging boom and thrashing jib, like a sloop in a blow, and fair rolled her brother and Magistrate Tripp on their beam-ends. I doubt not the Englishman had talked with her. He said she gave you a shot with her eyes as she left the room that was like to the flashes of a pair of rabinets from a privateer's rail."

Hugh laughed. "She spat at her brother like an angry kitten. I was fair put in stays, Israel, by her fury."

"Here is Benoni, Hugh," announced the dejected Stanton. "Speak a cheering word to your mother."

Hugh kissed Content, gripped Tom's hand, and moved toward the moping Israel. But the old sailor shook his head. "'Tis my watch on the Parade from noon till sundown! I stand by while none make free with you while you are fast in the pillory."

"Have a care, Israel, with that hot head of yours," warned Stanton.

"Rot me, I'll have a care! But woe betide any that abuses the lad."

So, headed by the drummer, Benoni Tosh, and Constable Painter, carrying his halberd, Hugh marched down Thames Street to the Parade, past gossiping groups of men and their chattering wives. The faces of curious women and children appeared at windows, and men stood at the doors of their shops as, with chin high, Hugh walked with his eyes on the broad back of Benoni Tosh. But the sensitive heart of the boy was raw with the shame that Ichabod Tripp had heaped upon him. Though his face gave no sign of the wrath that stormed through him, it would be many a day before Hugh Jocelyn forgot that march down Thames Street past the gaping faces of the people. For years the memory of it would return to sting his pride like the lash of a whip.

"See," cried a woman, "the mark of her whip on his face! What a stout lad he's grown!"

"'Tis a shame," said another, "for 'tis said that young Brinley ran him down with his horse and Hugh but stood his ground."

"'Twas but last year we were cheering him to win the race which he near did," added a sympathetic voice.

"He'll take it hard, that lad," said a fisherman. "I know him well. A hot temper he carries, and a high spirit. Some day Francis Brinley and Ichabod Tripp may pay for sending Hugh Jocelyn to the pillory for standing his ground."

"Be of good courage, Hugh," called little Jerusa Sugars from a roof on which he was working.

"Ay, no need of that, Jerusa," replied a man in the street. "He had it for a certainty when he dared lay hand on Francis Brinley's son."

But there were some waiting on the grassy Parade who bore Hugh no good will. From the gathering of spectators who surrounded the great cannon where the stocks, pillory, and whipping post stood, rose scattering jeers and catcalls when the little group halted. Then, while children ran from all directions and the crowd increased, the drummer beat the long roll. Sergeant Tosh drew a paper from his pocket and Constable Painter presented his halberd.

"Hear ye! Hear ye! People of Newport!" Tosh's big voice boomed across the Parade as he read. "Give you heed to the judgment of the Magistrates of the Town Council. For that one Hugh Jocelyn is charged and found guilty of mishandling Richard Brinley, on Dexter's Lane, Town of Newport, on the day last passed, the will of the court is that Hugh Jocelyn stand in the pillory from noon till sunset as punishment for his crime and example to all. God bless King James, our sovereign, and Sir Edmund Andros, Governor of the United Colonies."

There was a hush as Tosh unlocked with a great iron key the rusty lock securing the upper beam of the pillory, lifted the beam, and Hugh thrust his head and hands through the notches hollowed in the lower timber. The notched upper beam was lowered and locked, and the boy's head and arms imprisoned. Then Sergeant Tosh said in a low tone: "Give no heed to the sniggers, Hugh. 'Twill soon be sunset."

The drum rolled once more, and the Sergeant and Constable left the prisoner to the mercy of the tittering crowd.

In the cage, a few yards distant, stood the same old beldame, doing another day's penance for the looseness of her coarse tongue and the abuse of her neighbors. She pushed a long nose, carrying a large wart, which had pried overmuch into her neighbors' affairs, through the wooden bars and jeered at Hugh: "Heh! heh! Breath of Jesus! Hughie Jocelyn! A brave sight ye make with yer head trussed like a jib cat caught in a fence!"

Hugh turned his head and laughed at the picture made by the hatchet-faced Mercy Jiggles, wisps of gray hair hanging over eyes bright as a squirrel's as she cackled. But he wished no talk with the shameless old woman of tireless tongue and said: "Cease you, Mercy! 'Tis hard enough to stand here without hearing that gull's clack of yours."

"So ye soiled the gentry's clothes and dirtied their faces with the tar off yer sailor's paws! Heh! heh! But they put the goad on ye!"

"Shut that loose mouth!"

"Heh! heh! Afore sunset comes ye'll be that crazy in yer bones, ye'll pleasure yerself to gossip with Mercy Jiggles."

A shower of dirt from the rear of the assembled people put an end to Mercy's abuse.

"Well, Hugh," called a voice from behind a group of curious women, "where is Seeth Carr that she comes not to comfort you?"

That was Eph Greene, who swam in the race last summer, thought Hugh. He lagged far in the rear and hates me.

Then a small pebble struck him on his injured cheek, and his eyes glinted as he searched the crowd for the miscreant. Another and another small stone arched through the air from the rear of the chattering people.

"Shame!" cried a woman. "Were he not trussed, you'd take no liberties with that lad!"

"That was Caleb Cory!" Hugh muttered.

Again small stones rattled against the pillory, stinging his face. There were cries of protest from the crowd, and a blacksmith in his long frock and leather apron pushed back through the circle of spectators seeking the stone throwers. A shower of dirt stung Hugh's face, half blinding him. "I saw who cast that time!" he cried. "'Twas the young brother of Eph Greene."

Then, as voices of men and women rose in angry protest at the abuse of the helpless prisoner, a bellow, more like that of a bull than a human being, rose from the rear of the circle of onlookers. There was the noise of a scuffle, cries of pain and anger, and the beat of running feet followed by the appearance of a square-built figure shouldering his way through the crowd, each hand dragging a half-grown boy by the collar.

"Here be two of the slimy dogfish," roared Brandy, shaking the frightened boys. "Have a look at 'em, Hugh. Their big brothers were with 'em. One you beat in the race last summer. But they outsailed me with their two good legs. Rot my bones, but they lack the pluck of a weevil in a sea biscuit, to abuse a lad in the pillory!"

"Cast them loose, Israel," ordered Hugh, grown suddenly calm, after his first waves of anger.

"Cast them loose?" protested the sailor. "Cross my bow, but I hold 'em for their people to come for 'em, that I have two men to shake in the room of boys. Come on, Joe Cory and Henry Greene!" called Brandy to the murmuring men and women. "Come and dare take your measly spawn! You stood and marked them throw stones and dirt at that pillory and lifted no hand or voice against it. Now, pickle my guts, I'll lesson you to abuse that lad! Come!" roared Israel, his scarred face terrible in his rage. "Here be your filthy cubs!"

With peg leg and good foot spread wide apart, and gripping the helpless boys in his powerful hands, Brandy glared at the crowd. But no one accepted his challenge.

"Cast them loose, Israel," repeated Hugh. "I'll seek their brothers later. Cast them loose and calm yourself."

So, with a parting shake, Brandy flung the terrified boys from him and addressed the spectators. "Till sundown," he said, his voice rough with passion, "Israel Brandy stands watch over this lad whose hands may not defend himself. 'Twas low business to so abuse him!" He slowly rolled back the sleeves from his great, hairy arms. "But if there be those among you of a different mind, let them step out and speak like men."

"Good man, Israel," answered many voices. "You're right! 'Twas a shame!" But there were sneering faces and dark looks among some, who resented the manhandling of the boys whose sport had been spoiled. Yet no man voiced his resentment for, peg-legged though he was, Israel Brandy's strength was a tradition in the seaport.

Shortly, the curious returned to their homes and business, and the Parade was left empty but for a few playing children and the sailor on guard at the stocks shepherding the boy who stood with neck stiff and back aching, waiting for sunset.

The sun shone full in his eyes, and Hugh shifted from one foot to the other, seeking relief from his cramped position.

"I'm stiff as a plank," he muttered. "This head hole is too low for my height and my back is near broke."

At last finding a position of less discomfort, Hugh was fast falling into a doze when he heard a low cough, and opened his eyes.

With basket on arm, the graceful figure of a girl approached the pillory. Loosed from the confines of her red net hood, a cloud of tawny hair hung to the black whisk at her neck. She threw a swift glance at Israel's back and stopped in front of the pillory. Her green eyes darkened and there were tears on the black lashes as Seeth Carr gazed at Hugh's injured cheeks.

"Hugh!" she cried, her oval face etched with pain. "Hugh Jocelyn, what have they done to you? 'Twas not enough that that young Brinley and his sister put you here, but the scum must come and throw dirt at you when your arms were locked in the pillory. Oh, what beasts! And your poor face, Hugh! 'Tis such a pity!"

Hugh's ravaged face lightened. He had wondered if Seeth Carr had forgotten the evening on Brenton's Wharf. Since that time he had seen her but seldom, and then always in a mood. "Your Mr. Trelawney," she had said when they had last talked, "seems more pleasing than all the maids of Newport. You may have your Trelawney and your old books, Hugh Jocelyn!" And her eyes had been black with anger as she flung herself away. Hugh had thought that Seeth Carr had done with him, so moody had been her face when he had passed the house the day before on the way to the country; but here she stood, staring with those black-lashed green eyes shot with fire.

"I'm a sorry sight, Seeth, from the dirt they cast at me, but you are that pretty in your flowered dimity and red hood that were my face clean and arms free I would kiss the pout from that sweet mouth of yours."

"Heh! heh! heh!" chirped the crone, peering at the girl through the bars of her cage. "Here's a pretty kettle of fish! The boldness of the hussy!" A bony hand was thrust through the wooden uprights and a finger like the claw of a bird pointed in derision. "Look! She comes where all may see, with a basket to feed her fisherman! Heh! heh! Did your mother know where you are, you mincing doxy, she'd lay a whip to your behind!" Mercy Jiggles threw back her grizzled head and gave vent to her mirth in a maniacal cackling.

"Belay there!" stormed Brandy, stumping to the cage and glaring at its toothless prisoner. "Put a brail to that slack mouth or I'll warm yours!"

Ignoring the hag in the cage, the girl flushed furiously at the un-expected warmth of Hugh's greeting. "Why, Hugh Jocelyn, what has come over you?" she gasped. "I'd scarce know you! I brought salve for your hurt face, for the sun must burn it grievously."

"'Twas kind of you, Seeth. But 'tis all right. Content put salve on it."

She moved closer and her eyes were on a level with his, bent, as he was forced to stand, in the pillory. She opened her basket and took from it a leathern jack and a wooden cup. "This cider with a dash of rum will cool your throat, Hugh." Seeth filled the cup and held it to Hugh's dry lips.

"Ah!" he exclaimed. "That was good!"

"You are hungry, Hugh?" She took a piece of cake from the basket. "I made it myself this morning. 'Tis stuffed with wild strawberries."

Hugh was hungry and ate the cake she placed in his mouth. "Why did you bring this, Seeth? 'Tis sweet of you to think of me."

Her candid eyes probed his curious look. "Sweet to think of you, Hugh Jocelyn? Why, I think of little else, though you scarce give me a nod these days, so bent are you on reaching Mr. Trelawney and your books when the *Sea Gull* sails into the Cove."

A wave of self-reproach swept the lad trussed in the pillory. She had taken it hard, the swift lovemaking that May evening on Brenton's Wharf when she had returned his kisses with such frank abandon. There was something fierce and deep and wild inside her. And she was lovely, with those dark-browed eyes and that tawny hair ever escaping from her hood like the wild spirit of her.

"Seeth," he said, "you're the sweetest girl in all Newport. Shall we sit again on the wharf when my face heals and the sloop is back early from the shoals?"

Her eager face shone as she fixed him with a tense look. "'Twill be too long, Hugh. Wait not for it to heal." She turned and walked rapidly away.

Hugh watched her with thoughtful eyes as she picked her way between stray cattle, geese, and hogs across the Parade. Then he found himself comparing her with the self-assured Candace who had made his blood beat so when she had said, "I can wait till you learn more of lovin'!" That was three years ago, and he had since learned little of loving. Trelawney and Israel had seen to that. He wondered if Candace was still waiting. He had never seen her alone since that memorable morning at the Inn when the smiling sorceress had unveiled ever so slightly to the eyes of the awakening lad the mysteries of sex. The impression made that day on the fourteen-year-old boy by the amorous Candace with her smoldering black eyes had never been erased by the girls of his own age in the three years past. In the eyes of the growing boy, Candace stood for all that was feminine and desirable though she were wedded woman. But as Seeth's graceful figure in its flowered dimity faded into the distance, Hugh found himself comparing the two. And he vaguely realized, young though he was, that there was that in Seeth—depths and mystery and loyalty—of which Candace was as innocent as she was of love for her husband.

No, there was little likeness between Seeth Carr and Candace Prey. When younger, Seeth had been slim and angular as she grew tall, but now, at seventeen, she was as shapely as Candace, but with more grace of line and figure. And in a year her face had suddenly grown beautiful, with her dark-browed, greenish eyes and sensitive red mouth, that could pout so and yet could break into a smile that was like the sun bursting through the sea mist off Gay Head. Candace had spoken of his learning more of loving when he grew older. Hugh knew that with Seeth Carr one might learn much of loving but it would not be what might be lightly forgotten. With Seeth, love would go deep, like the water in the East Channel at the bay's mouth, and hold like a caught anchor. Seeth would never pass lightly, as did many of the maids, from one love to another. Once given, her love would be fierce and abiding, and all in all to Seeth Carr. Hugh shook his blond head in its wooden collar. Suddenly, to his youthful imagination, the mystery and allure of the girl grew so strong that it seemed there could be no resisting the fever she aroused in him. But there was Trelawney and his preachments, "Shun the women as you would the plague, lad, if you would go far—and with God's help you shall go far or my name is not Dick Trelawney."

What was he to do? Even though his books took much of his spare time ashore, a lad could not always hold the maids in scorn when they fevered him as had Seeth and Candace. What thought Trelawney he was made of? So fancy carried Hugh far as he shifted from leg to leg and tried to forget the misery of his cramped position and the sting of his injured face.

§21

THREE young men in riding boots and blue, green, and wine-colored broadcloth coats lounged at a table in the King's Head, smoking long-stemmed pipes and sipping Canary. It was mid-afternoon, and the noon patrons had returned to their warehouses and shops, wharves and rum distilleries, leaving the three scions of wealthy families, who were not famous for their industry, discussing the trial and sentence that morning of Hugh Jocelyn.

"When I heard of it, my blood boiled," Joe Brenton was saying.

"Trelawney swears that Hugh never struck Richard," said Arnold.

"'Tis not the first time Carr Newbury has perjured himself and 'twill not be the last," snorted Brenton. "He and Richard contrived the story."

"Lettice fair dazed Trelawney when she faced them all," said Sheffield.

"She has the temper of a wildcat, bless her!" chuckled Brenton.

"But what in heaven's name caused the minx to lie for Jocelyn after lashing him so savagely with her goad?" demanded Sheffield.

Brenton grinned. "Kit, he's caught the madcap's fancy. And by that Hugh has made an enemy who'll never forget or forgive," he said, "and one, as well, with brains."

Sheffield scoffed. "Brains Newbury doubtless has, but how does he use them? In the bubbling of his captains and crews out of full pay when the chance offers, the shipping of tainted cod and beef to Barbadoes, or the smuggling of Dutch and French cargoes into the colony."

"Carr Newbury has the business shrewdness of his father," insisted Brenton, "and the meanness of God knows whom!"

Arnold nodded. "If Hugh is wise," he said, "he'll forget Lettice while Newbury pays her court."

"Well said," agreed Brenton. "Newbury is deep and crafty—deeper than any of us dream. If he wants Lettice, he'll let nothing stand in his way."

"'Twill be nothing in the open Newbury will do," said Sheffield. "He works not that way."

"No, he'll secretly plot and scheme to avenge himself on Hugh for the shame she put on him today. He little relished being named liar by Lettice before them all. The memory of it will rankle in that fellow like a festering sore."

"True. He'll little relish Lettice siding with the son of a fisherman against a Newbury," added Sheffield.

The three drained their mugs. "I have business in Portsmouth," said Brenton. "Join me and we'll stop on the way through the Parade to hearten the lad who's been trussed up for standing on his rights."

They paid their score, dropped coins in the box which hung on the wall near the door for the benefit of the servants, and on which were painted the letters, T.I.P., which signified to the patrons, "To Insure Promptness," and mounted their horses. As they turned into the Parade from Thames Street, Brenton, who led, suddenly wheeled his horse and motioned to his friends. "Keep back, out of sight!" he warned. "Now, tell me who that may be on that black horse heading for the pillory!"

"Slay me, 'tis no other than that madcap Lettice Brinley," said Arnold. "I know the mare."

"'Tis she!" chuckled Sheffield. "I'll be bound but she goes to make amends. Brenton's right. The lad has caught her fancy and she cares not a jot for the faces which fill the windows up there."

As the three men watched from the lower end of the Parade, the black mare and its rider approached the pillory. Hugh was roused from a half doze by the beat of horse's hoofs. His eyes blinked in amazement as he recognized the girl, who stopped her mount in front of him.

"Hugh Jocelyn," she said in a low tone, glancing nervously at the averted head of the sailor lounging on the neighboring stocks, "I never may forgive myself for lashing your face that way. I—I knew not what I did, and I humbly ask your pardon."

In her embarrassment Lettice Brinley was very lovely. Her scarlet-lined riding hood hung on her shoulders, and the red in her wayward chestnut hair caught and held the sun like burnished copper.

"I owe you my thanks," said the startled boy, wondering at her daring in coming to the Parade, "for what you said to the Magistrate. 'Twas very kind."

Her mare stood so close to the pillory that Hugh could see the breast of the girl rise and fall beneath her habit as she struggled for words. At last she leaned toward the embarrassed boy and stared, seemingly fascinated by the welt which crossed his face. Then she burst into a torrent of words. "I—I did that to you? I'm so sorry, Hugh Jocelyn! And you laughed at me! When I turned and saw you standing in the path laughing, I hated myself, Hugh Jocelyn! You—you little know how proud you looked, standing there! I begged my father and brother, and Mr. Trelawney pleaded, but it didn't move them. Then Richard and Carr Newbury lied about you and I fair hated them."

The agitated girl caught herself up and the astonished Hugh thought he had never seen anything so lovely as her flaming face and brilliant hazel eyes.

"'Tis kind of you—Mistress Brinley," he stumbled, "to come here and—tell me this, you—a lady—and I—but a fisherman. I fear with the dirt they tossed at me my face is scarce fit to be seen. And you—you should have a care for the curious eyes watching you here talking with one in a pillory. Your father—"

"My father!" she cried. "Oh, how I hate him for doing this to you! And myself I hate worst of all—for striking you. You'll forgive me, Hugh Jocelyn? You'll not hate me for it?"

Suddenly she wheeled her black mare and left him, but as she rode away, she flashed him a smile that he remembered for many a day.

Shrill laughter and catcalls from the cage followed the girl on the horse. "Hey de dey! There she rides, all pert and coppet in her silk hood and green stockin's! Mistress Brinley, like a wagtail in the Butterfly tavern, after her sailor! Heh! heh! heh! 'Tis well for her his hands were trussed, or she'd not stayed long on her horse!"

"Brail that evil tongue of yours, Mercy Jiggles!" ordered Hugh, tired of the crone's babbling.

From the foot of the Parade three horsemen watched Lettice Brinley disappear into Spring Street. "If Francis Brinley hears ought of this, there'll be more trouble for Hugh, and he blameless," said Brenton. "Let us stop and hearten him. He must ache in every bone."

Shortly the horsemen were at the pillory where Hugh stood in a daze, thrilled by the boldness and the beauty of Francis Brinley's daughter. Joe Brenton swung from the saddle and grasped Hugh's hand.

"'Tis a shame to find you here, Hugh, for no other reason than that you are true Englishman and stood on your rights. But it seems you already have had heartening. There is one who forgot you not today, though but yesterday she left an ugly welt across your face."

Hugh reddened to his hair. "It was mad of her to come here, Mr. Brenton."

"'Twas not your fault, lad. She's wild as a hare and will brook no checkrein; but her heart seems sound, for they tell me she stood stoutly for you before the Magistrate. We three, Mr. Arnold, Mr. Sheffield, and I, bring you our good wishes."

With a wave of the hand, the three men rode away. As they left the Parade, they saw a horseman approaching from Thames Street.

"Who's that?" demanded Brenton.

"It looks like Newbury on his gray mare."

"I wonder if he saw her at the pillory," said Brenton. "If he did, he's doubtless beside himself. Israel Brandy'll take care of Hugh or I'd stay and see fair play."

"You'd likely insult him, Joe, and we'd have a duel on our hands," said Sheffield. "We're better out of the way."

So the three horsemen continued up Broad Street, bound for Portsmouth.

At the sound of horse's hoofs Hugh raised his eyes. Savagely whipping the air with his short riding goad, Carr Newbury stopped his mount before the pillory. "You scum of a fisherman," he spat out. "When Justice Brinley hears of this, he'll have you well lashed for your impudence."

Newbury's close-set eyes slanted savagely down at the boy, who watched him from the pillory, hot with rage at his helplessness.

"You'll pay to me for that word," Hugh bit off.

"I'm fevered to give you another cut across the face to lesson you to keep your hands off your betters," stormed Newbury, edging his mare closer to the pillory and viciously flicking his whip.

"You're a brave man," sneered Hugh. "Were I free, I'd show you how I'd manhandle my betters."

Suddenly, from the rear of the pillory sounded the beat of a peg leg on gravel and a hoarse bass roared: "Belay that horse goad! Touch that lad and, rot my bones! there'll be murder in Newport this day." Rolling back his sleeves, Israel stumped out between the pillory and the horseman.

"You dare threaten me, you pirate!" stormed Newbury.

Israel laughed, but his grotesque face was purple with blood and his mouth savage in his anger as he stood, hands on hips, in front of Hugh. "Stab my guts! 'tis a brave man who'd lay whip to a lad helpless in the pillory. Now put your goad on me, Mr. Newbury, an you dare!"

In sudden rage, Newbury whipped back his arm, then slowly let it drop as Brandy seized the bridle rein, jerked the mare forward and doubled a knotty fist. "Name of God! You buffle head of a sailor, you'll hear more of this," cried Newbury, backing his horse away as Israel released the rein.

"Heh! heh! heh!" cackled the hag from the cage. "'Tis well ye give room to that rake-hell, Israel Brandy, Mr. Carr Newbury! He'll eat ye alive—that pirate! Many's the Spaniard he's et in the warm seas, and yeller maid he's bedded. Heh! heh! Keep yer white hands off Brandy!"

Hugh grinned as the chagrined Newbury trotted away, followed by the caterwauling of the crone.

"'Tis well you kept your hands from him, Israel," said the boy. "We've had trouble enough."

"Newbury though he be," rasped Brandy, "had he touched you, I'd a-blooded his chitty face and gone to the whipping post for it."

"He was fair frenzical," said Hugh, "and aimed to cut me with his whip; but a cuff from you was not to his kidney."

"I trust no harm'll come from this," muttered the old salt. "Brinley rules here, and when he hears of it, that blue blood of his'll boil. Well, 'tis close to sunset, and Benoni'll soon be here to free you."

"Brinley's blood may boil but he'll send me to no whipping post," snapped Hugh.

Israel squinted at the sunburned face of the lad in the pillory. "How mean you?"

But Hugh made no reply. Shortly Benoni appeared, with Trelawney and Tom Stanton.

Once more secure—at least for the time being—in Tom Stanton's house, the three men and the youth sat quietly over mugs of flip and cider. Content hovered in the background, muttering, "To think they'd fling stones at my boy and he helpless!"

Trelawney, his sober eyes fixed on his mug of flip, at length said,

"Lettice Brinley rode into the Parade and talked with you, Hugh—and so did Newbury and Joe Brenton."

"I did not say so," Hugh answered.

"Israel told me, and it's important that I know all. Did Brenton and Newbury see her with you?"

"Yes. They came shortly after she left. She but came to say she was sorry for lashing me. I warned her people would see."

Trelawney scowled into his mug. "They said nothing of her to you?"

"Mr. Brenton spoke of seeing her, and Newbury called me scum and flicked his whip, but he had no stomach for trouble with Israel."

"Francis Brinley will never forget that she came to the pillory, nor will Newbury. They'll blame you, not her."

"But I had nought to do with it," objected Hugh.

Trelawney slowly shook his head. "You know him little. So proud is he that he'll scarce stop to further injure you because of his anger at it all. I must talk with Joe Brenton. He is your friend."

§22

BEFORE dawn the following morning Trelawney was pounding on Stanton's door. "Tom," he demanded of the surprised fisherman, who wondered at the gravity of the schoolmaster's face in the flickering candlelight, "is there a sloop sailing today for Boston or anywhere?"

"Why—yes," answered the puzzled fisherman, "the sloop, *Sea Flower*, Captain Beer, at dawn."

"Call Hugh, quick! There's no time to waste! Last night Francis Brinley went frenzical when he heard that his daughter had gone to the pillory. It will mean the whipping post for Hugh, though innocent. Call him!"

Stanton called to the loft. There was no answer. "Hugh! Wake up, lad!" he repeated, then mounted the ladder. Shortly the fisherman returned with a scrap of paper in his hand. He gave it to the anxious Trelawney, who held it to the candle and read aloud:

> I am shipping with Captain Beer. I'll take no whipping from Brinley.
>
> HUGH.

The two men stared into each other's fearful eyes. "Our talk last night drove him to it," said Stanton. "He must have sought out Captain Beer after we went to bed. He'd die before he'd be whipped!"

"Driven from home by Brinley and Newbury!" muttered Trelawney, the paper in his hand slithering to the floor. "What a fine justice exists in this colony! James is King; Andros, Governor; and Brinley, Chief Justice! Chief Justice of what? Bah! A pox on them all!"

At dawn, with a fair tide and following wind, the *Sea Flower* shook out her jib and brailed mainsail and slipped between Goat Island and Brenton's Neck. They passed the Dumplings, and across the channel the sun lifted over the chimneys thrusting above the tree-tops of Hammersmith, the home of the Brentons, the great landholders. As the roof of the large house reflected the lifting sun, a sudden hatred of all these rich landowners and their wide acres centered in Hugh's heart. Joseph Brenton had been his friend, but toward the rest, with their sheep and cattle, their wharves and rum distilleries, their silk and velvet clothes and curled periwigs and lofty airs, he bore a deep resentment. What cared they for justice when a lad could be put in the pillory for standing on his rights? And now Justice Brinley—Chief Justice Brinley!—because his daughter had demeaned herself by showing herself on the Parade in converse with a fisherman's son, needs must drive him from the port to escape the shame of the whipping post. Hugh's deep chest filled and his hands gripped a shroud where he stood at the chains watching Brenton's flocks of sheep grazing on the distant pastures. Some day, Hugh promised himself, he would again lay hands on that sprig of a young Brinley, and when he did, 'twould not be for the purpose of seating him in his saddle. As for the girl—with a thrill, Hugh smiled at the memory of Lettice Brinley's ardent face—well, he might lay hands on her, as well. From her actions at the pillory 'twould seem that that was what she wished. 'Twould be sweet revenge on the proud Justice Brinley! So ran his thoughts as the sloop rounded Brenton's Point and headed east.

The *Sea Flower*, a thirty-ton sloop, carried a crew of four men—three from Massachusetts Bay and a Cape Cod Indian. She had brought to Newport a cargo of merchandise from Bristol, England, which had been transshipped from Boston, there being little direct trade between the English ports and Newport. Her return freight was mostly country produce—Cheshire cheese, for which King's Province was famous, corn and salt beef, with pipes of wine from a brig just in from Madeira and the Canaries. Hugh was shortly as much at home on the larger craft as on the *Sea Gull*, for little had been overlooked by Israel and Tom in his training as an able seaman.

"How old are you, lad?" demanded Captain Beer when, without aid, Hugh hauled in and made fast the sheets of the long-boomed, loose-footed mainsail.

"Seventeen, sir, near eighteen."

"Seventeen?" Captain Beer's appraising eyes lingered on the wide shoulders and bared forearms of his new hand. "You have great power in that young back of yours. Always, before, four hands have done what you did with two."

"I am customed to hard work and much lifting."

"Ay, I believe you."

The wind was dropping, and as they passed Sakonnet Point with course set to round Cuttyhunk and enter Martin's Vineyard Sound, the eyes of the master anxiously watched the hazing sky to the south.

"You fish in this water," Beer said to Hugh, late in the afternoon; "what think you of this tricky wind and that bank of haze to the south?"

Hugh had been watching the weather all day and was quick with his answer. "'Twill be well to give the Sow and Pigs a wide berth. Before night we shall lie in a flat calm, in the fog, with a flood tide edging us northerd. In weather like this my father always heads south for sea room, for between the Sow and Pigs and the Devil's Bridge the Sound is fair dangerous to enter in a fog."

"Well spoken, lad! We'll bear sou'east while the breeze lasts."

Toward sunset the *Sea Flower's* long boom was swinging and the leach of her mainsail flapping lazily, but the fog bank to the south had not yet closed in. From the masthead—for she carried no square topsail—Hugh could make out a gray smear on the horizon. "Land! Nor'east! 'Tis Cuttyhunk!" he called to Captain Beer. "I can make out the slobbering of the Sow and Pigs! She rolls white over them."

Beer shifted his tiller and slowly worked the sloop's nose into the south. Occasional puffs of air barely kept her under steerageway. Then, as Hugh scanned from his perch the smoking sea to the eastward, a black hulk and a big mainsail suddenly loomed through the soupy haze. "Sail, ho!" he hailed the deck.

Slowly the strange sloop drifted down on the *Sea Flower*. Hugh slid down the shrouds and joined the crew at the rail.

"She's a coaster, like ourselves, likely bound for Newport," said Captain Beer.

"Why carries she so many men?" suddenly exclaimed one of the crew. "The rail's crowded!"

Hugh's blood suddenly leaped with excitement at what he saw. "Captain Beer!" he shouted. "She has guns! They're working at one on her starboard rail!"

"Guns? Name of God!" groaned the master at the tiller. "She's a pirate!"

The strange sloop moved down on the helpless *Sea Flower*. It was clear, now, why so many men crowded her rail. As the two sloops drifted within hailing distance, a puff of orange smoke leaped from a starboard gun port of the stranger, followed by the roar of a cannon, and a round shot hurtled across the *Sea Flower's* bow. "Heave to, damn yeh, or we sink yeh!"

The gray-faced Beer swung on his tiller. "There's nought to be done," he groaned to his frightened crew. "Put back that musket," he cried to Hugh, who at that moment sprang from the hatch with a cocked flintlock. "Her decks are full of men! Are you crazed? If we do their bidding, we may yet save our lives!"

"You'll not defend your ship?" cried the excited boy.

"Put back that musket, you fool!" ordered Beer.

"But the sweeps!" Hugh protested. "We might get away!"

"What sloop is that?" came the bellowing voice from the stranger's bow.

"*Sea Flower*, from Boston."

"What's your cargo?"

"Country produce and wine," replied Beer.

A cheer rose from the stranger's deck. "Stand by for our boat!" ordered the voice, again. "Have a care what you do or we'll rake your decks."

"Ay, ay!" called the frightened Beer.

The sloops were now drifting a hawser's length apart on a flat sea. A boat put off from the stranger.

A pirate! Israel's tales of the Spanish Main filled Hugh's young head as he watched the approaching boat. He had heard of stray pirates on the coast, men of New England birth. But they had never sought the small fishing sloops. Now, right here, in Vineyard Sound, was an actual pirate! The man who hailed was English, and the voices were English voices. Who could they be and what would they do when they had taken the cargo? Would they turn Captain Beer loose with his empty sloop or—? Hugh had heard of crews being murdered that they might carry no tales into the nearest port. Would that be their fate?

Of course, Captain Beer was right in not trying to resist. He had nothing but muskets. And yet, it seemed to Hugh, if he had been master he would have risked being hit, got out the sweeps, and tried to lose the sloop in the mist. A pirate, on his first voyage! Here was a tale for the ears of Israel Brandy!

Shortly, a bulky seaman threw a leg over the *Sea Flower's* rail, followed by four men brandishing pistols and cutlasses. "Where's the master?" he roared.

Beer stepped forward. "I am master. Caleb Beer is my name."

"I be Captain Samuel Bellamy, of the *Saucy Sally*. Burn me! you've heard of Bellamy? And you'll hear more. They'll soon know Bellamy from the Banks to Barbadoes. What carry you below them hatches?"

"Cheese, salt beef, and corn. And ten pipes of wine."

The big pirate smacked his lips. "Captain, you're a sloop after my own heart! Christ's blood, if you be not! I need cheese, beef, and corn, and plenty of wine for my thirsty lads, and you bring it me!" Bellamy staggered the frightened Beer with a clout on the shoulder.

His nerves alive with excitement, Hugh watched the pirate leader. He was a great bearded fellow wearing a beaver hat with a drooping feather. Beards were uncommon, and Bellamy's aroused Hugh's interest. Two pistols were thrust through the pirate's belt and a heavy cutlass, slung on a baldric, hung at his hip.

"I be a poor man," said Beer, sadly. "And I have a small interest in this sloop and cargo. 'Twill go hard with me to lose all for I have many mouths to feed in Boston."

"Boston!" roared the pirate. "Now there's a slimy town for you! Why, man, I was born in Boston! An honest man may not draw breath in Boston without leave of the filthy clergy, who live like leaches on other men's sweat. Church-ruled, is Boston! The people are but sniveling slaves to a shoal of long-faced old women!" Bellamy filled his chest and turned to his men for the nods of approval which he got.

It was evident to Hugh that the pirate was a man of some education. He seemed to revel in the sound of his own voice and the opportunity to impress his helpless prisoners. "Boston!" he shouted, with a sweep of his arm. "Pickle my guts! but I'd know what to do had I the Mathers, father and son, here on this sloop! They'd pray for no more stout lads a-sun-dryin' from gibbets on Nix's Mate!"

Hugh glanced curiously from the blustering leader to his four men. They much resembled the sailors he saw in Newport harbor. There was little about them to terrify anyone. Surely pirates were not so fearsome.

"Well," continued Bellamy, "we'll lay you board and board and take on your stores. I like not to rob a poor man, but the owners of these are rich and can pay."

Shortly the *Saucy Sally*, with the help of her sweeps, lay alongside, and the two crews started shifting the cargo of the *Sea Flower*, while Beer stood by mournfully watching. As Hugh slung a heavy bag of corn to his shoulders, his blood grew hotter and hotter at the thought of Bellamy and his crew living on the toil and goods of honest men. He was crossing from the hatch to the rail when one of the pirates lurched into him, throwing him off balance. He fell to his knees with the bag beside him. Before he could rise the pirate kicked him in the back.

"Out of me way, cod's head," bawled the sailor, as Hugh scrambled to his feet, hot with anger.

The pirate laughed at the furious boy confronting him and suddenly struck him full in the face, sending him reeling backward, to fall over the bag of corn he had dropped. The blow drove all thought of fear for his life from Hugh's head. A red Jocelyn rage stormed through him as he leaped to his feet and dove headlong at the sneering sailor. They went to the deck together, while the pirate crew formed a yelling circle around them. As they rolled and thrashed, straining in each other's arms, Hugh found to his surprise that he was quite as strong as his enemy. With a hunch, he freed a hand and clubbed the pirate's jaw again and again with his fist. Then an arm around him loosened and Hugh felt the other groping for his knife. But the boy gripped and pinioned the wrist before the knife was drawn. For a space they lay panting, while the circling crowd urged them on. And while they lay, Hugh burst into a cold sweat at the thought of the price he would pay—he, a prisoner on a pirate ship. Then, a voice bellowed over them.

"Belay! you sons o' rumpuncheons. Think you I'd lightly lose two men in a silly brawl? Let go or, slay me! I'll give you the flat of my cutlass!"

But Hugh feared to release the pirate's knife hand. Then, with a curse, Bellamy whipped the flat of his cutlass across the boy's back. He rose and leaped away as the pirate scrambled to his feet, knife in hand. Hugh backed against the rail and seized a handspike, to defend himself. Then Bellamy, with drawn cutlass, stopped the angered sailors closing in.

"Sheath them knives, you slit-throats," he roared. "I'll split the skull of any who touch that lad! Burn me! He was set on and only took his own part. Christ's blood! A stout pirate he'll make! How old are you, young rooster?"

Cold with the realization of how close to death he had come, Hugh gripped the spike, beside Bellamy, and faced the ring of hostile faces. "Seventeen," he said.

"Seventeen? Slay me! With that stout body and spunk, we'll make a rare pirate of you before you be full grown. Stab my guts, men, this lad goes with us. The man who harms him answers to me. Move lively, now, with the whip for them pipes of wine."

The crew of the pirate returned to their work of shifting the cargo, and Hugh felt suddenly cold and sick. They were going to take him—"force" him—as a member of the crew. What would become of Hugh Jocelyn now? When the cargo of the *Sea Flower* was stowed in the hold of the *Saucy Sally*, Captain Beer and his worried men waited while the pirates voted on the disposition of the captured sloop and its crew. Shortly Bellamy returned to the *Sea Flower* and announced the vote to the group of five men who, like prisoners after trial, listened with knocking knees and drumming hearts to their sentence.

"Damn my blood!" announced the garrulous pirate, "we be fair-minded men with no purpose to do a poor man mischief except it be to our advantage. Damn the sloop! She's but a tub and no use to us. Take her."

Tears of relief blurred Captain Beer's fearful eyes as he mumbled his thanks, while his crew of four men hugged each other in their joy.

"But damn ye, ye be but a sneaking puppy to bow to laws that rich men make for their own safety," roared Bellamy, with a sweep of his arm, while the crew of the *Saucy Sally* lined the rail to listen with grimacing faces to the oration of their chief. "Damn them, I say, for a pack of crafty rascals, and you, who slave for them, for a flock of chicken-hearted dolts! They rob the poor under cover of their laws while we plunder the rich under the protection of our own courage. Join us, Captain, and quit your slavery to the greedy rich."

Beer's face was gray with fear of the pirate's wrath as he meekly replied, "'Tis not in my conscience, Captain Bellamy, to break the laws of God and man."

Bellamy laughed loudly. He turned to his men. "Heard ye that, buckoes?" Then he addressed the trembling Beer: "So you're a rascal with a conscience, while I'm a free prince to live as I please! Damn me, there's no arguing with such sniveling puppies who suffer the high and mighty to kick their behinds at pleasure and who pin their faith on a pimp of a parson—a squab who practices not nor believes what he puts into the addled pates he preaches to."

There was a roar of approval from the crew of the *Saucy Sally* at this stilted invective, and Bellamy tilted his beaver hat at an angle and stroked his beard with evident satisfaction. Hugh had listened to the windy pirate's rodomontade with mixed feelings. He was overjoyed that Beer was to have his sloop. Word would then reach Newport that he was alive. But poor Content! How she would grieve for him! He felt cold and alone. What would be the end of Hugh Jocelyn now?

Before the ships parted, Beer came to Bellamy and made a last appeal for Hugh's release. "The lad is but seventeen," urged Beer. "He is over young for your uses. Let him come with me."

"Over young, eh?" cried the pirate. "He's as stout as a young bull and as spunky. He gave Jack Trigg all he could handle and more. What'll he do when grown? Stab me! he stays with us, and some day, when you hear of the deeds of a yellow-haired pirate on the Spanish Main, you'll have Samuel Bellamy to thank for making the lad a sea rover and a free man."

Hot with anger at his helplessness, Hugh bade good-by to Captain Beer and the crew of the *Sea Flower*. "You'll send word to Tom Stanton and tell them not to grieve for me?" he asked Beer.

"That I will, lad! 'Twill be known soon, in Boston, you were forced. I'll have it published at the taverns and will name you to the

court that you may come to no harm if Bellamy is taken. Keep your
heart up."

§23

BEER returned to his sloop, and shortly the *Sea Flower* drifted away
and was swallowed in the fog which blanketed Vineyard Sound. With
a last wave of the hand toward the vanishing sloop Hugh turned from
the rail. He was alone—alone on a pirate ship, bound he knew not
where. It might be many a long month—years, perhaps—before he
would again see Newport and those he loved. And mayhap—never—unless— Drenched to the bone with mist, the desperate boy shivered as he stood beside a brass five-pounder at the rail and thought of
home.

Content and Tom would be eating their evening meal now, for the
fog would have driven the *Sea Gull* home early from the Sakonnet
fishing grounds. Shortly, Israel would stump in for a cup of rum and
a pipe before he slept. Trelawney might stop on his way up Thames
Street to bring them the news from the taverns. Candles would flicker
in the houses, for the fog would hang thick in the narrow streets of the
little seaport. But none of this was for Hugh Jocelyn, forced man on
the pirate *Saucy Sally*. He realized that Bellamy would not dare linger
in the Sound but would soon put to sea, probably heading south for
the Sugar Islands. The Spanish Main! What chance of return from the
Indies was there for Hugh Jocelyn?

The aroma of cooking food drifted from the galley hatch to torment his nostrils. Maudlin snatches of song rose from the forecastle
where the pirates had broached a pipe of Canary. The flood tide had
been running two hours, and he knew that they were drifting northeast
toward the Sow and Pigs and Cuttyhunk. He heard Bellamy arguing
with the mate at the tiller. Then his name was called. Hugh went aft
and stood before the two men.

"Young Jocelyn," said Bellamy, "you say you fish this water?"

"Ay, sir," answered Hugh.

"Saw you land before the fog shut in and we happened on you?"

Hugh thought quickly. "No, we lay far to the south of Cuttyhunk
with plenty of sea room," he lied. "This flood is carrying us west of
the islands. The sloop is as safe as if anchored in a harbor."

"I told you there was nought to fret about," grunted Bellamy.
"Leagues of sea room and a broached cask of Canary below decks!
Stab me, but my throat is dry! We'll make a night of it. There'll be no

wind till daybreak."

"In weather like this," Hugh said, "the sea, here, lies flat for days." But in all Hugh's years with Tom and Israel he had never seen the sea between Gay Head and the Sow and Pigs lie flat for days.

"The young rooster knows," said Bellamy. "Burn me! he's a seaman. We'll stow our canvas and turn to on that pipe of Canary before them rascals hollering below have it drained dry."

The jib and staysail were lowered and the long-boomed mainsail reefed, while the sloop rode with the tide through a white pall of fog. Then, leaving a man at the tiller and a watch on deck, the captain and mate went below, and shortly Bellamy's bull-like voice was bellowing a song:

> On the Spanish Main the moon shines bright!
> Yo, ho, ho! And rot my bones!
> The maids are brown and the beaches white
> Where the trade winds drive and the flood tide moans
> And the stars wink down on the gray headstones!
>
> Oh, the Spaniards' ships ride deep with gold!
> Yo, ho, ho! And strike me dumb!
> They bring much joy to a pirate bold!
> For gold buys women and gold buys rum
> And opens the gates o' Kingdom Come!

"'For gold buys women and gold buys rum!'" bawled the mate. "Ay, Captain, 'tis the gospel truth! 'And opens the gates o' Kingdom Come!'"

There was loud laughter and the clicking of cups and Bellamy's bass voice roared again:

> Then gimme a brig in the West Indee!
> Yo, ho, ho! And slit my throat!
> With a black-eyed wench to bounce on my knee
> And a beaver hat and a gold-laced coat
> And wine in my guts, to hell I'll float!
>
> Some day we'll swing in the hot, hot sun!
> Yo, ho, ho! And let me burn!
> With a rope to our neck when our day is done,
> And dry as fish we'll twist and turn
> Till there's nought to eat for a starvin' worm!

"''Till there's nought to eat for a starvin' worm!'" roared the mate. "I drinks to that, Captain! But whilst we lives, we lives high. Christ's blood! we lives like kings, Captain, when we makes the Main and that Spanish gold and them brown and black maids a-callin' from the white beaches. Here's health to the Main and the wenches and gold that's a-waitin' fer us!"

"Jesus' breath!" bellowed Bellamy, "we'll bubble the worm, if it ever comes to that."

"Rot my guts! Captain, I like not the thought of swingin' a-sun-dryin' from some Spanish gibbet!"

"Nor I, mate," roared the captain. "They'll never take Bellamy alive. We'll blow her up first, and all go to hell together. A cup o' wine with you, matey!"

The boy who listened repeated, as the goose pimples lifted on his spine: "'With a rope to our neck . . . With a rope to our neck. . . .'" Yes, that was what Bellamy would take Hugh Jocelyn to if he could—a rope to his neck! They were bound for the West Indies and a life of loot and slaughter and rum and women, until—until some day their fate, in the shape of a Spanish or French ship of war, overtook the whiskered Bellamy and his crew and hung them from a yardarm or a gibbet, ashore, to swing in the wind a-sun-drying, as Israel called it. And with them would swing Hugh Jocelyn to-and-fro, twisting and turning in the wind until he was a withered carcass like a sun-dried fish on a beach. This was what they would take him to—if they had their way.

Hugh lingered at the starboard chains until he was called to take his supper with the mob of singing sailors, and a cup of Canary was thrust into his hands. But hungry though he was, he managed to avoid eating without being noticed by the drunken crew, for a full stomach would be the ruin of Hugh Jocelyn in the hours to come. Shortly he slipped away to the deck, and as he had been formally made a member of the crew, no attention was paid to him by those busy with their wine and maudlin songs.

As he stood barefooted, peering into the milk-white wall of fog which had soaked his shirt and canvas drawers, his ears strained to catch a familiar sound from the north, a low undertone of the sleeping sea he had often heard when the *Sea Gull* lay becalmed in this water on the same tide—a sound which had often driven him and Israel to the sweeps when the flood was running hard. But the low fretting of the Sow and Pigs did not reach his eager ears.

The watch changed, and four drunken sailors took the deck, carrying a large jack of Canary.

"Ho, youngster! A drink with you, lad," slobbered one, pushing the jack into Hugh's face. "Blood and guts! you be after my own heart. You tossed that rake-hell of a Jack Trigg like a man grown."

Hugh made a pretense of drinking, but little passed his lips, as the sailors pawed him and patted his back. "Christ's blood! what an arm for a lad of seventeen," cried one. "You'll make a rare one with a cutlass when we lay board and board with some Spaniard."

But the desperate Hugh had little to say, and soon tiring of the silent lad, the watch went forward with their jack of wine. In the cabin, the captain and mate were making a night of it. Still, Hugh knew that it might not be long before he would be accused by the drunken Bellamy of tricking him. And there would be no mercy, then, from the enraged pirate and his crew. He went cold at the thought and nervously shifted his position where he leaned at the rail beside a gun carriage and a rack of boarding pikes.

"There's no surf tonight," muttered the puzzled boy. "We've ridden this tide for near two hours and must be close in on Cuttyhunk beach. In a flat sea with the flood, the old Sow is ever muttering to her Pigs; yet I hear her not. What air there is moves from the east."

Again, for a long time, the boy bent over the rail and listened. Suddenly he sucked in a deep breath and expelled it with relief. "Ah! That will be the wash of the flood on the long beach. We are still far off, but I dare not wait." In an interval of silence between the maudlin chatter and lewd songs of the watch on deck with their jack of wine, came the audible splash of a body slicing the surface of the flat sea.

"Ho! What was that?" shouted a voice. "Ho, youngster!"

There was no answer as Hugh swam under water far out into the bank of mist, to rise, get his bearings from the blurred hulk of the sloop, and start his long swim for the shore. Behind him rose shouts: "Ho! Man overboard! Heave him a line! Toss the lad a line, he sickened from the wine and fell over the rail!"

Tearing his shirt from his back, Hugh settled down to his work. He heard the creaking of blocks as a boat was lowered, and he swam harder. They should not make a pirate of Hugh Jocelyn, this windy Bellamy and his crew. But what a shock awaited them when they heard the old Sow muttering to her Pigs, or the wash on the long beach! Were he on the sloop then, his life would not be worth a shell of Indian wampum.

Hugh swam for what seemed like a long time, then floated, to rest and listen for the beach wash, but no sound drifted through the white smother blanketing the sea. The water was not cold. He felt that he could swim for hours, and he knew that the flood would carry him ashore. Then a wave of fear suddenly chilled him. He felt cold and hopeless. Had he misjudged his course and wasted his strength circling or swimming across the tide? It was hard to tell. From the sloop's rail he had clearly heard the familiar sounds, but now he heard nothing. Was he being swept east, into the Sound, instead of toward Cuttyhunk? He changed his course and swam for what seemed like an hour. Then he stopped to rest and listen, but again heard nothing.

"Where am I?" gasped the panting boy, from whose heart hope was slowly fading. "I've swum miles. I've been circling! I should hear the beach wash! Name o' God, where am I?"

Moving blindly through the curtain of mist, wondering whether the tide was setting him closer to Cuttyhunk or sweeping him into the mouth of the Sound, Hugh fought on. As he swam he thought of the loved ones at Newport. How far home seemed to the boy lost out there in the gray wilderness of the pitiless sea! He could see Content's care-worn face and Tom and Israel's bleak eyes in the light of the supper fire. It was warm there, warm and dry. But it was cold in this sea water—cold and hopeless. And when, in the end, he had to give up and go down into the gray depths, there would be never a last look, as others had had, of the sky and sun, or the stars above him—only the white shroud of the fog.

As he swam he wondered if Seeth Carr's green eyes would weep for him. She was deeper than the others. She might remember Hugh Jocelyn. He had again stopped to rest and listen as he groped his way shoreward when, from the gray smother, a short distance away, came a loud splash. Icy fingers of fear clamped on the heart of the boy seeking the sanctuary of the shore. It was the thrash of a great fish. Hugh turned and swam hard. But again, squarely in front of him, a huge tail flayed the surface, and from the side and rear came the sound of churning water. "Name o' God!" They were all around him! Sharks! He was in a school of sharks! His heart slowed its beat. His tired limbs stiffened with the fear that lanced through him. "Sharks!" Shortly, toothed jaws would snap and tear and the water redden with blood. "Good-by, Hugh Jocelyn!"

The desperate lad swam as he had not swum since his race with the Lascar. At each stroke he fancied he heard the thrash of a great tail and saw a gaping maw as a black shape rolled beside him. But he swam on, unhurt. At last, far from the spot, he floated on his back to rest and fight for the control of his frayed nerves. "Grace o' God!" he panted. "I was fair mad with fear! Ugh! They were so near! Likely porpoises or blackfish, though I heard none blow, and not sharks after all! But the beach—where's the beach? I've already come a long way!"

Hugh was rapidly growing cold and stiff, and he started again on his hopeless search for the shore. "A mile or two more, Jocelyn," he muttered. "You can go a mile. Your father would keep on. Henry Jocelyn would never quit. He'd fight on till the last stroke. Come on, Hugh Jocelyn."

Suddenly the swimmer's body was entangled in a mass of clinging tentacles which wound around his arms and legs, stopping him dead. Their slimy touch sent a shudder through his body. But he threw himself on his back and, where another might have drowned, slowly freed his limbs of the drifting seaweed. As he circled away from the island of grass, his heart leaped. "What's that?" He stopped to listen, then cried: "I hear it! I hear it! 'Tis the beach! I hear the beach!" Hugh threw back his head and laughed through bloodless lips. As the blood flowed to the surface of his chilled body, strength returned with hope. "The beach! Name o' God! 'Tis the beach! I hear the tide wash!"

The half-delirious boy started to swim as if he had not already covered miles, but his reason soon returned and, saving his strength, he made his way slowly toward the shore he could not see, rode in on the low surf, and lay on the beach sucking deep breaths of the fog-wet air into his lungs.

"I beat him—the windy Bellamy!" he gasped. "I beat him—though the tide tricked me—and had me near waterlogged. This is not Cuttyhunk. Cuttyhunk is all stones. 'Tis Nashawena. What would I not give, now," he muttered with a shiver, "for a cup of that Canary I dared not drink!"

Now he should see Tom and Content and Israel and Trelawney again. And there was Seeth, with the tawny hair and the sweet, wild nature, to be kissed when he returned. For an instant Lettice Brinley's flaming face and telltale eyes returned to mock the boy who rested on the wet sand. The proud Brinleys! How he hated them! Hated—and yet Lettice had faced them all and told them her brother and Newbury lied. And then had come boldly to the pillory, defying the curious eyes. Though the act had driven him near to his death, the boy who sprawled on the beach in the bath of fog smiled as he remembered that lovely face, with its frame of chestnut hair, so close to his that day on the Parade.

But he could not stay there long shivering in the fog. He sat up and vigorously rubbed his stiff arms and legs. He must dig into the warm sand, back in the dunes, and rest until morning, then search for the shacks of fishermen or sheepherders, for he knew that there were fishermen's huts, sheep, and some small farms on Nashawena. For surely that must be where he had landed, carried by the tricky flood into the Sound. So he rose, made his way back into the shelter of the dunes, burrowed deep into the sand, heaped it over him for warmth, and quickly slept from exhaustion.

Some time later Hugh waked, shivering with cold. He opened his eyes to gaze up at a sky stippled with stars. Low in the west hung a pale moon. He sat up and rubbed the circulation back into his arms and legs and brushed the sand from his body. The wind had risen and wiped the sea of fog as a sponge wipes a slate.

"I doubt not I slept long," he muttered, stretching his stiff limbs. "Dawn will not be far away."

Hugh left the hollow and stood on the grassy shoulder of the hill of sand staring over the water into the west. "There it is!" he exclaimed as he gazed at a familiar knob in the distance. "'Tis Cuttyhunk, for a certainty!" Then his eyes shifted to the moon-bathed sea, broken with the wind bucking the ebb. He gave a start. "A sloop, on the Sow and Pigs! They're breaking over her! Name o' God! 'Tis the *Saucy Sally*! Bellamy, you'll drink no more Canary nor rob honest men."

It was clear to Hugh that the pirate sloop had ridden the flood in and struck. Now she lay rolling, with the ebb making fast and the surf, pushed by the rising wind, pounding her hull.

In his excitement Hugh forgot the wind on his naked body. Out there in the maw of the old Sow, whose black tusks, whitened by breaking combers, gripped her like a vise, the pirate sloop awaited her doom. The thirty who had flouted the laws of man and God had paid to the sea, for no boat or man could have reached the beach through the roaring slobber of the Sow and Pigs.

For an instant Hugh felt pity for the drowned men who had had such a grim awakening from their debauch, then his heart hardened. They were murderers, all, and had got their deserts. For a space he watched the sloop slowly breaking up in the distance; then, shivering from the flick of the chill wind on his bare body, he knew he must find a lee and wait until dawn before searching for the fishermen's huts. As he left the shoulder of the dune, he shook his fist at the doomed craft. "Pleasant voyage to hell, Captain Bellamy!" he cried. "You would take me to the Spanish Main and get me hung as a pirate, would you? Mayhap, with your windy tongue, you may cozen a good berth for yourself down below! The devil take you, Captain Samuel Bellamy!"

§24

IN the morning Hugh found the fishermen's huts and food. A week later he worked his way on a Cuttyhunk sloop bound for Westport Harbor on the mainland and loaded with the first run of bluefish. Stopping at a farm to work for his food and shelter and a shirt to cover his bronzed back, it was another week before the barefooted Hugh reached Pocasset, across the narrows from the Portsmouth shore. Then one evening he slipped through the fog-hung streets of Newport unobserved, for he had no intention of having his return known and of being trussed up and whipped before a gaping crowd on the Parade, to ease the anger of Justice Brinley. He stood outside the lead-paned windows of Tom Stanton's house and peered into the lighted room. A pang stabbed through him at sight of Content's face, drawn with sorrow, as she sat knitting in the light of a tallow dip. Tom and Israel sat smoking in silence, staring into the dying coals of the supper fire.

"They've got word from Boston, from Captain Beer, for never have I seen Content's face so sad nor Israel so silent," thought the boy at the window. "They love me—all three of them! Bless them!" He stopped to rub the sudden mist from his eyes, then, without knocking, pushed the door wide and entered the room.

Content saw him first. She dropped her knitting and rose, her pale eyes staring as if at an apparition. Then, with a glad cry of, "Hugh! Oh, my boy, my boy!" she was in his arms, crying out her joy on his heart.

Brandy and Stanton gaped in amazement at the returned youth soothing the sobbing woman. "By the great white whale, Tom Stanton, 'tis him!" at length roared the old salt, tears oozing from his winking eyes. "Pickle my guts, man, but 'tis our Hughie! Look at him! Damn that son-of-a-rumpuncheon pirate! He couldn't hold our lad! Not Bellamy! Burn me! Hugh gave him the slip. There he stands, barefooted, in shirt and drawers, with his yeller head and the blue eyes of him! Who-ree! Stab my guts! 'Tis a glorious night for us all!"

"Tom! Israel!" Hugh turned from Content, to grasp the excited pair by the arms. "I'm back! All the way from Pocasset and Portsmouth this day! I've a tale to tell 'twill make your eyes snap."

"Lad, lad! We had bidden you farewell, bound for God knows where!" cried Brandy. "Word come from Captain Beer you were a forced man on a pirate."

"And Trelawney?"

"He's fair pitiful, Hugh," said Stanton, "he so mourns for you." Tom's voice roughened with the tears in his throat. "Hugh, lad, there's been no smile in this house since the word come you were taken. Now you must be hungry, walking from Portsmouth, so first eat Content's supper while I heat the flip iron. Then you'll tell us how you escaped the sloop."

"Ay, that he will, and 'twill be a tale!" roared Brandy.

"When heard you from Captain Beer?" asked the thirsty Hugh, his face deep in a jack of cider, as Content placed on the table a trencher of steaming cod steaks and baked beans, and a huge loaf of rye-'n'-Injun bread.

"Beer spoke the sloop *Mary*, off Nantucket, bound for Newport, and sent word by her," said Stanton. "The *Mary* made Newport a week back. Head winds held her in the Sound."

"Saw they wreckage on Cuttyhunk beach?" asked Hugh, his mouth full of food.

"No, but we drummed up a crew of fifty men that day," answered Israel, stumping back and forth in his curiosity and excitement, "and mounted eight five-pound sakers on Tom Paine's big sloop. Tom made me gunner for old time's sake, and who think you I had serving one gun, lad? Stab me, but I laugh to think of it! Why, six men off the brig of the pirate Peterson, who now waits the pleasure of the grand jury Brinley called. He sent 'em and, burn my bones! we up and took 'em! And handy lads I found they were. There rose a great cry by some against their going, but we slipped away with 'em!" Israel roared with laughter.

"It takes a pirate to catch a pirate, Israel," grinned Hugh. "What then fell out?"

"Why, we hunted the Sound to the Cape and back, then headed south of Noman's and west to Block Island, but not a sign of Bellamy's sloop. He made for the Horse Lateetudes and the Bahamas when he got Beer's stores and wine, but—" Israel stopped to peer hard into Hugh's amused face—"but you gave him the slip before he left, lad? Now out with it!"

Hugh's twinkling eyes shifted from one to the other of the expectant group. Brandy thrust his face close to that of the boy, who laughed up at him from the stool. "Where, think you, I gave him the slip, Israel? From the Horse Latitudes?"

"Rot my bones! You laugh at us. What's the right of this?"

"Bellamy sailed not south, Israel. He sailed to—hell!"

"Burn me!" gasped Brandy. "What mean you?"

"Keep us no longer waiting, Hugh," begged Tom. "Content is well-nigh crazed to hear."

Content flashed an angry look at her husband as she stood beside Hugh's stool. "Tell Mother, Hugh," she coaxed. "How escaped you?"

So, finishing his mug of flip, Hugh told the story of the capture of the *Sea Flower* and of his long swim through the fog. As he talked, Israel's square jaw sagged lower and lower in amazement. The small eyes overhung by the mats of bushy brows glowed and snapped.

"Split my windpipe!" cried the sailor, when Hugh had finished. "'Tis hard to believe! For a certainty, 'twas the flood that saved you, but had you not crossed it and cut inshore, you'd be out there, yet, with the sharks!"

"Yes, I was carried east and, unknowing, crossed the tide and made Nashawena."

"And you clouted the pirate who kicked you!" roared Brandy. "Stab me! Clouted a pirate on his own ship and lives to tell the tale!" Israel wagged his shaggy head and slapped his good knee in his delight. "Tom, we've a young sea-bully on our hands! Rot my bones! Clouted a pirate!"

"'Tis a brave tale, Hugh," said Stanton, his gray eyes glowing with pride.

"And you saw the *Saucy Sally* in the moonlight hard and fast in the tusks of old Sow?" demanded Brandy.

"They were rolling white over her. She was breaking up fast. At daylight when I looked, there was no sign of her. For days the Cutty-hunk and Nashawena fishermen fetched the stores that came ashore. A pipe of Canary which was washed ashore, unbroached, held the islands foxed for a week."

"But they found not Bellamy?" asked Brandy.

"No. For days, bodies came ashore, but I saw not the bearded Bel-lamy."

"Well, burn my bones!" Israel's shaggy head bobbed. His face twisted in a grimace of satisfaction. "So Bellamy and thirty men went into the old Sow's belly! 'Tis not the first crew she's stomached—nor the last. But she got not this lad, eh, Hugh?"

Tom patted Hugh affectionately on the back. "I'm proud of you, boy! 'Twas a mighty swim! There's none in Newport could make it nor dare try. God be praised, He gave you back to us!"

Safe with those he loved, that night Hugh's emotions were close to the surface. As he looked into the candle-lit faces, home took on a deeper significance to the boy who had so nearly lost it. A great flood of happiness warmed his heart, and he swallowed hard as Content's toil-worn hand found his and his fingers closed around it. After a space he said quietly: "It was seeing you here, in this room, with the light on your faces, that drove me on when I was stiffening with the cold, out there in the Sound. Whilst I saw your faces I durst not give up. I had to come back to you."

Tom nodded, his eyes blurred with tears. "Ay, you're a true Joce-lyn."

"And the great fish?" shuddered Content. "Were you not in terror, Hugh, of their snapping jaws?"

Hugh laughed. "In terror? Never was I in such fear, Mother."

"They were porpoises, no doubt," said Tom. "Had they been sharks, God pity us!"

"Porpoise or no," grunted Brandy, "picture the lad a-swimmin' blind in that white soup of a fog with a shoal of them big, black devils for company!"

Content's arm crept around Hugh's shoulders. "He is home safe with us now, thank the good Lord!" she sighed. "And here he stays, with his mother."

Hugh kissed the lined face that bent over him. He turned to the men: "But if Justice Brinley hears I am back, what think you he will do? After the pillory, I will not stay to be whipped."

Israel exhaled a cloud of smoke and punctuated his reply with the stem of his clay pipe. "Trelawney tells us Brinley's heat has cooled since he learned he drove you into Bellamy's hands. He says you're safe."

25

IT was not until the following afternoon, on the return of the sloop from the Sakonnet nets, that Hugh saw Trelawney. The Englishman was waiting for them when the skiff slid into the gravel beach. As the barefooted Hugh leaped out, he realized to the full through what days of anxiety his friend had passed. The Englishman's joy at seeing him failed to fill the hollows in the lean face or erase the redness of his eyes from sleepless nights.

"I'm back for more schooling, you see," laughed Hugh. "Even a pirate might not hold me from your tasks!"

"Hugh, Hugh!" In his emotion Trelawney could only grip the lad's shoulders and stare into his brown face. At last he found his voice. "The sun went out for me, lad, when the news came you were forced by a pirate."

"Now I'm back, will Brinley haul me before a Magistrate?" asked Hugh, his face suddenly sobering.

Trelawney shook his head. "When the news came that you were in Bellamy's hands and had likely been carried to the Indies, Justice Brinley's anger cooled, for many people blamed him to his face. I have his promise that you are safe."

"'Tis a pretty pass," growled Brandy, "when a lad trussed in the pillory must pay for the wild fancy of a maid. Let Justice Brinley keep her at moorings where she may ride under his eye and can work no more harm to our boy!"

"Easier said than done, Israel," replied Trelawney as they walked to the house. "When Captain Paine returned from his search and reported that Bellamy had doubtless headed for the Indies, 'twas she who boldly accused her father of driving Hugh to his death some day on a pirate ship. She raved like a mad woman, calling Newbury and her brother sneaking cowards, which they are, and her father, a murderer. For days she refused food, and had her parents fair at their wit's ends. In the end I brought her to her senses, but she wrung the promise from Justice Brinley that if Hugh returned he should be safe."

A sudden glow of pride flowed through Hugh at Trelawney's words. This lovely madcap who had come to the pillory had done this for him—a fisherman's son! But what was to come of it?

"Hugh," said Tom Stanton gravely, as they stopped outside the house, "you are the foster son of a fisherman. You have no fancy for this maid of Justice Brinley's?"

"Have no fear of that, Father Tom," said Hugh lightly. "Once in the pillory is enough for me."

"I will talk with Hugh tonight, Tom," said Trelawney. "Harm, because of her, must not come again to him."

"Let Brinley keep his whelps from crossing the bows of our boy!" bristled Israel. "He was sailing a clean course when they first fouled him. And 'tis not his fault if the girl draws alongside when he's anchored!"

Trelawney shook his dark head. " 'Tis not so easy as all that, Israel. Brinley rules here, now. We must not anger him again."

That evening, after supper, Hugh and Trelawney sat on a string-piece of Coddington's Wharf in the long twilight. "Hugh," began the Englishman, "there is much of which I would talk with you. I was well-nigh desperate when we thought you lost. I know full well it's been hard at times, working at dull figures in the evening when the lads your age were dallying with the maids along the wharves."

"Yes, it has been hard," Hugh agreed, "but I wished to learn the use of the Davis quadrant and how to find latitude, as well as what went on in this world after Greece fell and the birth of Christ."

"You've been an apt pupil, Hugh, and little I've told you has escaped your memory. Today, near eighteen, you have more learning than any other youth and most men in Newport. And you shall soon know all I can teach you of the mathematics of navigation so you may be prepared for the future. But that is not what I wish to talk of."

As Hugh dangled his feet over the water, he guessed what was coming. It was Lettice. "You wish to warn me of that little tigress who refuses to learn her figures from you," he laughed.

"Yes, Hugh; you have guessed it. When we all thought you lost, I would no more start her reading than she would fling the book aside and ask: 'Think you he will ever return to Newport, Mr. Trelawney? Has he forgiven me for that lash across the face?' "

Hugh felt warm all over. It was pleasant to hear that so lovely a creature thought of him. He wondered how it would feel to hold her in his arms and kiss that ardent face and the wayward chestnut curls. But he knew that the high-born Lettice Brinley was not for the son of a fisherman, and said slowly, "Have no fear, Dick Trelawney."

Trelawney rested his hand on Hugh's shoulder. "Hugh, if you'll listen to me you'll go far in this port. But you must not see Lettice Brinley again, for it would lead to your ruin. Her father would hound you from Newport. He is all-powerful and the pet of the royal governor of New England. You give me your promise?"

Hugh threw back his head and laughed, and Trelawney's eyes lighted with pleasure. "Give you my promise? That is easy. How should my ways ever cross hers?"

"She will see to that. Little you know her. She's that headstrong she would send to you to meet her secretly. And I want your promise that you will not, for it would be soon known and Brinley would banish you. And that, lad, I could not bear, for you are all I have."

"Good old Dick!" Hugh's hand rested on the older man's arm. "Ease your mind; you have my promise. I'll not see your pretty scholar who will not learn her figures."

Trelawney gave a sigh of relief. "'Tis a heavy load you lift from my mind, lad. As for the other maids, 'tis but natural that you listen when youth calls. I would not have you a woman scoffer. 'Twould be silly! But, I beg of you, have a care lest you lose your heart and head when yet so young. It has ruined many a career. You will be master of your own ship, and more, if you but wait."

Hugh was thinking of Candace and Seeth. Suppose, some evening, he should meet Candace on a wharf. What would he do if those black eyes of hers flashed at him as they did that day in the tavern? He did not know, for the thought of her fired his blood. True, he had not talked with her since the race with the Lascar, and had seen her but seldom, and then at a distance, for he never went to the Blue Porpoise. Had she forgotten what she had said about waiting? He wondered. But seeing Candace was too fraught with danger to them both. It might mean the whipping post. And there was Content. It would break her heart. He must think of Content. No, it must not be Candace.

But Seeth, that was another matter. He had promised her at the pillory to kiss the pout from her sweet mouth. She would be waiting now that he was safe home again. And she should have as many kisses as her heart desired. The tawny-haired Seeth with the wild strain in her blood had taken a strong hold on his fancy.

"Have no fear," Hugh said, after the pause. "You've labored like a father with my dull brain that I might lift myself above the mass when I am grown man. I shall not fail you."

"No, you cannot fail me, Hugh. Of that I am sure."

At the Stanton house two young men standing in the dusk beside their horses waited for the approaching Hugh and Trelawney.

"We've come to shake the hand of the lad the pirate could not hold once he had taken him," hailed Joseph Brenton. "Welcome home, Hugh Jocelyn! The taverns are agog with the tale of your swimming ashore in the fog from Bellamy's ship."

Brenton and his companion, John Arnold, greeted Trelawney and warmly shook Hugh's hand. "'Twas a bold feat, Hugh, and we're glad to have you back in Newport," said Arnold.

"And glad I am to be back, Mr. Arnold," said Hugh.

Brenton turned to the Englishman. "There'll be no trouble from Brinley, Dick?" he inquired. "He's given his word, I hear."

"Yes," said Trelawney, "he has given me his word."

"Good!" said Arnold. "Were that slimy Ichabod Tripp to try any more tricks, I believe the people would do him harm."

The two friends mounted their horses and Brenton called as they rode off down Thames Street, "Good-night, and good luck to you, Hugh Jocelyn!"

Hugh and Trelawney found Content, Israel, and Tom awaiting them. "It was kind of Mr. Brenton and Mr. Arnold to come to our humble home to greet Hugh," said the pleased woman.

"Kind?" Israel Brandy scoffed. "Why should they not come to greet him? At the Blue Porpoise, last night, when I left you, I had the people with their mouths open, listening to the tale of Hugh's swim and the break-up of the *Saucy Sally* in the tusks of the Sow and Pigs."

There was the sound of feet on the gravel path outside, and Hugh went to the door. "Where's that pirate killer?" demanded a grinning youth, who seized Hugh's hand. "Evenin', Goodwife Stanton. Evenin', Tom, Israel! Brother John and I had to see the lad who slipped the pirate, then watched him break up."

Tom set stools for the Wanton brothers, William and John, somewhat older than Hugh, and hastened to heat the flip iron. It was in the shipyard of their father and elder brother that Tom, Israel, and Hugh worked when the fishing ceased in midwinter, and a warm friendship had sprung up between the Wanton boys and Hugh. The lad had to tell the story of his capture and escape in detail before the Wantons were satisfied.

"Hugh," said William, a well-made lad of nineteen, with a bold, dark eye and hooked nose that gave his high-cheekboned face the look of a hawk, "comes there another war soon, we are set to build the fastest, ablest sloop on this coast." The speaker finished his second mug of flip and went on: "She'll go ninety-ton and carry ten guns, and a crew of Newport and Portsmouth lads to sail and fight her. Count yourself signed up, now."

Hugh's blue eyes glowed. The enthusiasm of young Wanton was contagious. A privateer sloop, built by the Wantons, carrying big guns and a crew of lads from home! The thought of it stirred his blood.

"Avast there, William," growled Israel from his seat in a corner, "who'll be a-layin' of them five-pound sakers that their balls may sink into oak and splinter bulwarks and not splatter the whole sea about? Israel Brandy, and none else!" The irate old sailor stumped into the circle of young men and shook a stubby forefinger in Wanton's face. "Think you gunners are made in a day of young sprigs like you and Hugh, who never yet saw the red huff leap from the touch-hole of a privateer's gun, nor watched one jump and bust her breechin', nor smelled ought but musket smoke except from the old cannon on Goat

Island and the Parade?" Israel thrust his grimacing face close to Wanton's as his wide mouth twitched in his wrath.

All in the room except Content laughed heartily at Brandy's outburst. William Wanton laid a hand on Israel's heavy shoulder. "Captain Tom Paine says you're the best gunner in Newport, Israel," he said. "We could scarce sail without you to lesson the young sprigs like Hugh and me and John. Of course we'll have old heads aboard! You're signed up now as master gunner!"

"Of course, of course; and, burn me! you'll need me." With a cough of satisfaction the mollified Brandy resumed his seat.

As the Wantons left, the great hulk of Benoni Tosh, followed by little Jerusa Sugars and other neighbors, entered the room to welcome Hugh home.

Later that night Tom and Israel sat alone over their rum. "Master gunner!" chuckled Israel. "There be many a good fight left in these old bones still! And these young sprigs'll need Israel Brandy, gunner of the *Lady Bess*, that fit Spaniard and French and God knows who else, from the Bahamas to the Grenadines."

Tom looked quizzically at his friend. "You always keep a brailed tongue about the year before you and Tom Paine sailed into Newport with a chest full of Arabian pagodas and Spanish doubloons, and Boston wanted him arrested for piracy."

Brandy's small eyes twinkled as he grinned into his friend's face. "You'll never know from me, Tom."

"No, Israel, I'll never know from you, for you carry no slack mouth in your head and are bound to Tom Paine in long friendship. But I misdoubt that you and Tom let many craft, Spanish, French or Dutch, enemy or no, pass without a round shot athwart their bows. Name of God! I'll swear that you two sea wolves had a look into every hold for cargo that might bring hard money on the wharves of a friendly port."

Israel raised a calloused hand in protest. "Belay, Tom," he objected. "We scarce overstepped the law with intent—that is, leastawise, did we not carry grave suspicion. But in the days when all craft carried false papers and more than one flag, 'twas hard to mark enemy from friend."

"'Tis a marvel," Stanton laughed, "that you and Tom Paine ended not a-sun-drying on some Spanish gibbet."

Brandy gravely nodded. "Ay, 'tis a marvel—or on some English one as well."

26

THE fish were on the coast, and each day at dawn, the *Sea Gull* nosed out of Newport harbor bound east for the cod and halibut grounds. Often, wind and tide or lack of fish held the sloop to the eastward, but fresh fish brought higher prices than salted, on the wharves of Newport, and Stanton's nets and lobster pots in the Sakonnet River needed constant attention; so he was never long from home. Reaching the anchorage in the Cove in the evening after a long day's toil on the water, and facing the necessity of rising before dawn, Hugh had little chance of sitting on a wharf with Seeth Carr and watching the afterglow tint the harbor. But one evening, returning early, he went to her home.

"So, at last, you have remembered me," she said, as they strolled down to a wharf.

Hugh looked into her vivid face framed by its cloud of wayward hair. The dark-lashed green eyes, flicked with specks of black, gravely studied him as he answered: "Seeth, I've been ashore but to sleep only since my return. It's been out before sunrise and home after dark with the *Sea Gull* ever since I reached Newport. But as I stretched my tired bones at night, who think you I always thought of before I slept?"

A wave of color flowed up over her round throat to her cheeks. "Hugh, you mean it? You thought of me, Hugh Jocelyn, and not of that wretch who lashed you with her whip?"

Hugh's calloused hand found hers. "Seeth, you are the loveliest maid in Newport, and you have a way of looking through those green eyes of yours that fair starts the blood leaping in me. You were that sweet when you came to the pillory with cake and cider, is it strange that I think of you?"

The red lips Hugh had promised to kiss curled with pleasure. "I thought I should die, Hugh," she said, huskily, "when the news came you were a pressed man on a pirate."

"And when I was swimming in that fog, searching for the shore, Seeth, I saw your face. You smiled at me and gave me heart."

Her eyes fixed Hugh with a look so intense that he felt a sense of awe, almost of fear, of her. Seeth certainly did things to him that no one else had ever done. Candace had made him swallow hard as the blood pulsed in his veins at her touch, but Seeth stirred him far more deeply and in ways strange and bewildering. He wondered if he were in love with this girl who, in an instant, could run the gamut from laughter to tears. Then he thought of the shining eyes and the flushed face of Lettice when she came to the pillory, and he felt confused and ill at ease. This love the poets sang of was indeed a strange thing. How was one to know when it really came?

"Hugh, are you sure mine was the only face you saw, out there in that terrible fog?" she asked, quietly, but her throaty voice quavered.

His hand closed on hers and, drawing her behind a pile of lumber, where they were hidden from prying eyes on shore, he gathered her in his arms and kissed her eager lips. He felt the wild beating of her heart against his breast as she clung to him, madly returning his kisses. Suddenly she flung her head back, and her silk hood dropped from her hair as she fixed him with her green eyes.

"Why have you made me love you so, Hugh Jocelyn?" she demanded. "I was near mad when they thought you lost! Tell me you love me, if only a little! Oh, tell me, Hugh!"

Deep in her spell, Hugh drew the girl's yielding body close to his and his lips found her ear. "Of course I love you, Seeth! You are far sweeter than anyone I know. Of course I love you."

With a sigh she kissed his brown cheek and pushed herself away, for the people on an anchored sloop, not far distant, were watching them. Through the twilight the two sat on a stringpiece of the wharf and saw the afterglow turn to dusk. When night fell, Hugh took her in his arms, and knew that she was his for the taking, but wildly though his blood sang, some strange inhibition held the lad from taking what was so recklessly offered. It was not only his lack of experience in lovemaking that held him in restraint, but more than that, there was the knowledge that the love of Seeth Carr had not been lightly given.

As Hugh left Seeth at her gate, she said, "How long must I wait, Hugh Jocelyn, before Mr. Trelawney will grant you another evening from those old books?"

Hugh took her lifted face between his two hands and kissed her hair and eyes and mouth. "Do you think he or anything could keep me long from one so sweet?" And even as he spoke he knew in his heart that he did not dare see too much of Seeth Carr.

He was picking his way toward home, along the rutted surface of Thames Street, his blood alive with the fever of their last kiss, when he heard low voices behind him. There was no moon, and the street was black, for the candles in the houses had long since been put out. As Hugh kept on, at times feeling his way with his feet, to avoid stumbling into holes, he realized that someone was moving cautiously behind him. Thinking them neighbors on their way to the Cove, Hugh stopped. As he did so, two invisible figures reached him, and his greeting was cut short by a fierce light flashed in his eyes, and he fell unconscious.

Voices that sounded faint and far away, and the blurred faces of men bending over him holding a candlewood torch, eventually roused the stunned boy. He blinked up from where he lay in the street into the eyes of the watch.

"What happened you, Hugh? Are you sore hurt?" asked Jeremy Fitch, kneeling beside the dazed lad, his fingers groping in Hugh's long hair. "Ah, 'twas a club that laid you low! It lifted a lump big as a duck egg."

Fighting through the mists that clouded his brain, Hugh tried to sit up, but his splitting head and his weakness overcame him, and he fell back. Shortly, at the call of the watch, lights appeared in the windows of houses, doors opened, and Welcome Lawton, the second watchman, appeared with a cup of rum, which he poured down Hugh's throat.

"Can you think now, lad, how you got this clout on the head?" asked Jeremy, when he had raised Hugh to a sitting position.

In weakness, Hugh's yellow head sagged as the two men supported him. Slowly his disordered thoughts began to take shape. He had been on his way home—on his way home from Seeth. Yes, he had kissed Seeth and said good-night. Someone was behind him and he had stopped to speak with them. That was it. That was the last he knew. After that, all was black.

"Speak, lad! Who clubbed you?"

"Don't know!" muttered Hugh. "Two men—in the dark—behind me."

"Ay, 'tis strange business, for a certainty! Some of them foreign sailors, likely. Had you silver in your pocket, Hugh? Search his pockets and learn if he has ought now," ordered Jeremy.

In the pocket of Hugh's canvas breeches they found a pine-tree shilling.

"'Twas not for robbery, then, they clubbed him," said Fitch.

Hugh was given another drink of rum and his strength slowly returned. Then he said: "I was bound for home when I heard hushed voices and steps behind me. I stopped and hailed and, of a sudden, got this on my head."

"Ay, and a stout skull you have, Hugh, or 'twould be cracked with that clout! Now come and we'll help you home."

At the house Israel and Trelawney sat smoking with Stanton when they brought Hugh in.

"Stab my vitals! So they clubbed you in the dark of Thames Street without showing a flag or firing a gun?" fretted Israel, stumping to-and-fro, his wide mouth in action, while the worried Content powdered dried sprays of St.-John's-wort in water to heat for a dressing for Hugh's swollen head. "Now what make you of that, Mr. Trelawney?"

Trelawney lifted his periwigged head to the man squinting down at him and said gravely:

"I make this of it, Israel. Somebody has paid these miscreants to injure Hugh."

"It could not be that Joe Cory and Henry Green bear me a grudge because you shook their boys that day on the Parade, Israel," suggested Hugh, "and I pitched Eph Green into the harbor?"

Brandy shook his head. "They have no money to pay for having you clubbed, and they dared not do it themselves."

Trelawney turned to Stanton. "To me this thing points but one way."

"Points one way?" broke in Content, her pale eyes lit with indignation, as she bound Hugh's head with the dressing soaked in the liquor from the St.-John's-wort. "Who could hate him so? And for what?"

Israel placed a heavy forefinger against his broken nose and winked at the Englishman. "Cross my hawse! 'Twas Newbury and that sprig of Brinley's!"

"I fear you're right, Israel. Newbury was publicly called liar by the girl and, as he thinks, insulted by Hugh and you at the pillory. And Richard has never forgotten his sister's testimony and his humiliation at being pulled from his horse. He raved more than his father, even, when he learned from Newbury she had gone to the pillory."

Brandy's huge fists opened and shut as he stumped about the room in his wrath. "Stab me! Sailors they was, bought with Brinley and Newbury gold!"

"I believe Newbury is the prime mover in this, playing on Richard's stung pride. He has both the brains and the venom for it. They tell me he's ruthless and without scruple."

"I scour the taverns till I find who did this, for 'twas sailors, easily bribed!" growled Israel.

"Yes, that would be well," said the worried Trelawney.

"I'm off in the skiff for the Butterfly, now, for a talk with the Widow Moon. If a sailor talks in his cups in this port or shows hard money who seldom has it, she'll hear it and tell it me; for she put great store in Israel Brandy afore I sailed home with this face and one leg." With a chuckle Israel started for the shore.

"But would Newbury, because of what the maid said in court and her seeing Hugh at the pillory, go so far as this?" demanded Tom.

"Newbury fancies the maid, but she flouts him. His coming to the pillory that day proves how strong is his feeling. Hugh stands in his way."

"Then you fear he and young Brinley will go far to further injure Hugh?"

"I do. Hugh must keep the house at night."

"I'll not keep the house at night," said Hugh, holding his bandaged and aching head in his hands. "But when I go out, I carry that old cutlass that hangs over the chimney. I'd give much to run foul in daylight of that sailor who gave me this!"

§27

WHAT had prompted the deceased husband of the Widow Moon to call his small tavern the "Butterfly" the rotund widow could not clearly remember. It stood on an old wharf some distance south of the Cove and for years there had creaked in the wind above the door the rickety sign, weathered by sun and rain, on which had been daubed what purported to be a yellow butterfly but which might well have been mistaken for a flying fish or a golden eagle. The resort of sailors and of those who preyed on them, on more than one occasion the tavern had been the cause for grave consideration by the Town Council. For the widow's rum was fiery, and her rules of conduct liberal so long as her patrons paid. However, notwithstanding the frequent brawls in the establishment, and a stabbing or two involving the death of a sailor, it was generally agreed by the august body of family men that ruled Newport that seaports must have taverns for sailors and sailors would brawl in their cups. So the town fathers had never taken drastic action in the matter except, periodically, to instruct Sergeant Benoni Tosh to wait upon the lady with suitable admonition as to the conduct of her business. This duty Benoni never failed to perform in a most conscientious manner, consuming as he did on such missions hours of time in reminiscence and countless mugs of flip at the widow's expense.

Israel left his boat on the beach, went up on the wharf, and stumped into the small public room of the Butterfly. Flickering tallow dips on candle beams hung from floor joists lit the room, in which stood tables bearing the scars of many a hotly contested difference of opinion over the respective merits of a knife and a well-swung stool. Against a wall stood a battered dresser carrying an assortment of pewter and wooden cups, a waxed leather jack or two bound with copper, and some pewter tankards the worse for wear. On one table rested an overturned cup in a pool of ale. The sand on the floor was soiled with dirt and spilled beer, and the air of the room foul with stale tobacco smoke and the odor of ale and rum. Sole occupant of the room, there dozed at a table no less a personage than the widow herself.

With a shake of his shaggy head, Israel noted the stains on the bulging bosom of her Ozenbrig frock, and thought of the trim maid she had been thirty years before. He loudly cleared his throat, and she blinked at him from slits of eyes buried in cheeks round as apples and as red.

"Israel Brandy or I be no widow!" she laughed, her eyes twinkling with pleasure as her fat body shook like a stuffed pillow. She thrust out a bare arm from a sleeve that would have cased a cannon, and grasped his hand. "Rot my carcass, Israel, you be good for sore eyes! Sit you while Adam fetches a lick o' rum!"

Brandy seated himself beside her, and a black boy roused from a doze in a rear room shuffled in with the drink. Israel emptied the rum into his capacious throat, smacked his lips with a loud "Ah!" and said, "Betsy, you and me go back a-many year in this port." He stopped to chuckle at a memory. "Burn me! there was no sweeter armful of a maid in all Newport than you, nor warmer."

The widow tilted her head in a quizzical look at the sailor. "Israel Brandy," she rasped, "you ever had an oily tongue when you set sail for something. What's in the back of that ugly head of yours?"

A grin reached across Israel's scarred face from ear to ear. "'Tis not that you called it before that voyage to the West Indy when the Spaniard took my leg and left me this face," he countered. "My memory has it that a maid fair weeped her pretty eyes out the night afore we sailed, and gave me that to remember her by which pleasured my thoughts for many a day. Then I returned on a peg leg, with this slash athwart my hawse, and she—"

Suddenly down the mottled cheeks of the blowzy listener crept two tears. Her eyes all but disappeared as her mouth puckered in a sob. She raised a fat hand in protest. "Cease you, Israel," she choked. "Go not on that way. 'Tis more than I can bear to hear of the old days. I was overfond of you, lad, of which you had good proof."

"But when I hove into port from the Indy Sea with this face—" he chuckled, "you cooled, Betsy. You fair cooled, lass. Dost not recall it?"

For a space the Widow Moon was silent. Her brows pulled together as she seemed to search a rum-veiled memory for the truth of his statement. Then, evidently baffled, she found a solution in the age-old strategy of her sex. A flood of alcoholic tears streaked her ruddy cheeks as she sat hiccuping in the throes of an ephemeral heartache.

"There, there, Betsy," soothed Brandy, resting a hairy hand on her mound of a shoulder. "'Tis long forgotten, lass. I bore you no ill will that you found my face misshapen after that Spanish cutlass had done with it. But I seek not to bubble you when I say you was an uncommon sweet morsel of a maid. Stab me! who should know it better nor Israel Brandy?"

Misery was wiped from the widow's features as the sun wipes the sea of mist. Her teary eyes beamed with pleasure at his words. She called loudly to Adam to bring two cups of rum, and turned to her shameless flatterer.

"For a certainty, Israel, I was that fair, once, the sailors turned their heads when I passed. 'Tis true, Israel, I was that fair they did turn their heads—once? Say it, lad! Say it!"

"Turn their heads? Stab me! they followed you as bluefish follow herring. And many a one I had to clout before he gave up the chase to save his skin."

With a sigh of satisfaction she nodded, burying her chin in a roll of flesh. Again tears stood in her eyes, but they were the tears of pleasant memories. "Ay," she murmured, "they did turn their heads, I was that pretty."

"Betsy," he said, "never have I sighted a trimmer sloop nor you; nor one could sail closer to the wind." She bobbed her head as if, for an instant, her truant memory had recaptured the old days.

Her fat shoulders shook with her delight at his words. Then the smile suddenly left her face and she leaned toward Brandy and gravely demanded, as if fearing contradiction: "'Tis God's truth I was that fair, once, they did turn their heads? Say again 'tis the truth, Israel," she entreated. "'Tis so long ago, I fair misdoubt it."

"Burn me! they so did," gallantly insisted the sailor, and he swallowed a deep draft of the Butterfly's rum. He put down the cup and continued: "And 'tis little wonder, you, with your snappin' black eyes and cheeks red as apples, and legs as trim as a sloop's boom! They was fair mad after you, Betsy. You was handsome as a new-launched brig. And who could better know than me?"

His reply seemed to dispel her last doubts. She leered at him with a complacent grin and her button of a nose disappeared in her cup of rum. Suddenly she straightened, holding the cup suspended in air, as her brows contracted in two deep furrows. While he watched her narrowly, she deliberately placed the pewter cup on the table and drew a red hand slowly across her moist eyes as if banishing her memories, and returned to the present. "Now, Israel Brandy," she demanded sharply, "what brought you here this time o' night? Stab my vitals! Out with it!"

Amused at the sudden change in the atmosphere, Israel loudly cleared his throat. Then he got to the point of his mission. "Peterson's men are here, often, and the crews from them Barbadoes sloops and that brig from the Wine Islands?" he coolly asked.

She nodded.

Brandy lowered his voice to a whisper. "I seek for any sailors who have gold to spend, or too much silver. If any show gold and spend freely who had it not before, I needs must know. You'll do that for me, Betsy?"

She scowled as she pondered his request, her small eyes shrewdly probing his. "Why look you for men with gold to spend so long as they spend it here?" she demanded.

"I may not say, now, but will discover it to you later. For a certainty you can trust Israel Brandy, the lad who was once, on a time—"

The scowl faded as memory again returned. She smiled into Brandy's face thrust close to hers as he waited for her answer. "I'll do that and more, for the sake of old times, Israel, and no one the wiser."

"Good girl! Memories is memories, lass. Rot my bones! they may not rob us of ours, and sweet ones they be."

Again captive to the past, she thrust out her arm and caressed Israel's scarred cheek with her fat fingers. "And I was that fair—pretty you named me—that the men all turned their heads? You recall it, Israel? 'Tis true, lad, I was once that fair?"

"Slay me, Betsy! You had me fair frenzical with jealousy, watching lest the lads rob me of the sauciest little craft in this port, what with your trim bow and round stern and top hamper of black hair and snappin' eyes. You was that pert and coppet I durst not sleep o' nights from fear you might slip anchor and away on an ebb tide."

"Ay! You always had the tongue, Israel," she sighed. Then her red eyes leered up at him. "Kiss me, for old time's sake, Israel. Kiss me, once!" she pleaded.

Finishing his rum, Brandy rose, bent over her and delivered a moist smack, like the slap of a wave against a skiff, on her expectant mouth. "Gather me news of free spending, Betsy," he said. "I'll be back in a few days."

"Ay, lad, that I will," she promised, and waved a hand as he stumped from the room.

As the wily Brandy reached the skiff, he chuckled to himself: "Rot my bones! Betsy's ordinary is well named. She and the butterfly both like their honey."

Before he returned to the Cove Israel stopped at the three other taverns much frequented by sailors, the Break of Day House, the Sign of the Black Boy, and the Blue Porpoise, and obtained promises of aid.

§28

WITHIN a few days Hugh's bludgeoned head was as good as new. His rugged constitution had taken care of that. But the inquiries of Israel, alongshore, had brought no results. At none of the taverns had any sailors displayed a sudden possession of riches. Yet Trelawney, Tom, and Israel were convinced that the attack in the dark on Hugh was the work of men hired by Carr Newbury and young Brinley. Then, one day, when the *Sea Gull* returned to the Cove, Content handed Hugh a sealed letter. It was the first the lad had ever received, and he gazed in wonder from his name written in unformed, childish hand on the wrapping to Content's sober face.

"Who fetched this?" he asked.

"'Twas a black boy. From his good clothes I take he was sent by that madcap who lashed you across the face." Content impulsively grasped Hugh's arm. "Oh, Hugh, you'll not pay heed to her?"

"Never fear, Mother Content," said Hugh, his blood quickening with the thought of Lettice Brinley writing to him. "I've given my word to Dick." But his heart was pounding as he opened the letter and read:

DEAR HUGH JOCELYN—

I feared They had driven you to your Death. How I Hated Them. Now you are safe, Praise God. They scarce let me out of their Sight. But I could Contrive to ride into the Country with Aaron where I met you First and You laughed at Me if you'd but Come. Mr. Trelawney would Bear the Message did you But urge him Sufficient. Do Pleasure me Sir by writing what Day and Time You Will be at the Bend in the Road.

ONE WHO HURT YOUR FACE AND IS SORRY.

As Hugh finished the missive, waves of pride and elation flowed through him at the thought that the daughter of Justice Brinley had stooped to write a letter to the son of Tom Stanton. Flouting her high birth and the anger of her father, she was seeking a meeting in a secluded spot. She was fair mad. Trelawney would bear no message. Yet the thought of holding this proud child of the rich in his arms—of kissing her—started his heart drumming.

"What says she?" asked Content, quietly, though her mouth was firm with purpose.

"She would have me meet her on Dexter's Lane," laughed Hugh. "She is young and headstrong and fair spoiled. Fear not, Mother Content." Hugh tossed the note into the coals of the cooking fire and the look of solicitude on the face of the woman who watched him changed to one of relief.

"You know what would happen to you, Hugh, if Justice Brinley learned about this?" she asked.

"Only too well. I purpose not to be driven from home again."

"It pleasures me much to hear you say that," she said.

A few days later the *Sea Gull* sailed into Newport late in the after-

noon loaded with tautog, squeteague, and lobsters. While Tom and Israel ran alongside Coddington's Wharf to dispose of their catch, Hugh
took the skiff and rowed down to Ellery's Wharf, where he had noticed a gathering of people. As the skiff approached the end of the
wharf, he saw a ship's whaleboat alongside and, mounted as a swivel
on its bow, a bell-muzzled blunderbuss, or "murderer."

"'Tis Peterson's boat," thought Hugh. "But what passes up there?
Someone is speaking."

Hugh climbed to the wharf and joined the crowd of men and boys
gathered around a thickset man wearing a beaver hat from which
drooped a red feather. Long sandy hair framed hard-bitten features
typically Scandinavian. His yellow shirt, not overly clean, was caught
at the waist by a sash of parti-colored India silk, but he carried no side
arms. On his legs were loose canvas drawers and no stockings, but a
pair of shining gold buckles decorated his shoes.

"I vant five stout lad," said Peterson. "Already dere iss twenty
from dis islan' has shipped. Dere vil be var soon, and de brize money
vill mak' you rich."

Curious to see from closer quarters the reputed pirate who was
awaiting the action of the grand jury called by Justice Brinley, Hugh
was elbowing his way through the crowd when a voice behind him addressed the speaker. "Here's the lad you want, Captain! Hugh Jocelyn.
He slipped Bellamy and swimmed ashore."

"Vat? Vere iss he? I haf heard of him." Peterson's small eyes measured the tall youth who stood in front of him. "You are de lad who
mak' dat long swim?" he asked of the grinning Hugh.

The lad nodded.

Peterson deliberately studied Hugh, from his corded neck and
folded arms to the bare legs exposed by the loose canvas drawers.
Then his gaze lifted to the boy's smiling face. For a space, his hard
eyes searched those of the boy, who coolly returned his stare. Then he
turned an oblique look at a swart-faced man with gold rings in his ears
who stood beside him, and nodded.

"Are you so strong dat you look?" he asked Hugh.

"I'm stout enough for my age," Hugh replied, wondering what was
coming.

"Come vid me to de Blue Porpoise for a sip of rum. I wish talk vid
you."

With his dark-skinned mate, Peterson led the way off the wharf to
the Blue Porpoise on Thames Street.

Hugh was curious to hear what the pirate would offer, and he was
thinking of Candace. She might be serving in the big room. He might
have a chance to speak with her. And he wondered what she would
say. He felt suddenly warm at the thought of looking into her ardent

eyes. But he had avoided the Blue Porpoise and Candace Prey, and she might have no eyes for Hugh Jocelyn.

There were no customers in the ordinary when the three entered and seated themselves at a table. Peterson filled his long-stemmed pipe and lit it with flint and steel from a tinder bag he carried in his pocket. Then, blowing a cloud of smoke into the air, he leaned toward the curious Hugh. "You fish on small sloop, yah. You vork hard but mak' no money. You come vid me and in von—two year you come home vid pocket full of Spanish doubloon like dese." The speaker reached into his pocket and held a handful of glittering gold coins before Hugh's staring eyes.

Hugh had seen a gold piece but few times in his life, and the yellow metal in Peterson's hand fascinated him. Then he boldly said: "There is no war with Spain. How can you get this Spanish gold?"

Peterson's hard eyes and those of his swarthy mate met in amused smiles. He replaced the gold in his pocket and said, "My brass nine-pounder not know dere iss no var vid Spain."

Hugh smiled at the boldness of the retort. This reputed pirate was held now under a large bond for the action of the grand jury, and here he joked openly of his intentions. But Hugh's thoughts were suddenly diverted by a low laugh. He turned to look up into the smiling face of Candace Prey.

"Hugh," she said, her black eyes dancing as she looked down at him, "where have you kept yourself?" She turned, with a saucy grimace, to Peterson, whose small eyes were studying her. "Captain, if you think to sign up Hugh for a voyage to the Spanish Islands, you'll need my consent."

Peterson threw back his head in a loud laugh. "Ah, hah! So dat iss de vay de vind she blow! Yah, yah! He iss a lad for de eye!"

Hugh's nerves were tingling with the girl's nearness. As she took the orders for three rums, her hand casually rested on Hugh's shoulder and her knee pressed his thigh. He felt her touch down to his toes. 'Twas well he had kept his distance from Candace Prey.

She left to bring the drinks, and Peterson's face wrinkled in a broad smile as he nodded to Hugh. "She not like to haf you go, eh? V'en you come home you bring her gold for her ear and neck, yah!"

"She is wife of Landlord Prey," Hugh said, resenting Peterson's calm assurance.

Again the sailor laughed. "Yah, dat fat pig of a husband! She vas all eye for you, lad! I know! I know dem!"

Candace tripped back with the pewter mugs of rum. She reached across the table and placed them in front of Peterson and the mate, and as she did so, Hugh felt her breast touch his shoulder. Then coolly ignoring the company, she bent and whispered in Hugh's ear, "After this drink come to the kitchen. I'm alone," and left them, followed by Peterson's speculative eyes.

Although the privateersman and Da Costa, his swarthy Portuguese mate, painted a vivid picture of the Spanish Main and the Sugar Islands for the benefit of the boy they sought to ship, their eloquence fell on inattentive ears. Hugh had heard all this before from the lips of a more colorful artist, Israel Brandy. They moved to the door of the Blue Porpoise, and Peterson and his mate shook Hugh's hand.

"T'ink it over," said the sailor. "Dere iss blenty time. You are smart lad and vill go far. T'ink it over—de money you bring home in von—two year. Dere vill soon be noder var." Peterson reached into his pocket and brought out five shiny pine-tree shillings which he placed in Hugh's hand. "T'ink it over, den sail vid Peterson. He make you rich."

The two left, and Hugh turned and walked rapidly to the door leading to the rear room and kitchen of the tavern, where Candace stood waiting.

"I sent Martha upstairs," she said, her eyes shining with invitation, "and the men are out." She turned and led him into the kitchen, and Hugh heard his heart thundering in his chest. Aware of the danger of being caught in the kitchen with Candace, nevertheless the sight of her again swept away all caution. His blood was on fire.

She turned and was in his arms, their lips clinging in a long kiss. As he held her crushed against him, she lifted her burning face and laughed a low laugh of victory. "Hugh, oh, Hugh," she whispered, "I may love you, now. You are grown a great lad and, oh, what a lover you'll make!" Her hands were wandering over his hot face and neck. "Kiss me! Kiss me hard, Hugh, for the long months I have waited."

He lifted her and kissed her face and neck again and again. Gusts of passion swept over the uninitiated lad. He was mad with the intoxication of her clinging lips and the touch of her breasts and body.

They paused, and he set her on her feet. But she swayed giddily and he caught her to him. "Think you this may go on?" she whispered. "I am fair wild, but Martha is upstairs. I dare not!"

At the thought of their danger, Hugh's madness suddenly left him. "Prey and John, they may return," he said. "We must not be caught."

With a deep sigh she reached and drew his face to hers. Then, as they kissed, there was the sound of feet in the public room. "Quick, Hugh," she whispered; "out that back door. 'Tis they!"

The door closed softly behind him and Hugh made his way from the rear of the ordinary to the skiff. He had been mad to go into the kitchen with Candace. And now the thought of her round body in his arms would give him no peace! Here was a girl fair wild for him, as she said. 'Twas not as it was with Seeth—a maid, and such a sweet one, whom he must protect from herself. But what harm would it be with Candace, wed to that carcass of a Prey? What harm? Suppose they were caught? Did he want to see Candace at the whipping post? That might happen if Prey complained of her. But would he? And there were Content and Tom and Trelawney! How could he look them in the face if it were known that he and Candace— But what was a lad near eighteen to do? The other lads and maids sported on the wharves the summer long. True, many fell into trouble and were married out of hand. That must not happen to Hugh Jocelyn. Some day he would sail his own sloop out of Newport to Barbadoes. There would be time for loving, then.

Hugh found Tom and Content at supper. She filled two trenchers of boiled cod and beans for the hungry boy and placed a loaf of rye-'n'-Injun beside him. When he had finished, he took from his pocket the five shiny pine-tree shillings, minted in Boston, which Peterson had given him, and put them into Content's hand. "'Tis yours, Mother Content. Now you shall have the tammy for the new frock you need for church."

"Five shillings!" she gasped. "Why, Hugh, however got you that much money?"

Hugh told of his meeting Peterson, the pirate, and his mate. As he finished, Israel dropped in.

"So Peterson tried to ship you, and give you five shillings?" said Israel. "Where said he he was bound? The naval office will give him no papers and the grand jury sits on his case."

"I said there was no war with Spain, and he and his ringed-eared mate, Da Costa, laughed. He said his demiculverins knew not that there was no war with Spain."

"Burn me!" snorted Israel, "there spoke a true pirate and no less! But there be many Portsmouth and Newport lads already shipped, and the merchants were hot to buy the silver plate, Indy silk, and calicoes he brought in. He'll come to no harm, here."

§29

TRELAWNEY sat with his three friends, Brenton, Arnold, and Sheffield, at a table in the great room of the King's Head tavern. That morning a sloop in from Boston had brought the news from London of the birth of a son to King James, with the order of Governor Andros that proclamation to the people should be made forthwith, guns fired in salute, and bonfires lighted in celebration of the event. At the order of Justice

Brinley the drums had rolled on the Parade, calling for an assembly of the people. Benoni Tosh's deep voice had boomed the announcement of the birth of a royal heir to a scattering of citizens who had responded with a cheer so indifferent that Francis Brinley's handsome face colored with rage and mortification as he listened. A gun on the Parade, the two mounted in the little earthwork on the beach in front of Benedict Arnold's house, on Thames Street, and those of the small fort on Goat Island roared their salutes, but the people of Newport were cold to the news. They bore no love for the king who had ordered their charter seized and destroyed and had subjected them to the will and pleasure of a royal governor and a council sitting in Boston.

That day when the citizens of Newport met, their tongues were in their cheeks and their eyebrows raised in deprecation, for the rumor had already drifted from England that the pregnancy of the queen was a matter of doubt, and the heralded birth of an heir might be but a royal imposture.

"I had a letter from home by the Boston sloop," announced Trelawney, clapping his cup of malmsey on the table. "'Tis rumored that William of Orange may be asked to land on English soil with an army."

Brenton lifted his mug of Canary. "God speed the day!" he said. "A toast to William of Orange! With him king instead of his papist father-in-law, our charter which so miraculously disappeared may be as miraculously found again. But this child of the queen, Dick. Think you 'tis a trick on the English people?"

"I know not," replied Trelawney. "Trouble is doubtless brewing at home for the king. I believe his end is near. But I have troubles of my own here in Newport and have no ear for the self-made troubles of a Stuart. King James has been the death of too many good men, some my friends. Let him stew in his own juice."

"I drink to that," said Sheffield.

"How about that stubborn scholar of yours?" asked Arnold. "Truly, Dick, you doubly earn every pound paid you for your labors with those Brinley whelps."

Trelawney finished his cup of wine before replying. He shook his periwigged head as his mouth curled in a retrospective smile. "Since I told her how Hugh loved Will Shakespeare and the Elizabethans and was to start Latin this winter, that stubborn scholar of mine, as you name her, has fair startled me with her desire to learn. Her penmanship, which was once but unformed scratches like the tracks of birds in the snow, is now legible. And what think you she said when I commended her? Why, the minx, she coolly fixed me with those saucy eyes of hers and told me she would have shame if, some day, Hugh Jocelyn could not spell out what she wrote him."

"God's name!" exclaimed Brenton. "There's spirit in that minx!"

"Yes, she owns a will that will carry her far in her desires," agreed Trelawney. "Brain she has, too, would she but use it; and heart far beyond that vindictive brother. But her will will spell her ruin or—her triumph—I know not which."

"So she moons over Hugh, still," observed Sheffield. "Of course they do not meet?"

"I have his promise he will not see or write her, and he has not."

There were voices at the door of the ordinary and Justice Brinley, clothed in a wine-colored velvet coat and breeches, entered, followed by the lanky Peleg Sanford, and Richard Smith, of King's Province. Shortly, from the table where he sat, Brinley rose and, lifting high a pewter cup of Canary, smiled significantly at Brenton and his friends as he said in a loud voice, "Gentlemen, I give you the health of King James and the royal heir!"

Trelawney sprang to his feet and, raising his cup, drank to the toast. Brenton and the others rose with studied deliberation, touched their lips perfunctorily to their cups, and sat down. As he watched them, Justice Brinley's face crimsoned. He flung himself on his stool and talked heatedly with Sanford and Smith. Then, filling his cup, Joseph Brenton moved leisurely to the table of the three royalists, who raised hostile faces to the young man who smirked down on them.

"Your humble servant, gentlemen!" said Brenton, with an exaggerated bow. "I, also, would propose a toast. May King James, in his wisdom, make us an independent colony once more, under our old charter!"

With snorts of disgust the three men at the table turned their backs on the speaker.

"What?" cried Brenton, simulating surprise and chagrin. "You would not drink to that? That is most strange! Well, here's one, then, you will drink to! Gentlemen, I give you the Prince of Orange!"

Brinley was on his feet and glaring in amazement at the still leering Brenton. "What's your purpose in this? Are you mad?" he cried. "Why, your conduct is treasonous! You presume too far on the Brenton name!"

"So you refuse a toast to our gracious king's son-in-law? We've drunk to the king, but, Justice Brinley, it appears treasonous to drink to his daughter's husband? Explain me that! No? Well—be damned to you!" And Brenton turned on his heel and joined his worried friends.

"Have a care, Joe. You went too far bringing in the name of the Prince," cautioned Arnold. "Don't forget that Brinley is Chief Justice and Andros' friend. He could make trouble for that speech."

"Pah! No Brinley will ever dare try a Brenton in this port!" scoffed the other. "If he does, God save him!"

Fearing further unpleasantness, for Brenton seemed in a mood for trouble, and embarrassed because of his position as the Brinleys' tutor, Trelawney left the inn. At the door he passed Nathaniel Coddington and Benedict Arnold, uncle of John. The two joined Brenton and the others.

"What think you," announced Coddington, "the grand jury finds no bill against Peterson. Benoni Tosh who was with them so informed us as we passed down Thames Street."

"What? 'Tis too good to be true!" cried Brenton. "Brinley has not yet heard! I'll fetch him the glad news!"

Emptying his cup of Canary, Brenton rose and approached the table where Brinley, Sanford, and Smith sat with heads together. He bent low in a mock bow as they turned sour faces. "My respects to Justice Brinley!" he said. "Benoni Tosh announces that the grand jury refuses to indict Peterson."

Brinley was on his feet, his face purple with anger. "Where got you that?" he demanded.

"From Nathaniel Coddington, my lord!" And the half-intoxicated Brenton again bent low in an insolent bow, and returned to his friends.

"Well, what could Brinley have expected when half the jury are neighbors or kin to half of Peterson's crew?" laughed the elder Arnold. "Now the Swede will head for the Spanish Islands and I doubt not that he flies a red flag when he reaches them."

"I like not the idea of our Newport and Portsmouth lads shipping with him," said Coddington. "But how may one keep boys on the farms here when their heads are filled with these tales of easy riches on the Spanish Main? There's no war and 'twill be piracy to attack a Spaniard or a Frenchman, yet Peterson heads that way and, I believe, for no other purpose."

That afternoon all Newport was chuckling over the discomfiture of Justice Brinley and the necessity for the cancellation of Peterson's bond. Even the staid Quakers, who had shaken doubtful heads at the presence in the harbor of the brig of the reputed pirate, but who had been glad to buy his suspicious cargo and sell him stores at a handsome profit, shook hands in the privacy of their shops and storehouses in the general rejoicing over the defeat of the haughty Brinley. Yet there were many who asked what the growing port was coming to if, like the French-controlled Tortuga, in the West Indies, Newport was to become a clearinghouse for doubtful cargoes and a haven for the riffraff of the seas.

More than once that summer masters of deep-sea ships, tempting Hugh's imagination with tales of the fabled Spanish Main and the palm-lipped keys of the Windward and Leeward Islands, tried to ship him. But his love for Content and his loyalty to Trelawney kept him on the *Sea Gull*. Already, under the tutelage of the Englishman he had mastered the use of the backstaff, or Davis Quadrant, which had long since displaced the cross-staff and the astrolabe, and had learned to chart a course. And hunger to see the great world which lay beyond the horizons of his experience, Martin's Vineyard and the Cape to the eastward, and the bluffs of Block Island on the west, filled the boy with an ever-increasing restlessness. He now fully realized what it meant to be the foster son of a humble fisherman in a port where lived great landholders who counted their acres on either side of Narragansett Bay by the thousands; where the shipowners, distillers of rum, and the merchants, with their shops and warehouses dotting the wharves, and their sloops and brigs roving the seas, wore broadcloth, silk, and velvet, and lived in two- and three-chimneyed houses, with their black servants.

To please Content, Hugh sometimes went with her to the Second Baptist Church, but thanks to Trelawney, his training had been too liberal to permit him to stomach the theological absurdities and disputatious hairsplitting of the two hours of torture called a sermon. So he seldom listened except to marvel at the fact that a man could talk so long and say so little. It was on a long bench reserved for the humble, while, according to their station and wealth, the gentry occupied pews in front, that the hard and bitter facts of existence in a man-made world revealed themselves to the rebellious and unhappy boy conscious of his worn Kersey coat and locram shirt. He hated these smug, rich men in front, with their periwigs, fat stomachs, and superior airs, their broadcloth and velvet, and their wives and daughters in silk and taffeta, while beside him the simple Content sat in her worn linsey-woolsey, her red hands ungloved.

It was in church, oblivious of the droning voice of the preacher, that Hugh determined on a future far removed from the long benches of the poor. There would soon be another war and he'd sail the warm seas as Tom Paine had sailed them—ruthless and without fear; and he would return as Tom Paine had returned, with a fortune. Trelawney spoke much, and they read much in the poets, of honor and justice and ideals, but where, in Newport, the boy asked himself, could such be found? In many of those pews in front sat men who were known to have worked their bond servants to the bone, and haggled with their shipmasters and crews to the last penny. Some had bought their plunder from known pirates and resold it on the Newport wharves for triple the cost. Most of them flouted the law, and when the chance offered, broke cargo in a quiet cove up the bay rather than pay the King's duty and the entry fees to the naval office. They traded, schemed, and cheated, made laws to be lightly held or, as Trelawney said, made none at all, grew rich and sat in their pews in church, while he and

Content were given a long bench from which to admire. Name of God! how he hated them all.

And when, at last, the congregation had been sufficiently threatened with the wrath of God and the dire prospect of hell-fire and brimstone, and the occupants of the pews filed past the humble folk of the long benches, Hugh would flush with anger as he marked the raised brows of the maids when their eyes fell from his yellow head to his homespun coat and clumsy, untanned shoes. With passing interest they glanced at the lad who had made the long swim to escape Bellamy, then turned away. And the boy wondered why, in the House of God, the rich and the poor should be divided. Were they so in heaven? So it was seldom that Content could persuade the sensitive boy to join her in church, where his rebellious spirit made the hours one long torment.

"There's so much I might teach you, Hugh," Trelawney said, as they sat one night in his lodgings, "if we had but the time. Next winter we shall go far and fast if you do not leave us."

"But already I have mathematics and navigation, with much history. And we've read the old and new poets and their plays."

"Ay, but you forget the classics. I want you to have some Latin, at least. Stay with Tom and Content this winter that you may have a taste of Latin."

"Never fear, I shall stay. But 'tis hard, this poverty. And I'm fevered to see some of that world you talk of."

With a sigh Trelawney realized that he had educated the boy only some day to lose him. Hugh Jocelyn was clearly destined for the sea. For Shakespeare and Ben Jonson, Marlowe and Peele, Spenser and Chaucer, the old poet, Milton, and the new poet, Dryden, and many others had woven their spell. Already Hugh was dreaming the dreams that his teacher had promised him. And he was paying the price of the enchantment with ambition and aspiration, with unrest and discontent.

"Hugh," said the Englishman, lighting his pipe and clasping his hands over a lean knee, "your frame of mind, lately, gives me much cause for worry. Since your trouble with the Brinleys you've been beating your head against life—not facing it with wisdom and patience."

The blood moved up into Hugh's face. "You mean, I should love these people who sent me to the pillory—these rich who rule Newport?" scoffed the boy. "I'm wondering if your gentle birth warps your judgment, softens you toward them."

"There you go again! Always raving against the rich!" Trelawney was irritated. "Your quarrel with life is your poverty, and yet you never cease to rail at what you aim at, wealth!"

Consciousness of the justice of his friend's remark only served to feed the boy's mood. He got to his feet. "So you've turned against me as well," he stormed. "You give me the learning to measure these great men of ours for what they are, with their train of pickthanks and lickspittles, then you ask me to spare judgment—to scrape and bend the knee when they pass."

"No, lad; but as they rule Newport, one must look facts in the face."

"Name of God! I'm done with Newport, then," bit off Hugh, pacing the floor as he worked himself into a Jocelyn rage. "I'll ship out on the first sloop. I wish a war was on that I might sail on a privateer to the warm seas and see life!"

"And the taste of Latin?"

"What good will your Latin bring me?" flung back the unhappy boy. "I'm scum—son of a fisherman! What have I to do with Latin?"

"And Content and Tom?"

"I must leave them some day, why not now?"

"And a certain Dick Trelawney, who treasures you?"

Hugh ceased his pacing to stare down at the man on the stool calmly puffing his pipe. Suddenly his face softened. His mood melted, and he felt ashamed. "I'm sorry, Dick," he said. "I go hot all over when I think how unjust life is. I want to strangle—to kill. My hate gets beyond my control. I see red. I know 'tis jealousy. I want what they have." Hugh shook his clenched fist in his friend's face. "And some day, Dick, I mean to have it, if I have to loot and plunder as Tom Paine did in Florida and the warm seas!"

"Are you sure Captain Paine overstepped the law?"

"I know he did. Israel was with him and keeps a tight mouth on what happened in those days; but I know they plundered many a town. On their return, Massachusetts Bay urged their arrest, but the governor here turned a deaf ear. They pillaged the Spanish churches, but they waged no war on women and children."

"So did Henry Morgan, and they knighted him," said Trelawney. For a time the Englishman was silent. At last he asked, "Then you'll stay for the Latin, Hugh, this winter?"

"Yes, I'll stay. But don't ask me to give Newbury the road if I meet him. I'll pull him from his horse and—"

"Go to the whipping post for your pains!"

Hugh scowled at the man intently watching him. "Well, for your sake and Content's and Tom's and Israel's, I'll— Name of God! I'll let him—pass."

When the boy had gone, Trelawney sat drawing through his pipe stem. "'Tis a wild young stone horse I took to break! But I fear there's no breaking him. Life alone will lesson him. That high temper and hate of the gentry'll bring him much trouble. He's always been honest. But I fear this madness for wealth may undermine his integrity. In Newport he finds little scruple. 'Twould not be strange if he lost his—but what a pity! He hopes for the war, which is near. What will war and the warm seas do to Hugh Jocelyn!"

§30

NEITHER his old light o' love, Betsy Moon, nor the people of the taverns, whom he had secretly approached, had been able to give Israel the slightest clue to the mystery of the bludgeoning of Hugh. No sailor or other individual with the sudden possession of too much spending money had been noticed.

"Slit my windpipe!" growled Brandy, one evening on the return of the *Sea Gull* from the Sakonnet nets, "'tis a task for the devil himself. I be beat at it. Why, burn me! no other than that mud shark of a Newbury, with his sloops and his farms and his velvet coats and airs, was behind that clouting of Hugh, with young Brinley; but 'tis like huntin' for a worm in a ship's timber to prove it."

"Hugh carries his cutlass now," soothed Tom, "when he stirs abroad at night."

"Rot my bones! he must keep close watch. No man however stout may take the clout of an oak club without hurt. 'Tis that fevers me when he walks after dark."

"The lad may now take sight of the sun with the Davis Quadrant and chart a course," said Tom, proudly.

Israel blew a cloud of smoke from his wide mouth and grunted: "Captain Pease of the *Sea Flower* marveled at it but lately."

"Ay, he did. Hugh told it me," said Stanton.

"But the lad did not discover to us that Captain Scarlett, master of Brenton's brig, had Hugh aboard afore the *Swordfish* sailed for Jamaica, and Hugh's schoolin' from Trelawney in narveegation was such that Scarlett fair blinked his eyes."

"No, the lad told me not that," said Stanton.

"Nor me neither, but, burn me! Captain Scarlett did." Brandy spat into the embers of the supper fire and continued, "Then to prove how nimble he was, Hugh swarmed up the shrouds to fore and main tops like a monkey, slid down the back stays and dived off the jib boom."

"Ay, he would."

"When hauled over the rail by a man rope, Captain Scarlett said to him, 'When you be ready for sea, discover it to me.'"

"What did Hugh say?"

"He said he was stayin' on with Content and Tom and Israel. Mr. Trelawney had much to learn him this winter and time was fair short for it all."

There were pride and triumph in Stanton's weather-bitten face as he said, "A head and stiff will of his own he has, Israel, as you and I well know."

"Ay, that he has; and a temper like a speared swordfish. What with his broodin' over his poverty and his hate of the rich he has many times had me in a fret over his future. He sees life overhard and, built as he is, will find life overhard."

"'Tis true! Plenty of trouble he's bound to sight to wind'ard, but he'll never fall off and run! He'll face it with two hard fists and a clamped jaw."

"That he will!" growled Israel. "He'll buck every headwind with his top hamper groanin' and his rail awash. Frequent more is gained by lyin' to and ridin' her out, which Hugh has yet to learn."

"Ay, he's scarce learned, and will take much hurt in the learnin'."

A deep sigh whistled through Israel's teeth. "Ay, he will that! And 'twill be next year, I doubt not, he leaves us. He must not wait longer."

There was a long silence as the two friends puffed on their pipes and, avoiding each other's eyes, gazed bleakly into the dead embers of the fire.

After a time Stanton shook off his gloomy thoughts, to raise his eyes and find Brandy staring, open-mouthed, at the chimney above the lintel, where hung the two muskets, powder horns, and bullet and shot pouches. "What see you, Israel?" he demanded.

"Burn my bones, look!" cried the sailor, pointing. "There hangs the cutlass, now! In this light I saw it not. Hugh is barehanded. He carries not even a club."

"True," muttered Stanton. "I thought he had it with him."

"No doubt Hugh is with a maid on some wharf where the young sit in the evening. And someone who wishes him no good may be watchin' him," said Israel.

Tom nodded. "They could see him and wait for the dark, to strike."

"Ay. I like it not, Tom. And 'twill soon be dusk."

"Which way went he?" asked Stanton.

"I know not. Let us follow the wharves in the skiff. Stab me, I wish not the lad bludgeoned again, or knifed; for if set upon, he'll fight them with his bare hands."

Stanton's seamed face was taut with anxiety and his jaw clamped tight. He took his musket from its pegs, with a powder horn and bullet pouch. Israel drew the cutlass from its sheath and followed Tom down to the dory.

That evening Hugh had met Seeth Carr and strolled out on Brenton's Wharf, for the other wharves along the waterfront were peopled with young folk enjoying the barely moving air off the water. Over the flat surface of Cove and harbor drifted laughter and the sound of young voices. Along Thames Street people sat in their yards and gardens enjoying the serenity of the long evening and watching the creeping twilight banish the rose tints of the harbor water painted from the palette of the vanished sunset. Because it was the height of the summer fishing and the *Sea Gull* was often away over night or late in reaching her berth in the Cove, Hugh had seen little of the tawny-haired Seeth. But she had been much on his mind, the beauty and sweetness of her and her wild abandon on the night he had been attacked by unknown men. Yet the more he had thought of her, the more clearly he realized that to meet Seeth often would, in the end, mean the losing of his freedom. For she frightened him with the intensity of her emotions. She drew him as a magnet pulls metal, but young as he was, he knew that his dreams were over if he blindly followed the urge that tormented him. With his blood singing the eternal song of youth, nevertheless, Trelawney's hold on the troubled boy was clamped fast by the bonds of a deep gratitude and affection. For three years the Englishman had toiled with him that he might, later, climb from among the illiterates with whom he had grown. And Hugh but too well realized that once bound by obligation to Seeth he would marry her. For he could not take her lightly. She was too fine and her love too deep.

On this peaceful evening, Hugh and Seeth made their way around piles of pipe staves, lumber, and barrels of salt fish and molasses to the end of the wharf, where they might be alone and enjoy the light movement of air; breezes that carried odors of tar and fish, and ale and rum from the breweries and distilleries, mingled with the salt tang of the sea.

"'Tis overlong since we sat on a wharf end, Hugh," said Seeth, as she leaned against a bollard and smiled up into his bronzed face. "Four times, only, have you come to the house and sat in the garden, Hugh Jocelyn, since they put you in the pillory and you escaped from that pirate. It has seemed so long between your comings!"

His arm was around her lithe body now, and with a contented sigh, she tilted her tawny head back on his shoulder and pressed her cheek against his. "You know, Seeth," he said, thrilling to her touch, "we have been much away over night—sometimes for days. I have had little chance to come."

She drew down his blond head until their lips met in a long kiss. Then she said as she nestled against him, "But that makes it not the less hard waiting, sir, because you could not come."

His face was in the thick masses of her tumbled hair as he said, "Oh, Seeth, you little know how I carry you to sea with me every day we head out."

"And you, Hugh, I love you so it fair gives me fear for what may come of it. Dost love me? Say it! Say it, for I'll never tire of hearing!"

Hugh sat down on an oak timber and impulsively gathered her into his arms. "Of course I love you. You fair drive me mad with your sweetness, Seeth. You grow more fair every day, with those green eyes and their black lashes that shine and smolder and glow so when I kiss you; and your sweet mouth and your skin like silk, 'tis so smooth and soft. Could I help but love you?"

She lifted her flaming face and kissed his eyes, his bronzed cheeks, and his mouth, while his blood leaped at the touch of her lips. She was so sweet and desirable and so stirred him. They sat with little speech, contented in their nearness, until the twilight deepened over harbor and town and, here and there, like fireflies, lights winked on the anchored craft.

Suddenly Hugh rose and glanced around.

"Oh, Hugh, we're not going back to the house so early!" she demurred, clinging to his arm.

But the boy did not hear her. He was alarmed at what he had just seen behind some piled lumber. In the gathering dusk a man's head had surely bobbed out and then disappeared. There could be no doubt of it. His eyes had not tricked him. Someone was watching them. The warnings of Israel and Trelawney flashed through his brain. Someone had seen them from the water, landed on the wharf, and hidden behind the piled lumber. And the cutlass! He had always carried it since the night of the bludgeoning, but tonight, in his haste, had forgotten it. He looked about him in the fading light for a club, but saw nothing he could use.

"What has come over you, Hugh?" demanded the puzzled girl, peering into his eyes, which searched the piles of lumber beyond them rapidly blurring with shadow. "Why don't you answer me? What are you looking for?"

Hugh knew that he must act quickly, for the dusk was fast blanketing the wharf, and what occurred would not be seen from the shore. The presence of Seeth and the fear of her screams being heard must have delayed the attack on him. He had to get Seeth away safely before it came, for he knew it was coming. If she stayed, she would be hurt or thrown off the wharf, for they would show no mercy. He must wait there until she got well away, then he could fight or swim.

He bent and whispered in her ear: "Seeth, you must run, run fast for shore and call for help. We're being watched from that pile of lumber. I saw a head move. Someone's after me. Run, Seeth, and send aid!"

"But you, Hugh!" pleaded the terrified girl. "I'll not leave you to be hurt. Oh, come with me, Hugh!"

"If you love me, do as I say and call the watch," he roughly commanded.

With a sob, the bewildered girl started back over the wharf for the shore, while Hugh peered about in the dusk for a stick with which to defend himself. If the ruffians were armed, he could dive into the water, but he must stay on the wharf until Seeth was well away.

He did not have long to wait. Shortly he made out shadowy figures moving toward him from the pile of lumber. They were coming. He kicked off his heavy shoes and held them, one in each hand. As the blurred shapes moved closer, he hurled the shoes. There was a low curse as one man stopped. The other came on with a rush, and the boy stepped aside and swung with all his power. Like the blow of a club his fist caught the lunging man flush on the jaw, spun him around and sent him reeling over the stringpiece of the wharf, to fall with a loud splash into the water. As he struck his man, Hugh saw a knife in the thrusting hand that passed his face.

The boy whirled on the second man, who leaped at him with raised club. Diving under the blow, Hugh catapulted into the legs of his enemy and the club struck the pine planking with a dull thud. Then the two were down, thrashing over the wharf, locked in each other's arms. But Hugh had never grappled with such bulk and power. The man was enormous, and the boy knew that he was a Negro slave, by the fetid breath which nearly sickened him, and the strong odor of his body. As he fought to force the other toward the stringpiece, he felt the big muscles of the black man knot and swell. Powerful as Hugh was, it required all his strength and skill to block the Negro's groping fingers from his throat. And while he fought, in the back of his head lurked the thought that the man he had knocked into the water might soon be climbing back on the wharf, with his knife. As they thrashed and strained and wrestled over the pine planking, Hugh could hear the screams of the terrified Seeth as she neared the shore.

Hugh soon realized that in sheer strength he had met more than his match. If he were to win, it must be with his head. For it was evident that the giant Negro was using his weight to wear down and exhaust his agile opponent so he might silently put on a strangle hold. But Hugh's quickness and wrestling skill time after time balked the other in his purpose. Desperately he fought to edge the black man to the stringpiece of the wharf, but the slave was too strong. The Negro's breathing grew faster and faster with his efforts to strangle the lad who strained and twisted in his arms. Soon the black's body and arms, from which the shirt had been torn, grew so slippery with sweat that Hugh's hands could not hold a grip as he fought to protect his throat, and the struggling boy realized only too well that his only hope lay in outlasting his enemy.

Time after time as they battled in the dusk, now one on top, now the other, Hugh barely escaped the iron fingers seeking his throat. In his rage, the baffled black bit at the boy's shoulders and arms, to take in return the savage battering of Hugh's free fist in the jaw. But the Negro's jaw was made of iron.

The breaths of the tired wrestlers were filling and leaving their lungs in great gasps. The panting Hugh wondered how long he could hold out against the enormous strength of the man who gripped him in his thick arms. Then, of a sudden, the boy's blood boiled with a fighting fury. The strength seemed to double in his tired arms. He'd show these gentry how a Jocelyn could battle their hired scum! With a fierce wrench and the last ounce of strength he could summon, he rolled the Negro over the stringpiece and the two fell into the harbor water below.

Locked in each other's arms they went down into the blackness, but Hugh had sucked in a deep breath as they fell, while the Negro choked with water he had swallowed. They rose, and the boy fought to push back the other's head and free himself, but the arms of the frantic black clamped on him like a vise. Hugh knew that the slave would drown him if he did not soon break free, but he was held helpless as if trussed by hempen ropes. Then, again filling his lungs, the boy went limp and for the second time sank with his enemy. As they went down, his free hand touched and his arm reached and circled a barnacle-crusted pile, holding them under. At last, forced to break his grip, the drowning slave struggled upward for air, followed by Hugh. As the boy's head broke the surface, the Negro lunged for him, to take the vicious drive of Hugh's foot against his chest, pushing him away, and a swift back stroke put the boy out of reach. There followed a wild floundering, a choked cry, then silence.

Hugh swam to a bollard and climbed by a man rope hanging beside it up to the wharf, where he sprawled panting. "You ambush me—no more—for their dirty money—black man," he gasped. "But you near drowned me—with that strength—of yours!"

The exhausted boy lay on his back in the dusk while he recovered his wind and strength. His body and arms were sore and bruised from the mauling they had taken at the hands of the man down in the water below. And what a fool he had been not to carry the cutlass! With that he could have carved the man with the knife and the black man to ribbons. The man with the knife! Where was he? Drowned, or, if he could swim, perhaps waiting in the blackness behind the piled lumber with that knife.

At the thought, Hugh rolled over and got to his feet. Then, from the shore, lifting above Seeth's calls for help rose voices. Hugh started back to meet his approaching friends and find a club. If the man with the knife was still hiding on the wharf, they'd hunt him down as one hunts rats.

Suddenly he heard the pat of moccasined feet behind him. Instinctively he leaped to the side but, tripping over loose lumber, fell sprawling on his chest as a body struck his back and a knife was driven into the pine planking beside his cheek. Before the man on his back could wrench the blade free and strike again, Hugh's right hand gripped his wrist, then twisted the clutching fingers from the helve. A hand groped for Hugh's throat, but, reaching back over his shoulder with his free left hand, the boy seized his enemy by his long hair and, rising to his knees with the writhing body on his back, hurled it to the wharf.

Hugh recovered the knife sticking in the planking and knelt beside the sprawled shape of the unconscious man who had rushed him. He was an Indian, and his hair was clotted with blood.

"So you'd knife me from the rear, Wampanoag," muttered the boy. "But your head was softer than this planking!"

Alongshore, torches and lanterns were already bobbing and flickering. Shouts and the excited voices of approaching men reached the boy on the wharf.

"Seeth has called the watch!"

§31

THE pitch-pine torches and tallow-candle lanterns were moving rapidly toward the still breathless Hugh. Voices hailed, and he answered that he was all right. Then there was a rush of feet, and the frantic Seeth flung herself into his arms.

"Hugh! You're not hurt? But you're wet! You've been in the water! Where are those men, Hugh?"

"I'm all right, Seeth!" Hugh comforted the sobbing girl, who clung to him. "Don't cry, Seeth! It's all right now. I'm not hurt, Seeth!"

Then Shubael Painter, the constable, reached them with the watch, and Hugh told his story as they examined the Indian by the light of a candlewood torch.

"You nigh broke his head," grunted Painter, turning to Hugh. "Save trouble for all of us if we heaved his dirty carcass into the harbor, Hugh!" The Indian groaned and moved. "Thought he'd hear that," muttered the constable.

"If he gets well, he may have a story to tell, Constable Painter," said Hugh.

"True, this is the second time they've set on you, lad. You sure the black is drowned?"

"Yes. He near strangled me and I had to take him into the water to break his grip."

"You fish!" chuckled Painter. "Name of God! he set on the wrong lad. You took him into the water and drowned him like a rat. Heard you that, neighbors?" The constable turned to the two watchmen. "The lad drowned the black man like you drown a puppy."

"Ay, we did! He'll be bobbin' on the bottom along the wharves come the flood tide, and we can hook on to the slave and have a look," said a watchman. "Doubtless someone will know him."

"No," replied Hugh, "there is no slave on the island of his size and strength. They brought him from the Main to do this."

Shortly the wharf was crowded with chattering people insistent on hearing Hugh's story. Then Benoni Tosh arrived and had the dazed Indian taken ashore and locked up in the one-room jail on Prison Street, off the Parade.

Leaving the reluctant Seeth at her door, Hugh went home, where he found Israel and Stanton, who had reached Bremen's Wharf after Hugh and Benoni had left. With a cup of rum in his hands, Hugh stood before the freshened cooking fire, while steam rose from his wet canvas breeches and tattered shirt as he described his battle with the strange Negro and the attack of the Wampanoag. The room was full of sober-faced men, and the hovering Content, whose eyes and quivering mouth were eloquent of the fear in her heart, moved quietly in and about.

"This is the second time it has happened," Trelawney was saying, "and 'tis solely by the grace of God that it failed. It must not happen again."

"Stab me!" snorted Brandy, smashing a hairy fist into his cupped hand. "I'll draw the truth of this matter from that Injun's dirty tongue if I have to blister his feet with a hot iron."

"He's in the hands of Benoni Tosh now, Israel," objected Stanton. "Trust Benoni, and have a care what you say outside. Your tongue will bring you trouble."

In his rage the sailor stumped back and forth on his peg leg, waving his arms and growling like a caged animal. "Burn me! must we stand by, like a brig in stays, and see the lad murdered because Brinley's chief justice?" he roared. "Rot my bones! I'll go to the whippin' post afore I ease up on this matter."

"You think Newbury and that boy of Justice Brinley's are behind this, Mr. Trelawney?" demanded Stanton, the wooden cup in his hand shaking from the pent violence of his emotion.

Trelawney frowned, as his long fingers slowly stroked his bony chin. Then he said: "From what I know of Carr Newbury, he'd be well capable of it. The boy would follow his lead, for he nurses every grievance. But unless the Indian lives and talks, we shall never know. There's no proof yet against anyone."

There were voices outside, a knock on the door, and William Wanton burst in, followed by his brother John. "We had the news at the Blue Porpoise, Hugh," cried William, his keen face flushed with excitement as he shook Hugh's hand. "They little knew what they were about when they tried to drown Hugh Jocelyn."

John clapped Hugh on the back, while Stanton filled two cups with cider fortified with rum. "Drown him?" he laughed. "That's a pretty joke! They're saying in the taverns that Hugh held the black under till he choked."

Hugh smiled drily at the enthusiasm of his friends, whetted by the toasts they had already drunk to his health. "He near drowned me, John, he was that stout. I never met such strength."

"But the Injun, Hugh?" demanded the hawk-beaked William Wanton, his dark eyes snapping as he drained his cup. "He came back at you after you'd knocked him off the wharf?"

Hugh briefly told the story.

"Got his wrist and hair in those hands of yours and it was all up with that Injun," laughed John Wanton.

"We couldn't spare Hugh when the next war comes," said William. "Nor you, Israel," he quickly added.

"Ay, I goes as gunner, William," growled Brandy.

"Master gunner and no less, Israel," agreed Watson. "Captain Tom Paine told me but recent that Newport held no man could lay a demiculverin or a saker with Israel Brandy."

"Rot my bones! 'tis the living truth he speaks," said Israel, gravely nodding his shaggy head.

There was a loud knock and Tom opened the door on the towering bulk of Benoni Tosh. The massive red face of the Town Sergeant was sober as he stalked into the room. Nodding to the company, he said, "'Tis a pretty pass when a lad may not court a Newport maid on a wharf without being put to fight for his life!"

"Well spoke, Benoni," approved Stanton, handing the sergeant a cup of rum. "We were close to losing Hugh tonight."

"If the Court of Quarter Sessions do not hang him, forty lashes are little enough for that Injun, and Benoni Tosh swings the whip and no constable," growled the big man, tossing off his rum in one gulp.

"Is the Injun's head cracked?" demanded Brandy.

"No. When 'tis healed, the whip will make him talk."

Trelawney's dark face mirrored his doubt. "I'm wondering if he'll get the whipping post. There are those who might wish to stop his mouth."

The glances of the two men locked. Slowly Benoni's left eye dropped in a significant wink. "Schoolmaster," he said, "that, also, has been in my mind. There's strong talk and wild in the taverns tonight. The people are fevered over this thing. They say the lad has been marked to be got rid of. If not hung for attempted murder, 'tis the law that an Injun be proper whipped before sold as bond servant."

"Our law, now, seems but the will of a few men," sighed Tom Stanton.

"Mark me, as matters stand, the court will hesitate to flout the law and the people. Still, Andros is royal governor and Francis Brinley, chief justice, and we in this poor colony, now but a province of Massachusetts Bay, the dirt under their feet."

A heavy silence fell on the room. It was a bold statement for the Town Sergeant to make, but Benoni Tosh was a bold man and an institution in Newport. So strong was his hold on the people that not even Francis Brinley had dared to remove him. He knew that he was free to speak his mind to friends who hoped with all their hearts for a return of their former government under their hidden charter, and who detested the royalists and political toadies who constituted a majority of the higher court.

"Benoni," said young William Wanton, "we Quakers are with you, heart and soul."

Benoni laughed. "William, if all the Quakers were as good fighting and drinking men as your family, what a port this would be!"

A second cup of rum disappeared down Tosh's cavernous throat. He smacked his lips with a loud "Ah!", wiped his mouth on the back of a hand like a leg of lamb, clapped Hugh on the back, and with the remark "Well fought, lad!" left the house.

"Would we had more like Benoni in this port," growled Brandy. "Since Andros took our rights away and made Brinley our lord and master a man may scarce breathe in Newport but by leave of some lickspittle of a royalist who hates our charter."

"Strong talk, Israel," laughed William Wanton, "but proper fit from the mouth of an old buccaneer."

Brandy was off his stool and shaking a huge fist in the face of the roguish speaker. "Buccaneer, is it? You name me and Tom Paine buccaneers for that we harried the French and Spaniards afore you was sucking your mother's milk? Call Captain Tom Paine buccaneer when next you meet him and you dare! Stab my guts! Buccaneer!"

"Your pardon, Israel," soothed Wanton, his face sobering but his brown eyes twinkling at the sudden rage of the fuming Brandy. "My tongue did but slip. 'Twas privateersman I meant."

With a grunt, Brandy resumed his seat, his mouth twisting furiously. "Privateer I was and will be again, come there a war," he snorted. "But, rot my bones! no buccaneer, William."

Trelawney, Hugh, and the Wantons exchanged winks as Brandy's red face was lost to view in a jack of cider spliced with rum.

As Trelawney bade them good-night, he said: "We'll know more of this matter when the Indian is tried and sentenced and Benoni talks with him. Benoni has means of persuasion besides his whip."

"Burn me! he may dodge the rope, though he meant to kill our lad, but, rot my bones! if he be not whipped till he talks," snarled Israel, his small eyes burning savagely under his bushy brows and the veins bulging in his thick neck, "he'll sing a song for me when I find him, wherever they bond him out as servant in this colony, law or no law!"

"Spoke like the master gunner of the privateer sloop, *Flying Fish*, out of Newport, bound hell knows where!" chuckled William Wanton, as the brothers said good-night.

§32

BEFORE dawn the following morning, Benoni Tosh called at the Stanton house and found the men on the beach, about to shove off in the skiff.

"What is it, Benoni?" demanded Stanton, peering into the grave face of the Town Sergeant.

"When Constable Painter went to the jail this morning, what think you he found?"

"What should he find but a dirty Wampanoag with a broken skull?" growled Israel.

Tosh shook his great head. "He found the Wampanoag stabbed through the heart. The door had been forced. Now what make you of that?"

"A dead Injun tells no tales!" muttered Israel.

"So they feared the rope or the whip would make him talk," added Tom.

"From now on I carry a cutlass," said Hugh.

"That you do," answered Tosh. "And, remember, no more wharves after dark!"

"No more wharves, Benoni," replied Hugh as the Sergeant left them.

Two days later Dick Trelawney sat in the large garden in the rear of Francis Brinley's three-chimneyed house on Thames Street, with his pupil, Lettice. Trellises of eglantine, which a week before had hung pink with blooms, were now but a mass of olive green, but after the recent shower, the fragrance of their foliage hung in the heavy air. Ranks of stately hollyhocks marched with their multi-budded spears, a background for clumps of lavender cotton and honesty, gillyflowers and feverfew, and beds of patience and pitcher plant. The last clusters of pink, white, and red English roses nodded inside aromatic box hedges edging the gravel walks.

"'Tis a pretty story, but overtame, Mr. Trelawney, this 'As You Like It,'" said Lettice, who had been reading aloud from a volume whose sheepskin binding was much the worse for wear. "But 'tis over-hot this morning and the reading of this small print grows tiresome to the eyes."

Trelawney's dark features shaped a smile as he contemplated the girl's pouting red lips and her hazel eyes under their puckered brows. She dropped the volume on the seat beside her, stretched round arms, from which the loose lustring sleeves of her taffeta frock fell back from her elbows, and yawned.

"Your pardon," she said, patting her lips with shapely fingers. "I'm fair stupid this morning, with the heat."

"I fear that this enchanted forest of Arden, in dull print, casts but little spell over the fancy of Mistress Lettice Brinley," he laughed. "But could you see it played, as have I, by people of genius, you doubtless would succumb to its magic."

She smiled lazily through half-closed lids, but made no reply.

Trelawney realized that, as she matured, Lettice Brinley was growing more lovely. What skin she had! And those long-lashed eyes were fair dangerous, with that chestnut hair shot with red when the sun touched it, as it now did. Havoc she had already raised in the heart of many a Newport youth, but since her daring talk with Hugh Jocelyn at the pillory she had been held with a tight rein by her father and was patently chafing under it.

"Think you, Mr. Trelawney," she asked, after an interval, "that there is truth in this silly Phoebe's words, 'Whoever loved that loved not at first sight'?"

"There must be truth in it," replied the tutor, his eyes twinkling, "for it appears to happen—even in Newport."

A quick wave of color tinted her face, and then she swiftly regained her self-possession and boldly met his quizzical look as she said: "This lovesick Rosalind affects me not greatly, simpering and mincing in her doublet and hose. Where, indeed, were Orlando's eyes that he marked not her woman's legs? She doubtless fancied her shape, so donned the hose to make her case more sure. But she was overlong in getting to the point. What feared she?"

Ah, there spoke the true daughter of Francis Brinley. Trelawney was enjoying this talk. Lettice wore no whisk, and her disdain of a modesty cloth or kerchief revealed the loveliness of her neck and bust as she leaned toward him and shrugged her shoulders.

"One must grant the poet time and space to tell his tale or there is no play," he said. "True love may not run smooth, and lovers' hearts needs must bleed e'er they are united and live happily ever after."

"Pah!" Two white arms waved in protest, and from under the flowered taffeta skirt shot a red-heeled shoe and a shapely green-stockinged leg along the settee in an angry gesture of dissent. "These lovers of Arden were fair silly! They wasted time in idle talk!"

Trelawney threw back his periwigged head and laughed. Here, indeed, was a maid who would shoot straight for the mark, and already had. Young as she was, Lettice Brinley already possessed the force and directness of her father. She would fight for her heart's desire without quarter or scruple and with no concern for the consequences. "But, surely, you would not have had Rosalind overbold, unmaidenly?" Trelawney teased, guessing the answer he would get.

"Unmaidenly?" With a flash of white teeth, she burst into peals of laughter, rocking back and forth on the settee. "She airs her legs to the Arden breezes and the hot eyes of her lover! What call you that?"

"You think that immodest?" he demanded, wondering what she would say next.

"Immodest?" She shook her curly head. "Were her legs well turned, no! For how else was he to know what they were? I would name it an honest display of her wares before the bargain. Were they bowed or thin she would have been a fool. But by the custom of our day and in the sour eyes of old women 'twas overbold, though I see it not." The green-stockinged leg was jerked off the seat beside her and, with elbows on knees, Lettice leaned toward her amused tutor. Her face grew suddenly serious as she demanded, "What thought Hugh Jocelyn of 'As You Like It'?"

"Why, he was fair charmed with the tale."

"And he liked that sighing Rosalind, bleating like a lost lamb?"

"Yes, even in doublet and hose."

"Even, you say? I venture 'twas as much because of doublet and hose." A dimple dented her cheek as a corner of her red mouth curled.

"You forget, he saw her not but read of her, only," chuckled Trelawney. "But he loved the poetic fancy of the plot."

She gravely nodded. "Yes, you've learned him to understand and you'll yet learn me."

"You have the wit and could have the heart to feel the beauty of poetry, child, if you but cared to."

"I do care to." Then she startled him by suddenly demanding, "Mr.

Trelawney, who, think you, in this port, so hates Hugh Jocelyn that he'd have him hurt or put out of the way?"

"I wish I knew," said the tutor slowly, watching her closely.

"Well, I know!"

The amazed Trelawney stared into the girl's tense face, but her hazel eyes, shot with black, never wavered. "Are you certain?" he asked.

Her lips tightened as she nodded, then flung back at him: "Carr Newbury and Richard. Since I rode to the Parade that day, Carr's raved like a madman."

"But that proves nothing."

"'Tis enough for me. 'Twas my own affair, not his. First, to help Richard out he lied to old Tripp; then, because he was jealous and hated Hugh Jocelyn, he lied to my father. He—he makes love to me. Faugh! And my mother urges him on!"

"What makes you think Richard had a part in this?"

"Because he's worse than Carr, forever prating about my silly honor and the disgrace to the family. He's always betwitting me about my 'sailor scum.'"

Fearful that she might be overheard by the servants in the house, the Englishman raised a warning hand, but she went on impulsively: "Richard and Carr can't forget, nor my father, what I said to that cooper Tripp, and those wooden faces with him. Magistrates! Name of God! They looked more like the heads of two dried cod on fish flakes at the shore."

A red-heeled slipper kicked savagely at the gravel walk as Lettice scowled at her tutor.

"You forget that you're Richard's sister," said Trelawney. "This is a serious matter."

She laughed scornfully. "His sister! Why, this sweet brother of mine has fair hated me since the day I struck Hugh Jocelyn. On our way home I laughed full in his face over his manhandling by Hugh. I know him. Richard never forgets and never forgives. His sister! Pooh! He insists I dragged the fair name of Brinley in the mud." She flung her round arms above her head in a gesture of contempt. "Already he's sunk it deep in the mire if the truth were but known."

Trelawney wondered what the girl actually knew and what she merely surmised. And he was determined to learn, so threw out: "Surely, you're bubbling me, Mistress Lettice. Your brother and Newbury could not have been behind this attack on Hugh Jocelyn. 'Tis too monstrous!"

Her long-lashed eyes fixed his in a candid stare. Then her face hardened as she spat out: "You little know them! Those two are fair frenzical over my going to the pillory. You see, Carr Newbury's always hanging around. The family fret me to death about him. He swears he'll wait if he must, but he's bound to have me. He thinks to wear me down. Name of God! I'll die first!"

Trelawney was touched by the passionate outburst. The girl dabbed savagely at her eyes with a lace handkerchief as she regained self-control. Here, he thought, was spirit and will that neither Newbury nor the Brinleys might weaken. But he was no nearer the solution of the problem.

"You are right," he said, at length. "Hold hard to your purpose. No good could come of a loveless marriage. What is this Carr Newbury like as a man?"

"Like? You don't know him?"

"No. I've but seen him, and that seldom."

Lettice clasped her hands over a knee and rocked back and forth, her brows pulled together. "He's not handsome, as you know, for his eyes are too close set. But he has brains and a will of his own. Father says he's sharp—very sharp—in business, and will be a great land and ship owner, here, in time. But I feel he's not to be trusted. He loves money and himself too much. I—I'm sure he has little heart, though he swears he'd die for me." She stopped, then finished passionately, "I hate him!"

Trelawney watched her lovely face darken with her emotion. What a wild, impulsive creature she was! What charm and fire! "That's a strong word," he said.

The blood moved up past the heartbreaker, curled below a small ear, to her cheeks. "Am I not as pretty," she savagely demanded, "as that Seeth Carr who may sit with Hugh on the wharf? How I wish I'd been with him that night! But I, because I'm a Brinley and you refuse me your aid, may not!" She leaned toward the man who was studying her. "Mr. Trelawney, you know everything. Father says you and Doctor Lodovic are the most learned men in Newport."

Trelawney laughed. "You flatter me. But what is it that leads you to say that?"

"Since I went to the pillory I've been treated like a child. Yet I've more wit and spirit than that brother of mine. 'Tis so! You've said it yourself. Why, then, should I take orders from him?" Biting her underlip in her anger, the girl clenched her hands, then rose from the bench and shook her fists in Trelawney's face. "I'll not stand it! Some day I'll—"

"Tut, tut!" he soothed. "Be calm, Mistress Lettice! Let us sit and talk this over quietly." They were wandering from the matter uppermost in Trelawney's mind. He must learn what she had in the back of her small head. "You have a quick wit," he said, "and have pleasured me much, this summer, with your desire to learn."

Her cheek dimpled in a pleased smile. "I've done your bidding and strived to learn because—because—well, no matter the reason, while my brother's wasted his time prowling around Portsmouth."

Ah, they were on the track again! "How mean you, prowling around Portsmouth?" he asked.

"I've had him followed by my black boy, Aaron, and know he meets Carr Newbury and rides somewhere into the country." Lettice Brinley's mouth tightened. Her dark brows met as her eyes flamed with anger. "I'm sure these two had a part in bringing those men here to hurt Hugh Jocelyn."

Her underlip quivered and her hands shut as she met Trelawney's startled look. She had never seemed so lovely to him as now under the stress of emotion—this willful girl who so resembled her father. "You must have a care," he warned. "This is a grave matter. Though your father is judge, Newbury and Richard are not outside the law. The people of Newport are aroused. And what you suspect is felony. Think what you say, child."

"Child?" She tossed her chestnut head and laughed, but the laugh was without mirth. "There it is again! Child, you call me, who am past seventeen and grown woman, with a mind of her own."

"Ay," he agreed, "with a mind of your own. But turn that mind to what you are saying against Newbury and your brother." The Englishman probed her passionate face, wondering how much more she knew.

"My brother!" she sneered. "A pretty brother, indeed! I've already told my father about Portsmouth."

"And what said he?"

"He scolded me for a fool, but it startled and fair sobered him. He acted stunned."

"Has he talked with Richard?"

"Yes. One night they quarreled. Mother and I heard them from our beds. Father warned Richard that his actions were suspicious—that he might bring disgrace on the family and ruin upon himself. He had a heated talk, later, with Carr Newbury, who is here much. But Carr has courage and does not fear Father. He seems to have little fear of anything, so vain he is. He denied everything and dared Father to show proof. They were both in a rage. I heard them."

The beat of horses' hoofs on the road leading to the stable checked her. She placed a finger to her lips. "There's Father, now," she whispered, picking up the discarded book and beginning to read aloud.

"Ah, Mr. Trelawney," presently called a voice, "how behaves your pupil this warm morning?"

Trelawney rose as Francis Brinley approached over a gravel path. "Your servant, Justice Brinley!" Trelawney bowed. "Mistress Lettice is somewhat critical of Will Shakespeare's comedy we are reading," he laughed. "She finds it tame and the lovers overtimid."

Dressed in blue broadcloth and riding boots, his handsome face beneath his brown periwig stippled with moisture, Francis Brinley frowned down at his daughter, as he removed his high-crowned beaver hat. "So you find Shakespeare's lovers overtimid?" he observed. "You might well copy them, Lettice."

The girl coolly smiled into her father's face. "But I have pleased Mr. Trelawney, Father, with my progress in reading. Most of the long words I now name at sight without faltering. Is it not so, Mr. Trelawney?"

"She has indeed shown great advancement," praised Trelawney, "and will shortly write a hand with any lady in Newport, sir."

Brinley sighed. "God be praised that one of my children has the sense to profit by your teaching," he answered. "I am well pleased at what you say." He turned to Lettice, who was narrowly watching him. "Know you where your brother went this morning?"

"No, Father, he rode away early."

"I hear he was seen with Carr Newbury on the Portsmouth Road."

The lids of the girl's eyes flickered as she glanced furtively at Trelawney's sober face. "He likely rode to the big farm," she said.

Brinley savagely struck his booted leg with his riding whip. "Yes, yes!" he muttered, his face black with anger. "I doubt not he went to the farm. He had business there of mine."

The Chief Justice left them and, shortly, Lettice said, as Trelawney took his leave: "When that precious brother of mine shows his face back in Newport today, he'll have to answer to Francis Brinley. Father is fair frenzical."

"But think you he actually links Richard and Newbury with this attack on Hugh?" Trelawney boldly asked.

"I know not, but I hazard 'twill be many a day before Richard again rides to our farm in Portsmouth." Then she reached impulsively and grasped the tutor's hand. "Oh, tell Hugh that I am glad—so glad he escaped harm!" she said in a low voice.

"I will."

As Trelawney walked up Thames Street, his thoughts were of the black face of Justice Brinley when Lettice mentioned the big farm. "I'd give much to learn who those two meet at the big farm," muttered the puzzled Englishman; "and if Richard's father knows anything definite or only suspects."

ONE night, a week or so after the attack, the small public room of the Butterfly, hazy with smoke and reeking with the fumes of rum and stale beer spilled on tables and the sand-strewn floor, was noisy with the voices of drinking seamen. Nodding at a table near the door leading to the small kitchen in the rear, an empty cup beside her, sat the Widow Moon. But little escaped her red-lidded eyes, deep in bulbous cheeks, as her unkempt head rolled and bobbed on her fat neck. While the black man, Adam, shuffled in and out with wooden cups of fiery rumbullion, kill-devil and blackstrap laced with spirits, those furtive eyes were busy in a restless patrol of the crowded tables.

At one gossiped three ringed-eared Portuguese sailors off the lately arrived wine ship from Fayal, in the Canaries, swart faces close together. At another, four weather-bitten colonials and a Cape Cod Indian, the crew of a Boston sloop, their hair chopped below their ears, the open collars of their rough Ozenbrig shirts baring hairy chests, were rapidly drinking themselves under on rum and hard cider. At a third, argued four local fishermen. But it was a table near the door of the small tavern which had in reality claimed the furtive attention of the seemingly drowsy eyes of Betsy Moon. There, for some time, three strangers to the Newport waterfront had smoked long-stemmed clay pipes, drunk, and talked in low tones. And, as yet, their liquor had had no visible effect. The oiled leather breeches, locram shirts, and homespun kersey coats of two of the men marked them as landsmen. They were tall, and their heavy shoes with wooden heels had never trod a ship's deck. But the third, who was short and dark, wore the loose canvas breeches and open shirt of a sailor, and his legs were bare. The faces and speech of the three strangers were English.

When Betsy Moon waddled to their table to collect for each round of drinks, she told herself she had seldom looked into harder or shiftier eyes. However, hard faces and scarred were common coin at the Butterfly. What first had caused her curious eyes to flicker with surprise was the bulging deerskin wallet from which one of the farmers was paying for the drinks. For among the pine-tree shillings with which it was stuffed, she had caught the yellow glint of gold.

"Name o' God! Gold!" she had breathed, as she shuffled back to her stool. "The news of this will fair put Israel in a fever! Where got these sons-of-rumpuncheons gold, and a bag near choked with silver? They are off no pirate craft hiding in the bay, for two are landsmen.

Could it be, they— No, 'twas but last week it happened. They scarce would dare—so soon!"

Her frowzy head busy with suspicion of her three guests, Betsy Moon watched customers drift in and out, while the air of the room thickened with smoke and stank with the reek of ale and rum. The drunken Portuguese were singing now, urged on by the maudlin crew of the Boston sloop. But the men near the door drank and talked, heads together, ignoring the carousing at the adjacent tables.

"Israel must have word of them," she told herself, "but I scarce may reach him tonight. How came these three to Newport, by ship or over the Path? Mayhap on a Providence shallop. But what do they here so soon after—" The pouched eyes of Betsy Moon grew grave as she nodded. "He treasures that lad like a son! But no, they scarce would dare—not with the people in such a fever!" She shook her head and the fat rolled about her buried chin. "But Israel shall know before the *Gull* leaves at daybreak."

It was late, and the Portuguese and the Bay sailors had reeled out, leaving the three strangers alone in the room. A shrewd look suddenly spread over the Widow Moon's red face. Her loose lips curled. With much effort and many grunts she got to her feet and waddled over to the table by the door. She stumbled and almost fell, laughing loudly as she regained her swaying balance, and wiped her mouth with the back of a fat hand. As she teetered uncertainly beside their table, the strangers ceased their low talk and glanced curiously at their tipsy hostess.

"Mates," she said, thickly, "since the trouble—here—last week—the Town Sergeant—is overstrict!" Betsy hiccuped and grinned. "The Butterfly—stands you—a last cup o' rum!" She called to the rear room, "Adam!"

The strangers leered at the teetering mountain of flesh. "Sit with us, mother," urged the sailor, "and we'll drink much health to you and many lovers."

A sudden rage stiffened Betsy where she stood. For an instant the fatuous grin was wiped from her face, as a sponge wipes a slate, then as swiftly returned, as she plumped heavily down on the vacant stool and giggled: "Lovers I've had a-plenty in my time, mates. And some could break any of you in their bare hands, such men they was!"

"Ay," soothed the sailor, "a blind man could see a rare piece of flesh you was once." Grimacing at the others, he reached an arm around Betsy's bulging back, for waist she had not. As she roguishly pushed him away, her searching fingers touched the bone haft of a knife hung between his shoulder blades, under his loose shirt.

"Rare I was and no doubt!" she roared, slapping a huge thigh and rocking back and forth on her stool, while the strangers roared with her. "But I was overfond of beer and rum, and now look at me!" Adam placed filled cups before them and Betsy lifted hers, spilling rum on her bulging bosom. "Godspeed, mates!" she laughed, "to whatever port you sail, be it hell or Boston! There be small difference. Now, how reached you Newport, by sea or land?"

As she drank, Betsy caught the warning looks exchanged by the three men. "Mother," said the sailor, "we steered a course over the Plymouth Path to buy Portsmouth sheep."

"Ah," nodded Betsy, slapping down her cup, "it is for that you bring the fat purse!"

For a swift instant the sailor's hard eyes searched hers, but seemed to find only a woman fuddled with rum. "Yes," he answered, "we buy for a great landowner in Plymouth."

"Ah!" She gravely nodded. "There be no better sheep in the colonies—nor grass—than here on Rhode Island. 'Tis a sweet country; but the lads stay not on the farms but are ever away to sea. 'Twas so in the old days. My lad went for a privateersman and hove into Newport one day on a peg leg and with a cutlass slash athwart his face—like that on your hand!" She pointed suddenly at the sailor's maimed hand.

With a quick movement he thrust it beneath the table, blood coloring his face as he shot an oblique look at his friends. But Betsy Moon was so patently drunk that they smiled indulgently at their garrulous hostess. "Yes, mother," said the man with the heavy purse, "Rhode Island sheep be the best; 'tis why we're here."

Betsy raised a fat finger in warning as she swayed unsteadily on her stool. "But, look you, mates! There be shagrags along this waterfront who'd slit your throats and drop you over a wharf for that gold and silver you carry!" She belched loudly, then giggled: "And plenty of drazels in this port to help you spend it. Buy your sheep tomorrow, lads, e'er 'tis too late!"

They rose, and she waddled after them, hiccuping. At the door the sailor clapped her on the back. "We came not to Newport to leave our gold but to take it away," he laughed. "That is, the value of it in fat sheep, eh, lads? There be fat sheep, mother, for the shearing, on this island! Sleep you well!"

Betsy Moon stood at her door as the strangers made their way over the dark wharf to the shore. "They thought me well whittled," she chuckled, "so were overbold in their talk. Too much money they carry in that wallet for honest men. No man would trust his gold to faces such as those to buy sheep. What meant they by 'there be fat sheep for the shearing on this island'?" she muttered. "And I like not that hidden knife, neither! Israel must hear of this."

But when Adam brought Israel to the Butterfly at daybreak, and on hearing the story, he, Hugh, and the two Wantons searched the port, no trace of the three strangers was to be found.

§34

LATE that summer tautog, squeteague, and striped bass were so plentiful alongshore, and the run of bluefish, cod, and haddock so heavy in the Sound, that the Newport market was glutted. Then at sunrise one morning, Tom Stanton found more lobsters in his pots at the mouth of the Sakonnet than he could hope to sell on the home wharf in a week.

"Too many have taken up fishing," lamented Stanton to Israel, as he ruefully surveyed the heap of milling crustaceans confined in a gill net on the forward deck of the *Sea Gull*. "More than half these will be left on our hands with nought to show for our toil!"

When he had made fast the sheet of the mainsail, which filled as she headed for home, Hugh turned to Stanton at the tiller. "There's a stiff south wind making. By noon 'twill blow half a gale. Why not pick up some barrels of salted cod and with these lobsters head for Providence?"

"Why Providence?" asked Tom.

"I talked with a man on Easton's Wharf last night who said they have salmon and sturgeon in the spring but lacked salt cod there, and always they have a sweet tooth for lobsters. They have much corn, peas, and dried apples for barter."

"I'll give it thought," answered Stanton.

Under her jib and bellying mainsail the *Sea Gull* heeled to the stiffening south wind as she passed, in turn, Sachuest and the beaches, and headed for Coggeshall's Ledge, off the cliffs. It would be a straight run to Providence at the head of the bay and a quick one with this wind.

Stanton glanced at Brandy, whose squinting eyes were searching the southern horizon. "Plenty wind in that sky, Tom," said the sailor, "and the flood'll be with us most the way. They see few lobsters in Providence. The lad is right."

"Peas, corn, dried apples, and candlewood we need for the winter," said Stanton. "'Twill be as well to risk a load of lobsters in Providence as to have them lie stinking on the beach, food for the gulls."

So it was settled. Stopping at the Cove to pick up the barrels of salt cod, the *Sea Gull* slipped between Goat Island and the Point, cleared Coasters Harbor Island, and pointed her stub nose up the bay past Gould Island, riding the flood with the freshening wind behind her.

Following the Prudence shore they passed the Narrows and Bristol Harbor and the long Popasquash neck. It was Hugh's first trip to Providence and the upper bay, and he watched the wooded eastern shores claimed by Plymouth Colony with interest.

"This Prudence Island over there to the west was a godsend to Roger Williams in the early days, Hugh," commented Stanton, as the sloop plunged her nose into the long swells from which the wind cut the white spindrift in showers. "There he kept his swine and goats and sheep safe from the wolves and the Injuns."

"When King James was Duke of York," laughed Israel, leaning on the tiller as the sloop yawed and rolled in the running seas which broke under her quarter, his shaggy hair whipped about his grotesque face, "he gives this Prudence Island on our larboard to a friend with the name of John Paine. Now, burn me! this Paine was to sit pretty, on the island, right in the heart of this colony, the lord of Sophy Manor, which was what they named it."

"But how might that be?" objected Hugh, watching the curving leech of the mainsail, while his yellow hair fluttered like a flag about his head. "There were already plantations there."

"Well spoke, lad! Nor could it be! When John Paine hove into Newport and sent word to the farmers on the island that he was now their lord and master by virtue of the Duke's patent, rot my bones! they sent a shallop to Newport with word for him to come and take the island and bring plenty men and muskets if he was in earnest."

"What did he do?" asked Hugh, glancing back at the cultivated fields and the pastures of the island to the west.

"Stab me, what could he do? He had no stomach for such a fight for his island, and the colony would not put him on his throne, so Prudence stayed Prudence and the King of Sophy Manor hauled down his flag and went back to the Bay Colony."

It was late afternoon when the *Sea Gull* reached the Narrows and sailed up the Salt River of Roger Williams. It passed the little settlement on the natural meadows at the mouth of the Pawtuxet and its cove and, at last, when Fox's Hill lifted from the water ahead, where the Seekonk joined the Salt River, forming Providence Neck, Hugh caught his first glimpse of the settlement Roger Williams had planted in the wilderness fifty years before.

"Where's the anchorage?" he asked, in surprise, as the *Sea Gull* sailed past shores on which lay canoes and open shallops but which boasted no wharves. From the long lane following the river shore, over which, at intervals, gates barred passage, up over the hill to the east ran the narrow home lots of Pardon Tillinghast, Wickenden, Power, and others. Behind their story-and-a-half houses, with huge chimneys at the end, set back from the street, stood their barns and orchards on the abrupt western slope.

The surprised boy turned to Stanton. "There seem few people here. Their houses are scattered, and there are no wharves for ships."

"There are not many people and there is little shipping. 'Tis all farming."

The sloop skirted the shore at the foot of the hill, with its narrow home lots. They passed the Narrows and hove to while they brailed the mainsail, bucking the slight ebb, now running, with the jib. Beyond, to the northwest, reached a large cove dotted with grassy islands. To the northeast a small river emptied into the cove. Entering the river, the sloop dropped anchor below some low falls near which stood a gristmill and a sawmill. Above the falls the river was crossed by a crude bridge. Opposite them, on the long street which followed the river shore, huddled a group of buildings from which a lane followed the bed of a brook back over the hill. At intervals in the rutted street, where poultry scratched, hogs wandered, and an occasional yoke of oxen stood before a rude cart, public wells had been dug and curbed. Hugh counted but three small sloops anchored off the shore, and nowhere were there wharves with their storehouses thrusting into the stream, as at Newport; only landing places. His gaze followed the narrow lots reaching over the hill from the long thoroughfare, and he turned puzzled eyes on Tom Stanton, busy with the skiff, alongside. "Where live all the people of the town of Providence, Father Tom?" he asked.

"You forget, Hugh, that little more than twelve years past, all the houses were burned by the Narragansetts, except two or three garrison houses where thirty men stayed with Roger Williams while the rest fled to Newport with their families."

"I see."

"After the war, 'twas a bitter struggle to start life anew, with their homes gone and their cattle driven off. There is a gristmill and a sawmill above here by the falls of the Moshassuck. The large house over there on Towne Street is Turpin's Inn, from which Dexter's Lane runs back over the hill to the Seekonk Ferry, and there are a few merchants."

"What a pity, all their toil wasted!"

"All are farmers, here, but they grow no such crops as do we on our island, for they have not our soil nor grass lands. And they own no ships. Providence is a poor town."

"Stout Roger Williams!" commented Hugh. "Fifty years of toil and planning brought to nought! How had he the heart to rebuild?"

Stanton shook his grizzled head. "He was a great man and a bold. It needed more than that to dishearten Roger Williams. He brought freedom to worship according to one's own conscience to these shores. His name will never die."

"No, 'tis true. 'Twill never die!" echoed Hugh. "He was indeed a great man."

Stanton and Israel went ashore and soon returned with two of the town magistrates, William Turpin and John Smith, the miller, who agreed to take the cod and lobsters in barter for corn, peas, dried apples, and pork. When the fish had been put ashore and the grain loaded on the *Gull*, the crew ate their supper, then made their way to Turpin's ordinary, the largest house on Towne Street, where the governor and council met and the Court of Trials sat. In the great room, with its huge chimney at the end, its spit, and its copper and iron kettles suspended from the lug-pole, men sat at tables on the sanded floor over their rum, beer, and cider, and gossiped of the latest news brought over the Boston Path. The entrance of the sailor with the scarred face and peg leg, the tall youth, and the older man caught the attention of the drinking farmers. There was still feeling in the struggling little hamlet against the Newport Quaker government which had left Providence to the mercy of Canonchet's raiders. Men who had lost their all and been forced to rebuild their burned homes held bitter memories. So the entrance of the Newport fishermen was greeted with unfriendly looks from more than one table.

Seating themselves, the Newporters ordered drinks. Shortly, from a neighboring table rose a hulk of a man, his face flushed with rum, who advanced uncertainly and faced Israel and Hugh with truculent, outthrust jaw and bloodshot eyes.

Brandy scowled darkly at the Providence man, who teetered back and forth on the heels of his boots, while Hugh surveyed him with a wide grin.

"Newport men, be ye?" began the stranger. "Twelve year ago ye slept snug on yer island and left us to the Narragansetts!"

Hugh got to his feet, and faced the farmer. "My father died at the Swamp Fight, stranger," the boy said, hoarsely. "Were you there?"

"Careful, Hugh!" warned Stanton, as Israel rose, his face filled with blood.

The intoxicated farmer avoided the thrust of Hugh's glittering eyes and turned to the peg-legged sailor. "Where got ye that face?" he sneered.

The veins stood out on Brandy's bull neck but he did not answer. He grimaced horribly as he rolled back the sleeves from his thick arms and measured the man leering at him. "Stab my guts! you be foxed, farmer. For that, I gives you leeway," he rasped. Then, with a contemptuous shove of his open hand against the other's jaw, he sent the drunken man reeling backward.

There was a roar from the adjoining tables, and protesting men quickly surrounded the three fishermen.

"Heave out the Newport scum!" shouted a voice, and a farmer reached for Hugh, to thrust him aside, when the boy's open hand clubbed his jaw with the smack of a jib filling with wind, and he staggered back into the circle of menacing Providence men.

But the tension had been too great for the former privateersman. In spite of the warnings of Tom Stanton, he could no longer contain himself. As two men menaced him with their fists, he bellowed: "You fished for trouble and we peaceable! Well, burn me! here it waits. Come aboard, you dogfish!" With a quick movement, he seized the men facing him by their collars and flung them back against the excited onlookers.

The room was in an uproar. But Brandy's exhibition of strength and the tall youth's cool handling of the man who attacked him had made an impression. There was no move to accept Israel's challenge as the three Newport men waited, shoulder to shoulder.

"We are fishermen, from Newport," cried Stanton, gripping his heavy stool, "and seek no trouble here."

"Ay, we seek no trouble," added Brandy, "and, as yet, no Providence face has felt Newport knuckles. But slit my throat! lay hand on us and you'll learn what the fist of Israel Brandy, gunner of the *Lady Bess*, feels like! Now take your choice!"

"The *Lady Bess*, Tom Paine's privateer sloop!" warned a voice. "Have a care! 'Tis Brandy, Tom Paine's master gunner!"

"Ay, 'tis Brandy," Israel replied, with a broad grin. "Brandy, of the *Lady Bess*, that put fear into the Spaniard from St. Augustine to the Grenadines! You do well to remember Brandy and Tom Paine!"

Then William Turpin, the landlord, pushed his way through his arguing patrons and called for silence. "What foolishness is this?" he stormed. "These men, here, are honest fishermen from Newport, off that anchored sloop. I traded with them this day. They were set on and stood for their rights. Put this fool, Peleg, out, Restcome," Turpin ordered his brawny serving man. "He's foxed and the air may cool his thick skull."

Following the words of the landlord, muttering men resumed their seats, and the room was again filled with talk. During the argument, two men had sat across the room watching the proceedings with unconcealed amusement. Dressed in worn and greasy deerskin, wearing knives and hatchets thrust through leather slings at the back of their belts, powder horns and skin bullet pouches slung from their shoulders, their two long flintlocks resting against the wall beside them, the strangers brought the color of the northern frontier to the farming village. Summer though it was, they wore tattered fox-skin caps, the tails drooping behind over their long hair. Their hard-bitten faces, tanned by sun and wind, were lean and lined.

When Turpin had got rid of his drunken guest and the hum of voices and the smoke of pipes filled the once-more orderly great room, one of the skin-clad men rose and approached the Newport men's table.

"Friends," he began, "I am Giles Slocum, fur trader. I mark you are sailors and strangers here. I mark as well that you lack no schooling in the use of your hands."

Brandy's suspicious eyes coolly surveyed the raw-boned speaker, from tangled hair to moccasins, while Hugh studied curiously the stranger who was patently fresh from the forest country to the north. "We be fishermen, from Newport," grunted Israel.

The man in deerskin grinned and thrust out a bony paw. "My hand on it, stranger! 'Twas fair pretty the shaking you gave the farmers. The big lad, here, pleasures me, he was that cool about the cuff he dealt one of them with his weight behind it. He so closely bears the look in eye and build of a lad I once knew that I'm fevered to learn his name."

The scowl was wiped from Israel's face as the wind wipes the sky of clouds. He reached a hairy paw and shook the stranger's hand. "Sit you down and join us, friend, in a cup of rumbullion," he urged, "and bring your partner."

The eyes of the man in deerskin focused on Hugh. "Stand up, lad!" he said. "I would see how high you reach. You are that broad I may not judge."

Hugh laughed and rose from the stool, while the fur man took a step backward and measured him with narrowed eyes, from yellow head to feet, then confidently nodded, as Hugh's friends stared with curiosity.

"Like as two bear cubs," grunted the woodsman, while Hugh probed his sober face. "Younger by some years. Yaller hair 'stid o' tawny. Blue eye 'stid o' gray. But the very look and build of him." The stranger suddenly seized Hugh by the shoulders and cried, "God's blood! your name's Jocelyn or I'm the son of a Nipmuc!"

Hugh's jaw dropped in amazement as Israel and Stanton straightened on their stools. "How did you know?" demanded the surprised boy.

The man in deerskin threw back his head and laughed, as he slapped his thigh. "How did I know? How could I mistake the son of Henry Jocelyn who lies in the long trench at Cocumcussoc with forty others? Why, the look in your blue eye, lad, and the big bone and build of you! Younger you are nor he was, and not full-meated yet, but wild Henry Jocelyn of Plymouth stands out all over you! You're his own flesh and blood or I'm an Injun!"

A lump swelled in Hugh's throat as he listened to the excited trader. His heart quickened, a wave of blood reached his face, and mist suddenly clouded his eyes as a thrill of pride shot through him. This man had known his father! "Yes," he answered slowly, "I'm the son of Henry Jocelyn."

The stranger again gripped Hugh's shoulders and tested his thick arms as he devoured him with squinting eyes. "I was with Davenport's company, from Sudbury, and cut to pieces we were when we first went into that stockade before Major Treat scaled the rear wall with his Mohicans. But Henry Jocelyn followed us in with the Plymouth men, smashed in the doors of flanker and blockhouse with an oak stick, and saved our scalps. God's name! you have the living look of him, though so young."

Shortly the two men in buckskin were drinking at the table. They were fur buyers on their way to Boston with pack horses, and had come across country from the Connecticut. "Your health, young Jocelyn!" said Giles Slocum, the spokesman, lifting his wooden cup of blackstrap. "May you grow as good a man as your father!"

Slocum's companion, a lank woodsman by name of Sampson Batty, added: "I was with Captain Moseley that day, and I saw your father show skill beyond belief with the war hatchet. From thirty paces he buried his belt ax in the neck of one of the hounds which was worrying an Injun child." The speaker stopped to laugh. "Then a sailor with us thought to chasten him—chasten that wild Jocelyn!"

Hugh leaned toward the trader. "And did he chasten him?"

"Ho! ho! ho!" the latter roared. "What? Chasten Henry Jocelyn? As well chasten the devil that day. Why, Jocelyn broke the sailor's pike over his iron hat and clubbed him senseless with his fist."

For a time Brandy sat listening with dropped jaw, but at last he tired of the praises of the man he never knew. With an explosion like a musket shot, he cleared his throat. "Look you, friend," he sputtered, "Henry Jocelyn was a bold man and an able. That we all know. But the lad, here, reached eighteen only this summer. Three years more and whatever Henry Jocelyn was, that his son shall be and more."

Slocum rocked on his stool, roaring with laughter. "Well spoken, friend Brandy. 'Tis plain your heart lies in the lad."

"Ay," Israel agreed, gravely. "My heart is in the lad."

"What news bring you of the north country?" asked Stanton.

The leathern features of the trader sobered. "I fear there's trouble brewing on the border. We trade with French Indians from the St. Francis who trap the Connecticut headwater country and plant corn in the upper intervales. They're restless, and say there's talk among the French of a war with the English in the spring."

"Trelawney says there scarce can be a war while James is king," spoke up Hugh, "for he is a papist and friendly with King Louis of France."

"Ay, but if William of Holland lands in England with an army, as 'tis rumored he may, and the people rally round him, war there will surely be here in the colonies," insisted Stanton.

"True words, friend Stanton," agreed Slocum. "And the people of Northfield, Deerfield, and Turner's Falls, on the Connecticut, are already nervous, for they will be the first struck by raiding parties from Canada."

Israel's face lighted. "And then the Wanton boys will build that ninety-ton sloop and we go to sea, Hugh," he said. "I'm fair frenzical to squint down the black back of a nine-pounder again."

As they bade good-by to the traders and left the ordinary to board the sloop, Israel sought a private word with Landlord Turpin. "Have you chanced to cast eyes on a big black man and a Wampanoag in tow of a seaman, passing this way in the last month, landlord?" he asked.

"A big slave and an Injun?" Turpin scratched his head as he probed his memory. "A big slave—why, yes; there was such a pair come in over the Boston Path and set sail in a shallop for Bristol, some weeks back."

Brandy's mouth worked with excitement. "And was a sailor with a scarred right hand minus a forefinger with them?"

"The sailor was here. I talked with him. He said he was for Newport to buy sheep, and the slave and Injun were to drive them over the Plymouth Path."

"Ah-hah!" Israel nodded to Stanton. "Showed the sailor a wallet choked with silver?"

"That he did, when he paid his score. I liked not his face. He had more the look of a pirate than a sheep buyer."

"Landlord Turpin," fumed Israel, scowling savagely, his scar swelling with his anger, "the slave and Injun will never take the Plymouth Path; they're already in hell. And my fingers itch to grip that sailors' throat!"

§35

ONE evening, a week or so later, Hugh stood on a wharf throwing a war hatchet at an upright plank placed against a storehouse. He had heard so much of his father's skill at hurling the belt ax that from the time he was strong enough to handle one he had practiced until he could sink the thin, narrow blade into plank or bollard with uncanny accuracy. For two years, as well, he had been coached by Israel in cutlass play, using the hatchet in the left hand as a guard.

"Israel says that when a man slips on a wet or bloody deck, a belt ax in his left hand may save him from a split skull or from being pinned by a pike," said Hugh, to himself, as he drew back his arm and hurled the hatchet into an upright pine plank twenty paces distant.

He practiced until the approaching twilight stopped him, then sat on a stringpiece of the wharf and watched the last of the afterglow tint the harbor water as the light air carried odors of clam flats and salt marshes, tar from ropewalks and shipyards, rum from distilleries and of fish from the flakes alongshore. To his nostrils drifted, alike, the stenches of a colonial port and the salt tang of the sea. When dusk finally blanketed harbor and town, Hugh made out a dark object moving slowly over the flat water toward the wharf. It was a boat, evidently rowed by someone unaccustomed to oars and he thought of the night he was surprised with Seeth. But he had his cutlass and belt ax, now, and called confidently, "Ho, the skiff!"

The answer came in a woman's voice. "Hush, Hugh! Would you wake all Newport?"

Candace Prey! She had seen him and was coming to him. The blood leaped through Hugh's veins. Unleashed passion swept him in waves. Candace was coming out there in the night to him. She had waited long, but he knew her waiting was over. Candace was coming to see if he had learned ought of loving! The boy's blood was afire as he huskily spoke her name.

"Candace! Is that you?"

The skiff bumped against a bollard and Hugh reached and lifted her from it as if she were a child. Then, holding her in his arms, kissed her lips and hair and eyes.

"Oh, Hugh," she whispered, "I saw you out here and had to come."

The boy sat down, took her on his lap, and kissed her hot neck and shoulders from which he thrust the loose frock she wore.

"Hugh," she murmured, clinging to him, "I've waited so long, so long! You've never come near me, Hugh! You've kept away from the tavern where I might speak with you! And when they tried to kill you I was that frenzical! But I knew that—some day—"

He covered her breasts, which his groping hands had bared, with kisses. "Candace, I've learned nought of loving," he whispered, "but you shall teach me, now!" His heart thundered in his throat and the realization that she was there, alone with him, with no one to disturb them, filled his brain with madness. She wore no stays, and her soft body clung to his. His eager hands wandered over her warm flesh, while the suppressed desires of youth broke their leash as a swollen river bursts through a dam.

"Oh, Hugh," whispered the love-hungry girl, "I've wanted you so! I've been fair mad with thinking! Hold me close that I may know 'tis no dream! Kiss me! Kiss me hard!"

And so, in the dusk of the wharf, the untutored boy learned of loving from the wedded Candace Prey.

At last, with a sigh, she checked his wandering hands and stood up. "'Tis growing late. I must get back. I said I was sick and took to my bed, then let myself out of my window by the ladder. The customers will be leaving and Prey must find me in bed. There'll be other nights, Hugh!"

"Think you, Candace, I've made a good scholar in loving?" laughed the boy, as he placed her in the skiff.

She flung her round arms about his neck and gave him a lingering kiss. "Oh, Hugh, I shall dream of this night forever! What a sweet lover you are you will never know, for you've never been the wife of a human pig like Prey! Good-night, lover, you've brought me that which I never dreamed of! Oh, we must live it again, soon! I will send you word."

Like one in a dream, Hugh watched her boat fade into the gloom. At last, it had been Candace! What a mad creature she was to take such risks for love! And what a mad lover she was! The memory of her warm body and her reckless abandon sent hot waves over his flesh. Then, of a sudden, a revulsion of feeling swept him. He thought of Content and Tom and Trelawney—and was ashamed. He thought of the devoted Seeth who would have given him all as had Candace, but who loved him from the depth of her wild heart as Candace could not. This was not the love of which he and Trelawney had talked and read—this wild orgy of the senses. This was but the love of the body—this mad ecstasy with Candace. And yet one could not well live without this love. The thought of it and the lack of it had fair driven him mad. Torn between a sense of shame and the vivid memory of the girl's unleashed passion, Hugh walked ashore and made his way home through the dark streets of the sleeping port.

§36

It was April of the year following, in Newport, and the taverns were crowded with excited men discussing the news brought by horse messenger over the Plymouth Path and the ferry from Pocasset. William of Orange had landed with an army in England, King James had fled to France, and the people of Boston had risen and thrown Governor Andros into prison, while his English troops in the fort and the castle had surrendered.

The great room of the King's Head was a babble of heated voices. Around the news board, hung on the wall at the door, fresh arrivals crowded to read the message. At the tables sat groups of men whose names bulked large in the history of Portsmouth and New-port—Nathaniel Coddington and young Benedict Arnold, Jahleel Brenton, Joe's uncle, John Easton and Caleb Carr, and the former governor, the little Quaker, Walter Clarke, and John Coggeshall, with old Henry Bull. In the excitement and rejoicing, staid Quakers clicked pewter cups with periwigged men in silk and broadcloth and colored waistcoats. Citizens of known sobriety drank recklessly to the success of the Dutch son-in-law of King James. Newport had gone mad with joy, for the hated Andros was through. Francis Brinley's Court of Quarter Sessions would be abolished and the old government restored under the hidden charter. Never had Landlord Timothy Whiting done such a business as on this April day of the year 1689.

"'Tis the happiest news our ears shall ever hear!" cried the purple-faced Joseph Brenton, clapping his stocky friend, John Arnold, on the back. "A cup of malmsey with you, John; and you, Kit! Long live William of Orange and—England!"

Arnold and Sheffield drank to the toast. "'Tis surely a great day for the colony, Joe," said Arnold.

Brenton laughed. "Mark you our Chief Justice over there wears a face as sour as a green apple!"

"And well he may," replied Sheffield. "With Andros in jail and that lickspittle royalist, Dudley, stripped of his power, Francis Brinley must feel like a gib cat on a dark night."

Brenton rose, holding his cup of wine, and before his friends could check him, was standing at the table where Brinley and his party talked, heads together.

"Your servant, gentlemen!" Brenton bent his back in a bow of mock civility. "But recent I offered you the health of Prince William of Orange, and you refused it. Again I offer it to you, Francis Brinley, and to you, my noble kinsman, Peleg Sanford." Then with a roar, Brenton challenged, "Now refuse it and you dare!" He raised his cup high above his head. The men at the adjacent tables ceased talking, wondering what was coming. "Justice Brinley and Peleg Sanford," Brenton shouted, "I give you King William of England!"

The speaker, still holding his cup above his head, leered down at the black faces at the table. A ripple of laughter and applause ran through the room as the onlookers gloated over the discomfiture of the royalists who had lately been their masters.

"Come, come, gentlemen!" cried Brenton, grimacing at the surrounding tables. "Do you refuse before this company to drink the health of the future king of England? 'Tis no less than treason!"

"Ay," agreed many voices, " 'tis treason!"

Men left their tables and stood in silence, watching the outcome of the baiting of the proud Brinley by the intoxicated Joseph Brenton.

But Francis Brinley proved equal to the occasion. With a dry smile and glittering eyes he rose, followed by Peleg Sanford, raised his cup, while men held their breaths, and replied, "I drink to the King of England—whoever he may be!"

For a space the room was hushed, then a roar of jeers and protests greeted his words. "Stand to your guns, Francis Brinley," shouted Coggeshall. "You are for King James! Why do you forswear him?"

"Peleg Sanford, the turncoat!" cried another. "Now that Andros is jailed and Dudley taken in Narragansett, you are hot for the old charter, no doubt!"

With faces drained of blood, the two royalists, followed by the others at their table, emptied their cups and took their seats, while the room was filled with jeers, laughter, and shouts of "Out with the Court of Quarter Sessions! Down with Brinley, the royalist! Give us back our old charter and our Governor, Walter Clarke! Long live William of Orange!"

Back at his table, the incorrigible Brenton was leading in a song of his own making:

> Stout-hearted Prince William he sailed o'er the sea,
> And the papist King James into France had to flee!
> Give a rouse for King William and Mary, his Queen,
> Who'll restore us our charter, that'll shortly be seen!

Following Brenton's lead, Quakers and Baptists, old antinomians, Sabbatarians, and men favoring the Church of England, sprang to their feet and joined in the song, keeping time with the click of their pewter cups. Amid a chorus of jeers, catcalls, and curses, the enraged Brinley and Sanford left the room.

Men who never before had been seen drinking to excess vied with each other in pledging the health of William and Mary and the restoration of the charter. At last, lifting the protesting Walter Clarke in his arms, Joe Brenton placed him on a table and demanded a speech. Raising his hands for silence, the former governor said:

"Freemen of the Colony of Rhode Island and Providence Plantations!" (Cries of "God bless Rhode Island!" rocked the room.) "God has been good to us! A call will shortly go out to the towns for our old Assistants and Deputies and all freemen to meet at Newport to hold an election and resume our ancient government under the charter from King Charles."

The smoke-filled room echoed with cheers. Men stood on their stools and shouted themselves hoarse. Some rolled from their seats to the sanded floor, where they lay temporarily ignored by their excited friends.

Raising both hands for silence, the purple-faced Joe Brenton, who, to the amusement of the older men, had become a self-appointed master of ceremonies, cried: "Confess, Walter Clarke, you have the lost charter there, in your pocket! Show it us!"

"Show us the charter, Walter Clarke!" was demanded from all sides.

The weazened face of the former governor flushed and he shook his gray head. "Our young friend Joseph," he replied, "is forehanded. The charter rests not in my pocket but—"

"But 'tis in safekeeping!" roared Coggeshall.

"Ay," laughed Clarke, his black eyes snapping; "mayhap with diligence it might be found!"

"Ay, 'twill appear when needed," insisted Brenton. "Never fear!"

"Take good care of it, Walter Clarke," cried Coggeshall. "We shall soon put it to use!"

So, far into the night at the King's Head, the merchants, landholders, and shipowners of Newport celebrated the good news from Boston, and many, unable to walk, were carried to their doors on the backs of their friends and delivered to their startled wives.

Shortly the freemen of Rhode Island assembled in Newport, issued a declaration of their reasons for resuming the charter government, and sent an address to the King. Clarke refused to accept his late post, but Coggeshall, with several of the former Assistants, boldly resumed their functions. Connecticut followed, under her long-hidden charter. Plymouth took the same course. And Massachusetts voted to reorganize its government but hesitated to assume its old charter.

Then in May a ship arrived in Newport, from Boston, with the news that William and Mary had ascended the throne, and the new monarchs were proclaimed in the nine towns of the colony amid the rolling of drums, the lighting of bonfires, and the general rejoicing of the people. The reign of Brinley, the royalist, and his hated Court of Quarter Sessions was over.

3. An Able Seaman

§37

A MONTH after the spring fishing had opened the news had come from England. To Hugh Jocelyn and the Wanton brothers the landing of William in England had meant much more than the restoration of Rhode Island's charter. It signified eventual war with France and the building of the privateer sloop, *Flying Fish*, of which they had dreamed. For war with France meant the harrying of the New England coast by privateers and the pressing need of ships and men for its defense.

One spring evening Trelawney sat in Tom Stanton's house, pulling at a long-stemmed clay pipe while they talked of the news from England.

"From New London to the Cape, the watch fires are heaped high ready for lighting when war breaks out," announced Stanton.

Israel shook his grizzled head. "'Twill go hard with the poor folk of Block Island and Martin's Vineyard," he lamented, "when the French privateers show their colors off this coast."

Hugh's face lit and his eyes sparkled at the mention of privateers. "The Wantons will lay the keel of the *Flying Fish* this autumn," he said. "Their father agreed to it today, William told me."

Israel straightened on his stool and drew a deep breath into his barrel chest as he shook a thick finger. "Six sakers and four nine-pounders I want for that sloop, and no less," he announced. "I lean to the heavier metal, but demiculverins weigh a ton-and-a-half and will be over-heavy for the sloop in a blow if we carry more than four."

"The Wantons have already ordered sakers and demiculverins from Boston," said Hugh. "And they mean to have falcons for swivels and plenty of murderers."

"Ay," agreed Brandy, "the paterero is a handy tool to clear a deck of boarders or a whaleboat of pirates." He laughed at a memory. "I well recall a shot I made in a calm off Surinam at a boat packed as thick as a school of mackerel with black-faced devils. It was all up with us if they reached us, for we carried but a crew of six and no cannon. I waited behind our rail till they were a boat's length away and then let 'em have two murderers loaded with cut nails. When I got up off my back, where the kick of the second shot sent me, I looked, and the pirates' boat carried a cargo of dead men chopped to pieces like fish bait!"

Hugh's eyes were glittering. Good old Israel! "And so you got away?" he asked.

Israel scowled. "Got away? Be I here, now, talkin'? But it was them murderers we carried that saved our hides. Yes, the blunderbuss is a handy tool, close to and proper loaded. We'll carry plenty of old nails and bits of iron as well as lead balls for the swivels and the murderers when we sail on the *Flying Fish*."

"What carried away your leg, Israel?" asked Trelawney.

Brandy scratched his shaggy head as his eyes closed. "I was never certain. We was off Hispaniola, lying board and board with a big Spaniard. I was on our rail about to leap to their deck when fair in our faces one of their guns blew to pieces from an overload. Something took my foot off clean as a whistle!" Brandy suddenly turned to Hugh and asked, "Does Israel Brandy still stand on the Wantons' roster as master gunner?"

Hugh slyly winked at Trelawney. "They say that Brandy's their man if he's not afraid of the French," he said gravely.

With the snort of a maddened bull Israel rose, his bushy brows bristling as his mouth twisted savagely. "Feared of the French?" he roared, his face filling with blood. He glared about him while his friends with difficulty kept straight faces. "That sprig, William Wanton, says I'm feared of the French? Rot my guts! No man in this port will look me in the eye and tell me that!"

"No, Israel," Hugh soothed, "you must have heard me wrong. William said it not nor thinks it. He still names you master gunner, remember. It seems that someone told him you liked not the French privateers. They shot too straight and fought too hard."

With difficulty Hugh maintained his gravity, while Trelawney shook with inward laughter.

"Liked not the French—" In his rage Brandy stormed back and forth across the room, waving huge fists in the air. "Stab my vitals! Shoot too straight and fight too hard, do they? Put me in range of a Frenchman with that ninety-ton sloop and a crew of Newport lads at my back and, burn me! I'll show William I love the French like a brother!"

Tom Stanton put an end to the baiting of the old tar. " 'Tis that devil, Hugh, who would tease you, Israel. You know he means not a word of what he says and would fight the man who belittled you. Sit down and put a cup of cider laced with rum into your stomach."

Brandy scowled at the grinning Hugh, then shook his head. "Were you not that stout and big that it would upset the room and the spinnin' wheel and send Content after me with her broom, I would spank you over my knee," he chuckled, reaching for the cup of stonewall that Stanton handed him.

One night in early June the Stantons had a caller.

"My cargo is stowed and I sail in the morning," announced Captain Beer of the *Sea Flower*, as he shook hands with Tom, Israel, and Hugh. "But one of my crew is sick, and I need an able seaman."

Stanton glanced at Israel and the latter nodded. "There is little in the fish this summer for the lad," he said. "Let him go."

True to his promise, after the last flights of geese and swan had left the brown Sakonnet marshes and the December cod and mackerel fishing ceased, Hugh had worked hard through the preceding winter with Trelawney. Now he knew that his hour of release had come.

"I'll ship with Captain Beer," he said, tingling to his toes with excitement.

Content Stanton stood beside her spinning wheel, a fluttering hand at her throat. So it had come at last! Hugh was going to sea.

"Ay," said Beer, "I'll take you. Come aboard at daylight."

Before dawn, with his small sea bag, Hugh swung over the low rail of the *Sea Flower*, bound for his first view of the world. Pausing, his eyes swept the sleeping town. The harbor mist still hung in wisps above the wharves. Back on the hill the sails of Benedict Arnold's stone windmill thrust skyward. The odor of malt from a brewery and of fish from flakes on the shore fused with the salt breath of the bay. It was a big moment to Hugh Jocelyn. It had come—the great adventure!

That afternoon, with a fair wind, the *Sea Flower* passed the slobbering jaws of the Sow and Pigs and headed up Vineyard Sound. To the southwest, reflecting the sun, the bold headland of Gayhead, its clay cliffs striped with gray, rose, and ocher, lifted from the sea—a giant beacon warning passing ships from the rock fangs of the Devil's Bridge thrusting out from its foot. Into Nantucket Sound and over the shoals past the Bishop's and Clarke's and the Old Rose and Crown, past Nanemoy, and into the blue sea off Wreck Point and the Nonset bars, the sloop headed east, held up, at times, by head winds. At last she cleared Race Point on the hook of the Cape, headed across Massachusetts Bay, and sighted the beacon, with Point Allerton to the south, marking the entrance to the ship channel leading into Boston Harbor.

The excited Hugh scrambled up the ratlines to the crosstrees for a better view of the port. Rounding Nix's Mate, where the sun-dried bones of a pirate swayed in the wind on the gibbet erected as a warning to all passing seamen, the *Sea Flower* reached up the ship channel for Castle Island, off Dorchester Neck, with Governor's Island on the starboard hand. The boy's eyes widened and his jaw dropped as he caught his first glimpse of the spires of Boston Town, the anchored ships and the wharves, the buildings and houses reaching over the hills behind them.

"Newport is no such port as this!" gasped Hugh, his amazed eyes roving from the mole and battery at Fort Hill to the Meeting House and the South Church beyond, then on to the Long Wharf, which reached far into the harbor, with the Town House in its rear, while to the north rose the spire of the North Church.

From Wind Mill Point on the west to the North Battery, wharves, shipyards, and warehouses lined the shores, while sloops, ketches, brigs, and ships lay at anchor awaiting berths. To Hugh, Boston on her low hills was a revelation. Newport and her four hundred houses on her snug little harbor faded in comparison with the busiest port of the colonies, rich from its commerce with England, the Mediter-ranean, and the West Indies. But as his eyes swept the distant city, bristling with church spires, Hugh thought of what Trelawney had said: "Church-ruled and smug they are. A prayer ever on their lips but their eyes ever on the shilling. They left England, these Puritans, for freedom of worship, but here in the New World they grant freedom of worship to no man. One must ask the Mathers for leave to breathe, in Boston."

For a day Hugh wandered the streets of the strange town, from Fort Hill to the Common and from Beacon Hill to the Charlestown Ferry.

"'Tis a huge town," he observed, as he returned to the *Sea Flower's* berth at Scarlett's Wharf, "and Trelawney tells me that de-spite their piety, these good merchants and shipowners would fleece one of his last shilling, but given the chance. And they hung Quakers here; while in Newport half the people are of that faith."

One morning late in September, on Hugh's third trip to Boston, the *Sea Flower* eased in to Scarlett's Wharf. Eager to stretch his legs and obtain a close view of two three-masted Bristol ships which lay at the Long Wharf, Hugh walked up Ship Street and on to the Three Mariners tavern at the head of the wharf. Entering, he ordered a cup of ale and sat observing the activity of the tavern, where sailors from far ports sought ease and refreshment. At a near-by table a group of bronzed seamen, talking excitedly, aroused Hugh's interest.

"So Captain Pickett was taken at Holme's Hole by the pirate Pound, you say?" demanded a new arrival at the table.

"Ay, 'tis said he now lies in Tarpaulin Cove overhauling for a cruise to the West Indy."

"The Council has commissioned Captain Pease to take to sea in the sloop *Mary*, in search of Pound. They drum up for volunteers today!"

Hugh's heart jumped a beat. Volunteers! They want volunteers! Then his straining ears heard a thickset sailor with a bold eye say, " 'Tis true. I go as Leftenant."

A pirate at Tarpaulin Cove, and they want volunteers! Hugh thought of the long swim in the night that a pirate had forced him to make. He rose to approach the table, when the roll of a drum was heard in the street outside the inn.

"There's the drum!" said a sailor.

"Ay, Captain Pease loses no time. We sail today, when the shot and powder is stored, the ports cut for the three-pounders, and the gun carriages rigged."

Ports cut for the guns! Hugh's mind was made up. A pirate and they needed men!

The long roll of the drum drove the customers from their tables to the street. Hugh touched the arm of the man addressed as Leftenant Gallop. "You seek volunteers?" he asked.

The stocky sailor turned as he was leaving the tavern and looked at the boy who was speaking. His eyes slowly measured Hugh, from his yellow head to his feet. "How old are you and where from?" he demanded.

"Nineteen, from Newport, on the *Sea Flower*!"

In the street the sound of the drum fused with the cheers of the gathering crowd.

"Can you aim a musket and use a boarding pike and cutlass?"

"Ay, sir. I shoot geese and swan in the fall and am well trained in the use of the cutlass by an old privateersman," answered Hugh.

Gallop grinned as he reached and felt of Hugh's thick arm. "You look it, lad! You'll do. Come outside and we'll talk to Captain Pease."

In the street the crowd was increasing. A tall seaman standing in the center raised his hand and called for silence. "Citizens of Boston!" he announced. "I am Captain Pease, late commander of the King's ship *Fortune*, twelve guns. The Governor and Council have named me master of the sloop *Mary*, which sails today in search of the pirate Pound, reported lately at Tarpaulin Cove, Martin's Vineyard Sound." There were cheers from the listening stevedores, seamen, and artisans. "I seek a crew of thirty able seamen. Some must be gunners. You'll be well paid with prize money if we take the pirate. Now, who's the first to step up?"

"I, sir!"

Captain Pease turned at Hugh's voice, and his gray eyes squinted at the face and measured the wide shoulders of the yellow-haired youth who towered beside him.

"He'll do, Captain!" said Gallop. "I talked to him inside."

Captain Pease nodded to the waiting Hugh. "Now, who's the next man?" he asked of the sailors milling about him.

Men clapped Hugh's shoulders and shook his hand. He tingled with pride at the thought that a Newport boy had been the first.

At the repeated rolling of the drum, men hurried from all directions to join the excited crowd. But Captain Pease and his mate, Gallop, refused all but the most daring and able-looking. Shortly Pease had his picked crew of thirty men, and made preparations to sail.

The sloop *Mary* lay at Wentworth's Wharf, taking on stores and arms. The six three-pound minions mounted on their carriages already stood at their ports. Four half-pound rabinets, perched on iron crutches on the after-rails. Racks of boarding pikes and axes stood handy. A quick glance at the *Mary* convinced Hugh that Captain Pease, the Governor, and the Council meant business. Returning to the *Sea Flower*, he quickly obtained his release from Captain Beer, and reported back to Leftenant Gallop on the *Mary*.

§38

FOR weeks the pirate Pound, in the captured sloop *Good Speed*, had been harrying the coast shipping. Armed sloops had sailed from Salem and Boston to hunt him down but had missed him. Now he was back in his old haunts of Martin's Vineyard Sound, through which the coasters must pass.

Under her topsail, staysail, jib, and mainsail, the *Mary* proved a fast sailer, rounded Cape Cod and Nanemoy, drove over the Nantucket shoals and, one morning, rose Wood's Hole. Here Captain Pease learned that Pound was still in Tarpaulin Cove.

Shortly the sloop was heeling to a beam wind as she headed into the Sound. Perched as lookout on the crosstrees under the bulging square topsail, Hugh gripped a topmast stay as his eyes followed the Naushon shores in the distance. Sheets of spray drove to leeward as the sloop buried her stub nose and bowsprit stays in the running seas. Her three-pound minions, trussed to eyebolts in the deck by heavy preventer and train tackles, side tackles, and breeching, strained in their creaking harness, while the eyes of Codman, the master gunner, never left them. For, once loose on a pitching deck, a twelve-hundred-pound gun became an engine of terror and destruction. Under the driving of the officers, the decks were alive with hurrying men.

"Load all muskets and the swivels!" Pease ordered. "Get up and stow the balls and powder cartridges for the minions. Station the gun crews and stand by to ease the tackles and breechings. We may surprise her in the Cove."

"Ay, ay, sir."

The deep voice of Codman spurred the excited gunners to their work. Racks of three-pound iron balls were rushed from the hold and stowed near the guns, and barrels of paper powder cartridges lashed and covered with wet tarpaulin. Horns of priming powder hung from the gunners' shoulders, and matches of twisted cotton wick, soaked in lye, were set in tubs of sand, ready for lighting, with sheepskin sponges and wooden rammers within reach. On the forecastle a detail of men under Leftenant Gallop was stationed with loaded muskets, cutlasses, and boarding pikes. Extra pikes and boarding axes stood in racks along the rails. Captain Pease, former master of a twelve-gun ship in the King's service, knew his trade. From the poop his restless eyes checked the preparation for the battle with the pirate.

A man was sent aloft to relieve Hugh as lookout, and he slid down a backstay to join the gun crew to which he had been assigned because of his strength in handling the iron crow and handspikes when the gun was laid.

Stripped to the waist, watching the gray shores ahead, Hugh leaned against the rail beside his three-pounder, his long yellow hair, whipping about his face, wet with spray, in the stiff southeast breeze, his blue eyes dark with excitement. Shortly he would see a ship's guns in action! Shortly he would be living one of Israel's tales of the Spanish Main! He wondered if he would be afraid. He had never been afraid of a fight. He had not hesitated to take the long swim for Cuttyhunk. He had not feared to battle the giant Negro. It was his life he had fought for and he had had no time for fear. But this was different. He wondered if he would sicken at the sight of men sliced into shreds by splinters or smashed by round shot, with their blood smearing the deck and trickling into the scuppers. Then, with a shrug of his shoulders he put his mind on other things.

On the sail from Boston he had often practiced serving the gun with its crew, but to save powder it had not been fired. He was keen to see the black tube on its heavy carriage lift from the deck when the match fired the priming powder at the vent and the muzzle spewed orange smoke as the minion roared its challenge to the enemy. He knew he must leap from the recoil as the gun jumped and bucked back into its breeching. And he itched to see the round shot smash the pirate's bulwarks, scouring the deck with splinters. Here, at last, was adventure of which he had dreamed. A fight with a pirate!

He thought of Israel's tale of the fight off Hispaniola, when he lost his leg. Would Hugh Jocelyn lose his leg? The horror of it gripped him in the middle. He could see his mashed and bleeding stump. What would life be then? Life on one leg—a cripple! For a time the wind on his face seemed cold—bitter cold.

Shortly the two sloops might be lying board and board and the *Mary's* barefooted men scrambling over the pirate's rail with cutlass and pike. Would he flinch from that—the smoke and thunder of guns, the hail of lead, the cold steel? Would he play the coward? Who knew? Before the next turning of the sandglass in the Captain's cabin Hugh Jocelyn might be lying, torn by flying splinters or mangled by a round shot, the red life oozing from him—the life he'd but just begun to live. He shivered as he greeted the ugly thought with a raw laugh. It was war! Others had gambled. He'd have to take his chance. Yet he wished desperately to live—oh, so desperately. Life could hold so much, and he'd lived so little of it.

Then the sudden memory of Bellamy and the long swim through the night stung the boy with a fierce desire for the coming fight. He was hot to see round shot smashing into the pirate's hull and the grappling irons flung, holding her in a grip of death. How they'd scramble aboard with pike and cutlass and avenge the heartless looting of the little coasters which, for weeks, had fallen prey to the brutal Pound, whose stolen sloop lay in the Cove ahead.

Suddenly the lookout at the masthead hailed: "Sloop, ahoy! They've seen our tops'il! They're standing out of the Cove to the sou'west!"

All eyes on the *Mary* strained at the bold shore ahead which masked the Cove. Presently the sloop cleared the point, the Cove opened up, and they saw their quarry, a half-mile away, heading out under full sail. To the cheers of her crew, the King's Jack was run to the *Mary's* forerigging and the chase was on.

On the poop, beside the two straining sailors at the long tiller, Captain Pease watched the fleeing Pound, through a battered telescope, as the *Mary* plunged in pursuit. Then he called the mate aft and said, as he handed him the glass: "The dirty coward! Her deck is black with men and she carries six big carriage guns, yet he makes a run for it! But he can't outstep us with that weight on his deck; not if I know this sloop!"

Gallop nodded as he gazed through the glass. "Right, sir! By the look of his deck he's fitted for a cruise to the West Indy. Besides them big guns which look like sakers, I count four patereroes on his after-rails."

"Name of God! he'll need them all when Codman gets to work on him with the three-pounders. They've got no gunner like Codman! But I aim to board him at the first chance, as he outguns us and may do us much damage."

"Ay, sir! We have a crew of stout lads for close work."

Down the deep water of the Naushon shore, past Robinson's Hole, little Pasque Island, and Quick's Hole, raced the fleeing pirate. But the *Mary* was slowly overhauling her enemy. They reached the long beach of Nashawena and were so close that the excited crew of the Bay sloop could follow the movements of the men on the pirate's deck. Taking the weather gage, the *Mary* at last drew up abeam. Doubtfully shaking his head, Codman waited for the command of the taut-faced Captain on the poop. The stiff southeasterly breeze was heeling the sloop so far over that her starboard guns could not bear on the pirate two hundred yards off except on the lift from her roll.

"Put a shot across her bow, gunner!" called Pease, from the poop.

Codman sprang to Hugh's gun. "Knock out two coins, men, and raise her muzzle!" he ordered.

Two men pried up the breech with handspikes, while with blows of his crow Hugh drove out the upper coins supporting the breech of the three-pounder and the muzzle was raised. Codman sighted the gun, then ordered, "Fire on the lift when she rolls!"

A gunner sprang to a tub of sand where a lighted linstock sputtered, while another poured priming powder from his horn along the channel to the vent on the gun's breech. "Fire on the lift!" cried Codman.

Hugh leaped back from the breach. The sputtering match fired the priming powder as the gun's muzzle rose with the sloop's roll. There was a flash; the minion roared as she belched a cloud of orange smoke and leaped from the deck into her straining breeching and side tackle. A red huff of escaping gas spat vertically from her vent as the round shot plunged on its way. A gunner clapped the lead apron over the vent.

The ball plowed into the sea off the pirate's bow, kicking up a column of spray, while the crew of the *Mary* watched. Then a crimson flag fluttered to the masthead of Pound's sloop.

"There she shows her true colors, lads!" cried Pease. "Mark the bloody rag!"

"Reload!" ordered Codman. "They're waitin' for shorter range before they let go them sakers!"

Hugh and his mates sponged the gun, drove the powder cartridge home with its wadding of rope yarn, and rammed in the three-pound ball. A gunner thrust a priming iron through the hot vent to break into the paper cartridge, primed, and the three-pounder was run up to the port by its side tackles.

Pease was closing in. At one hundred yards there was the rattle of musketry on both sloops, while three puffs of yellow smoke leaped from the pirate's ports. There was a splitting crash and the oak bulwarks beside Hugh's gun were ripped into splinters as a round shot smashed through, hurling two mangled lumps of flesh across the deck. Dazed, Hugh picked himself up and stared with wide eyes on death. Two men of his gun crew who, a moment before, had stood beside him, a smile on their bronzed faces, were now bloodied heaps. He gazed curiously at the great blobs of blood spattered on his naked arms and chest. He might well have been one of those mashed bodies. Death was as close as that! Then he vomited.

"Belay, there!" roared Codman. "There's no time for that! Back to your gun!"

The humiliated boy wondered if he had been marked as a coward by the master gunner and his mates. With a sob he picked up the crow he had dropped and reeled to the minion, where he was joined by two of the larboard gun crews. Codman laid the three starboard minions and cried, "Fire on the rise!"

The guns belched flame and acrid smoke, which the wind scattered, while their crews' straining eyes watched the hull of the pirate. But so great was the *Mary's* list that the shots plunged short, into the sea, kicking columns of spray high into the air.

With a curse, the infuriated Codman leaped the shattered body of a gunner and reached the poop ladder. "Christ's blood, sir!" he shouted to Pease, standing beside the tiller men, "we can't work the guns with this list! She heels too hard!"

The taut-faced Captain nodded. "Luff!" he cried to the helmsmen.

From the bow, Gallop and his musketmen poured a fierce fire at the enemy, but the pirate's crew were shielded by her high weather rail, while the list of the Bay sloop exposed the men on her decks. As the *Mary's* bow swung into the wind, another salvo from Pound's sakers tore through her mainsail and top hamper. The Bay sloop fell astern, and a cheer lifted from the pirate.

"They think we're through, do they?" cried Codman, his face black with powder stain. "Drive in them spare coins to lift her breech!" he ordered Hugh. "We'll soon lie on her lee! God's blood! Then we'll show Pound!" He ordered the two dead men rolling in the scuppers carried forward, and a piece of canvas thrown over them.

As he stared at the mangled bodies, Hugh was again gripped by nausea. Then, as the broken shapes were carried away and the bloody deck swabbed with sea water, a black Jocelyn rage boiled in the youth who, for the first time, was looking upon violent death. His hands shook as they gripped his iron crow. Pound should pay for this! Pound and his rabble of renegades should pay!

The reason for Pease's maneuver was plain to his crew as the *Mary* again swung her nose in pursuit. Once on the lee of the pirate the tables would be turned and the Bay sloop's high weather rail would serve as a shield from musket fire and enable her to use her guns. Finally, off Cuttyhunk and the foaming Sow and Pigs, as Pease drew up, a cheer lifted from the pirate's deck.

"What are they cheering for?" Hugh demanded of Codman.

"The bastards fancy we're goin' to strike to 'em," laughed the gunner. "'Tis naval custom to drop to lee'ard when you mean to strike your flag. But, as they run from us, why do they think we close on 'em to strike? They're fair frenzical!"

"Name of God!" cried the excited boy, "we haven't begun to fight yet."

Codman's face, streaked with powder stain and sweat, relaxed. There was approval in his hard eyes as he looked at Hugh. "Never fear, you'll have your fill of it, lad, when we lay her board and board!"

As the *Mary* slowly nosed up and crossed the counter of the pirate, her minions and muskets raked Pound's deck, while the pirate's sakers were useless. But at the short range, he poured a merciless swivel and musket fire into the Bay sloop's bow. Then, in a break in the firing, a tall figure stood on the pirate's poop, a beaver hat, from which fluttered a feather, jammed on his head. Brandishing a huge cutlass, he bellowed, "Do you strike?"

"Strike yourself!" shouted Gallop from the sloop's bow. "We'll give you good quarter."

"Board us, you dogs!" roared the pirate, shaking his cutlass. "Damn you! we'll give you quarter by-and-by."

There was a burst of musket fire from the decks of both sloops, and Pound reeled and pitched forward on his face. Again the larboard guns of the *Mary* spat their iron balls at point-blank range, and the splinters flew on the pirate's exposed deck, taking their toll of the men firing at the sloop closing on them.

Blanketed by the big mainsail of the *Good Speed*, the *Mary* fell back on her quarter. Bracing himself against the after hatch coaming, his face smeared with blood from a scalp wound, Pease shouted, "Stand by with the irons!"

Men crouched in the *Mary's* bow with iron hooks made fast to lines, as Pease drove his sloop in on the pirate's beam. There was fierce exchange of musket shots as the end of the *Mary's* jib boom crashed its way between the *Good Speed's* mast and starboard shrouds. Frayed by shot, her straining main sheets parted with the report of guns, whipped back on the poop like writhing snakes, and smashed two swivel gunners and a tiller man to the deck. The sloops swung into the wind, and grappling irons were heaved and made fast. Firing their muskets, Gallop and his barefooted boarding crew leaped through clouds of acrid-tasting smoke for the pirate's rail, with cutlass, pike, and ax, while musket balls spattered around them like rain; and the bitter hand-to-hand battle was on.

Leaving the swivel men with Pease on the poop, Codman and his gun crews raced forward to join their comrades in the wild melee on the pirate's deck, where men battled with clubbed musket, cutlass, and pike. Outnumbered Gallop and his men fought savagely to clear the bow and drive the crew aft, where Pease's swivels could rake them. But Pound's renegades were desperate, for capture meant the gibbet on Nix's Mate off Boston Harbor.

Over the deck of the pirate sloop, littered with shattered gear, splinters, wounded and dead men, the battle raged. With drawn cutlasses the barefooted Codman and his gun crews, naked torsos smeared with powder stain, leaped the bulwarks and hurried to Gallop's aid. As he rushed into the melee, Hugh was faced by two burly pirates who had whirled to meet him. His heavy cutlass hacked at the shaft of a pike lunged at his chest. The pike was beaten down, and Hugh's war hatchet parried the slash of the second man's cutlass. He leaped aside to avoid another slash, and his belt ax battered the pirate's skull, bringing him to the deck. At the same instant the pikeman again lunged, and only by a desperate side leap and twist of his body did the boy avoid the iron-pointed shaft aimed at his chest. A wild Jocelyn rage stormed through him as he circled his man. Again the pirate lunged savagely with his pike. Hugh missed the parry with his cutlass but drove his ax deep into the other's outthrust arm. With an oath, the pirate retreated, his left arm useless. Whipping back his blade, Hugh leaped at his man, but his bare feet slipped in blood and he sprawled helpless on his chest. With his good arm the frenzied pirate poised his pike for the thrust. The desperate boy tried to fling himself aside to avoid the lunge, but his hands, still gripping ax and cutlass, slid in blood, and he flattened on his face. Here was the end!

But at the instant the wounded pirate shifted his feet and started the thrust which would pin the prostrate lad to the deck, Hugh drove with a desperate upward lunge with the point of his cutlass into the man's belly and he pitched forward on top of the boy, his pike quivering in the deck beside Hugh's face, pinning a lock of his long hair. Pushing the screaming pirate aside, Hugh tore his hair free, scrambled to his feet, and sprang forward to the battle in the waist of the sloop.

With clubbed musket, cutlass, and boarding pike, the infuriated Bay men were driving the pirates back to their after deck. The battle-mad Gallop and his men would not be denied as they fought over sprawled dead and wounded to the poop, where the last of the ship's crew rallied to make their stand. As the Bay men closed in and started to scramble up through the open rail and over the poop ladder, Codman shouted: "Down, men! Flat on the deck! The swivel!"

Hugh saw, screened by the rabble of desperate men facing them, two pirates working madly to train one of the mounted blunderbusses on the *Mary's* men as they reached the poop.

At the warning, the Bay men flattened on the main deck, covered by the raised poop, as the foremost pirates leaped aside, exposing the pointed swivel. There was a red flash, a loud explosion, and the overcharged murderer blew into a hundred pieces of ragged iron, killing and maiming the men around it.

With a yell, Codman leaped to his feet and, waving his bloody cutlass, bellowed: "Come on, men! Give 'em the steel!"

The Bay men leaped to the poop and charged the last of Pound's dazed crew huddled at the after rail among their dead and dying.

"Quarter! Quarter!" they whined.

"Do you surrender?" roared Gallop, looking more like a black than a white man, with his face and naked torso powder-smudged and streaked with blood.

"Ay, we surrender! Christ's blood! Give us quarter!"

"Drop your arms! We'll give you good quarter!" snarled Gallop. "But, damn you! 'twill do you little good. You'll all swing at Nix's Mate!"

Muskets, pikes, and cutlasses fell from the pirates' hands, and they were herded into the forecastle and the hatch battened, while Gallop's men looked to their own wounded.

In the cabin lay Pound and many others badly hurt, and here Gallop had the rest of the wounded pirates carried, while their dead, weighted with iron, were dropped over the side, and the decks cleared.

But, to their grief, back in the cabin of the *Mary*, Gallop and Codman found Captain Pease unconscious on his bunk, bleeding from wounds received early in the fight, when a swivel had scoured the *Mary's* poop. They twisted tourniquets on his leg and arm and packed the hole in his side with cobwebs. Then they had their own wounded carried to the cabin. Soon they put the prisoners, under a guard of musketmen, to work with the crew, reeving new rigging and making temporary repairs to the mainsails and top hamper of the two sloops.

Later, under the fair wind and tide, the Bay sloop, followed at a distance by the limping *Good Speed*, sailed by its prize crew, headed for the Sakonnet River, bound for Portsmouth and surgical aid. It was a grim and silent crew that dropped anchor that night in the Pocasset Narrows off two farmhouses on the Portsmouth shore. They carried their captain and the other wounded to the houses, and Gallop sent a horseman to Newport for doctors.

That night the tired Hugh sat in a farmhouse. Across the fire room, Pease and others lay on pallets, fighting for life. Women summoned from neighboring farms busied themselves rolling dressings and watching kettles, in which were boiling the bitter tansy blossom, and St.-John's-wort, and comfrey, to be used both internally and on wounds. Never in his life had Hugh so desired anything as he then craved to see Content and Tom, and Israel and Trelawney—but ten miles away in Newport! He had come through the greatest adventure of his life, had looked death in the face, and though fearing to die, had not been afraid. He had seen men die and their blood run into the scuppers; and fought in self-defense. Nothing would ever seem the same to him again. He felt sick and cold as he remembered the agony of those they had carried on stretchers to the farmhouses, where kindly women bathed their wounds. And he would never forget the ashen faces and staring eyes of the dead. While the fight on the sloop lasted, he had been in a frenzy of rage to beat to the deck these renegades who had raised their red flag against honest men. But now that it was over, he felt dazed and strange and lonely. The heat of battle and the triumph of victory had left his blood. He wanted to see Content's lined face and feel the touch of her hand.

The mate and master gunner entered the house and looked in silence at their captain, raving in fever on his pallet. Then, sadly shaking his head, Codman turned away. His glance fell on Hugh, squatted in a corner. The drawn face of the gunner lighted.

Ashamed of having been seen by Codman when the sight of the mangled bodies of his mates had sickened him, Hugh had avoided the master gunner since the fight. Blood stained his face as his doubtful eyes met those of the older man.

"Ho, youngster!" greeted Codman, "that first shot through our rail capsized your stomach, did it? Thought you was goin' to strike your flag, you was that white! But you turned to and worked that minion and drove in them coins cool as a shipwright drivin' tree nails! You'll make a gunner yet!"

Hugh breathed with relief. After all, he was not thought a coward. But he wondered if the master gunner had guessed how much he had feared mutilation and death—how much he had wanted to live.

Leftenant Gallop nodded. "The lad paid his way! He was fair handy with his ax and cutlass."

As the officers left the room, Codman said, "There'll be prize money for you when we make Boston and the *Good Speed's* condemned and sold by the admiralty court."

Prize money! Hugh thought of the silk hood and gown he would buy in Boston for Content, and the gift for Seeth; yes, and for Candace, too, for he owed her at least that much thought.

Late that night three chirurgeons, Caleb Arnold of Portsmouth, son of Benedict, and the Huguenots, Peter Ayrault and Norbert Vigneron, trained in Europe, reached the wounded in the farmhouses at the Pocasset Narrows.

"What chance has he?" asked Gallop of Doctor Vigneron, when

the latter had labored long and in vain to check the hemorrhage in Pease's torn side by the use of cobwebs.

"None, whatever!" was the answer. "He slowly bleeds to death internally and there is nought I can do."

At dawn Captain Pease joined those of the desperately wounded who had died in the night.

When the dead had been buried, the two sloops were to start for Boston, leaving the seriously wounded in Portsmouth. Hugh longed to return home; but duty demanded he stick with the sloop, for Gallop needed him to help work the *Mary* around the Cape, and he might never see the prize money owed him if he once left his ship. So, much as he longed to walk in on them that evening at Tom Stanton's little house, take Content in his arms, shake Tom's hard hand, and make Israel's and Trelawney's jaws drop with the tale he had to tell, he was forced to wait.

§39

IN BOSTON the news of the arrival of the *Mary* and the captured *Good Speed*, with wounded and prisoners, brought men running from the taverns, shops, and shipyards to Wentworth's Wharf. There the aged Governor Bradstreet and men of prominence in the city welcomed the victorious Gallop and his crew. The wounded Pound and his mates were jailed, to await trial, and within the week the *Good Speed*, with her stores, was condemned and sold in the admiralty court. Hugh learned that the *Sea Flower* had already sailed with a cargo, so with a leather wallet full of shiny pine-tree shillings, allotted by the court as his share of the prize money, he shipped on a small ketch bound for Newport.

One October evening he walked in on the little group gathered in Tom Stanton's living room.

"Hugh!" First to see him, Content flew into the open arms of her foster son. "Oh, 'tis good to have you back safe and unhurt!" she cried, kissing his brown cheek.

"Welcome back, son!" exclaimed Stanton, in his excitement snapping his clay pipe stem into bits between his teeth as he sprang to his feet.

"Ahoy, Hugh Jocelyn!" With a bull-like rush, the bulky Israel reached the boy, as he stood with his arms about Content, and clapped him on his broad back.

"Pickle my guts!" cried the excited sailor. "What mean you by sniffing your first sulphur and saltpeter in the smoke of a ship's gun without Israel on your beam to steady your nerves? Sink me! But you played me a scurvy trick, shipping on the *Mary* and laying board and board with that slimy Pound, and Israel not there with his cutlass! We got the news from Portsmouth the day after the fight."

Hugh grinned into the grimacing face of the sailor as he reached and gripped Brandy's hairy paw. "Israel," he said, "I was that scared when the saker balls began pounding us I could have jumped into the sea!"

"Not a man in the crew but was scared inside when the fight started!" said Israel. "Every son-of-a-rumpuncheon was scared! But that passed when their blood heated, the same as with you. Belay that talk! Now I'm bustin' to hear how you served them three-pound minions!"

So, in detail, Hugh told the story of the fight in Vineyard Sound. Later, Trelawney, Benoni Tosh, and the Wanton boys burst in to welcome their friend and hear the tale retold.

When Israel and the guests had left and Hugh was alone with Tom and Content, the boy opened his sea bag.

"Why, whatever have you there, Hugh?" Content's pale eyes widened as she stared in amazement at the shimmering gray silk frock Hugh held for her inspection.

"What think you of it?" demanded the smiling boy.

"'Tis the beautifulest silk frock I ever did see!" she gasped, stroking the glossy fabric with her rough hands. "'Twill mightily become Seeth, Hugh! And she will be that pleased!"

Hugh slowly shook his blond head as he smiled into her fascinated eyes. "'Tis not for Seeth Carr," he said, "but for the best mother boy ever had, to wear on the Sabbath to the meeting house."

With a faint cry of "Oh!" and a bewildered look at the amazed Tom Stanton, Content took the gown and, crushing it to her breast, rose on her toes to kiss the boy smiling down at her. "Hugh! Hugh!" she laughed in her joy, "'tis the first silk frock ever I had! I will feel like a queen when I wear it, next Sabbath!"

Hugh again reached into his sea bag and brought out a gray silk hood lined with blue, while Content watched him with open mouth. "And here," he said, "is the hood to wear with it."

"A silk frock and hood! Oh, my lad! My dear lad," she cried, winking back the sudden tears. "But the money they cost you—your wages?"

"They were bought with prize money, not wages. See?" Hugh showed her his bag of shiny shillings. "I have most of it still left for you to hide for me in the chimney."

It was a happy Content and a still happier Hugh Jocelyn who parted that night at the foot of the ladder reaching to the sleeping loft.

§40

THE flight of swan, gray geese, and brant were on the coast. Islands of mallard, black duck, and blue bills dotted the bay and the Sakonnet River. But powder was too valuable to waste on duck. While Hugh waited for the return of the *Sea Flower* from Boston, he hunted the yellow and saffron reaches of the Sakonnet marshes for the great honkers and whistlers from the north. The geese and swan they did not sell were salted for the winter. Because of the price, beef, mutton, and pork were strangers to the humble table of Tom Stanton, except when he got them in barter for fish. But of fish there was plenty. Barrels of pickled sturgeon, eels, salt cod, haddock, and halibut carried the family through the winter.

As yet the stolid oxen of Farmer Dexter, who lived off the Portsmouth Road, had not lumbered into Newport with the last loads of firewood and pitch-pine candlewood Stanton had ordered. So one morning Hugh started for the Dexter farm.

He was a different-looking lad from the one who, the year before, had walked the same road. Taller and many pounds heavier, Hugh had thrown aside his seaman's canvas and sea doublet, and wore a homespun suit, red woolen stockings, and heavy shoes. His cutlass hung from a baldric slung over his right shoulder. He had considered long that morning before giving up the idea of wearing his new broadcloth suit with the pewter buckles and buttons, which fitted him so well, for in passing down Thames Street, through the Parade, and up Broad Street to the Portsmouth Road, he knew he would meet the gaze of many a pair of feminine eyes, and the young man was proud of that new suit. But the roads were dusty and the broadcloth was too precious to soil with country dirt. So Hugh started on his long walk in the mellow November air with his yellow head high, but in his heart the realization that he would pass more than one lifted brow belonging to son or daughter of merchant or landowner, wearing silk and velvet and broadcloth, who would secretly snigger at his rough clothes.

"Why is it," he asked himself, "they cannot take me for what I am and not for what I wear? Trelawney says there is no lad in Newport, not even among those who have been schooled in Boston, and they are few, who has my reading. In fact, he names on his fingers the men here who have it. Yet these sprigs of the rich, though they speak to me in church, sit in pews reserved for the mighty, while Content and I, because we are poor, needs must look from a long bench and admire."

Through the Parade, where he had spent that eventful afternoon in the embrace of the pillory, Hugh picked his way among foraging chickens, dogs, and rooting swine, strayed from the Common beyond, and passed up Broad Street. The benison of a mellow autumn day lay on forest and farmlands. Haystacks and shocked corn stippled the brown fields. A film of haze hung low in the oaks, still holding their ocher leaves; but the flaming flags of the maples and the birches' yellow banners had been struck in surrender to the frost, leaving a lacework of naked branches. From the stone chimneys of the story-and-a-half farmhouses, smoke curled lazily upward; while in the fields ruminating cattle stood in groups enjoying the warmth of the sun, sheep still grazed in the dun meadows, and hogs rooted in the woods.

Hugh enjoyed his walk through the drowsing farmlands of the island, with their sweet odors and the feeling they gave of security and permanence and abundance, but he was grateful that his lot had not been cast among them. He loved the wild appeal of the ever-changing sea, with its menace and its challenge to the stout heart and the restless spirit. He thought of the Dunbars on their farm in Somerset. It seemed so long ago that he had sailed there in the shallop, after losing the swimming race.

Absorbed in his thoughts, he walked on past rolling meadows and corn land. He wondered what life held for him! But of one thing he was sure, he would fight free of the poverty in which he had grown up. War would soon come, and the *Flying Fish* would scour the seas in search of French shipping. Then, with his prize money he would buy a share in a sloop and sail as her master. Captain Hugh Jocelyn! It sounded sweet to the ears of the dreaming youth. And Seeth? Would he marry Seeth, then? He did not know. She would not want him at sea. Yet the sea should be his fortune. Someday they would not cock their brows when Hugh Jocelyn entered the King's Head. 'Twould be Captain Hugh Jocelyn, privateersman, owner of shares in sloops and a farm. Yes, there would be a farm for Tom and Content's old age. A farm with a square house and an upper story, like Tom Paine's. Someday Newport would wake to find Hugh Jocelyn a man of property, fit to sit in the King's Head with the gentry—someday!

Before he was aware of it, he had reached the winding lane that ran west from the Portsmouth Road. He turned in, and when he came to the bend where he had met the Brinleys and Lettice had lashed him across the face, he stopped. It was here that the spitfire had turned in her saddle, with her bright hair flying, and flung back that look as he stood in the road and laughed at her. What a hot head she was, and how lovely she looked the day she came to the pillory! Hugh wondered what would have come from his meeting her as she had begged in her note. Had her father learned of such a meeting, he doubtless would have had Hugh whipped in the Parade on some charge or other, for he had been all-powerful under Andros. But times had changed. Francis Brinley was king no more.

Hugh walked on to the Dexter farm, where he was told that Stanton's oak, maple, and candlewood would shortly be delivered. Early afternoon found him again approaching the bend in the lane through the oak woods. His dreams of the future ran the gamut from voyages to Barbadoes to sea fights with French privateers off the New England coast in the *Flying Fish*. But they were suddenly broken by the sound of horses' hoofs beyond the turn in the lane. The horses were swiftly approaching, and as Hugh reached the bend, with a cry of surprise a girl in a blue riding habit reined a black mare back on its haunches as she stared at the tall figure standing in the road facing her.

"Hugh Jocelyn!" Her lovely face framed by a scarlet riding hood, Lettice Brinley stared at the youth who stood smiling up at her. "Wherever did you come from?"

"Your servant, Mistress Brinley!" Hugh bowed, with a smile, his heart starting to race. " 'Twas here, I believe, we first met!"

The girl swallowed twice before she could control her voice. Hugh stood so close to the restless mare that he noticed how her gloved hands trembled as a wave of blood pushed up over her neck and face. Her hazel eyes, flecked with black, were dark with excitement. "Hugh Jocelyn," she repeated, and her voice was throaty with emotion, "to fancy I should meet you here, today, when I rode this way because—because 'twas here I lashed you with my whip!"

Hugh glanced inquiringly at the black boy who had stopped his horse some yards behind his mistress. "Is it wise," he asked, "for you to talk with Hugh Jocelyn? 'Twill be reported."

She impatiently shook her head, and the hood fell from the cloud of chestnut hair, to her shoulders. "Aaron would die for me. He is safe." She turned to the young slave. "Aaron, ride back to the Portsmouth Road. I will meet you there."

The black boy wheeled his horse and disappeared. Then the girl smiled down at the youth standing in the road, wondering what this wild daughter of Francis Brinley had in her mind.

"Mr. Trelawney would not suffer you to meet me," she said, with a toss of the head, "but it seems that fate has been kind to us today."

Her words drove a swift flow of blood through Hugh's veins. He felt strangely disturbed, and yet elated. His gaze wandered from the chestnut ripples of her hair and her shining eyes, to the red mouth and its trembling lower lip, and the white roundness of throat. This lovely daughter of the Brinleys who was stooping to the foster son of a fisherman strangely stirred his blood.

"Mistress Lettice," he said, tightening his folded arms on his chest and fighting for control of his voice, " 'tis overrash of you to have words here with a fisherman's son. Think of your family, what—"

She leaned toward him. "Damn my family!" she spat. "Name of God! Hugh Jocelyn, should you think of them when they have twice tried to injure you?" She edged her pony closer to the youth in the road, and he did not move, as the blood beat in his throat. Then she leaned from her saddle, while his arms gripped his chest in an effort at self-control. "Why, you're trembling, Hugh Jocelyn!" She laughed in her delight. "You're trembling! You're not made of wood, after all!"

Her face was very close as her hand touched his shoulder and her challenging eyes searched his. As flood waters burst a dam, Hugh's pent emotions suddenly broke their bonds. He reached and swung the girl from her saddle, and holding her high, crushed his lips to the red mouth, that passionately returned his kisses. He was drunk with the mad sweetness of holding Lettice Brinley in his arms, while his lips wandered from her fragrant hair to the soft roundness of her white throat.

"You do—you do find me—nice?" she murmured in his ear, her arms circling his neck. "Oh, I've dreamed of this! 'Tis why I rode here today, Hugh Jocelyn; to think of you!"

"Why do you ask me? You know well how—how lovely you are," he said thickly. "But your father would have driven me from Newport had I met you as you asked and he learned of it."

"Set me down," she said, "that I may straighten my clothes and catch up my hair. 'Tis a fright!"

Hugh placed the girl on her feet. "You were never more beautiful than now, with your hair tumbled about your shoulders and your frock awry." He caught her to him and kissed her, then held her at arm's length while he devoured the beauty of her flushed face as she laughed up at him. His blood raced wildly at the touch of her.

Leaning backward, with a toss of the head, she took his two hands in hers and surveyed him from beneath long lashes. "Come, let's sit on this bank and talk," she urged, leading him across the lane. "I'm so trembly I scarce may talk or think."

"Let's not think," he murmured.

She flung herself on the grassy bank and drew him down beside her. "You were foully set upon—almost killed! But you were too stout for them," she said. "How I envied that Seeth Carr—hated her that she was with you that night! Think you she's more pretty than I?"

A twinge of shame shot through him. He had forgotten Seeth. Yet he was too deep in the spell of Lettice Brinley to turn back now. Gathering her up in his arms he kissed her again and again, while she fiercely clung to him, returning his caresses. But her lack of all restraint sent a flicker of uneasiness through him. This headstrong daughter of Francis Brinley would brook no curb to her impulses. What she desired she would take without a thought. She was as untamed as some wild creature. And she was fair ravishing with that scented cloud of chestnut hair, those dancing hazel eyes, and skin like satin.

"And you've been in a sea fight with a pirate," she chattered on. "Mr. Trelawney told us how you fought. Even Father said you seemed without fear. But Richard," she laughed, "went green and left the room, refusing to listen."

His arm tightened about her. "I love the smell of your hair!"

A wave of blood pulsed to her temples. "If you'd but be kind and listen, we could make these oak woods our Forest of Arden, Hugh," she said, through half-closed eyes, her head on his shoulder, as her white fingers toyed with a long lock of his yellow hair. "I, too, have read 'As You Like It' with Mr. Trelawney."

"Was it not beautiful—that forest and those lovers?" he asked.

Her red mouth shaped a pout and her dark brows drew together. "We could make this more so if you'd but consent to meet me here, sometime, when ashore."

Hugh was silent as he pushed back the lustring sleeve from her round arm and kissed it from the wrist to the cup of the elbow. With a shiver she drew it away. "Don't!" she whispered. "You fever me! But we could make this our forest," she went on, her short upper lip curled above her white teeth. "I'd waste no time, though, with silly doublet and hose, however it became me. Think you Orlando guessed not who she was, with those woman's legs? Faugh! He was fair blind, did he not!"

"You'd make a lovely Rosalind," laughed Hugh, "in doublet and hose."

"But straight though they are and well shaped, my legs would betray me." To Hugh's amazement, Lettice calmly drew her skirts to her round knees, thrust out a small riding slipper and symmetrical leg cased in scarlet silk stocking, and laughed as she wiggled her foot. "Would that deceive your man's eyes, Hugh Jocelyn?"

His heart thundered in his throat. "No, 'tis too rounded and pretty for any boy's," he laughed.

Lettice continued: "And my woman's hips! Had this Rosalind the straight flanks of a boy to so deceive him? If so, she were not desirable."

Hugh's right hand moved from her waist to the rounded hip below. "I'd never mistake these hips for a boy's, Lettice Brinley, but in hose they'd adorn any forest. The birds and beasts would be your slaves."

Her long-lashed eyes were serious as they probed his. "You think I'm comely, then, and shapely?"

He drew her close as he kissed her white throat and the nape of her neck beside which a long heartbreaker curled, then pushed down her frock and crushed his lips against a white shoulder. "You are more ravishing than any Rosalind, and more dangerous," he murmured.

The girl sighed and lifted languorous eyes. "I feared you hated me for what my brother and father did to you."

"I never forgot how you stood for me against Magistrate Tripp, nor your coming to the pillory."

She was again all smiles. "I could not stay away," she whispered, then lifted smoldering eyes to his, and her arms tightened about his neck as she crushed her lips to his mouth.

In a gust of passion, Hugh's hands wandered over the satin flesh of the girl's body as she lay in his arms. She was offering herself to the son of a fisherman, this daughter of the proud Brinleys. Intoxicated with her perfumed loveliness, Hugh drifted fast toward the brink of the emotional maelstrom which awaited them. His promises to Trelawney, his own decision that intimacy with Lettice Brinley could only bring disaster, were forgotten in the mad appeal of the reckless girl to his senses. His brain reeled with the knowledge that this lovely aristocrat was his. He crushed her yielding body until she cried out from the pressure of his circling arms. "You hurt me, Hugh! You are so strong!" she gasped. "Don't you—don't you—want—me?"

"Name of God! You know I do," he whispered. Then, of a sudden, the flame in him died as a candle is snuffed by wind. Again his ears caught the distant beat of a horse's hoofs. The girl's curious eyes opened wide, searching his set face. "What is it? What is it you hear?" she demanded.

"I hear a horse's hoofs! Someone's coming this way!" He lifted her to her feet and threw the baldric carrying his cutlass over his shoulder. Near them Lettice's mare was leisurely cropping the grass. "Quick! Ride for the Portsmouth Road and meet your black boy," he ordered. "We must not be seen together here—your family would—"

"But I don't want to go, Hugh," protested the girl, grasping his arm. "I won't go! 'Tis but some farmer."

"You must go! Quick! You must get away before we're seen. It may be someone who knows you and will tell your father he caught us here, alone." He carried her to her horse, swung the reluctant girl into her saddle and slipped her riding shoe into the stirrup. But it was too late. The horseman was at the bend in the lane. Lettice glanced back and the color left her face as she said under her breath, "Name of God! 'tis the Newburys' head farmer, who knows me."

The farmer reached the girl and the sailor standing beside her horse. His eyes widened as he recognized the daughter of Francis Brinley. With a mumbled greeting he removed his hat, then glanced quizzically at Hugh and his cutlass, to meet the thrust of a stare so cold that his eyes shifted and he turned his head.

From her horse, Lettice looked helplessly into Hugh's grave face. "He'll tell Carr, and they'll pack me off to Boston to that Misses School," she spat out, angrily. "Oh, why didn't I go! Why did I stop to argue!"

Hugh's mind was a whirlwind of confused thoughts. Newbury would hear of this and tell the Brinleys. How Richard would abuse his sister and her sailor scum! She had been caught as if at a planned meeting and would pay dearly. As for himself, he did not care. Francis Brinley had lost his power and could fume his periwigged head off. But the reckless girl beside him! They'd take it out on her proud spirit. But they'd never break it—not hers! What fools they'd been not to hide! But then, there had been her mare and the side saddle. The farmer might have stopped to investigate. Poor Lettice!

He looked into the girl's tempestuous eyes and she smiled down on him. "You must find your black boy and go home," he said.

"Kiss me, Hugh," she commanded. "Hold me and kiss me good-by." She leaned toward him and he took her in his arms and kissed her eyes and mouth and tumbled hair.

"Good-by, Rosalind," he said. "I'm sorry for this. Twill all come on you."

The girl's face was radiant as she straightened in the saddle. "Sorry? Name of God! I'm glad it happened! Glad, Hugh! Glad! I've wanted to see you so—to have you take me in your arms!" Her face clouded. "But we've lost our Forest of Arden. They'll guard me like a prisoner after this, and send me away. God knows when I'll see you again, Hugh Jocelyn!"

With a wave of the hand she cantered away, then turned and blew him a kiss as she disappeared down the lane.

§41

For days, the thoughts of Hugh Jocelyn were a confused medley of surprise and youthful pride in the infatuation of the patrician Lettice Brinley for a fisherman's son and an uneasy searching of the heart concerning his real feeling for Seeth. In Lettice Brinley there were rare magnetism and personality. She had been as intoxicating as wine, had swept him far out on a heady sea from which he had not wished to seek the shore. Hugh was disturbed and unhappy. He was worried too about Lettice. Their encounter with the farmer had put the girl deep in the power of Newbury and her vindictive brother. She would be packed off to Boston. For himself, there was little to fear, for Justice Brinley was no longer powerful, and Hugh Jocelyn could not be publicly whipped on a trumped-up charge, nor could he be driven out of Newport.

Through the winter events of vital importance to the colony had galloped upon each other's heels so rapidly that the people of the port had been kept in a state of constant excitement. In February the reply of the Crown to the petition of Deputy Governor Coggeshall and the Council for confirmation of the charter had been proclaimed throughout the colony in a week of rejoicing. To the cheering people of each town, summoned by drumbeat and the firing of muskets and cannon, the Town Sergeants read in the light of great bonfires the answer of the King: "Never having been revoked but only suspended, the charters of Connecticut and Rhode Island remain in full force and effect."

While Francis Brinley and the other royalists raged and wrote letters of protest to the Board of Trade in London, the General Assembly had convened for the first time in four years, old Henry Bull had been elected governor, and a new seal with the anchor and the motto "Hope!" had replaced the one ordered broken by Andros. Thus the bold attitude of the patriots had secured the freedom of the colony.

And now word had come over the Plymouth Path, relayed from Boston, that war had been declared between England and France.

In May, 1690, the Assembly gathered, the lost charter was produced and read, and the Quaker, John Easton, was elected governor. War now raged with the French and Indians along the frontiers, and the little ports of New England hastened to prepare for attacks from the sea. From Nantucket to Block Island the farmers and fishermen waited with fear in their hearts for the coming of the French. Even Newport waked from its smug Quaker complacency, for shortly the coastwise trade would be at the mercy of French privateers, and craft bound out or returning from Barbadoes, Jamaica, and others of the Sugar Islands would be compelled to run a blockade of enemy ships. Late in the month good news arrived from Boston. Sir William Phips had made an easy conquest of Port Royal, Acadia. As yet the French had not plundered the coast islands, and the people of Newport breathed easier.

With the outbreak of war, Hugh had become uneasy and in doubt about what to do. After the taking of Port Royal, news had come from Boston of the fitting out of an expedition under Sir William Phips, against Quebec. He and the Wanton boys talked of going to Boston and enlisting, but their father and elder brother held them to their work in the shipyard. In the autumn the *Flying Fish* would be launched and ready, and the war would be long. But an attack on Frontenac and

Quebec! The very thought of the adventure they were missing stirred the imaginations of the three restless Newport boys as they made plans for the future.

One night that summer, ruddy-faced, thickset John Arnold, the incorrigible Joe Brenton, the genial Kit Sheffield, and Trelawney met to discuss the latest news, and to pass on a recent importation of rare Canary by Landlord Whiting, which had slipped past the French privateers.

Brenton repeated what had been known for months, that from New London to the Cape watch fires were already heaped high and ready for lighting. "Captain Tom Paine also tells me," said Brenton, "that today he dispatched a sloop to warn Block Island to keep close lookout and light their fire on Sandy Point at sight of the French. 'Twill not be long before they show their teeth."

"From Nantucket to Block Island the poor devils of farmers will lose everything," deplored Sheffield, who had relatives on Block Island. "In three months there won't be a cow, pig, or sheep on an island, or hardly a sack of corn. The French will leave nothing but the fish in the sea."

"'Tis cruel hard," agreed Arnold, "but that is war. And it hits hardest the poor islanders and the frontier villages, which can least afford it. They say patrols are already being sent from Providence to watch for Indian war parties from the north."

"Colonel Church will have his hands full now, with the Maine savages spurred on by the French," added Brenton. "What a tough old fighter he is! Once Massachusetts slighted him; now he's their man."

"Hugh and the young Wantons are fair wild because Joseph Wanton was too busy with orders for other craft to finish the *Flying Fish*," observed Trelawney, smacking his lips over his cup of Canary. "And Israel Brandy rages like a wild bull. Last night he stumped the floor at Tom Stanton's, his sleeves rolled back from his great arms, twisting his big mouth and bellowing: 'Stab my vitals! these French'll be in Newport a-takin' their pick of our women and a-swillin' our wine and rum afore them Magistrates wakes up! And there lie four ninepounders and six fives, brought from Boston last fall, as sweet cast and as true as any tubes I ever laid on a pirate, fair eatin' their hearts out for no craft to mount 'em on and no gun crews to work 'em!'"

Laughter greeted Trelawney's rendition of the old salt's tirade.

"Name of God! Israel's right," cried the impulsive Brenton. "Tom Paine tells me he sat with the Town Council when the news came in, and those pinchpenny Quakers hemmed and hawed over the cost of buying more powder and balls in Boston, arming two sloops, and paying the wages of a crew to work the guns at King's Fort on Goat Island. Tom told them if they wanted their wharves and shops plundered under their eyes and their women raped, they'd better do nothing."

"So they've finally decided to put the two guns in the earthwork on the shore in front of your place, on wheeled carriages," said Sheffield to Arnold.

"Yes, they're at work on them, now."

"But don't these woodenheads realize that Newport would be the richest kind of plum for a fleet of well-gunned privateers?" demanded Sheffield. "Hammersmith would be the first they'd strike on their way up the East Passage. We could never reach there in time to save it. And the town never returned the two guns they took during King Philip's War from your uncle, Jahleel."

"No, they still lie at the Pocasset Narrows. I wish my grandfather were alive," sighed Brenton. "He'd make those chitty faces listen. They were all afraid of William Brenton. God's name, what a man he was in a temper!"

Newcomers entering the tavern drew the young man's attention.

"Benoni! Captain Paine!" called Brenton, waving his hand. "Here are two stools for you on which to rest your bones and cool your throats!"

The hulking Town Sergeant, followed by a thickset, barrel-chested man, his grizzled hair chopped off at the nape of his thick neck, approached the group, nodding and joking with the occupants of tables as they passed. "Your servant, gentlemen!" said Benoni. Captain Tom Paine, of Conanicut, retired privateersman, nodded to the younger men, who placed a stool for him beside them.

"Captain Paine," said Arnold, when the newcomers were seated and had ordered their drinks, "how soon, think you, before the French will be on the coast?"

Paine's gray eyes squinted into the cup of stonewall grasped in his thick fingers, as his mats of brows pulled together. His pock-marked face, weathered to the hue of old leather, was grave. Then his eyes, from which radiated a network of deep lines, lifted and met the expectant looks of the younger men.

"The French will be here before we've waked to our danger," he answered. "'Tis well known that Newport has little defense for a strong attack from the sea. The guns at King's Fort and the culverins on the shore, here, could not save Hammersmith, Mr. Brenton. Half the gunners of the port are at sea, and most of those here, save Israel Brandy, have forgot much of what they knew, in the long peace."

"The Governor and Assistants from Newport and the Town Council think the French will not dare attack us," suggested Sheffield, "but will plunder the islands and pick up the coasters."

Paine's agate-hard eyes bored into those of the speaker. There was a smoldering fire in them like sun behind fog. "Well, will Rhode Islanders sit meekly down like sheep and watch the French fill their bellies with Block Island cattle while they destroy our commerce?"

"God's name, no!" snorted Benoni. "We'll man our ships and go out and sink 'em!"

Lights danced in Paine's eyes. "That we will, Benoni!" he snapped, clapping his pewter cup hard on the table. "Captain Godfrey and I are already taking means to fit two sloops for what may come."

"That's good news, Captain Paine!" applauded Joe Brenton. "I am no seaman, but there are few better shots with pistol or musket in Newport. When you call for volunteers, count me among them."

"And me! And me!" cried Arnold and Sheffield. "We can handle musket and pistol as well as Joe, here," added Sheffield, "but he won't admit it."

Paine smiled good-naturedly at the amateurs, whose fighting spirit was superior to their experience. But from boyhood they had hunted geese, brant, and swan on the south shore, and deer and bear in the forests of the mainland, so were familiar with firearms. "'Tis gunners we'll need to work the five- and nine-pounders. Israel Brandy goes master gunner on my sloop, and with him Hugh Jocelyn."

"Our brig, the *Swordfish*, now doubtless in the hands of the French," regretted Brenton, "is a good sailer. She would have been useful if here and properly manned and armed. 'Tis a pity the Wanton sloop is not off the stocks and rigged."

"Ay, you are right, Mr. Brenton," said Paine, puffing on his long-stemmed pipe. "Sweeter lines I never saw in a sloop's hull. 'Twill take a lively Frenchman to show her heels to her, and William Wanton, though young, is a smart seaman and a bold one."

"You say Israel Brandy sails with you as master gunner?" said Arnold.

Tom Paine's gray eyes lit as if with sudden memory. He rubbed a stubbled chin with a brown hand through which a bullet had once passed, leaving a lumpy, blue scar. "Stanch old Israel!" he chuckled. "We were shipmates when he lost his leg off Hispaniola. He could lay a demiculverin with the best I ever saw, and with a cutlass would slash about him like a swordfish in a school of mackerel, bellowing the while like ten bulls."

His hearers laughed at Paine's description. "Though near fifty, he's no man to trifle with today," added Brenton.

"Ay, you're right! Stout he is beyond most men. But he's young no longer, nor am I. Still, there's many a good fight left in Israel Brandy and, I hope, in me."

"We set great store by him," said Trelawney.

"There's no better man, peg leg and all, in this port today," agreed Benoni, as he audibly gulped his fifth cup of ale at his friends' expense and, with an "Ah!" of satisfaction, wiped his wet lips with the back of a huge hand.

Brenton was staring at the entrance to the room. "What's this?" he exclaimed. "By the look of his face, Constable Painter has news for us!"

With a grunt, the red-faced Town Sergeant lifted his three hundred pounds from the stool and his thick finger beckoned the constable to the table. The hum of talk suddenly ceased as the curious people in the room watched.

"Your servant, gentlemen," exclaimed the excited Constable. "A shallop is in from Block Island. 'Tis reported from the south shore that for two days strange sail have been seen standing off and on. 'Tis likely the French!"

The room was suddenly filled with the hum of voices as the news traveled from table to table.

Tom Paine's hard-bitten face expanded in a smile as he blew a cloud of smoke from his wide mouth. "Good!" he grunted. "Now these Newport pinchpennies will wake up, for many have craft at sea and now in danger of loss to the French."

"That's what'll move them to loosen the town purse! Damn their grasping souls," snorted Brenton. "When it hits their pockets, they jump like a man treading barefoot on a live coal."

Paine rose from the table, followed by the others. "Captain Godfrey and I," he said, "must look smart to fitting the sloops, for the gun ports are not all cut and the guns in their tackles. The French will come some day soon. 'Tis a pity the *Flying Fish* is not off the stocks and rigged!"

The stocky former privateersman left the others at the door and hurried up Thames Street to the Wharf called the Queen's Hithe, at the foot of Queen's Street, where lay the two sloops, the *Neptune* and the *Royal Stede*.

§42

On a July night in 1690, the skies were suddenly illuminated by a great signal fire on Sandy Point. The French had come! The lookout on Point Judith saw the light across the eight miles of sea separating Block Island from the mainland. From New London to Sakonnet Point, and on to the Cape, watch fires took up the message and blazed through the night, warning the people that the enemy was on the coast.

The following day Newport was delirious with excitement. Men stood in the streets discussing the threatened safety of the port. Frightened women gossiped from open windows across the narrow streets. The two rusty culverins that had been taken from the Brenton place during the Indian war and mounted at Pocasset Narrows were hastily loaded on a sloop and ferried around the island to the harbor, where they were set up in King's Fort beside the four already there, and gun crews were detailed to work them. The taverns were filled with nervous and excited citizens. That night, at the King's Head, the new governor, John Easton, talked with Captain Tom Paine, Benedict Arnold, and Major John Greene of Warwick, Deputy Governor. Their faces were grave with uneasiness and foreboding, for little or nothing had been done by the May Assembly toward strengthening the defenses of Newport. In accordance with the tenets of their faith, the Quakers in power had deprecated active preparations for war and, ostrich like, had hidden their heads in the sands of their hope that the French would not dare attack the little seaport. In the same way, fifteen years before they had callously left Providence and Warwick to their doom, refusing to send Roger Williams aid. But now that their own property and families were threatened they had suddenly waked from their stupor and were listening, ill at ease, to the loud-voiced condemnation of their fellow citizens, stimulated and barbed by frequent insertion of noses into pewter cups. Soon the room was a bedlam of heated controversy. Men came to blows and had to be separated.

At length Governor Easton rose and addressed the wrangling assembly. His bony face, framed by graying hair hanging to his neck, was accented by eyes that were bleak. "Citizens of Newport," he began, "'tis known that Nantucket and Martin's Vineyard have been robbed by the French, and today Captain Paine brings word from Block Island that five French ships landed men, took cattle and sheep, wounded some farmers, and disappeared into the fog. 'Tis not known whither they sailed, but it well may be Newport they will next seek to plunder."

"Whose fault is it we are ill prepared, John Easton?" called an angry voice.

"You Quakers will fight now that your warehouses are in danger!" called another.

"'Tis God's truth!" was roared from many tables.

Ignoring the interruptions, Easton continued: "At sunrise Captain Paine sails to learn if the enemy is in sight. Captain Paine commands the sloop *Royal Stede*, and Captain Godfrey the *Neptune*, which are being armed. Later, at the Parade, they will call for volunteers to man them."

"High time, Governor Easton!" sneered Francis Brinley from the table where he sat with his son, Richard, Carr Newbury, and Peleg

Sanford, "and likely too late!"

"Ay, high time!" called another. "Now we are threatened, you Quakers grow warlike!"

There were cries of "Shame!" followed by shouts of "No, 'tis God's truth!"

Then the barrel-chested Tom Paine stood up. Suddenly the room became silent as the agate-gray eyes in his scarred face slowly traversed the men at the tables, who strained forward to hear his words. Tom Paine, of Conanicut, was known as a fighting man and a daring seaman, with years of privateering on the Spanish Main, and the hushed room waited with tension. He cleared his throat and his stiff lips moved.

"Citizens of Newport," he rasped, "you've been asleep! Ten years ago, in French Tortuga, I heard pirates over their cups talk of a raid on Newport and of the fat loot that was here."

Murmurs of doubt and surprise filled the room.

"Yes, I tell you, in Tortuga, the filthiest port in the Indy seas, where the French West Indy Company outfit pirates and divide their plunder, I heard it," he roared, shaking a huge fist. "The Block Islanders say the five craft off our coast are not privateers but pirates from the West Indy. They are after Newport and will spare neither man, woman, nor child if they come. Half of them are mustees and blacks—the scum of the Spanish Main. Men of Newport, if you love your homes, wake up!"

The tavern was in an uproar. Drink-flushed faces suddenly went gray. Men searched each other's startled eyes. Paine raised his thick hand, obtained silence, and went on: "The watch on Beaver Tail and Brenton's Point will have horses, tomorrow, to carry the news if the French are sighted. Citizens, look to your muskets and powder, and listen for the signal of the drum, at night, from the Parade. If the drum beats, man the wharves, for the French may attack at any time."

The room became a riot of arguing men. But as Paine resumed his seat, there was a commotion at the entrance of the inn, and a stranger, his drawn face smudged with dirt and streaked with sweat, his clothes filthy from hard riding, burst into the room.

"A messenger from Westerly!" shouted a voice. "He brings news!"

Men crowded around the newcomer, whose eyes, red from dust, blinked in the light of the tallow dips. They led him to the Governor's table.

"The French have attacked New London," the youth panted. "I took horse—from Westerly over the Pequot Path—and crossed by the ferries."

"Did they take the town?" demanded Paine, handing the messenger a cup of rum, which he drained at a gulp.

"No!"

"How came you by the news?"

"A horseman brought it from Groton—to Westerly. I was—sent—by Captain James Pendleton," the speaker panted. "The people from the back country rallied—at New London harbor. The French feared to land—and sailed away." The exhausted youth teetered on his feet, his head nodded, and his red-rimmed eyes drooped.

"Which way did they sail?" asked Paine, seizing him by the shoulders and shaking him until his heavy-lidded eyes blinked.

"Five ships—passed Fisher's Island—sailin' east."

The messenger slumped on a stool, dropped his head on his arms sprawled on the table, and fell asleep.

Paine turned to the listening room. "Heard you that?" he cried. "The French headed east! It may be Newport—tomorrow!" He whispered into the ear of the taut-faced Easton, and left the room.

"Captain Paine goes to gather his gun crews," Easton explained to the circle of men surrounding the table. "In the morning he calls for volunteers to fill his roster. There's no time to waste. We're in grave danger."

The realization that the following day might find them defending their homes and families from ruthless sea robbers drove many from the inn to look to their powder and muskets, while others lingered to debate the news.

There were voices outside, and Joseph Brenton stood in the doorway, with Arnold and Sheffield. The three young men were clothed in the blue serge uniforms, piped with red, and the jack boots of the Newport troop, swords slung from baldrics and pistols in holsters on their belts. In place of the clumsy periwig, all three wore campaign wigs, short, curled close to their heads, and tied in the rear, on which were set beaver hats, cocked on one side. Brenton's roving eyes rested on Francis Brinley and his party. Approaching the table at which they sat, Brenton, with amused eyes, surveyed the seated men, who continued their conversation, ignoring his presence.

"Your servant, gentlemen," began Joe, with a low bow. "Good-day to you, Carr Newbury, and to you, Richard, my lad!"

Newbury swung angrily on the speaker. "Who invited you to this table, Joe Brenton?" he rasped.

Brenton grinned down into Newbury's inflamed face. "I invited myself, Mr. Plotter! And I suggest if my presence offends you, you proceed to remove me!"

Crimson with rage, Newbury got to his feet, while Brenton leered at him, hands on hips.

"Name of God! you're overfree with your talk," stormed Newbury. "What mean you by calling me plotter?"

"You know what I mean!" Brenton's eyes glittered.

Newbury returned his stare with unflickering lids. There was nothing in his face to show that the charge had struck home. Carr Newbury possessed both nerve and self-control. But Richard Brinley was narrowly watching his father's face, as if he feared for the outcome of the quarrel.

"Come, Joe," urged Sheffield, laying a restraining hand on Brenton's shoulder. But the aroused Joe pushed his friend away.

"I know not what you mean and care less," said Newbury, his cold blue eyes stabbing at Brenton. "Why do you come here where you're not wanted?"

The horse-faced Sanford rose and turned savagely on Joe. "You're foxed, as usual, and know not what you say—if you ever know," he snarled. "We wish no words with a man in his cups."

Brenton laughed uproariously. "Ah, Sir Pickthanks, the doughty captor of Andros, whose boots you once stooped to lick! Neither do I wish words with you, turncoat! I speak to the gentle plotters, Carr Newbury and Richard, here."

The furious Newbury started to raise his clenched fist, but Francis Brinley rose, pushed him aside, and confronted Brenton. His face was purple with anger. Beads of sweat stippled his forehead under his periwig. "Are you crazed or whittled?" he demanded. "What's all this you hint at?"

"Ask Richard, there, and Carr, the injured innocents who've fair pulled the wool over your eyes, Francis Brinley!"

Brinley turned to Newbury. "What means he?" he demanded.

"No more than he ever means," sneered Newbury. "He's been at the wine again."

Brenton's fist went back, but Arnold and Sheffield had his arm and forced him away. As he left, he flung back over his shoulder, "They're bubbling you, Francis Brinley, that boy of yours and Carr Newbury—bubbling you!"

§43

THAT same day Hugh Jocelyn had worked with William and John Wanton, aiding Israel in rigging the breechings, preventer, side and train tackles of the newly mounted demiculverins on the *Royal Stede*. An able hundred-ton sloop, out of Barbadoes, and pressed by the authorities for the emergency, extra gunports had been cut through her bulwarks for the four nine-pounders Tom Paine had obtained for her and the *Neptune* from the Town Council. In addition to the six five-pound sakers, they already carried four rabinet swivels mounted on iron crutches with shanks let into supports on their poop rails. Not until evening had the hurrying shipwrights finished sinking the last eyebolts in the *Stede's* deck, and the garrulous Israel, happy as a quahog in high water, got the breechings hitched over the cascabels with a cut splice and run through the ringbolts of the heavy carriages and so to the eyebolts of the deck.

Throughout the day seamen had bent sails, spliced ropes, reeved new running rigging, and loaded barrels of powder and racks of iron balls for the guns. Now their work was done. The sloops *Royal Stede* and *Neptune* were ready to give the French marauders odds of three to one and ask no quarter.

As the dusk fell, the sky was slowly smothered by clouds blanketing the harbor with a pitch blackness. Only a few dim candle lanterns were lit on anchored shipping. Hugh and his friends still remained on the wharf, talking of the fight to come.

"You know, from the talk of these Block Island fishermen, Israel has the idea he once met the leader of these French slit-throats," said Hugh.

"Who thinks he he is?" demanded William Wanton.

"'Tis but a guess. Still, the big, swarthy fellow who came ashore and took the cattle and sheep was monstrous like a buccaneer he once knew. It seems he wore rings in his ears, a green silk shirt, flapping breeches, and fancy colored boots they'd never seen the like of. His yellow sash was stuffed with pistols, and he swore mightily while he shook a big sword with a gold hilt."

"He sounds like a pirate out of one of Israel's tales," laughed John Wanton.

"That's just what Israel thinks he is," answered Hugh. "The fishermen said the pirate kept bawling something in French which I make out to be, *ventre du biche*, belly of a fish. He had no left ear and his neck was badly scarred. Israel near burst with laughing when they described him. 'Stab me!' he roared. ''Twas my cutlass that took that ear or I'm a mackerel. I slipped or I'd a split him to the eyes!'"

"You believe it, Hugh?" laughed William Wanton. "Or was Israel bubbling them?"

"He swears he knows the man by the '*ventre du biche*' and his lost ear. His name is Pekar or Picard, and Captain Paine knows him, as well. It seems this Picard lost his ear in a little dispute with Israel at a tavern in Granada."

"What did they quarrel over?" asked John Wanton.

Hugh chuckled. "At first Israel was mum about that. I had to pry it out of him as one opens an oyster. The cause of the dispute seems to have been a lady, or rather, a bird, a Spanish quail, as Israel named her. And after slashing Picard and near beating him to death, Israel got the lady. Trust him for that! He says this Picard is as cold-blooded a rumbullion, as ever scuttled a ship."

"And now he's here to plunder Newport," said William. "Well, he'll know he's in a fight if he tries!"

Blackness thick and impenetrable as sea fog lay over the harbor. And still the three boys sat on the cap log of the wharf and talked of what the next few days might bring.

"Some have already taken their families to Portsmouth," said John, "but 'tis said the Brentons, who are most in danger, refuse to leave Hammersmith."

"Even the girls will not move to their winter house on Thames Street," added William. "They say they'll not leave till they see the pirates' ships in the East Passage."

"You ever see Serena, Hugh?" asked John.

"No."

"Hugh has no eyes for any except the sister of his dear friend, Richard Brinley, since she came to the pillory," laughed William.

Hugh thought of the day on Dexter's Lane and did not reply.

"This young Serena," went on John, "bids fair to be the handsomest maid in all Newport. Tall, with hair like a blackbird; and eyes—"

"You hear that?" broke in William.

"Yes," said Hugh. "Sounded like oars—muffled!"

The three boys stiffened where they sat, and listened. Again the low sound drifted to their ears.

"Men from the fort coming ashore, likely," said John.

"We'd hear them talking on a night like this and their oars would click on the pins, wouldn't they?"

"You don't suppose—" William Wanton suddenly checked himself.

"Don't suppose what?" demanded his brother.

"Don't fancy that boat is from outside?"

Hugh Jocelyn already had his friends by the arms and was pushing them toward the *Royal Stede* lying at the wharf. "Quick!" he said. "Get your muskets, and we'll drop into that skiff, alongside."

"Name of God, we should sound an alarm!" urged John, as they slipped into the skiff and shoved off. "Shouldn't we call the watch? They're on the poop by that lantern, likely asleep."

"No. Suppose we're wrong? Captain Paine would murder us for giving the people such a fright."

Sculled noiselessly by Hugh, the skiff moved out through the wall of murk toward King's Fort, while, stiff on the thwarts, gripping their muskets, the Wantons listened. Halfway across the narrow harbor Hugh let the skiff run while the three strained their ears for a repetition of the measured thump of wrapped oars on tholepins. Shortly, from the direction of Brenton's Cove, drifted the scarcely audible sound fused with the faint splashing of water.

"They must have slipped in between the island and Brenton's Neck," whispered Hugh, unshipping his scull and reaching for his musket. There was no doubt in his mind, now, that Picard had taken advantage of the black night to enter Newport harbor. Was it a scout boat or the leading craft of an attacking party?

"Shall we fire and rouse the town or—wait?" asked William.

"Wait," cautioned Hugh.

"Why?"

"Because if we hold our fire, they may report back to Picard that the town may be easily surprised, as it is unguarded. Then some night, when they come in force through the gap, we'll blow them out of the water."

"Right," agreed William.

The ebb carried the skiff down toward Brenton's Cove while the three boys listened to the approaching beat of muffled oars.

"There seems but one boat," whispered John. "I hear but few oars, and those from one direction."

"It may be a scout boat in the lead, with others following." If that were so, Hugh realized that they were endangering the safety of Newport by waiting to give the alarm. If Picard were attacking in force, the pirates would be swarming over the wharves and into the sleeping town before the people were aware of their danger. The crews on the anchored craft seemed asleep, and the gunners on Goat Island as well. Still Hugh waited, wishing to be sure.

"They're pretty close, Hugh," William warned, at last. "They're doubtless headed for the wharves."

The rhythmic thump of wrapped wood on tholepins grew louder. On a night like this a single boat could fire the wharves, possibly burn the *Royal Stede* and the *Neptune* before aid could be summoned. Hugh now knew the watch on the sloops were asleep. The safety of the armed sloops lay in the boys' hands.

"They've passed us, Hugh, headed inshore," whispered William. "We've got to stop 'em!"

"Right," answered Hugh. "Fire!"

Three spurts of yellow flame stabbed the murk as the muskets roared blindly from the skiff. Curses and frantic orders in French broke from the gloom beyond the boat as the boys hastily rammed home the balls dropped from their mouths into their gun muzzles. Then came the swift beat of oars tearing at the flat water. Lights suddenly winked on the anchored shipping and in houses and taverns. The guns on Goat Island and in the earthwork in front of Arnold's house boomed as the startled gunners, waked from sleep, fired into the harbor. There was a great splash, and the water leaped high into the air, to spray the boys in the boat and rock the skiff.

"Give 'em a volley and get out of here," urged Hugh, "before these crazy gunners at Fort William sink us!"

"Christ's blood, we put fear into those French!" cried William. "Hear them over there? They're headed for the East Passage."

Another ball from the fort plowed the water beyond the skiff. Again the muskets spat orange flame in the direction of the beating oars, and the Wantons rowed for the wharf.

"Look!" cried Hugh, as the oarsmen settled to their work. "The town is up!"

The long roll of a drum fused with the staccato explosion of muskets on the shore. Candle lanterns and lightwood torches bobbed along the wharves. An occasional woman's scream mingled with a bedlam of men's voices.

"They think Picard has come," panted William, as his oars bit at the water. "Guess they'll keep watch after this! Wonder if that boat was going to fire the wharves?"

"No," said Hugh. "I think they sneaked in to learn how easy it would be or hard to attack at night in force. Now Newport has learned its lesson. And so have that damned watch on the sloops. Captain Paine will see to that."

William and John rowed the skiff back to the *Royal Stede*, where candle lanterns lit her poop. The boys climbed aboard to find Captain Paine, with Godfrey of the *Neptune*, talking with a group of excited citizens armed with muskets and cutlasses. Paine eyed Hugh sharply.

"Was it you three who fired from the harbor?" he rasped.

"Ay, sir," answered William, with a grin at Hugh.

Paine's pitted face went savage in the yellow light of a lantern. "You young fools! You scared Newport out of a year's growth. I thought you had sense, William Wanton."

Wanton looked at Hugh, then at his brother. "It's Newport that lacks sense, Captain Paine," he answered with spirit.

A grunt of disgust rumbled in Paine's throat. "What did you fire those muskets for?" he demanded. "The people thought Picard was here."

Hugh stepped forward and dropped the butt of his piece sharply on the deck as he coolly surveyed the circle of scowling faces in the half light from the lanterns. "Captain Paine—he was."

Paine's wide face filled with blood. He thrust his heavy jaw toward Hugh, who coolly returned his scowl. "God's name! You boys heard a fish break or a night heron squawk and you fired and turned the town out of bed with cold shivers and goose pimples up their backs and knees knocking."

Hugh looked down on the shorter man and smiled. "Captain Paine, Picard's boat came into the harbor tonight with wrapped oars. We heard them from the wharf, but your damned watch on the *Royal Stede* was asleep and did not. I can see by their faces now, over there, 'twas they put it into your head that we fired at ghosts!"

There was a low muttering as the men of the watch scowled savagely at Hugh.

"Go on," ordered Paine. "I'll tend to the watch, later."

"We put out in our skiff," continued Hugh, "to learn if it was a single scout boat or an attack in force, before we gave the alarm. When they passed us, we clearly heard the splash of their oars and the thud on the pins. The watch on this sloop were asleep or they'd have heard it. The gunners on Goat Island and the shore were asleep. Every stupid fool in Newport was asleep, and here was Picard sneaking into the harbor and, but for us, he could have burned the town and got clear. We fired twice and they turned and made for the gap and the East Passage. We heard them cursing in French when they passed. Now, believe that or not!"

For an interval Paine's hard eyes searched the candid blue ones of the angry boy. Then he turned to Captain Godfrey. "These lads are not light heads but have more than once proved their mettle. I believe them. We owe them amends. But ten lashes are due every man on duty tonight on Goat Island, the sloops, and ashore! And the Town Council sees they have it or I leave for Conanicut in the morning and this port can go to the devil!"

From Benoni Tosh's bulk, towering behind Paine, came a chuckle. "Ay, Captain. And I'll see to the laying on of them lashes. Were it not for these boys the French could come and go and we none the wiser till we rolls out of our beds with smoke in our noses and the town in flames. Ay, the jail'll be full this night or my name's not Benoni Tosh!"

§44

EARLY the following morning the roll of drums brought the people to the Parade. When a call for volunteers had been made by the Governor, Captain Paine mounted the stocks. Deep lines furrowed his forehead. The hard eyes in his wind-bitten face squinted at the upturned faces.

"We want thirty young men, unmarried," his deep voice boomed. "Stout, mind you; stout and customed to the sea; who won't spill their breakfasts when we roll to the ground swell off Beaver Tail or go green under the gills when we sight the French. Thirty sailors. Who's the first to step up?"

He stopped and rubbed his stubbled chin with a thick hand as his restless eyes surveyed the crowd. "We want thirty seamen, young and able," Paine went on. "And we want forty, seamen or no, who can shoot, and when the French board us will not turn green as apples while their knees knock, but will devil them with cutlass and pike."

"Ay, ay, Tom Paine," called voices, "they are here for your asking!"

"My gun crews are filled," continued Paine, "and most are trained men. Now I want stout lads who'll keep their powder and breeches dry and their blades swingin' when them ringed-eared monkeys come screechin' over the rail. Come on, you Newporters! Come on!"

From a group of sober-faced men wearing steeple-crowned hats and somber clothes, who had gravely watched the proceedings, stepped two youths, tall and well built, with faces tanned by sun and wind. "Sir," said one, "we would join the musketmen. My name is Daniel Campanal."

Cries of approval burst from the spectators. Paine's corkscrew eyes searched the serious face of the speaker. "You are son of the Jew, Mordecai Campanal?"

"I am. My brother and I have sailed thrice—to Surinam, Tobago, and Barbadoes—on our father's sloop. We are able seamen and know the handling of muskets, as you shall see."

Paine nodded at Godfrey. "You and your brother look stout and able," he said to the eager boy. "I have friendship with your father and uncle, good citizens and honest merchants. I take you."

The crowd was pleased at the loyalty of the youngest Jews to their adopted colony. They were sons of Mordecai Campanal, who, with other Jews, had fled the Inquisition in Brazil and had moved on from New York to Newport, where they had become respected merchants and traders. The youths were known as capable seamen on their father's sloop. Thirteen years before, Campanal, Moses Pacheco, and others of their race had bought land for a cemetery—their Beth-Chayin, Abode of Life—at the union of Griffin Street and what, thereafter, was called Jew Street. Now the wanderers who had found sanctuary in the free land of Roger Williams were offering their young men for the defense of the seaport.

Shortly, Paine had the men he required, and the two armed sloops at Long Wharf were alive with activity, the last rope reeved, gun lashings adjusted, and the craft made ready for sea.

All Newport crowded Long Wharf, the neighboring wharves, and anchored craft, to wish Godspeed to the crews of the *Royal Stede* and the *Neptune*. Israel stumped from forecastle to poop and back again, making a last inspection of the lashings of the demiculverins and sakers, his face split by a grin as he patted the black tubes of his beloved guns as a trooper caresses the flanks of his horse.

From the poop, Tom Paine stopped from a last check of the top hamper of his craft to smile at his master gunner. "Name o' God, Israel," he called, "you're as hot to touch a match to the vents of them demiculverins as you were that day in the Mona Passage off Saint Domingue when the pirate took to his boats to board us!"

"And remember you, Captain, how my third shot raked that pirate whaleboat from stem to stern?" laughed Israel. "I can see them lift in the air now, like flyin'-fish with a barracuda after 'em."

On the wharf Seeth Carr stood with the Stantons and Trelawney, waiting to say good-by. The girl made no effort to veil her emotions, her eyes solely on Hugh. Tom Stanton and Trelawney gripped the boy's hand and turned away, leaving him to the two women who loved him.

Seeth choked back a sob and impulsively took Hugh's hand in both of hers. "Goodwife Stanton," she said to the woman at her side, "you—you think me overbold to—wait to say good-by—with you, his mother?"

Content smiled at the girl whose blurred eyes and quivering mouth betrayed her heart. She rested a hand on her arm. "I know, Seeth!" she said kindly. "I know! 'Tis but natural. We both love him."

Hugh's throat tightened as he gazed into the two faces turned to his. Oblivious of the onlookers, he impulsively reached and took both women in the sweep of his arms and kissed them. "Watch for us in a few days," he laughed. "We'll soon drive these French from New England water."

Captain Paine bellowed through his trumpet from the afterdeck of the *Royal Stede*, "Look lively! Tumble aboard, you lads! We're off!"

Seamen cast off the warps from the bollards, while Hugh leaped to the sloop's rail and waved to the two women watching from the wharf. The square topsail and the jib filled with the light breeze, and the bow of the *Royal Stede* swung from the wharf, followed by the *Neptune*, from whose chains the Wanton boys called "Good luck!" to Hugh.

As the two sloops shook out their mainsails and left the harbor, the guns of Fort William on Goat Island and those on the mainland roared a salute. The people on the wharves cheered and waved until the craft came about and, slipping between Goat Island and Brenton's Neck, headed for the East Passage and the sea.

The *Royal Stede* was off the Dumplings, plunging her dolphin striker into the ground swell and lifting it in a shower of spray as she caught the freshening sea breeze, when Joe Brenton suddenly called from the bow: "There they are! That's Serena's white apron! She's signaling us from the big meadow!"

A half-mile distant on Brenton's Neck, beyond the chimneys and roofs buried in the treetops, something white fluttered from a great meadow where sheep grazed. On the poop beside his tillermen, Paine lifted a battered telescope. Then he sent it forward by a seaman to Brenton, while Hugh watched with interest from the waist, where he leaned against the black breech of his nine-pounder.

Brenton raised the glass to his eyes. "There they are!" he said to Arnold and Sheffield, standing in the bow beside the windlass. "Serena promised to wave from the big pasture and there she is, bless her! with little Bess and Desire." He raised his musket and returned the salute of the tiny figures on the far hill.

As he watched, Hugh wondered what this young cousin of Joe Brenton's was like. The Wantons knew her and often spoke of her hair, black as a crow's wing, her vivid coloring, and mischievous eyes. She had a tongue, they said, they could not keep pace with, so quick it was and ready at retort. But the Brentons lived most of the year at Hammersmith, the great house William Brenton had built on the top of Brenton's Neck, and Hugh had never seen her.

Passing Beaver Tail, the two sloops bore away for the blue smear of Block Island on the horizon fifteen miles to the southwest. With a lookout in the crosstrees, Captain Paine put his gun crews through a long loading and firing drill, aided by his master gunner, Israel Brandy, while Leftenant John Cook, second in command, worked forward with the musketeers. Along the rails, boarding pikes were set in racks, together with war hatchets. Barrels of cloth-cased powder cartridges covered with wet duck were lashed near the guns; lockers of iron shot were stowed, with tubs of sand holding linstocks, ready for lighting; and copper-bound rammers, with sheepskin sponges, lashed to stiffened rope on the opposite ends, were placed handy for use. Hugh and his crew drilled in elevating and lowering the breech of the nine-pounder by knocking out or inserting coins with handspikes and crow. With the side tackles they ran the ton-and-a-half piece up to the port for firing, then with the train tackles eased it back into its breeching. Israel, his face wreathed in a perpetual grin, stumped forward and aft, directing the work of the gun crews, most of whom were experienced men. Time and again he bent and squinted along a black tube at an imaginary target, then grimaced, with a satisfied nod of his shaggy head, as the sloop drove on her way.

The last crew finished its practice and Tom Paine called "Belay!" to the swivel men on the poop, who had been loading charges of lead balls and scrap iron and swinging the three-hundred-pound pieces, set on iron crutches let into the rails, to sight at imaginary boat crews of boarders.

"Stab my guts," cried Brandy, "give us another day to shake down this sloop's crew and, burn me, this Picard'll soon be hull down for the Indy Sea!"

"Remember, he outguns us, Israel, and outnumbers us two or three to one," said Paine. "He sails a ship with twenty guns and a big sloop with twelve, the Block Islanders say. And his smaller craft carry minions and swivels, and are packed to the rails with slit-throats. They'll doubtless try to lay us board and board and smother us with numbers!"

The veins in Brandy's thick neck swelled. His hairy chest bulged. "Board us?" he roared, shaking his head as his small eyes burned. The old privateersman reached, drew his heavy cutlass from its scabbard, and cut the air with vicious slashes, the thews of his thick arm swelling and rippling with the effort. "Stab me! Captain, we're as stout a crew as ever cleared Beaver Tail for the open sea! These lads were well picked or I'm a blackfish. Look at 'em. Young and tough, with the devil in their eyes and hell in their hearts."

Paine's eyes twinkled as he looked at his master gunner. "Israel, no odds ever dampened you," he laughed. "I've seen you with your back to the rail and four ringed-eared mustees stabbing at you while you laughed in their faces. But these French are the scum of Tortuga and Saint Domingue and have seen much blood let. Like starving dogs, they're snapping their jaws for the women and booty of Newport."

Followed by the *Neptune*, the *Royal Stede* neared the sand cliffs of Block Island, but the French fleet was nowhere in sight. Paine sent a boat ashore, but got no news. The French had not been seen since they headed west for New London. So the Newport sloops stood off and on through the day waiting, while the officers drilled their men at the guns and in methods of repelling boarders.

Late in the afternoon the lookout in the crosstrees of the *Stede* hailed the poop. "Sail ho! Royals of a ship off the weather bow!"

Paine seized his leather speaking trumpet. "All hands stand by!" he shouted to the sailors in the waist and the musketmen lounging in the forecastle.

A signal flag was run to the top to warn the *Neptune*, a mile astern, and with a brisk south breeze abeam, the sloop headed for the enemy.

Shortly the lookout hailed: "Big sloop with the ship and three smaller craft!"

Israel Brandy filled his barrel chest with a deep breath, hitched his canvas breeches, and spat on his hands. "Gun crews stand by!" he bawled, his mouth working furiously in his eagerness for the fight.

At No. 2, starboard demiculverin just forward of the poop, Hugh watched the excited Brandy stump forward to the six sakers, to check the matches set in the sand tubs ready for lighting, the shot lockers of painted iron balls, the powder barrels protected by wet canvas from sparks. To avoid slipping on his peg, Israel had lashed a piece of sheepskin to the end of the maple support, and he hopped around the gear on the crowded deck with the agility of a boy.

"They've sighted us and changed their course!" called the man in the crosstrees.

Hugh stripped his shirt from his brown back and waved to Brenton, who stood with the musketmen and Chirurgeon Rodman in the bow, listening to the instructions of Leftenant Cook. The crews of the two nine-pounders and the four swivels mounted on the poop watched Paine beside the tillermen, checking the set of his square topsail and the pull of his jib and staysail. Then, with his glass at his eye, he studied the five sails bearing down on them.

The breeze was easing and, with little list to the heavy sloop, there was no need of raising the starboard gun muzzles when Paine took the weather hand of the approaching fleet. So Israel waited, his squinting eyes shifting back and forth from gun to gun as he folded his great arms across his chest and sucked his teeth with satisfaction.

Hugh thought of the fight with Pound in Vineyard Sound and of his fear of betraying his dread of death before the round shot tore the splinters from the rail and turned two of his mates into shapeless lumps of bloody flesh. This fight that Captain Paine was so coolly sailing into would be bloodier than that with Pound. Thirty-two guns the Block Islanders reported the French as carrying on the ship and big sloop alone, many of them twenty-pound culverins. Thirty-two heavy guns against but twenty—nine- and five-pounders—on the *Stede* and *Neptune*. And Picard's smaller sloops carried minions and perhaps sakers. The odds were too great. And yet the thickset privateersman on the poop was watching the enemy as calmly as he might follow the grazing cattle on his Conanicut farm.

Hugh's eyes traversed the expectant faces of gun crews, sailors, and musketmen, and wondered how many of them would be alive when, that night, the sun would be drowned in the sea off Fisher's Island. He glanced at Ward and Potter, of his own crew, two older men with experience on privateers, and at a boy who had never looked death in the face. The boy, red-haired Jeremy Mott, chosen by Israel because of his strength and reputation for courage, had left a weeping mother on Long Wharf. Hugh wondered if she had said a last farewell that morning to the big lad who now grinned back at him from a face stippled with freckles, his blue eyes shining with excitement. And there were Joe Brenton and his friends, with everything to live for. What if they should return minus an arm or a leg, as Israel had—or perhaps not return at all! Hugh thought of himself. What if a splinter should tear through the brown chest he looked down at! What if the arm he doubled should be sheared off by an oak splinter and he were left to grope through life a maimed man! Would Seeth still love him? And how about that madcap Lettice, the thought of whom made his nerves tingle? Seeth would still love him, he was sure, but the other— However, it mattered little, for he would never talk with her again.

§45

HUGH was roused from his thoughts by the order from the poop deck: "Ease her a point!"

Foam breaking from their bows, the French came on, the ship and the big sloop in the lead. It was evident that the enemy were also trying for the weather gauge, but the ship could not point with the sloop and they fell apart, while Paine, followed by Godfrey in the *Neptune*, worked the *Stede* steadily to windward, then bore down on the approaching craft. From the maintop of the ship was broken out a blue ensign powdered with yellow fleur-de-lis; and from the sloop's peak fluttered the French naval flag. At the same moment Paine and Godfrey hoisted the red ensign, with white canton bearing a red cross and a red globe in its first quarter, the colors of New England.

With her guns run out to their ports, the *Royal Stede* drove down on the big sloop. As the two sloops came within range of one another, a cloud of orange smoke broke from the enemy's starboard ports. There was the ripping of canvas aloft as a shot tore through the *Stede's* mainsail. Off her quarter columns of white water lifted into the air where the high-aimed shots of the French sloop plunged into the sea.

Working desperately with crows and handspikes, Paine's starboard gun crews pried the demiculverins and sakers to bear on the enemy. Crouched at the breech of the poop nine-pounder, Brandy sighted at the Frenchman's hull, a gunner standing by with a lighted match.

Israel straightened and stepped away from the breech. "Fire on the lift!" he bellowed to the starboard guns.

Hugh leaped sideways from the coming plunge back of his piece. The matchman touched off the train of powder in the groove of the breech leading to the vent. There was a sputtering of powder along the starboard rail. Red huffs of flame shot from the vents as the demiculverins and sakers roared and, jumping from the deck, bucked back into their breechings, belching clouds of acrid, yellow smoke.

"Stop your vents!" yelled the master gunner. Lead aprons were clapped over the reeking touchholes to confine the escaping gas. "Stab my guts," Israel bawled, "we hulled the bastard! I see the splinters fly!"

There were shouts from their comrades in the bow as the barebacked gun crews strained at the train tackles, eased in the creaking gun carriages, and drove the sheepskin sponges into smoking muzzles. Powder cartridges were inserted with ladles, followed by hemp wadding and iron shot, and the charge rammed home. Hugh drove the spiral priming iron in his hand down through the vent, to break the cloth cylinder of the cartridge. Then, with the side tackles, the crew heaved the ton-and-a-half gun up to its port.

Again the Frenchman vomited a broadside at the sloop bearing down on her. There was a tearing of oak planks as a shot crashed through the *Stede's* rail. A huge oak splinter hurled two men of a saker crew forward against the water cask and foot of the mainmast, shapeless heaps of mangled flesh. Fresh men sprang to take their places. A volley from the Frenchman's swivels raked the *Stede's* bow, but Cook and his men had flattened on the deck and the shower of lead rattled over them, wounding but two, while the answering volley from Cook's musketeers sheered the enemy's poop of men as a scythe cuts grass. Then the *Stede's* starboard guns roared and, sweeping her deck with flying splinters and torn rigging, round shot raked the Frenchman from poop to stem as the *Stede* crossed her stern. Her tiller unmanned, the big sloop swung into the wind to shudder in stays, her guns useless, when the *Neptune* drove past her bow, pounding her with a broadside.

"We got her, lads! We got the rumbullions!" bellowed Brandy, as the topmast of the French sloop swayed, sagged, then with a tangle of shrouds, spars, and stays slumped alongside into the sea.

Paine headed for the ship, which had come about and was attempting to beat to windward to reach the scene of action, while the three small sloops hovered to leeward. Working frantically, the crew of the disabled French sloop chopped at the debris which hung over her rail, as Godfrey jibed and drove past her stern, hammering the impotent craft with another barrage of iron.

"William and John are giving her hell!" Hugh called to the smoke-smeared Brandy, watching the action astern. He turned and waved to Joe Brenton with the musketmen in the bow. "All right, forward?" he shouted.

He felt suddenly sick as his eyes rested for an instant on the canvas-covered heap at the foot of the mast, from which trickles of blood oozed across the deck and into the scuppers. For a moment the fear he had known on the *Mary* gripped him. The thought that he might not measure up in the fight to come sent a cold shiver through his body. Again, as at the fight in Martin's Vineyard Sound, he wondered if splinters would rip and tear his brown body—if an arm or a leg would be the price Hugh Jocelyn would have to pay. He looked curiously at the other men of the gun crew, but their faces, taut with strain, masked their thoughts. Then he glanced at Jeremy Mott, who stood, with his crow, staring in wide-eyed horror at the heap under the smeared canvas from which protruded a bare foot. The boy's face was gray and drawn, and he winked hard, while he bit his lip, drawing the blood. Hugh knew how Jeremy felt. He was suffering the same torture that had been Hugh's before the Pound fight. Violent death and blood were strange to his young eyes. But Jeremy was as sound at heart as a Rhode Island oak. He would measure up when the time came. In thinking of Jeremy, Hugh forgot himself.

A cheer turned the youth's thoughts from the broken shapes under the canvas. He glanced astern and saw a white flag fluttering from the peak of the French sloop. Godfrey had finished her! But there was still plenty of work ahead for the Newport craft. They had no men they could spare for a prize crew, so left the shattered Frenchman astern.

Then Tom Paine's rough voice roared through his leather trumpet as the *Stede* drove down on the ship. "We've made a good start, lads! Look sharp, now! The sloops may lay us board and board when we close with the ship! And they're loaded with men!"

The barefooted gun crews, faces and naked chests stained with powder, cheered. Among the musketeers in the bow, his campaign wig tossed aside, and almost unrecognizable in his cropped black hair, stood Joe Brenton in his linen undershirt, sleeves rolled to his elbows, talking excitedly to the smudged-faced Arnold and Kit Sheffield.

But Hugh had no idea that the old sea fighter, Tom Paine, would attempt to board the ship while those sloops, packed with ringed-eared cutthroats, hovered in the offing.

"Stand by to jibe her!" ordered Paine. The long boom was eased across her deck by three men on the sheet, the jib and staysail thrashed, then filled with the report of muskets, and she pointed to cross the bow of the ship now a half mile distant to leeward, and headed west. "We may not give and take broadsides with this one! She carries culverins! We'll cross her bow and rake her!"

"Ay, ay, sir; that we will!" answered Brandy.

Hugh and his gun crew leaned on the rail, watching the two-hundred-and-fifty-ton three-master on which they held the weather gauge. He counted her ten gun ports with the black muzzles thrust through them. Those were eighteen- or twenty-pound culverins, while the largest guns Paine and Godfrey carried were nines. Those big guns were capable of smashing through the oak bulwarks of the *Stede* and crippling her with a broadside. A ten-gun broadside against a five! One-hundred-and-twenty pounds of iron against a mere thirty-three from the *Stede's* demiculverins and sakers! True, as Paine said, they could not swap broadsides with the Frenchman. How, then, did he dare close with the ship?

As the craft approached one another, Hugh made out black figures in her tops—musketeers set to snipe at the enemy's decks. To leeward hovered the three sloops, no doubt carrying minions and sakers and plenty of men to swarm over the *Stede's* rail with pike and cutlass when the chance offered. According to Tom Paine they were outnumbered three to one. And yet, up there on the afterdeck stood the square-built privateersman, watching the ship through his battered telescope and joking with Israel as if the *Royal Stede* were working up the East Passage to her anchorage in the harbor instead of sailing into the jaws of what would soon be a hell of flying iron shot, lead and more deadly splinters.

Not that he would not work his nine-pounder until she was too hot to load, or that he feared this ringed-eared scum so long as there was room to swing a cutlass or chop with a war hatchet. But the chances against them seemed too great to the youth, who had never seen Newport privateersmen give odds of three to one and win. Yet he took heart when he saw the peg-legged Israel pointing with a knotty paw at the ship's top hamper and chuckling into the ear of the leather-faced captain, who grinned back at him. Hugh wondered what these two found to laugh at in those tops filled with musketmen and those black muzzles at the open ports. Then Brandy stumped down from the poop and stood at Hugh's shoulder.

"What think you, young one, of that school of buckeroos packin' her foc's'le like herrin' choke a river?" demanded Israel, clapping Hugh's bronzed back. "I says to Tom Paine, the more of 'em they be, the more we'll hit!"

"I can't yet make out the rings in their ears, Israel," laughed Hugh, whose heart was pounding madly against his ribs, "but I can see the mustees' dirty brown faces and the red and yellow kerchiefs on their heads, and I itch to send a nine-pound ball into them."

Israel nodded, smacking his thick lips in anticipation of the fight as if he were about to sit down to a toothsome dinner. "'Tis more than likely that the sloops in her wake plan to lay us board and board when the ship has softened us with her big guns. They're doubtless thick as flies on their decks, waitin' to finish us with the cold steel. But Tom Paine'll show 'em a trick or two."

Young Jeremy Mott's blue eyes bulged and his spine felt cold as he listened. The boy wondered whether the others noticed the goose pimples on his bare back, and if they were signs of cowardice; and his jumping nerves were a warning that he would not play the man.

"Do you favor the short chop or the full slash with the steel?" the boy asked Brandy, simulating a cool assurance belied by his white face and hammering heart.

Israel's twinkling eyes measured the big-shouldered lad with the freckled face and arms, whose eyes were dark with excitement. There was power in that young body and plenty of spirit, but the boy was naturally nervous before his first fight. "That rests on how many you face, lad. In a jam, the short chop and jab with the point. But with sea room, the wide slash with your weight behind it brings them to the deck. In your left hand a war hatchet, well handled, stops a cut on your larboard beam and guards one when off balance from a missed blow."

Israel winked at Hugh. "Jeremy, here, has yet to smell blood; but, stab my vitals, he'll smell it today!"

"All hands stand by!"

Tom Paine's voice sent Israel scrambling back to the poop. The crews leaped to their guns and the seamen to their stations. In the bow the musketmen crouched behind the starboard rail. The *Stede* was holding a course which would take her across the ship's bows. Hugh gripped the rail beside the gun port as he watched, his heart thundering in his throat. "Name o' God," he cried to Jeremy Mott, "we can't cross her bows! She'll sink us! And if we bear off now, we'll take her broadside!"

"It looks bad to me," muttered Jeremy, his underlip twitching as his fearful eyes watched the forefoot of the oncoming ship pushing aside a mound of foam.

Hugh glanced at the square figure on the poop beside the tillermen. Neither doubt nor hesitation lay on the bold features of Tom Paine as his squinting eyes shifted from the ship to his square topsail, the leech of his bellying mainsail, his straining jib, then back to the ship whose course and that of the sloop would shortly meet.

"Tom Paine must know what he's doing," thought Hugh. "But we're set to take a broadside if they don't sink us!"

The *Stede's* crew instinctively stiffened where they stood, waiting, gripped in the tension of fear. Beside Hugh, Ward, Potter, and Jeremy held handspike, linstock, and rammer, the muscles of their faces, arms, and bare torsos rigid. The vessels were within range when the command was roared from the leather trumpet on the poop.

"Stand by to jibe her!"

Seamen sprang to the jib, staysail, and main sheets as the strain of waiting was broken. The tillermen threw the long stick over. As mainsail and jibs thrashed across deck and bowsprit and filled, and the sloop's bow swung to the bite of the rudder, orange smoke burst from the Frenchman's ports and a broadside of round shot swept past and plunged into the sea close on the *Stede's* larboard quarter.

"Name o' God," gasped Hugh, gaping into his mates' faces, "he tricked 'em! Before they sensed what he was about, the old fox drew their fire and bubbled 'em with the jibe! 'Twas a close deal!"

"Larboard guns! Fire on the lift!" roared Brandy. As the sloop crossed the ship's counter, red huffs leaped from the vents, and the larboard battery belched flame and smoke. A great tear opened in the ship's spanker. Flying splinters from her afterrail swept the poop of men as the iron shot smashed through gear and bulwarks. From the *Stede's* bow roared the muskets. Like bags, two sprawling shapes fell from the ship's mizzen top. Again, with spare muskets, the Newport goose hunters poured a hail of lead into the ship's crowded deck as the sloop drove on.

A wild cheer rose from the *Stede's* crew. Israel Brandy was frantic with joy. "Stab me, Captain," he roared at the taut-faced Paine watching astern the Frenchman he had outmaneuvered, "'twas the same trick which you foxed the Spaniard with that day in the Windward Passage! Burn me, 'twas neat!"

While his larboard gun crews were loading, Paine jibed his sloop again and followed the slower sailing ship. A mile to leeward Picard's three sloops stood off, holding a parallel course. Bearing down from windward drove Godfrey in the *Neptune*, after giving the crippled French craft a last broadside. Paine ran a signal flag to his top, and Godfrey changed his course to cross the ship's bow.

Hugh's crew fretted as they stood at their gun. "The larboard guns are having it all!" Jeremy protested. "We outfoot the ship! Why don't we stand to windward and give him a volley on his quarter?"

"Wait," said Hugh. "We have three sloops filled with men to leeward. Our time will come."

The *Stede* gradually overhauled the ship and, hauling her wind, held a course out of range on her weather beam, while the *Neptune* drove on to cross the Frenchman's bow. Not daring to exchange broadsides with the ship's heavy guns, Paine waited for his ally before closing on the enemy's stern. On came the *Neptune* before the wind. Shortly Godfrey would be in position to rake the ship without taking a shot in return. On the Frenchman's weather beam Paine angled in just out of effective range.

All eyes in the *Stede* were on the *Neptune* as she drove close in across the ship's course, when suddenly the Frenchman's bow swung into the wind. Like monkeys, men swarmed up her rigging. Her yards were braced to go about. And as Godfrey crossed her bow and his guns roared, the swinging ship's starboard battery bore on him, and a broadside smashed into the sloop too close to sheer off.

Hugh's face went gray. A sudden nausea gripped his stomach as he saw the *Neptune* shudder from forefoot to counter with the weight of iron that crashed into her hull. He thought of William and John in a hail of shot and splinters. He glanced at the poop where Paine and Israel stood at the rail, faces tight with apprehension.

Turning from the rail, Paine raised his trumpet. "Stand by, larboard guns!" he roared.

The main and jib sheets were eased as the tillermen swung on the long stick and the sloop plunged down wind. With handspikes and crows, the larboard crews pried the rear wheels of the carriages so the sakers would bear on the ship's stern, and the gunners sighted along the black tubes. Israel hopped across the poop, thrust the gunner of the larboard poop demiculverin aside and sighted. Then, as the sloop crossed the counter of the ship in stays, Brandy roared, "Fire!"

The priming powder sputtered at the vents of the larboard battery. There was a roar along the sloop's rail as five guns at a distance of fifty yards vomited smoke and flame, the vents spat red huffs into the air, and the cannon jumped from the deck and bucked back into their breechings. The *Stede* heeled from the kick of her guns as the round shot tore through the ship's mizzen rigging and splintered the bulwarks, where men worked to brace the yards, raking her from stern to stem. A volley of lead from the muskets on the *Stede's* bow spattered the ship's crowded decks and was answered by the French. Picking up spare guns, the goose hunters on the Newport sloop raked the ship's mizzen top, from which men fell like ducks riddled with bird shot.

Paine sheered off, avoiding the starboard guns of the ship, and passed out of range, heading down wind for the crippled *Neptune*, whose gaff sagged and whose jib and staysail were fluttering ribbons.

As they drove to leeward, Jeremy seized Hugh by the shoulder. "Look! The sloops! They're making for the *Neptune*!"

The three French sloops, which had held off, were now headed for the drifting *Neptune*, whose crew were feverishly working on her rigging.

"They aim to board her," said Hugh. "Thank God we can give them iron for iron!"

"But the ship will soon be down on us! What then?"

Hugh went cold at the thought. Unable to maneuver, the *Neptune* was doomed when the ship joined the battle. "We'll fight her so long as we can work a gun," he muttered.

On the poop Israel was talking excitedly with Paine as the *Stede* drove to leeward in aid of the *Neptune*. Paine lowered his brass-bound telescope. "Godfrey's in a bad mess," he said. "He'll need to work fast to reeve new peak halyards and set a stays'il so he can handle her. The sloops aim to board him, and they carry plenty men!"

"Did he lose any guns?" asked Brandy. "That broadside fair plowed into his guts!"

Paine nodded grimly. "Her starboard bulwarks are all smashed in. I doubt if he can work a gun. The French are pointed to get the weather of him and board on his smashed beam."

Brandy spat on his hands and hitched his canvas drawers. "We'll be in that fight, Captain!" he growled, and returned to his gun.

While the *Neptune's* crew worked desperately to repair her damaged gear and rigging, the French sloops rapidly closed on her. It was clear that the three enemy craft meant to board her, and counted on the ship to follow the threatening *Stede* and put her out of action before she could smash them with her heavier guns. Tom Paine's gray eyes glittered in his pitted face as he raced the privateers for the helpless sloop.

"Stripped of his fores'ils, Godfrey can't bring his larboard guns to bear," he said to Israel, with a shake of the head. "With his starboard guns smashed, they'll run past, give him all they've got, then come about and lay him board and board."

Israel's eyes flamed with anger as he thrust his face close to Paine's. "And what will the *Stede* be at?" he demanded.

Paine smiled. He glanced at his bellying mainsail and bulging jibs as the *Stede* drove on before the wind. "They may think we'll hold our fire to save hitting the *Neptune* and durst not board with the ship soon on our heels."

With a snort, Brandy reached and clamped on Paine's arm with iron fingers. "Tom Paine," he cried, "the safety of Newport hangs on the next turn of the glass. The wind already sets east'ard. We'll soon be in a soupy fog. She's drivin' in now. Look at her come! Now what do we do?"

Paine's cold, agate eyes coolly met the fierce stare of his master gunner. "Israel, we'll pound them sloops to kindlin'! Then we'll board, and chop them ringed-eared scum to fish bait! If the ship reaches us, we'll board her, fog or no fog!"

"Ah!" Brandy's face stretched with a maniacal grin. "You be a captain after my own heart! But, stab my guts, them slit-throats don't know this, nor do you! Tom Paine, when we passed that ship, I put a nine-pound ball into her sternpost. Her rudder's jammed. She can't follow us. Christ's blood, she can't reach us!"

Amazement lifted Paine's thick brows and his jaw sagged as he stared at his master gunner. He raised his glass and studied the laboring ship, in irons, to windward, then turned to Brandy. "Name o' God, Israel, you're right!" His thick hand clapped a resounding smack on

Brandy's bare back. "Them rumbullions on the sloops don't know the ship's rudder's jammed! Now we give 'em red hell!'"

§46

THE two large sloops of the enemy were closing on the starboard beam of the *Neptune*, whose crew fought desperately with the sweeps to head her around to bring her larboard battery to bear. Time was too short to reeve halyards and set a new jib, and Godfrey was driving his men at the long oars. But as the *Stede* drove down wind to Godfrey's aid, it became clear to Paine that the swinging *Neptune* would be raked by the French sloops as they crossed her bow. The long sweeps tore the water as Godfrey's men battled to swing their vessel, but the leading French sloop crossed her bow and raked her with her minions, while Godfrey's poop was masked in a cloud of smoke as his swivels and muskets replied.

With sober faces Paine and Brandy watched as the broadside hammered the swinging *Neptune's* hull.

"Burn me!" cried Israel, his mouth twisting in a grimace. "She took it hard, then. Pull, you bastards! Pull!"

Godfrey's sweepmen strained desperately to head their craft over before the following sloop could hammer them and pass without a reply from the *Neptune's* larboard guns. The *Stede* was rapidly bearing down on the leading French sloop, which luffed to bring her loaded larboard guns to bear on the approaching enemy. But the Frenchman moved too late. Paine was on her like a gull on a herring, and struck.

"Stand by, starboard guns!" he roared. Crossing her bow, he shot between the swinging Frenchman and the *Neptune*, and his starboard battery spat flame and smoke as he raked her. Holding his course, he headed for the second French sloop, and before her starboard guns bore on the *Neptune* Paine hauled his wind, swung across her bow, and gave her a broadside from his larboard battery, while the goose hunters in his bow poured a rain of lead on her decks. Then, before the Frenchman reached the *Neptune*, Godfrey's sweepmen had her head around, the wind caught her bow, and her larboard guns covered the approaching sloop. Simultaneously two broadsides roared as the Frenchman passed the *Neptune*, and yellow smoke smothered the two sloops.

"Good for Godfrey!" cried Paine. "He gave more'n he got that time! Mark the Frenchman's afterrail and mains'il!"

"She's cut up like a lobsterman cuts bait," laughed Israel. "Now, which one, Captain?"

The second sloop drove on. "Ah!" said Paine. "She aims to board Godfrey on his smashed beam, trustin' we'll follow the other to leeward and dodge the ship."

"What do we do?" demanded Israel, his grinning gargoyle of a face betraying that he already knew Paine's reply.

"Master gunner," growled the other, thrusting his pock-marked face with its squinting eyes and outthrust jaw into Israel's scarred features, "we crowd hard in her wake, give her a broadside as we pass, jibe, and lay her board and board 'twixt us and Godfrey when she grapples him. And God knows the rest!"

Brandy's face lit with an unholy joy. "Stab my guts, Tom Paine, you be a fightin' man!"

"Stand by to tack!" roared Paine, to his waiting crew. The tillermen put the rudder hard down, and with a flapping of jib and staysail the sloop swung, and the mainsail filled on the new course as the *Stede* drove after the French sloop.

Paine's crew were alive with excitement. Her guns reloaded, the crews hung over the rail watching the chase.

"Will the Frenchman run? She rocked on her keel when we gave her that broadside, and the *Neptune* fair hulled her!" said Hugh to Jeremy Mott.

The excited boy was gripping his crow until the muscles bulged in his thick forearms. He turned questioning eyes to Hugh. "Were you scared when we took that first broadside? I closed my eyes and hunched when I saw them fire. I was that cold in my bowels! Poor Clark and Sisson! I near puked, I was that sick to see what bloody messes the splinter left them."

"We were all scared, Jeremy," said Hugh. "Don't think we were not! But you'll grow used to it. Don't think of the blood! Just think what we're fighting for. Think of your mother and sister if Picard takes Newport. That should steady you and make you fight. Think what it means if we lose! We can't lose, lad! We dare not lose!"

Young Mott's round face was gray with tension. "I—I can't help but think of the blood and the maimed men, Hugh. I'll fight— Name o' God! I'll not play the coward—but I'm awful scared—scared of being cut to pieces by a splinter and bleedin' to death."

"You're not scared any more than I am, Jeremy. We all feel the same way! But hadn't you rather be here, today, in this fight for Newport, with the chance of being hurt, than to die in bed of old age or smallpox?"

A light suddenly glowed in Jeremy's eyes and the color returned to his face as his jaw shut. He rested a hand on Hugh's arm and said, "Name o' God, Hugh, you've talked the goose pimples right off my back!"

Hugh slapped Jeremy on his heavy shoulders. "Just think of what you're going to do with that cutlass of yours for Newport, Jeremy, when we lay board and board with that sloop!"

True to Paine's guess, the French sloop paid off, and as the *Stede* passed her, boldly exchanged broadsides.

But the Frenchman's gunnery was poor and the iron shot plunged high and astern, while the *Stede's* larboard guns hulled her. As they passed, Hugh could see the swart faces of the men on her decks. He looked at the ship in the distance curiously, maneuvering in circles, and wondered what Paine meant to do.

There was a voice at his shoulder, and he gazed into Israel's grinning mask. Over the gunner's naked right shoulder hung the leather baldric of his cutlass. "Sling your cutlass, lad, and stick that hatchet through your belt. If you leave it loose, there's no knowing who may grab it when we lay board and board with 'em."

"She's going to board the *Neptune* on her smashed beam," said Hugh, glancing at the French sloop. "She'll rake them. They can't head her around in time!" He thought of William and John and the others desperately toiling at the sweeps. There would not be time to swing the *Neptune* before the Frenchman was on them.

"Ay, she'll board 'em and she's full of men—but we'll be hard on her heels!"

"Stand by to jibe!" shouted Paine, and the *Stede* plunged in pursuit of the French sloop, now bearing down on the drifting *Neptune*.

"But the ship'll be hammering us soon, Israel, grappled on to that Frenchman! She'll smash us to splinters, and what'll happen to Newport?" cried Hugh, chilled to the bone with the thought.

Brandy clapped the boy's heavy shoulders, while Jeremy looked on with fearful eyes. "Pick up your cutlasses, lads, and spit on your hands," laughed the gunner. "We're goin' over the rail of that sloop, and in the turn of a half-hour glass we'll have Godfrey out of trouble." Israel jerked his thumb toward the distant ship. "I put a shot into the sternpost of that craft. Mark how she yaws and swings, like a swordfish with a lance in his lungs."

The two boys looked. "Come on, Jeremy," cried Hugh. "Sling on your pig-sticker, lad! There's hot work ahead, but no fear now of a broadside of eighteen-pounders in our backs when we swarm over her rail."

Evidently counting on the swift aid of the ship, the French sloop boldly bore down on the smashed starboard beam of the *Neptune*, fired her minions, passed on, and came about to drive in and heave her grappling irons. But the *Stede* was the faster sailer, and her broadside shook the sloop to her keel, as Paine passed within a ship's length, the muskets blazing from his bow. When the smoke, which made his eyes smart and tasted bitter in his mouth, cleared, Hugh looked back to see the decks of the Frenchman crowded with swart-faced men, heads wound with red and yellow kerchiefs, brandishing their cutlasses as they cursed and grimaced.

"Christ's blood," bawled Brandy, from the poop, "the scum of Tortuga! Look on 'em! Brown, yeller, and white, puked up by Guadeloupe, Martinique and Saint Domingue! Beauties, ain't they?"

As Paine brought the *Stede* about, the Frenchman angled in and drove the end of her jib boom into the fore rigging of the drifting *Neptune*, and the sloops swung together, a yellow cloud of musket smoke blanketing their bows. Paine ran his sloop close to the locked craft. "Stand by! Larboard guns!" he bellowed. "Shoot low for her ports!"

The *Stede's* broadside smashed into the Frenchman's ports and bulwarks as she passed, and Hugh heard the shrieks of stricken gunners, mangled by splinters and iron shot. Paine went on, tacked, and ran alongside, while his musketmen poured a volley into the backs of the pack on the Frenchman's bow fighting to board the *Neptune*. Grapplings were thrown and the two sloops lay locked.

With a bull-like bellow, Israel Brandy stood balanced on his good foot on the *Stede's* rail, gripping a backstay with his left hand, his cutlass in his right. "Come on, lads! Give the dogfish the steel!" he roared, as a wave of French wheeled from the rush to board the *Neptune* to the defense of their own deck. Joe Brenton and the musketeers poured a volley into the mass; then, like tide over a reef, Brandy and his men fought their way over the Frenchman's rail. Slashing at red and yellow heads, chopping with war hatchets and thrusting with pikes, the Newport men drove the French toward their bow. But the white and half-caste rabble fought savagely. On their poop men worked desperately to swing two murderers to bear on the *Stede's* deck. Seeing the danger to his mates, Brandy, with Hugh and Jeremy, wheeled and made a rush for the afterdeck. A huge mulatto swung at Israel, engaged with two others, to have his cutlass caught on Jeremy's guard. Like a flash the lad recovered and drove his point through the half-breed's throat.

"Stout lad, Jeremy!" panted Brandy, slashing the skull of a Frenchman with a chop of his blade. Then, with a leap to the poop, they were on the gunners about to spray the *Stede's* deck with a hail of bullets. Here Israel's long schooling of Hugh in cutlass play proved itself. For a time there was a vicious milling around the swivels, but the three Newporters, fighting shoulder to shoulder, at last cleared the poop of standing men. They turned to join their mates forward but were faced by a French officer with six ruffians who were scrambling through the poop rail to head them off.

"Gimme room!" roared Brandy, thrusting Hugh to one side. "I want sea room when they rush!" Gripping his ax in his left hand, with his right Israel waved his heavy cutlass in a wide arc before him, grimacing like a gargoyle. At the sight of his powerful body, smeared with blood and powder stain, and his scarred face horrible in its grin, with two brawny youths flanking him, the attackers hesitated. Then a pistol exploded, and Hugh felt a sharp sting in his temple. For an instant he thought he would fall, but he shook the momentary dizziness from his brain, reeled back to Brandy's side, and the fight was on.

"All right, lad?" cried Israel.

"All right!" was the answer.

The maddened Brandy and the two beside him cut and chopped and slashed at the yelling rabble who charged them. Time and again Israel's peg leg slipped in blood and he went to his good knee, to be jerked to his feet by one of the lads beside him. Time and again the French rushed to overwhelm the three Newport men, only to be driven back by sweep of cutlass or chop of war hatchet. At last but three remained on their feet and, shaking his shaggy head, the battle-drunk Israel roared, "Clear the poop of the slimy scum!"

Brandy lunged at a huge Frenchman, but his peg leg slipped in a pool of blood and he sprawled on his chest. The other's cutlass was whipped back for a chop at the helpless man at his feet when an outthrust hand gripped his ankle, jerked him off balance, and the point of Israel's blade drove up through his stomach. With a scream he doubled forward, gripping the steel which impaled him as a lance stabs a swordfish, to have his skull bludgeoned by Hugh's ax. The latter dropped his hatchet, jerked Israel to his feet with his left hand, recovered the ax, and the cutlasses of the three cleared the poop. The retreating French officer leaped to a dead man sprawled on the deck, tore a pistol from his sash, and wheeled on Israel, who was nearest. As the Frenchman leveled the cocked flintlock, Hugh yelled a warning. Then his left hand whipped back and his ax whirled end over end, to bite into the face of the pirate. The pistol exploded, burying a bullet in the deck as Brandy's cutlass crashed on the reeling Frenchman's skull.

"Handy work, lad!" panted Israel, as they ran forward to join their comrades.

The *Neptune's* crew were battling the French on their own bow when the *Stede's* boarding party, swarming over the bowsprit, took the enemy in the rear. Back and forth the fighting raged among groups of men when, suddenly, the hoarse voice of Tom Paine boomed above the clamor: "The Frenchman's sinkin'! *Stede's* men stand by aboard the sloop!"

The fog had shut in until those who looked across the gray smother to the *Stede's* poop could barely make out the square figure of Tom

Paine standing with his trumpet. Cries for help rose from the wounded on the French sloop, whose rails were settling below the bulwarks of the craft between which she lay. Swallowed somewhere in the mist, her companion sloops had deserted her.

"The Frenchman's goin' down!" cried Leftenant Cook, from the *Neptune's* bow. "All hands stand by on the *Stede*!"

The disheartened crew, cut off from retreat, dropped their arms. Driving their prisoners before them, the *Stede's* men boarded their craft, while the *Neptune's* crew seized sweeps and fought to push their bow clear of the jib boom of the sinking Frenchman.

Across the doomed sloop Tom Paine called through his trumpet, "Ahoy, the *Neptune*!"

A voice answered through the mist, "Ay, ay, Captain Paine!"

"Are you hurt below water, Godfrey? Do you need help?"

"No!"

"Can you get clear of her?"

"Yes!"

"Make for Sandy Point, Block Island. They'll be on our backs tomorrow. This fight's just started."

Through the white drift floated the voice of William Wanton. "Hugh, are you all right?"

"Yes! How about you and John?" answered Hugh.

"Nothing but scratches! See you tomorrow!"

With their sweeps, the *Stede's* crew pushed off from the wallowing French sloop. Through the mist they could see the *Neptune's* bow swinging clear of the Frenchman's jib boom. As they were swallowed in the fog, they sent back a cheer.

With the aid of a fair tide and the light air, the *Stede* groped her way southeast toward Block Island. In Paine's cabin Chirurgeon Rodman and an assistant, sleeves rolled to their elbows, were working on the wounded. The crease from the bullet across Hugh's temple had bled so profusely that his face and chest were streaked with blood. Back on the *Steed*, Brandy solicitously pushed back the boy's thick hair and examined the furrow.

"Stab my vitals, lad, by the blood on you I'd think you were all chopped up had I not seen you laying about you like a wild man!"

"'Tis but a scratch; yet it colored me well!" laughed Hugh.

Brandy thrust out a big hand and took Hugh's. "Had it not been for your helpin' hand when my peg played me false, and that ax, they'd have reached me! There be few men walkin' a deck with the strength of arm to parry that slash of yours with your weight behind it. You pleasured me, lad, today."

Hugh was busy examining the hairy torso of his friend, smeared with blood and grime. "You took two cuts on your shoulders, Israel," he said.

"Ay," grunted the other. "They were spent blows and of no account."

"But we must have them dressed when the badly hurt men are taken care of."

"What fevers me is not the scratches," grunted the privateersman, "but this waitin' for Tom Paine to tap that cask of rum down below. My throat is dry as a hung pirate!"

When the seriously wounded had been cared for, Hugh and Israel reported in Paine's cabin to the surgeon. As they entered, Hugh saw a still shape lying on a bunk, with Joe Brenton and Kit Sheffield sitting beside it. The unconscious man was swathed in bandages. Hugh touched Brenton's shoulder. The latter's worried eyes met his as Brenton slowly nodded.

"Yes, it's John," he said. "Left arm shattered. Had to be amputated. We hope, Hugh," Brenton muttered. "We hope! That's all we can do."

Nodding to the silent Sheffield, Hugh turned away. So it had come to the merry Arnold to face life, if he lived, a maimed man. Hugh glanced down at his own body. He had come through what might well have been mutilation or death, with only a bullet sear across his temple and scratches on shoulders and legs. God had been good to him! He thought of Content and Tom back at Newport—poor Content, waiting with fear in her heart—and was glad. For the moment he had forgotten. There was another day coming. Tomorrow he might not be so lucky. Tomorrow night he might lie, as John Arnold now lay, with a mutilated body; or, mayhap, a round shot might leave him a bloody mess on the deck.

Hugh heard his name called, and Chirurgeon Rodman washed the gash across his temple and put a bandage on his head. Then he went to the rail beside his gun and bathed himself with buckets of salt water from overside.

Cleaned up, and refreshed with a supper of cold salt beef and ship's bread, washed down with rum, Hugh, Brandy, and Jeremy stood beside Hugh's gun carriage as the *Stede* slipped through the fog.

"Well, Jeremy, did your knees knock together as you said they would when we went over that rail thick with ringed-ears?" teased Hugh.

The boy's freckled face went sober. "My heart was fair leapin' out of my mouth," he replied, "until—until I saw poor Jack Albro take a slash clean to his eyes. Then I was too mad to have fear."

"Good lad, Jeremy!" Hugh placed his hand on the other's shoulder. "You laid on with that cutlass like an old hand. I'm proud of you, lad."

"Proud of me? You think me not a coward—then?"

Brandy snorted as he clapped Jeremy's broad back. "Lad, there ain't a cowardly drop in your veins. Your father shall hear from me what a stout cutlass man you be!"

Jeremy's blue eyes were sober as he swallowed hard. "It pleasures me much what you two say."

In an hour Paine sent men forward to start heaving the greased lead, for he knew he was close in on the Block Island beach, and familiar with the nature of the bottom, he could thus estimate his position. With barely sail enough for steerage way, he groped through the soup-thick fog while the leadsman called the depth and reported on the sand or mud which adhered to the lead. At last the water suddenly shoaled, and the *Stede* worked around Sandy Point, with its shallow east shore, and anchored, waiting for daylight and the arrival of the *Neptune*.

§47

Day broke clear on a flat sea where, close to the east beach of Sandy Point, rode the anchored *Stede* and *Neptune*. On the arrival of the crippled sloop, Tom Paine and Godfrey had laid their plans for the coming day. With the loss of but one of their fleet, the French were sure to renew the attack. The big sloop that had struck her colors, although sheared of her topmast, could doubtless be handled under patched jib and mainsail to aid the ship with her heavy guns when the latter's rudder was cleared and working. And the two captains had no doubt that the French could clear their rudder. The *Neptune*, with a makeshift rig and three guns smashed, could not be counted on in a running fight. Over their rum the two captains took counsel.

"Captain," said Paine, "'tis certain as death they'll attack tomorrow, and 'tis equally certain they'll lay you board and board if you're under sail, with the *Neptune* clumsy and slow on her rudder and shy three sakers in her starboard battery."

"That is so," agreed Godfrey.

Paine blew a cloud of smoke sucked from his long-stemmed pipe into the air, rubbed his stubbled chin with thick fingers, and said, "What I suggest may appear fantastical to you, but I believe it will work."

"What is it?" demanded the leather-faced Godfrey.

"I advise we anchor, stern to stern, close to the beach, cut ports, and shift our guns so all bear seaward."

Godfrey's face was blank with amazement. His heavy jaw sagged as he stared at his friend in an attempt to digest the proposed plan. Then he demurred, "He's bound to board us, anchored."

"With her draft, the ship durst not. The sloops may try it, but the odds will then be fair. Anchored close in shore as we'll be, they can't surround us but will have to pass by to seaward and take the fire from all our guns."

Godfrey's eyes closed as he considered Paine's plan from diverse angles. "Can we cut ports, sink ringbolts in the deck, and shift and rig our guns before Picard attacks?"

Paine nodded. "He's got his rudder to free if he can, and that smashed sloop's gear and running rigging to refit and reeve, and he'll need light to do it, as we will. We'll have time."

Godfrey smashed his fist on the slab table at which they sat. "Tom Paine," he exclaimed, "I believe 'tis our only hope!"

"From the prisoners we took 'tis clear what a rabble of West Indy slit-throats he carries—the scum of the French islands. If that crew of pirates once land in Newport, God help our families! They'll fire the town even if they're beaten off!"

Godfrey agreed.

"Good! There's light enough to start work, now. We'll anchor in-shore, and put all hands to shifting them guns and the ballast to balance their weight."

As dawn broke on the flat sea, anchored stern to stern in line, in eight feet of water, the two sloops were alive with busy men. Between the starboard guns of the *Stede*, carpenters were cutting gun ports for the larboard battery and sinking eyebolts in the deck. Seamen shifted ballast in the hold to balance the weight of the guns when moved and prevent a list. Gun crews rigged blocks and tackles with which to ease the ton-and-a-half demiculverins and sixteen-hundred-pound sakers across the decks and into place at the ports. Israel Brandy and a crew of men swung the forward saker of the starboard battery into the *Stede's* bow and cut a port through the bulwarks beneath the bowsprit stays, sank eyebolts in the deck, rigged her breeching over the pompillion and adjusted her side and train tackles.

"What's this for, Israel?" asked the sweating Jeremy. "The French will pass to seaward and this gun may not bear on them."

Brandy looked at Hugh, who was assisting, and his left eye slowly closed. "Wait, my lad," he said. "It may be that this gun'll bear on many of 'em before the day's over."

Because of the three smashed sakers of her starboard battery, the *Neptune* lay stern to stern with the *Stede*, her larboard guns bearing seaward, with the addition of the two starboard demiculverins. The guns shifted to their new ports and lashed in their tackles, the powder barrels and shot lockers made handy, with the unlit matches in their sand tubs, Tom Paine and Godfrey waited for the French craft lying a mile to the west. Late in the morning, Paine, who was watching them through his telescope, suddenly announced: "Here they come!"

The lounging musketmen, gunners and seamen on the *Stede* were on their feet. Led by the ship, the French fleet was heading southeast for the two sloops, anchored, with their sails brailed, off Sandy Point. The master gunner stumped along the starboard rail for a last inspection of the rigging of the shifted guns.

"Mark you," he warned each gun captain as he passed, "if she passes close, shoot for her ports to smash her guns! Keep your shots low!"

Standing beside their nine-pounder, Jeremy and Hugh, with Ward and Potter, watched the French approaching slowly under the light breeze. There was no doubt of himself on young Mott's face today; only a fierce eagerness in the blue eyes.

"How do you feel, Jeremy?" asked Hugh, resting a hand on the boy's freckled shoulder, for they were barefooted and stripped to the waist.

A slow wave of blood spread over Mott's round face as he grinned. "I'm fevered with the thought of it, and my heart is fair beatin' like a drum, but my back is free of goose pimples, if that's what you mean."

"After yesterday, Jeremy, have no doubt of yourself. No one of us but has fear of splinters and round shot."

On came the French, the big sloop following the ship, the remaining two in their wake. But the watchers on the *Stede* laughed as they noted the sloop's crudely patched mainsail and makeshift rigging.

"She took a rare beating, yesterday," chuckled Paine, to Israel, his telescope at his eye, "but her decks are full of men and her starboard guns run out through her ports, which are well smashed."

Slowly the ship moved up abeam of the *Stede*, and the crew waited tense for the orders.

"Aim for her ports!" shouted Israel, sighting along the black tube of his demiculverin.

There was the thud of handspikes on wood as the breeches of guns were lifted by driven-in coins.

"Fire!" roared Israel, hopping away from his breech as the matchman touched the mealed powder of the priming with his linstock. Red huffs leaped from the vents and flame burst from the *Stede*'s ports, followed by a cloud of acrid orange smoke as the guns roared, hunched from the deck, and bucked back into their taut breechings.

"Stop your vents!"

As the lead aprons were clapped on the escaping gas, the French ship was smothered in yellow smoke and round shot whistled over the *Stede*, to plunge into the shallows inshore, flinging water and sand into the air.

"Reload!" yelled Brandy. "Well over us and we hulled 'em!"

Then the guns of the *Neptune* roared as they bore on the moving ship. As his gun was run in to load and he rammed home the nine-pound shot, Hugh breathed with relief. No eighteen-pounder had smashed his rail that time! No splinters and blood and death! But the ship would come about and give them the other broadside, and then—

The *Stede's* nine-gun battery was run out and sighted as the slow-moving sloop finally came abeam. A hail of nine- and five-pound shot battered the sloop's hull and rigging as she passed. In return, two shots crashed into the *Stede* at the water line, but no men were hit.

Israel Brandy hopped about with delight. "We hurt 'em, lads! Hurt 'em bad!" he cried. "Keep them shots low!"

Evidently having little relish for the sixteen-gun broadside of the anchored craft, the small sloops in the rear sheered off and fired high over the *Stede* and *Neptune*, their shots ricocheting over the water in-shore and kicking high the sand on the beach. It was clear that the French held the Newport gunners in respect, but with his superior numbers, it was only a question of time when Picard would try to take the Newport sloops by boarding, and the fight would be bitter.

The ship wore around, followed by the others, and bore in close to the anchored *Stede* and *Neptune*. As she approached, her decks seemed, to the less than one hundred men who watched her, to be alive. Did Picard dare risk grounding in order to spew that horde on the decks of the anchored craft? More than one cheek grayed at the thought. But the Frenchman sheered off, and as he came abeam, mus-kets spat lead from the *Stede* and *Neptune*, and they heeled to the kick of their guns. Hugh saw splinters fly from the ship's smashed bul-warks, then came the answer.

Waiting in the choking smoke of their own gun, Hugh's crew held their breaths. There was a roar in Hugh's ears and he was knocked flat on his back by the wind from a shot which lunged past. He rose, dazed, to learn what had become of his gun crew.

"Name o' God, that was close!" he gasped to the bewildered Jere-my, who was fumbling at his arms and legs to learn if they were still a part of his body.

"I—I thought I was hit, Hugh!" muttered the dazed lad, swallow-ing hard on the lump in his throat.

"All right?" Hugh asked the stunned Ward and Potter, who had got unsteadily to their feet.

They nodded, but their faces were gray with shock.

Again Picard had taken severe punishment and given little. As the breeze drove the smoke seaward, a tall figure in a yellow shirt ap-peared on the ship's poop and shook his fist at the anchored craft.

Paine swung his glass on him and called to Brandy, busy with his gun crew: "There he is, Israel! Jules Picard, or I'm a dogfish!"

Paine dropped his glass and raised his leather trumpet. "Ahoy, Jules Picard!" he bellowed. "'Tis Tom Paine! Board us and I'll give you what you got off Hispaniola!"

The man on the poop of the ship moving away raised a glass and looked long at the square-built figure on the *Stede's* afterdeck. Then the smoke from musket shots from the *Stede's* bow shut the ship from sight.

Israel was fidgeting at Paine's elbow. "'Twas Picard?" he asked.

"None else!" chuckled Paine. "Yellow shirt, big mustache, long hair, and his sash full of pistols. 'Tis Picard!"

"I was sure when the islanders pictured him to me," answered Israel. "If he dares board us, I'll take his other ear!"

Following the ship came the big sloop, but the sixteen guns of the *Stede* and *Neptune* were served by better gunners from the steady aiming platform of anchored vessels, and the French were badly battered.

"What are they up to now?" queried Israel, as the ship and sloops hove to at a distance and boats could be seen passing between them.

Paine's glass was at his eye, while his men waited at their guns. At length he turned to his master gunner who stood at his elbow. "Damn that French fox!" he muttered. "He's nobody's fool!"

Failing to inflict damage on the anchored sloops and taking a hammering himself, the wily French buccaneer had hit on a plan of attack which might well be successful.

Israel's face split in a grin as he nodded his shaggy head. "I looked for it, and I'm ready!"

"You were right, Israel, in moving that saker! He's found our weakness! While the ship and sloops pound us from the sea, he aims to send them longboats along the shore and board us on the bow and beam where we have no guns."

Brandy took the glass and studied the distant ships. He saw five long boats loaded with men leave and head for the shore at Sandy Point. His face turned grave, his wide mouth working nervously. "They've got more'n a hundred men in them boats—no less. On the *Stede* there's scarce forty fit to fight. We need thirty to work the guns and keep off that big sloop and the others. That leaves ten men to man the rail when they board." Israel's small eyes bored into Paine's. For a space the two taut-faced men were silent as they read each other's thoughts. They were thinking of the *Stede's* forty men fighting desperately as the big sloop lay alongside and the longboats spewed their boarders over the bow where the poop swivels might not bear on them if they used the bowsprit stays.

Then Paine's heavy jaw shut hard, and lights flickered in his agate-gray eyes. "When was three to one too big odds for a Newport crew, Israel Brandy?" he rasped.

Israel's hand struck Paine's. "Rot my bones! Never, Tom Paine! We'll beat 'em yet!"

But the situation was desperate for the anchored *Stede* and *Neptune*. If Picard could once reach their decks with his men, the odds would be almost hopeless. Their only salvation was to beat off his sloops with their guns.

Following the beach, the long boats approached in line while the ship and sloops hung off, evidently waiting until their boats were near enough the anchored *Stede* to strike. Brandy chose Hugh and his gun crew to assist him with the bow saker. The old privateersman clapped Jeremy on his broad back.

"Now, lad, you'll soon see why we cut this port and shifted the gun."

"'Tis clear enough," said the boy. "But a longboat is a small target."

Brandy laughed. "Ay, a small target!" he chuckled, patting the black tube of the gun as he bent and sighted. "But not too small for Israel Brandy."

The range was long for a saker, and Hugh wondered if Israel's sighting the gun was not intended more for the encouragement of the men aft, who watched, than with any hope of hitting the leading whaleboat moving under many oars along the beach.

Squatted at the breech of the saker, Israel finally ordered, "Shift the breech a little to starboard."

With crow and handspike, Hugh and his men eased over the rear wheels of the gun carriage as directed. Brandy again sighted along the cast-iron tube. "Now," he said, "a shot for range and to let 'em know we're alive!"

He stepped back and ordered, "Fire!"

The vent flared up and the saker roared and jumped back, while the entire crew of the *Stede* watched the whaleboat. A column of water lifted to seaward and astern of the leading boat black with men.

There was a muttered "Oh!" of regret from some of the musketmen.

Israel turned on them fiercely. "Burn me! You fools! I'm tryin' for range! Wait!"

The longboat, still far out of musket range, continued close to the beach, outside the low wash, followed by the others. Israel had a coin driven in under the breech to lower the gun's muzzle and shorten the range, and again took a careful sight. "She shoots to starboard, mind you," he said to the crew. "Shift her a little more!"

The rear of the gun carriage was pried over by the spikes and crow.

Again Brandy sighted on the nearing boat. "There she is! . . . Fire!" The iron shot plunged into the water directly in the course of the target, showering the boat with spray. There was a shout of applause from the *Stede's* crew. The rowers stopped as if in confusion. It was clear that the gunnery of the *Stede* had made them wary. The longboat following came abeam of the first, and it lay close, while there seemed to be uncertainty among them as to their next move.

"That's what I'm after!" chuckled Brandy, spitting on his hands and hitching his canvas drawers. "I aim to bunch 'em, then I'll turn the bastards into shark's feed!"

Israel sighted his gun and ordered, "Lower her muzzle! Quick!"

The coin was driven in, Brandy glanced along the tube, jumped away and shouted, "Fire!"

While forty men on the *Stede* held their breaths, the round shot hurtled toward the bunched boats. There was a wild cheer! The iron ball smashed into the bow of a boat packed with men. Splintered planks, men, and water rose into the air as the shot plowed its way the length of the craft, to leave on the surface a debris of kindling wood and struggling men.

Hugh hugged the bare shoulders of the grinning Brandy. "You did it, Israel! Name of God, you gutted 'em!"

The saker was quickly reloaded as the unhurt longboat sheered off from the shore. Then the four boats started for the *Stede's* larboard rail, their oars tearing the water.

"There comes the ship!" cried Jeremy.

Led by the ship, the four French craft were bearing down on the anchored sloops. Again Brandy shifted the saker to bear on the four approaching longboats. But the leading boat was in close now, and the gun overshot. Again the sweating crew reloaded, and Brandy aimed and fired at the two rear boats as they bunched. A cheer rose from the *Stede* as, cut in two by the plunging shot, the bow and stern of a longboat lifted into the air. But the ship was moving into range, and Hugh sprang back with his own crew to his demiculverin while others took his place.

The three remaining longboats were now working in close on the larboard quarter, and the desperate Brandy had his muzzle lowered and shifted but could not bring his saker to bear, so fired wildly. The plunging shot hurled a column of water high in the air between two of the boats and they sheered off.

The ship moved up abeam, to take a broadside from the *Stede*. Hugh plainly saw his nine-pound shot crash through the rail, opening a jagged gap between two gun ports. Then the ship was shut from sight by orange smoke. A plunging shot bored across the *Stede's* deck and smashed through her larboard rail, but the smoke cleared, and Hugh found his crew unhurt. They reloaded, and Hugh sighted on the waist of the slow-moving sloop coming abeam. The nervousness which had swept him like a cold wind before the ship's broadside had gone. He glanced at Jeremy standing beside him with his handspike, and the boy's powder-smudged face shaped a confident smile. The begrimed faces of Ward and Potter were taut with determination. He gave the order to fire, and a thrill swept him as he saw a great tear in the sloop's bulwarks where his shot had swept her deck with a hail of splinters. Badly hurt, the clumsy sloop drifted past, but the small sloops were now swinging in straight for the *Stede*.

"They mean to lay us board and board! Rake the first one as she comes!" roared Brandy from the poop.

Hugh wondered about the longboats full of pirates, close in on their bow, as he sighted his demiculverin to rake the deck of the sloop bearing in on them. The *Stede's* guns belched fire and acrid, yellow smoke at the craft as she came. Desperately, Hugh's crew brought their gun in, sponged, reloaded, ran her out, and fired again at the sloop, not a hundred yards off their beam. Like a tree struck by an ax, the sloop shivered from the hail of round shot that hammered her, sheered off, and the *Stede's* gunners saw through the smoke that she was using her sweeps. Then her mast swayed and fell overside, while her crew fought with axes to clear away the top hamper which clung to her. Mercilessly the *Stede's* guns pounded her again as she drifted past to take the broadside of the *Neptune*.

"All hands stand by the bow!" bellowed the voice of Tom Paine through the smoke.

As Hugh and his men seized their cutlasses and ran forward, followed by Israel and the gun crews on the poop, they met the musketmen fighting with clubbed guns, cutlass, and pike against a swarm of men pouring over the bow and bowsprit stays from the boats.

"Lay into 'em, lads! Drive 'em into the water!" With furious sweeps of his heavy cutlass, Brandy drove back three swart-faced pirates who had reached the windlass. Beside him, Hugh, Jeremy, Leftenant Cook, and the musketmen fought to hurl back the human tide that flowed over the rail. As he struck and slashed, Hugh wondered where Sheffield and Brenton were.

The rush of Brandy and his gunners held the first wave of boarders at the foot of the bowsprit, but the larboard rail was lined with French, some carrying cutlasses in their teeth while they pulled themselves up with their hands. Hugh's foot trod on a body on the deck and he glanced down to look into the white face of Joe Brenton with a smear of blood on his forehead. Poor Joe! Then a huge Frenchman cleared the rail and rushed him. The shock of Brenton's gray face whipped Hugh into a frenzy. He parried the slash aimed at his blond head, and with his left hand drove his war hatchet with all his power. The thin blade bit into the skull of the pirate and he rolled at Hugh's feet.

The fate of the Newport sloops and the safety of the town hung by a hair. Along the larboard rail the *Stede's* men fought savagely with clubbed musket, cutlass, and windlass bar against the horde of boarders from the boats alongside. If they once gained a foothold on the deck the battle would soon be over, for the French outnumbered the *Stede's* crew three to one.

Not daring to fire his poop swivels for fear of hitting his own men, Tom Paine shouted above the melee: "Clear the rails, lads! Knock 'em into the sea! You're fightin' for Newport!"

The cutlass of the old privateersman parried and slashed and his pistols spat as he urged on his crew. His blade snapping as it rang with a missed blow on the cascabel of the forward saker, Hugh seized a windlass bar and bludgeoned heads as they bobbed above the rail. At his side, Jeremy Potts fought like a wild man. At last, clearing the bulwarks in front of him, the frenzied Brandy stood, for an instant, panting like a beast at bay. Suddenly his bloodshot eyes glittered as a yellow-bound head and evil face showed above the rail.

"Stab me!" roared Brandy. "I've seen your slimy face before!" Whipping his cutlass far over his back, with a savage sidesweep Israel struck. Driven by all the tremendous power his thick arm could summon, the heavy blade caught the pirate full on the side of the neck. The keen edge sliced through muscle and into the spine. The yellow head, with its grimacing face, slumped, hanging from the body sprawled over the rail, to smear the deck with a gush of blood. Brandy pushed the body from the rail and it fell with a splash into the water. "I left you for dead, once, at Fort-de-France, French Louis!" he bellowed. "Burn me! You're dead, now!"

Then men ran to the rail with lockers of nine-pound shot and hurled them into two of the crowded boats alongside, smashing through their planking as if through eggshells. One by one the Newport men drove the last of the boarders back over the rail. There, floundering in the water, they were picked off by the musketmen as the third boat was rowed away in a hail of shots from the stern swivels.

His face black with powder stain and his tattered shirt smeared with grime and blood, Tom Paine stood on his poop, telescope at his eye. "They're abandonin' the sloop we dismasted," he panted to Brandy, beside him, still gripping his smeared cutlass.

"Looks to me, Tom Paine," said the man whose hairy torso was streaked with blood from two surface shoulder cuts, "that Jules Picard is makin' ready to kiss us good-by!"

The ship had picked up the men in the sole surviving longboat, and with the two sloops was heading west, leaving the dismasted craft behind.

A smile lay on Paine's powder-black face. "Jules Picard came here to loot Newport and the coast. But he's takin' back a belly full."

"We got a prisoner, here, from one of the boats, with a story," chuckled Israel.

"What is it?"

"He tells us that when Picard saw you on the poop when the ship passed us the first time, he cursed and took on fair frenzical. '*Vente du biche!*' he yelled, ' 'tis Tom Paine! I fight the devil sooner nor Tom Paine!' "

Paine laughed loudly. "He remembers the drubbin' I gave him off Hispaniola!"

"Yes! And, Tom Paine, I have more news, the thought of which fair strangles me."

"What is it, Israel?"

"That sloop lying off there is loaded with Canary, malmsey, and brandy from the Wine Islands." Israel licked his dry lips as he spoke.

Tom Paine instinctively ran his tongue across his parched mouth. "What? She's a wine ship?"

"Ay, a prize they took off New York! Are there orders, Tom Paine?" demanded Brandy, sucking his lips in anticipation. "She may sink before we reach her if we dally! Stab me! I'm dry as a dead fish on a beach!"

"Take the whaleboat and board her," said Paine. "And waste no time swillin' on board but load this boat with all you can carry."

Shortly Brandy was standing in the stern sheets of the sloop's longboat urging on its all-too-willing crew.

In the meantime, Hugh and Kit Sheffield had carried the bludgeoned Joe Brenton to Chirurgeon Rodman, working in the cabin. In a bunk in Paine's cabin, the bandaged John Arnold lay groaning.

In the distance the French fleet were headed west. "Bound for some cove on Long Island, likely," said Paine to Leftenant Cook, "to lick their wounds and refit. But they've had their fill of Newport lads! And it's good-by to Picard!"

Pushed through the water by Brandy's thirsty crew, the longboat neared the dismasted French sloop.

"If you fancy wettin' your tongues with a taste of prime Canary, put your backs into it, you rumbullions," urged Israel, swallowing hard on his dry throat and licking his lips. "She rides perilous low in the water!"

The longboat shot alongside the battered sloop, and her crew scrambled aboard and into the forehold. There were cheers while handspikes smashed in the head of a cask of Canary and the thirsty men drank like horses, their faces in the wine. Filling a leather jack he found in the cabin, Israel buried his nose in the fragrant Canary. Then one of the crew dropped through the hatch and spoke to him.

"She's settlin' fast, sir!"

"What?" Wine dripping from the corners of his mouth, Israel lowered the jack and turned a stricken face to the speaker. It was as if he had heard his death sentence. He gulped and shook his shaggy head in protest at the bad news.

"She's makin' water fast in the afterhold. She'll go down afore we get a cask into the boat if we don't hurry!"

"Stand by!" bellowed the master gunner to the men around the broached wine cask. "Avast swillin', you swine, and lend a hand with this small cask, here! She's settlin' under our feet!"

Swiftly rigging a tackle, willing hands hoisted the small cask of Canary through the hatch to the deck and lowered it into the boat. With frequent recourse to the half emptied jack in his hand, the disappointed Brandy superintended the operation. "Now, lively, after the mate to this one," he ordered. "I doubt not from the look of it 'tis brandy."

With shouts, the men scrambled back into the forehold, for the sloop was rapidly filling.

"Lively, now, you sons of rumpuncheons!" bellowed Israel, standing at the hatch. He emptied the jack and handed it to a boy. "Fill that from the broached cask," he ordered. The boy disappeared. "What think you Tom Paine and your mates will do to you if you bring them not that brandy?" he cried. "Her stern's awash! Heave up that brandy, men, afore we all go down with her!"

Up came the brandy cask through the hatch, to be eased into the boat alongside. "Stand by the longboat, you in the hold," bawled Brandy from the stern sheets of the whaleboat, the refilled jack in his hand.

Wiping their dripping mouths with the backs of their hands, the last of the reluctant crew left the hold, tumbled into the boat, and pushed off. Gradually the sloop began to wallow, then in a swirl of foaming water she went down.

"Silence!" roared Israel, holding his jack aloft as he would a flag.

At Brandy's command the groans of regret and disappointment, as the sloop disappeared, died away.

"Men," said the master gunner gravely, his eyes bright from his potations, "bow those frowzy heads of yours and every rumpuncheon whisper a prayer to the repose of that there wine we lost! We fought hard and we earned it! Now, the Almighty has seen fit to take it from us. 'Twill serve but to feed the fish! Sink me! who'd not be a fish and live in that sloop the rest of his life? Give way, all, and keep your dirty paws off that brandy cask in the waist. 'Tis the property of Tom

Paine."

The returning boat found the decks of the *Stede* and *Neptune* alive with busy men. The guns and ballast were shifted, decks cleared and made shipshape, and damaged rigging spliced and reeved for the return. Had his sloops been in shape to take up a pursuit, Paine would have followed the retreating French with the purpose of cutting out a laggard or two and thus obtaining prize money for his men. But the limping French fleet was already hull down in the west from the *Stede's* masthead.

§48

THE people of Newport rushed to the wharves when the *Stede*, with patched mainsail and jib, and the battered *Neptune*, sheered of her topmast, slid into the harbor that evening as the sun hung low over Conanicut. Shortly the guns of King's Fort on Goat Island and those mounted in the earthwork on the shore near Arnold's Wharf boomed their salute, for flying at the *Stede's* masthead was the red signal of victory Paine had promised the Governor he would hoist on his return. The beating of drums and the cheering and shouts of the townspeople who swarmed over the wharves sent a thrill through Hugh as he watched at the rail with Israel. Tom and Content would be there, and Seeth and Trelawney.

To the cheers of the gathered townspeople, the two sloops dropped their peaks and eased in on the flood to their wharves. The Governor and leading citizens scrambled aboard to congratulate Paine and Godfrey. Standing at the rail, Hugh eagerly searched among the rejoicing men and women for Tom and Content. But they were not there, nor was Seeth.

When the sloops were made fast with lines to the bollards, and the sails brailed, wives, mothers, and sweethearts rushed to greet the returned crews. There was much kissing, embracing, and laughter. Then, suddenly, silence fell on the people crowding the wharf. A line of stretchers moved slowly from the *Stede* and *Neptune*. The low cries and sobbing of women broke through the hush as the bodies of broken men, some groaning, some still, were brought ashore by their mates, to be met by their families and taken away. Then—for Tom Paine had sworn that no man of his should be buried at sea—ten motionless shapes, sewn in canvas, were carried from the sloops on planks and laid side by side on the wharf. Stricken women and men knelt beside their dead.

Hugh and Israel went ashore. They stopped for a moment to clap Jeremy on the back and shake his father's hand, while his mother wept in his arms. Hugh's eyes roved the milling crowd alongshore and on the two neighboring wharves in search of Content and Tom and the tall figure of Trelawney. He wondered where Seeth was. He felt cold and alone and deserted.

"Where are they, Israel?" he asked, his voice thin with emotion.

"Likely too late to get a place here. They'll be on Brenton's or Easton's."

Hugh and Israel stood talking with Benoni Tosh and the Wanton boys, who had come out of the fight unhurt, when two stretchers, surrounded by men and women whose clothes marked them as of the upper class, slowly approached. A voice called, "Hugh Jocelyn!"

Standing, with Jahleel Brenton, beside a stretcher, was Kit Sheffield, beckoning. "Joe wants to speak with you, Hugh!"

The elegantly dressed woman and young girls, in lace love hoods, dimity, and lustring, who were with Brenton and Sheffield, made Hugh suddenly conscious of his canvas drawers and tattered locram shirt. He flushed beneath the soiled bandage which bound the gouge across his temple.

"Here, Hugh!" called Sheffield. "John is in a fever and knows no one, but Joe wants to see you before they take him to Hammersmith."

The woman and girls were Brentons, Hugh thought, struggling with his embarrassment and desire to flee. He had never seen them to know them, but the Brentons were dark. This one with the cloud of dark hair and the brilliant black eyes must be Serena, and she would laugh at his seaman's canvas drawers, his scratched legs, and torn shirt.

Jahleel Brenton, Joe's uncle, the head of the family, shook Hugh's hand and said: "Hugh Jocelyn, Joe tells me great things of your gallant conduct with Captain Paine. I am happy to see you home safe."

Hugh mumbled his thanks.

"I wished to say good-by to you, Hugh," said Joe Brenton, turning his bandaged head, as Hugh stood beside him.

"How do you feel, Mr. Brenton?" asked the embarrassed boy, conscious of the scrutiny of four pairs of feminine eyes.

"I'm still too dizzy in my thick skull to walk, Hugh, but will be all right soon. Poor John!"

"'Tis a pity, Mr. Brenton! But Chirurgeon Rodman has strong hope for him."

"Yes, I know. 'Twould scarce be the same world without old John," sighed Brenton. Then his face lightened. "You yellow-haired devil, Hugh!" he broke out. "The last thing I remember before I was cracked on the head was seeing you slashing at three yelling Frenchies and using that ax in your left hand!" Brenton chuckled at a memory, then he beckoned the listening women. "Aunt Mary, Serena, Desire, Bess—this is my friend, Hugh Jocelyn."

Scarlet to the bandage on his forehead, Hugh bowed low and mumbled, "Your servant, ma'am!"

The older woman came to his rescue, while the girls' eyes took Hugh in from feet to yellow hair. "'Twas a great victory. We are all so grateful that Joe returned safely. Poor John Arnold!" she rattled on. "Joe has told us much of you—the pirates and that long swim fairly took our breath away. Your head—I trust 'tis not serious?"

"Oh, no, ma'am; 'tis nothing."

The man on the stretcher laughed. "What think you of him, now, my curious little cousins?" he flung out. "Do you blame Lettice Brinley for going to the pillory?"

A frown lay on Jahleel Brenton's dark face as he shook his head. The two younger girls tittered, but the taller and older one intervened: "Pay no heed to Cousin Joe, Hugh Jocelyn. His hurt head boldens his tongue. He is your loyal friend and talks much of you. We are pleasured to meet you and glad that you returned sound, save for that hurt on the forehead."

As she spoke, the girl's sloe-black eyes hovered for an instant on Hugh's wide shoulders, then candidly lifted to his eyes. She seemed little more than sixteen, though tall for her age. As she threw back her dark head and looked him full in the eye, he noticed the straight nose, sensitive mouth, and the roundness of her white throat where it joined the black lace whisk at her neck.

"She'll bubble you with that smooth tongue of hers, Hugh, if you heed her," broke in Brenton. "No one ever knows when Serena's serious."

Color flushed the girl's face, as angry lights danced in her eyes. "'Tis Cousin Joe who is seldom serious," she countered.

Brenton took Hugh's hand. "You have never seen Hammersmith," he said. "When my head stops buzzing, I'll ride down with an extra horse and show it you."

"Thank you, Mr. Brenton." Hugh bowed low to the ladies and Jahleel, with a mumbled, "Your servant!" and left, followed by the appraising eyes of the girls.

"Well, Aunt Mary," said Brenton as they started for Thames Street, where saddle horses and one of the three coaches in Newport waited, "what think you of my young fisherman?"

"He must be very poor—the son of a fisherman. And he badly needs a fresh bandage on his head and a whole shirt to his back to shield his nakedness from the eyes of our maids."

The man on the stretcher snorted with disgust. "There you go! Of course he's poor; but in learning, thanks to Trelawney, he's far richer than any of us, young though he is." He held his forehead in his hand as if to clear his brain, then went on: "As for his shirt, he's fought two days for Newport in those clothes. It ill becomes you to notice them. But that tattered shirt failed to conceal from the gaping eyes of our modest maids a rare pair of shoulders!"

"Joseph! Your language is unfit for our ears," demurred his aunt. "You said you were bringing him to Hammersmith. Think you it wise to so humor a fisherman's son? He would presume upon our friendliness."

Jahleel Brenton frowned at his sister-in-law, while the man on the stretcher grimaced at Serena, whose black eyes snapped fire: "Mother, if the French had not been beaten by men with tattered shirts or no shirts, you might now be screaming for their aid, unmindful of their clothes or lack of them. Could you not see that the poor lad was painfully ashamed to meet us? 'Twas Cousin Joe and Kit Sheffield who insisted."

"Yes, Mary," added Serena's uncle, Jahleel, "the boy is barely off the sloop. What matters his shirt? Tom Paine's was worse when he landed."

Sheffield had returned from Arnold's stretcher, which was being carried away, to hear Serena's remark: "Of a truth, I insisted that he come," he said. "Joe wished to see him. And, Serena," Kit's eyes twinkled, "now that you've met him, you understand Lettice throwing her Brinley pride to the winds?"

"I wonder at nothing Lettice Brinley may do, Kit Sheffield," retorted the girl with spirit, her black eyes brilliant with sudden anger. "Your friend, Hugh Jocelyn, is well enough—for a sailor!"

Aware of the fierce pride of the tall girl who faced him with threatening eyes, Sheffield did not reply but smiled and turned to his friend on the stretcher, his brows lifted in a significant look.

"You've had your answer, Kit," chuckled Brenton. "Poor Hugh! He's well enough for a sailor. Well, despite all his reading, that's what he aims for, a ship of his own under his feet. 'Twas too much to expect Serena to understand what I see in a poor fisherman's foster son in canvas drawers, torn shirt, and a bullet wound across the temple, taken while fighting for the safety of Newport!"

Joe Brenton's eyelid fluttered as he looked hard at Sheffield, then at the girl who had turned her back and was watching the people leaving the wharves. She swung round at the remark. "I meant not what I said about a sailor," she impulsively threw at them. "You think—you think 'tis because he's poor that I spoke that way. But you're wrong! 'Twas because I tire of hearing Mr. Trelawney talk of how fearless he is, what learning he has, of Hugh Jocelyn this, and Hugh Jocelyn that.

I doubt it not. I grant it all," she went on vehemently, while her mother raised her hands in helpless protest. "But I entreat you, cease talking of him! I've heard enough!"

"Come! There's the coach!" said Dame Brenton. "We must get Joseph home and into bed."

As Sheffield left, his friend Joe Brenton drew him down and whispered in his ear. "What thought you of Serena's pretty tirade?"

"I thought what you thought," answered Sheffield.

Brenton nodded. "I see you know her. She has her grandfather's pride."

"And spirit!" added Sheffield.

§49

"OH, my lad, my lad!" Hugh suddenly heard, and there were Content, Seeth, and Tom, who had been searching for him. With a wide sweep of his arms, he met them. "God was good to us, Hugh!" said Content. "You are safe! But the bandage! What happened to your head?"

"'Tis nothing. I hardly knew it, Mother, when I got it. Seeth, girl, don't weep!" He sought to comfort the girl, for she was shaking with great sobs. "I'm only—weeping—Hugh," she answered, between gusts of tears, "because I'm—so—happy!"

"There! There!" Hugh patted her shoulders. "'Tis all right, now! 'Twas but a scratch!"

As they walked slowly home, Hugh told the story of the fight off Block Island. Then leaving Tom and Content, Hugh went on with Seeth to her house. On a bench in the garden she removed the bandage, bathed the red furrow on his temple, and rebound his head with fresh linen.

"You mother me so," he laughed, taking her face between his hands and kissing her. "You fair spoil me."

The gray-green eyes lifted to his grew dark until they were almost black under the long lashes. "And why should I not mother you when you are my life, Hugh Jocelyn?" she whispered.

He looked into her lovely, oval face, framed by the tawny hair. Her eyes burned into his with the intensity of her feeling. Impulsively he caught her to him. "Seeth, you are the sweetest maid in all Newport," he murmured.

"And you love me, Hugh? You do love me?" she asked, her lips at his ear.

"I do, Seeth! How could I not, with you so sweet?" And yet, as he said it, he half wondered if it would not have been kinder to remain silent, for he knew that he could not fully return the devotion of Seeth Carr.

At length she said: "They are celebrating tonight, in the taverns. You, who fought so bravely, should be there with Israel and the Wantons. They are waiting for you."

"It is nice here with you, Seeth," he demurred.

"No, you must join them. William Wanton told me at the wharf that we women should not keep you."

So Hugh said good-night, and returned home, where he found Trelawney waiting. The Englishman's eyes were bright with pride as he laid his hands on the boy's shoulders. "They've told me, Hugh—Israel and Jeremy and Captain Paine. I'm fair proud of you, lad!"

Trelawney waited for Hugh to wash, eat dinner, comb his long hair, put on his broadcloth suit with the pewter buttons and buckles at the knee, and sling the baldric with Tom's cutlass over his shoulder. Soon they were on their way down Thames Street, past lighted taverns, from the open windows of which drifted cheers and laughter. That night a light-hearted and grateful Newport was giving itself up to the celebration of Tom Paine's victory.

Hugh stopped and looked through the open door of the Blue Porpoise, while Trelawney kept a firm grip on his sleeve. Gray with tobacco smoke through which blinked tallow dips, like sun through thinning fog, the room was filled with chattering men and women drinking with members of Paine's and Godfrey's crews. Jonathan Prey and his man, John, their red faces dripping with sweat, hurried back and forth carrying foaming, copper-bound jacks from which they filled the wooden and pewter mugs on the tables.

"Come, Hugh," urged Trelawney. "Israel's in there, bellowing like the bull of Basham as he tells them of that lost wine and brandy. The thought of it will parch his throat to his dying day. If they see you, they'll not let you go. The Wantons are waiting for us at the King's Head!"

As Hugh looked curiously through the door, he saw a young sailor of the *Neptune's* crew leering into the black eyes of the woman who served him. The sailor's hand circled her waist, then dropped to her hips as she bent to set the drinks on the table. As she pushed away his arm, her dark eyes smoldered invitingly into the boy's inflamed face.

With a laugh and a shrug of his heavy shoulders, Hugh turned to his friend who still gripped his sleeve: "Candace is having her hands full with the lads, tonight! And one, there, is having his hands full of Candace."

Trelawney was relieved at Hugh's tone. There was no tinge of jealousy in it or of regret. Evidently Candace had long since passed from his thoughts. "You have no objection to going to the King's Head tonight?" he asked.

The young man gave a hollow laugh. "I'm still a fisherman's son and, no doubt, in the eyes of many, broadcloth ill becomes me. But the man who cocks his eye at me tonight will have it blackened. I've changed, Dick. I'm through being hurt and stung by life. I have a different look at things. Fisherman or no fisherman, I'll wear what I can pay for and go where it pleasures me. If this be not to the taste of certain Newport gentry, so much the worse for them. I'm quit taking shame at anything. From now on I fight for my rights."

Trelawney stared at his friend in amazement. "Hugh, what has come over you? You're so changed. And yet I'm glad—glad of your resolve. You've brooded too much and nursed your grievances too long. Now you've proved your worth in defense of Newport. No one may belittle you."

"Whatever I've proved to others, I've proved one thing to myself," Hugh answered. "One deserves what one can seize and hold. From now on, that is my motto. In the future I take what I can get and ask no quarter."

"I wish there were not so much bitterness in you, lad," said the Englishman, with a sigh. "Life is not all head wind into which you must forever plunge your bow. But I understand."

Bursts of laughter and a babel of high-pitched voices floated from the open windows of the King's Head as the two friends approached the door. The smoke-filled room was packed with men in all stages of alcoholic inspiration. Trelawney and Hugh stood at the entrance, searching through smoke wreaths from long-stemmed pipes for the Wantons. Judging from the calls of clamoring customers, the utmost exertions of the sweating landlord, Timothy Whiting, his white servant, and the black boys had failed to relieve the drought which had stricken Newport throats. Not since the news of the landing of William of Orange in England, when Joe Brenton had become master of ceremonies and had led the singing, had the King's Head witnessed such rejoicing. For the coast had been cleared for the time being of the French, and worry was wiped from the minds of shipowners and merchants. As half the business of the port was in the hands of Quakers, many of the sect were joining their Quaker governor, John Easton, in the celebration.

Guests of honor, Captain Tom Paine and Captain Godfrey sat at a table with the Governor, Jahleel Brenton, Benedict Arnold, and John Coggeshall.

Hugh entered the room with Trelawney, to be welcomed by exhilarated citizens who, a week previous, would have raised smug brows at his presence. He was highly amused when some even clapped him on the back. He had helped save their precious property, so tonight he was welcome. But, nevertheless, it sent a thrill through him to have these older men greet him, drunk though they were. Penniless fisherman he was, but he knew that the fight with Picard had given him standing among the men of Newport. Hadn't Tom Paine told him so and personally thanked him after the fight?

"Where did you disappear to, Hugh?" demanded William Wanton. "We looked for you when we landed but you slipped us. Doubtless you found a maid waiting and forgot your friends."

"I was called to the stretcher by Mr. Brenton," said Hugh.

William Wanton's dark eyes twinkled. "Ah, so you had words with the black-eyed Serena?"

Trelawney glanced quizzically at Hugh, for he had not mentioned this meeting to his friend. "I was that ashamed," said Hugh, "with my poor shirt and drawers half covering me, before Mr. Jahleel Brenton and those ladies!"

William and John roared. "Did the maids cover their faces with their hands and look through their fingers at you?" demanded John. "But not Serena, not she! I doubt not she looked you fair in the eye with those black snappers of hers."

"John has her right," laughed William. "Serena would scarce drop her eyes for any man, shirt or no shirt."

"I give you Mistress Serena Brenton!" said John, raising his cup of Canary, "who fears no man, coated or shirtless."

Trelawney listened with an amused smile to the Wantons, who were feeling their wine, then William, whose sunburned face was mottled from drinking, poked Hugh in the ribs, "And was there no hazel-eyed madcap there at the wharf to greet you, Hugh?"

While Trelawney's foot found Hugh's under the table and pressed it, the boy looked blankly at the speaker. "I know no hazel-eyed madcap," he replied.

There was silence as Trelawney's warning look caught William's eye, and the conversation changed to the fight with Picard. But the mention of Lettice made Hugh strangely restless. He wondered if she too had been at the wharves when the sloops returned.

At the urging of the Wantons and spurred by the revelry and jubilation at the surrounding tables, Hugh drank until Trelawney laid a warning hand on his arm. "You're too big and heavy for me to carry, lad," observed the wily Englishman. "'Twould be fitter if you carried me."

"You mean I show my wine?"

"'Tis more, doubtless, than you ever before drank. I feel mine, so let us ease off and carry the Wantons home, rather than they, us."

Hugh grinned sheepishly in acquiescence. He glanced at William and John, already far in their cups and roaring an obscene sea doggerel with two friends from a neighboring table. Here and there men slipped from their stools, to lie snoring on the sanded floor, ignored by their riotous companions. At one table a tipsy merchant stood on his stool, propped by two patient friends. His periwig was askew, baring the bald skull beneath, and his flowered waistcoat was splashed with wine from a cup he held aloft. With a wave of his lifted cup, which spilled half the wine on his periwig, he loudly congratulated Tom Paine, who was neither listening nor could hear him, on the glorious victory. Greeted by shouts of applause from those who had neither heard the speech nor cared to the speaker gravely bowed and slid to the floor, where he lay snoring on his back in the soiled sand.

As he watched the hilarity, Hugh's inflamed eyes marked more than one citizen whose fat rear he longed to kick, and who, in the past, had treated with scant courtesy the son of a fisherman in patched locram shirt and bare feet. But tonight they patted his back and shook his hand for having fought with Tom Paine in defense of their property and homes. Well, some day, he promised himself, Hugh Jocelyn should have his own property to defend and the devil could look after theirs.

The casualties of the battle of the King's Head were gradually being removed by friends, or by retainers sent by foresighted and experienced wives, and the crowd was thinning. But the Wantons were still enjoying themselves and refused to leave, so Trelawney and Hugh remained to look after them. Finishing a song which would have horrified his Quaker father, William slapped his cup on the table and stared hard across the room.

"Look what's beating up against the wind, loaded to the hatches with a cargo of wine!" he cried.

The others followed William's eyes. Groping his way unsteadily between the tables, like a blind man, tacked and teetered the former Magistrate, Ichabod Tripp. Hugh's fingers itched to close on the red rolls of flesh that bulged over the soiled neckband of the man who had sent him to the pillory. Yawing like a dismasted sloop in a blow, on came the cooper whose hammer, at the order of Andros, had broken the ancient seal of Rhode Island.

William and John burst into roars of laughter as the purple-faced Tripp, battling for his balance and his dignity, jibed and veered between the lines of tables. Stung with the bitter memory of his humiliation, Hugh watched the approach of the fuddled cooper. Then William suddenly swung on his stool and leaned across the table to speak to Trelawney. At the same instant the zigzagging Tripp stumbled against William's thrust-out foot and sprawled on his face on the sanded floor, where he lay helpless and retching, with his head jammed between the legs of a stool.

Before Hugh and the Wantons could rise, a bulky shape towered over the drooling cooper on the floor. "Name of God," grunted Benoni Tosh, bending over the helpless Tripp, "'tis a hard pillow you've picked for yourself, Ichabod! And you'll find that sand in your mouth poor chewing."

While Hugh and the rest watched with undisguised delight, Benoni turned over the limp cooper and freed his bald skull from the legs of the stool.

"Now, Ichabod, you know how the lads you put in the pillory felt," Benoni chuckled, lifting the inert Tripp to his unsteady feet and clapping his soiled periwig crosswise on his hairless head. With his arms over their shoulders, two of landlord Whipple's men started with Tripp for the door.

"Good-night to you, Ichabod," called Tosh. "Keep your head up, that the wine trickles not from your ears. 'Twould be sad to waste it."

"I could scarce keep my hands from him, Benoni," fumed Hugh.

Benoni stroked his chin as he essayed a scowl at the innocent-appearing William Wanton. "William," he said, "'twas doubtless only by chance that your foot found itself thrust in the path of our former Magistrate. But had he not been foxed, he might have took serious hurt."

"Benoni," replied Wanton, with an injured look, "you do me grave wrong. Think you I would seek the fall of so great a man and toady as Ichabod Tripp?"

Benoni squinted down his huge, red-veined nose at the lad whose eyes danced as they met his, and his great body shook with inward laughter. "William, you devil, I would put nought beyond you—not even the murder of that slimy Tripp who, since Brinley is no longer our ruler, nuzzles the hands of those he once abused."

Hugh placed a hand on Tosh's shoulder and scowled into his twinkling eyes. "If Tripp had broken his neck, Benoni, what would you, the Sergeant of this town, who saw it, say to the grand jury?"

The Town Sergeant's expansive features suddenly sobered as he reached and coolly seized the cup of wine in William's hand, drained it in a gulp, smacked his lips, and gravely surveyed his waiting audience. "Hugh," he replied, "as the sworn Sergeant of this town, named by the freemen to uphold the law and see justice done between man and man, if Ichabod Tripp lay there dead on the floor from the thrust foot of one William Wanton, rake-hell, skip-jack varlet, devil's crony, and French killer, I would, under my sworn oath, have to swear—" Tosh's heavy features set hard as he scowled at the surrounding faces and gravely finished—"'twas an accident!"

THE tidings of Paine's victory over the French fleet went galloping over the horse path to Plymouth and on to Boston, where Sir William Phips was preparing to sail with a fleet for his long-delayed attack on Quebec. With her own men and ships little Rhode Island had cleared the coast of the marauding French from Cape Cod to Long Island Sound, and men breathed easier in every port. Paine's victory aroused a naval spirit in the people. The Bay Colony and Plymouth joined Rhode Island in rejoicing. The farmers and fishermen of the coastal islands could now, for a time, sleep free from fear of landing parties of swart-faced plunderers carrying torch and cutlass. The coastwise trade around the Cape was resumed, and merchants and shipowners were happy.

But along the frontiers the war with the French and Indians raged savagely, and even from little Providence patrols roved far into Massachusetts territory scouting for red raiding parties from the north.

While the one-eared Jules Picard had been sent, a much-chastened pirate, limping back with his shattered fleet to the West Indies, it was but a matter of time when French privateers would reappear off the southern New England coast, and Block Island and Vineyard sounds would again become dangerous waters for the little Newport fishing fleet and the coasters. As a matter of caution, most of the deep-sea fishermen now cautiously followed the shore. As a consequence the price of cod and mackerel steadily rose on the Newport wharves, and the *Sea Gull*, boldly continuing to fish her old grounds off the Vineyard and Noman's Land, reaped a comfortable profit. In the words of Israel Brandy: "We might as well be bobbin' fathoms deep on a mud bottom a-feedin' the fish, as short o' cod. For without cod we may buy no rum, and without rum we are worse nor dead!"

Then one September evening Captain Scarlett, of the Brentons' brig, the *Swordfish*, knocked at the Stantons' door.

"We're sailin' with a cargo of cod for Barbadoes, privateers or no," announced Scarlett to the interested Stanton, Israel, and Hugh. "Mr. Brenton has his letters of marque, and six sakers to arm the brig await us in Boston. Israel, I want you as master gunner and you, Hugh, as mate."

Hugh tingled with excitement from head to toes. Israel's face expanded with delight. "Stab my vitals, here be your men!" he shouted.

Stanton shook his grizzled head. "The best season in years and no crew to work the *Gull*!" he said.

"'Twill be full December afore we head for Barbadoes," Scarlett explained. "We've cargoes for New York and the guns to take on in Boston. The cod will be through by the time we sail."

So it was arranged.

Barbadoes and the Spanish Main! The thought thrilled Hugh to the bone. The fabled isles of the West Indy, with their palm-girt keys and shining beaches, their dark-skinned people, their white houses with red roofs lifting above the harbors! His imagination had often run riot with the tales of Israel. The Sugar Islands—Antigua, Barbadoes, St. Lucia! The Dutch Surinam on the mainland! Jamaica and the Windward Passage, where the pirates waited! The Gulf of Honduras with its mahogany and logwood, the old haunts of the buccaneers! And the storied Spanish Main, New Grenada, Darien, and Panama, with their cities of fabulous wealth and the golden galleons and plate ships. He wanted to touch this world of romance and adventure, of black deeds and outlawed men—to walk the streets of exotic ports on far islands whose beaches were washed by the lazy turquoise sea of the West Indy.

Early in December the *Swordfish* lay at Wentworth's Wharf, in Boston harbor, where, under the supervision of Scarlett and his master gunner, Israel Brandy, six five-pound sakers were being hoisted aboard, mounted by their trunnions on their carriages, and their harness adjusted to eyebolts in the deck at the new ports cut in her rails.

One afternoon the crew were working at the guns and stowing powder and racks of round shot in the brig's hold when a rumor, running through the port like fire before wind, reached the wharf. A sloop had just arrived with the news that Phips had failed in his attack on Quebec. Storms had wrecked many of his ships, smallpox had broken out among his men, and the scattered survivors of the disaster were making their way south from the Gulf of St. Lawrence.

Hugh and Brandy stared soberly into each other's faces. "Name of God, Israel," gasped Hugh, "'tis lucky the *Flying Fish* was not ready! Think of all those ships and men, lost! We well might have been among them!"

Shaking his shaggy head and scowling fiercely as he mumbled to himself, Brandy resumed his splicing of the breeching on the cascabel of a five-pounder, while Hugh waited for his reply. Then the master gunner gave vent to his disgust:

"Stab my vitals, lad, there was nought but sad bunglin' and beatin' 'gainst head tides about it all! They dillydallied and waited to sail until August and caught the fall dirty weather, when the time to head for the Gulf is May or June. All seamen know that. And they sail short of powder and shot for the big guns and, by the report, fiddle-faddle weeks before they attack that old fighter, Frontenac."

"But Admiral Phips was reputed a good seaman," demurred Hugh.

"A shipwright, he was; nought else," scoffed Brandy. "On his return he'll be no great man as he was."

Anxious for further details of the story of the defeat of New England ships and men at Quebec, Hugh obtained leave of Captain Scarlett to run down to the Three Mariners tavern at the head of Long Wharf, where talk of Phips's fiasco would be on every man's tongue.

At the Three Mariners Hugh found the tables in the public room filled with sober-faced men, stunned by the news, who talked in hushed voices; for many had sons and relatives with the ill-starred fleet. A crowd of recent arrivals milled and argued around the newsboard hung on the wall at the entrance, reluctant to accept the truth of the report. Using his height and weight, Hugh worked his way to a spot where, over the heads of excited men, he could read the scrawled writing on the sheets of paper fastened by nails and tacks to the board. On a large sheet was the heavily inked report, brought by the sloop, of Phips's failure to take Quebec and the scattering of his fleet by storms, with great loss of life. There was no news in this to Hugh, and his eyes wandered curiously to legal notices, mention of the arrival and sailing of ships to and from Bristol, England, the West Indies, and the Wine Islands, offers of goods, livestock, and slaves for sale, and rewards for the return of lost animals and escaped bond servants. Then, of a sudden, Hugh's bronzed face was drained of blood. He felt sick and numb and cold as he read:

Horse messenger over the Plymouth Path brings the news that Small-Pox rages in Newport. Many already dead. People fleeing the town to escape the Plague.

Smallpox in Newport! The world went dark for Hugh Jocelyn as he read and reread the ghastly news. Many already dead! Content! Seeth! Tom! Trelawney! At that very moment they might be dead or lying sick with the plague. The stunned boy roughly pushed his way through protesting men, reached the door, and started on a run for Wentworth's Wharf. They must sail at once. He and Israel and Scarlett were needed in Newport. If Captain Scarlett would not sail that night, he, Hugh, would start over the path on a horse. But where would he get a horse, and who would trust a penniless sailor? Then he would walk. But it would take days over the Plymouth Path and the ferries. No, Scarlett must sail that night. He too had a family in Newport. He would sail. With a good start around the Cape and the wind holding in the north they could make a quick run to Newport—quicker than walking, for the brig was fast before the wind—and he would then have Israel with him for aid and counsel. He had to reach Content and Tom, and reach them soon, to learn if they were in need of help and nursing. Perhaps they would be beyond the need of help and nursing!

The rich would fly for safety to their country homes, but the poor would have to stay and face it—face the scourge that filled the grave-yards of colonial ports. Tom and Content, Trelawney, and Hugh Jocelyn were poor. If he found them alive, they would face the plague together. As Hugh ran, he thought of the pock-marked faces in Newport left by earlier epidemics. Thus far his generation had escaped, but now the young would have to pay—pay with the hateful scars. Seeth and Candace might now, if they lived, have to carry through life the dreaded pits marring their fair skins. But the daughters of the rich—Lettice, the Brentons, and others like them—would be in the country, safe from infection. It was always so. While the rich escaped, the poor paid, with sweat and toil and hunger and blood. So ran the thoughts of the desperate boy as he hurried to Wentworth's Wharf.

Hugh reached the wharf and found Israel and his men working on the harness of the last saker. The startled Brandy gazed in amazement at the anxious face of the boy who leaped from the cap log of the wharf, over the rail, to the brig's deck.

"There's smallpox in Newport!" Hugh panted, seizing the puzzled Brandy by the shoulders. "'Tis posted in the Three Mariners. The town is filled with the plague. Tom! Content! They may be down! If Captain Scarlett won't sail on this ebb, I'm walking the Path."

Israel's jaw sagged. "Smallpox—in Newport?" he gasped. "Rot my bones, lad, 'tis sad news you carry!" The master gunner wagged his head from side to side. "'Twas there when we sailed—and no one knew it—for it takes some days to bring them to bed! And the dead, Hugh? Are they many?"

"Yes; the notice said many are dead. Israel, I'm sick with fear!" Hugh's eyes were suddenly blurred, as his voice broke. "If Content and Tom or Trelawney, or—" He did not name Seeth, but Israel knew.

"Easy, lad! Tom has doubtless taken Content to live on the sloop out of harm's way! Trelawney will be with 'em if he's not with Joe Brenton at Hammersmith. Captain Scarlett will be worried about his family and will sail tonight, as our cargo's aboard. Never fear!"

"If he will not sail, I leave by the Path!"

A great hand reached for Hugh's shoulder. "Trust Israel to see that Scarlett sails tonight," soothed Brandy. "'Twould not do to have you reach Newport alone. We go together, lad. Whatever comes, we face it, you and Israel, shoulder to shoulder, as we met the French."

As if in an attempt to banish the fear which sickened him, Hugh took a deep breath and expelled it. He smiled into the scarred face he had loved since he came as a little boy to live with the Stantons. "Yes, shoulder to shoulder," he said. "Always shoulder to shoulder, Israel! You and I! We needs must be men whatever may come. But every turn of the glass while we round the Cape and head up the Sound for Newport will be hell!"

§51

ONE morning a few days later, when the sun had burned through the mist smothering the coast, the brig *Swordfish*, giving the dangerous Brenton's Reef a wide berth, reached up the East Passage with the southeast wind, past Brenton's Neck, came about, and nosed in behind Goat Island. To the crew whose anxious eyes marked the deserted wharves, the scattering of anchored sloops and brigs and the absence of moving small craft, the once busy little port seemed dead. The smoke of breakfast fires rising lazily from chimneys was the sole evidence of life in the stricken town. Newport, with its four hundred houses and twenty wharves, lay prostrate in the sinister grip of calamity.

Gray-faced with anxiety, Hugh stood at the rail with Israel, searching the Cove in the distance for the familiar hull and mast of the *Sea Gull*. He found the sloop, but wharves and buildings blocked the view of the little house on the shore which he called home.

"They must have sighted us, Israel," he cried. "Where are Brenton's men? Where's Jeremy's father? He's Brenton's head man and this is a Brenton brig! Where is he?"

Brandy's mournful eyes traversed the deserted wharves. "There must be many sick, and all trade seems dead, by the look of the town. Brenton's men may be underground already, but the Brentons themselves lie snug at Hammersmith, where no plague can reach them."

Under her jib and spanker the *Swordfish* slipped up the harbor past the deserted wharves, came about in the lee of Brenton's, brailed her spanker, and the tide eased her into her berth. There two men appeared, to handle the lines cast from the brig and make them fast to the bollards. There were sober greetings between the few men who were on the wharf and Captain Scarlett and his crew. Then Jeremy Mott's father appeared and called: "You heard the news in Boston, Captain Scarlett? The port is down with the plague."

"My family?" demanded the fearful master.

"They're all well, still."

"And mine, Goodman Mott?" cried the anxious Hugh. "Have you word of Content and Tom Stanton and Mr. Trelawney?"

"Tom took his wife to live on the sloop, Hugh! I saw them when they passed last night from the Sakonnet grounds. Mr. Trelawney is at Hammersmith."

"God be praised!" gasped the relieved boy. "They're not sick, Israel! Tom's still fishing! Do you hear, Israel? They're alive and well!"

"And my sister, Jane?" demanded Brandy.

"Your sister, stout as ever, was here yesterday, seeking news of you, Israel."

Then Hugh turned to Mott on the wharf and asked in a thin voice, "And Jonathan Carr's family?"

"I have not heard. People fall sick every day. Many have gone to Portsmouth and some to Jamestown. The Carr family may be there."

Israel placed his hand on Hugh's shoulder as the youth turned his head to hide the anxiety in his face. "I—I want to see Content and Tom—then I must learn if Seeth Carr—" A flood of tenderness and remorse engulfed him. He swallowed hard against the tightening of his throat, crossed the brig's deck, to stand beside a demiculverin and look with unseeing eyes across the water.

Seeth! What if Seeth had been stricken! Already she might lie dying in the house on Thames Street. Or she might live, to meet life with her lovely skin marked and scarred. He recalled many of the older women in Newport who wore scarred faces from the last plague. Branded though they were, they had had to face life gallantly and conquer it. And the men! There was Tom Paine, who got his scars in Hispaniola, in a French prison, and there were many others. With men, the marks were a hazard of life. But on the delicate skin of a girl they meant ruin to beauty. It must not be so with Seeth! She was too lovely to be marked for life—too moody and reckless and intense to endure it.

In a small skiff they borrowed at the wharf, Hugh rowed Israel to the *Sea Gull* moored in the Cove. Curled around her shrouds hung the wood smoke of Content's small breakfast fire on the iron grate of the cramped galley, that used the forehatch as a vent.

"Ho, the *Gull*!" called Hugh.

Tom Stanton thrust his head through the cabin hatch, then ran to the low rail.

"Hugh! Israel! They told you at Brenton's we lived aboard the sloop? Content is here, for safety. Every third house in Newport has the sickness. But we and Mr. Trelawney are well, Hugh."

"Thank God, Father Tom! But Jonathan Carr's family—Seeth!" he cried. "Have you news of her?"

Stanton's face sobered. His eyes wavered before the boy's searching gaze. And Hugh knew. Seeth, for whom he had prayed every turn of the glass doubling the Cape and driving up the Sound for home—Seeth was sick with the plague!

"Hugh! My lad! You're back, sound and well!"

Dazed by Stanton's words, Hugh turned at the sound of Content's voice, to be comforted by her glad smile. "I've been frenzical lest you carried the sickness away with you on the brig. But Tom scoffed at it. And you're well? Oh, my son, my son, praise God for that!"

"And thank God you and Father Tom are untouched! But Seeth, Mother? Seeth is sick. Is she—dying, Mother? Have they hope for her? I'm going to her—now."

Stanton and Israel moved forward, leaving the two alone.

"Hugh," explained the troubled woman, "Seeth and her father are sick, but Chirurgeon Vigneron says they have passed the worst of it. The fever and the ache is lessening and the pus is now hardening into scabs. She will not die, Hugh."

Yes, Seeth would live—live with that lovely skin scarred with pits. "I'll go to the house—now," he said.

"Grace of God, no, Hugh! I beg you not to go. You may not see her. Goodwife Carr and her sister, who nurse them, let no one into the house. 'Tis the order of the Town Council and the chirurgeons. The plague lies in the air of the stricken houses. You must not go."

"I'm going, that she may know that I'm not afraid and have not deserted her in her need."

"But if they let you in, she would have shame for you to see her with the sores on her swollen face and arms," argued Content.

"She would see, then, if she can see, or they tell her, that I—love her," he said quietly. Then he gently removed Content's restraining hands, and before she could summon help from the men, was overside in the skiff and pushing off from the sloop.

"Hugh, lad!" bellowed Brandy, stumping aft. "You would not desert Israel? You forget I have a sister to look after. I go with you."

Hugh backed the skiff alongside, and Israel dropped into it. Wringing her hands in her fear and helplessness, Content stood with the silent Stanton and watched until the skiff reached the shore and Hugh and Israel disappeared into Thames Street.

As the two reached the street, a yoke of oxen, drawing a low cart on which rested two rough slab coffins, passed them, followed on foot by black-garbed mourners.

"Tom says not a day passes but they take someone to the Common Burial Ground on Farewell Street," said Brandy, as they stood with bowed heads until the funeral procession passed.

Here and there on Thames Street shops were open, and sober-faced men and women listlessly came and went about their business. The anvil of a blacksmith's shop rang to the blow of a hammer. To the nostrils of Hugh and Israel drifted the familiar odors of malt and brewing beer, and of a rum distillery on a wharf. A cart passed, carrying country produce from Portsmouth; another, with wood. Driving milk-cows to the common, a town cowherd crossed the Parade where children played in the grass. In the rutted streets chickens scratched, hogs foraged, and dogs wrangled over bones. But to Hugh and Israel the hush of death hung over Newport. People still ate and slept, traded and worked at their tasks, for while the sick died, the strong needs must live. But ever at the hearts of the strong lay a great fear—dread of the day when the grim specter of the plague would knock at their door.

Hugh stopped to speak to Israel's sister, then went on to the Carrs' house. For a moment his eyes rested on the garden in the rear, now bloomless and dead, where he had sat with Seeth. Now she lay inside, perhaps dying; if she lived, her lovely face marked for life. What had Seeth done to merit this agony? Then he lifted the iron knocker.

He heard voices inside and sensed that he was being observed from a window, but there was no response to his knock. He knocked again and waited. Again he heard voices, but the door remained closed. Then a diamond-paned window opened over his head and he saw the haggard face of Seeth's mother.

"Hugh Jocelyn, we are a stricken house," said the woman. "Jonathan and Seeth are sick. Are you mad that you come here?"

Hugh lifted his anxious face to hers. "Seeth—will she live? Tell me—tell me, will she live?"

"Praise god, Chirurgeon Vigneron says they are both past the worst."

"Does she suffer? Does she know you?"

The white face in the window shaped a faint smile. "The fever and ache are lessening," she said. "She knows me, now, and understands what I say. God has been good to me, Hugh. He has given me back Seeth and Jonathan."

Two tears made their way down Hugh's uplifted face. Then a swift thought poisoned his joy. When she grew stronger and could think, Seeth would not care to live. He must hearten her—give her courage and hope and happiness. He must see her—see her now; let her know that he loved her in the way she had always craved. She must know—now—that the scars on her face would mean nothing to Hugh Jocelyn.

Goodwife Carr started to close the window. Hugh raised his hand, and his face was stone hard with purpose. "I must go to her—let her see me," he insisted, and the woman who looked down into his fierce blue eyes and clamped jaw was afraid.

"No! No! 'Tis forbidden, Hugh!" she cried. "Would you catch the plague?"

"Have you caught it?"

"No."

"She loves me."

"Yes, Hugh, she does."

"She'll not wish to live when she's strong enough to think about her face. I know her. She'll want to die unless I can hearten her, Goodwife Carr; make her see that the plague cannot separate us—that I love her and am not afraid."

"I know; but I dare not, Hugh."

"I will but stand for a moment at her door so she sees me."

"I dare not."

"Name of God," warned the desperate youth, "then I push the door in. For see her I will! Come down before I put my shoulder to it."

The window slowly closed, and shortly Hugh heard a bolt being shoved from its socket and the latch lifted. The door opened and he stepped inside. The trembling Goodwife Carr whispered:

"She's awake, in the north room. Make no noise on the stairs to disturb Jonathan. He's asleep. God forgive me, I tried to keep you out! I tried to stop you!"

With heart thundering in his throat, Hugh tiptoed up the stairs. He looked through an open door. In the high four-poster bed of the small room lay a girl. On her pillow, a cloud of tawny hair framed her swollen face, stippled with eruption. The air of the room was heavy with a strange odor.

He opened his arms and said, shortly, "Seeth, 'tis Hugh!"

Her heavy eyelids lifted, and she stared fixedly at the boy in the doorway as if at an apparition.

"Seeth," he repeated, "I love you—Seeth! Courage, my sweet! Keep a brave heart and get well soon. I am waiting for you!"

As he spoke, the staring, gray-green eyes softened and lit with recognition. He saw her dry lips move with the effort to shape his name. For a moment he smiled into her glowing eyes, then, blowing a kiss with his hand, said, "I love you!" and left her.

Seeth's mother was waiting at the door. "Did she know you?" she asked. "Oh, I'm so afraid for you, Hugh! And 'twas against the law!"

"Law? No law could keep me from seeing her when I love her. Tell her again and again that I love her. Keep telling her. Do you understand? There was such happiness in her eyes when she saw I had come to her I could scarce fight back the tears. Tell her I wait for her."

Hugh made his way like a drunken man back to the skiff on the shore. If love could make her whole again she should have all the tenderness and devotion she craved. Since the shock of hearing the news in Boston he had had no doubt of his love for Seeth. But, had he doubted, it would have been the same.

He and Israel rowed to the sloop, where Content and Tom awaited them. "You—you saw her, Hugh?" asked the incredulous Content, while Tom and Israel watched him in silence.

"I saw her and she will live, praise God! Before you touch me, let me take a dive into the cold water and wash myself."

Hugh disappeared through the forehatch and reappeared in a pair of short canvas drawers, carrying the clothes he had worn and dropping them on the deck. He plunged into the icy water of the Cove and swam out to the main harbor, while the two older men conversed in low tones.

"He must have forced his way into the Carr house," muttered Israel. "There's no stopping that lad when his mind is set."

The worried Stanton sadly wagged his grizzled head. "He was there but a short space, and the bad time for taking it from Seeth and Jonathan is passed. Yet I shall fear for him until the time has run for him to show it."

"He was but in the house and out," demurred Israel. "I've had shipmates down with it and lived among them for weeks and never took it. I set no store by the tales that the air carries it. Cease your worry for the lad. He did but look at her and go."

Smoke began to rise from the forehatch. "What's that stink comin' from the hatch?" demanded Stanton.

"She's burning his clothes," replied Brandy.

The sting of the cold salt water was a refreshing antidote to the fever of worry which for days had run in Hugh's veins. As he rolled and splashed and reveled in the refreshing bath, tingling to the wash of the icy water over his brown body, his heart beat high with thankfulness and hope. Tom and Content had escaped, and Seeth, they said, would live. He turned and started back to the moored sloop.

As for the danger to himself, Hugh ignored the risk he had run that day. Seeth had needed him. He knew from the look in her eyes that he had brought her happiness and the desire to live—had given her courage, secure in his love. That was all he cared about or wished for—to save her from herself.

He swam up to the manrope Tom tossed him, drew himself up hand over hand, and threw a leg over the rail. Going forward, he called for Content's kettle of soft soap, and after lathering his head and scrubbing his face and body, plunged naked into the Cove and returned to the deck by the bowsprit stay, where he stood and squeezed the water from his thick hair, then whipped his tingling shoulders with his arms. In the last year he had not grown much in height, but Israel, who was closely watching him, noted with the eyes of a connoisseur the symmetry and power of the body.

Hugh got into canvas breeches and a shirt, and, barefooted, joined the men. "Mother Content threw away my shoes," he said ruefully. "I have now but my sea boots and the one best pair I save to wear with my broadcloth suit. 'Twas a pity to sink the shoes!"

"What need have you for ought but sea boots on the sloop?" asked Brandy. "It's on the *Gull* you stay, for we head at daylight for No-man's. We'll fish with Tom till the brig sails for Barbadoes."

Hugh swung on his heel and left them. Barbadoes! There would be no Barbadoes for Hugh Jocelyn that winter! He was needed in Newport. Seeth needed him, and Content and Tom. There would be no West Indy sea with its palms and white beaches and red-roofed towns and French privateers. He would stand by and face the plague with the others.

§52

At a table at the King's Head, where men came to drown the dread which lurked in their hearts in wine, rum, and metheglin, sat Joe Brenton, long since recovered from his head injury, a white and shaken John Arnold, wearing an empty sleeve, and a subdued Kit Sheffield, with Hugh and Trelawney.

"'Tis a shame, Hugh," said Brenton, "that you will not sail with Scarlett. You have never seen Barbadoes."

Hugh examined the pewter cup in his hand, his dark brows pulled together, while Trelawney pointedly shook his head at the speaker. "Mr. Brenton," replied the young man, "while the plague lasts my place is here, with my people."

Brenton already knew from Trelawney of Hugh's anxiety over Seeth Carr and did not press him. He turned to the pale-faced Arnold. "John, 'tis good to have you with us tonight. You're looking better every day."

"I give you gallant John Arnold, musketman on the *Royal Stede!*" cried Trelawney, raising his pewter mug of malmsey. "'Twas as glorious a fight and against odds as great as the doughty Drake or Henry Morgan ever fought! Gentlemen, Dick Trelawney, exile, gives you John Arnold, bless him! and the fighting men of Newport!"

The toast drunk, Hugh said impulsively:

"Mr. Brenton, I've had no chance to tell you what a shock I got that second day when I stumbled over you on your back in the *Stede's* bow with a broken head."

"I trust I was not in your way, Hugh," laughed Brenton. "They tell me that Picard's longboats near got us. Captain Paine could not use his swivels for fear of hitting his own men."

"There were but two things that blocked those boarders getting a foothold on our bow that day," said Sheffield, "Israel Brandy's cutlass and that windlass bar of Hugh's."

"And John and I flat on our backs to miss it!" lamented Joe Brenton.

Hugh's blood quickened to the praise of the older men. "It was fair hot while it lasted," he laughed. "Tom Paine was worth ten men, alone, and Israel was a roaring bull."

Brenton laid his hand on Hugh's shoulder. "Hugh, you have never seen Hammersmith, nor Cherry Neck and Rocky Farm. Some day in the spring I'll lead over a spare horse and you must ride back with me."

Hugh colored with pleasure at Brenton's renewal of the invitation to see the great estate on the Point. "It would pleasure me greatly to see Hammersmith, but—"

"But what, lad? You have no fear of my cackling aunt and her three chirping offspring you met the night the *Stede* returned from the fight? They are but children and look on you as a hero. They'll not bite or scratch you—if they do, at times, spit at me like kittens!"

"Yes, Hugh, you should see it," added Trelawney. "'Tis a beauty spot with a noble view down the East Passage and of the town."

"Sometime it would pleasure me to go with you, Mr. Brenton."

"When spring comes, then, I'll ride down for you with an extra horse, unless—" he hesitated—"unless the plague reaches Hammersmith this winter, which God forbid!"

"There's been no burial in three days, so Benoni tells me," said Sheffield. "Thank God for that! It may be lessening."

"Here, here!" objected the quiet Arnold. "'Tis hard enough to carry an empty sleeve. Let us not talk on this evening together of what is on every tongue in the port and chills every man's blood."

"Right, as always, John. 'Twas my fault to break our rule," said Joe. "Now for less gloomy thoughts. And before I forget it, Hugh, let me tell you there is one at Hammersmith who fair envies you."

Hugh's brows drew together in a puzzled look. "One at Hammersmith who envies Hugh Jocelyn?" The boy shook his head. "I can scarce believe that, Mr. Brenton."

"Dick will bear me out because he's her tutor and she adores him and he knows her heart's secrets. Little Desire, whom you saw that night, declares you have no right to such yellow hair—yellower than her primroses."

"What amends can I make for the fault?" laughed Hugh.

"This, my lad! She fair hates her black locks and threatens to color them. 'Twould greatly pleasure her to learn if you'd shear yours off that she might have them for a wig."

A burst of laughter greeted the remark. "The little devil!" chuckled Sheffield. "Name of God, she's a real Brenton!"

"'Tis true, Hugh," agreed Trelawney. "Mistress Desire is in earnest. She told it me, too. She was bewitched by your yellow head and hates her black tresses."

"So there seems nought for you to do, Hugh," said Sheffield gravely, "but to shear that mop of yours to the skull and present it to the lady."

Hugh's eyes twinkled as he met Joe Brenton's grin. "If you're in earnest, and your aunt, Dame Brenton, is willing, Mistress Desire may have my yellow thatch, now." He drew the cutlass he now always carried and pushed the handle at Trelawney. "Shear it off, Dick, and take it back with you!"

Trelawney, laughing, pushed the weapon away, and Hugh sheathed it.

"You mean to say the child was really serious?" demanded John Arnold, his pinched face lighting with interest.

"You little know her," said Trelawney. "Though her crow hair is lovely and wavy, she loathes it and craves yellow locks. Since she saw Hugh, she's given me no peace."

Sheffield's square, good-looking face shaped a grimace. "These Brentons are a stubborn lot and a greedy. If they see anything they want, they either take it or angle for it, for have it they will."

With a chuckle Joe clapped his cup of malmsey on the table. "Hugh," he replied, "Kit speaks the truth. You are already a scalped man. A Brenton is like an Indian. When she covets your hair, 'tis as good as lost. That minx, Desire, will have it yet."

So the friends bantered as they drugged with wine the fear within them.

When Hugh had left them for his skiff on the shore behind the tavern, to return to the *Sea Gull,* Sheffield turned to Brenton. "How about that young lady of spirit and temper, the fair Serena?"

A corner of Brenton's mouth curled as his amused eyes met Sheffield's. "You possess a good memory, Kit, and a greater curiosity," he replied. "But I admit, in this case, 'tis only natural. Serena, unlike little Desire, carries a cautious tongue. She keeps her thoughts well hid in that pretty head of hers, but I have my own private opinion of them as had you, that night, when they carried me on a stretcher off the *Royal Stede.*"

For Hugh the weeks following were days of hope and doubt, of mingled joy and apprehension. For Seeth Carr's recovery was slow, and it puzzled Chirurgeon Vigneron. More than once the doctor had asked Goodwife Carr if her daughter had some secret sorrow, some fear which harassed her, for she seemed constitutionally strong and when the disease left her should have fast regained her strength.

Following Hugh's first mad storming of the Carr house, Seeth's mother, with the help of Benoni Tosh and the doctor, had persuaded him not to try to see the sick girl until she was better. He knew that his coming had given her joy and courage, something to live for, a desire to recover, but until she was well and could talk with him he was forced to stay away. Each day he was ashore he left a letter at the Carr house—a letter filled with plans for their future and of devotion and love for the girl he knew was fighting a secret battle with gloom and despair.

Then came the afternoon when the *Gull* returned from a four days' absence, and Hugh found a note from Seeth tucked under the door of the closed Stanton house. It was written in an unformed hand and, in the manner of the day, many words were spelled with capitals. It read:

HUGH DEAREST,

Before You stood in the Doorway Y^t Day desire to Live had left me & all I wished was to Drift away to Forgetfulness. B^t seeing you, Hugh, was like— Well—was like a Starving man seeing Food. I thought You had done with Seeth Carr when You learned she had caught the Plague, and would have Fear to come. For You Knew my Face would be Pitted for life. The Scars are there now, with Hateful Red Spots. B^t my Sweet, naught kept Hugh Jocelyn from seeing me, though they refused Him, and Loving me and making me Wish to Live.

Chirurgeon Vigneron says all Danger is past. Mother will admit You, now, if You come to the House. I am up and stronger every Day in the Thought of Your Love Y^t I have always so Craved. Oh, You may never know W^t beats in my Heart of Love for You.

SEETH.

Hugh read and reread Seeth's letter. All the tenderness and affection in his nature went out to her, the sweet and gallant and loyal Seeth. In his heavy sea clothes he hurried to the Carrs'.

That evening Jonathan Carr was back at his cooperage and the door was opened to Hugh's knock by his wife, who smiled a welcome and left. On the settle, before the fire, Hugh found Seeth waiting.

"Seeth!" He ran to her and knelt with his arms around her trembling body, while her tawny head bent and she kissed his yellow hair.

"You made me whole, Hugh, with your love for me," she whispered. "When did you learn to love me so?" She searched deep into the eyes he lifted to hers, as if to find her answer there.

He took her face between his two hands and kissed her eyes and mouth. "When I learned in Boston that the plague was here I knew then how much I loved you, Seeth."

Her eyes glowed with joy as she stroked Hugh's head. "It was your coming that gave me back life—knowing you still cared—with my face marked."

He sat beside her and laughed as he lifted her into his lap and looked boldly into her happy eyes blurred by tears.

"I see no marks. But what do I see?" he demanded. "I see a girl who will soon be pert and coppet and bursting again with health. She has a cloud of yellow-brown hair that will not suffer a hood to prison it but seeks ever to curl and tumble about the sweetest brows and little ears. I look into a pair of eyes with the longest of dark lashes. They are gray-green, and often almost black, and again all a golden flame. I see a straight little nose and as red and warm and lovely a mouth as God ever gave woman, and a maid who wears in her breast the gallantest and truest heart."

With a swift catch of the breath she cupped his mouth with her hand in protest. "This is candlelight, but daylight always comes."

He held her at arm's length and frowned into her eyes. "Think you my love is like mist before the rising sun, to vanish with the light?"

"Why, you're a poet, Hugh! You talk like your Shakespeare!" she cried.

She threw back her head and laughed in sheer joy as he caught her to him. With a contented sigh she nestled in the big arms that held her, and together, in silence, they watched the flickering glow of the oak sticks on the hearth.

"They wished to ship me to Barbadoes on the Brenton brig," he said, holding her close to his heart. "But I'm telling them all that Seeth Carr and I are to wed, soon, and I may not ship deep-sea till she gives me leave."

§53

WHEN the ice stopped the cod fishing and the squadrons of geese and swan had passed south, Hugh returned to the shipyard to work on the neglected *Flying Fish*, which the Wantons planned to launch in the spring. Meanwhile, it was with reluctance that Israel Brandy had sailed on the *Swordfish* on her hazardous voyage to Barbadoes, but the

Brentons had persuaded him that they needed him as master gunner on their armed brig.

In the warming sun of Hugh Jocelyn's devotion Seeth Carr had rapidly become her old self. The color had returned to her face, and she had regained her lost weight. Often, to tease her, Hugh warned that he'd have no fat wife like some he knew, and she had better look to her eating. In her happiness that winter, she bloomed with health, and now, on Hugh's insistence, never spoke of the scars which disfigured her skin.

Hugh's prize money from Pound's captured ship, together with savings from wages and his share from the sale of fish, was still safe in the chimney, but he would need much more if he were to make a decent home for Seeth Carr. So, with reluctance, she agreed that their marriage should not prevent his sailing as boatswain on the *Flying Fish,* for a few lucky cruises on a privateer would provide them with a home and money, and Seeth was practical. To Hugh's surprise she had insisted on his continuing with his study of history and Latin with Trelawney.

As for the Englishman, he had watched the sudden shipwreck of his plans and hopes for Hugh's future with a secret grief and a public approval, for his loyalty to the youth never wavered. During the weeks of Seeth's illness, while the plague was at its height, he had seen little of Hugh, owing to his residence at Hammersmith, where he carried on his tutoring of the children of many of the wealthy families. But in their few talks together he came to view the situation through Hugh's eyes. He realized that Hugh's loyalty had lifted Seeth from black despair to happiness, and he understood. The Englishman's heart was large and his perception keen, and he saw the futility of attempting to dissuade Hugh from doing what, in the end, he feared would embitter his life. For marriage with Seeth was bound to lead to Jonathan Carr's cooperage, as the girl was so deeply in love she would never agree to the long separation involved in privateering voyages to the warm seas. Yet privateering, alone, offered Hugh the quick road to the wealth and power on which he had set his heart. And Trelawney wondered if, in the future, the young man's affection and pity would assuage the bitterness of broken hopes and balked ambition. For Hugh had time and again, to Trelawney's doubt and misgiving, sworn that he would carve a fortune for himself with his cutlass, own his own sloops, and out-bubble the crafty merchants of Newport at their own game. Now, how was that fierce spirit to be tamed to the prosaic ways of Jonathan Carr's cooperage?

Yet it was characteristic of the delicacy of the fine-grained Englishman that, when Joe Brenton expressed regret at Hugh's decision to marry and the possible ruin of his career at sea, Trelawney should avoid all mention of the sudden blasting of his hopes for Hugh's future.

It was a winter Newport would not soon forget, for the plague dragged on with processions of ox carts and sleighs carrying wooden boxes to the Common Burial Ground from forlorn and shuttered houses where grief and terror dwelt and memories and loneliness would follow through the years. At the cemetery, fires constantly burned to rid the ground of frost, that graves might be dug. But the greatest toll the dread disease had taken was from among the children. Week after week, on men's shoulders, little coffins found their way to freshly dug graves on Farewell Street. Some families fled to the country, but those that stayed in the seaport worked stoically on at their daily tasks and prayed for spring. On the streets the pitted and red-spotted faces of those who had gone down into the valley to return, disfigured for life, became a commonplace. Braving the contagion, men still went to the ordinaries for news of the French war and of privateers rumored off the coast, and to find in the anodyne of the cup surcease from the terror that stalked their footsteps.

In February the exhausted doctors announced that the plague was on the wane. The Governor, who in November, because of the smallpox, had met with the Assembly in Portsmouth, now announced that he would call a spring session in the seaport.

The haunted look gradually faded from the eyes of those on the street, and again men laughed and women smiled. When the ice cleared the harbor, the trade with Boston and the small New England ports, which for a time the plague had ruined, swiftly revived.

There had been times in December when the thoughts of Hugh Jocelyn traveled far south in the wake of the *Swordfish* carrying Israel to Barbadoes. He often wondered if the brig had passed the doldrums of the horse latitudes, had left the Bahamas and the Salt Islands, the rendezvous of the Turks Island salt rakers, and was now feeling the pull of the trades. Often Trelawney noted a secret restlessness and absence of mind in Hugh when they read together, and his heart went out to the lad who was fighting his lonely battle against the dreams of youth.

One evening Hugh went directly from the shipyard to the Carrs', as Seeth's family were to be away and they were to cook their own supper. As he entered the yard, in the early dusk, the windows of the fire room glowed with the light from the hearth and the candles. Stopping at a diamond-paned window, he looked in to surprise her. Beside a table, spread with a red Turkey carpet, on which stood a tallow dip, Seeth sat gazing intently at something in her hand which he could not see. She moved, and the thing in her hand caught the glow of the fire, and he saw that it was a small steel mirror.

A groan of protest left his lips. "She promised not to do that—not to brood over it! Oh, why does she do it?"

The girl's shoulders shook as she laid the mirror down.

Through the window Hugh called, "Seeth! You promised!" But the tears were gone as she quickly threw wide the door and opened her arms to him. As he held her to his heart, he sensed the desperate wildness of her mood. Then she lifted her face and said: "Forgive me—forgive me! I know 'tis wrong and I promised. But I may not help it! They are so hideous—those—"

He closed her lips with his hand and held the distraught girl tightly. "When will you put this from your mind? You promised! You are your same dear self to me, with your lovely hair and eyes and sweet shape! It matters not! Is it not enough to know I love you?"

"Yes! Yes! I know, Hugh! I promise!" She shivered as if in an effort to throw off her depression, then smiled up at him. "Now I'll be happy and forget, like a good maid!"

They sat before the fire and ate their supper of fresh rye-'n'-Injun bread, a broiled cod steak, succotash, and a cake she had baked that day. There were, too, cranberries from a Sakonnet bog and cheese from Narragansett. And as a surprise, she lifted a pewter pot from a trivet on the hearth and filled his cup with a thick, brown liquid and added muscovado sugar.

"Know what it is?" she asked.

Hugh tasted the sweetish beverage in his cup and shook his head.

"'Tis the new drink they name chocolate. There is another named coffee, made from grinding roasted beans and boiling the meal. I like it not so well."

Side by side the two sat before the fire and finished their meal.

"Open your mouth and shut your eyes!" she ordered, and stuffed Hugh's gaping jaws with a huge piece of her cake. She laughed hysterically as he chewed in mimic desperation on the cake, while she patted his bulging cheeks with her two hands.

To Hugh's relief the mood in which he had found Seeth had passed. They cleared the table, brushed the crumbs into a voider, washed the dishes and placed them with the spoons on the great dresser against the wall.

Then the lovers sat and watched the fire while they talked of the future. Suddenly she turned in his arms and fixed him with her graygreen eyes, and Hugh thought he had never seen the lights in them dance so madly. "Think you, Hugh," she asked, "I might love as deeply as that Juliet we read of in Mr. Trelawney's book, who took the poisoned draft because of love for her Romeo?"

She trembled in his arms, awaiting his reply, while her eyes searched his.

"There is much in you of Juliet, Seeth!" he replied, thrilling to the fire in her smoldering eyes. "You have a wild sweetness about you and a great power of loving. When you wish it, the very touch of you kindles the blood in my veins."

With a glad laugh she cried: "You still want me? Then I can give as she gave!" Her arms circled his neck and her lips passionately found his. From the depth of her bitterness she had been swept to the height of exaltation by the knowledge that she still stirred him as a woman—that it was not pity. The reckless mood which suddenly possessed her swept them into a whirlpool of emotion. They belonged to each other and had suffered much. And they were young.

Later, at the door, his face in her tumbled hair as she clung to him, she whispered: "Now nought may take you from me, not even death! You are mine—mine! Oh, I'm so happy, when before you came tonight I was near despair!"

His arms tightened tenderly about her. "And you are mine, forever, sweet—Juliet. You will never again brood as I found you today? For I love you! Promise me!"

"I promise!" she whispered.

§54

In March Hugh was offered the berth of mate and master gunner on an armed sloop, the *Wild Duck*, in the coastwise trade, and, because of the money it would bring, accepted with Seeth's consent, for they were saving every shilling for their marriage in May. A month later, after runs to New London, Boston, and Salem, on which they saw no signs of the French, he returned to Newport. As he left the wharf carrying his sea bag, with gifts of a gown, hood, and stockings for Seeth, he met and stopped to shake hands with Jerusa Sugars, the carpenter.

"Have you seen Content and Tom?" asked Hugh of the little man, who seemed strangely silent as his grave eyes avoided Hugh's face.

"Ay, Content and Tom are well," was the laconic reply.

Hugh turned up Thames Street on his way to the house of the girl who would be waiting. He pictured her shining face and the joy in her eyes as she flew to his arms. He could already feel the warmth of her clinging body and the beating of her heart against his. Seeth! With the wild strain in her that so thrilled him, and the sweetness and loyalty.

He neared the Carrs' house and searched the windows for her face, for the news of the arrival of the *Wild Duck* that morning must have reached Seeth and her mother. But she had not heard, and her tawny head was not visible. Goodwife Carr answered his knock. The eyes in her drawn face were circled with shadow. Her quivering lips were pitiful in her effort at control as she looked hopelessly at the stunned boy.

"Goodwife—"

"Hugh, oh, Hugh!" she cried. "You poor lad! You poor lad!"

The sea bag in his hand slumped to the threshold of the door. Numbed and speechless, he stared at the softly weeping woman as the blood drained from his face. Seeth! Name of God, something had happened to Seeth! He reached and took the inarticulate woman by the arms. "Tell me! Tell me!" he cried.

"Seeth—" she murmured—"is . . . gone!"

Gone? Seeth gone? Something seemed to explode in Hugh's brain. It was not true! His Seeth! He held the sorrowing mother at arm's length and searched her eyes. "Seeth—you say—is—"

"Come inside, Hugh."

He followed her into the fire room and flung himself on a stool, as she told the pitiful story. For a fortnight after Hugh had left on the sloop Seeth had been cheery and had talked much of her coming marriage and her plans for the little home near her father's house. Then her mood had changed, and almost daily her mother had surprised her gazing into her mirror. The efforts of the older woman to banish the girl's melancholia had been useless, and one day, the week previous, Seeth Carr had disappeared. Later they had found her floating in the Cove.

The first paroxysm of Hugh's grief passed, leaving him numb and silent. With his agony had come remorse—a vague sense of responsibility for this ghastly thing. She had not dared hazard the future with him—had not believed he would always love her, that in his eyes her face had never changed. Dry-eyed, he gazed hopelessly into the fire, while Goodwife Carr left the room. She returned, and her hand lingered on Hugh's yellow head as he stared blindly at the burning oak logs.

"She left this for you, Hugh," said the woman, placing a folded sheet of paper, sealed with wax, in his hands.

He stared at the missive, turning it over and over, fearing to open it. Then he steeled himself, broke the seal, and read:

BELOVED:

It was no Use. I have been so Happy these Few months. Happy beyond my Dreams. For, at last, We belonged to Each Other. But it was no use. You see, Dearest, Whom I have Loved with all my Soul and Heart, I am a Woman and Know. You would never discover it to Me but I know what a Cross it would be to You—a Wife with a face pitted with

Small-Pox. You have made me so Happy with your Love, I
durst not Risk losing it in the Future. Forgive me, Hugh. I
tried to Hope but it was no use. No one will ever give you
her Soul and every Breath of her Body as have I.

Good-by, Hugh.

SEETH.

The paper fell from his listless fingers to the floor. In her hour of
need he had failed her! He had tried so hard to comfort her—to convince her, but in her heart she had doubted—had not dared to face the
future. The scars on her lovely face had hemmed her in with a wall of
doubt and fear beyond which she dared not pass. Rather than someday
to discover pity in his eyes where love had dwelt, she had preferred
not to live.

Hugh found Content alone when he entered the Stanton house.
She looked up, and the anguish in his eyes drained her face of the joy
which for the moment had lighted it. "Hugh! My poor Hugh!" She
held the silent boy to her heart. "You have been to the Carrs'?"

"Yes," he said, and shivered as his smothered grief sought to voice
itself. Then the tears burst their bonds and he cried as he had once as
a little boy, on the sanctuary of Content's comforting breast.

That night, hearing of Hugh's return, Trelawney rode in from
Hammersmith. "Will you sail again with the *Wild Duck*, Hugh?"

"No, I shall work at the yard until the *Flying Fish* is launched.
Then, when Israel returns, we're off to make our fortune."

Content's heart fell as she listened, for she knew how reckless and
desperate Hugh Jocelyn would now be.

"God help the French," laughed Trelawney, "when you and Israel
and the wild Wantons start after them!" He lifted his cup of flip. "Success to the *Flying Fish*!"

"Unless the *Swordfish* has met with mishap she should be standing
up the East Passage one of these days with a fine cargo of sugar and
molasses," observed Tom.

"Joe Brenton is fair anxious about her," said the Englishman, "for
a sloop has brought word into Boston that the French have taken many
of our craft in the West Indies."

Hugh accompanied Trelawney outside when he left. The arm of
the older man stole around the shoulders of the stricken boy. "My
heart went out to you, lad, when I heard. I know how you have griev-
ed."

They stood in the moonlight and Hugh faced his friend. "You felt
all along that I had done with dreams—was headed for a commonplace cooper and your toil over me thrown away. I saw it in your
eyes."

"No, Hugh, you do not state it fairly. Such steadfastness and devotion could not be lightly trampled underfoot. I understood. But now you must not brood or blame yourself. You were stanch to the end. You have your life to live. Treasure her memory, lad, but keep your eyes on the stars."

"But—but I do blame myself. If I had—"

"No. You are wrong. Have done with brooding and show the world a brave face."

"I mean to show you yet that you have not wasted your time on me," Hugh said. "But I will long carry a sore heart."

"I know, but a gallant one as well, Hugh Jocelyn."

Drugging the pain of his grief for Seeth in the hard labor of shaping oak and white pine with ax and adz and in the strain of long hours in the saw pit, Hugh lived for Israel's return and the launching of the graceful hull which was rapidly taking shape on the stocks on Easton's Point. Then came a May day when the patched top hamper of the overdue *Swordfish* was sighted off Beaver Tail, and soon the brig sailed into Newport harbor, minus her foretopmast and with her rails ragged from gunfire. She berthed at Brenton's Wharf, where a crowd welcomed the craft many had thought lost.

The news reached the Wantons' shipyard, and Hugh dropped his adz and ran through Shipwright Street to Thames, and so to the wharf. There, as he approached, he saw the bushy mane and square body of the man he loved.

"Ho, Israel!" called Hugh, and pushing through the excited men surrounding Brandy, ran into the sailor's open arms.

"Stab my guts, Hugh," cried Brandy, "you missed a sweet fight, lad! But we brought our cargo home if we did leave our foretopmast and some rail splinters to the sharks off Guadeloupe!"

The two friends wrung each other's hands. " 'Tis good to have you home again safe and sound, Israel!"

"Who-ree! Burn me, it pleasures me to sight that yeller top of yours, Hugh!" Brandy held the boy at arm's length and squinted up into his brown face. "Thank God, the plague passed you by! And Tom and Content, and my sister?"

"All well, Israel."

"Well, you son-of-a-sea-gunner, tonight I'll spin you a yarn 'twill make that long hair stand on end," laughed Brandy, stumping off the wharf, arm in arm with Hugh.

"You met up with a Frenchman?"

"No less! And 'tis lucky for Scarlett he had Israel Brandy for gunner!"

That evening, with clay pipe in one hand and a cup of beer laced with rum in the other, Israel sat with the Stantons and Hugh and told his story.

"We worked through the Horse Lateetudes without much delay and made a quick run past the Bahamas, sightin' but two or three Turks Island salt rakers and a forty-gun English ship o' war which boarded us, scanned our papers, and warned us to give Guadeloupe and Martinique plenty sea room on our course to Barbadoes."

"When did you make Barbadoes?" asked Hugh.

"In February we sails into Bridgetown—as short a run as ever I heard of. But the *Swordfish* is a lively craft, and the weight of her eight guns was no harm to her on the wind."

"She rode pretty low, I thought, at the wharf," said Hugh.

"Ay, but owin' to the need of it here, Scarlett put in every hogshead of molasses, sugar, and indigo she'd carry, and that's heavy stuff."

"Barbadoes!" said Hugh, with a sigh. "How often I've dreamed of sailing into Bridgetown, Israel, and seeing the palms and the white houses and the hibiscus!"

"And layin' your tongue to some of that heavy, red rum that puts fire into your veins," added Brandy, smacking his lips. "They makes a rare rum in Bridgetown!"

"When did you run into trouble?" asked the interested Hugh.

Israel calmly drained his cup, relit his pipe, and said, "Who's tellin' this yarn?"

"I hoped you were," replied Hugh, glancing slyly at the smiling Stanton, "but I see I needs must get it from Captain Scarlett or one of the lads of the crew."

Israel's brows met in a fierce scowl. His small eyes blazed as he thrust his craggy chin at Hugh. "Captain Scarlett and Mate Drury was flat on the deck—wounded by the first shots fired—and stayed there. Only the bo's'n and Israel Brandy, who sailed and fought her, can tell that story!"

Properly reproved, Hugh waited for Israel to knock out and refill his pipe and begin.

"We was some days out of Bridgetown, off Guadeloupe, and makin' slow work of it crossin' the trades, good sailor though she be. Not a Frenchman had we sighted off Martinique, though they warned us at Barbadoes that the Wind'ard Islands was thick with 'em huntin' English ships. Then one mornin' the sun lifts on a flat sea and no air." Israel stopped to wag his shaggy head and chuckle. " 'Twas my watch, and with the light, what think you I made out lyin' a mile astern of us but a long, low slimy craft they calls a peeragua, with her canvas hangin' limp from her yards. I calls Captain Scarlett. 'If that be not a Tortuga pirate with French papers, I'll eat my hand,' I sez.

"He hands the glass to me with a sour look. 'I like not the look of her, Israel,' he sez.

"She carried only six guns, but what looked bad was, her decks was black with men and she had three boats in the water alongside.

"'Captain,' I sez, 'with the wind dead, them boats'll soon swarm over us like flies after sugar. We'd best tumble up the men and clear for action.'

"'Ay, Israel, we'd best!' sez he."

"Was she privateer or pirate?" interrupted Hugh.

Israel grinned. "How was we to tell at that distance? There was no fair wind to carry the smell. She showed no colors, but pirate or privateer, we was fair in a clove hitch if we let 'em board us, for she carried many men, as the glass showed. We got up and stowed our powder and ball handy to the guns, and loaded the swivels and small arms. Then the French put out their sweeps and headed for us, towin' the three boats. 'Twas plain they meant to board us on both beams."

There was the crunch of gravel on the walk and a knock on the door.

William and John Wanton walked in and warmly welcomed Brandy home.

"Israel," said William, "'tis good to have you back! Captain Scarlett tells us the French gave you a drubbin' off Guadeloupe and you got off by a hair. We're fevered to hear the story."

The old sailor's face clouded with anger. He glared at Wanton's guileless countenance, his mouth twitching as the veins in his neck swelled. "Took a drubbin', did we? Slit my windpipe, William Wanton, what call you a drubbin'? We leaves the galley settlin' from the water in her hold and—" Brandy swallowed hard on his irritation, paused a moment and cannily changed his tack. "William, when once I clears the wharf and shakes out my jib and mainsail, I heads for sea and comes about for no late comers. Batten your hatch while I finish my story."

William grinned at Hugh and Stanton with surreptitious delight. "Right, as always, Israel! Let her run!"

Brandy drank noisily from his cup, wiped his lips with his tongue, and started: "As I was sayin', before a certain party I could name crossed my hawse, the galley starts for us with the sweeps, and just out of range fills the three boats, to board us."

Israel stopped and surveyed his intent audience. "Well, young sprigs, what was we to do then?"

Lights danced in William Wanton's keen eyes. "Why, with Israel Brandy sighting the guns, blow the longboats out of the water!"

"Well spoke, William," agreed Israel, nodding gravely. "But the boats wouldn't bunch, and sweet shootin' 'twould take!"

"Were your crew scared?" asked Hugh. "Did you trust 'em?"

"There was green faces among 'em, but I heartened 'em with the promise to cut them boats to fish bait. The galley was still out of range but movin' in under her sweeps."

"What happened then, Israel?" demanded John Wanton.

Brandy coolly relighted his pipe with a coal, blew a thick cloud of smoke from his mouth, and fixed John with his squinting eyes. "What think you happened?" he asked.

With a glance at Hugh and William, John innocently replied: "Why—why, the master gunner of the *Swordfish* missed the longboats and the French swarmed over her rails and—and not a soul lived to tell the tale!"

Rocking on their stools, Hugh and William choked back their laughter at the savage scowl which darkened Brandy's face as he thrust his square jaw at John. Then Israel rose and stumped about the room growling like a dog, while the others waited for him to cool. Shortly he wheeled, and standing over John Wanton shook a thick finger in his red face. "Stab me, John Wanton," he rasped, "did I not respect your father and brother Joe I'd have you over my good knee! Burn my bones! If all died on the *Swordfish*, how comes it she lies now at Brenton's Wharf with her cargo safe? And how, if I missed the French boats, be I here tellin' the story? Answer me that!"

"Tut—tut, Israel!" soothed Tom Stanton. "The lad but sought to speed your tale. He is that fevered to hear it he scarce can wait."

"Go on, Israel," urged Hugh. "I'm hot to hear how you beat them off."

Israel looked at John's guileless round face. "John," he chuckled, "young roosters was made to listen to the old and wise and not crow afore their tail feathers is grown. This is what fell out. The galley hangs off out of range and breaks out the French colors, while her longboats headed for us. They come within gunshot, when the galley starts with her sweeps. Four of 'em aimin' to surround us. I sights the starboard demiculverin and the sakers and lets the galley have it full in her guts, smashin' half the sweeps on that beam, and she stops rowin'; but the boats kept comin'. It was plain that we was in for a lively mornin'. But we was poundin' the galley hard, and the French shot mostly over us."

"Did you hit the boats?" asked Hugh.

"I made no fair hit on the longboats till they was close, and the third boat headed for our bow and we couldn't bear on it. Our guns pounded the galley, but she got her sweeps goin' again and was sheerin' in to board, with her decks full of howlin' mustees. It looked bad if we let 'em close with us—they was too many. We figgered they had close to a hundred men, and if they reached our decks it was all up with the *Swordfish*. Then somethin' happened."

Brandy rose, leisurely knocked out his pipe and helped himself to the beer, while his impatient audience chafed at the delay.

"What saved you, Israel?" demanded Hugh. "Did you cut up the longboats with the swivels? Did the galley board?"

"Yes, and what became of the boat off your bow?" asked William.

"Couldn't you stop the galley with the six-pounders?" clamored John, walking back and forth in his excitement.

Israel's wide mouth stretched from ear to ear as he calmly contemplated his aroused listeners. He took a deep, leisurely draught from the cup, and evidenced his satisfaction with a loud "Ah!" It was his turn now, and he was making the most of it.

"Come, Israel," urged Tom Stanton. "How did you beat them off with no wind to move you?"

Israel turned on them. "Who said there was no wind?" he bellowed. "Stab my guts, 'twas me see it comin' over the flat sea! When I see it, I give them boats the swivels and yells to the crew to stand by.

"Scarlett and Drury was down and I took charge. The boat off our bow was in close when the puff hit us and we picked up steerageway. Smashed as she was, they had rowed the galley close in on our beam when that blessed breeze struck. The jib and stay sail filled and her bow swung, then the fore and maintops'ils bellied, and we was off!"

Deep sighs of relief filled the room.

"The longboat makin' for our bow started to sheer off. That give me my chance. We put the tiller over hard and had 'em on their beam! Our boys give 'em a volley with the muskets, then our forefoot rolls 'em under. 'Twas like breakin' an egg with a knife, the way we crunched that longboat to kindlin' under our keel!" In his excitement, Israel rose and shook his empty cup. "And who think you was flounderin' alongside, like a speared whale, among them screamin' mustees? I see his ugly face plain while he churned the water bellerin' for help. No less nor our friend Jules Picard, one ear and all!"

"Picard? Christ's blood! Are you certain, Israel?" gasped William.

"Certain? I'd know him in hell! He'd dropped down in the world some since we give him his bellyful off Block Island—down to a peeragua he was, a slimy galley."

"What happened him?" demanded Hugh.

"I could a sunk 'em all with the poop swivels but, instead, wishes him a pleasant cruise to hell! We give the wallowin' galley a last broadside as we passed, and later I see one of the boats pickin' men out of the water. It may be Picard was not drowned, but he never got to board the *Swordfish*!"

"Name of God, Israel, you played in luck to have that puff of air hit you!" said Hugh. "Did the breeze last?"

"Yes; and the last we see of the galley through the glass she was settlin', so Picard had a long row back to Guadeloupe."

As the company broke up, William Wanton said to Brandy, "The *Flying Fish* will be launched and ready for sea in June and we'll need our master gunner." With a grimace Israel stiffened, threw out his big chest, and waved a salute.

"Ay, ay! Your master gunner reports for duty now!"

"Good! There's plenty to do yet. See you at the yard in the morning!"

4. The Call of the Warm Seas

§55

JUNE CAME and the graceful hull of the *Flying Fish* stood in the stocks near completion. Often, as the Wanton shipwrights, aided by Brandy and Hugh, worked on her bulwarks and poop deck, seamen and townsmen came to the yards to inspect the craft which had been so long in building but of which so much was expected. She was a ninety-ton sloop, one hundred feet over all, with a long run, and built for great speed on the wind; but the lines of her bow and bilges were so easy that she looked longer. As she was to carry a weight of ten tons in guns, her deck was low slung, with a deep sweep; her beam wide, but her bulwarks were high and heavy. The critical eye of Captain Tom Paine had pronounced the *Flying Fish* the fastest-looking sloop ever built in Newport. But there were sailors in the port who shook shaggy heads, doubting her ability to carry ten heavy guns in a cross sea without rolling her rails under. But William Wanton and his brother John desired a craft quick in stays and able to outfoot the more heavily armed brigs and ships she would meet, and gave little thought to the doubters.

With the passing of spring, the plague had left Newport. Women again leaned from windows to chatter across narrow streets, and men laughed and shouted at their work, for fear had left their hearts.

One day early in June, Joe Brenton rode down with a spare horse and took Hugh from his work for a day at Hammersmith. It was not without much misgiving that Hugh put on his broadcloth suit and his shoes with pewter buckles and rode off down Thames Street beside Brenton. Eyebrows lifted in surprise as merchants stood at their doors and watched Hugh Jocelyn, the fisherman, astride a horse in such company.

The memory of his meeting with Dame Brenton and her daughters was still vivid, as was Joe's reference to Lettice visiting the pillory, which had brought the blood to his face and embarrassed him. He wondered if those imps of maids would again measure him with the bold scrutiny of two pairs of black eyes, as they did when he stood before them on the wharf that night after the fight, with bandaged head, and in tattered shirt and canvas drawers. Should he see the eldest, Serena, who had taken his part when the irrepressible Joe had asked them if they blamed Lettice Brinley for going to the pillory? It had been as though she pitied the son of a fisherman who had chanced to cross their path.

Hugh had always wished to see the great Brenton estate, whose three farms reached from the East Passage to the first of the white sand beaches of the south shore. From the deck of the *Gull* he had often watched the grazing cattle, horses, and great flocks of sheep. He had heard of the fruit trees and flowers brought from England by the first Brenton, and had wondered, as he passed in the sloop, what the great house set in the trees on the hill looked like near at hand. Now he was going there, and eventually he forgot his diffidence over meeting Dame Brenton and her daughters in his interest in Hammersmith.

"I want you to see," Joe was saying as they rode down Thames Street, "why we Brentons hold so fast to our home in the country and regret coming into town for the winter. But the road goes bad and the girls need tutoring and the company of their kind and age, so we come to the Thames Street house."

"I am little customed to the company of ladies, Mr. Brenton, and hope my manners will not displease them."

Joe Brenton glanced sidewise at his companion and laughed. "Trelawney has schooled you well, Hugh. You need fear the company of no one nor the learning of any. 'Tis they who will be awed by your size and good looks."

"You bring the blood to my face with talk like that!"

"Pah! You know you fill the eye, lad. Don't belittle yourself!"

They passed Cannon and Brewer's streets, reached Mile's End, and left Newport, to skirt the harbor on the Hammersmith road. Circling Brenton's Cove, which cut deeply into the rock ledges of the high shore, the horsemen entered Hammersmith Farm. On the hilltop, ahead, towered the great house with its four stone chimneys and its balustraded promenade walk on the roof commanding a view southwest down the East Passage to Beaver Tail and the sea, north past Goat Island and Conanicut, and east over the harbor to the shipping and wharves and the four hundred houses of Newport. They turned into a long avenue and rode between columns of English and native elms, fresh in their young leaves. Surrounding the house, graveled walks flanked by hedges of fragrant English box ran hither and thither past settees and diminutive summerhouses bowered with eglantine, pink with bloom. In the background nodded white syringas and clumps of pink and white laurel; and everywhere were beds of gillyflower and feverfew and patience, with stately rows of hollyhocks thrusting up behind them not yet in bloom. At the foot of the garden was a lily pond, its shores banked with blooming sweetbrier, and near it, a large sundial of bronze set on a buried boulder.

Beyond, reached the herb garden, enclosed in an aromatic box hedge: St.-John's-wort and comfrey, used for wounds; tansy for tea and spring tonic, and prized as a stimulant for the sick; goldenrod and gentian, hyssop and pimpernel, for drawing thorns and splinters; sage for tea, and Solomon's-seal for broken bones; fragrant thyme, and rosemary, which aided the memory.

They rode to the stables, where a groom took the horses, and then wandered over the garden. Never had Hugh seen such a riot of flowers. In place of stools, the summer houses contained chairs shaped in the round and built of cedar with the bark left on, from which one might watch the glittering waters of the East Passage.

"My grandfather, William Brenton, planned all this," said Joe, with a sweep of his hand. "It took years of hard work, for 'twas mostly wooded. He brought flowers and shrubs and trees from England. There are few places like it in the New England colonies."

"'Tis all so beautiful it fair takes my breath," said Hugh.

The beat of horses' hoofs sounded on the graveled roadway, and three girls, followed by a black boy, trotted up to the two men. Wearing red, blue, and green silk hoods and riding capes, and safeguard skirts to protect their clothes from the brush, the flushed-faced maids stared in surprise at the transformed Hugh.

"Serena, Desire, Bess, I have torn Hugh Jocelyn from the Wantons' shipyard to see Hammersmith."

"Your servant!" Hugh bowed, embarrassed but secretly amused at the surprise on the girls' faces.

The sailor with bandaged head and tattered shirt had been transformed into a presentable young giant in broadcloth, with white band and cravat circling his brown neck. Thirteen-year-old Desire stared with open mouth and envious eyes at Hugh's yellow hair. The black eyes of little Bess roved in surprise from his neckband to the shining pewter buckles of his shoes. Serena nodded; but there was little warmth in her voice as she said, "Welcome to Hammersmith, Hugh Jocelyn!"

Joe Brenton and the groom aided the girls in dismounting at a horse block, and the black led their mounts away.

"Where have you been this morning?" asked Brenton.

"Down past Cherry Neck to the Spouting Rock. The sea is beautiful!"

As Serena led the way up the path with Joe Brenton, Desire and Bess dropped behind Hugh to stare with unconcealed envy at his hair. The uneasy young man watched the older sister's vivid face as she bantered with her cousin. With an impatient toss of her head she threw back her scarlet hood from the masses of her crow-black hair ruffled by the breeze. Hugh realized that she was taller than he had thought, but her cape concealed her figure. Curiously he watched her dark eyes flash and her teeth gleam in a smile, as she joked with her cousin. Though but seventeen, Serena Brenton could hold her own with that quick tongue of hers. And handsome she surely was with her cloud of hair, sloe-black eyes, and fair skin. Hugh turned to the small maids beside him.

"'Tis a most beautiful home you have, Mistress Desire," he opened with.

Desire smiled up at the sailor who towered above her black head. "Yes, Hugh Jocelyn," she boldly answered, "but I would gladly trade it for your hair!" She blushed furiously, but her fascinated eyes clung to the head of the surprised Hugh.

"I would never think to part with such lovely tresses as yours, Mistress Desire," he said. "They are fair beautiful, and so wavy."

The girl gaped into Hugh's amused face. "You are honest about my hair? Why, I hate it!"

"'Tis lovely, I think," answered Hugh, recalling Joe Brenton's tale of Desire's wish to have a wig from his hair. "It becomes your pretty eyes, Mistress Desire. Never would I part with that beautiful hair were I you."

Desire's round face grew thoughtful. "If—if I were to have a wig of your hair, Hugh Jocelyn, my eyes and brows would still be black," she gravely considered. "They would not match, would they?"

"Of course not, and I'd not think you half so pretty," added Hugh.

Roguish eyes lifted to his. "You think me pretty, then?"

"Of a surety! Most pretty and—charming."

Catching the remark Brenton wheeled around. "Here, here, Hugh!" he demurred. "You'll have this maid fair out of her silly head with your compliments. She's barely thirteen and already spends too much time before her glass."

Serena turned to Hugh with quizzical eyes. "Our guest should be merciful. He'll find Desire too easy a conquest for his proven talents."

It was like the flick of a whip on raw flesh. The blood moved up over Hugh's neck and face as he met Serena Brenton's enigmatical smile. She was thinking of Lettice.

"Fair ladies," announced Brenton, "Hugh and I are off to the horse and cattle barns, then over to Rocky Farm. We'll meet you at midday meal."

The two men rode past fields of corn and barley and lush Rhode Island grass, past great flocks of the famous Brenton sheep grazing on the upland meadows, then down to the ledges of the broken south shore. They passed the cherry orchards of Cherry Neck, started from seedlings brought from England, and went on to the big lily pond and the Spouting Rock and cliffs of the east shore. To the north lay the two long white beaches divided by Easton's Point and, farther on, Sachuest. Out at sea, Cormorant Rock, white with gulls, lay off the mouth of the Sakonnet; and east of it, across four miles of water, Sakonnet Point thrust its rocky fangs into the ocean.

"'Tis a sweet shore, this," said Brenton, "with its cliffs and coves and white beaches. There's nought like it on the whole coast."

"No, there is no island 'twixt here and Cape Cod so beautiful," said Hugh. "I long to see the keys and the palm islands of the West Indies to learn if they outshine it."

"Before this war is over you'll see them, Hugh. We need you in our trade with Barbadoes."

Returning, they found Dame Brenton and her three daughters waiting for them in a rustic summerhouse, where the midday meal had been spread on a table laid with a red Turkey carpet. A tall, silver standing salt, brought from England, was in the center. At each shining pewter plate was a silver sneak cup and taster, a knife, spoon, and fork. Rare in Newport, the forks were the first Hugh had ever seen.

In the eyes of the embarrassed young man, Dame Brenton was an impressive figure in her flowered tabby frock and black lace whisk. Though a widow in her forties, a heartbreaker curled coyly at the base of her matronly neck, below which a lace modesty cloth but imperfectly shielded her fair and plump bosom from profane eyes. Serena and her younger sisters had changed from broadcloth riding habits into dainty lustring frocks with puffed virago sleeves, caught in love knots by colored ribbons that matched their blue, green, and crimson stockings. On their feet were shoes with red and white heels.

Overcome by so much female elegance, Hugh bowed over Dame Brenton's plump hand, murmuring, "Your servant, ma'am!" as his hostess greeted him.

"Welcome to Hammersmith, Hugh Jocelyn," she said. "Joe tells me your family escaped the terrible plague. 'Tis a blessing!"

From behind Hugh's shoulder Joe Brenton frowned and pointedly shook his head at his aunt.

Glancing at Serena, who was watching him, Hugh thought that her dark eyes pictured her sympathy as the thought of Seeth flicked him with pain. "Yes, my—family escaped," he answered.

Joe Brenton led the talk to happier things. "We are expecting great deeds of the *Flying Fish*, Hugh. When do the Wantons plan to launch her?"

"Soon, they hope. Then we're off for a fling at the French."

"Is it because you're so strong and fearless that you love a fight?"

Hugh met the candid eyes of the girl who leaned toward him

across the table. Unlike her mother, she wore no modesty cloth below her black whisk and the youth's eyes caught the flawless modeling of her neck, marked the tint of color which flowed to her cheeks, and the raven brush strokes of brows above her brilliant eyes, which seemed to search through him for her answer.

"Why, Serena," demurred the older woman, while Joe Brenton scowled his disapproval, "what a strange question!"

Serena Brenton's eyes were so honest that Hugh was disarmed. "We are at war, Mistress Brenton," he replied. "I do not love a fight, but war means fighting. 'Tis not pretty, I grant you. In your eyes, no doubt, 'twould be cruel and loathsome."

Serena's eyes snapped with dancing lights. Her color deepened as she replied, "So that is what you think me, Hugh Jocelyn, too frail for the sight of blood—a weakling!"

The girl's resentment was so marked that Hugh reddened to his ears. "I crave pardon," he stammered. "I meant no such thing. But war is not for the eyes of ladies. I am certain you could face—face anything. I know you have courage, Mistress Serena. But did we not harry the French, they would stop all trade on our coast. That would ruin Newport. I am poor, and in privateering there is chance for gain. Is that a crime, to be poor?" Under the fire of her searching eyes Hugh hardly knew what he was saying. He only realized that he could not fathom her, that there was something baffling about this girl.

But Joe Brenton burst out indignantly: "Name of God! Is this the manner my family treats my guest—to betwixt him? What's got into you, Serena?"

Serena's level gaze never left Hugh's face as her cousin exploded. When he had finished, she smiled, though her lower lip quivered, and Hugh sensed the struggle she was making to control herself. Then she quietly said: "I crave your pardon, Hugh Jocelyn. I meant nothing unkind. All Newport knows you are brave. If I've offended, I'm sorry."

"'Twas a fair question, Mistress Serena," said Hugh, moved by the girl's frank apology. "There's nought to be sorry for. To be honest, I'm fair sick before a sea fight with thought of the blood and the maiming. But when it once starts, one forgets to have fear. It makes one feel alive."

Then to the surprise of Joe Brenton and the horror of her mother, Serena impulsively burst out with: "'Twould thrill me to see men fight—fight when all hope was gone! Fight like those heroic Greeks at Thermopylae Mr. Trelawney tells us of. I'd like to see men fight like that, not for gain or glory but—for—for their right!" With a choked sob Serena Brenton rose and left the table.

"Why—why, whatever has come over her?" gasped Dame Brenton, watching her daughter's retreating back. "She's fantastical!"

Joe Brenton smiled mysteriously. "Don't mind our Mistress Impulse, Hugh. Serena's that way—always surprising us with some wild fancy, then leaving us to wonder at it. She meant no unkindness, but she's deep and feels strongly. She has too much heart."

Desire gravely turned to Hugh. "Pay no heed to Serena, Hugh Jocelyn," she admonished. "'Tis but one of her burst outs! She'll seek comfort from her spinet, and when she has twanged it sufficient her sulks will be over."

The dazed Hugh had no answer, and presently from the house there drifted the thin tinkling of the virginal.

"There she goes!" laughed Desire. "Now, Mother, may we eat?"

From the kitchen, black maids brought broiled chicken, with young peas and beets and delicate corn muffins. Potato was unknown, but there was the new drink, chocolate, and Canary wine, and strawberries buried in cream. In the colonies pudding was commonly served first at meals, but Dame Brenton had heard that it was now no longer done in England, so it was omitted.

Never before had Hugh sat at such a table, or used a fork, and he became suddenly aware of the size of his brown hand as it grasped one doubtfully. As he watched the plump white hands of his hostess, he thought of Content's, red from washing and rough with toil, and the latent resentment he bore toward the rich for an instant rose to the surface. Then he caught the merry eyes of Desire and Bess furtively watching him. He returned their smiles, but was inwardly hot with embarrassment.

Joe Brenton came to his rescue. "A table fork is doubtless strange to you, Hugh, as it was once to me. I, myself, fancy a knife and fingers, but forks seem in fashion in London and we needs must follow. To my mind a fork is but poor aid in eating."

"They are the first small ones of silver I've ever seen," Hugh said, watching how the others held and used theirs.

Waiting impatiently for Hugh's initiation, Desire and Bess giggled.

"Pay no heed to the silly imps, Hugh," Joe comforted. "When Desire first tried to use one she dropped it on the floor."

The objects of Joe's banter rocked with laughter. Reddening to the ears, Hugh said, "I trust I prove not too clumsy." He lifted his fork and attempted to spear the half chicken as he would stab a swordfish with a lance. The chicken slipped from the plate and, to the delight of the young watchers, the fork left Hugh's uncertain fingers.

"That's exactly what happened to Desire, Hugh," laughed Joe to the mortified youth. "Pay no heed to the twittering of these sparrows!"

"Children, children!" reproved the girls' mother. "Where are your manners?" Her arched brows lifted still higher as she contemplated the humiliated sailor at her table.

Hugh raised embarrassed eyes. "I—I crave your pardon, Dame Brenton," he stumbled.

Then the delighted Desire and Bess burst into uncontrolled laughter, in which Joe and Hugh joined and the ordeal was over.

Later, as the horses were led from the stables, Desire came flying from the house.

"Why, Desire, what fevers you so?" demanded Joe.

Clutching a pair of scissors and rosy with color, the girl approached Hugh. "Hugh Jocelyn," she said, pulling at his sleeve, "I've come to snip a lock of your hair to see if it becomes me. Would you give it me?"

"In God's name!" gasped Brenton. "What a brazenness! I warned you, Hugh, the minx would scalp you!"

With a laugh Hugh insisted: "Lock for lock, Mistress Desire. If you'll shear me a plume of those black ringlets, you may have one of mine. Is it a bargain?"

"But what will you ever do with it?"

"Wear it on my heart, fair lady."

He dropped to one knee beside the delighted maid. A red tongue appeared at a corner of her small mouth as, reaching, she snipped off a lock of her crow-black hair and placed it in his hand. Then with an "Oh!" of delight she ran her fingers through his blond mane and cut off a handful.

"'Burn me!' as Israel Brandy would say," laughed Brenton, "but you two have gone frenzical! Now, Desire, when your mother misses that lock, remember you forced it on Hugh!"

With a farewell wave of the hand, the excited Desire sped back to the house and the privacy of her room, to learn from her mirror the effect of framing black brows and eyes with a mop of yellow hair.

On the way back to town Hugh found himself wondering as to the cause of Serena Brenton's strange action and of her seeming dislike of him. He had felt it in her manner, and often a veiled hostility seemed to lurk in her eyes. Was it the natural aloofness of her patrician blood to the foster son of a fisherman? Lettice Brinley was as high born, and she had found his poverty no bar. Yet Serena and Dame Brenton both seemed to look askance at him. The sensitive youth was stung to a fierce resolve to prove to this haughty Serena that one of humble birth could travel far, could someday shoulder his way as an equal among those who now looked down on him.

THREE years had passed since the last attack on Hugh and he had put it from his mind. Nevertheless Israel, with the secret aid of Betsy Moon and Tobias Bump, proprietor of the unsavory Break o' Day house, had not ceased in his efforts to unearth proof that Carr Newbury and Richard Brinley were back of the trouble. The Break o' Day, located, like the Butterfly, on a small wharf, enjoyed the doubtful distinction of having been the scene of more than one sudden death from knife thrust or swung stool. But however much the Town Council frowned upon the brawls and the easy morals of the ordinary, for it catered to the dregs of the water front, the closing of the tavern meant burdening the town with the support of Tobias Bump, his hawk-nosed wife, and a numerous progeny; then, too, a seaport must provide taverns for its sailors. So, with an eye half shut to the loose behavior of its patrons, Benoni Tosh, under the advice of his thrifty superiors, tempered the enforcement of the law with the mercy of an easy good nature.

A close study of the sign which hung over the entrance of the weather-battered building perched somewhat precariously on its wharf disclosed the evident intention of the artist to paint daybreak over a flat, blue sea. But time and the elements had transformed the rising sun into something more closely resembling a moldering Wickford cheese sinking for the third and last time into an azure cow pasture. However, those who sat at Tobias Bump's battered tables and drank his bitter ale and fiery rum were undisturbed by the artistic limitations of the masterpiece creaking over his door.

One June evening Israel made his skiff fast to a bollard of the wharf, hoisted himself up the ladder, and entered the Break o' Day. It was early, and as yet there were no customers. At a table near a rickety dresser, which held leather jacks, tankards, and rows of battered pewter and poplar-wood cups, sat the one-eyed Tobias Bump and his hatchet-faced consort, Godsgift. Bump's single eye blinked from a fatuous red face framed by sandy hair. He was stout, and he wore over his greasy linen shirt and leather breeches what had once been a white locram frock which reached below his knees. The lean face and hunted eyes of the frowzy Godsgift Bump were eloquent of the weary years she had spent in the effort to keep Tobias from the hands of the authorities and the Break o' Day from dissolution. For the latter had long been a rendezvous for the sailor-hunting drazels and doxies of the port. Not that the hard-working Godsgift had ever attained to the importance and status of a maquerelle, for, be it said in her favor, she exploited neither the harpies who drank at her tables nor the sailors who were their quarry.

"G'd-e'en to you, Tobias and Godsgift!" greeted Brandy.

Goody Bump wiped her bony hand, wet with beer, on her soiled apron and took Israel's big paw.

"Christ's blood, Israel," cried Bump, already mellowed with his own rum, "you be good to look at from my one eye and that none too sharp. Sit you down, man."

"And how fares the virtuous Godsgift and her deck-load of children?" chuckled Brandy.

The woman's lined face relaxed in a smile. "Israel, 'tis the first peep I've had of your ugly snout since you landed from Barbadoes," she answered. "When do you launch the *Flying Fish*?"

"The sloop tastes the water shortly. Then we're off for the French."

"There be six sloops and two brigs, no less, fittin' in Newport for that purpose," said Bump.

"Ay, and you have many strangers here, nights?"

Bump nodded. "I have not forgot your search, but have seen nought of the sailor with the maimed hand."

Godsgift left, to bring Israel rum, and his fingers closed on Bump's arm. "There's gold in this for you, Tobias—Brenton gold—if you learn ought of what I seek."

Bump's fishy eye lit with interest. "Joe Brenton, eh? He's behind you?"

"Ay, and young Arnold and Sheffield. We want the right of this. There be scum in this port today who would do murder for gold. It may be someone will offer it them. Keep your ears open for waggin' tongues, Tobias. There's gold in it for you."

Godsgift returned with three cups of rum. Wiping her red hands, she sat down, and Israel paid for the drinks.

"Now I'm anchored awhile tonight, Godsgift," he explained, "and afore you knows it, will be whittled to my gills. Pay no heed to me if I snores with head on table or joins with strangers in a song. Money I have and will spend it, lass, and think it not strange if a few cups of rum loosen my tongue or edge my temper. Pay no heed, I say."

The dour-faced Godsgift nodded. "Though I've yet to see your head on a table or under it, Israel," she chuckled, "I'll vow you've been here since midday, and carry a cargo."

"Good lass! You'll lose nought by it. Now, both of you, attend. If strangers ask my name, I'm a Vineyard fisherman and bear the name of Tom Swallow. Mind you, I'm in port on a Vineyard cod-fisher."

So, sprawled at a table, Israel soon bore the familiar symptoms of a man far in his cups, as he guzzled and slobbered over his rum while the tavern filled with patrons. At adjoining tables girls with flushed, pitted faces and eyes hard from the hunting of men drank with strangers off sloops refitting as privateers. At another table four raw-boned whalers from Nantucket, boys hardly out of their teens, caroused. Beyond, two Newport fishermen, having vainly urged Israel to join them, left him to his muttering. It was not until late, when the room was deserted, that two men who entered the tavern and seated themselves at the next table aroused Brandy's curiosity. They were sailors off one of the privateers and strangers to Tobias Bump, as he whispered to Israel when he filled his cup from a jack. From between his thick fingers as he supported his bushy head on a hand, Brandy furtively studied the late arrivals. In their faces, weathered by sun and wind, and in their bold, hard eyes there was the unmistakable look of men who had sailed far and gazed on strange scenes; such men as were common in the deep-sea trade and might be met in the ports of the Leeward Islands or in Dutch Surinam and English Tobago, in the Grenadines and French Tortuga and Fort-de-France.

"Now how came you to Newport, my fine lads?" Brandy muttered. "There is that in the cut of your jibs that leads me to wonder if you ever rambled and sailed on the account. But now that there is war, privateerin' is safer."

The two sailors were making a night of it and showed the effects of the strong rum. True to Israel's surmise, their loud talk was filled with familiar names—Hispaniola, the Bay of Honduras, the Virgin and the Mona passages, and the Sugar Islands. After a time the younger of the two tossed off his rum and broke into a song.

In Boston Town the quails are white.
Heave ho! Heave away, my lads!
They rob poor sailors every night.
Then heave away, my lads!
They bites your shillin' for fear 'tis lead,
And they says their prayers afore they bed.
May they sleep with the devil when they are dead.
Oh, heave away, my lads!

In Dutch New York the maids are fat.
Heave ho! Heave away, my lads!
But they wear six skirts in spite o' that.
Then heave away, my lads!
Their hearts be warm if their legs be cold,
Their fingers itch for a sailor's gold,
But they'll all be dead afore they're old.
Oh, heave away, my lads!

In old Charles Town the nights are dark.
Heave ho! Heave away, my lads!
'Tis a pleasant place for a sailor's lark.
Then heave away, my lads!
There be wenches brown and wenches black,
The rum is hot and the law is slack,
And a sailor wakes with a knife in his back.
Oh, heave away, my lads!

Israel bobbed his head and pounded his cup on the table, roaring his applause. "Christ's blood," he guffawed, "was you ever in the port o' Charles Town? That song takes me back a-many year."

"Ahoy, stranger! Come aboard!" urged the singer, winking at his companion.

Israel rose unsteadily and the two men surveyed him, from his canvas breeches and peg leg to the massive shoulders, enormous, bare forearms, and grinning mask of a face. The elder of the strangers, whose face carried a blue-white scar, laughed: "You and me needs must be friends as we both were kissed hard by the same wench—the blue steel. Where got you that?"

Israel lurched forward and rested his hairy hand on the other's shoulder. "One day off Hispaniola," he replied. "And the leg, I left to the sharks in the Mona Passage."

"Sit you down, friend, and give us the tale of it." The speaker closed one eye. "Were you—a—on the account?"

Brandy grinned in recognition of the term. "Nay, nor one of the Brothers of the Coast," he laughed. "She was a Spaniard we boarded from a New England privateer." Shortly he was deep in his tale of the fight, and as he talked he studied the two sailors, who listened, roaring with laughter at the salty humor of the adroit storyteller. He finished and sighed into his cup of rum: "But them was happy days long dead, lads. Now I fish for a livin' and the lads on the wharves snigger at my face and peg leg as I pass."

"There's bigger game nor fish afloat these days," remarked the older stranger, mysteriously.

"Ay, but though a master gunner I be, there's no berth for me here in Newport. 'Tis the young sprigs they ship." A maudlin tear left one of Israel's eyes to wash his scar. "What sloop is yours?" he asked.

"The *Primrose*, out of Boston. We wait for our papers from Deputy Governor Greene—and no naval office! They are quicker got here if you have the gold."

"Ay, ay! If you have the gold!" Israel mournfully nodded. "Gold! 'Tis what fevers our blood but we seldom see."

The quick eyes of the two strangers met. "We hear there is gold to be had here, in Newport, by one not too tender of his neck," said the younger man.

"Here in Newport?" Israel's bleary eyes blinked. "How, in God's name? I sore need it."

"You know this port—fish from it?"

Israel shook his head. "I be a Martin's Vineyard man and am here on a cod-fisherman."

"You may not tell us, then, who finds the gold for the sailor with the maimed hand?"

Israel tingled to his toes with a fierce joy. At last he had uncovered something. The sailor with the maimed hand! These men had met him! "When saw you a sailor with a maimed hand?" he demanded. "I had talk with one in Boston."

"'Twas in Boston we met him," said the man with the scar. "When he heard we were for Newport on the *Primrose* he offered a fair price in gold for the business, but 'twas scarce to our liking."

Israel leaned forward. "Why not?" he demanded.

"'Twas risky. A big lad, stout as a bull whale, and a wild man with a cutlass, which he always carries, and hatchet-handy as well. 'Twould mean a nasty fight and go hard in Newport with strangers, if caught."

"Ay," grunted Israel, "'twould be more than that, my friend. 'Twould be a pair o' strangers so chopped up their mothers might not know 'em. I doubt not I know the lad you mean. He's that stout there's none in Newport dares lay hand on him."

The two strangers exchanged looks and nodded in agreement. "'Tis what we hear," said the younger.

"Where, in Boston, met you this sailor? And why wishes he to harm the lad?" asked Israel.

"'Twas at the Crown Tavern, near Clark's Wharf. He would pay high to have the lad pressed on a privateer—disappear from Newport. He did not say why."

"He was alone?"

"Ay."

"Was it from Newport that the gold comes?" asked Brandy.

"We guessed 'twas secret business for someone in Newport. He would not say, but he'd pay gold for it."

"Ah! But the risk, not the business, held you?" Brandy's small eyes drove fiercely into the stranger's.

The sailor shrugged. "The risk was too great."

"That I know," said Brandy, his fingers closing on the seaman's arm until he flinched with pain.

"We were wise not to touch this money," agreed the older sailor.

Brandy threw back his head and laughed. "Stab my vitals, you were wise, my friend! I've seen the lad you speak of handle timber at Wanton's yard you might not stir." Israel's eyes pointedly measured the shoulders and arms of the other. "He would break you in two, mate, with his bare hands."

"Ay, we were wise."

"But you know not if the sailor with the maimed hand found his men for the business?"

"No."

At that instant Israel caught the single eye of Tobias Bump who nodded toward the door. Leaning against the jamb, his bloodshot eyes sullenly surveying the men in the room, stood a swarthy stranger who wore loose seaman's drawers and canvas shirt. From his shoulder hung a leather baldric carrying a short cutlass. He scowled as his eyes came to rest on the scarred face and heavy shoulders of Israel Brandy, who had risen.

The sailor with the scar muttered, "Stab me, but there stands the man who offered us gold at the Crown Tavern in Boston!"

"Ay, 'tis he, for a surety," answered the other. "So he comes to Newport himself for that business!"

A thrill of delight shot through Israel as he watched the scowling sailor, who seemed in doubt about entering the room. Brandy motioned to him. "Come aboard, mate," he called. "We're all friends here!"

The newcomer, who also appeared to have been making a night of it, moved uncertainly toward the table, his sinister eyes on Brandy. Tobias Bump placed a stool for him, and Israel ordered drinks. While they waited, Brandy studied the stranger's swart face, seamed with lines, which carried a half-sneer. The rum was brought and Israel resumed his seat and lifted his cup. "Fair wind to you, mate, and what craft brought you here?"

From half-shut eyes the short man savagely searched Israel's grinning mask, then turned to the others with no sign of recognition. "Who is this scar-face?" he rasped.

"Stab my guts," Israel bellowed, "who think you he is, a Newport Quaker? I be Tom Swallow, fisherman from Martin's Vineyard!" Brandy leaned and snarled into the other's face: "Now, burn me! who be you?"

"Fair enough!" agreed the sailors.

The venomous eyes of the newcomer coolly met Israel's stare. He reached for his cup and the hand that lifted it was deeply scarred and minus the forefinger. He drank deliberately, clapped the cup on the table, then bit off, "Mate of the *Sea Horse*, waitin' for our papers."

Lights flickered in Brandy's small eyes as his mouth twitched. He thrust out his square jaw and demanded, "What's your name, mate?"

For a moment the stranger studied Brandy's inflamed face with its livid scar, then answered, "John Creach." He turned and called, "Ahoy, landlord!" And Bump stood at the table. "What name bears this man in Newport?" he demanded.

Brandy's mouth was twitching furiously. His thick fingers closed in two ponderous fists. He cautiously drew his peg leg beneath him so it would not slip when he rose on his good right. The two sailors moved their stools back, narrowly watching the men facing each other, and the right hand of the scarred sailor left the table and slowly moved to the knife in his belt. Tobias Bump's stubbled jaw dropped as he gaped from Brandy to the stranger.

"Slit my throat, tell him, landlord!" roared Brandy.

"In Newport?" said Bump. "How mean you in Newport? This man is a Vineyard fisherman and they calls him Tom Swallow."

Creach grunted, his face sour with disappointment. He drank again, glowering venomously at Israel over his cup, as if suspicion still lurked in his mind. Then sneered, "Be there another scar-face with wooden leg in this port?"

Ho, ho! surmised the gunner. So this Creach had heard of Israel Brandy! Well, he'd hear more of him shortly. "A-plenty of 'em, Mate Creach, or Screach or Smeach, or whatsoever you calls yourself for the time bein'," retorted Brandy, stiffening to iron where he sat.

Creach's face went purple with blood. He was on his feet and had whipped his cutlass half out of its scabbard when Israel's lunging hand reached his wrist and jammed the cutlass back into its sheath. With the other, he jerked Creach forward and down, forcing him, struggling savagely, to the sanded floor, where he fell heavily on top of him.

But Creach was not through. He squirmed, managed to reach beneath his shirt behind his neck with a free hand and had a knife. With a roar Israel pinioned the knife hand of the straining sailor to the floor, twisted his wrist until his fingers relaxed and the knife fell from his grasp, then drove a knee into his stomach. His wind knocked from him, Creach lay gasping for breath in Brandy's hands.

"Pull a knife on me from your shirt, would yuh?" snarled Brandy, while the two sailors stood back, watching. "I was lessoned in that trick by a Spaniard!" Brandy got to his feet with the limp Creach in his arms and hurled him halfway across the room, where he crashed head-long into a table and lay stunned, while blood from a cut on his fore-head trickled over his face. "Mates," cried Israel, whirling on the two silent witnesses who had watched the swift action with open mouths, "you heard what this Creach said? Christ's blood! He fished for trouble and caught it! Now, stab my guts! be I right or wrong?"

Brandy's inflamed face was frightful in its grotesque grimace. The strangers stared at the master gunner as if hypnotized, then one said: "Sink me, mate, 'twas his blame! Breath o' Jesus, you're stout as an ox but ten times as quick!"

The other added: "Now what to do with him? He looks more whittled than hurt. That cut on his skull is little for the tough one he is."

Israel was in a quandary. Here was the man he had long sought, lying helpless in his hands. He could have Bump call the watch, charge Creach with assault with a knife and insist he be put in the jail to await the action of the magistrates. Then he might be made to talk. But would he? The magistrates would likely call it only a tavern brawl and refuse to listen to Benoni. If Creach denied knowing Carr Newbury or Richard Brinley, there were only the stories of Betsy Moon and these two sailors, if they would talk, to fall back upon. And their tales in no way involved Newbury or Richard Brinley directly. The men behind Creach were unknown to them. So Israel decided to wait for advice from Benoni, Brenton, and Trelawney. There would be ample time, as Creach's sloop would be in port for days.

"What do we do with this sailor?" again demanded the scarred stranger.

"Will you carry him in your skiff to the *Sea Horse*?"

"Ay, we will," agreed the older sailor. Then he squinted hard at Brandy and asked: "But who is this peg-legged one with the scarred face that Creach has doubt of?"

"'Tis plain who he fears," chuckled Israel, catching Bump's single red eye. "'Tis the master gunner of the *Royal Stede*, who sails with the privateer sloop *Flying Fish*. Israel Brandy they calls him. 'Twas lucky for Creach 'twas me he met this night and not Brandy, or the *Sea Horse* would lack its mate. Why, mates, this Brandy is that hot-headed he would split this Creach, now, with his own tool, as a fish knife splits a cod!"

"Why fears he this Brandy?" asked the man with the scar.

The hot blood beat in Israel's throat as he choked back his rage. He glared at the two who watched him, and his words sliced the smoke-filled air like the slash of a cutlass. "Because Brandy'll kill the man who harms Hugh Jocelyn! 'Tis he Creach is after!"

The room was thick with silence. Brandy's menacing eyes locked with the surprised stares of the strangers as his ponderous fists shut hard.

"Has Brandy the mate to that arm?" asked the younger man, pointing to the bulging thews of Israel's forearm.

Israel chuckled. "Why, Brandy could toss me like a child. He's that stout he could break his own back."

So the sailors carried the limp body of Creach out and started in their skiff for his sloop, the *Sea Horse*, while Israel rowed up the shore to the house of Benoni Tosh and roused him.

"I will seek a warrant in the morning and arrest him, Israel," said Tosh when he had heard the story. "'Tis but on suspicion of a plan to press or injure Hugh, but we have the story of Betsy Moon, Landlord Turpin, of Providence, and these two sailors you speak of, to put fear into him, and he may talk. But I doubt it. You did well not to cripple him or call the watch. 'Twould look like a personal brawl, only."

In the morning, when Benoni, armed with a warrant, started with the wrathy Israel and two constables for the *Sea Horse*, she was gone. Men on neighboring sloops said she had sailed at dawn. Investigation at the Naval Office by Tosh and Joe Brenton revealed nothing except that one Gibbons, of doubtful antecedents, master of the *Sea Horse*, out of Boston, had applied for a privateering commission and was awaiting the action of Deputy Governor Greene. The man with the maimed hand who called himself Creach had slipped them again.

Except for the precaution that he always carried his cutlass at night, Hugh gave little thought to Israel's recent meeting at the Break o' Day with Creach. Of course, Carr Newbury and Richard Brinley would have been glad to have him shanghaied or pressed on a privateer, especially since they had learned from Newbury's farmer of Hugh's meeting with Lettice. The knowledge of that meeting, which had resulted in the sending of Lettice to a Misses School in Boston, must have bitten deep into Newbury's pride and added new vitriol to his jealousy of the penniless sailor who had caught the fancy of a Brinley.

But if Hugh, still sick at heart over the death of Seeth, was little affected by the happenings at the Break o' Day, Trelawney, Joe Brenton, and the others were aroused. Creach, the man who might, under pressure, have exposed Carr Newbury, had slipped through their hands.

The exasperated Israel blamed himself for not having taken the law into his hands and crippled Creach with his own knife when he attempted to draw it. That would have brought the watch and the constables and have thrown the whole matter into the open. An airing before the magistrates, even if Creach had remained loyal to his secret employer and refused to betray him, would have frightened Newbury into inaction and involved Brinley in trouble with his father. But what Joe Brenton and Trelawney sought was actual proof, and so far that had escaped them.

§57

At last the hull of the *Flying Fish* was finished. From bowsprit to sternpost she was a thing of strength and beauty. Built of heavy Rhode Island white oak to withstand the battering she would someday have to take from French guns and the sea; with low freeboard and deck doubly reinforced with oak knees to carry her four demiculverins and six sakers; and with poop rails extra heavy to seat the shanks of the swivel crutches, the *Flying Fish* was, nevertheless, as graceful in her lines as a gull. On the day of her launching, the friends of the Wantons gathered to watch the sloop slide down the greased ways from her cradle and into the water. Tom Paine sailed across from his Conanicut farm. Joe Brenton, John Arnold, the red-cheeked Kit Sheffield, and Trelawney joined Israel, Hugh, and the Wantons for the occasion.

"There she stands, Captain Paine!" said William Wanton. "Is she too fine forward? We wanted her extra quick in stays."

Tom Paine's agate eyes squinted back and forth over the calked and freshly painted hull which stood shored up in her bilgeways waiting to slide into the water. He took a position off her bows where he could observe the sweep of her bilges. "Her long run and lean buttocks'll make her fast on the wind, William," he said. "She's fine, forward, and should be as quick in stays as a swivel swinging on a poop rail."

"I aimed to give her no bluff bows, like a snub-nosed brig," replied William; "and we eased her bilges and gave her a long run. If she's not too tender with that ten ton of iron on her deck, I'll be happy!"

Tom Paine studied the hull from many angles, rubbing his stubbled chin, with a thick hand, then slowly nodded his iron-gray head. "William," he said, with finality, "with a proper large mains'il to push her, she'll show her poop to ought that sails this coast!"

William grinned with pleasure, for the approval of Tom Paine stamped his labor with success. From a great jack of waxed leather bound with brass he filled the cups in the hands of the assembly with rum. As the blocks were knocked from under the sloop and she left her cradle and stocks to slide slowly down the greased ways and plunge stern first into the water, a cheer lifted from the throng of well-wishers.

"Success to the *Flying Fish*!" shouted Joe Brenton, as the trim stern of the sloop took the water with a splash. "May she send many a prize into Newport!"

"Success to the *Flying Fish* and the Wantons!" rose from many throats properly moistened with strong rum.

"A sweeter sloop never left the ways! She'll point into the wind's eye," said Tom Paine to Brenton, as the hull was eased to the wharf, where her mast waited to be stepped, her topmast seated, and spars, shrouds, and stays rigged. In a neighboring shed lay her freshly painted nine- and five-pounders with their carriages, and six one-pound brass falconets, with a pair of blunderbuss murderers.

Israel Brandy joined the group and stood watching the Wantons' men making the hull fast to a wharf. "But I doubt, William," went on Paine, with a jerk of his head toward Brandy, "your master gunner can lay those nine- and five-pounders. He'll be jumpier nor a grasshopper. You see, William," said Paine, as Brandy slowly wheeled and eyed him darkly from beneath his bushes of brows, "he needs lessoning and the sight o' blood to harden his nerves and cut his eyeteeth."

Brandy sniffed. A growl rumbled in his thick throat. "William," he snorted, "you ever heard of that old man who claims he was buccaneer or pirate, but I believes was a Turks Island salt raker, or a turtle fisher, and who was driv' out of the Indy Sea by the blacks and mustees and took to Conanicut to live where 'twas safe and quiet?"

"Of a certainty," answered William, catching the twinkling eyes of Brenton and Trelawney. "He was powder boy to Israel Brandy on the *Royal Stede*?"

"That's the old barnacle! Name of—name of—now what's his name?" muttered Brandy, scratching his craggy chin. "Ay! Paine! Tom Paine! He took fear of the sea and now is nurse to sheep and hogs and chickens and suchlike harmless brutes, over on the island."

The amused crowd moved closer to listen to the verbal battle between the old sea dogs.

"Well, William," went on Israel, his mouth screwed in a grimace, "this farmer, Paine, has recent spoke doubt of the best master gunner what ever laid eye to the black back of a culverin. To show him how straight them sakers on the *Flying Fish* can shoot when they're rigged and tidy, let us anchor off the island and knock the chimney off his house."

"No, no, Israel; you'd have the best gunner on the *Flying Fish* lay the guns," objected Paine.

"Of course I would. Who think you would lay them but Brandy?"

"I said you'd have the best gunner," dryly insisted Paine. "I'll not have Hugh Jocelyn knocking my chimney down!"

"Hugh Jocelyn?" roared Brandy. "Why, I brung that sprig up from so high, and all he knows I lessoned him! Best gunner? I'm the best gunner on that sloop—but, burn my bones, Hugh Jocelyn'll be the best man!" Israel winked at Hugh, spat on his hands, hitched his belt, and continued: "Do you mind a longboat—ay, two on 'em—smashed to kindlin' one day off Block Island, Tom Paine, when you was down in your cabin prayin' while we men was doin' the fightin'?" he chuckled.

"That I do, Israel," laughed Paine, slapping Israel on the back. "And I treasure my chimney too much to have either you or Hugh shootin' at it!"

When Hugh returned from the launching he found Content holding a folded sheet of paper sealed with wax. "Hugh," she said, as she handed him the letter, "this but just arrived by a black boy. You promised once; will you still promise, Hugh?"

"You know who sent it, then?"

"'Twas the same black boy who came before."

Hugh took the letter. Lettice! Trelawney had told him shortly after his meeting with her on Dexter's Lane that she had been sent to the School for Misses in Boston, and that she had been kept there during the plague. Now she had returned and was writing. He glanced at the worried face of the woman who watched him. "Yes. Mother Content, I promise," he said, and broke the seal.

DEAR HUGH JOCELYN

When I returned from that School for Misses where They Sent me when They learned of our Meeting I Needs must put Quill to Paper. I saw Your sloop return last summer from the Fight and how Proud I was yt Hugh Jocelyn had once Held me in His arms. Mr. Trelawney writ me in the Winter that you had Escaped the Plague. Thank God your face is Unmarked. I Have never Forgot yt Day. Have you Forgot, Hugh? Oh, if that Day could come again. It might Well if You but wished it. Dost not wish it? I am all a tremble at the Thought of it. Carr Newbury came to Boston, Last winter, But I would not see him. Mr. Trelawney tells me yt my Writing and Spelling are greatly better and yt I Read surprising Well. 'Tis all because I wished You not to think me a Dunce Hugh Jocelyn. I have read Much from your Shakespeare this winter though 'twas forbid at the School as unfit for Maids. Pah! Did they but know how few Maids Were there. Yet I borrowed it and Read. Please, please make Mr. Trelawney Bear me an answer.

LETTICE.

Hugh stood frowning at the written sheet in his hand, but his blood warmed to her words and the memory of that afternoon in Dexter's Lane which seemed so long ago. Then he grew suddenly cold at the thought of how near they had come to a wild recklessness that would have changed the whole course of his life. It would have killed Seeth as surely as her desire to live was killed by the plague. A deep sense of shame and remorse flowed through him and he turned to the anxiously waiting woman.

"I promise, Mother Content," he said, and tossed the letter into the supper fire.

Trim and fresh as a Newport maid starting for church, the *Flying Fish* lay at her wharf, rigged and gunned, ready to sail against the King's enemies. With the loving care of a mother for her child, Israel had labored with the lashing of the nine- and five-pounders into their harness at their ports, while Hugh had worked with the shipwrights in stepping her long mast, seating her topmast and jib boom, bending sails, running stays and shrouds, and reeving lines through blocks. Extra sails and spars were stowed on top of the ballast in the hold, along with powder barrels, shot, small arms, and provisions for a two months' cruise to the Gulf of St. Lawrence. When the sloop was ready, she had been taken on a trial trip, outside, to test her sailing qualities, and had pointed so close in a stiff southwest wind that the Wantons, Israel, and Hugh were confident of her future.

"She'd fair crawl into the wind's eye, William," Israel had chuckled as the sloop drove her stem and her bowsprit stays into the seas and a belt of milk-white foam swept past her lee rail, on a tack toward Block Island. "That ten tons of iron on her deck fails to souse her lee bulwarks even with the ballast she carries. She's stiff as a man with a boil on his neck and, burn me, some livelier!"

"Israel, there's no Frenchman on the coast may point with her."

"Ay, William, there's good prize money waitin' the crew that works the *Flying Fish*. I never see a craft could sail so small."

The busy little seaport in whose harbor lay craft fitting out as privateers or waiting for guns, to sail with letters of marque for the Sugar Islands, was suddenly alive with rumors of French ships on the coast. Over the Plymouth Path came word that ships recently arrived in Boston from the West Indies reported that French privateers infested the seas of the Leeward and Windward Islands, that trade was at a standstill, and Tortuga pirates, carrying French commissions, were raiding the harbors and shipping of the southern colonies. As New England depended on the sugar, molasses, logwood, and indigo of the Barbadoes and Jamaica trade, and the islands needed the salt cod, beef, pipe staves, and lumber of New England, the growing triangle trade between the colonies, the West Indies and Europe, and between New England, the Guinea slave coast, and the Sugar Islands was threatened. While the French and Indians raided the frontiers from Montauk to Newfoundland, unarmed New England fishermen and traders were falling easy prey to privateers and former pirates sailing under French commissions.

And now that the French were again on the coast and the farmers and fishermen of the islands were at their mercy, young William Wanton, master and part owner of the privateer sloop *Flying Fish*, with John, Israel and Hugh, packed their sea bags for the great adventure. William had had little trouble in obtaining the choice of the daring youth of Portsmouth and Newport for his crew. Many had fought Picard the previous summer, under Paine and Godfrey. Israel's gun crews had been hand-picked from a throng of eager applicants. Rated as boatswain, because of his skill as gunner Hugh also acted as captain of No. 1 poop nine-pounder, with Jeremy Potts and the two Campanal boys, Daniel and Isaac.

The *Flying Fish* made a trial trip to New London, carrying much-needed sugar and rum. On the night after her return to Newport, the watch on Point Judith saw, across the eight miles of flat sea to the southwest, a red glow suddenly illuminate the sodden sky. Shortly, the heaped driftwood at Point Judith was flashing its red warning to the coast guard at Watch Hill, and east to Beaver Tail. Then, in succession, from one headland to another up the coast to the Cape, blazed the signal fires. The news, carried into town by one of the watch at Brenton's Point, riding a Brenton horse, threw the little seaport into a fever of excitement. The French were again plundering the coastal islands and no ship at sea was safe.

Late that night a shallop from Block Island groped her way into Newport harbor with the news. A big three-masted Frenchman, carrying twenty guns, had landed shore parties, abused the people, butchered cattle, sheep, and hogs, and when last seen was headed east, probably for Vineyard Sound. Of the armed craft in the port, fitting out and waiting for papers, but one besides the *Flying Fish* was ready to sail in defense of the coast, and she was a stub-nosed, Boston-owned brig armed with six sakers.

At daylight, when the *Flying Fish* got up her anchor and beat out of the harbor past the brig, Israel said to William Wanton at the tiller, as he watched the crew of the Boston craft shaking out her brailed canvas, "William, we'll sight Cuttyhunk afore that floatin' horse-trough clears Brenton's Reef beatin' into this baby's breath of a breeze."

The *Flying Fish* rounded Brenton's Reef and, with the light air, started its long beat to Cuttyhunk, which lay almost in the wind's eye. For the French privateers, when on the coast, haunted the narrow Vineyard Sound through which all coastwise shipping passed. Through the day Israel sweated his gun crews at the grueling toil of rolling the creaking carriages back and forth by their train and side tackles, shifting the breeches of the nine- and five-pounders with handspike and crow to bear on a target forward or abaft the beam, and knocking out and inserting coins to raise or lower the muzzles. Barrels of powder cartridges, racks of balls, and sand tubs were lashed in place near the guns, and against the high rails of the sloop stood racks of muskets, pikes, and boarding hatchets. William Wanton and his master gunner were taking no chances on the *Flying Fish* being caught unready for action by suddenly sighting the French ship behind Cuttyhunk or Nashawena when the sloop had put the bold knob of the former on her lee and slid into the Sound. For, unless the fog rolled in before night, in the narrow waters of Vineyard Sound they might sight the Frenchman at any time.

As the day wore on, the watch with his battered telescope, under the square topsail in the crosstrees, hailed the poop that it was so thick to the south he could see but a few miles. And as the sloop slipped lazily through the smoky sea on her long tacks against the light air, the sharp eagerness which at daylight had kindled the bronzed young faces of the crew was replaced by disappointment and uneasiness. Grouped along the weather rail and gun carriages, they watched with shaking heads the thickening weather and argued as to what their young captain would do when he reached Cuttyhunk. The black bank of fog still hung in the southeast beyond the Vineyard and Noman's Land, which were now gray smears on the horizon. In order to put plenty of water between her and the Sow and Pigs, which thrust a mile and a half of black fangs into the southwest from Cuttyhunk, the sloop was forced to make a long leg to the south. As they passed the buried ledges of the reef and cleared the island, all hands were straining their eyes for a glimpse of the top hamper of a three-master in the Sound, but saw nothing.

On the poop, beside the two tillermen, William Wanton stood with Hugh and Israel. "John was for running in behind Cuttyhunk and dropping the hook for the night," he said. "That would mean that the Frenchman, if she's in the Sound, could slip through to the Cape when the weather clears, and we might lose her."

Israel scratched his head, damp from the drip in the air. "Now,

Captain, as you ax my opinion, I say she had less nor a full day's start on us. She's a clumsy square-rigger and may point but little into the wind. You can burn me if she's in the Sound, with wind scarce lively enough to ruffle the hair on your arm!"

Wanton turned to Hugh. "Bo's'n, what do you think?"

"You're captain, William! Just now I'm getting up the long sweeps from the hold."

"You think we'll need them?"

"I know we shall if we try for Tarpaulin."

Wanton's lean face, with its bold eyes and aquiline nose, sobered. "I still believe she's ahead of us and we ought to go in," he stubbornly insisted.

"Whatever the captain orders!" Israel growled. "But that ship ain't in the Sound."

Hugh was secretly wondering at the young captain's daring in gambling the safety of the craft on which for two years he had centered his hopes. Wanton studied his doubtful face. "What is it, Hugh, Cuttyhunk or Tarpaulin Cove?"

With a shrug Hugh answered, "Tarpaulin or sink!"

"Tarpaulin it is then!" cried William. "And devil take the fog! This Frenchman'll never slip out of the Sound and over Nantucket Shoals to the Cape if the *Flying Fish* can fight as well as she can sail!"

§58

To the north the gray shoulders of Cuttyhunk were slowly fading into the drift settling on the oily sea when the tiller of the *Flying Fish* was put over and she came about and headed into the treacherous Sound. With the light air almost abeam, it was a straight ten-mile leg to Tarpaulin Cove, and in Hugh's opinion, in which Israel privately joined, it would not be long before the fog moving in from the south would blanket Sound and islands. Then they would be sailing by compass alone, with only the lead to warn them off the beach and keep them clear of the dangerous set of the flood through Quick's Hole as well as Robinson's Hole. To Hugh it was a rash move of the impetuous William to attempt to head off the French ship in such weather, but William was part owner and master and wanted to take the chance, so there was nothing else to do.

"Gun crews stand by! Pass the word to the foc's'le!" bawled Israel's deep bass.

"Musketmen stand by!" shrilled John Wanton's tenor.

There was the rush of bare feet as musketmen and gunners tumbled up through the forehatch and, joining those on deck, took their stations. There was much chatter and shaking of bushy heads. Captain Wanton was taking the sloop into the Sound after the French ship. To most of the sixty men of the crew the move seemed hare-brained when a safe anchorage lay behind Cuttyhunk. But William Wanton, at twenty-two, already bore a reputation for daring and seamanship. He was doubtless headed for Tarpaulin Cove, and Wanton luck and Wanton nerve might make it. Failing that, they could anchor and wait for clearing weather.

While Israel stumped the length of the sloop, speaking to each gun-captain in turn, Hugh leaned against the breech of his larboard nine-pounder talking to Jeremy Potts and the two Campanals. Across the poop lounged the crew of the starboard demiculverin, with the men detailed to the six swivels mounted on their trunnion crutches by shanks let into the massive supports of the rail.

Jeremy sidled up to Hugh and whispered, for William Wanton stood beside the two tillermen, not ten feet away: "He thinks they're ahead of us in the Sound?"

"Ay, Jeremy; but we're making for Tarpaulin to wait out this fog."

"You know this water. Can we make it blind with the compass?"

"The tricks of the tide around these islands make a compass poor aid with which to hold a course. Tarpaulin Cove now bears east-nor'east, but before the glass is turned in the cabin an east-nor'east course with the suck of the tide might put us on the Pasque beach or into the rocks of Robinson's Hole."

"If we run into her in the Cove in this thick weather and light air," objected Jeremy, "they might sink us with a broadside before we could show our heels."

Hugh placed his hand on Jeremy's wide shoulder. "If we blunder on her in Tarpaulin Cove, Jeremy, William aims to drive straight in and lay her board and board before they know we're there. Then you and I go over her rail as we did at Block Island."

At the words, Jeremy's blue eyes snapped. His voice cracked with excitement. "Name of God, Hugh, 'twill be two to one against us, but with Israel bawling like a bull caught in a stump fence, while he lays about him, we'll run them French robbers into their hold!"

"That's the talk, lad. If William lays us aboard the devil's own ship, we'll scramble over her rail and take her!"

"That we will!"

With what there was of the light air abeam, for two turns of the glass in the cabin the *Flying Fish* slipped through the smoking sea, gunners at their stations, though the chances of running into the Frenchman were not one in a hundred. But William Wanton had no intention of being taken by surprise. Gradually the thin drift thickened, and Nashawena, on their lee, faded. At last the sloop was barely making steerageway in a pea-soup fog.

Hugh went forward and started heaving the greased lead, for he and Israel knew the bottom around the islands better than any of the crew. He heaved, hauled, measured the wet line with extended arms, and examined the lead.

"Five fathoms, and mud!" he shouted to Wanton on the poop. He heaved again. "Four, and mud!" he called. Once more he heaved. "Three fathoms!" he warned, running aft. "We're headed into Robinson's Hole!"

"Stand by to tack!" cried Wanton. "Put her hard down!"

The bow of the *Flying Fish* swung lazily to the drag of her rudder. The staysail and jib sheets were let go, and she hung for a moment; then as the bow of the sloop fell off, the jib sheets were hauled in and the mainsail slowly filled.

Forward of the chains, Hugh was rapidly heaving the lead, while he and Israel inspected the bottom sticking to the grease. Suddenly he dropped the lead on the deck and ran aft. "Short three fathoms, sir!" he cried to Wanton. "We're making sternway! This flood'll land us on the ledges or on Nashon beach!"

"Man the sweeps! We're goin' ashore!" shouted Wanton.

"Stand by the sweeps!" cried the mate, seizing a twenty-four-foot oar and running it over the rail between the heavy tholepins.

"Lively there, you rumbullions! You want to lose the sloop?" roared Israel, shipping another.

Forty men rushed to ship the long oars. Shortly the water boiled under the beat of six blades, as Israel's bull-like bellow called the stroke. Again Hugh heaved the lead into the white wall of fog. He hauled and measured the depth. "A scant three fathoms!" he shouted, and the men laboring at the sweeps bowed their backs and pulled until their joints cracked.

William Wanton leaped from the poop to the main deck. In the light air her canvas was giving the sloop little aid, caught in the set of the fresh flood over the shoals of Robinson's Hole between Pasque and Nashon. "We're off Nashon beach, with the flood makin' and pushin' us toward the ledges!" he shouted to his panting men. "You want to leave your bones here? Heave, you sons o' drazels!"

Brushing aside a tired man beside Israel, Hugh flung his weight and power on the pine shaft until it bowed with their united heaves, while Wanton stood like a slave driver in a Roman galley calling the stroke, his thrashing arms marking the beat. "Ah! . . . Heave! Ah! . . . Heave!" cried the desperate young captain as the sweeps bit at the flat sea in unison.

The man heaving the lead forward called, "Short o' three fathom!"

"Christ's blood! You hear that? Lift her!" implored Wanton. "Ah! . . . Heave! . . . Ah! . . . Heave!"

With his weight and thrust on his powerful good leg while the peg kept his balance, Israel was pulling like a horse beside the straining Hugh and the others on the sweep that churned the water to foam as it struck. But the tide was stiffening against them and the air barely toyed with the sails. It looked hopeless. The rush of the flood would carry the *Flying Fish* into the funnel of Robinson's Hole and on the ledges, or land her on the bold Nashon beach; for there was no holding ground for an anchor.

Again the leadsman called, "Short o' three fathom!"

The sloop was barely holding her own, but the thirty-six desperate men sweating at the long oars and the young captain who called the stroke fought doggedly on. Fresh men sprang to spell those already exhausted, who dropped panting to the deck. The sweeps settled into a rhythmic beat. The breaths of the oarsmen whistled in unison through their open mouths at the finish of each stroke, led by the grunting "Huh!" from Israel's deep chest.

Then the leadsman shouted, "Three fathom—full!"

There was a cheer from the men waiting their turn at the oars.

"Name o' God, lads," cried Wanton, "you've got her runnin'! Ah! . . . Heave! . . . Ah! . . . Heave!"

The heavy sloop was beginning to respond to her sweeps. Shortly the leadsman called, "Four fathom!"

A roar went up from the men standing by the sweepsmen.

"Four fathom! She's runnin', lads! She's runnin'! Give her hell!" cried the half-delirious Wanton.

Encouraged by their shouting mates, the heartened men on the sweeps redoubled their efforts. Hugh and Israel, standing shoulder to shoulder, threw the last ounce of their weight and power into each lunge of the long oar, backed by the brawny Jeremy and the three men facing them. Against the young flood the sloop was crawling through the wall of fog into the safety of deeper water.

The leadsman called, "Six fathom!" And the gasping Hugh knew that they had broken free from the grip of the making tide which had sucked them in toward the rock shoals in the narrow mouth of Robinson's Hole. Then the sails lazily filled with a sudden puff of air. Fresh men leaped to the sweeps, and the *Flying Fish* headed into the open Sound and was clear.

Standing at the poop ladder, William Wanton called to his exhausted sailors in a voice cracked by emotion: "You cleared her, men, by your guts and your stout backs! My thanks to you! Name of God, no Frenchman can beat a crew of Newport and Portsmouth lads like you!

Now for some prize money!"

"Ay, ay!" roared many throats. "Prize money! Show us the French-man!"

The sweeps were stowed and the sloop had slipped lazily into the fog bank on an east-nor'east course for a turn of the glass, when William called Hugh and Israel to the poop. "We're in ten fathoms, and likely handy to Tarpaulin, for the Cove is less than four miles from Robinson's Hole and we've been moving east-nor'east for a turn of the glass and the tide with us."

Brandy rubbed his wet head, for he disdained both the Monmouth cap and tarpaulin hat worn much by sailors. "Captain William," he said, "with ten fathom under us we might be anywhere twixt Tarpaulin and the Vineyard save over the shoals. With the tricks this flood can play on a craft in the Sound, that compass is as useless as a sailor with sore feet. You won't find the Cove."

Wanton turned to Hugh.

"With the night, 'twill be too black to work the sloop," said Hugh, "and there'll be no air. We'd better anchor till she clears. We've had our lesson."

"I favor bearing easterly past the middle shoals, where the tide runs too strong, and dropping the hook inside," said John.

So the sloop's course was changed. Riding the flood, with bare steerageway, she was moving through the fog, when the lookout in the bow suddenly called: "Ship, ho! Starboard bow!"

"All hands stand by!" cried William Wanton.

"Gunners stand by!" roared Israel, leaping to his poop nine-pounder.

There was a rush of bare feet to the guns and the snapping of steel on flint as the candles were lighted to ignite the dry matches, and the guns were freshly primed from powder horns. The square sails and black hulk of a ship broke through the curtain of fog off the starboard bow. The chatter of voices and shouted orders in French reached the crew of the *Flying Fish*.

Muscles tight as strung wire, Hugh, and Jeremy with his sputtering match, stood at the gun waiting for Israel's order, for there was no time to lay the nine-pounder. The craft were so close that a broadside from the ship's heavy guns would pound the sloop into a derelict. Yet the gun crews and the musketmen in the bow stood at their stations like statues, facing the coming barrage of iron. The sweat of the dread of a hovering death burst from foreheads and drawn faces, but their hearts pounded with the pride of fighting Englishmen who would show no fear.

Then, as they drifted abeam of the black bulk of the ship, Wanton's order rang in their waiting ears, "Fire!"

Red huffs from the vents stabbed the mist, and the five guns of the sloop's starboard battery spewed their iron shot into the ship's bulwarks. At the same instant twenty muskets spat a hail of lead into the ship's poop, followed by a second volley from spare guns. Clouds of acrid, yellow smoke hung over the choking gunners straining at their train tackles to run the guns in from the ports while they waited for the orange flashes and answering roar from the ship. But the blurred bulk of the enemy faded into the fog without reply.

"Christ's blood! Caught hard aback, with their breeches off!" yelled the jubilant Brandy, whirling on the young captain who stood peering into the fog, astern. "The fools' matches and primin' was too damp to take fire and they couldn't work a gun!"

Wanton grinned. "Now, Israel," he jeered, "did that Frenchman head us into the Sound?"

"Burn me, no!" grunted the master gunner. "She was fair in our wake, as I said, and the fog blanketed 'em as it did us. They was brailin' their main and mizzen canvas and makin' ready to anchor when we sighted 'em. I marked men on her yards."

"That means they've dropped their hook, and so does the *Flying Fish*. Stand by to tack!" shouted Wanton. "Put over the tiller!" The sloop slowly swung in the light air.

"Clear the anchor!" called William.

Men sprang into the bow and stood by the coiled anchor line and the windlass.

"Let go the anchor!"

The anchor lashings were cast off and the heavy weight of iron splashed into the sea while the line played out through the hawsehole. When the anchor was holding, William Wanton called a council of war in the cabin.

"The ship was making ready to drop her hook and wait for the weather to clear when we ran into her," began William. "And my guess is she dropped it right where we left her, for they figure they can blow us out of the water and we durst not board them. What do you think, Hugh?"

Hugh ran his fingers through his yellow hair, pushing it back from his forehead. His heavy brows met as his eyes half closed above his high cheekbones. "If we get wind in the morning or next day to handle her, and the weather clears, you're going to see what the *Flying Fish* can do to a two-hundred-ton ship carrying twenty guns and, likely, over a hundred men."

"Right," said William.

"Although the sloop will sail circles around that ship, William, 'twould be cruel hard to have her fresh paint scraped and her new oak bulwarks and bilges smashed by a few lucky shots from those French culverins."

Israel scowled with impatience. "Think you we'll give 'em a chance at a broadside? The sloop is too nimble and William too good a seaman."

"What's in your mind, Hugh?" demanded John Wanton, a puzzled look puckering his round face.

"Yes, Hugh," added William with a grimace. "When you start running your fingers through that mop of yellow hair, I know there's a plan buried in that thick skull that pistol balls may not dent."

"That ship rides at anchor not a quarter mile distant," said Hugh.

The three listeners nodded, their faces alive with curiosity.

"Can we find her in our light skiff in this fog?"

"I took her bearing when the fog swallowed her," said William, "and we moved little before we anchored. 'Twas west-sou'west."

"Good! How much cod line do we carry?"

"Cod line? You aim to fish for the ship?" laughed William.

"We stored plenty for need off the Maine coast and north," answered John.

"Sufficient, spliced, to make—say—two hundred fathoms?"

"Yes, and four hundred," answered the puzzled mate.

"Good!"

Israel cleared his throat and his mouth worked up and down with impatience. "Puke it out, lad! We're waitin'! What's the plan?"

"If the ship lies not too far away, I'll jam her rudder!"

"Jam her rudder?" exploded William.

"So that's what you want the cod line for?" cried John. "With one end fast to the *Flying Fish* you'll pay out the line from the skiff so she may find the sloop on her return without firing muskets?"

"You think you can put the skiff under the ship's counter and jam the rudder somehow without being blown to fish bait?" demanded William.

"Put me close enough in the skiff to locate the ship and I'll swim to her, pushing two pine sticks, with a short piece of rope to bind them," Hugh answered. "If we can't make her out, we'll hear the watch talking. The French are always chirping."

Israel shook his head, his mouth twisted in disapproval. "When you left the ship's rudder, if you ever did, you'd scarce find the skiff, swimmin' in this pea soup, unless there was noise made, and that would draw their fire. Rot my bones! I won't agree to it! Them French'll murder you in the water!"

"How do you aim to locate the skiff?" asked John.

"In two turns of the glass," said Hugh, " 'twill be so black on the water that the skiff can slip with wrapped oars within a ship's length of the Frenchman's stern and the tide should be about dead. I'll make a cod line fast under my arms and when I've swum over and jammed the rudder, I'll jerk the line and you'll haul in the biggest cod you ever hooked."

"No!" insisted William. "Name of God, Hugh, you'll drown tangled on that line in the murk or they'll hear you working on the rudder from the ship's cabin and spray you with lead from a blunderbuss."

"Right, Captain William; right!" growled Israel. "I've lessoned, e't and slept with this lad from so high, and I ain't done with him yet!"

"It sounds mad to me, Hugh," protested John. "How do you think to jam a piece of pine between her rudder and sternposts from the water with no purchase?"

"'Twill be more than that! Pass the word for the carpenter."

"No, Hugh," protested William, "I can't have you drowned at the end of a cod line."

Hugh's deep-set eyes met Wanton's in a look his friends well knew. "Pass the word for the carpenter!" he repeated.

Brandy sat hunched on a bunk hopelessly wagging his head as he surveyed a huge bare foot. "'Tis no use, William," he muttered. "Pass the word for the carpenter." Suddenly he rose and thrust his head and shoulders through an open port while the others watched curiously his broad back.

"Name of God, Israel, what you listening for?" demanded William.

Brandy withdrew his head and shoulders and warned with raised hand: "Batten your mouths! I hear 'em! I hear 'em for a certainty!" Then again he leaned through the square porthole.

The Wantons stared at each other. Was it the French Israel heard? Hugh grinned back into their questioning eyes. With a satisfied look Brandy turned from the port. "I thought I heard 'em after we let go the hook, but wasn't sure. But I hear 'em now," he said cryptically.

"What, in the name of God, do you hear?" demanded William.

"Crickets!"

"Crickets? Then we're lying close in on the Vineyard beach!" cried William.

"We are! Hugh and me has heard 'em on a dead night like this near a half mile off the beach. Now 'twill make findin' them Frenchies easier. We'll keep the skiff always in sound of the crickets so we can't work too far offshore. For the Frenchman lies as close in as we do or I'm a dogfish."

"Israel, you're a seaman!"

Brandy grinned. "I told you, you young sprigs needed an old hand aboard."

§59

ALBRO, the sloop's carpenter, appeared and Hugh explained that he wished two heavy, eight-foot sticks of squared pine, each notched around the center to take and hold a number of turns of tarred rope. Shortly the carpenter returned, and in the shielded light of two candle lanterns Israel and Hugh lashed an end of the line to one of the sticks while the carpenter left, to slice a third piece of pine into a thin wedge, three feet long.

"The wedge'll work loose from between the pintles," said William, "even if you're able to jam it between the stern and rudder posts. You can reeve the end of the line, holding one stick through the play between the posts, but how are you going to lash it, from the water, to the second stick so 'twill hold when they start to work that heavy rudder?"

Hugh smiled doubtfully but he said, "If this works, it may save the lives of Newport and Portsmouth lads asleep in the foc's'le. That's worth trying for, William."

Wanton's keen eyes suddenly met Hugh's look. "But how about Hugh Jocelyn's life? 'Tis worth more to us than a dozen others."

The loud clearing of Israel's throat filled the small cabin. The master gunner reached and bowed his broad back, pretending to test the lashing of the line to the pine stick.

Two hours later, when the tide was barely moving past the anchored sloop, the light skiff put off into the ink-black night. Israel sculled noiselessly from the stern, while John Wanton payed out the spliced two-hundred-fathom cod line made fast to the sloop's rail, where it was handled by Jeremy. With one end of the thirty-fathom line fast to a leather sling beneath his arms, the other end lashed to a thwart, Hugh knelt in the bow, stripped. Beside him were the wooden wedge and the eight-foot pine timbers, one lashed to the tarred rope. Around his waist was strapped a belt carrying a razor-edged sheath knife. Aft of him, William Wanton sat on a thwart holding the blades of two wrapped oars tossed above the water, ready for instant action.

Although checked by the sloop's compass on a course west-southwest, for they had no boat's compass, Israel had said when they started: "If we locate the Frenchman, 'twill be like findin' a dropped shillin' on a sand beach. The crickets is the only thing will hold us inshore."

"Their ports may show lights, for they'll have no fear of the sloop that fired into them," said John. "They likely think they're well rid of us, so we'll hear talk if they've prize wine and rum aboard her."

"Ay, we'll hear talk if we find her," muttered William, "but I doubt we find her."

"A light won't glimmer twenty fathom in this soup," grumbled Israel. "'Tis only by their French love of singin', if they be foxed, we'll reach her, and we scarce will or I'm a sperm whale!"

Hugh was silent.

Pushed by Israel's noiseless scull, the skiff crept through the murk. Like a black pall, the fog and the night lay on the sleeping sea.

"How much line is out, John?" whispered William, after an interval.

"About half," came the low answer.

Stripped as he was, in the dripping fog Hugh began to feel cold and rubbed his arms and legs to start the circulation. William reached and covered his shoulders with a wool sea jacket.

"The water's warm," Hugh whispered. "I'm fevered to get at that rudder."

"We'll never locate her, Hugh," muttered the anxious captain.

"Don't lose heart yet."

On went the skiff, exploring the murk, while John payed out the line. Often Israel stopped sculling while they sat rigid, ears straining for the sound of French voices. But the flat sea was blanketed with silence except for the measured monotone of the crickets, which drifted to them from the shore.

At length John whispered to Brandy, "She's near all out!"

"Change your course again, Israel," suggested William.

"Change my course?" Israel's throat rumbled. "I likely do little else, steerin' blind. We'll land fair inshore of the sloop afore we're done. Were it not for the crickets I'd a bin boxin' the compass for a half-turn of the glass."

"Lie here and listen for a time," warned John; "the line is most gone."

But out of the black vastness which walled in the skiff there came no sound. Israel started sculling in a new direction. They had gone but a short time, blinking into the gloom and listening with nerves taut as harp strings, when Hugh touched William's back.

"I heard something!"

For a space the four men sat stiff as wood. Then, in disgust, Israel muttered: "There's little sense in Hugh's shivering longer. We'll have the ebb soon and the line may part afore we reach the sloop."

"That's what I—"

"I heard it again! 'Twas the French, laughing!" broke in Hugh, cutting William short. "Listen! All of you!"

From the depths of the blackness to starboard came the faint sound of laughter.

"Christ's blood, there she lies!" murmured Brandy, swinging the skiff's bow and laying his strength into the scull. "Rumbullions for luck—these Wantons!"

While John took in the slack of the cod line, the skiff moved in the direction of the sound. Hugh sucked in deep breaths of relief while he chafed his stiff muscles. Action, at last! He might fail in his attempt to jam the rudder but he'd give it a good try. To his personal safety he gave little thought. If the French heard him at work they might spray him with a blunderbuss from the afterrail, above, before he could dive and swim away. Once he cleared her stern they could never locate him, and their shooting would be blind. But as the plan was his, his pride would be stung if he failed; and pride was a dominant trait in Hugh Jocelyn.

Handled by the skillful Israel, the skiff edged through the gloom nearer to the anchored ship as the sound of voices grew louder. Then two yellow smears burst through the wall of fog. Nearer and nearer moved the skiff. Now the lights glowed, like the eyes of some huge beast.

"Belay!" whispered Hugh. "We're close enough."

"'Tis the cabin ports over her counter we see, and they're open. We're dead off her stern," whispered William. "They're deep in their wine and will hear little."

Hugh tingled with the itch for action. "I'm casting off from here," he said in William's ear. "The line on me'll reach her stern; if not, I'll jerk it and you move in to give me plenty of play in which to work."

Hugh let himself into the water over the bow and William eased the pine sticks and the wedge, lashed together, after him, then picked up the short cod line by which Hugh could keep contact with the skiff.

"Luck, Hugh!" whispered William. "We'll stand by till they blow us out of the water!"

"You'll do it, Hugh! You'll do it!" said John.

Brandy added, "If the line parts and you may not find us, keep hollerin', lad, for Israel'll be waitin' with the skiff so long as she floats!"

The skiff lay directly astern of the anchored ship, on which no lights showed except the two blurred, yellow squares of her open cabin ports. As he swam, Hugh's ears caught snatches of song and maudlin laughter. He hoped that the French officers were making a night of it and were already well foxed. Otherwise, he might be heard working in the water below, for the shaft of the rudderpost would thrust up through the cabin to the poop and the whipstaff. The sea was not cold, and the wash of the salt water over his body was refreshing after his long inaction. But he moved with great caution, fearing the ears of the deck watch. He had planned in detail his procedure when he reached the rudder with his timber; but success or failure would depend largely on chance, and he had to work fast. Success might mean saving the life of many a Newport and Portsmouth lad in the coming fight and avoidance of damage to the *Flying Fish* from the ship's culverins. Hugh's heart beat hard with the will to win.

He swam up under the counter, pushing his small raft of pine, and reached the rudder. Through the lighted ports, little more than ten feet above his head, drifted the voices of the revelers in the cabin. With great effort, for he had no purchase in the water, he worked the narrow wedge as far as it would go into the free play between the stern and rudderposts, above a pintle. So long as it held its place, it would help to jam the rudder. Then with his knife he cut the cord binding the eight-foot pine sticks, thrust the end of the tarred rope through the play below the pintle and pushed the length of the rope through so that the timber floated at right angles to the sternpost and alongside and parallel to the deadwood and the plane of the rudder.

"So far, so good," he thought. "Now I've got to lash that loose stick on the other side fast, with the rope, to this one."

Hugh swam around the rudder with the loose stick and took two turns of the rope he had thrust through the play between rudder and sternpost, around its notched center so that it lay floating parallel to the stick on the opposite side. Then, suddenly, the hum of voices ceased to drift through the open port above his head. He clung to the rudder and listened. Had they heard him working? The shaft of the rudderpost passed through the cabin where they sat. If they suspected where the noise came from, a hurricane of lead from a blunderbuss would shortly spatter down on him. He floated, hugging the barnacle-crusted deadwood, hardly breathing. The water suddenly seemed icy cold, and a shiver shook him. It was not so much that he feared the death that hung over him by a hair, as the slow drowning, wounded and helpless, in the blackness.

Then he heard a low muttering, and knew that a Frenchman was leaning through a port. There was a curse and the click of steel on steel. The Frenchman had a musket or blunderbuss and was listening for the boat he thought he had heard. But the night was too black to see a yard. Would he fire blindly down at the rudder on a chance? At the thought, Hugh inhaled a deep breath and sank beside the deadwood. His groping fingers found a pintle, and he held himself under. When his tortured lungs seemed about to burst, he rose to the surface and listened.

Then on the thick silence broke a drunken laugh and rapid talk. The laughter grew and the talk continued inside the cabin. Cups clinked. Hugh drew a deep breath of relief into his lungs and expelled it. Thank God! The French had given it up as a false alarm and were again at their wine. He returned to his work of lashing the two sticks fast on either side of the projecting deadwood and the rudder.

Gripping the rope, with one foot braced against the rudder and the other against the sternpost, Hugh bowed his back and by repeated hunches and wrenching took up the slack between the timbers afloat on either side. Forcing the second piece of pine in against the two flat surfaces, he lashed it fast in position.

Unless the knots and rope gave under pressure, he had made the ship's rudder useless. A wave of exultation flowed through his bare body as he stopped to rest. "You'll sing another song up there, Frenchies," he chuckled, "when the weather clears and the *Flying Fish* bears down on you!" With a kick of his feet, he floated silently away from the ship's counter.

Hugh had left the skiff astern of the ship, and he swam out with a bearing on the cabin ports. Then he remembered that he had not given William the agreed-upon three jerks on the cod line when he started back. So he rolled on his back and slowly hauled on the line, keeping afloat with his feet. He had run thirty or forty feet through his hands when, like the thrust of a knife, a chill of fear shot through him. Something had happened! The line had parted! It still sagged deep in the water! He had lost the skiff! He would never find her in that baffling blackness! He could hail Israel and William, but that would only draw a spray of lead and chopped iron from the Frenchman's swivels. And they, in the skiff, not aware that the line had parted, might have drifted far. Yet they had always had the cabin ports as a range! Where were they? What was the trouble?

In the black water Hugh thought of his despair on his swim to Nashawena beach from Bellamy's sloop. But he was riding the tide then, and now the ebb was but just starting. Why hadn't William hauled on the line and, finding it parted, hailed him, even if it drew the Frenchman's fire? He knew that without the line he was lost.

Then, with the cabin ports as a range, the desperate Hugh swam straight away from the ship's stern. When he was far enough, he would hail the skiff and Israel would be sure to answer. But suppose the skiff was not there? Before he realized it, Hugh found himself swimming hard. He had not moved far when the line lashed to the sling on his back suddenly tightened. Hugh whirled in the water, grasped the line, and jerked hard.

"The line's taut!" he groaned. "It's fouled the bottom! I'll have to cut it!" He reached for the sheath on his belt and had the knife in his hand when the line lashed to his body tightened, then eased, tightened, then eased.

"Name of God," he muttered, "what's on this line?" But he did not slash the line as he trod water, waiting. Again the line was pulled hard—and suddenly he had the answer to the mystery.

"God's name! 'Tis William! The line's not parted, but the skiff moved up on me, making the sag. They're out there waiting for me not a ship's length away!"

Hugh jerked hard, then swam in on the end of the taut line, and shortly was alongside the skiff. A big hand reached and seized his long hair.

"Stab my guts, I bin near frenzical with fear! Be you all right, lad? I'll hold my grip till I'm sure you won't slip through my hands. Be you all right?"

"All right, Israel."

"You did it, Hugh? You jammed her?" demanded John. "We got no jerk from you that you were finished and were coming, and the line sagged till we thought we had lost you. Then we knew we had drifted in on you."

"Yes, I got the sticks lashed," said Hugh. "I hope they'll hold."

He worked his way to the bow and drew himself in over the gunwale, where William wrapped the sea jacket around him. The calloused hand that found Hugh's dripping one was shaking. "Name of God, I'm glad you're back, safe! I fair blamed myself for letting you go."

"When you moved in toward the ship so the line sagged, then tightened, I thought I was foul of the bottom. But I jammed the rudder, William, unless the lashing gives way."

"That cooks the Frenchman's goose," chuckled Wanton. "Hugh, there's none in Newport enough of a fish to do that, save you!"

§60

THE following afternoon, off Tarpaulin Cove, the French three-master *Diomede* was falling off, then hauling into the brisk southwest breeze which had cleared the sea of fog, then lying in irons, only again to fall off and circle into the wind, while the *Flying Fish* repeatedly crossed her stern at fifty yards, to rake her with a burst of musket fire and a withering broadside. Unable to bring her heavy guns to bear on the elusive sloop, the ship was being fast hammered into a derelict, her top hamper ripped to ribbons by the langrel chain and bar shot from the sloop's sakers, and her poop bulwarks and guns smashed from the battering of the *Flying Fish's* nine-pounders.

"There she goes!" shouted William Wanton to the smoke-grimed

Hugh and Israel, standing with their crews at the poop demiculverins, as the sloop sheered in to pass the ship's stern. "Name of God, there goes her mizzen!"

A wild cheer rose from Wanton's bare-backed gunners as the *Diomede's* splintered mizzenmast sagged and, with a tangle of ragged sails, shrouds, and spars, lurched overside. Men on the Frenchman's deck worked frantically to chop clear the wreckage over her rail as the *Flying Fish* reached down to cross her counter.

"Aim for her riggin'!" shouted Israel.

With their handspikes, the starboard crews knocked the coins from under the breeches of their pieces to further elevate the muzzles. Gun captains sighted the black tubes, then came Wanton's barked order, "Fire!"

Sputtering matches touched off the priming, and red huffs flashed skyward as the thundering starboard battery belched its flame and orange smoke. Langrel and bar shot tore through shrouds, stays, and sails the length of the French ship. Her main yard broke free and fell, crushing like flies a group of musketmen firing at the sloop. The deck of the privateer which had looted little Block Island was a shambles and a litter of rigging and gear.

The *Flying Fish* drove on, while her starboard gunners ran in, sponged and reloaded their pieces.

"Stand by to tack!" ordered Wanton. The sailors sprang to their stations at the cleats of the mainsail and jib sheets and the topsail braces. "Put her hard down!" he shouted to the men straining at the long tiller. The sloop swung to the bite of her rudder, came about, and ran past the counter of the stalled ship, spewing another broadside, then tacked and headed in, close hauled, for the *Diomede's* stern.

"Stand by with the grapplings, forward!" roared Wanton. "Boarders stand by!"

There was a rush of bare feet as the crew raced to obey. Pikes and war hatchets were seized from rail racks, cutlasses caught up and muskets hurriedly primed. In the bow men stood with iron grappling hooks, ready to hurl them and lash the sloop to the ship. The *Flying Fish* sheered in, thrusting her long jib boom over the enemy's counter, and the grapplings were thrown. There was a roar of muskets and, led by the Wantons, Hugh, and Israel, a mob of boarders scrambled up the bowsprit and over the bow rail to the ship's poop. But on the smashed afterdeck there remained only a bloody litter of the sprawled bodies of the dead and wounded and wrecked gear, for the French had fled forward as the howling pack of Newport and Portsmouth lads swarmed over their splintered rail with pike and cutlass. On the main deck a few turned to make a stand, only to go down under the charge of the cutlass men led by Israel and Hugh. Driven down their fore and main hatches, the covers were battened on them and the French made prisoners below.

The panting William Wanton sheathed his cutlass and turned to look for his scattered officers among the cheering groups of boarders, surprised at their easy taking of a ship supposed to carry over a hundred men. Near the main chains he saw Israel and John standing with Hugh, whose face was gray beneath sweat and powder smear.

"Hugh!" cried the captain. "You've been hit!"

Making his way over the littered deck, past dead men mangled into bloody heaps by splinters, and whimpering wounded crying for water, William reached the group, where Israel was tightening a belt as a tourniquet around Hugh's arm below the shoulder.

"Only a musket ball, William! I'm lucky 'twas not a splinter!"

Israel turned a grimy face to the captain. "He was hit on our deck but boarded with us, his left arm hangin' while he laid about him with his good right. The bone is sound, but there's much bleedin'. Send Chirurgeon Arnold with a bandage afore he touches the slimy French."

Wanton passed the word for the surgeon of the *Flying Fish*, who was attending to the wounded men of her crew, then detailed a guard for the hatches and started clearing the decks of the battered ship. The French wounded were carried aboard the sloop, which was leaving at once for Newport, and put in charge of Chirurgeon Arnold. The dead, including the captain and mate, were wrapped in pieces of tattered sails, weighted, and sunk. Shortly the guards at the hatches announced that the French below decks were clamoring to surrender. So they were disarmed and set to work under guard clearing the ship's deck and repairing her rigging.

"Captain," said Israel, when he had seen Hugh aboard the sloop with other wounded and half the prisoners, "I make no sense to the jabber of these frenzical French, but carry strong suspicion that there be plenty rum and wine in her hold with other prize goods they took since they sailed from Port Royal. The cabin fair stinks with stale wine and rum from the drinkin' of last night."

William grinned at his master gunner, whose smudged mask and hairy torso, stained with powder smoke, gave him the look of a gorilla. "Israel," he laughed, "I thought the smell of rum and wine was fair sweet to your nose. Never before have I heard you belittle it."

Israel's small eyes twinkled as he licked his lips. "Nor do I, Captain, when 'tis sailin' a straight course for my own throat where 'twill be put to good use," said the gunner. "But this was spilled about the cabin by them swinish drunkards of French and wasted, while the tongues of honest lads aboard the *Flyin' Fish* was dry as a hung pirate."

"Well spoke, Israel! When you search the hold, fetch up a jack or two of wine to moisten our throats before we sail."

In the ship's galley Israel and John Wanton found the freshly dressed carcasses of Block Island sheep and hogs. There, when John's sign language brought from the sullen cook and his helper a fluttering of hands, shrugging of shoulders, and a barrage of French, but no action, Israel stumped forward, thrust a ferocious face into the cook's, and, with the growl of a bear, sent him sprawling to the deck with a cuff beside his ear.

"Tumble to on them sheep, Frenchy!" he roared, pointing to the hung carcasses. "Run that spit through 'em! Lively, now! Stir that fire and get 'em to roast or I'll fry your ears!"

Although his English was wasted on French ears, Brandy's terrifying appearance and ponderous fists brought instant response from the frightened cook and his helper. Shortly the sheep were roasting over the open wood fire on the iron hearth of the galley.

To Israel and John's delight, when they dropped through the hatch to the hold they found a cargo of prize goods that would find ready sale on the Newport wharves—bales of cotton cloth and silk, hogsheads of sugar and molasses, indigo, logwood from the Bay of Honduras. And Israel shouted in glee when the flickering light from their candle lantern disclosed pipe after pipe of Canary and malmsey stowed alongside barrels of rum and brandy. It was evident that the privateer had taken ships bound in to Boston from Spain, the Wine Islands, and the West Indies.

"Stab me, but we'll divide a pretty haul of prize money if we can keep her out of the clutches of the pimps at the Naval Office!" chuckled Brandy.

"Governor Easton and the Council sitting as Prize Court shall condemn her," said John. "We'll not have the slimy hands of the Vice-Admiral's Office in Boston or their Naval Office in Newport touch her. Deputy Governor John Greene will have her sold with cargo before the news reaches them."

A cask was broached, wine brought on deck, and the noses of the sloop's crew were soon deep in jacks as they were passed around, while the French prisoners licked parched lips.

Leaving John, Israel, and a prize crew to patch the *Diomede's* sails and rigging and work her into Newport, Captain Wanton sailed that night, with his wounded and half the prisoners. At daylight the sloop slipped into the harbor and was made fast to Long Wharf. Shortly the news had spread through the sleeping town. Roused by the watch, a drummer led a parade of shouting men and boys through Thames Street to the wharf. Through opened windows, across the narrow streets, women chattered excitedly over the news. Muskets were fired.

The shore battery and the guns of King's Fort on the island roared their salute across the harbor to the returned *Flying Fish*. Soon the running people crowded the wharves, and Governor Easton and leading citizens were wringing William Wanton's hand, while the crew were hugged, kissed, slapped on the back, and cheered. Hugh, with heavily bandaged arm and shoulder, left the sloop with the other wounded, to be met on the wharf by the hurrying Tom and Content. Keen as a knife, a pang shot through him as he thought of the day when Seeth had waited with Content on the wharf at the return of the *Royal Stede*.

"Don't weep, Mother Content," Hugh comforted. "'Twas only a musket ball through the arm, and the wound is clean, so Chirurgeon Arnold tells me. But I'm a little weak from loss of blood and will need to keep quiet till the fever passes."

Content reached and placed her hand on Hugh's flushed face.

"Why, you're fevered now, Hugh! Have you strength to walk home? We can go by skiff. Note his face, Tom! 'Tis hot!"

Hugh circled her waist with his right arm and half carried the anxious Content while she pleaded with him to wait for a skiff.

"He's fevered, but give him his way, Content. 'Tis not far. 'Twas a great victory, Hugh, for a sloop to take that ship," said Stanton, as he walked proudly beside his foster son, back over the wharf to the shore through the chattering and excited people who pressed around them, cheering the bandaged Hugh and offering their sympathy.

Two days later the *Diomede* came limping in under jury mizzenmast and makeshift top hamper. In the meantime, the Wanton family had not been idle among their influential friends. Ignoring the protests of the Naval Office, the Governor and Council, acting as a Court of Admiralty, condemned and sold the *Diomede* and her cargo. And John Wanton carried to Hugh the news that when the previously agreed-on shares were distributed to owners, officers, and crew, he and Israel would each be the richer by the sum of two hundred pounds.

"Well, Israel," said the happy boy that evening, as he lay on a pallet near the fire, on which Content was cooking supper, "what are you going to do with your riches?"

"I think to buy a new sloop for Tom and me, for I'll soon be too old to go privateering with you young sprigs," chuckled the master gunner.

"Why, you're the best cutlass man and gunner in all this port and—you know it!" exclaimed Hugh. "Let any tell you you're too old to go privateering and he dare!"

Brandy grinned down at the big-limbed youth. "As good a lad with a cutlass as ever sailed out o' this port lies right here," he said soberly, pointing a finger at Hugh and then turning on Tom Stanton as if he expected a denial. With deliberation Israel reached and drew from his belt a leather pouch, which he handed to Stanton, saying: "Put that with Hugh's savings in the chimney hole. 'Tis the start of his fortune."

Content and Tom stared in wide-mouthed surprise at the gunner. "You mean—you want Hugh to have it, Israel?" asked Tom. "You give it to him?"

Brandy nodded. "Stab my vitals, for a certainty! He's tugged at the strings of Israel Brandy's battered old heart since he was that high. My savin's and his savin's lie board and board, shipmates, in that chimney hole. If I ever need ought of it, he'll not deny me. But 'tis his for all time."

Hugh's eyes were winking hard. "No, Israel!" he demurred, raising himself on his elbow. "You worked hard for it. I will not take it. 'Tis yours and 'twill always be!"

"Belay!" growled the sailor. "You be the sole sprig I've got to waste my heart on—or my prize money. Burn me, I'm a free man and do with both as I see fit! Content, put that gold with Hugh's against the time he buys into his first brig."

§61

It was a sad Hugh who bade good-by to the *Flying Fish* and his friends as, a week later, she sailed out of Newport to continue her patrol of the coast in search of marauding French privateers. But Chirurgeon Vigneron, who had been called in by Joe Brenton to examine Hugh's arm, had prescribed absolute rest for a month until the gunshot wound healed to his entire satisfaction. So, with bandaged arm in a sling, Hugh had seen his friends off from the wharf. He was walking slowly back up Thames Street when from behind him came the sound of horses' hoofs, and he stepped to the abutting wall of a house to give the animals ample room to pass. Ahead of them, seeking safety, fled a pig and her squealing offspring, followed by flapping geese and chickens. Turning, Hugh looked into the black eyes of Serena Brenton. For an instant their eyes met, then she turned her face without recognition and urged her horse into a canter. The blood leaped to his cheeks as he watched the red hood ride on toward Passage Street. Following, came Desire, her jet-black hair breaking from the confines of her yellow hood and, after her, a black groom brought up the rear. With a cry of recognition, the young girl reined in her mount.

"Hugh Jocelyn!" she exclaimed. Then sympathized: "Oh, your poor shoulder! I hope 'tis better and mending. You were hurt in the sea fight! Cousin Joe told us about the rudder," she chattered on. "What a trick you played on the French! And you did it alone!" From under the cloud of ebony hair Desire's eyes were feasting on the yellow head of the tall youth who laughed up at her. Then she shot a puzzled glance at her sister's retreating back. "Why did Serena not stop? 'Tis very strange!" With a parting wave of the hand she flung back as she started her pony: "I have that lock of hair! Have you yours? Come and see us soon, Hugh!" Was it the difference in birth between a fisherman's foster son and a Brenton that led her to pass him by without so much as a nod?

He entered the house and lay down, for pain stabbed his wounded arm and shoulder. He felt weak and hot with fever. Chirurgeon Vigneron had ordered him not to leave the house, but he had had to see the *Flying Fish* sail. He had to. Wrestling with the mystery and the hurt pride which drove him to dreams of the day when no proud patrician of Newport would pass Hugh Jocelyn on a street with a turned face, he fell into a troubled sleep.

Hugh's arm had been pronounced well on the way to recovery by Chirurgeon Vigneron. Some days later Trelawney asked Hugh to join him and Joe Brenton for an evening of talk at the King's Head with Doctor Lodovic, a learned Dutchman who had lately come to Newport from Boston and was sharing with Trelawney the conduct of the school and the tutoring of the children of the wealthy. In the great room of the tavern, with its low, oak-timbered ceiling from which hung candle beams with their flickering tallow dips, men sat over frothy sillabubs, a mixture of hard cider, sugar, and nutmeg, with cream slowly stirred in. Here and there were notables of the town, staid Quakers wearing their own hair and sad-colored clothes, and younger Quakers sporting periwigs and blue and wine-colored velvet and broadcloth coats with brocaded waistcoats, like their fellow townsmen of other persuasions. Half of Newport was Quaker but, following the lead of the dead Governor Coddington, not half the Quakers, men and women, affected the somber garb of the sect.

As Hugh entered the tavern he felt none of his former embarrassment at his invasion of the private domain of the gentry. From some tables there were friendly calls, waves of the hand, and inquiries concerning his wounded arm; at others there were lifted brows and surprised stares. But the young sailor was learning to harden himself against the world. The stares no longer infuriated him. He coolly returned them in kind and followed Trelawney to the table where Brenton waited, with a fat, red-faced man.

"I've been telling Hugh about some of your experiences in Boston, Doctor," said Trelawney, after they were seated. "He could scarce believe me when I said that the Harvard Library at Cambridge Town held not a line of his beloved Shakespeare or of Ben Jonson, nor of any other loose and immoral English poet of good Queen Bess's time or later."

Chuckling with merriment, the Dutch savant threw back his red face, deeply pitted from smallpox, and topped by a rusty, black wig, too small for his great round head. Past fifty and stout, educated at Leyden and Leipzig, the credentials he carried credited him with an astounding erudition in the classics, philosophy, and history as well as familiarity with the sciences. "I viewed vat dey gall de library at Harvard, and ven I looked for your great Chaucer and Milton, Shakespeare and Dryden, Lord Bacon, Locke and Hobbs, de long-faced tutor reddened like a maid. He swore dey harbored no such brofane and obscene writers in deir sacrozanct halls."

"Well, what did those horse-faced Puritans harbor?" laughed Joe Brenton, tossing off his sillabub.

Lodovic guffawed. "Horse-vaced Buritans! Dat is a bretty description of dem, Mr. Brenton! Dere vas a limited gollection of Latin classics, less of Greek, and no French, no history or philosophy, but much, oh, very much, teology of de subernatural school of Buritan writers which I cannot read for it is de nonsense of unscholarly men and fanatics."

Hugh listened with mingled amusement and wonder. "You mean to say, Doctor, that you found none of our great English poetry or drama at Harvard?"

"None vatever. It is not known dere or missed. Dey have only a narrow, egglesiastical curriculum bare of any addemdt at a liberal culture. Dat is natural, for de bresident and fellows have it not demselves."

"Well, Hugh," said Trelawney, "you believe me now, I hope. Their Harvard College seems designed solely for the training, in their crackpot doctrine, of aspirants for the ministry in the Puritan Church which rules the Bay Colony. Liberal culture they're as ignorant of as a shark of fleas."

"Why, I wouldn't swap Will Shakespeare for all the doctrine in the world!" bridled Hugh.

"Vell sboken, my lad," agreed Lodovic, puffing on his long clay pipe and nodding his head so vigorously that tufts of untrimmed reddish hair protruded from the sides of his black wig.

"Name of God," sneered Trelawney, "a Harvard student today is lucky to survive the holy heat and pious delirium of that nitwit teaching without impairing the mental powers he entered with; that is, if he had any, which perhaps most do not."

Joe Brenton poked the Englishman in his lean ribs. "How long, Dick," he demanded, with a wink at the company, "were you in Boston Town before they feared you a menace to the youth, with your rake-hell manners and morals of the court of merry King Charles, coupled with a dangerous familiarity with English poetry and drama?"

The Englishman closed his eyes and gravely stroked his chin with a lean hand. "'Tis an unhappy experience to recall, Joe. I was fair lonely and sick at heart. They gave me but a year, and then the Mathers had me up on charges."

"Charges? What kind of charges?"

"As you know, I tutored sons of the rich and gave instruction at a Misses school, as well. It appeared from the charges that I had been heard to quote the saintly Cotton Mather with my tongue in my cheek. I had poked fun at his warning that playing cards were the devil's picture books, and I had sniggered, 'twas said, at his silly remark to the effect that the practice of physic by the clergy was 'an angelical conjunction.' It seems I had also laughed obscenely at his boast from the pulpit that when one of the clergy entered a house it was as if 'an Angel of Light' had appeared!"

"You vere bold, my friend," laughed Lodovic, "to bull de beard of de Buritan lion, or I might say de dail of de Buritan ass, in his own sdable." Draining his pewter cup, the Dutchman smacked his lips with a loud, "Ah, dat vas gut!"

"So was your remark," chuckled Trelawney. "Wasn't it, Hugh?"

"So good," said Hugh, "that it makes me itch to get my hands on one of the reverend toads that so treated you, Dick."

"Boston Town would be no place for you, Hugh, with that fighting blood of yours," said Brenton. "That hot head would soon have you in trouble. You'd be strangling constables, the clergy, and even the governor." He turned to Trelawney. "You were fair reckless, Dick, to bait the Mathers and the official pickthanks who sit cheek by jowl with them."

"Yes, I was headstrong and unwise if I had wished to stay, for I drank hard and talked freely in my cups. They also accused me of deriding their sending of Puritan missionaries to convert the lost heathen of the Church of England in Virginia."

"You mean to say the Puritan Church did this?" demanded Brenton.

"They did, out of their abysmal ignorance and conceit. I had insisted that there be a fair exchange and that missionaries from the Church of England in Virginia be sent to convert the Puritan bigots in Boston."

"No vonder dey banished you!" chuckled Lodovic.

"'Tis a wonder you were not whipped as were the Quakers!" said Joe.

"They doubtless would have done so but for my brother, who had the ear of the King. They so hate the Church of England that I heard from Boston that Phips's fiasco before Quebec, last autumn, was laid to the founding of the new King's Chapel by Governor Andros."

"It seems they blame everything but their own thick pates for their mistakes," commented Hugh.

"Yes, and these gallant Boston clergy have a weakness for claiming the women responsible for every evil predicted by the prophet Isaiah—fire and war, poor harvests and caterpillars, even baldness and bellyache."

"Dot is right! Dot is right!" agreed Lodovic, bobbing his black-wigged head and reaching for his refilled mug.

"One night," continued Trelawney, "I was overheard in an ordinary mimicking the Reverend Increase Mather in a windy sermon of his I once tried to listen to until I sickened and left. It seemed that I repeated his warning to the men that wigs were horrid bushes of vanity—although his son shortly wore one—and that the dames of Boston walked, as he put it, 'with outstretched necks and wanton eyes, mincing as they go.' I remarked that, despite Increase Mather, Boston dames still stretched their necks, wantoned their eyes, and minced as they walked, to say nought of pleasuring themselves with livelier matters. That was the last straw. As the clergy and laymen draw their law from the Old Testament and there is no knowledge of, or respect for, English law in the Colony, I was expelled from Massachusetts Bay."

With a grimace, a shrug, and a wide sweep of his long arms, Trelawney finished to the laughter of his friends.

"I give you the dames of Boston!" cried Joe Brenton, lifting his mug. "May they mince and wanton to their hearts' content and the content of their swains, and devil take the clergy! But what was Boston's poison, Dick, was our sugar! God bless you!"

"Ay, it was a happy day for me," said Hugh, resting a hand on Trelawney's lean shoulder. "Had not Dick Trelawney come to Newport, I had grown up an unlettered cod's head."

"Like myself and John and Kit," grinned Brenton; "who have lacked the wit to profit by Dick's learning as have you, Hugh."

"Now," said the Englishman, "you have a man to listen to whose learning dwarfs mine as the moon the stars."

Lodovic's red jowls bulged with his chuckle as he raised a fat hand in protest. "My friend, you are kind vid your flattery."

"They shall see when they have heard you talk. You must explain to Hugh, Doctor, your theory of middle-parallel sailing. Already he knows more astronomy and navigation than any master who sails out of this port. Now, Joe, two sillabubs are all an honest man should drink—they are too tame. But if you hanker for sweetness in a drink, I'll have Landlord Whiting mix a lamb's wool for us."

"Name of God, a lamb's wool? What devilish London drink is that?" asked Brenton. "Have you ever thrust your nose into such a doubtful-sounding potation, Doctor Lodovic?"

Lodovic's small eyes twinkled. "If it is so good as your sillabub, I vould dry one, yes."

Trelawney left the table and found the landlord in the back room off the kitchen, where drinks were mixed. Later a black boy appeared with four pewter mugs in which floated a white pulp, powdered with nutmeg. Lodovic, Hugh, and Brenton tasted their drinks.

"What's this white mush in the ale?" demanded Joe. "However, 'tis a nice blend, though mild."

"That's the pulp of roasted apples, joined with ale and sugar and a sprinkle of nutmeg. 'Twas just new in London when I left."

"It is gut!" said Lodovic, with a smack of his thick lips.

"'Tis strange to the colonies and well enough, but I feel inclined to get foxed tonight, since I marked Carr Newbury and Richard Brinley enter with that burly henchman of his father's who conducts his Portsmouth farms. I have suspicion of that farmer."

Hugh glanced across the room to meet the vindictive stare of Newbury. For a space the eyes of the two met, then Newbury turned away. "He hasn't forgotten that meeting on Dexter's Lane," thought Hugh.

"Don't get foxed, Joe," pleaded Trelawney. "Stick by the lamb's wool."

Brenton flung a look at the Newbury table and answered, "No, I want a strong cup of metheglin on which to nourish my bile while I poison my eyes on Richard."

"Vat is dis metheglin you sbeak of?" asked the Dutchman.

"'Tis made from yeast and honey and is headier than it tastes," said Trelawney, shifting his gaze from Brenton's brooding face to the Brinley table. "It has the strength of kill-devil or rumbullion."

The Dutchman roared. "Vat names! Vat names you English gif your trinks!"

"They gave me a drink in Boston I venture you've scarce heard of, Mr. Brenton," said Hugh. "They told me 'twas common in New Hampshire—'whistle-belly vengeance.'"

"Whistle-belly vengeance!" Brenton exclaimed, screwing his dark face into a grimace. "In God's name, what vile mixture is in that?"

"I scarce know, but 'tis a man-killer. Rum and cider and spirits, with egg and sugar, they told me. A few of these and a man would kill his own brother."

"I doubt you not, Hugh." Brenton tossed off his metheglin, then swung on his stool and glared at Newbury and Brinley, who ignored him. But the big farmer, whose powerful body filled his kersey coat as corn fills a bag, coolly returned Brenton's stare.

"I like not the look of that square-jawed sheepherder and ox prodder," growled Brenton. "'Tis said he beats and drives his hands hard and keeps none long save the poor Wampanoag bond servants who may not leave. And now here come Francis Brinley and Peleg Sanford."

Brinley and Sanford were seating themselves at a table adjoining Newbury's. Trelawney glanced at Hugh and gave him a warning shake of the head as he pressed the sailor's shoe with his foot. Joe Brenton was drinking himself into an ugly mood. That meant he would be over at the Newbury table before the evening was done and there would be words.

"Francis Brinley told me but lately that he would return to Boston could he sell his Conanicut and Narragansett lands," said Trelawney. "He despairs of good government in Rhode Island."

Brenton snorted with disgust. "And what sort of government had we when Andros was royal governor and Brinley sat in the saddle? A fawning, lickspittle Court of Quarter Sessions ruled by Boston! Have you forgot how his tagtail, Tripp, sent Hugh to the pillory for standing on his rights and ruffling the hair of that precious whelp of a Richard?"

"William Wanton made Tripp eat sand for that," laughed Trelawney. "He was bedded for a week from that fall on the floor, here, from William's thrust foot."

"I have not forgot what the Brinleys did to me, Mr. Brenton," said Hugh.

Brenton's black eyes twinkled. "Ah, but there is one Brinley who is your friend. I talked with her about you but recent. She's the sole Brinley who bears me no ill will. She seems to hate her brother and," Brenton lifted his black brows and smiled roguishly at the fast-reddening Hugh, "I fear, has a weakness for this big privateersman of ours."

Trelawney was scowling and shaking his head at the incorrigible Joe, already feeling his strong metheglin; while the blood pushed through the bronze of Hugh's neck and face in his embarrassment. Then he thought of the slight from Serena Brenton and said, "The daughters of the gentry scarce stoop to privateersmen and fishermen's sons, Mr. Brenton."

Brenton looked sharply at the speaker, "Are you serious? She's fair mad about you. Cease belittling yourself. We know your worth, as does all Newport. Why, you've fair captured my little cousin Desire's heart, already. Were she grown, I should fear for you lest she married you out of hand."

"And what would the proud Brentons say to that?" laughed the confused Hugh, thinking of the cold eyes of Serena when last he saw her. "They'd have me expelled the colony."

"This proud Brenton, as you name us," said the flushed Joe, vehemently, "would count it an honor!"

"Tut-tut!" interposed Trelawney. "Enough of this! Now I wonder what Richard Brinley is chirping into that steward's ear that so sours his ugly face."

Brenton swung on his stool and stared at the tables across the room. Then he burst into laughter. "Doubtless that great brain of his itches with some scheme to get Hugh out of Newport."

"Put it from your mind, Joe," urged Trelawney. "And heft that cutlass which Hugh took on the French privateer."

Hugh drew the cutlass at his side from its scabbard slung to a baldric and handed it to Brenton.

"Name of God, 'tis sufficient heavy to fell an ox!" said Joe, returning the blade. "But what goes on at the Newbury table? Richard and the steward, Gill, sit with heads together looking poison our way. I like not the ugly snout of that cattle nurse of Brinley's and am fevered to so tell him!"

Before Trelawney could stop him, Joe Brenton had risen and stood beside Newbury and Richard Brinley, while the occupants of adjoining tables suddenly ceased talking and awaited curiously the outcome. "Come, Hugh," urged the Englishman, "we must get him away before there's trouble!"

Young Brinley and Newbury had turned their backs on the man who stood at their table, but the farmer Gill glowered up at him as Francis Brinley called to Trelawney, who had Brenton's arm, "Mr. Trelawney, will you remove your whittled friend? Mr. Newbury and my son have nothing to say to him."

"Oh, yes, I have," sniffed Newbury, rising and facing Brenton. "Go back where you belong, with your sailor scum, Joe Brenton, and your fat schoolmaster," he sneered, "and leave gentlemen alone!"

Choking back his anger, Brenton deliberately surveyed Newbury from his silver-buckled shoes to his curled periwig, then jeered, "Ah, 'tis the slippery and scheming Mr. Newbury, I believe!"

"Name of God, I warn you for the last time to leave us, or—"

"Or what?" demanded Brenton.

Before Newbury could reply, the farmer Gill rose to his feet. As he did, Hugh moved toward the group, watching him, while Landlord Whipple hovered close by, wringing his fat hands in helpless uncertainty. His fists doubled, the big steward stood glaring at Brenton.

"Come away, Joe," urged Trelawney. He turned to the elder Brinley, who had now left his table. "He's not himself, Mr. Brinley, as you may see."

"'Tis not the first time he's insulted members of my party in a public place," stormed the exasperated Brinley. "He'll answer to me for this!"

"Ay, and he'll answer now!"

With a quick movement Gill pushed Joe Brenton back into

Trelawney's arms. At the same instant there was the rattle of steel as Hugh stripped the baldric from his shoulder, dropped it with the cutlass to the floor, shouldered Brenton aside, and faced the steward.

"Hugh! Hugh! Name of God, man! Your wounded arm is not yet strong," cried the Englishman, pushing between the two. But a sweep of Hugh's good arm brushed him back.

There was the confused murmur of voices as men rose from their seats and crowded around the Newbury table. "Hugh's but lately wounded! Have a care, Hugh! Shame! Keep out of it, Hugh!"

Lights like the glitter of sun on March crust danced in Jocelyn's eyes as he measured the man who threatened him with clenched fists.

"Don't, Hugh! Stand back! You're a wounded man!" pleaded Brenton, as Hugh forced him back, then turned on Gill, who waited with hunched shoulders and outthrust jaw.

"Now, farmer," said Jocelyn, "you're primed with good rum, loaded and laid full on your target; touch off the match!"

With a grunt Gill made a wild swing, but Hugh stepped inside, taking the blow on the shoulder of his left arm, stabs of pain shooting through the healed wound. Then with his right hand he struck Gill full in the face. And his weight was behind the blow. Gill reeled back, recovered himself, and lowered his head for a rush. As he did an oak stool in the hands of a square-built figure crashed down on his skull and he sagged to the floor.

"Christ's blood, will you see a recent wounded man set on by a whittled lout without lifting a hand?" stormed Tom Paine, facing the circle of excited men.

Bending over the bludgeoned man on the floor, Richard Brinley was pleading: "Get up, Gill! Get up and hit him! Down the scum of a sailor! Smash the dirty upstart!"

But Gill was beyond hearing. Hugh smiled as the aroused Tom Paine glared into the flushed faces of the protesting Newbury and Francis Brinley. As Richard straightened from the limp Gill, he was smacked on the cheek by a heavy hand and knocked back against his father. "You'd set your man on a lad wounded in the service of Newport, would you, you bufflehead!" snarled Paine.

"Name of God, Captain Paine, you're overfree with your hands!" cried Brinley, stepping between the privateersman and his son, who nursed his slapped face as he backed away from the inflamed sailor. " 'Tis none of your affair!"

With a shrug of his heavy shoulders Paine shook off Brinley's restraining hand. "None of my affair? You stood by while your man Gill, there, set on a lad with one good arm. For you thought he'd be bested by your bully!"

"Ay, he did!" agreed voices from the circle of onlookers.

"That's a lie!" exploded Newbury, confronting Paine. "Neither Francis Brinley nor I had a part in Gill's attack on this sailor! Gill's foxed! It was his own doing! But you went too far in striking Richard Brinley!"

"You name me liar, Mr. Newbury?" Paine's agate eyes glinted savagely. But Newbury stoutly held his ground and gave Paine look for look.

"No, Captain Paine, I name you no liar! Nor would any man in Newport dare to! What I say is that Francis Brinley had no part in this attack by his farmer."

Paine's breath whistled through his teeth as his eyes twinkled. "I scarce thought you'd name me liar," he said. "No Newbury would and keep his bones whole!"

Be it said to his credit, Francis Brinley faced Hugh's amused stare and the taunts of those surrounding the group with courage and dignity. He turned to Hugh. "My man was foxed. I had no part in his attack on you, and I apologize for my son's conduct. But I am warning you, here and now, keep your hands off my family."

The thrust went home. Francis Brinley knew. In silence Hugh recovered his cutlass, while Landlord Whipple whined: "Gentlemen! Gentlemen! We've had enough brawling! Please, Mr. Brinley, take your man out. He's bloodied my sand sufficient already!"

Brinley turned to Whipple. "Joe Brenton came to my son's table and insulted him and Carr Newbury. I will have my man removed."

With the aid of black boys, the dazed Gill was lifted to his feet and the Brinleys, with Newbury, left the tavern.

Seated again at their table, with a cup of rum in his hand, Hugh said to Brenton and Trelawney: "You heard what he said. I'm scum and upstart! Because I'm the foster son of a fisherman. I'm not fit to mingle with gentry! Mr. Brenton, you're fair reckless to sit here with scum and upstarts!"

Brenton impulsively reached and closed Hugh's mouth with his hand. "Stop that woman's talk, Hugh Jocelyn! 'Tis unworthy of you!"

"But I'm not gentry! I'm scum! My people were humble farmers! I've been fisherman all my life! What meant Francis Brinley when he warned me to keep my hands off his family? He meant my hands of a sailor were unfit to touch gentry, even in a blow."

"Name of God, Hugh," protested Trelawney, "have done with this nonsense!"

"You two are of the gentry and may laugh," said the sailor, who had been cut to the marrow by the epithet hurled at him by young Brinley. "But it seems, though I have learning, I am still scum, unworthy to—"

"Circle the waist of a high-born maid, which you already have, you rascal, and will again! And I envy you!" broke in Joe Brenton, poking Hugh in the ribs. "Now enough of this. You are oversensitive. The Brentons will always hold you an honored guest."

But Brinley's scorn had knifed deep, and the blood leaped to Hugh's face as he answered, "There is one Brenton who takes shame to speak to Hugh Jocelyn because he's not gentry!"

Trelawney looked in surprise from Hugh to Joe, on whose face lay a frown as he slowly shook his head. "Desire told me, Hugh," muttered Brenton. "The reason for the strange action of a strange maid I do not know, but I do know 'twas from no cheap snobbery. 'Twas from something else, and I am sorry."

§62

Weeks passed and the *Flying Fish* did not return. Then one day, as the *Sea Gull* needed new shrouds and stays, Hugh started for the rope-walk. He walked up Griffin Street, past the widely spaced houses and their gardens, and was approaching the ropewalk when he heard behind him the beat of a horse's hoofs. He did not turn but continued on his way, wrapped in his thoughts. The beat slowing from canter to trot sounded close behind him, and a familiar voice exclaimed: "Name of God!"

With a pulsing of blood through his body, Hugh turned to face the radiant Lettice Brinley, her blue silk riding hood tossed from her wavy chestnut hair, her hazel eyes shining, as she reined in her horse.

"Your servant, Mistress Lettice!" Hugh swept off his beaver hat with a low bow. She had seen him at a distance and had followed him.

The girl's brilliant eyes caressed the man who stood in the road-way, from his yellow head to the buckles of his heavy shoes. The color crept up over her fair skin to her temples, and her lower lip trembled. "Come near me, Hugh Jocelyn," she ordered softly. "It has been so long! No one may see us here, for the trees!"

Hugh stood beside the horse and she stripped off her glove, reached, and her fingers touched his cheek and chin as he smiled up at her, strangely elated. Here was a patrician who thought it no conde-scension to speak with scum and an upstart.

He caught her hand and pressed it to his lips. The hand trembled as she drew it away. "Why did you not answer me, Hugh Jocelyn? Why have you kept me hungry for a word with you? Think you I might easily forget that day?"

As she bent from her saddle and her hazel eyes shone into his,

Hugh thought her lovelier than he had ever seen her. Though they might be noticed from a distant house, he battled with a fierce desire to sweep her from her horse and crush her in his arms—this delectable morsel of the gentry. He glanced back down the street for her black groom.

The girl read his thoughts. "Have no fear of Aaron," she laughed down at him. "I bid him stay at Ann Street when I sighted you in the distance walking this way. He worships me and would die rather than tell."

"Your father would doubtless send you back to Boston did he learn of this."

She shrugged, and her long-lashed eyes darkened with anger. "You had words with them at the King's Head. And Tom Paine put that brute Gill on the floor. When I heard, I laughed at them for thinking to beat Hugh Jocelyn. Father cursed you for a common brawler. And I laughed at him again. 'Who sought the brawl?' I asked. 'Did not Richard set Gill on Hugh Jocelyn?' "

"Your brother named me scum and an upstart," said Hugh, resting a hand on her horse's neck and standing so close that he saw the blood pulse in her neck.

"When, oh, when will you meet me on Dexter's Lane?" she whispered. "I'm all a-tremble at the thought of it!"

His right hand grasping her left, rested on her rounded thigh, and he felt her shiver. "You would meet with an upstart, you—a lady?"

"Meet? I'd go fair mad if you'd consent!"

"When shall it be?"

"Soon, oh, soon! Tomorrow I can be there! I've never forgot that day, Hugh Jocelyn!" She leaned toward him, her breast rising and falling with her quick breathing, and he caught the faint perfume of her hair.

Intoxicated by her nearness and the touch of her, Hugh burned his bridges. The Brinleys might do their worst. He would meet her. "I'll be there tomorrow," he said.

"Oh," she murmured, "you've made me so happy, Hugh Jocelyn!" She suddenly leaned nearer, her arm circled his neck and her lips found his.

Giddy with her sweetness and the passion that stormed through him, Hugh forgot their danger from prying eyes. Then his reason returned. "'Tis too dangerous, beautiful," he said thickly. "Not here, where someone will see. Have a care!"

She straightened, her darkened eyes languorous with her emotion. Then hoofbeats sounded from beyond the turn of the road where it met Jew Street.

"Someone's coming!" warned Hugh, moving back from her horse.

"Damn them!" muttered the girl, impatiently thrusting locks of wayward hair beneath her silk hood.

Shortly a horse turned the bend at the ropewalk and approached down Griffin Street at a canter. Lettice looked at the horseman and gasped, "Name of God! Richard!"

"Yes," said Hugh, folding his arms across his chest, his face wearing a look of amused anticipation. "It seems that you are surprised by your brave brother talking with one of the lower classes—an upstart. I'm sorry, Lettice! 'Twill bring you trouble."

Reining in his mount, young Brinley stared open-mouthed at the girl on horseback and the man in the road. Then his anger broke loose and he turned on the girl watching him with sullen, defiant eyes.

"Lettice!" he cried. "Have you no shame—no pride? You—"

"Wait!" Hugh's voice was as cold as ice and as hard as he moved toward young Brinley, who drew back in his saddle as if he feared bodily assault. "Have a care what you say! I had business at the ropewalk and met your sister by chance. If there be fault, the fault is mine. I stopped her and would not let her pass."

Brinley turned on his sister and glared into her unwavering eyes, as his lip curled in a sneer. "You—you fancy I believe that?"

Hugh moved to the side of Brinley's horse. "What you have to say, say to me. 'Tis true that I, one of the scum, have been so brazen as to speak with your sister, of the quality. That is a grave crime! But what are you going to do about it?"

Richard Brinley choked with rage, fidgeting with his riding whip. He glanced down at the braided goad, then at the towering Hugh Jocelyn, who watched him with amused eyes. At last he found his voice: "I have nought to say to you! 'Tis my sister I'd speak to!" He backed his horse away from Hugh and moved toward Lettice, who sat toying with her riding whip. "You shameless huzzy!" he exploded. "You'll pay dearly for this to your father!"

"Cease your chirping, you pitiful fool!" spat out the infuriated girl. "Pay to my father, shall I? Then you'll pay, too, for what I've learned of your goings and comings in the last month!"

Richard Brinley crimsoned to his ears. "What do you mean? Threaten me, will you, you quail—you drazel—you—"

There was a whir, as a whiplash snapped in the air slashing the red face of the horseman.

"Oh! You—"

Again the braided lash of Lettice's goad whipped across the face of her whimpering brother. "Name of God! You'll call me drazel, will you, you sniveling coward!" she cried, as her brother started his horse and moved out of reach, nursing his face with a hand.

As his horse broke into a canter, Brinley turned and flung back at the girl, who stiffly sat her mount, gripping her riding whip, her blazing eyes picturing her scorn, "You and your sailor scum will regret this day!"

Never had she seemed so lovely as, chin tilted and red lip curled above her small white teeth, she watched her brother gallop away, his hand at his face. She turned to Hugh. "God's name," she cried in disgust, "what a jackanapes for a brother!"

Hugh went to her where she sat, her hair, escaped from her hood, framing her face in a chestnut cloud. "Well struck, Lettice!" he laughed. "'Twas full as savage as that you once gave me!"

Her flaming eyes softened and filled with tears as she looked down at the man beside her. "Kiss me good-by, Hugh!" she sobbed. "There'll be no tomorrow in our Arden. They'll have me watched for a month. Will you write me?"

"Yes, I'll make Trelawney fetch it."

"Oh, take me in those big arms and kiss me hard, Hugh Jocelyn," she murmured, "for you carry my heart away with you in your hand!"

§63

EARLY in December the *Flying Fish* reached Newport, convoying a French ship she had taken in the drifting ice of the Gulf. After condemnation by the Governor and Council, the prize money was divided and Israel Brandy's share was added to the common fund in the hole in Stanton's chimney.

The winter was closing in early and there would be little enemy commerce afloat off the northern coast for three months; so the Wantons, not wishing to spend the winter in the warm seas of the West Indies, laid up the *Flying Fish* for overhauling.

In the spring, after a successful cruise off the coast, William Wanton sent two French prizes of the *Flying Fish* on to Newport for condemnation in the prize court and headed into Boston to purchase balls and powder for his guns. With her stores aboard, the sloop lay anchored in the stream off Scarlett's Wharf, her jib and foresails set and her mainsail shaken out of the brails, waiting for the ebb. Leaving John, the mate, in command, William Wanton, with Hugh, Israel, and Jeremy Potts, went ashore to the Green Parrot, a tavern on Ship Street, to read the latest news from the Indies and London posted on the newsboard. The four seated themselves at a table and were served their rum and hard cider, called stonewalls. As they sat talking of the cruise, a group of men entered the ordinary. Two who carried halberds, insignia of a constable's authority, and wore swords, were soon talking in loud tones with men who joined them at the next table.

"He died in his sin, refusing to confess his wrong," said a burly minion of the law.

"What had he done to be hanged, he, one of the clergy?" demanded another.

"Done?" snorted the second constable, a beefy hulk of a man with small, pig-like eyes and a doublet stained with food and spilled beer. "He denied witches! He preached to the people at Wells that such never was! God's name! 'Twas treason to the Church and the Magistrates!"

Hugh looked at Israel and lights flickered dangerously in his eyes, while the sailor's tufts of brows pulled together in a scowl.

"Oh, but 'twas a pity," broke in a third man. "The Reverend Burroughs meant no disrespect to the Magistrates. I had it from a man from Wells, in the crowd on the Common who watched the hanging of him, that he but sought to quiet the fever for hunting witches among his people."

With a snort, the big constable turned on the speaker. "You cod's-head! Know you not that Reverend Mather spurs the people to rout the witches from our midst? Already twenty have hanged as did this chitty-faced Burroughs today. Confess he would not, and he got his deserts!"

"But the people who saw were that wrought they near took him from the hangman. There were tears in many eyes to see that good old man go to his death with a smile of faith on his face."

The other constable reached and cuffed the speaker on the ear. "Keep your sniveling to yourself or, Name of God, I'll smite you for a friend of witches!"

As they listened to the talk, the blood of the four Newport men grew hot. Israel's face was black with anger. His small eyes met Hugh's in a significant look as his paw of a hand opened and closed beside his cup.

The slapped man meekly took his chastening from the constable in silence; but another said: "The Reverend Cotton Mather sat near me on his horse as the hangman swung off the Reverend Burroughs and the crowd groaned and many wept. He turned to the doubtful people and said, 'The man there is not of the ordained clergy! Cease your sniveling, for know you not that the devil oft appears as an angel of light?'"

"Burn me, the devil was the one sittin' the horse!" exploded the deep voice of Israel Brandy as he whirled on his stool and glared at the startled group, his mouth twisting savagely and the veins swelling in his thick neck.

The pig-eyed constable was on his feet, his heavy face red with wrath. "How now! What say you, sailor?" he stormed, rising and moving toward the squat man on the stool. "You call the Reverend Mather devil?"

Hugh and Israel got to their feet, followed by William and Jeremy, and in the hands of Hugh and Jeremy were their stools, hanging beside their legs. The occupants of other tables stopped their talk and closed in on the strangers.

Israel hunched his head between his massive shoulders as he faced the two angered constables. "I calls devil whosoever sneers at a dying man, constable or whatever you be!" he snarled, slowly rolling the sleeves back from his huge forearms.

"I'll lesson you in respect for your betters, sailor!" exploded the other, reaching across his body for the handle of his sword. "I'll lesson you foreign scum!"

With a quick movement Hugh had the right wrist of the constable pinioned and forced the blade back into its sheath. His hands closed on the latter's arms as his eyes burned into the blood-mottled face of the man, who winced under the power which held him helpless. "Draw that blade," Hugh snarled in his ear, "and, Christ's blood! constable or no, I'll break it over your fat head!"

Straining vainly to free himself, the enraged constable writhed in the vise of Hugh's hands. With a cry, his companion leaped back, drew his sword, and called to the circle of men from the surrounding tables closing in on the four strangers. "Help! Arrest these sailors! They make light of our clergy and Magistrates! Show 'em there's law in Boston!"

"Come on, lads," ordered Wanton. "Make for the door before they cut us off!"

"Flatten the cod's-heads with your stools!" roared Brandy, brandishing the heavy oak above his head. "All hands stand by to board!"

There was a rush for the Newport men and the fight was on. Hugh hurled the fat constable in his hands crashing back over a table, picked up his stool, caught the slash of the second man's sword on its oak seat and battered him to his knees as Israel and Jeremy opened a path to the door. Hit with flying cups, tankards, and stools, the four privateersmen beat their way through the circle of men blocking their escape. With a last desperate rush they made the street. There a huge longshoreman brought William to the ground by a blow from a stool. "They're off the *Flying Fish*!" he yelled. "Down with the Newport dogfish!"

With the bellow of a charging bull, Israel bludgeoned the longshoreman while Hugh jerked the bleeding William to his feet and they fought on toward the shore.

"Who wants more of the same kind?" roared Brandy, guarding

their rear, as he brought a man to his knees and stood swinging his stool in a wide arc as he would his cutlass.

"Make for the skiff, Israel!" ordered Hugh as a flung stone opened his cheek, and he again jerked William to his feet, his face smeared with blood. "Make for the skiff! Don't stop to fight!"

Shoulder to shoulder the four friends broke for the beach through the shouting men who barred their way. Sticks and stones battered them, but the fighting Newporters kept their feet and pushed on. Hard at their heels the yelling rabble followed the four to the skiff.

While Hugh and Israel whirled on the pack and beat them off with a barrage of stones they picked up from the shore, William and Jeremy slid the skiff into the water and seized the oars. Plunging in to their knees, Israel and Hugh dove into the skiff and she moved away, followed by a volley of stones and execrations.

"John'll have to chop her hawser and step lively or the Naval Office will have a boat after us! But I'll blow their damned craft out of the water before I'll put my sloop and crew into the slimy hands of Boston Magistrates!"

"Well spoke, William!" applauded Brandy, wiping blood and sweat from his face. "After today the crew of this skiff'll be wanted men in Boston Town!"

"They can burn in hell before I'll bow to their clergy and their witch hunting!" exploded Hugh, tearing a strip from his shirt to stanch the flow of blood from his cheek. "I was fevered to murder that fat constable when he sneered at the death of that old minister! 'Twould have pleasured me to beat his face to lobster bait!"

The people on the shore seemed to have no desire for a fight on the water, for no boats followed the skiff. As it approached the *Flying Fish*, Wanton called: "Cut that hawser, lively! Call all hands to stand by!"

The crew of the sloop, who had seen the skiff leaving the shore followed by showers of stones, were already at their stations. As the four went over the rail, axes cut the last strands of the hawser, the bow swung, and the flapping sails filled with the light air. From the shore and Scarlett's Wharf an angry crowd hurled epithets at the departing sloop.

"Name of God, what happened to you?" demanded John Wanton of his brother. "Your face is beaten and your nose bleeds! We saw you followed by a pack to the skiff, so I called all hands to stand by!"

Standing at the afterrail, William Wanton bowed low to the town they were fast leaving. "Fare thee well, Boston Town!" he shouted derisively, his thumb at his bloodied nose. "Hang your witches as you hung the Quakers, but your louts of constables will not soon forget the clouting given them by Newport lads!"

§64

THREE days later the sloop sailed into Newport, but a horse messenger over the Plymouth Path from Boston had arrived two days before with a dispatch from Governor Phips to Governor Easton of Rhode Island. At the summons of the latter, William, Hugh, Israel and Jeremy waited on the sober-faced Quaker in his warehouse on Easton's Wharf.

"Captain William Wanton," began the Governor severely, fixing William with a pair of cold gray eyes in a face lean and ascetic, whose soberness was heightened by his sad-colored clothes, "Governor Phips has dispatched me a message which grieves me deeply."

For an interval William's black eyes studied the face of the old man before he replied. "I make no doubt, Governor Easton, that they have contrived a pretty pack of lies over their murderous assault on us in the Green Parrot tavern," he said, with the pained expression of injured innocence.

"Here is what he writes." The Quaker read with some difficulty from the paper he took from his desk:

> For that one Captain Wanton, of the sloop *Flying Fish*, of Newport, an Evil Faced, one-legged Sailor, a Giant of a youth with yellow hair, and Another, did at the Green Parrot tavern in the presence of many, Sneer and Snigger at the Boston clergy and did Assault, Abuse, Manhandle and Mistreat the Officers of the Law, to wit, Two Constables who would Restrain them from their Evil Purpose. All this to the grievous Breach of the Peace of this Town and Collony, the Shame and Dishonor of our Clergy and the Righteous Wrath of God, most High, our Lord and Master. Therefore, under my Sworn Duty, I do hereby Request and Demand, in the name of the above, that the said Captain Wanton, of the privateer *Flying Fish*, the Yellow Haired youth, the peg-legged Sailor and their Companion in this monstrous assault on the Citizens of Boston and the Sanctity of the Clergy, shall be Suitably Punished for their Crime and report Thereof dispatched to me, forthwith.
>
> Your humble and obliged Servant,
> SIR WILLIAM PHIPS
> *Governor of the Collony of Massachusetts*

The sharp eyes of John Easton probed in turn the guileless faces of the four offenders. Then he demanded drily, "What is your answer to these charges?"

William flung a warning look at his friends and replied: "Sir, our answer is the cut on Hugh's cheekbone from a flying stone, the great bruise on Israel's temple from a tankard, Jeremy's battered chin and my broken and swelled nose. The Boston constables, foxed with rum, sought trouble with us, naming us Rhode Island Quaker swine and fit only for the rope which had been given Mary Dyer and other Quakers in the Bay Colony. They set upon us in a body, roaring for Quaker blood, and followed us, unresisting, to our skiff and stoned us. 'Tis like they would have murdered us, as they did Mary Dyer, had they caught us."

Hugh's brows lifted in surprise and admiration as he followed William Wanton's adroit appeal to the Governor's prejudice in his astonishing picture of the meek submission of the Newport men. Catching the ludicrous twitching of Israel's mouth, he was forced to turn his face.

"So they mistreated you for Newport Quakers, did they?" rasped the fuming Governor, his gray eyes glittering as his mouth shut hard. "They set on you and beat you, sitting civilly in this tavern?"

William's hawk-like face pictured the terror of a remembered danger. "Sir, they beat us cruel! 'Twas solely by the grace of God they had not killed us!" replied the wily captain of the *Flying Fish*. "It appeared they thought us Quakers and for this attacked us!"

The Governor of Rhode Island scowled. His eyes snapped as he rubbed his bony chin in thought. With inward amusement Hugh watched the color come into his face as he considered William's statement.

"Return in the morning and I will have my reply to the high-handed Governor Phips," said Easton. "There may be that in it which you would amend."

The four meek-faced and unwarlike privateersmen filed out. "William, you devil," chuckled Hugh, as they walked over Shipwright Street to the Wanton yard. "You'll hang some day for that faulty and misfit memory of yours! But you played on the Governor like a maid on a spinet."

"'Twas cruel hard to listen to such a chicken-hearted tale of sound blows struck on Boston skulls," grunted Israel, "but, burn me, William's chickens'll come home to roost or I'm a mud shark!"

The following morning the four met in Easton's warehouse to hear the Governor's reply. Gravely, John Easton bade them sit down while he read from the paper in his hand. Following the customary greeting, he continued:

Captain William Wanton and the three members of the Crew of the *Flying Fish* have been Quizzed by me as to the Charges made against them in your Honored and Esteemed Dispatch. Were these Grave Representations possible of Belief they would give me Grievous Hurt y^t Newport sailors should conduct themselves in so Unseemly a Manner. But I fear y^t Your Excellency has been sadly misled by over Zealous Tale Bearers. Captain Wanton is the Son of a pious Quaker father, esteemed in Newport and opposed to all Violence, and has soe Nurtured his son. 'Twould be Monstrous to believe that Captain Wanton did aught but Defend his Life for he has long borne a name in this port for Civil Conduct and Sobriety. The peg-legged Sailor you name is but a Poor Cripple, scarce able to move on his one Good Leg, a man of Good Repute, God-fearing, never known to Brawl or Wrangle and a Hater of Strong Drink. The Big Youth with the yellow hair is of so Mild a Conduct and Bearing y^t I misdoubt he would strike an Officer of the Law. The Fourth is but a Boy, Puny and Unwarlike.

The Grievous Wounds and Hurts carried by the Bodies of these Men on their arrival in Newport, which were had from the hands of the Constables and Others, proclaim the Hard Handling they, though Innocent, took from Boston men. Therefore, Your Excellency, I Desire that you look deeper into this Untoward and Cruel Beating that the Truth may Prevail to the Glory of God and the Peace of our Collonies.

Your Obedient and Obliged Servant,
JOHN EASTON
*Governor of the Collony of Rhode Island
and Providence Plantations*

Easton ceased and lifted eyes cryptic and baffling to the men who listened. Brandy's face was black with anger. Wanton's dark eyes swung to the inwardly convulsed Hugh watching Israel's patent resentment of his clean bill of health at the hands of the Governor. One of Wanton's eyelids fluttered as Hugh glanced obliquely at him. Then Brandy's sense of humor seemed to overcome his wrath at the characterization of "poor cripple" and "hater of drink," and his throat swelled with strange noises.

"Governor Easton," said William, his face stiff as a parson's, " 'tis a most just and seemly reply and tastes stoutly of the truth."

Easton's level gaze covered the four men in turn. He cleared his throat as if about to speak, then suddenly turned and gazed out of the window at the harbor. A sidelong look from William's twinkling black eyes caught Hugh's as his mouth drooped in a grimace. Then the Governor turned his lean face.

"They hanged Mary Dyer and others," he said bitterly. "They flouted us and called us savages for that we suffered men to worship as their consciences impelled them. They have been fevered to swallow this colony as they have swallowed Plymouth. They envy our rising trade and hate the Quakers." Again he cleared his throat, and Hugh felt that he was about to smile, but his face abruptly stiffened. "William, it grieves me that you turned not the other cheek to them, but it would shame me and your father if you had. Governor Phips and the Mathers will take this letter hard, but I will not have meek and peaceable Newport sailors misused by brutal Boston constables!"

On the rigid face of the Governor hovered the ghost of a smile as he watched his listeners. "Boston will scarce welcome you, William, after this," he said.

"Sir, we thank you for your belief in our story," said the shameless captain of the *Flying Fish*, grasping the Governor's hand as they left.

Easton's flickering eyes met Wanton's sober face. "William," he said, and a corner of his thin mouth twitched, "the Lord shepherds his own!"

The four friends walked off the wharf, fighting for the control of their laughter. Well out of sight of the warehouse, Israel turned on the others. "Stab my guts," he snorted, "I be no hater of rum!"

"Nor fear you God or man, as the Governor would have it!" roared William.

Hugh seized Wanton and shook him. "Name of God, William Wanton, you'll come to no good end, thinking to bubble the Governor with your Quaker craftiness! But he needed no bubbling. He saw you for the liar you are, but will have no orders from the high-handed Phips and took joy in naming us pretty innocents."

"I knew not Israel from his picture," laughed Wanton. "God-fearing, no brawler, enemy of rum!"

"Burn me, I be no brawler!" growled Brandy. "Leastawise not till proper pressed, as in Boston. But I near guffawed when he named Hugh meek, and you lovin' sobriety, and Jeremy, here, puny. Bless his Quaker bones!"

"'Twill always madden a Quaker to mention Mary Dyer," said William. "But my father sat with Governor Easton last night and I knew we were in good hands."

"Governor Phips will need rise early to fuddle a Newport Quaker," said Hugh.

"Ay, the old man near bit off his tongue, so deep had he it in his cheek," chuckled Israel. "But though cripple I pass over, I like not hearing William and me named haters of rum. Therefore let us stop at the Sign of the Black Boy and wash away that slimy charge."

Which they promptly did.

§65

THE summer was a prosperous one for the *Flying Fish*, and the little hoard of coin in the chimney hole at the Stantons' grew in size when the prize goods and two French ships, taken off the coast of Acadia, were condemned and sold on the Newport wharves. But in October, when Hugh suggested to William Wanton that the winter might be well spent in the West Indies, where the French had become a scourge to New England shipping, and that the Leeward Islands and Barbadoes were clamoring for New England pipe staves, cod, and beef, he found William cold to the idea.

"Hugh," said his friend, "there is a certain maid whom you know who says I may not go to sea this winter."

Hugh nodded, attempting to conceal his disappointment. "So at last you have her consent?"

"Her family are set against the Quakers. Mine are set against the Congregationalists. We were in a pretty pass and scarce knew what course to sail."

"How did you contrive it, then, if she has consented?"

William's black eyes snapped. "I said, 'Ruth, your family will not have you marry a Quaker, mine will not have me marry a Congregationalist. As we love each other, there's nought to do but join the Church of England and go to the devil together!'"

"And she agreed?" chuckled Hugh.

"Agreed like the spirited maid she is. But I had spoke of the warm seas, and she added: 'William Wanton, I will not be kissed between cruises and married to a man I seldom see who may make me widow before I'm little more than wife. If you want me, you stay this winter in the shipyard!' Hugh, I want her, so I stay!"

"Then the sloop will lie up? John will not care to take her to the warm seas?"

"John is in the same case as I," said William.

So the disappointed Hugh shipped as mate with Captain Scarlett on the *Swordfish* for Barbadoes.

At the news, Trelawney blew a breath of relief through his teeth.

"You've settled it, then, with Joe?"

"Yes, today. They worry over the privateers and ship a large crew to work the guns. Israel and Jeremy go with me."

Trelawney rubbed his chin in thought, then said, "While at Barbadoes, Hugh, I wish you would visit my brother's plantation and talk with the overseer."

"Yes, I hoped to have a look at it."

"It is his chief source of income since he suffered The Towers to be so encumbered and mismanaged. He writes me that he is near sunk with debt. 'Tis his gaming that's brought him to the brink of ruin," said Trelawney, with a sigh, "and the company he keeps at court, a hard-drinking, dissolute crew of carrion crows."

"But he stands high at court."

"That pays no gaming debts nor buys jewels for soulless mermaids."

"Is the Barbadoes overseer honest and able?"

"I believe so. The income has been good. But I wish to know how things look and how this steward shapes to your eyes."

"I'll do my best, Dick. For someday it will be yours."

A week later the *Swordfish* lay at the Brenton Wharf ready to sail. The whip, rigged to the main yard, had swung the last barrel of cod and pickled beef, Narragansett cheese, and dried peas into her hold. The oak pipe staves and the lumber had been stowed. Content and Tom Stanton had said good-by and left the wharf. Arnold, Sheffield, and Trelawney stood talking with Hugh, waiting for the appearance of Joe Brenton, while his uncle, Jahleel, was in his office giving parting instructions to Captain Scarlett.

At last they heard the beat of hoofs, and three horses stopped at the wharf. Joe Brenton, followed by two girls, hurried out toward the group.

"There come Mistress Serena and Desire with Joe, to bid you good-by, Hugh!" said Trelawney, watching Hugh's face. " 'Tis kind of them to ride over."

Why should Serena Brenton come? wondered Hugh. Joe and Desire were his friends, but the proud and haughty Serena! What had she to say to the sailor, Hugh Jocelyn?

"I've come to wish you Godspeed, Hugh," said Brenton, "and have brought two who would join me!"

Hugh bowed low, with a "Your servant!" to the girls. In lustring frock, her jet-black hair caught in a loose, yellow silk hood, black eyes dancing in her flushed face, Desire impulsively grasped both of Hugh's hands. "Hugh Jocelyn," she cried, "how handsome you are in your new sea coat and Monmouth cap!" As the others laughed at Desire's artlessness, the embarrassed Hugh held the maid's hands as she stood on tiptoe beaming up at him. "You have not been to Hammer-smith all summer! What kept you away?" she continued with a pout of red lips.

"I've been off on the *Flying Fish*, Mistress Desire. You grow more bewitching every day."

Hugh was conscious of the calm inspection of the eyes of the older girl as he spoke.

"You still fancy my black hair, then?" demanded Desire, flushing with delight.

"No other color would suit you."

"I wish you a successful voyage, Hugh Jocelyn," said Serena, giving him her hand.

"My thanks for your good wishes, Mistress Serena." To Hugh, the candid eyes of the girl seemed to search his very thoughts, while he wondered what had led her to show this civility. Her scarlet, tiffany hood was flung back from her ebony hair, and a long heartbreaker curled beneath a small ear.

A faint flush of blood tinted her throat as she said, "Cousin Joe and Desire demand that I tell you that I was fair uncivil when last I saw you on Thames Street, so I have come here to make amends."

Beneath the long lashes Serena Brenton's eyes held so level a gaze that for an instant Hugh was almost convinced of her sincerity. Then a wave of resentment swept him. "'Tis for ladies of the quality to choose when they shall be civil to sailors," he replied sarcastically, with a mock bow.

The startled Desire stared wide-eyed from one to the other, while his thrust left Serena seemingly unembarrassed. A wraith of a smile crossed her face and the corner of a red lip curled. "So it touched the pride of our paragon?" she said. "I meant it to," and turned away, while the angered Desire caught his hand as he drew in a deep breath.

"Hugh Jocelyn, pay no heed to Serena," she exclaimed with a stamp of her small foot. "She—she—oh, I know not what frets her so to say such things! But you shall always be my good friend."

"Yes, I shall always be your good friend," returned Hugh.

Joe Brenton joined them. "Uncle Joe," spat Desire, as Hugh watched the retreating back of her sister, "Serena has been spiteful to Hugh! And he's been saying foolish things about ladies of quality and poor sailors. We are his good friends. Make him believe it!"

Brenton threw an amused look at Serena's back and turned with a grin. "More of Serena's didos? Give them no thought, Hugh. Of course, Desire, we're Hugh's good friends. 'Tis silly even to talk of it! We'll expect to see you in the early summer, Hugh. 'Twill go hard with this maid, here, if ought happens to Hugh Jocelyn."

Desire's black eyes were winking hard as they clung to Hugh.

"Come back soon, Hugh, and remember, bring me a green parrot!"

"A green parrot you shall have if there's one in the West Indies."

Trelawney, who joined them, with Sheffield, added: "Green parrot or no, don't let the French take you, Hugh. Remember those who treasure you and come back to us."

"Let the French have the Brenton brig, first," said Sheffield.

"Yes," laughed Joe, "rather than lose Hugh we'd give 'em two brigs; eh, Desire?"

The small girl impulsively reached and again had Hugh's hand in her two. "Rather than lose Hugh Jocelyn," she cried, "I'd—I'd give them Hammersmith!"

"And that," remarked Brenton, as they parted, "is true measure of her devotion."

Later that day as the brig reached down the East Passage, with yards braced, Hugh leaned against the afterrail, his glass leveled at two objects on a distant hill. They proved to be horsewomen, and appeared to be watching the *Swordfish* on her way to sea. Hugh lowered the glass, loaded a falcon swivel on the rail, and fired a parting salute. Shortly there was a flutter of white from the distant group.

"'Tis no kerchief, that!" he laughed. "It must be a petticoat, to show so clearly. Sweet little Desire and Bess! They rode down to see the last of Hugh Jocelyn bound for Barbadoes and God knows what!"

§66

PASSING BLOCK ISLAND and clearing the coast without meeting a Frenchman, the *Swordfish* headed south across the Gulf Stream. Daily, Israel and Hugh trained the large crew of thirty men which the Brentons had shipped to defend the brig. Their letter of marque gave them authority to take enemy vessels, but the Brentons' primary purpose in arming the brig and shipping a fighting crew was to insure the safe carriage of her valuable cargo.

The brig passed through the doldrums of the horse latitudes, where ships were often becalmed. Giving the Bahamas, the century-old haunt of pirates, a wide berth, she picked up the pull of the trades and drove on far to the east of the coast of Hispaniola and the island of Tortuga, long the nests of French sea rovers, avoiding the dangerous Windward Passage and the Mona Passage, now patrolled by privateers. Except for an occasional Turks Island salt raker or a turtle hunter, the *Swordfish* had passed no sails.

Off the Bahamas, Hugh had caught his first glimpse through the glass of the lazy lather of surf along foam-washed keys and, beyond, the palm-lipped beaches of small islands. His reading, buttressed by the tales of Israel and Tom Paine of the fabled Spanish Main, the plate ships, the galleons, the buccaneers, and the pirates, spurred his lively imagination. For two centuries men had sailed these seas, leaving in their wake a history of blood and violence and greed for gold. For a hundred years the Spanish, French, and English islands had pillaged and preyed upon each other in numerous wars, and in the intervals of peace privateersmen turned pirates had infested the seas.

The gray wastes of a sullen New England sea in December had given way to warm skies, a hot sun, and a world of turquoise-green water in which floated curious gulf weed of many colors, and swam fish of brilliant hues. Off Antigua and the Leeward Islands the brig headed south on its dangerous passage, past French Martinique, Guadeloupe, and Marie Galante, where the privateers ranged the trade routes to the English islands. Here, far from shore, the swift and tireless frigate, or hurricane, birds drove past in the wake of the fishing gulls and Cayenne tern, to rob them of their catch. Often, resting on the flat sea, the brig stirred rafts of vivid white birds, the size of pigeons, with red bills and long red spikes of tails, called "bo's'ns" by the sailors, and commonly known as "tropic birds." Crossing from island to island, long lines of pelicans traced the cloudless skies. Pursued by voracious barracuda and swift dolphin, swarms of flying fish burst from the water in silvery lances of light, fins fluttering like wings as they skimmed the tranquil sea. On cod lines the sailors caught the graceful dolphins arching around the bow, and their flesh was most welcome after long weeks of pickled beef and salt cod. Hugh never ceased to marvel at the beauty of their azure heads, their sleek brown backs stippled with gold and scarlet spots, and their bellies of beaten gold; a beauty which faded swiftly after death.

Then one day the watch in the fore crosstrees hailed the deck: "Land ho!"

"There she lies!" called Israel to Hugh, pointing to a cobalt smear floating in the haze of the western horizon. "She looks little like Guadeloupe nor the Leewards with their blue mountains!"

As the brig drove on, pushed by the steady trades, the low island the first Portuguese explorers had named Barbadoes, the Isle of Bearded Figs, lifted before them, a brilliant green, rimmed by its foam-washed keys. Through his glass the excited Hugh made out rows of sentinel cabbage palms lining white beaches, their globe-like fronds nodding in the trade wind. On the shoulders of low hills the long arms of windmills turned lazily, grinding the cane in sugarmills.

Skirting the south shore the brig kept on until Carlisle Bay opened before them. In the distance lay Bridgetown, with its anchored shipping and rows of plaster houses buried in foliage reaching back from the blue harbor, flanked by shore batteries and the stone fort.

Screaming gulls and tern circled the *Swordfish's* top hamper, escorting the brig. There was much shipping in the harbor, and on the careening grounds, at the mouth of a small river, two sloops lay on their beam-ends, having weed and barnacles scraped from their foul bottoms.

"There seems scarce water enough under her; will she ground?" asked Hugh, gazing over the rail into the transparent green harbor water, as the brig hung in stays while her square canvas was brailed and she worked in under jib and spanker.

Israel laughed. "The water is that clear it bubbles you, but we'll hardly make the wharf on this tide. What think you of Barbadoes, lad? Your eyes have fair bulged out of your head like a squeezed herring for a half-turn of the glass."

Hugh gazed beyond the warehouses, wharves, and shore batteries to the white plaster houses, buried in greenery, which reached back over the low rise, and on to the rounded fronds of the cabbage palms nodding on the skyline. "When I've seen it closer, I'll tell you," he laughed. "I can catch a whiff of the rum distilleries already, and what smells like molasses. But I miss the odor of fish and the ale breweries, of tarred rope and oakum and the clam flats of our New England ports."

"Ay, you will! 'Tis a rum and wine-drinking port, and they build no ships nor dig clams here. There be sea eggs and green lizards in the room of clams. The women alongshore carry a knife in their stocking when they wear one and strapped to their leg if not, and they use it sudden when foxed." Israel sighed as if over a memory. "Always mark well those with Spanish blood. Like the men, they're slow except with a knife in their hand."

Hugh laughed at Israel's warning. "They're brown or mestees, I suppose, and the look of them would capsize your stomach."

"Not all, lad. There be Spanish and French in the West Indy, carrying a dash of black blood, that'll make your eyes melt to gaze on. Those of Martinique are fair handsome, built as pretty as dolphins. But they're pizen. When your money's gone, they spit in your face."

Hugh's amused eyes watched Israel's sober features. "You speak from experience, Israel, no doubt. But have no fear. I want none of them."

The *Swordfish* let go her anchor in the shallow fairway off the wharf and warehouse of the Brentons' agent, Elisha Sanford, brother of Peleg Sanford, of Newport, where a group of men gathered to wave a welcome to the brig carrying the much-needed cargo of salt fish, dried peas, beef, and lumber. At anchor, off the small wharves with their whitewashed buildings, lay armed sloops and brigs, some with top hamper and bulwarks ragged and battered from recent brushes with French privateers. Two privateers and an English twenty-four-gun frigate were moored off the fort.

Hugh went ashore with Captain Scarlett, to report to the waiting Sanford and deliver the instructions, invoices, and mail.

"You have arrived in good time, Captain Scarlett," said the agent, dressed in sloppy white cotton which hung from his lanky frame in folds. "We are in sore need of your cargo and 'twill bring a pretty penny. Did you meet any French on the passage down?"

Hugh studied with interest this Sanford, sallow skin tight over cheekbones, pale eyes cold as glass, who offered Scarlett a limp hand.

Scarlett laughed. "No French, Mr. Sanford. And I worried little, for I have the two best gunners in Newport aboard. This is my mate, Hugh Jocelyn."

Thin lips devoid of expression, Sanford coldly scrutinized the young mate as Hugh took his moist hand, clammy as the touch of a fish. "You are overyoung, Mate Jocelyn," he said drily, "for the berth in a Brenton brig."

"He already has more learning in navigation than I," said Scarlett, "and is a seasoned gunner and privateersman. He was a right hand of Tom Paine in the Block Island fight with Picard."

Sanford made no reply but arched his brows in a supercilious look, as his thin lips tightened. It was evident that Paine's victory, which had saved Newport ships and the town itself from possible attack, had made little impression on this exiled Rhode Islander. Hugh felt a violent dislike for this sapless effigy of a man, with narrow face and fishy eyes so resembling his brother's. He made him think of a sun-dried pirate he had once seen hanging from the gibbet on Nix's Mate in Boston harbor. And he wondered if the Sugar Islands sucked the blood and the heart from all northerners who lived there too long.

§67

IMPATIENTLY fingering the manifests, invoices, and letters which Scarlett handed him, the factor waited, glancing pointedly at Hugh. Taking the hint, the mate left. Outside he found Israel, and the two proceeded along the waterfront. Familiar only with the look of the New England ports, Hugh was all eyes. At storehouses along the wharves half-naked slaves—the backs of many seared with red welts left by the whip and their faces often hideous with open sores—unloaded hogsheads of molasses and muscovado sugar from clumsy ox carts, to the curses of white overseers and the merciless crack of goads. From distilleries drifted the ripe odor of rum. Fat Negresses, with pock-marked faces and clad in dirty slips, their heads bound with red and yellow kerchiefs, offered for sale baskets of avocado pears, limes, lemons, small oranges, yellow and aromatic guavas, papaws, and juicy mangoes.

Beside wicker cages from which rose a bedlam of raucous chatter, shrill screams, and squawks, sat a withered Demerara Indian from the mainland, soliciting trade. There were great hyacinth macaws from Brazil, cobalt blue except for yellow throats and rumps; gaudy, scarlet macaws, tails and backs splashed with blue and yellow; green Amazon parrots and garish birds from Guadeloupe with flame-colored heads, backs, and breasts, wings shot with red, yellow, and blue, and long scarlet tails.

In amazement, Hugh marveled at the delirium of color worn by these tropic birds. "I am to bring one back to Mistress Desire," he said to Israel. "Which are the best talkers?"

"The green Amazons," said Israel, pointing. "But I've heard them painted French doxies of Guadeloupes chatter and curse a-plenty in their own lingo."

"When we sail, a green Amazon it is, then."

From the open doors and windows of low white taverns drifted song and laughter, the strumming of stringed instruments, and the stench of stale liquor and tobacco. Ears ringed with gold hoops, mulattoes and quadroons, garish with color, some with faces pitted from smallpox, all with the stamp of their trade, leaned from windows, laughing and beckoning to the tall sailor with yellow hair and eyes like deep-sea water.

Blond seamen from the ports of Bristol and Rotterdam; swart, ringed-eared slit-throats from Madeira, Fayal, and the Wine Islands; swaggering privateersmen, wearing heavy cutlasses and pistols in belts, from Jamaica and the Leeward Islands, turned to look curiously at the young man and his squat, peg-legged companion with the great shoulders and the scarred face. Once or twice when men stared hard at Hugh's impressive physique, Brandy grinned back as if to say, "Fill your eyes, mates, with the lad I lessoned!"

"Enough of this waterfront with its grimacing brown doxies who sicken my stomach, its rum-making and whipped slaves loading sugar," said Hugh at length. "I would see how they live in those plastered, white houses back on the hill near the government house, smothered in palms and casuarina trees, as they name them. I wish to see the gaudy hibiscus and jasmine and the seedy pomegranate."

Israel shook his head. "But those streets be not for sailors, by the Governor's orders," he demurred. "They are the houses of planters and government people."

Lights danced in Hugh's deep-set eyes. "Gentry, you mean! Sailors are scum! Why don't you say it?"

"Belay, lad! This is Barbadoes, not Rhode Island. Here there be ten blacks to one white and they draw the line hard even against sailors unless they be shipmasters and owners."

"Unless they are rich, you mean," said Hugh, bitterly. "But we go on! We'll not poison their air!"

The two followed a street where the heavily spined lime hedges gave both protection and privacy to the white houses half hidden in the masses of feathered casuarinas, like great ferns or weeping willows, bearded figs, papaws, and pomegranates. They had not gone far when, at a gate in the hedge ahead, Hugh saw a splash of yellow against the vivid green of the limes. A girl in a clinging slip which boldly outlined her figure was watching their approach.

There was a squawk, a hoarse chuckle, then a cackling from the depths of the lime hedge, and a voice called, "Bon jour! Bon jour, m'sieu'!"

Hugh stared in surprise at Israel, then glanced at the smiling girl at the gate. She was very dark, with the brilliant eyes and coloring of a mestee, and in her crow-black hair was a yellow jasmine. As the men drew nearer, a raucous "Prettee sailor! Prettee sailor!" greeted them.

"God's name!" gasped Hugh. "'Tis not the girl! What is it?"

Israel shook with laughter as he watched Hugh's perplexed face. The girl in yellow silk, bare feet thrust into yellow slippers, exposing a round leg, flashed white teeth in an amused smile. Then, with a flapping of wings, a flame-colored macaw with mottled blue, red, and yellow wings and a scarlet tail lit on her extended arm, gravely nodding its fiery head and clicking its beak.

"God's name!" muttered Hugh. "A parrot!"

They approached the girl at the gate, and her black eyes lazily surveyed Hugh from his long hair to the heavy cutlass at his side. "Deed René frighteen the pretty sailor boy?" she laughed, with a tilt of her dusky head.

From the corner of his mouth Israel muttered the warning: "A French mustee! The English planters favor 'em highly. 'Tis likely this one belongs to a great man of the island. Sheer off, lad!"

Hugh was both interested and amused. He smiled into the sloe-black eyes challenging his. "Bon jour, ma'm'selle!" he said, doffing his canvas hat and bowing low, while Israel noted how the octoroon's gaze lingered on the boy's yellow head. "'Tis a beautiful bird!" said Hugh.

"Va-t'en, mon petit!" With a flirt of her wrist the girl shook off the gaudy bird, who flapped noisily back into the garden, squawking his rage: "Ventre du biche! Ventre du biche!"

She threw back her dark head and laughed. "René ees from Guadeloupe! He ees not polite! M'sieu' ees a privateer? Oh, la, la! What a beeg boy and what bee-uteeful hair and blue eye! Is eet not?"

Israel pulled at Hugh's sleeve. "We'll have trouble on our hands! Belay, lad!"

The octoroon slanted an angry look at the peg-legged sailor, then her eyes smoldered into Hugh's as she purred up at him. "You are veree nice privateer man, so beeg and strong! I like you, veree much! Tonight you weesh to come? I weel be alone and ze scent of jasmine weel perfume ze moonlight."

Hugh bowed and boldly met her challenge. "A'voir, ma'm'selle! It is tonight, then!"

The two men moved on, while Israel vented his displeasure in a hurricane of oaths. A white-garbed planter rode past them and leered at the girl, who still watched Hugh's back from her gate.

"Stab my vitals!" spat out Brandy. "What meant you bubblin' that quail of a mustee? She's fair set on you! 'Twas clear she see us comin' before that pretty play with the parrot!"

Hugh poked the irritated Brandy in the ribs. "Israel, 'tis my first cruise to Barbadoes. Think back to your first voyage to the West Indies. What was your conduct then, you old rumbullion?"

Israel gravely nodded. "'Tis true! I was wild as a blue shark! But—but you are my own chicken! I may not let you come to harm. You marked that planter who passed? He saw you chirping with the mermaid. We seek no trouble for Captain Scarlett."

Hugh patted Brandy's broad back. "Have no fear, Israel. I will play no Romeo in her garden when the jasmine perfumes the moonlight and the amorous lady makes love to strangers."

Brandy's breath whistled through his teeth with relief. "'Tis well! By the look of the place she's private property. To meddle with her means trouble."

The two friends returned from the secluded residential section of the wealthy shipowners and planters to the slums and busy waterfront and went aboard the brig.

The following day, when the *Swordfish* had been warped to her berth and was unloading, Sanford beckoned Hugh to his office in the warehouse.

"Mate Jocelyn," began the tight-lipped factor, his pale eyes glittering, "it was discovered to me last night that you were so frenzical as to be seen, yesterday, talking with a certain person well known in Bridgetown."

Hugh's blood heated at the manner of the Brenton agent. Sanford was not his keeper, and the off time of a mate on a vessel was his own.

What did this sourface mean by such talk?

"While viewing the port with our master gunner," Hugh said, "I was spoken to by a woman at a house on the hill and was civil to her. Speak out, Mr. Sanford! What are you coming to?"

Sanford's thin-lipped visage soured. His pale eyes were eloquent with irritation. "I'm coming to this," he snapped. "That harlot is not to be spoken with by captain or mate of a Brenton ship. She is—is the friend and under the protection of Governor Kendall. Name of God! Do you wish to make difficulty for me?"

Hugh's anger cooled. "Have no fear on that score. She stopped us and I was civil, which I would be to any woman—governor's doxy or no."

At the reply, Sanford patrolled the room in his rage. "You keep away from that Guadeloupe octoroon they name Ma'm'selle Jasmine!" he rasped. "She was fetched here a prisoner, on a privateer, and is under the Governor's protection. She's private property and above the advances of common seamen. 'Tis my duty to report your conduct to Mr. Jahleel Brenton."

"Report to Mr. Brenton? Christ's blood! Report what?" stormed Hugh, rising. "Report that I replied civilly to a stranger's greeting?"

Sanford's upper lip lifted over yellow teeth. "You dallied at her gate. You were seen sniggering with her. 'Tis no fit conduct for a Brenton mate and, besides, too dangerous to me."

Hugh broke into mirthless laughter which brought the color to the yellow face of the agent. "Name of God, man, the waterfront here is lined with hot houses and taverns where drazels drink with sailors! You dare not forbid the Brenton crews to sit there with the scum of the port! They'd laugh at you! But you think to condemn the innocent conduct of a Brenton mate! Write to Jahleel Brenton what you will! He's no master of mine nor are you, you sniveling hypocrite!"

While Sanford gaped in white-faced surprise, Hugh stormed out of the office. When he informed Scarlett of his talk, the master shook his head. "Hugh, I carried a letter here to Sanford from his brother, and I doubt not what it held has much to do with his talk with you. He asked me why the Brentons had shipped such a brawler and rakehell as you. I told him that you were respected greatly in Newport for your courage and seamanship. But he only laughed his sour snigger. His brother, Peleg, is at the bottom of this!"

Hugh nodded. "Yes, I can imagine what kind of a credit that horse-faced royalist, Peleg, would give me."

"But, Hugh," went on Scarlett, soberly, "Israel has told me of your meeting with Ma'm'selle Jasmine, as they name her here. Have no traffic with her, Hugh. There'll be trouble if you do. 'Tis already known that you were seen at her gate—however innocent it happened."

Hugh gave Scarlett his hand. "Have no fear. I shall not see her again."

§68

LATER, when the cargo was ashore and the brig waited for her return load of sugar, molasses, indigo, and logwood, Hugh and Israel had a day off. Hiring horses, they rode back into the undulating interior of the island to inspect Lord John Trelawney's sugar property and talk with the agent. Tall cabbage palms lined the roads which wound through the plantations of tasseled cane waving like fields of northern corn. Long arms of windmills endlessly turned in the trade wind, grinding the cane into pulp to be drained into the sugar vats. Everywhere half-naked African slaves sweated in the cane fields under the hard eyes of swart overseers carrying whips. Here and there the plastered houses of planters shone white in the hot sun behind hedges of limes and feathered casuarina trees and surrounded by thickets of mahogany, of pomegranate with scarlet blossoms, of gaudy pink and rose hibiscus, the yellow jasmine, with the fragrant and lovely frangipani. On trellises against the white walls of the houses bloomed masses of magenta bougainvillæa.

They found the Trelawney plantation and were welcomed by the steward, who impressed them as honest and efficient. With him they rode through the cane fields and inspected the sugar windmill. To Hugh's eyes the Trelawney property seemed in good hands and prosperous. Seated in the shade of an arbor of pomegranates, they sipped long pewter beakers of rum, sugar, and lime juice, gossiping of the war and the trade. After a time they took their leave and rode on.

The two horsemen stopped on a hill overlooking a white beach edged with palms, sea grapes, and the poisonous manchineel tree, with fruit like apples, and guarded by a reef over which the sea broke lazily in a lather of foam. Beyond the beach, at their feet, the pale-green water reached out, deepened to emerald, then to sapphire, and, last, to maroon as it met the moaning reef. Scavenger buzzards, grim harbingers of death, hovered overhead, and in the distance a parade of pelicans crossed the blazing sky.

Hugh and Israel sat for a while in silence, enjoying the cool drive of the trade wind in their faces. Something made Hugh glance sidewise at Israel's face. The old sailor's small eyes seemed to be searching beyond the northern horizon, and his head was cocked as if far-off sounds drifted to his ears.

"What do you see and hear, Israel?" laughed Hugh.

"I'm lookin' on a gray sea rollin' under a sou'easter, with the surf boomin' high over the rocks, throwin' the spray in showers, and an arrowhead of gray honkers crossin' the black sky."

"Homesick?"

"Yes, there be times when I'm overfed with the warm seas, though the rum be good and the life easy. I likes to think of how the sun bursts like a gunshot through the mist behind Noman's, and to fancy I hear the gulls squawk as the bluefish hunt the herrin' over the shoals. To-day 'twould pleasure me to hear the old Sow a-gruntin' to her Pigs, and the surf a-roarin' like demiculverins on Nashawena Beach."

Hugh stared at his friend in surprise. "Why, I've never heard you talk like this, Israel. You're fair poetic in your fancy."

The sailor's eyes still clung to the northern horizon. "I can see the whale and blackfish roll and spout off Gay Head, gaudy as a Guade-loupe doxy, all pink and rose and brown in the western sun, while the old Devil's Bridge boils at her feet."

"Ay, and so can I."

"I can make out the gray nose of old Cuttyhunk pokin' through the fog, and Block Island adrift on a smoky sea."

For a time Israel was silent, while Hugh waited. Then he said: "Can't ye hear the swan and brant droppin' down on the red and yeller Sakonnet marshes when the first frost bites the air? And the clatter of the duck as they rise? And the whistle of the yeller-legs and the scream of the sea eagles? Ay, that's the sweet country—not these slimy is-lands what rot a man's bowels, lives he here long enough!"

A wave of nostalgia flowed through Hugh. Home was call-ing—the gray New England coast and those he loved there. He reached and touched Israel's shoulder. "Belay, Israel! You make me homesick. What would you give now for a big lobster, boiled red, with a trencher of clams and fried oysters beside it? And some crisp, brown journey cakes, and rye-'n'-Injun, and a taste of Content's cranberry sauce, and her strawberry cake? I'm fair sick of these sweet, painted flying fish and the tart fruit that fills your face with juice when bitten. I long to set my teeth into a sound Rhode Island apple!"

Israel grinned and smacked his lips. "You have me fair slobberin' at the mouth!"

One evening Israel and Hugh went ashore to a tavern frequented by the better class of masters. As they entered, Israel's eyes widened and his jaw sagged as he stared toward the end of the low-ceilinged room filled with smoke and the fumes of stale rum.

"Rot me, 'tis the old rumbullion to the life!"

Alone, at a table, sat a dark-haired man of medium size, a baldric carrying a cutlass slung over the shoulder of his white cotton jacket dressed with buttons of yellow Spanish doubloons. From the black sash worn as a belt protruded the brass-bound butt of a pistol. He wore no wig, and his black hair fell to his neckband. As he gazed moodily out of a window at the shipping, he puffed on a long-stemmed clay pipe.

"Who is the privateersman, Israel, that so surprises you?" asked Hugh, as Israel moved toward the table where the stranger sat, a frown on his weather-burned face.

Israel turned a beaming countenance. "Stab me, an old shipmate! He was with me that day I left my leg with the sharks in the Mona Passage. I heard on my last cruise here with Scarlett that he was master of a ship with Admiral Hewetson in the attack on the French at Marie Galante."

"But who is he?"

"That barnacle with the long face lookin' out the window is Captain William Kidd, master of a privateer in the service of Barbadoes."

The two reached the table and the seaman turned. His face lit with recognition. "Burn me! Israel Brandy! I feared you was dead!"

His mouth splitting his face in a grin, Israel thrust out a calloused paw and seized Kidd's hand. "Captain, I be still lively as a dolphin and a sight tougher!"

The privateersman's face wrinkled with pleasure. "Sit down, Israel, with your young friend, while I ease my eyes on you. How came you here? On a Boston brig?"

"Boston?" Israel growled. "Rot me, no! Out of Newport we be—the Brenton brig *Swordfish*, eight guns and thirty men."

Hugh was aware of an intense scrutiny from the candid eyes of the man at the table as they swung from Israel. "Your shipmate?" asked Kidd.

"Our mate, Hugh Jocelyn, Captain Kidd," said Brandy. "Slip your eye over his bilges and top hamper. Twenty-one he is, and already a gun layer near equal to Brandy himself!"

"Mate Jocelyn," said Kidd, with a chuckle, as they shook hands, "when Israel admits you have an eye for laying a gun, 'tis high praise, indeed."

Israel leaned toward the speaker. "And mark you, Bill Kidd, the make of him—all white oak and double braced! I lessoned him with the cutlass from a boy."

Kidd winked at Hugh. "If he's half the man you are, Israel, he'll clear many a deck." Suddenly Kidd's face sobered as an idea seemed to take shape in his brain. "Goodmen and loyal are hard to find down here, Israel. While ashore, at Antigua, three years ago, my crew deserted me and turned pirate, out of hand. You can trust no one, so set are they on gold and loot."

Israel nodded. "I heard that, here, last year. Slimy scum they were!"

"Slimy scum is what we have to ship and fight with in these seas." Kidd slapped his pewter mug on the table and leaned toward the men who listened. "Let me tell you a story. I am just back from London. While there, I was sent for by one Lord Bellomont, close to the Whig ministry of King William. He told me he spoke for Lord Somers, the Chancellor, the Earl of Orford, the Duke of Shrewsbury, and others who sought a privateer captain they could trust with a voyage to the Indian Ocean. Owing to my services with Admiral Hewetson at Marie Galante and later, they had heard of me from Governor Codrington, Vice-Admiral of the Leeward Islands and Governor of Antigua. They said they'd obtain a commission from the King himself, and would buy, arm, and outfit a ship in Bristol, to sail a year from next summer. That would be in '94, for there's a large sum to be raised."

"How about Long Ben Avery and his pack of Maddeegasco pirates? You were to attack them?" demanded Israel.

"Yes, all enemies of the King. But it was the French East Indy Company with their rich cargoes they had most in mind."

"Hum!" Israel doubtfully shook his head. "Captain, you'd be a lone blackfish among a school of sharks. Steer clear of them Maddeegasco pirates!"

"Tom Tew returned to Newport with much booty from the Indian Ocean," commented Hugh.

"Yes, and he was one of Long Ben's crew," said Israel.

Kidd refilled and lit his pipe, then continued: "The French East Indy Company and the Great Mogul send many ships from India to Arabia and the Red Sea. 'Tis these ships that Lord Bellomont seeks to attack. For years Avery and others have been fillin' their bellies on them. Now it seems the King's ministers are fevered to have a share in this booty."

Israel grunted. "Ay, if they can take it and hold it from Long Ben's paws."

"A three-hundred-ton ship, heavy-gunned, and with the King's commission! My fortune is made, Israel!" Kidd probed Brandy's unwinking eyes. "Will you join me?"

Hugh tingled with excitement. The Indian Ocean! A quick fortune! He thought of Tom Tew as he searched the inscrutable features of his friend.

"Bill Kidd," said Israel, drily, "there be too much you've left untold. You take the hazard for these great gentlemen but what do they offer Captain Kidd as his share?"

Kidd's eyes clouded at the question. "'Tis true they overreach, as do all these fine people in high places. Because of the King's commission and their protection they ask too much."

"Rot my bones! The King's protection!" sneered Brandy. "And what worth would that have if he forswore it? Out with it! How much?"

"They offer me and my crew one share in five, with the ship to be mine if I bring her back."

"What do you offer Hugh, here, and me, if we join you?"

"I'm so set to have you join that I'll name you master gunner and Jocelyn mate, and give you a third of my share."

Israel threw back his head with a roar of laughter. "Now give ear to this. Back in Newport lies the ablest sloop that ever wet a keel. That sloop Hugh and me aims to buy and head right back here to the warm seas. In two-three year we'll sail into Newport with our fortune. We'll fight for ourselves, not for jukes and lords who'll hog most the prize money. We'll take the risk and, if we win, we'll take the gold. I like not the smell of this thing, Bill Kidd, and I warn you go slow! They'll use you and cast you aside like a dead cod."

"Why, Israel," objected Kidd, vehemently, "there's richer booty to be had in the Indy Ocean in a month than you'll find here through the whole war. 'Tis gold and silver, silk and gems, man! Sleep on my offer!"

"Ay, and what'll Long Ben Avery be doin' when he hears of you out there with the King's commission a-pokin' your bow into his private water? He'll hunt you down like a barracuda hunts flyin' fish."

Kidd sneered. "With a twenty-four-gun ship I'll drive his pack from the seas!"

"But he's too strong! He's got a fleet of pirates out there, says Tom Tew, and Tom ought to know; he was one."

So they left it, promising to talk again with Kidd before they sailed. On their way to the wharf Hugh said, "Israel, I wonder if we could get a commission for the *Flying Fish* in the Indian Ocean."

Brandy stopped dead and faced his companion. His mats of brows met in a scowl. "Hugh Jocelyn, what's eatin' your vitals?" he growled. "Bill Kidd's fair frenzical to put trust in them English lords! And you'd be worse to sail for the Indy Ocean. The scum of the seas foregather there, and no honest governor in the colonies would commission you. 'Tis said Fletcher, of New York, will sign one for five hundred pounds. Where would you get that? We can't even raise Wanton's price for the sloop."

"Israel," insisted Hugh, "Tom Tew returned with a fortune in two years. If we could only obtain a commission to privateer in the Indian—"

Brandy roughly grasped his friend's arm. "Belay! Do you aim to turn pirate? They all do who sails there! And few make their home port again. I thought you aimed for a brig and a farm and a family!"

Hugh laughed, but his eyes were serious. "You old buccaneer! You would preach to me? Here's a chance for a quick fortune and you turn churchman."

"You'd ship with Bill Kidd and fill the purses of the King's ministers and take a beggar's share?"

"No, but if I owned the *Flying Fish* I'd go after a commission for the Indian Ocean to attack the King's enemies."

"And end by swinging from a rope at the yardarm of a King's ship!" scoffed Brandy.

"As well that as dying in a poor man's bed."

To Kidd's disappointment, Israel and Hugh gave him no encouragement when they bade him good-by. They frankly told him that they did not like Bellomont's offer and, besides, were only waiting to buy into the *Flying Fish* and return to the warm seas. On their way back to the brig Israel said: "It may be, Hugh, tonight we have lightly put by the chance for a fortune. Kidd is a good seaman and a stout fightin' man. I make no doubt that some day he'll sail into New York rich, as did Tom Paine into Newport."

With her cargo of sugar and molasses, logwood and indigo, the *Swordfish* was driving north across the trades. From a bulkhead in the captain's cabin, shared by the mate, hung a wooden cage containing a green Amazon parrot. Hugh had bought a young bird that would be easy to teach, and he had set a task for himself as the homebound brig stood across the steady winds from the east and then up through the horse latitudes. Daily, on his watch off, Hugh labored with his charge. It was not long before the bird became tame enough to have the freedom of the cabin, while over and over, each day, between squawks and chatter and much nibbling at his hands, Hugh repeated the words "Desire" and "Bess." At length, somewhat to Captain Scarlett's confusion, on entering the cabin he would be greeted with the squawked names of his employer's nieces. Then, in time, it became "Pretty Desire! Pretty Bess!" But the bird had not been taught to say "Pretty Serena!"

With the exception of a fight with a privateer sloop off Guadeloupe, which was beaten off by Israel's gunnery and gave up the chase when her top hamper was brought down by langrel from the demiculverins, the brig had left the warm seas and cleared the Bahamas without adventure. But one day, when they were riding the Gulf Stream north, Scarlett stumbled over a train-tackle eyebolt and broke his ankle, and Hugh Jocelyn, at last, had his first command.

From there on, into Newport, the brig was his, and he reveled in his new responsibility, grinning widely into Israel's unwinking eyes as the master gunner gravely touched his tousled forelock and reported for orders.

Day after day the *Swordfish* companioned the spring north, sails bellying in the southwest breeze that snored through shrouds and rigging. Never before had Hugh had the leisure to explore his own mind as on that long voyage home. And the more he thought, the more determined he became to wrest a fortune from the present war. Kidd's picture of the opportunity offered in the Indian Ocean had left a lasting impression. The Bellomont offer was niggardly, but a commission for the *Flying Fish* might be obtained from Governor Fletcher of New York. If they could find the money to buy the Wanton sloop, they might join Kidd. True, the hazard was great. There were the Madagascar pirates. Tom Tew admitted he had sailed with them. It would mean many a nasty brush on those pirate-infested seas. But there sailed no pirate sloop that could outfoot the *Flying Fish* nor outfight her. And the ships of the Great Mogul were rich prizes. One or two, and Hugh Jocelyn's fortune was made. Israel was against it, but Israel would go, the old buccaneer, if they could buy the sloop.

Ten years before, Tom Paine had come back with a fortune. With a ship of his own Hugh Jocelyn could do the same. Schooled by Trelawney though he was, he was still a sailor, the foster son of a fisherman, and not fit companion for gentry or gentlewomen. That was the hard code of the colonies. So long as he was poor, he was an inferior. But once he owned a sloop and a home farm or a city house, those who could scarcely spell out a letter and owned barely a book or two but bore one of the old names of Newport would suddenly find him fit company for themselves and their mincing women.

Day after day as the brig plunged her dolphin striker into the running seas and a lather of wool-like foam ran past her bilges, while shrouds and stays chattered and blocks creaked above his head, Hugh paced back and forth between the two tillermen and the eyebolts of a poop demiculverin, wrestling with his discontent. The war would be long! The war would be long! Men were making names and fortunes for themselves. What would the war leave to Hugh Jocelyn? Perhaps a peg leg or a scarred face! Perhaps a fortune! Who knew?

He often thought of Lettice, and of her family who had been so intent on his ruin. Israel and he had no doubt that Carr Newbury and Richard Brinley would never cease their secret efforts to avenge the insult of a sailor to the proud Brinley name. For they certainly knew of that meeting in Dexter's Lane. As for Lettice and the future, Hugh dared not think. There was no denying her capture of his senses, her fascination. What would come of it?

And then his thoughts would leave Lettice and the memory of her kisses, to dwell on the mystery of Serena Brenton. That day at Hammersmith when she had betwitted him with a love for fighting! What had meant this strange girl, with those baffling wells of black eyes stippled with lights like the reflection of fireflies over water? She was no doubt beautiful, as they said, but it was not her dark loveliness which had drawn his interest but the mysterious reserve which walled her in. At Hammersmith she had frozen him, while Desire fair ate him up, then had flung herself from the table with that parting shot. An unfathomable maid, this Serena Brenton, and a lovely, but clearly steeped in pride of birth and station, though Joe said not.

How different was that minx of a Desire, all impulse and heart and friendliness! He could see her black eyes shine when he gave her the parrot and hear her shrieks of delight at the "Pretty Desire! Pretty Desire!" he had spent so many hours teaching the green-feathered chatterbox.

"Pretty Desire!" had been achieved by weeks of daily drudgery, but it was not until the brig was nearing the New England coast that the bird would scream, "Pretty black hair! Pretty black hair!" How Desire would dance on her toes at that!

It had been not without misgiving that Hugh had taught the parrot to repeat the name "Serena." "Pretty Bess" had been simple, but "Serena" had been a knotty task for that thick Amazonian tongue and grotesque beak. But Hugh had doggedly persevered, and one morning, on entering the cabin with the parrot's breakfast, he was greeted with "Se-re-na! Se-re-na!" in staccato squawks as the bird flew to his shoulder and nibbled the lobe of his ear.

"This may be taken amiss by the haughty Mistress Serena," Hugh laughed. "For a Brenton sailor to make so free with the sacred name of a Brenton maid fair deserves the whipping post. But come what may, the vile deed is done."

It was a bright spring day, when the sea was a glittering panorama of dancing blue water, that the lookout in the fore crosstrees made the landfall. Crude as was his Davis quadrant in determining latitude, and with the longitude always a matter of guesswork, Hugh had sighted the low smear of Montauk and sheered to the east to make out the southwest cliffs of Block Island. As the brig drove on past the island, headed for Beaver Tail and the East Passage, the man on her poop who watched her bellying jibs and square sails as the sea boiled past her bilges was strangely cold to Israel's greeting when he joined him. The eyes of the young captain were bleak as they shifted to the distant coast.

"Burn me," exclaimed Brandy, "you're as glum as a gull with the bellyache! And here you are close to dropping the hook in Newport harbor."

"Why not?" returned Hugh. "A fortune lies behind us in the warm seas had we the money to buy the *Flying Fish*."

"You'll not take the brig back to Barbadoes if they ask you? Scarlett's ankle will be long in mending."

"They'll not ask me. Scarlett carries a letter from Sanford to Brenton that will doubtless picture me a wild rake-hell and no fit man to master the brig."

Israel squinted quizzically at the bold profile of the man whose somber eyes were eloquent of the doubt and unrest in his heart. "Bill Kidd's talk still fevers you?"

Hugh did not reply as he gazed at the distant Beaver Tail and the gray ledges of Brenton's Point, on which the brig was rapidly closing.

§69

THE evening following Hugh's return, he and Trelawney joined Joe Brenton at the King's Head. When Hugh had finished his story of the voyage, Brenton surprised him by announcing:

"The *Swordfish* is now yours, Hugh."

To the surprise of his friends there was reflected in Hugh's face little pleasure at the promotion. "But Captain Scarlett?" he asked.

"Scarlett's lying off while his leg gets strong. He will command our new brig the Wantons are building. It's Captain Hugh Jocelyn of the *Swordfish*, if you please."

"Have you talked with your uncle since he read Sanford's letter we carried him?"

Brenton's face darkened. "I'll talk with you later of that. Now I drink to Captain Hugh Jocelyn and matters more pleasant."

"I'll talk with you later of that, also," replied Hugh. The eyes of the disturbed Trelawney shifted from one to the other as Hugh went on: "I have the Amazon parrot I promised to fetch Mistress Desire. Will you take it to her?"

"Does the bird talk?"

"A little."

"Name of God, Desire will dote on you more than ever!" laughed Brenton. "But these tropic birds learn paw words from the sailors. I trust my saintly aunt will find his chatter fit for virgin ears?"

"He knows no paw words in English. I got him from a Demerara Indian."

"Good! I'll ride down with a spare horse and you shall deliver your present in person. Desire was fair leaping out of her bodice when we saw the *Swordfish* standing up the East Passage."

Outside, in the unlighted street, Trelawney left Brenton with Hugh. "Name of God, what happened in Barbadoes?" Joe demanded. "I had a bad hour with Jahleel today."

So Sanford had lived up to his promise. "What said the fishy-eyed brother of the horse-faced Peleg?" Hugh demanded.

"Why, he called you rake-hell and what-not—claimed you had been seen leaving the house of the mestee mistress of the Governor, and it had caused him trouble."

"He lies!" Hugh swallowed hard on his rising wrath. "I had brief talk with an octoroon who hailed us from her gate or, rather, her parrot hailed us—Israel and me. I never saw her again. Sanford made a great ado about it. It all came from the letter his brother Peleg sent him by Scarlett, to injure me."

"That's what I told Jahleel. But though he greatly respects your metal and ability, he's been poisoned by someone."

"Then why does he consent to my taking the *Swordfish* to the warm seas?"

"He freely admits there's no stouter fighting man nor better seaman in the colony."

"So he would use my seamanship but doubts my character?" sneered Hugh. "Then he would object to my coming to Hammersmith where beauty and innocence breathe untainted air! I will have the parrot carried to Mistress Desire."

Joe Brenton impatiently gripped the heavy shoulders of the man who faced him in the darkness. "Grace o' God, Hugh Jocelyn, listen to me! You are coming to Hammersmith with me as my honored friend! You think I'll suffer the sly tongues of Brinley and Sanford to poison my family? 'Twould break Desire's heart did you not bring her that parrot yourself."

"You can carry my regrets and respects to her."

"No! You little know those maids! Do you know who rode down to the high meadow to watch the *Swordfish* when you left for Barbadoes?"

"I saw Mistress Desire with Bess, and fired a swivel in salute."

Brenton thrust his face close to his friend's. "The two you saw were Desire and—Serena! And 'twas Serena who helped Desire strip off her white petticoat to signal a farewell!"

So it was the aloof Serena and not Bess who had stood that day on the hill with Desire, wishing him Godspeed!

"But Dame Brenton?" Hugh demanded. "She must be turned against me."

"She's a fool! But my uncle bade me bring you. He will not be there. And Desire would fair raise a rebellion did you not come."

"As you wish, then," said Hugh, reluctantly. "It shall be but long enough to pay my respects and present the parrot."

Brenton left, and on the way up Thames Street Trelawney exclaimed, as he gripped Hugh's arm: "Captain Hugh Jocelyn! I salute you, Captain Jocelyn! I'm happy tonight! My heart is fair full!"

Hugh said little. He was thinking of Jahleel Brenton and of the hostility of the Sanfords.

" 'Twill be some time before you sail with the *Swordfish*?" asked Trelawney.

"I do not sail with the *Swordfish*, Dick," said Hugh.

"What? You cannot mean it!"

"I'll serve no man who is glad to use my cutlass and seamanship to bring his cargoes safe into Newport but believes what the lying Sanfords say of me!"

A few days later Joe Brenton brought Hugh again to Hammersmith. The two men swung their horses between the stone pillars, buried in ivy, that flanked the elm-arched entrance. On Hugh's saddle-bow rested the cloth-covered cage holding his gift to Desire. His eyes traversed the young green of the planted fields, the meadows with their grazing sheep and cattle, and the woodlands of the great estate splashed with the white of flowering dogwood, then moved out to the gray sentinels of the Dumplings guarding the sunlit sweep of the East Passage. The horsemen reached the gardens, where the lavender of lilacs and the pink of scattered clumps of azalea stippled the green background with color, and the bowers of eglantine were heavy with buds. The fragrance of hyacinths and lilies-of-the-valley mingled with the aroma of the box hedges.

An air of serenity lay upon the great square house with its four chimneys and balustraded roof looking on the sea from its green setting, its tranquillity belying the confusion, the violence, and the agony of a world at war outside. To Hugh, Hammersmith was of another world—something aloof and inviolate, beyond the reach of the havoc of war and destruction by human hands. There was a feeling of permanency about it, of immutability. It seemed as stable as its rock ledges washed by the East Passage. Somehow he felt Hammersmith would always be there.

Privateers and captured ships shorn of topmasts, bulwarks splintered by round shot, sails ripped, and rigging frayed by chain and langrel, had from time to time moved past up the East Passage, eloquent witnesses to the savage struggle between William and Louis XIV. A war which had turned New England frontiers into charred villages and abandoned farms, and had kindled its coast with watch fires. But the peaceful acres of Hammersmith, of Rocky Farm and Cherry Farm, with their drowsing woodlands and pastures of grazing sheep, had known no touch of war, of the terror that harried the hearts of the islanders and the crews of the coast shipping. Yet, heaped high on every headland in the colony driftwood awaited the torch, and from deck and beach restless eyes ceaselessly patrolled the sea for French sails. For it was spring, and as Frontenac's red raiders of the forest were already taking the trails south to ravage the English frontiers, so the sea wolves of King Louis would soon bare their fangs and strike along a thousand miles of coast.

As the two horsemen followed the gravel horsepath, edged with box, to the stables, the thin, tinkling notes of a virginal drifted from the house. Then the shrill voice of a girl hailed from an open window:

"Hugh Jocelyn! Welcome home! 'Tis he, Bess! Welcome to Hammersmith, Hugh Jocelyn!"

"There she is, the moppet!" chuckled Joe. "All a-flutter, and doubtless has been watching for a turn of the glass for our coming!"

Hugh doffed his beaver hat to the girl who, half out a second-story window, was excitedly waving. "Your servant, Mistress Desire!" he answered. "I have something for you from Barbadoes!"

"Oh, 'tis my parrot! See the covered cage, Bess! 'Tis my blessed bird! Fetch it me, Hugh! I'm in a fever to see it!" she called.

A groom took their mounts, and Hugh followed Joe to a rustic summerhouse to which two maids, blown hair streaming behind them, taffeta skirts tossing from red- and blue-stockinged legs, came running. Black eyes shining her welcome, Desire seized Hugh's hand in her two. "Hugh Jocelyn, 'tis good to see you! And you've fetched it? You've fetched me the parrot?" she cried, beaming her delight into his bronzed face.

Smiling, he removed the cloth covering of the cage, and the green Amazon blinked a yellow eye, fretted for a moment in low gutturals, then cocking his head, squalled: "Pretty Desire! Pretty Desire! Pretty black hair!"

Eyes and mouths round with amazement, the two startled maids stood speechless.

Again the parrot blinked, chattered incoherently, then laughed mockingly: "Pretty Desire! Pretty Bess! Ha—ha! Pretty Desire!"

"Oh, hear him!" The enchanted Desire danced on her slippered toes in her excitement. "He talks! He spoke my name!"

"And mine too," shrilled Bess.

Joe Brenton shook with laughter as he watched his young cousins. "Name of God! Pretty Desire! Pretty black hair! Now, you minx, will you make light of your jet tresses?"

"Oh, Hugh Jocelyn!" Desire's eyes shone as she clung to Hugh's arm. "You lessoned him for me! And he's mine—my parrot! He knows my name!"

Hugh handed the girl the cage. "He is yours!"

"How can I ever thank you?"

"You have thanked me enough by your pleasure over him. Feed him yourself and he will soon tame and fly to your shoulder and nibble your ear."

The little Amazon nodded and blinked at the two pairs of black eyes that inspected him curiously through the wooden bars of the cage. To the girls' delight, he repeated, "Pretty Desire! Pretty Bess!"—stopped for an interval, then screamed in a maniacal staccato that filled the garden, "Se-re-na! Se-re-na!"

Again the two girls squealed with laughter. In the house the spinet was suddenly silent. Shortly, from an open window, a girl's voice called, "Who named me in that frightful voice?"

"Serena! Hugh has come! We're here in the garden!" answered Desire.

The tall figure of a girl in white dimity appeared at a door and approached. As she reached them, Hugh noticed how the scarlet ribbons of her virago sleeves of lustring set off her ink-black hair and fair skin. There was curiosity in her eyes as he bent over her extended hand with a "Your servant, Mistress Serena!" and she replied:

"Welcome home from Barbadoes safe and—"

"Se-re-na!" squawked the parrot, and the girl flashed her white teeth at the man who doubtfully watched her.

"It seems the bird has been well lessoned," she said, her black eyes twinkling.

"I plead guilty," admitted Hugh. "As he was to find a home at Hammersmith I felt 'twas fitting he spoke the names of the family."

With a curl of her short upper lip she threw back derisively: "So he's been lessoned to say, 'Pretty Desire!' 'Pretty Bess!' but not 'Pretty Serena!' That, sir, was fair cruel!" She laughed, but it was a laugh without mirth.

"God's name," burst out Joe Brenton, "she has you there, Hugh!"

A slow color flowed up over Serena Brenton's face but she coolly met Hugh's embarrassed eyes.

"Mistress Serena," he said, "if you will but grant me the liberty of plain speech, the bird's tongue labored for weeks over 'Lovely Serena!' but could not accomplish it."

"Ha—ha!" cried Joe. "Will you venture to trip a privateersman again with your quick tongue, my fair cousin?"

It seemed to Hugh that Serena Brenton's candid gaze was searching his very thoughts. "I am fair flattered that one so versed in women's looks intended me such compliment," she said, with a bow. "You have my thanks. I hope to see you at Hammersmith again before you desert us for Barbadoes."

She swung on her red-heeled shoes and left them. Brenton

watched her retreating back with a quizzical frown. He met Hugh's questioning eyes and shook his head.

When Hugh had advised Desire as to proper food and care of the parrot, he said good-by and followed Brenton to the stables.

"Pay no heed to Serena," said Joe, as they mounted their horses. "She was taken aback by your neat reply and was embarrassed. When surprised or embarrassed, Serena is apt to spit. She meant nothing."

Hugh made no reply, and in silence the two started back to Newport.

5. The Gold of the Spanish Main

§70

IT WAS the summer of 1693 and the war with France raged in all its fury. To the surprise of Jahleel Brenton and the disappointment of Joe, Hugh had refused to take the *Swordfish* to Barbadoes. William and John Wanton would not make a summer cruise north in the *Flying Fish*, for they were freshly married and anchored to Newport, and the price of one thousand pounds which the elder Wantons were asking for the sloop and her guns was double the hoarded savings in the Stantons' chimney hole. Hugh was growing desperate. Precious months were slipping by. Then the Wantons gave him the command of the sloop for a summer privateering cruise on shares, to northern waters. But he took no prizes of value and the cruise barely paid expenses. On his return, when he approached men of means to take a half share in the *Flying Fish* for a two years' cruise to the warm seas, he found that vague rumors of a voyage to the Indian Ocean had already reached their ears, and this had left them cold. Finally, in an attempt to aid Hugh by borrowing money from his uncle, Jahleel, Joe Brenton had met a stone wall. Bitter with unrest and frustration, Hugh faced a winter in Newport, while the gallant *Flying Fish* lay desolate at the Wanton yard, her guns wrapped in tarpaulin, their muzzles plugged with wooden tampions, and her sails stored in the hold.

From Lettice, whom her family had packed off to Boston on Hugh's return and had kept there during the winter, Hugh received two letters by the new post from the Bay to Virginia. But she warned him not to answer, for his letters would never reach her and only cause trouble.

"Was I young, Hugh," said Tom Paine, one day as, together with Israel, they sat before the oak logs and the wind whined in the chimney of the farm on Conanicut, "I'd waste little time in northern waters with a ten-gun sloop like the *Flying Fish* and a proper crew of Newport and Portsmouth lads."

"Neither should I, Captain, had I money to buy the *Flying Fish*.

But Joseph Wanton holds to a high price and I'm seeking someone to put up half."

Paine nodded. "My own spare money is tied up in new land or I'd take a half share, for I have faith in you and Israel. But if you ever do get her and you'd bring back a fortune from the slippery West Indy, you must harden yourself."

Hugh grinned good-naturedly. "Israel thinks some of my schemes are over hard. Let go the main sheet, Captain! I'm listening."

Paine blew a cloud of smoke from his mouth and said: "Women and rum will scarce wreck you. I know that, though there be some in Newport who hold to the contrary. But in the West Indy every governor has an itching palm and no memory or conscience. They're all mad for gold. Trust one of these fortune-hunting Englishmen and you're lost."

"Ay, 'tis the naked truth!" grunted Israel.

"You must drive hard bargains, Hugh, and keep the islands in need of your sloop and guns. Weaken, and when things go amiss they'll turn on you and see you hung as a pirate, or leave you to rot in a French or Spanish prison without the quiver of an eyelid."

"Ay," growled Brandy, "'tis as true as there's comfort in rum. We'll let no English governor bubble us with fair talk and a shifty memory. Hard bargains they'll be and no trust."

Hugh's face stiffened. There was a glitter in his eyes as he answered: "Captain Paine, I trust no man of them! If I get the sloop and reach the islands, we're sailing home with a fortune or we're leaving our bones on a sand beach."

"All of which I signs my mark to," added Israel.

While Hugh chafed through the long winter, in his leisure moments Israel Brandy moved among the sailors who caroused at night in the taverns. The coming and going of swaggering and insolent privateersmen from up and down the coast, barring Thames Street, at night, to the use of all honest women, had given Benoni Tosh, the constables, and the watch little rest. But interested though Tosh was in Israel's attempts to obtain evidence against Carr Newbury, he had failed to unearth anything.

Early one evening Israel stumped into the Butterfly for a talk with Betsy Moon. Perched on its wharf, convenient to much of the anchored shipping, the war had brought prosperity to this unsavory haunt of thirsty seamen and the harpies who preyed on them. In fact, Betsy had been doubly fortunate. It was her boast that of the four murders of seamen in Newport in the past year, none had occurred within the chaste precincts of the Butterfly. To be sure, the mate of a Salem sloop had been followed from the tavern after a brawl and stabbed, but Betsy refused responsibility for that, and Benoni Tosh, after profound consideration of the facts, buttressed by frequent and gratuitous assaults on her fiery rum, had absolved her from all blame, although the Town Council had been severe in its reprimand. However, there had been many a dispute over the respective merits of Boston and Newport wenches as sweethearts, and concerning the ability of Newport-built sloops to outsail and outfight those launched north of Cape Cod. Tables had been smashed, stools swung, and heads battered against the peace of the port, but no skull was known to have taken mortal blow in the Butterfly in the past year, and the Widow Moon was justly proud of her record.

"Sink me, Israel," she chuckled, as Brandy entered the vacant room, for it was pudding time and she served no meals, "what brings you out betimes?"

Israel seated himself beside the blowsy Betsy, the bulging bosom of whose ozenbrig frock carried eloquent souvenirs of past dinners and spilled rum. "Betsy, I was fair fevered for a look at that saucy face of yours."

Her button of a nose and small eyes narrowly escaped burial in her bulbous cheeks as she laughed, "Israel, what's on that slippery tongue of yours, the same old story?"

"Ay, the same old story. Have your ears caught, lately, ought of what I seek?"

Narrowing her eyes in thought, the Widow Moon groped for her chin with fat fingers, but the embedded feature eluded her. "No; but we now have in the port some who doubtless would turn an honest penny by slippin' a knife betwixt a man's ribs."

"Brinley's man, Gill, has not stuck his nose, flattened by Hugh Jocelyn's fist, in here of late?"

"Nay, not since summer."

"Captain Bill Mayes of the brigantine *Portsmouth Adventure*, and Jack Bankes of the *Pearl*, wait for papers from the Deputy Governor, with as likely a company of slit-throats as ever I see in the West Indy."

Betsy nodded. "They are here much, and I have listened; but drunk or sober, their talk is only of the Indy Ocean and Maddeegasco."

"How shape they to your eye?"

"If ever I glimpsed a pair of pirates, 'tis them!"

"And while they cool their heels on the Governor's pleasure, they might listen to an offer from Gill?"

Betsy shook her head. "'Twas but lately I heard them use your name and Captain Jocelyn's in open talk. It seems they are after Tom Tew to leave his Portsmouth farm and join them for a last cruise. And they say 'tis their purpose to add the *Flying Fish* and the two best gunners in the port to the fleet."

Brandy's heavy brows lifted. "Pickle my guts, that may only mean me and Hugh!" he gravely announced.

Betsy nodded. "If they name you that and plan to urge you to join them, they'd scarce have ears for Gill's offer."

"No. But I'm fevered to have Gill approach them and they tell me of it. Gill is the dogfish I'd set my teeth in."

Voices sounded outside and three men entered the Butterfly. "Rot my bones, here they be with Tom Tew, now! Look you, Betsy! I nurse my rum, here, while you serve them and get their talk of me, before they hail and have me at their table. I'm fair fuddled, you understand, and pay them no notice."

Betsy left Israel huddled over his rum, and waddled toward the newcomers. "G'd d'en to you, mates!" she greeted.

Beaver hat, caught on one side with a silver buckle and cocked at an angle on his black periwig, Tom Tew was a rakish young man, wearing a blue camlet coat, bright with yellow Arabian sequins for buttons, and a red fustian waistcoat. Tew clapped Betsy on her mound of a shoulder. "Slay me, Betsy," he laughed, "but you grow easier on the eyes every day. We'll sit at that table in the far corner, where flapping ears may not catch our private talk."

"Ay, Captain, the table is yours. When the seamen and their wenches drift in, I'll shove 'em off your beam."

Tew's bold eyes focused on Brandy's back, hunched over his table. He turned to the men with him, who wore sailors' Monmouth caps and, beneath their duffel sea jackets, cutlasses slung on baldrics. "Stab me, there sits Tom Paine's peg-legged gunner who sunk Picard's longboats at Block Island."

Tew's companions stared at the broad back and tousled head of the man at the far end of the dingy room, as he sat in the flickering light of the tallow dips hung on candle beams. Then the sandy-haired Bankes muttered to the swart Mayes, "Ay, 'tis Brandy, the gunner!"

Mayes nodded, and his hard eyes lit with interest. "He's the devil with a cutlass—worth a dozen men on a ship's deck. We'll speak with him shortly," he added, to Bankes.

The three sat down, and when Betsy returned with their drinks, Mayes lifted his pewter cup: "A quick voyage to us all and speedy reunion, Captain Tew!"

Tew slapped his cup on the table. "Breath of Jesus, Bill Mayes, we've got no papers here as yet, and you talk of quick voyages! John Easton refuses my five hundred pounds with the whine he knows not where I'm bound. I tell him I'm bound where he'll never hear from me. When fitted out, I'm for New York with the *Amity* sloop, where Governor Fletcher will ask no questions."

"We have good hope, here, of our papers," said Bankes, "but lack men of proper stuff. There sits one slobbering at that table, and Captain Jocelyn is another, could we get him to join us with his sloop."

Tew's black brows met as he drummed on the table with a big hand which carried on the little finger a massive gold band set with an enormous emerald. "Young Jocelyn!" he mused aloud; then asked, "Have you talked lately with this Gill?"

Bankes laughed. "But recent he pressed me at the Blue Porpoise with his secret business. I was near to ending the job Jocelyn started on his ugly snout."

"What mean you? Did he offer again?"

Bankes nodded. "He was hot to bind a bargain till I told him I hoped to sail in company with the *Flying Fish* and he could look elsewhere."

"What's behind it all?"

"Young Newbury—no less! I hear 'tis Brinley's daughter and Jocelyn."

"Think you Jocelyn could be got to take the *Flying Fish* to the Indian Ocean?" asked Tew.

"'Tis said he's off for Barbadoes."

"There sits his gunner, Brandy, who should know," said Bankes.

"He's over-whittled to talk now," said Tew, turning to glance at Brandy talking with Betsy Moon.

"Hail him and see," suggested Mayes.

Israel turned as Bankes stood beside him and called him by name.

"Ay, Jack Bankes!" he said, licking his lips and rolling a wild eye on the speaker.

"Come aboard, Brandy! Captain Tew wishes talk with you!"

Israel lurched to an upright position which he seemed to maintain with difficulty. "When Captain Tom Tew, the pirate, orders, I obey!" he jeered, with a sweep of his arm, while Betsy Moon narrowly watched him.

Bankes scowled darkly. "Stab my guts, you're overfree with your talk. Captain Tew sails only with proper papers, as you know!"

Israel seized Bankes by both arms and leered into his face. The vise of his grip made the other wince with pain as they faced each other. "Jack Bankes or Crankes or Shankes," laughed Brandy, "I was boardin' Spanish and French ships when you was suckin' milk! If it pleasures me to name Tom Tew pirate, I'll answer to Tom, here and now!" He pushed Bankes roughly aside and stumped to Tew's table.

"Ho, gunner Brandy!" greeted Tew, as Bankes joined them, rubbing an arm.

"Captain Tew," said Brandy, swaying on his good foot as if giddy from drink, "I named you 'the great pirate, Tom Tew' to Jack Bankes, here. Be I right or wrong?"

Tew laughed loudly. "What care I what you name me so I sail as privateer with proper papers? Sit and drink with us while we talk."

Israel sprawled on a stool and grinned into the faces of the three men. "So you head again for the Indy Sea?" he boldly queried of Tew.

Tew tipped his cocked hat and threw a quick glance at the scowling Bankes and Mayes: "You are bold with your talk, gunner. 'Tis not where I sail but what I bring back. They say the *Flying Fish* is off for the Sugar Islands."

"Ay, we have our papers and sail soon," Israel glibly lied.

"Captain Jocelyn no doubt seeks his fortune from French shipping?" Israel nodded. "And, stab my vitals, he'll find it!"

Tew leaned forward and tapped Brandy's arm. "He'd find more if he joined us."

Israel blinked stupidly into Tew's serious face. "More of what?"

"Stab me, more of fortune! 'Tis but heavy cargo he'll take in the West Indy, which needs must be condemned and sold and the outcome milked, like a cow, by the thieving governors and crown officers. With us, gunner, 'twill be gold and plate and jewels and rich Indy silk, which we keep. The western islands are a waste of a good man's time."

"Ay," muttered Brandy, "'tis so! 'Tis so!"

"With a sloop like the *Flying Fish*, sailed sweet and fought hard as Jocelyn would fight her, he'd return rich from Maddeegasco."

Israel seemed the soul of sincerity as he grunted: "'Tis true! Tis true!"

"I would talk this matter with Captain Jocelyn," continued Tew. "Fetch him to my farm soon."

"That I'll do, Captain," promised Israel, while Bankes and Mayes nodded with satisfaction.

"You'll be made for life if you join us," said Tew.

"You brought back plenty, 'tis said."

"Slit my throat, and I'll bring more this voyage!"

Brandy scratched his head and his tufts of brows knotted as he suddenly demanded: "Have any of you ever clapped your eyes on a sourfaced sea rat named Creach? When last I nailed him here in Newport he was mate of the brig *Sea Horse*."

"Creach! Creach!" muttered Bankes. "Ay, I have him, now; and a prime shagrag he looked. Short, with the face of a poisoned dogfish. 'Twas in the Crown tavern, Boston Town, I drank with him."

"Spoke he of Newport?" demanded Brandy, his small eyes glittering.

"Rot my bones, now I venture he did! 'Twas some secret business there that fevered his blood. Gold a-plenty, from a high place, for the man who would finish it."

"Finish what?" snapped Israel.

Tew caught Bankes's eye. "Why"—he went on lamely—"finish the business. But I was for the Sugar Islands and asked no questions. 'Tis said in Boston that Creach has gone on the account."

"Ah!" Brandy's breath whistled through his teeth. "Now, since you dropped anchor in this port have you chanced to foul one Gill, a farmer?"

Bankes shot an oblique glance at Tew, and the latter nodded. "Ay, I know this Gill. Why do you ask?"

Israel leaned and shook a heavy finger in the speaker's face. "This is why, Jack Bankes!" he snorted. "Gill is Brinley's man. For years young Brinley and Carr Newbury have held a grudge against Hugh Jocelyn. Creach was the go-between. But I cracked his skull one night and he sailed away. Now 'tis Gill who handles the matter. Has he sought you?"

Again Bankes received a nod from Tew. "Gill talked of plenty gold, gunner, for the man to do a job," he answered; "but," he added, "never of Captain Jocelyn."

"Why?"

"Because certain who he meant to injure, I swore we hoped Jocelyn would sail in company with us."

"That shut the rumbullion's mouth!" laughed Israel.

"Well," said Tew, "you see, gunner, how we hang with our friends? Now ride out soon to the farm with Jocelyn, where we may talk without brails on our tongues, and I'll make him forget the West Indy."

The room was filling with seamen and women, who stared in unabashed admiration and envy at the handsome Tew, known to have returned rich from the Indian Ocean. There was no more to be gained from Bankes at present, so Israel bade them good-night, promising to bring Hugh to Portsmouth; for he was keen to learn more about these worthies and their intentions. Warning Betsy to linger near their table and pick up the talk, he stumped out.

But there was more than one problem on his mind as he made his way up Thames Street. First, they had to find the money to purchase the *Flying Fish*. And that would not be easy. Hugh was already fair desperate over it. If financial aid was not forthcoming soon, Israel feared the boy would do something reckless. His heart was in taking the sloop to the warm seas. He had lived for it. If they lost the chance to buy her, Brandy would not put it beyond the headstrong Hugh to insist on taking ship for Bristol and joining Kidd. For Kidd's offer had been fermenting in Hugh's brain and it was that summer that Kidd was to sail. To this Israel would never agree. He put no trust in princes—or in kings' ministers. And he knew what happened to most men who sailed for the Indian Ocean. Eventually they flouted the law and their commissions, attacked all shipping, and became outlaws. No, there should be no Indian Ocean if Israel Brandy had his way.

As for going to Tew's farm in Portsmouth for a talk, would it be wise? Both Israel and Hugh were curious concerning this man who had made two successful voyages and was now planning a third. And Israel was interested in Bankes's story and hoped, somehow, to tie Newbury in with the offer made to him by Creach. But would Tew paint so glowing a picture of easy wealth that Hugh would be tempted? Hardly. Hugh knew the breed. Yet the tales might fever his blood to join Kidd, for the young privateersman was mad to make his fortune. If he could obtain a commission to attack the King's enemies in the Eastern Sea, he might consider it.

In the end, Israel decided to accompany Hugh to Tew's farm on a fishing expedition. They would listen, and might possibly learn something.

§71

BEFORE HUGH and Israel made their call at the Tew farm, a ray of hope slanted across the horizon. One Samuel Stafford, Quaker, who owned land, sloops, and a wharf, sent word to Hugh that he wished to see him. In his small office on his wharf Stafford lost no time in coming to the point.

"Captain Jocelyn," he said, "'tis reported that you seek funds with which to buy the Wanton sloop, *Flying Fish*."

Hugh's eyes lit with interest. "If ownership in the sloop were divided into eight shares, I have sufficient to buy four," he said. "The remainder I must raise."

The Quaker cleared his throat. He was a lean, dry-faced man of middle age, somber of dress and manner, with a thin-lipped mouth and cold eye. "I have some funds at my disposal," he said; "what do the Wantons ask?"

Hugh contemplated the wooden face of the man who spoke. He knew that Stafford was a sharp trader, and was on his guard. But the thought that at last the sloop might be bought and headed for the warm seas quickened his pulse. "The Wantons ask one thousand pounds for her as she stands, gunned and geared, with her spare sails. Besides, we'll need to buy powder, shot, and stores."

The Quaker cleared his throat. "That seems a high price for a hundred-ton craft."

"Not for that sloop! 'Tis low, as you well know, because of my friendship with the Wantons. She's the fastest sloop on this coast."

"Yes, I know; I know. Under the Wantons she's made good voyages."

"She's paid for herself many times over."

"Had I not confidence in your ability, I would not risk a pound in her. What do you ask for your share and the crew's?"

Hugh was irritated. It was established custom for the captain and crew of a privateer to take half the winnings. "You well know the usage of this port," he said. "After crown and admiralty charges and costs of stores have been met, all privateering agreements allot half the prize money to captain and crew."

Stafford smiled weakly in assent. "You have a commission to cruise in the West Indies, issued by Governor Easton, to run two years?"

"I have."

"I should insist that you return and make an accounting of the prize money and expenses by one year."

"That would kill the venture. It leaves too little time in the islands." Hugh was annoyed at the Quaker's attitude. Stafford had something up his sleeve and was edging toward it.

For a space the wharf owner drummed with his long fingers on his desk, as if considering his next move. Then he raised shifty eyes. "'Tis much money to hazard in a doubtful venture. I run the risk of your not returning at all."

The blood pushed up over Jocelyn's face. He leaned toward the speaker and the thrust of his eyes drove down the other's sly look. "You're treading dangerous ground, Mr. Stafford! You're suggesting that I'm—"

"Oh, no, no! No offense was meant!" Stafford raised his bony hands in protest as Hugh glared into his sapless face. "The fact that I sent for you proves my confidence. But you know 'tis a tricky venture. If you lose the sloop, I have lost my money."

"Well, what's your point?"

"I suggest that we make out papers allotting captain and crew forty per centum of the return and the owners sixty."

"No! 'Tis not the usage and you know it! And I refuse to agree to return before two years!" Hugh feared that he had burned his bridges. For an instant the eyes of the two men locked.

Then Stafford said with a sigh, "You drive a hard bargain, Captain Jocelyn."

"I seek only my rights!" retorted Hugh.

In spite of his haggling, it was evident to Hugh that Stafford intended to advance the money; so he held his ground. In the end it was agreed that he should return home within two years for an accounting;

also that his share and that of his crew should be half the profits.

So Stafford advanced five hundred pounds for a half-interest in the *Flying Fish* and the sloop was purchased.

Two days later Hugh and Israel dismounted at the large farmhouse which Tew had bought on his return from his second voyage to the Indian Ocean. The door was opened by a black boy. Loud voices and snatches of ribald song drifted from the fire room. His dark face flushed from drink and wig awry, Tom Tew welcomed them, dressed in a shirt of yellow silk and a pair of loose Oriental trousers heavily embroidered. His waist was circled by a green sash. It was apparent that he fancied himself in the garb of the East and enjoyed startling the simple farmer folk of Portsmouth with his garish costumes.

"Captain Jocelyn!" he cried, seizing Hugh's hand. "It pleasures me to welcome you and Gunner Brandy! Some friends and old shipmates of mine will also greet you—Jack Bankes, Bill Mayes, and Captain Gillam. Rum for Captain Jocelyn and Gunner Brandy!" he shouted to the black boy standing at the door leading to the kitchen, from which issued the aroma of a roasting sheep turning on a spit.

Hugh and Israel followed Tew into the smoke-filled room, where five men sat drinking before the hearth, above which the wall was decorated with Arabian scimitars, Malay creeses, and Indian swords, the hilts of which were inlaid with pearl and gold. "Gentlemen," announced Tew, "Captain Jocelyn and Gunner Brandy!"

"Ho, Captain! Come aboard!" called Bankes, raising his cup, followed by the others.

From a quick survey of the carousing men it was evident to Hugh that they had been at their rum some time. Another lay snoring on the floor, over whose body the black boy stepped on his way to and from the kitchen. Bankes, Mayes, and Gillam in turn shook Hugh's and Israel's hands, and they sat on the settle with Tew. The faces of two of the company bore the familiar pits of smallpox, but from ear to collarbone the open throat of the red-haired Gillam carried the blue-white cicatrix left by the slash of a cutlass. From the look in the hard eyes which met his, it was clear to Hugh that these same eyes had looked on scenes in the past of which their owners would hesitate to speak in Newport.

"Well, Captain Jocelyn," began Tew, emptying his cup, "you doubtless wonder at the company here today on a quiet Portsmouth farm; but the reason is this. For a year these old shipmates of mine have been laying board and board of me, chirping for another cruise to the Indy Sea. At last I've agreed. Deputy Governor Greene has already commissioned Jack Bankes and Bill Mayes, but John Easton refuses me, whining he knows not where I go. Therefore I'm for New York in the *Amity* sloop to my friend Governor Fletcher."

"You sail soon?" asked Hugh.

"Yes, with Jack and Bill here. But we name no names and we loose no talk of our purpose."

"Gunner Brandy, here, tells us you're for the warm seas," said Mayes, spilling rum over his chin, which he wiped with the back of a hairy hand. He leaned toward Hugh and shook a thick finger. "Christ's blood, Captain, why the Sugar Islands and the chance of a rope at the yardarm of a French ship when there's Arab gold and Arab women ready for the takin' by a crew of stout New England lads?"

Hugh laughed. "You make it sound easy, Captain Mayes! But how about Long Ben Avery? 'Tis said he's king out there, though they've put a price on his head."

Israel was watching Hugh curiously from under half-closed lids.

Mayes winked. "True, Long Ben sails without the proper papers which we carry, but we have—"

Tew stopped the speaker with a warning hand, two fingers of which carried huge emerald and pearl rings in Oriental settings. "Captain," he said to the interested Hugh, while Israel's small eyes shifted from one to another of the drinking men, "the French East Indy Company are the King's enemies. The Great Mogul is the King's enemy. His ships carry rich cargoes, and though heavy-gunned are easy taken. Join us with your sloop and you'll sail into Newport a rich man!"

Israel tossed off his rum and nodded. "Ay, Captain Tew, I believes your story. 'Tis the Indy Ocean for a quick fortune. But though easy got 'tis hard held, as you say, on your return. Since Governor Easton refuses you papers they'll scarce let you bring your prize goods and gold into Newport."

Tew laughed heartily. "But Robert Livingston and others will be on the wharf to welcome us in New York, and the wharf and arms of Colonel Pierson of Long Island will be open. If Newport's cold, we'll find warm friends in New York."

"How long were you away on your last voyage?" asked Hugh, and Israel looked at him sharply.

"'Twas less than two years, and a tidy fortune I brought back."

The swart-faced Bankes broke in: "Join us, Captain! 'Twill make three able sloops in our fleet and we'll sweep the sea. If you do, you're rich in a year and New York'll take your prize goods and no questions asked."

Israel noted the rising color in Hugh's face and the glitter in his eyes as he listened to the urging of Tew and his friends.

"If your last voyage was so successful, why risk your neck in seeking more?" suggested Hugh.

Tew leered in his face. With a sweep of his arm he included the company. "Out of fat winnings these rake-hells have scarce a pound left. Rum and women took it. I need no more but they give me no peace, and were my shipmates."

"So you sail for a last fling at the Great Mogul?" laughed Hugh.

Tew emptied his cup and burst into a song, while his friends beat time with their clicking cups and the man on the floor snored an accompaniment.

> 'Tis ho for the Indy Sea, lads!
> We'll slant athwart the trades
> And fill our hold with Arab gold,
> Our bunks with the Mogul's maids!
>
> 'Tis east-sou'east and round the Cape
> And up the Afric shore,
> Then home we'll come when our fortune's won
> To sail the seas no more!

"Ay, to sail the seas no more!" roared Tew—"until these rumbullions have not one shilling to rub against another and they'll head for Portsmouth to bubble me into another voyage! Hi, mates?"

As they left, Tew said: "If Governor Easton'll not give you papers for the Indy Ocean, it can be arranged in New York. My friend Governor Fletcher'll see to that!"

"But the price?" Hugh demurred, curious of the answer. "I'm at the end of my means."

"The price? Tom Tew'll look to it!" cried the pirate, clapping Hugh on the shoulder. "Think it over and we'll talk more in a day or two, when sober. With the *Flying Fish* and two sweet gunners like you and Brandy, it's a fortune in two years and ease for life! Chew on that till I see you."

§72

HUGH and Israel had not ridden far when the old privateersman checked his horse and turned to the man at his side. "What's churnin' in that head of yours? I see your eyes light up when Tew talked of easy prize money. You frettin' to head for the Eastern Ocean with that school of slit-throats?"

Hugh turned dreaming eyes on his friend. "Israel," he said, "I'm fair tempted. If I could get proper papers and arrange with Stafford— But he'd never agree. And we've no money left for a commission."

Israel sucked his lips with satisfaction. "Then why fret your mind about it? Pirate stands out on that crew we just left as scales on fish.

You'd scarce swim with that school of sharks?"

"I know what they are as well as you, Israel. They're nothing but sea wolves sailing with the sheep's clothing of a governor's commission. And once in the Indian Ocean we're done with them. We join up with Kidd. I was dreaming of the sure fortune to be made."

A sour look spread over Israel's face. "Long Ben Avery rules down there. There's no half way. You'd play his game or—"

"The *Flying Fish* can take care of herself."

"You'd have to join him, I tell you, or you'd never see Newport again. You're fair fantastical, moonin' over the Eastern Sea."

"Likely I am, Israel. But I'm fair set for a fortune. If we could get papers for the Indian Ocean and you and the crew'd join me, I'd—I'd—"

"Belay! You forget Stafford. But where you goes, I go, even to hell!" Brandy's voice was rough with feeling. "You goes nowhere without Israel. But I see nothin' but trouble with Tom Tew as I saw it with Bill Kidd."

"Stafford would overlook the breach of agreement once he saw his prize money."

"I tell you they're all slimy pirates out there, and few lives to return," insisted Brandy.

"The two buccaneers, Paine and Brandy, returned from the Spanish Main!" taunted Hugh.

So they argued as they rode back to Newport.

A few nights later Hugh sat in Trelawney's room. "'Tis a great adventure, Hugh, you are setting out on, a challenge to fate such as our friends, the Elizabethans, often flung. Well, lad, I've given you what I had to give and am proud of my labor."

"You've made me what I am, Dick," Hugh replied. "I owe you everything. Whatever I capture from life will be but your gift to me."

For a time Trelawney was silent, then said, "Israel has told me of your going to Tew's."

"Yes?"

"He's worried, Hugh. You know how he lives in you. You're like a son."

"Yes, I know."

"He fears that Tew has put the Indian Ocean into your blood, that you might try to get papers from Governor Fletcher of New York, and—"

"And what?" Hugh demanded, nervously pacing the room.

Trelawney rose and placed his hand on the other's shoulder. "You wouldn't think of heading for that hell-hole of pirates and proscribed men, Hugh? No honest privateersman can long sail those seas—'twould be ruin for you."

"Captain Kidd sails this spring with the King's commission," retorted Hugh.

"I know, but Tom Tew is known to have been a pirate. You'd not join him?"

"I'd not play his game, no! I'd attack the ships of the King's enemies only. But I might use his help to get a commission from Fletcher, of New York."

"I wish I could make you see how mad 'twould be for you to sail with Tew. They're not your kind—Mayes, Bankes, Gillam, and the rest. Their company'd damn you in the eyes of honest men."

"Honest men? Are there any left, Dick?"

"Yes, and there always will be, as you well know."

"Dick, I'm venturing my all on bringing back a fortune. If I fail, Newport has seen the last of me."

"How about us who love you?"

"'Tis life, Dick! I'll not return empty-handed. 'Twill be hard on Content and Tom and you, whose love has meant so much to me. But my purpose is fixed."

"And you'll not promise me you'll not join up with Tew at New York?"

"I promise nothing, Dick; I'm sorry."

The morning Hugh sailed, Content could not bear to go to the wharf, so bade him farewell at home.

"Hugh," she said, as he held her in his arms, "it may be this is our farewell. If it is, I want you to know what joy and sunshine you've brought to my life, lad."

He stroked her graying hair. "No son ever had better mother. From the time you first took me to your big heart I've treasured you, Mother Content. Down there in the warm seas I shall think of you and Tom in the little house on the Cove. The money I've left in the chimney hole is yours. 'Twill help to ease you through the years if I come not back. But if that falls out, don't grieve. Think only of the happy years we've had, you and I."

At the wharf, among the friends and families of the crew waited Trelawney, with Joe Brenton, Arnold, Sheffield, and the Wantons. They had given Hugh, Israel, and Jeremy Potts a last handclasp and slap on the back, and had left the deck of the *Flying Fish*, when there was a clatter of hoofs, and a girl's shrill voice called from the shore: "Hugh! Hugh Jocelyn!"

"God's breath!" exclaimed Brenton. "She's ridden alone from Hammersmith to say farewell!"

The rider urged her horse through the chattering people on the wharf and reached the sloop, where men already stood at the bollards to cast off her lines.

"Desire!" laughed Brenton, swinging his panting niece from her saddle. "What kept you?"

The girl's anxious eyes roved the sloop's deck. "Where's Hugh?" she gasped. "I must speak to him before he goes!"

"Here he comes," answered Arnold.

Hugh joined the group and smiled into Desire's flushed face. Here was one who had not forgotten him. "Your servant, Mistress Desire. I count it sweet of you to ride down this morning to see us sail."

Desire impulsively took his hand in both of hers and her eyes were very bright as she said: "Oh, Hugh, I shall watch the East Passage every day next spring for your sloop! 'Twill fair vex me if you stay beyond the spring! I'm going back to Hammersmith, to the high meadow, to be the last to wave to you!" Her unabashed eyes shone into his. Then, with a catch of the breath, she turned, mounted her horse, and rode off the wharf.

The men exchanged smiles. "She's near a woman, now," said Arnold. "Once she coveted your hair, Hugh. Have a care or 'twill soon be your heart!"

"Desire is still a child, and a sweet one," answered Brenton. "Hugh won her everlasting friendship with the parrot."

So, with last farewells, the *Flying Fish* under jib and staysail swung from her wharf. Her big mainsail was broken out from its brails and she moved away to pass behind Goat Island, headed for the tropic seas.

Later, from the high meadows of Hammersmith Farm, a white petticoat fluttered in the stiff breeze where Desire and Bess stood beside their horses. From the big sloop driving down the East Passage leaped a puff of orange smoke and flame as a demiculverin roared Hugh Jocelyn's farewell. A mile away, on Brenton's Point, from which reached the white thrust of the reef, with Beaver Tail in the west across the East Passage, a girl sat stiff on her horse, waiting. At last, with square topsail, jibs, and big mainsail bellying with the northwest breeze, the sloop appeared and stood out to sea. While her horse fidgeted with impatience, the girl watched until the sloop reached the far offing. A half-frown lay on her face, while in her eyes were both pain and bewilderment. Finally the sloop faded into the sea haze. Turning her horse, the girl rode slowly back to Hammersmith.

§73

BANKES and Mayes had already left Newport, and the day the *Flying*

Fish sailed, Tew's sloop, the *Amity*, slipped out of the harbor. To the gossips in the taverns, that evening, the sailing of the two sloops seemed to confirm the rumors which had circulated along the waterfront to the effect that no one knew where Jocelyn was bound. True, he carried the governor's commission for the West Indies, but it was known that he had visited Tew's farm and that the latter was headed for New York and the Indian Ocean. It looked as if they had sailed together, to obtain papers from the complacent Governor Fletcher. So the tongues wagged.

"There surely can be no truth in this," Brenton said to Trelawney as they sat alone at the King's Head.

The Englishman nervously rubbed his chin. "In Barbadoes Hugh was urged by Captain Kidd to join him on a venture to the east. Kidd sails from Bristol this summer. But I can't believe Hugh would go. As for his sailing with Tom Tew, 'tis silly."

"Where did he finally raise funds to buy the sloop?" asked Brenton. "It was a sore disappointment to me I could not spare or find the money. None I spoke to dared take the hazard on so long a cruise; and, you know, by some he's named rash and headstrong."

"The Quaker, Stafford, put it up," said Trelawney.

Brenton's eyes widened. "Stafford? Why, he's closer than hair on a dog and cautious as a cat. 'Tis unbelievable!"

"Yet he did."

Tom Paine came in and sat down at their table.

"You've heard the rumors, Captain Paine?" said Brenton.

"You mean of Hugh joining up with Tew?"

"Yes."

Small lines radiated from the corners of Paine's twinkling eyes. "There'd be a quick finish to such a partnership. Hugh and Israel would end by sinkin' him. Dogfish and blues don't school together."

"But Hugh has no papers for the Indian Ocean; he's commissioned for the Spanish Main," insisted Brenton.

"And that's where he's steerin'."

"I hope so," said Trelawney.

Yet, for months, to those who so anxiously waited, there came no news of Hugh Jocelyn and the *Flying Fish*, and many in Newport believed he had sailed to the eastern seas with Tew.

One night Trelawney sat with his friends at the King's Head. "He's been away eight months now," he said, "and no word. There have been ships into Boston from the Sugar Islands this winter. Had he reached Barbadoes we would have heard from him. I fear he's with Kidd."

"There's still a chance he's in the West Indy," said William Wanton. "Two Newport and some Boston craft bound home from the Windward Islands have been taken by the French. His letters may be lost."

But the gloomy Trelawney would not be comforted. He alone knew with what fierce determination to bring home a fortune Hugh had sailed out of Newport—what years of unrest and discontent lay behind his mood. Had he recklessly burned his bridges and joined Kidd for the Indian Ocean?

Thus they talked and argued concerning Hugh Jocelyn, privateersman, somewhere roving the tropic seas or lying beneath them.

It was the spring of 1695 and there was still no news of the *Flying Fish*. At Hammersmith, one April evening, Joe Brenton sat alone in one of the great parlors with Serena. It was chilly, and a fire burned in the huge chimneyplace. The mahogany furniture of the room had been brought from Barbadoes, where it had been made by one of the island's famous cabinetmakers. On the pale blue-green tinted walls hung the portraits of old Governor Brenton and his wife, painted by a roving English artist.

In the center of the room a Turkey carpet covered a mahogany table on which stood a massive silver tankard with tray and cups, the work of Barbadoes silversmiths famous in the colonies. Contemplating the fire, a cup of Canary on a small table at his elbow, Joe was smoking a long-stemmed clay pipe. He shifted his gaze to the girl at his side, who was seemingly deep in reverie as the fire-glow touched the dark masses of her hair. He studied the courageous black brows and long-lashed eyes, the straight nose, and the curves of mouth and chin, and thought there was no lovelier face in Newport. Yet she was known as the cold Serena Brenton. Fire she surely had, as Joe more than once had learned to his regret when pressing his teasing too far. But although many Newport swains had paid their court, to the dismay of her mother she had cooled them with her quick tongue and ridicule. A strange girl, Serena, Joe mentally commented—deep, deep beyond ordinary probing. And down there in the depths behind those baffling eyes which danced or clouded, ever masking her inmost thoughts, dwelt an ardent nature, could any man but reach it.

"What's in that pretty head tonight, Serena?" asked her cousin. "Why so silent? You've been blinking into the fire like an owl for a half-turn of the glass."

"I've been thinking about what they are saying about your friend, Captain Jocelyn."

"What mean you? There's been no word of him."

"That is not what Richard Brinley said at the Newburys' last night."

"What did that gentleman say? He knows nothing."

"Why, he said that Captain Jocelyn had turned pirate, for he had not reported to Stafford, a half-owner in the sloop. He said 'twas no news to him, for he had always thought Hugh Jocelyn had the making of a rare pirate."

"Name of God!" stormed Brenton. "Did no one dispute that? Had I been there, he'd not have dared open his silly mouth! I'd have beaten him, the coward!"

Serena laughed at her cousin's vehemence. "Cool yourself, Cousin Joe! Hugh Jocelyn numbered many friends."

"What said they to the coxcomb?"

"I said that the wish was clearly father to the thought, as no word of Captain Jocelyn had been received by anyone."

Brenton's eyes widened. "You said that? I fancied you had scant liking for him."

Her eyes clung steadfastly to the fire as she replied: "I told him—and the company shouted—that a pirate at the least needed courage and a stout right arm, both of which he himself sadly lacked."

"You told Brinley that, Serena? Name of God, I'm proud of you!" Brenton chuckled his satisfaction.

"Then others added that Hugh Jocelyn might return some day and make Brinley eat his words." Serena laughed. "Poor Richard!"

"When Hugh Jocelyn turns pirate," said Joe, "I turn Quaker and wear straight hair!"

It was autumn. More than a year had passed with no word from Hugh. Little hope now lingered in Content's heart. Then, one night, William Wanton burst into the house.

"Goodwife Stanton!" he cried to the startled Content. "A letter—a letter from Hugh by the brig from Surinam arrived today! He didn't sail with Kidd. He's in the warm seas—the Sugar Islands!"

Content's knitting slid to the floor. She reached for the letter William waved at her, and two great tears ran down her thin face. "Hugh! Oh, my Hugh! He lives! He lives!"

"Of course he lives!"

Tom Stanton shook with his emotion, his gnarled hand fumbling as if to free the lump which tightened his throat. Content greedily fingered the letter, whose address she could not read, then returned it to William. "Read it, William! Read it us!"

Wanton broke the wax seals and opened the heavy folds of paper addressed in Hugh's script-like hand.

DEAREST MOTHER CONTENT AND FATHER TOM:
I wrote You last Autumn and again in Winter, also Dick, Joe Brenton, and William, by different ships. But many Craft have been taken by the French so you may have heard Nothing. We have been over to Hispaniola, where Pirates are thick, in the service of Jamaica, and up to Antigua.

Fortune has been Good to us for we have taken and had condemned many Prizes, some Rich. But Four of our Men have been wounded and none killed, thanks to Israel's gunnery. Two have died of fever in Antigua.

The Sloop has become Famous for her Speed and Gunnery. The French governor at Martinique sent two ships of war to hunt us. One found us. After a six hour Fight we took her into Barbadoes and had her condemned. Now, we hunt the French. The Story spread from Barbadoes to the Bahamas. Your son, Hugh, now dines with Colonial Governors when in port. But I trust Few of them for They seek only to enrich Themselves and I have driven Hard Bargains for they need me.

While my body is far away, Mother of Mine, my Heart is Always with You in the little House on the Cove. Father Tom must not take Risks with the Sloop. Take Good Care of each Other. Do not Despair of me if you Receive no Word. My love to Dick, Joe Brenton, William and John, and All who remember me Kindly.

The Small Boy You Loved and who Loves You.

Hugh.

Content and Tom stood speechless in their joy. "He lives and will come back to us," sobbed Content. "God has been good!"

When the *Swordfish* returned from Barbadoes the following spring, two years from the sailing of the *Flying Fish*, Captain Scarlett brought the tale of Hugh's adventures in the warm seas. At Brenton's invitation, Hugh's friends gathered at the King's Head to listen to Scarlett's account of his meeting with the captain of the now famous black sloop.

"We was lyin' at the wharf in Bridgetown," said Scarlett, setting down his cup of rum and lighting his pipe with flint and steel from his fire bag, "when a big black sloop come drivin' in afore the trade. I'd know her in hell by her fine lines for'ard, her big mains'il, and the oily way she crawls through water, kickin' little white from her bow. That night Hugh, Israel, and me sit till daylight, while I listened."

"How does he look, Captain?" demanded William Wanton.

"A leetle older about the eyes and sober-faced, for he's sailed and fought wide and far; but hard and sound as new oak. Why, he's fought that sloop from the Grenadines to the Windward Passage, and the French hate him like poison. At French Tortuga, Fort-de-France, and Port Louis they call him 'Captain Yaller Hair,' and for a year now they've tried to take him. If they do, they'll swing him from a yardarm, for they name him pirate."

"Oh, no, not that!" protested Trelawney.

"But he's commissioned privateer and is no pirate," objected Brenton. "He attacks French commerce legally, as we do here in the north."

Scarlett snorted. "You little know what them French governors are in Guadeloupe and Martinique. He's hit their pockets cruel hard and they're wild for revenge. He's taken two rich cargoes of wine and brandy and silk bound out from Bordeaux. They've sworn to have him, dead or alive."

"Good old Hugh! God bless him!" cried William Wanton. "A health to Hugh Jocelyn and the *Flying Fish*!"

The company rose and drank the toast.

"When does he plan to return?" asked Arnold.

"When he's made sufficient to buy a brig, a farm, a new sloop for Tom Stanton, and has enough to keep him for life, he says."

The company laughed.

"I wish he'd come home with what fortune he already has," said Trelawney. "His luck may not always hold."

"To my mind, you'll not see that lad, Mr. Trelawney, till the war is over," said Scarlett. "He's cheek by jowl with the new Governor Russell, and this has made him enemies, Elisha Sanford among them. He bade me warn you to put no weight in any tales Sanford may write to Newport."

A frown lay on Brenton's dark face. "True, he's made enemies, for Deputy Governor Stoughton has writ from Boston advising Walter Clarke to arrest Hugh and search his sloop on his return."

"That's Stafford's work," said William Wanton. "He claims he's written Hugh to return and has received no answer. So he calls him a pirate."

"Doubtless Hugh will have need of his friends when he returns," said Brenton.

"Name of God," exploded William, "he'll find them with him, shoulder to shoulder!"

"Ay, he will!" asserted Trelawney.

§74

TRELAWNEY sat with Lettice Brinley in the large garden behind the spacious house on Thames Street. It was June, and the bowers of native wild roses and English eglantine were masses of pink bloom. The scent of flowers and of freshly turned earth and the fragrance of the box hedges filled the air, while the serenity of the morning was broken only by the low drone of bees and the occasional note of a bird.

To the gratification of her father, Lettice had continued with her reading of the poets with Trelawney and the general improvement of her mind. But aside from her fondness for the society of the clever Englishman, her underlying purpose was not the pursuit of learning but the pursuit of news of Hugh Jocelyn.

As she sat on a cedar settee, frowning on a small volume of Wycherley's collected plays, Trelawney studied the face of the girl whose indomitable will and hot head had been the despair of her parents. Her long-lashed eyes followed the printed lines, and her lips moved with each word, for she had never learned to read without their aid. Meanwhile the Englishman contemplated her loveliness. He envied Hugh, as his eye rested on the wavy chestnut hair framing her flawless skin and the lush red lips as they moved. She disdained a modesty cloth, and the low-cut dimity frock revealed the round symmetry of her throat and neck. From beneath her flowered skirt an impatient foot swung in the air, exposing a daring reach of blue-stockinged leg.

She waved away an exploring bumblebee. Then her eyes idly followed the uncertain flight of a yellow butterfly, to turn eventually to those of the attentive Englishman. With a sniff, she dropped the volume on the settee. "This Restoration drama fair tires me with its endless pursuit by wives and husbands of someone else, and the sly tricks they play to attain their desire."

"You disapprove of unfaithful wives and husbands?" he roguishly hazarded.

She violently shook her head. "Name of God, why disapprove if they tire of their own? A man or woman lives but once and seldom finds happiness. But 'tis all so petty, these silly capers, in compare with the meaty drama of the Elizabethans; and so mincingly writ. There's neither poetry nor life in this sly stuff."

"Mistress Lettice, I'm proud of your taste and discernment. You do your tutor honor."

She clasped her hands behind her head, and her ribboned virago sleeves fell from her round elbows as she tilted her chin and gazed into his amused eyes. "What think you my blessed brother taunted me with last night?"

"Nothing so wise as your remark on Shadwell, Etherege, and Wycherley, my dear!"

The arms came down and the girl's eyes flamed. "He said 'twas reported by Sanford, in Barbadoes, that a beautiful Martinique mestee sailed with Hugh Jocelyn wherever he went. Do you think that truth?"

"If it were truth," ventured Trelawney, "why should Mistress Lettice Brinley give it much heed?"

The girl's hands closed until her knuckles whitened. Blood stained her tense face as she caught her breath, then flung at him, "Why should I give heed to ought Hugh Jocelyn does?" She tossed back her chestnut head and laughed mirthlessly, while Trelawney was awed by the intensity of her feeling. "You ask me why, who know me and him? You ask me why?"

"Have a care or you'll be heard!" he warned. "Lower your voice."

Her white teeth bit at her lower lip, then she desperately flung her arms above her head. "I'll tell you why, Mr. Dick Trelawney. 'Tis because since the day I lashed him across the face and he laughed at me I've been frenzical over him! And you know it!"

In her unabashed abandon to her emotion, the girl's eyes were almost black as they burned into the embarrassed Trelawney's. Defiant and unashamed, she was stripping bare her heart, and a great pity stirred in him. "I know—I know!" he murmured.

"You doubt 'tis true?" she demanded. "I can't bear thinking of his having an octoroon on his sloop! It fair boils my blood! Oh, I know 'tis jealousy—just jealousy! It seems I can't have him, so I hate those who can!"

An admiration for the naked candor of the infatuated girl grew in Trelawney. He had never liked her so much as he did that moment in the reckless revelation of her passion. "Mistress Lettice," he said, "you have grown much today in my estimation. But you know what your family thinks."

"God's name, man, speak not of my family! My family can burn over it! But this tale they mouth, is there truth in it?"

Trelawney shook his head. "No, Hugh Jocelyn sails with no mestee. 'Tis the venom of his enemies."

She gave a deep sigh and rose, then smiled steadily into Trelawney's solicitous eyes. "After Hugh those Boston men were but dolls. No man—" She broke off suddenly, rose and walked rapidly into the house.

It was the autumn of 1696, almost a year since Captain Scarlett had met Jocelyn in Barbadoes. That was the last that Newport had heard of Hugh. At Hammersmith, after a period of tears and mourning for her friend, Desire now spoke of him as dead, although Joe Brenton stoutly refused to abandon hope. He often talked with Serena of the man who had lost himself in the wilderness of the tropic seas. But she invariably walled herself about with reserve. One thing he had noted: that summer she had ridden much on the path that led down to Brenton's Point and the sea, and she had ridden alone.

The lean Trelawney had grown noticeably leaner. Although he doggedly insisted that the craft carrying Hugh's letters had been taken by privateers, anxiety as to whether Hugh were dead or a prisoner in a French dungeon tortured his thoughts. Content's hair was growing white, and while Tom kept steadily at his fishing, Benoni Tosh and Jerusa Sugars one night left the house with the comment that, over three cups of rum, Tom had spoken only when questioned.

One day the *Gull* was back early, and Tom reached the house to find the fire room empty. Kettles already simmered over the supper fire, and the odor of burning bread caused him to take the wooden peel and lift the scorched loaves of rye-'n'-Injun from the chimney oven. He surmised that Content had stepped over to a neighbor's house and had forgotten her oven. She had been growing fair queer of late. There was a look in her eyes as if she were seeing things far away, and often she failed to answer when spoken to. Several times she had burned the bread or allowed the water to boil out of a kettle. And nights she tossed and murmured in her sleep.

Tom slouched on a stool and stared bleakly at the fire. Life would be cruel hard with Hugh gone! Hugh and Israel dead—or prisoners, which would be worse! Jeremy Mott's family had long since abandoned hope, and so had the families of most of the crew. Since the outbreak of the war a number of Newport ships had sailed never to return, and now it had come to Hugh. The creaking of boards in the floor of the loft above his head roused him from his painful reverie, "Content! You up there, Content?"

"Yes, I'm here," came the low answer.

"What busies you? You forgot your bread and I lifted it."

"I—I came up to—look around," came the muffled answer.

Slowly shaking his head, Tom climbed the ladder to the square, hatchlike opening in the floor of the loft, and looked. In the dim light from the small window under the eaves, Content knelt beside the pallet bed, holding a worn-out kersey coat of Hugh's. Beside her were a pair of old shoes, an outgrown sea doublet, woolen stockings and ozenbrig shirts and drawers. A wave of tenderness pulsed through him as he watched Content's bowed back.

"What—what are you doing?"

"Just looking for dust, and keeping them shipshape against his homecoming."

"Homecoming!" groaned Stanton.

The kneeling woman turned a face almost fierce in the intensity of her emotion. "Yes—his homecoming! Did I not believe in it, I'd scarce find strength to go on!"

"Ay! Ay!" murmured Stanton.

Content returned the clothes to the wooden pegs from which she had taken them, smoothed the blankets and small pillow on the pallet, and followed Stanton down the ladder.

75

ONE evening, in the late summer of 1696, a long, black ten-gunned sloop with an enormous mainsail carrying patches over gunshot tears slipped into the Bridgetown anchorage, Barbadoes, saluted the fort and batteries, and let go her anchor. While the crew were brailing the big sail and stowing jib and staysail, a longboat put out from her, bound for the government wharf.

"There should be letters from home," said Captain Jocelyn to his master gunner. "Some have doubtless been taken by the French, but 'tis eight months since we left Barbadoes. There should be word from Newport."

Brandy's wide face, tanned by the tropic sun to the color of mahogany, broke in a grin. "Like as not Stafford's orderin' us home for an accountin', now the two years is passed."

The eyes which looked into Israel's hardened. "Think you I'll lose months carrying Stafford's prize money to Newport? He can wait."

Israel chuckled. "'Twas in the papers."

Over Jocelyn's high-cheekboned face spread a dry smile. "We'll have to break our word with Mr. Stafford. But when he learns what we took for him by hard fighting, he'll forgive us. Trust his money-grubbing soul for that!"

At the Naval Office there were two letters. One bore the familiar script of Trelawney; the other was from Stafford. Hugh read the latter's letter aloud to Israel. It was not pleasant reading. Following the demand that Hugh return at once for an accounting, it stated that there were rumors adrift to the effect that his conduct had been irregular. And Stafford feared for his prize money. It might be seized by the authorities.

"What think you of that, Israel?" Jocelyn's face was flint-hard as he awaited Brandy's answer.

Israel scratched his mop of hair, while his mouth worked industriously with the problem. Then he spat out: "Rot that Quaker's bones! There's more behind this. The friendship betwixt you and Governor Russell is well known. You have his commission and good will. I name no one but that conger eel, Elisha Sanford, as the man. And his brother, Peleg, has spread it in Boston and Newport."

Hugh nodded. "Doubtless Sanford has painted us black while we were after the French in the Windward Passage," he replied, and opened Trelawney's letter. It read:

My dear Hugh:

No word from You since Scarlett met you last winter and we are in despair. If this finds you Living, in God's name send us word by different ships that it may reach us. All here are well but mourning You. Stafford is making a great ado about Your not coming Home. Ignore him. He is a slick Quaker and has thought for Naught but the Shillings.

We devoutly hope that no Harm has Come to You and that You will return soon with that Fortune. Content and Tom are Well but sadly Missing You as do we all and send our best love. We are Very Proud of You. Come Home soon. God Keep you!

DICK

Two weeks later, a battered ship, followed by a big, black sloop, entered the long, narrow harbor of St. Johns, Antigua, capital of the Leeward Islands. The ship carried only her courses, topsails, and a jib, for her mizzentopmast was gone and top hamper badly damaged. Her bulwarks were stove by cannon shot, and poop rails carried away. Passing through the narrow entrance to the long harbor, the ship and sloop saluted the batteries on rocky Rat Island, over which flew the red English ensign. In the distance the white houses of St. Johns crawled from the wharves up over the low hill, where a white government house, surrounded by hedges of limes and pomegranate, stood among cabbage and coconut palms.

The battered ship with its accompanying sloop fired a second salute from their swivels, and dropped anchor off the Naval Office on the stone government wharf. Aroused from their siestas, townspeople came running to the shore. Landing at the wharf in his skiff, Captain Hugh Jocelyn was met by a group of excited men.

"Name of God, Captain Jocelyn," greeted a bulky, red-faced Englishman in a white linen uniform heavy with gold braid, "what have you brought us!"

"A wine ship, Governor Codrington, the *Bonneaventure*, out of Bordeaux, for Fort-de-France. We took her off Marie Galante from under the nose of a French sloop of war, twenty guns. Already I had a prize crew aboard her when the Frenchman appeared, and we coaxed him to wind'ard, lost him off Grande-Terre, and picked up our prize again at Redonda."

The group of officials stared open-mouthed at the speaker.

"That was clever work, Captain," laughed Codrington, clapping Hugh on the back. "But we expect it from Captain Jocelyn! That deserves a toast in French wine which, by God's grace! you've brought us. But lacking that, at present 'twill be rum and lime, for the war has dealt hard with us. Will you join us at the Naval Office?"

The group left the blazing sun and entered the cool shade of the white stone building, where a black boy was busy mixing coconut milk, lime, sugar, and rum in tall pewter mugs. Hugh was introduced to Captain Edwards, Collector and Surveyor of the port, and to two officers, Colonel Swift, a yellow-faced regular, already wearing the indelible stamp which drink and the climate etched on the faces of those who stayed on the Islands too long, and his young aide-de-camp, fresh from England, Sir Wilfred Strait.

The company enthusiastically drank Hugh's health, for the French privateers had deprived the Leeward Islands of luxuries and a wine ship was a godsend.

"What else besides wine does she carry?" asked Codrington, smacking his thick lips in anticipation of the coming treat.

Hugh had met the great man once before, and the Vice-Admiral had then vividly recalled to his mind Tom Paine's warning: "In the West Indy, every governor has an itching palm and no gratitude or conscience." Jocelyn answered, "There are brandy, olives, figs, and many bales of silk, Governor."

Codrington's heavily pouched eyes lit as his fat face expanded. "Wine—brandy—silk! What a cargo! 'Twill bring a handsome sum from the rich planters on condemnation. Captain Jocelyn, you're a seaman after my own heart. Why send your prizes into Barbadoes when you've good friends here?"

"With French ships of war scouring the seas for us, our prize crews must make for the nearest English port or be taken."

"Yes, I know, but you've been most successful, they tell me. Russell, down at Barbadoes, has been good to you, but I could be even more useful."

There was a subtle suggestion, an inference in the remark, which set Hugh to thinking. "Governor Russell is my friend. I sail under his commission."

The red-lidded eyes in the florid face of the Vice-Admiral lingered suggestively on the speaker. Hugh caught Colonel Swift's oblique look at the Collector of Customs. What had he fallen into in Antigua?

As there was much to do before the condemnation of the prize, Hugh presented his papers and those of the captured ship, made arrangements for the taking over of the crew, then left, to have Israel warp the *Bonneaventure* into a wharf where her cargo could be surveyed and set out for the "vendue." Later he sat with Israel and Jeremy Potts, his lieutenant, in the cabin of the *Flying Fish*.

"Israel," he said, "I like not the look of things."

Brandy frowned. "You mean you smelt somethin' ashore today?"

"I heard nothing but I felt it. There are itching palms in Antigua."

"Where are they not in these slimy islands?"

"Jeremy," Hugh turned to his strapping second in command, whose freckled face beneath his mop of red hair was grave, "I want you to learn the strength of the Rat Island batteries, in men and guns; what shape they're in, and how commanded. This Colonel Swift appears to me a man half dead from drink and the climate. I doubt he's a good officer."

"You think we'll have trouble getting our prize money after the sale?" asked the surprised Potts.

Hugh nodded. "Row down there for a social call on the fort and use your eyes. Mark the size of the guns and the number, and the look of the men."

Two days later the *Bonneaventure* was condemned by the prize court and she and her rich cargo of wine and silk eagerly bought by the merchants and rich planters of the island. When the figures from the "vendue" were assembled by the clerk, the total, after port and Crown charges, came to eight thousand pounds. As they sat at a table in the Naval Office, Hugh watched the color deepen in the Governor's florid face, while his fat fingers nursed his chin and his pouched eyes half closed in thought when Edwards announced the amount of the proceeds.

Then, with a smile, Codrington turned to the privateersman. "Name of God, Captain Jocelyn, a handsome day's work for your sloop, and she but a fortnight out of Barbadoes! A tidy fortune you'll carry to Newport when the war's ended."

There was a glint in Jocelyn's blue eyes and his face stiffened. "We've fought hard for it, Governor, from the Bahamas to Barbadoes, and saved much English shipping. You now drink wine in Antigua for the first time in a year."

"And tonight you'll join me at Government House to test some of that wine?"

"'Twould pleasure me, sir," answered Hugh, deciding to await the outcome of the dinner before attempting a settlement with the Naval Office.

He returned to the sloop and called Jeremy and Israel. "The sale brought eight thousand pounds," he announced, "but if I know men, Codrington's set to make me a proposition tonight after he's fed me sufficient wine and softened me for the slaughter. He never intends to pay us our full share of the prize money. Now, Jeremy, you say there are twenty demiculverins mounted on carriages in the earthworks and some 24-pounders in the stone batteries on Rat Island?"

"Ay, but the men appear none too happy, and half are sick. Still they could easily sink the sloop did we try to run past them, for the range is short."

"A shot from a culverin on our water line would be our ruin," growled Israel.

"Here are the orders," said Hugh, ignoring the comments. He gave detailed instructions to his mate, then finished with: "Israel and two men will stand by with the skiff off the Naval Office. Sharpen your ears for my hail, Israel; 'twill not be early."

Brandy and Jeremy listened with bulging eyes. "Rot my guts! What—what think you will fall out?" demanded Israel. "You talk like trouble at the Government House! Christ's blood, lad, trouble with the Governor makes us proscribed men, no less! How can we fight him?"

"We fight no one! 'Tis a matter of one man's greed."

"But he might arrest you if there's trouble," objected Jeremy. "If he throws you in his jail, we're comin' after you."

Hugh's eyes glittered. "He'll not arrest me—he's no fool, this fat Governor Codrington!"

"Lad, I like not the smell of all this," snorted Israel. "If you have trouble over the prize money, he'll name us pirates. Better to leave some of our gold in his filthy palm than be named pirates by the Vice-Admiral of the Leewards!"

Hugh's bronzed face tightened as he leaned toward his friends and bit off through stiff lips: "No governor will touch our prize money if I can stop it! And I think I can—tonight."

In his anxiety, Brandy stumped back and forth in the low cabin. "Hugh, was it in fair fight and I be with you—but what can we do if they take you? We may not fire on Englishmen."

"You've got your orders—both of you. Send me that French prisoner we hid in the hold."

Presently a young Frenchman, not a sailor, entered the cabin. "M'sieu' Dupree, I promised to set you ashore on Guadeloupe if you would write me a letter," Hugh began.

"Yes, M'sieu' le capitaine!"

"Sit here and write what I tell you!"

The Frenchman sat down at the hanging table, dipped quill in inkhorn, and wrote as Hugh dictated.

"Sign it Honoré St. Jean, Captain of His Catholic Majesty's Ship *Amethyste*!"

The young prisoner looked up at Hugh with a quizzical expression. "M'sieu' le capitaine is clever," he said. "He would deceive someone?"

"We will land you as I agreed on Guadeloupe," said Hugh. Taking the paper, he went ashore.

76

IT was a gay dinner party that night at the white Government House, set within its pomegranate hedges, where the air was heavy with the fragrance of passion flowers and carnation trees. Colonel Swift and his young aide lost no time in starting on the champagne from the captured *Bonneaventure*. Because of the war, no wine had reached the thirsty throats of the officers of the garrison in months, and they made the most of it. But it soon appeared to the suspicious master of the *Flying Fish* that the bibulous Swift was overplaying the Governor's hand. In his endeavor to lead Jocelyn into a drinking bout, he himself was fast growing whittled.

They talked of the long war with the French and of Hugh's taking, the previous year, the ship sent to capture him.

"Captain," said the Colonel, rising unsteadily and raising his cup, "I drink to your future success. Hereafter, bring your prizes into Antigua, and no questions'll be—"

Codrington cut the speaker short with a loud cough. The Governor scowled darkly as the Colonel slumped back into his seat with a fatuous grin and finished, weakly: "Bring us more of this good wine, Captain Jocelyn!"

Hugh grinned at Swift's embarrassment and relieved the situation with, "Colonel, you do not agree with Gonzalo in Will Shakespeare's 'Tempest' when he cries, 'I would fain die a dry death!'"

There was a roar of laughter from Codrington. "Well spoke, Captain Jocelyn! A wet death for Swift! I see you know your poets."

Then Hugh flung back as he held the Vice-Admiral's pouched eyes. "I fear the Colonel would 'hoist himself with his own petard.'"

For an instant Codrington's eyes flickered as he caught Hugh's meaning. Swift's yellow face filled with blood. "How now, Captain!" he rasped. "You speak in riddles!"

Codrington abruptly raised his hand. "Take Captain Strait to the game room, Colonel, and learn if your luck with the dice is better than your knowledge of the poets."

The whittled officers left Codrington with his guest. Hugh's muscles tightened as he waited. The Governor was about to show his hand.

"Captain Jocelyn," he began, clapping his empty cup on the mahogany table, "'tis a great pleasure to meet a man of parts, one who knows his poets and the Latin and history as do you. One scarce expects to find it in privateersmen. You say you are not of Oxford or

Cambridge?"

"No, I owe it all to a friend who was of Cambridge."

"What a friend!" Codrington's red eyes stared into the stiff face of the privateersman. He leaned forward and added, "I, also, could be a friend to you—a friend most useful to one of your profession."

It was coming. "My profession is an honorable one. Without us, you would have been taken by the French, here in Antigua, for they are very near."

"You forget our fort. No ships can pass it."

Hugh smiled. "As yet they have not tried but soon will."

"Nonsense! And as for the privateers, though useful, they must depend on our prize courts for a living, and that's what I'd speak of now."

Hugh took the bull by the horns. "I wish to sail tomorrow. I have a rendezvous with two New England craft. Will you instruct the Naval Office to make payment of the prize money in the morning?"

Codrington's heavy features shaped an insinuating smile as he shook his head. "I fear tomorrow is too early for a settlement, Captain."

"Why?"

"Because we have not yet agreed on terms."

"On terms?" In simulation of shocked surprise, Hugh's brows lifted as he glared at the other. "What terms are there but the legal crown charges and port costs?"

"Captain, you disappoint me!" sighed Codrington. "I mistook you for a man of brains. I've offered you my friendship and—a—aid. We could be most useful to each other in this war."

"You mean, then, Governor, that you wish a share in the prize money?"

Codrington's eyes hardened. "I mean just that, in return for my issuing you full clearance and proper papers. Otherwise, you might—"

"You know this is contrary to English law?"

Codrington brushed the protest aside with a laugh and a wave of his heavy hand. "Captain, do you realize that word has already gone to Boston from Barbadoes that your conduct was most irregular last year—in fact, piratical, and that your arrest has been ordered on your return? That added to my own report to the crown officers might make it difficult for you to hold the fortune you hope to take home—in fact, it might make it impossible for you to keep a rope from your neck."

Hugh laughed icily as the Governor closely watched the effect of his words. The evening was, indeed, proving interesting. "Governor Russell has already cleared me in reports to the crown," he answered. "But, Governor, what are your suggestions as to an understanding between you and me?"

"To further our friendship and fix the terms of distribution of all prize money in the future, I will see you paid four thousand pounds tomorrow morning, Captain. I will issue you a commission which you'll find most useful. Bring your prizes here, of any nature, and no question of flag will be raised."

"And if I refuse that offer?"

Codrington shrugged his heavy shoulders. "Then you lose your sloop, your prize money, and when you are tried for piracy, Captain, your neck!"

"I believe you said my sloop, Governor?"

"I did. The guns of the batteries will sink her if she tries to leave!"

"But, Governor, she has already left."

"Left? How mean you? She lies off the wharf!"

"No, Governor Codrington, she now lies anchored outside. She passed the batteries this evening, with her sweeps wrapped, for there's been no firing, and your foxed Colonel Swift drooling in the next room over the dice and wine has, indeed, served you well."

So purple grew Codrington's face that Hugh feared he would burst from shock. "You lie!" gasped the great man. Then he got control of himself and sneered, "But Captain Jocelyn and eight thousand pounds of prize money are still in St. Johns, where we have a stout prison."

"Yes, Governor, but not for long. I've been looking over your batteries on Rat Island. With half the men sick and discipline gone, under your able commander in the next room, St. Johns will be an easy morsel for French ships of war to swallow."

"French ships? How mean you?"

"You might read this—or have it read if French is foreign to you." Hugh took a folded paper from his pocket and handed it to the other.

"Where came this from?"

"I found it on a passenger in a shallop we took off Guadeloupe. He was carrying the message to a French ship of war off Grande-Terre."

The stunned Codrington called to the gamesters in the next room. "Captain Strait, you speak French—come and read this!"

Strait appeared, walking uncertainly, followed by Swift.

"Can you see to read, you whittled dolt?" demanded Codrington, his former calm and assurance gone. "Christ's blood! Stand by the candles here and read it us."

Sir Wilfred Strait looked stupidly at Codrington and Hugh; then took the letter and blinked over it, his lips moving slowly as he deciphered the French script. The color left his flushed face. "Yes, sir, I can—read it! 'Tis most astounding!"

"Name of God, read it then! What's in it?"

"Bad news! Bad news!" cried the frightened Strait. He read in a broken voice:

Count Louis de Brisson,
Commander His Catholic Majesty's Ship *St. Nazaire*.

With sloop *Niobe* and ship *Amethyste* I sail from Fort-de-France, Wednesday, six days hence for rendezvous at Redonda rock, and attack on St. Johns. The fort is poorly manned and will be easily reduced. The colony is rich. One of our captured merchant ships with cargo of silk and wine lies there now.

Respectfully and Obediently,
HONORÉ ST. JEAN,
Captain, His Catholic Majesty's Ship Amethyste

Codrington's flushed face turned a sickly yellow. Deep furrows etched themselves between his nose and the corners of his mouth. Beneath his wig sweat burst from his forehead as he stared helplessly at Hugh.

"It seems, Governor," said Hugh, with a dry smile, "that you are about to lose that wine, silk, and prize money to the French."

"And you held this message from me? Why?" demanded the outraged Codrington.

"We discovered it on the Frenchman only today."

"Not an armed ship in the harbor! We have but the batteries to stop them!" bewailed the harassed Governor. "Christ's blood! And you, Colonel Swift, have fifty men sick out of the hundred to man the batteries!"

The hiccuping Swift was swaying back and forth on his heels, unable to grasp the situation. Codrington turned bloodshot eyes to Hugh, who stood, arms folded over his chest, grimly watching the proceeding.

"Antigua will be a rich prize for the French, Governor," Jocelyn said.

"You said you—you were meeting two privateers?" demanded Codrington.

"Yes."

"When?"

"In two days." He paused significantly, then added, "There is just time, Governor."

"You mean you'll aid us?"

"If a pirate may offer a suggestion to a governor, I would advise that you send a messenger to rouse Captain Edwards of the Naval Office, go there with me at once, pay me eight thousand pounds, which I will stow in my skiff which waits for me and join my sloop."

"Yes! Yes! Go on!"

"With the twenty-gun brig and big sloop I'm meeting, I'll find the French and lead them a chase to the south. When we have battered them—and we shall—they'll head into Fort-de-France to repair before they sail for Antigua again, if they ever do. This will give ample time for help to reach you from Nevis and St. Kitts."

Codrington reached and gripped Hugh's hand. "Christ's blood, Captain, 'tis a way out! 'Tis a way out!"

"Then you'll accompany me to the Naval Office, now, and settle my account? My own skiff waits for me at the wharf."

Codrington heaved a deep sigh as his circled eyes measured the man who waited for his answer. "Captain Jocelyn," he said, "you are a brave and resourceful seaman and in position to do me great service. Let us forget what has passed. I will see you paid in full."

Packing off Swift and Strait to their sleeping garrison, Codrington roused the Naval Office, where Hugh's prize money was delivered to him in bags of coin which Israel stowed in the skiff.

"There's one matter yet to settle, Governor," said Hugh. "You spoke of charges against me dispatched to Boston. Will you be so kind as to give me now, in addition to a full clearance, a certificate of character and good conduct in the matter of the condemnation of the *Bonneaventure*?"

Codrington nodded. "'Tis no more than fair," he mumbled, "if you're to fight for us, that you get it." He wrote rapidly with a goose quill on a paper, signed and sanded it, added the great seal of the colony, and handed it with the clearance to Hugh, who read it and placed it in his pocket beside the French letter he had taken from Captain Strait. Then he bade the Vice-Admiral of the Leeward Islands farewell.

"Good luck to you, Captain!" called Codrington, as Hugh's skiff left the wharf. "I'm sending to St. Kitts and Nevis for aid, but I count on you to save Antigua. Remember, I am always your friend!"

"Have no fear, Governor," Hugh replied. "The French will not take you this time."

On his way down the harbor, past the Rat Island batteries where lights blinked and flickered as Swift aroused the garrison, Hugh told Israel his story.

When he had finished, Brandy gasped: "I thought never to be raisin' up such a liar when I took you to nurse! Burn my bones, that French letter you had the lad write, which bubbled Codrington, was a stroke worthy of Henry Morgan! Tom Paine'll be proud of you when he hears."

They reached the anchored sloop and Hugh laughed to find the demiculverins and sakers run out to the ports in their side tackles, the big mainsail shaken from its brails, and Jeremy and the *Flying Fish* ready for whatever might come.

As they left the black smear of Antigua behind them in the murk and headed south, Hugh said to Jeremy and Israel: "The air of Antigua will doubtless be unhealthy for a sloop called the *Flying Fish* if Codrington learns that he was bubbled out of his pretty little scheme by a false letter. We'll give it sea room in the future, but I have his certificate and clearance on the *Bonneaventure* over his name and seal, and he may sing whatever tune that frets him."

§77

FOR two years and a half the *Flying Fish* had patrolled the warm seas, and the bags of gold and silver coin on deposit in the strong room at Government House in Barbadoes had slowly increased in number. Of all the governors and officials with whom Hugh had come in contact in the course of the condemnation of prizes, Russell was the one man who had won his entire confidence. From New Providence, in the Bahamas, to Trinidad, crowding the coast of the Spanish Main, Hugh had met English officials of many stripes—wastrels seeking to retrieve fortunes lost at home; cold-blooded, hard-bitten adventurers hungry for spoils; indolent dolts, whom the rum, women, and climate of the islands were assisting to a short life and a merry one; and a few honest men. But Russell, alone, had won his friendship. It was Russell who had issued his new commission, when the two-year term of the old one of Governor Easton, of Newport, had expired and Hugh had written Stafford refusing to return. And it was Russell who held Hugh's prize money and his will, which left Trelawney a legacy and the rest to Content and Tom.

As the years of his roving had left their indelible imprint on the bronzed features of the young captain, so had they wrought a change in his philosophy. He had sailed from Newport with a heart full of bitterness and revolt, determined at whatever cost to wring a fortune from the war. His hatred of the gentry as a whole, his resentment of their attitude of smug superiority, and his contempt for their unlettered complacency had become an obsession. And the allure of the Indian Ocean had been strong. On clearing Newport he had come near putting it to a vote with his crew as to whether they should head for Bristol and join Kidd. But his sense of responsibility for the lives of the lads who had shipped with him and trusted his leadership had won. And there had been the memory of his last talk with Trelawney. So he had set his course for the Windward Islands, and Israel's battered face carried a smile of relief.

In the ports of the islands he had met and tested many men. And gradually his fierce resentment of the unfairness and injustice which permeated Newport life—and life everywhere, as Trelawney insisted—faded to a more sane point of view. He realized, at length, that he could neither change life nor men, but himself he could mold and adjust to meet whatever faced him. He would cease driving his bow into the head seas of a blow when it was wise to lie to with shortened sail. 'Twould be the fault of Hugh Jocelyn, not of the world, if he failed. And he should not fail.

He had fought the *Flying Fish* from the salt Turks Island fifteen hundred miles south to the shoals of Surinam. The French had learned to respect the big black sloop that could slide to windward like a frigate bird, and whose demiculverins were laid by a peg-legged gunner with an uncanny eye. In Guadeloupe they had honored him by putting a price on his head, calling him pirate. He had become famous. And unless his luck changed, in a year or two his fortune would be made.

It was the second morning out of Antigua, after the Codrington dinner, and Hugh was far on his way to Barbadoes to deposit his prize money in the strong room at Government House. As he leaned against the brass falcon on the poop and watched the loose-footed mainsail fill to the warm caress of the trades, while the sun burst in a golden flame over an indigo sea, he dreamed of fog-hung Cuttyhunk and the wail of the gulls over the smoking Sound. In the distance the violet silhouette of Dominica lifted sheer from a sea now turquoise. A long line of pelican flapped lazily across the hot sky, and hurricane birds drove past in eager pursuit of cayenne tern and the fish they carried. But the dreaming eyes of the privateersman saw a rock-rimmed shore where gray combers burst, and his ears caught the faint, far whistle of swan riding the November wind. Nearer, now, a vast cathedral shape whose spires were mountain peaks, thrust up from the sea, a wrinkled mass of blue and green and gray. But the picture Jocelyn saw was a long white beach buttressed by dunes, capped by waving grasses, while he listened to the piping of yellowlegs and the peep of skittering sandpipers.

With a sigh, he expelled a deep breath and said to the two men at the long stick of the tiller, "A year more, lads, and we head for home!"

The eyes in the tanned faces lighted. "Ay, sir!" one replied. " 'Twill be good to sight old Beaver Tail and set one's teeth into fresh cod or a blue, after three years of these painted bait of flying fish skippin' out there."

Arriving at Barbadoes, Hugh took his prize money at once to Government House for safekeeping. He was frank in talking with Governor Russell about the taking of the *Bonneaventure*, but concerning the trouble at Antigua he maintained a studied silence. And soon the *Flying Fish* put to sea again. Avoiding the Leewards, where a fuming Vice-Admiral would be plotting vengeance if he were as yet aware of the trick played upon him, the sloop pointed for the Mona Passage on a long cruise north.

Early one morning, three months later, the sloop was approaching a great, gray mountain shape whose sheer cliffs lifted almost perpendicularly from the sea.

"St. Croix," Hugh said to Israel, as they watched the vapory bulk of the volcanic island whose topmost peaks were edged with a green glow. " 'Tis a five-hundred-mile run to Barbadoes, and we may sorely need the sloop's speed on the wind, for the French are hunting for us. I dare not risk it without careening her, for her bottom is filthy with weed."

Israel nodded in agreement. "Scrapin' she must have and calkin' of her sprung seams, and I knows just the island, with a narrow cove and a shelvin' sand beach."

"In the Virgins?"

"Ay, not a day's run north of here; near Tortola. Tom Paine careened the *Lady Bess* there twice."

"Can we run in without being seen? We'd lose her if caught in a cove hove over on her beam-ends and the guns ashore."

"What think you our guns would be doin' from the shore if they followed us in?"

"True, but they could ruin her hull with cannon fire and then where would we be?"

"We won't let the pigs pass the narrows! Trust Israel Brandy for that."

The following morning the *Flying Fish* sighted a small island which lifted two smoke-blue, truncated cones of mountains from the sea.

"The cove lies betwixt them two mountains," said Israel, pointing. "The trees grows thick right down to the shore except at the head of that cove, where a sweet sand beach shelves into deep water with nary a rock."

"Could you see the beach from the outside with the sloop on it?" asked the cautious Jeremy.

"That's the beauty of it," said Israel. "The narrows cut in on a slant and a cliff shuts off the view. She can't be seen from the outside."

"How's the water in there?"

Israel scowled. "Tom Paine careened the *Lady Bess* there and she drawed five feet more nor the *Flyin' Fish*."

So, after a careful survey of the flat sea with the glass, Hugh headed the sloop for the distant break between the mist-green mountains around whose truncated summits clouds still hung. She reached the island, and under light sail crept in through the narrows between the cliffs capped by cabbage and coconut palms, and dropped her anchor off the sand beach. As Israel had said, the beach shelved into deep water without rocks or stones to stave the planking of the sloop. Hugh lost no time, for the danger of being caught with a careened boat was very great.

Moving the sloop with the sweeps back to the abrupt shore of the narrows, a whip was rigged from the mast, and the four demiculverins, each weighing more than a ton, were swayed to the cliffs. After them followed the fifteen-hundred-pound sakers and the poop falcons, with racks of shot and powder barrels. Stripped to their brown backs, under Israel's driving the sweating crew, working with axes and bars, soon had the guns, concealed by foliage, in position to rake the entrance to the cove. Then the sloop was rowed to the sand beach and lightened, hove over on her beam-ends by tackles rigged to trees, and the slow process of scraping the weed from her bottom begun. Following that there was oakum to be picked, pitch melted, and the strained seams in her bottom calked. For two days, from daylight to dusk, the crew sweated in the tropic heat, shut off by the hills from the trade wind, while with them, stripped to the waist like the rest, toiled their young captain, Jeremy, and Israel.

The danger which the *Flying Fish* faced was a very real one. If the watchful eyes of an enemy had seen them, from a distance, approaching the island and entering the cove, it would not be long before they would be attacked as easy prey. So Hugh drove his crew to the limit of their strength. On the afternoon of the fourth day the work was nearing completion. Oakum was being picked and calking hammers were rapping on the clean bilges of the careened sloop, while the black smoke of boiling pitch rose from kettles on the shore. Suddenly a gunshot reverberated between the cliffs high above the narrows where a lookout was stationed.

Ordering the rest of his weary men to follow in the longboat, Hugh manned the skiff and started for the battery position where Israel stood guard with a detail. Scrambling up the precipitous shore to the camouflaged guns, he found Brandy talking with the sentry who was reporting.

"There's two galleys in the offing, sir," the sailor announced as Hugh reached them.

"How far away?"

"Pretty far toward that other island. There's little air and they're usin' the sweeps."

Taking his glass, Hugh climbed with the sailor to the shoulder of the cliff. Still miles distant, two long, low craft, with sails set but using their sweeps, were approaching the island. Hugh rejoined Israel and Jeremy at the gun positions. "Call all hands to stand by," he ordered Brandy. "Two galleys are headed this way."

"How are they rigged?"

"Piragua rigged with short masts. They're doubtless French privateers or pirates."

Shortly the crew of the sloop was assembled at the hidden guns. Hugh ran his eyes over the lean faces and sweating brown torsos of his men who for days had worked with little rest. He knew them all so well, these boys from home. They had taken the sloop lying there on the beach in all the symmetry of her long lines through many a hard fight, and they would not lose her now, caught helpless on the shore, while they had the strength to serve a gun or slash with a cutlass.

"We're fair caught aback, men," he said. "A small boat alongshore must have seen us come in and carried them word. They're doubtless pirates, black, brown, and white, but who has forgotten what Tom Paine gave Picard at Block Island!"

"Let 'em come, Captain!" shouted the boatswain, who had fought with Hugh on the *Stede*. "The blacker they come, the louder they yelp when they feel the steel!"

"They'll outnumber us two or three to one," went on Hugh, "try to land and rush the guns. Make every shot tell! Sink them in the narrows! Look at that sloop down there on that beach. Did you ever see anything sweeter? Do you want to take her home to Newport next year, with your prize money? Then don't let them get by!"

There was a hoarse roar of "Ay, ay, Captain! We'll take her home!"

"I know you will. No galley pirates will beat the crew who took the *St. Louis* with cold steel!" Hugh smiled into the eager faces of the gunners, dripping with sweat. In a group with Jeremy stood twenty musketmen, cutlasses and war hatchets at their belts, cool confidence shining in their eyes. "There may be a hundred—two hundred—of these ringed-eared slit-throats who stand between us and home next year. Do we let them pass and take the sloop?"

"No!" The cliffs flanking the narrows tossed back and forth the echoed reply.

Hugh gripped the hand of each man in his crew, then turned to speak to Brandy.

"Draw the loads of No. 2 and No. 3 sakers and load with chopped iron from that barrel!" ordered the master gunner.

With their iron worms, the saker crew drew the loads of round shot and rammed in the scrap iron. Ranged in a line beside them stood the six brass falcons from the poop of the sloop, the shanks of their trunnion crutches braced in the ground and buttressed with logs. The falcons were loaded with cut nails, bullets, and scrap iron.

The sentinel on the cliff above again fired his musket and shortly appeared. "Captain," he panted, "there's another galley, a small one, joined the two! They're a mile offshore headed straight for us!"

The eyes of Hugh and Israel met. "Rot my bones, I misdoubt that'll make close to two hundred of the slimy mustees!" muttered Brandy. "It'll take a heap o' shootin' to stop 'em if they come with a rush in the small boats."

Jocelyn nursed his chin in a hand. Two hundred! Odds of three to one! At sea in the *Flying Fish* he would have laughed at the galleys, for she would have outsailed them and hammered them at will, but if a hundred pirates could make a landing with their small boats—and they doubtless had many—it would be a stark fight with the steel on that steep shore. Suddenly he thought of the remark of Serena Brenton at Hammersmith so long ago. She had said she would like to see men fight against hopeless odds as had the Greeks at Thermopylae. Hugh's eyes glittered as he smiled at the memory. Mistress Serena should be here today!

At last the first of the galleys hove in sight off the entrance to the narrows. She flew the French flag—blue, powdered with yellow lilies. Through his glass Hugh saw that she carried six guns and that her deck was crowded with men. Somewhere near the island there must have been a pirate rendezvous to have brought this horde upon them. Following the first galley came a second, also under sweeps. In the rear followed a third. There was little talking among the sixty men hidden in the lush growth of tamarind and mahogany of the high shore. A tension filled the heavy air. Men heard each other breathe as they waited beside the guns, gripping rammer and crow and musket.

Entering the mouth of the narrows, the leading galley crept slowly on under her sweeps. Then a cheer rose from her decks as her crew discovered the careened sloop. Brandy was busy with the guns. He squatted and sighted each of the four demiculverins and four of the six sakers to bear on the course of the approaching piragua when she came abreast. The two sakers loaded with langrel he was saving for the small boats in tow of the galley. Nearer moved the long, low craft, while the men on shore waited.

At the short range, the plunging fire of the shore guns would be cruel. Hugh stood beside Jeremy and Israel watching the galley, which was now barely moving. Suddenly the blue flag at her masthead was lowered and the red ensign of piracy took its place.

"Christ's blood, look at the slimy rag!" chuckled Israel. "Now they fly their true colors!"

"They can't make out where we are and are worried," said Jeremy. "They see no target for their guns."

"But they'll have one when we fire!" growled Israel.

"There's a big fellow on her poop in a yellow shirt searching the shores with a glass for signs of us," said Hugh. "They smell something."

In the man who stood, stripped to his waist, beside his guns, with baldric slung over a brown shoulder and ax in belt, there was little of the excited boy who had vomited, years ago, at the sight of blood in the fight with Pound. The dread of being maimed was still there, and the desire to live; but the years had given him an iron self-control. He wanted desperately to go on with life, but the ice in his eyes gave little hint of his thoughts. On the lip of success after the years of struggle, his life was doubly dear to him, but the men who had boarded the *St. Louis* at his back would have laughed at the idea of their captain fearing death or mutilation. As he watched the approaching galley he could not help wondering if the years of toil and aspiration under Trelawney's guidance, the hopes and dreams, were to be buried that day in a lonely cove of an island in the warm seas—if Newport was never again to see the black hull of the *Flying Fish* slide into the harbor. A foreboding of disaster, which he had never before felt, hovered in his brain. What had come over him? For an instant the faces of Content and Tom and Trelawney crossed his vision. Then, to his surprise, the dusky eyes of Serena Brenton flamed into his as she said, that day, "I would see men fight when all hope was gone!"

He inhaled a deep breath of the humid air and expelled it through his teeth, then with a shrug of his heavy shoulders returned to the present. Curious of their thoughts, he glanced at the men at his side. The eyes in their taut faces were intently watching the approaching galley.

The craft would shortly be abreast of the concealed guns, and Israel hopped from one to another for a last sight. Squatting behind a demiculverin, he waited until the gun bore on the target, then snarled: "Fire!"

Matches sputtered, powder flared in the vents, red huffs leaped into the green foliage above, and the roar of eight guns filled the entrance to the cove with echoes. Gunners choked and coughed in the acrid fumes which smothered them as they peered with smarting eyes through the smoke.

"Christ's blood! Hulled her for fair!" cried Brandy, as the gunners sponged their pieces.

Hardly two hundred yards distant the shattered galley was alive with shouting men. Shrieks of the wounded drifted to the shore. Then her guns replied blindly at the orange smoke hanging in the timber. Now men were filling the boats she had in tow.

"Load all sakers with chopped iron!" yelled Brandy. "Wait for the boats when they bunch!"

As the galley fired aimlessly at the concealed shore batteries, the sloop's demiculverins belched flame and smoke, and iron shot plowed into the piragua, hurling splintered sweeps and bulwarks into the air. Then four longboats, jammed with a mob of screaming mestees and white men, heads wound with colored kerchiefs, who brandished pikes and cutlasses as they urged on the oarsmen, moved for the shore. Behind them the second galley was firing at the clouds of yellow smoke in the treetops. The boats were within a hundred yards when Israel's voice lifted above the bedlam: "Sakers give 'em hell!"

The six sakers spewed their murderous charges of scrap iron into the approaching boats, and four wooden shells filled with dead and dying drifted helpless. Torn with holes, two filled and sank with their mangled human freight. Then the musketmen on the shore opened on the survivors. Brandy's demiculverins were fast turning the leading galley into kindling, but the following piragua had now got the range of the shore batteries and a round shot plowed into one of the saker carriages, killing two of the crew.

"Watch the last galley!" warned Hugh, as the third boat angled sharply in and approached alongshore, hugging the cliff. "Musketmen stand by at the water's edge!"

The picture had suddenly changed. The muzzles of the guns above could not be depressed to bear on the piragua inching along the bold shore. Crowding her deck, a howling rabble of blacks and mestees waited to land and charge the guns.

Israel's bass rose above the racket. "Stand by to up-end the swivels!"

Frantically men worked to reset the shanks of the trunnion crutches of the falcons in order to depress their muzzles and cover the shore below them. The demiculverins and sakers were steadily pounding the second galley and had already sunk two of her boats loaded with men while her guns searched the shore; but the danger from the galley moving under protection of the cliff along the narrows was great. Her decks were full of men, and if they once reached the shore and rushed the guns, the fight would be bitter. Nearer she came under a hail of slugs from Hugh's musketmen concealed in the scrub. But the task of setting up the falcons to bear on the approaching enemy was trying Israel's soul. The tropical undergrowth which smothered the precipitous shore balked all his efforts. He could not sight the falcons. Shortly the clamoring mob of murderers on the galley's deck would be swarming ashore and on them.

Doggedly the demiculverins and sakers pounded the second galley and the boats she had launched, while Hugh, Jeremy, and Israel fought with the men to reset the swivels. Then a frenzied cheering broke loose in the narrows, and a musketman scrambled up the cliff to the guns. "They're landin', Captain—swarms on 'em!" He panted. "They'll soon be on us!"

Hugh slid down to the water's edge and looked. Not a hundred yards distant in the deep water alongshore the galley was spewing out her deck-load. "Back to the guns, men!" he ordered. "We'll make our stand there!"

He joined the sweating Israel with his gunners. "They're ashore!" he announced. "It's the steel, now!"

But the aroused Israel would not accept defeat. "Stand by, you rumbullion!" he roared. "We'll swing these falcons and rake 'em as they reach us from that brush!"

Smeared with sweat and grime, Israel and his gunners lifted and strained at the three-hundred-pound swivels, swung them into position and braced them with timber, then hacked branches from young tamarinds and concealed them. The curses and yells of the rabble cutting their way along the steep cliff through the tropic undergrowth filled the ears of the men who silently waited. Israel crouched behind the concealed swivels with his gunners. There was wild elation in his eyes as he patted a brass falcon as he would a dog. Outwardly cool but at heart in grave doubt of the outcome, Hugh moved back and forth encouraging his men crouched in the tangle of undergrowth. "Stand by the guns!" he warned. "Don't separate! Watch each other in this thick growth! They'll come with a rush, but when they get the steel they'll cease their caterwauling!"

As the pirates approached, Hugh again felt the premonition of disaster. After their years of success, were his Rhode Island lads to find graves on a nameless island? He glanced at the taut faces around him and the cold blue and gray eyes focused on the forest growth in front. He saw jaw muscles bulge, where teeth ground under the tension, and fingers close on ax helve and cutlass or grip musket barrels while they waited. He was proud of these lads who could face death with fearless eyes. Death! Was this, then, the end of his dreams?

With a yell, the leading pirates broke through the undergrowth and into the cleared gun positions. Seeing no enemy and surprised at the silence, they stopped, peering suspiciously around them. But Israel held the fire of his musketmen and the falcons. More followed, black and brown and French; grotesque, with yellow- and red-bound heads and ringed ears, many faces pitted by smallpox and horribly scarred. When the cleared ground in front of the concealed guns was jammed with men, the falcons and muskets belched flame and smoke and the rabble was cut down as a sickle shears grass. Then the crew of the *Flying Fish* charged, and the pirates were driven off the shoulder of shore. A second rush followed the first, as the galley now lying alongshore at the foot of the cliff spewed out more men. Outnumbered, the crew fought savagely around their guns. At last, led by a wild man with yellow hair, the Rhode Islanders drove the mestees and blacks back to the water's edge where the galley lay. Here, boats from the second galley were also landing to join the battle. Rallying on the shore, the pirates again started up the cliff to overwhelm the men who stood at bay beside their guns.

Then a voice roared: "Lend a hand on this saker!"

With iron crows and six-inch mahogany sticks, men gathered around Israel.

"Come on, you sons o' doxies!" cried the desperate Brandy. "Over with her!"

With the mahogany levers and the crows, they edged and pried the damaged saker to the lip of the cliff. "Over with her!" roared Israel. "Heave, you sons o' drazels!"

Hugh, Jeremy, and the rest lifted till the veins on their necks and arms stood out like whips.

"All together! Heave!" grunted Israel. With a united effort the men at the levers bowed their backs, and plunging down the precipitous cliff tore the fifteen-hundred-pound gun and its carriage, to flatten all in its way. Catapulting through the galley's deck like a stone through glass, it crashed through her bottom, breaking her back. Following the gun bounded boulders and rocks on the heads of the climbing pirates, sweeping them into the water. On the heels of the rocks leaped wild-eyed furies with cutlass and belt-ax. Into the water and down the shore they drove Negro, mestee, and white.

Hugh and Jeremy reached the water as a boat from the second galley was landing. Standing in the stern, a red-kerchiefed ruffian in a yellow shirt brandished a cutlass and screamed in his desperation at the rout of the pirates. Howling, "Ventre du biche! Ventre du biche!" he leaped into the water, following his men. There was a savage fight on the shore. Bringing a mulatto to his knees with a slash of his cutlass and bludgeoning another with a short chop of his ax, Hugh turned his head at a warning cry from Jeremy, to take the spent blow of a cutlass on his left cheekbone. The yellow pirate had a pistol leveled at Hugh's chest when Jeremy's cutlass bit into his head and the pistol exploded into the water. Reeling forward, the pirate pitched into the shallows. Shortly, the fight at the boat was over. The crew had been wiped out by the enraged men who saw their captain's face and chest smeared with blood.

"You hurt bad, Hugh?" cried the anxious Jeremy, examining Hugh's opened cheek.

Hugh worked his jaw under the cut, which bled profusely. "Only a surface cut. I turned my head when you yelled and took the end of a weak slash."

One of the crew appeared with a roll of linen bandage, and Israel and Jeremy, who were only scratched and bruised, wound it about Hugh's head and jaw to close the cut and stop the bleeding.

Filled with water, the broken-backed galley lay on the bottom alongshore. At the entrance to the narrows the last of the pirates were putting off in a longboat, followed by slugs from Hugh's musketmen. Under a few sweeps the battered second galley was retreating seaward, while the dismasted hulk of the leading piragua drifted, abandoned in the cove. The crew of the *Flying Fish* filled the narrows with their cheers. The sloop, lying on her beam-ends on the sand beach, was safe.

On the shore by the sunken galley, where brown and black bodies crushed by the gun and the rocks and slashed with cutlass and belt-ax sprawled in the water and out, the boatswain assembled his men. "Captain," he cried, to their bandaged leader, "the crew of the *Flyin' Fish* will take her home!"

In his relief and joy over the victory and pride in his men, Hugh mumbled through the blood-stained linen which swathed his face, "Name of God, lads, I knew you would!"

Suddenly, Israel, who was running his eye over the dead on the beach, burst out: "Stab me! What's that bobbin' there in the water like a speared shark? Mark you the lack of an ear on the larboard side?" He waded in and turned the dead man over. "Well, I'll be burned!" he gasped. "Look! Look at this!"

Jeremy and Hugh splashed into the water and gazed down at the glazed eyes staring up at them.

"Who done this and robbed me of my right?" fumed Brandy, glaring at the surrounding group. "Mark that missin' ear!"

"You don't mean to say that's—" began Hugh.

"Rot me, none other! So they picked him up, after all, off Guadeloupe!"

"Picard!" exclaimed Hugh.

"Christ's blood!" gasped Jeremy. "Picard, the pirate!"

Standing on peg leg and good foot in the water, resembling, with his shaggy head and hairy torso smeared with powder stain and blood, a man more wild than civilized, Israel bowed gravely to the dead man. "Bon soir, M'sieu' Pekar! I take your ear at Grenada! I meet you polite at Block Island! I could drown you but let you go off Guadeloupe! But, stab my vitals! I now see you dead as a cod in the Virgins! Bon soir, my friend! May you rot in peace and poison the fish!"

§78

A FORTNIGHT later the *Flying Fish* dropped anchor off the shore batteries in Bridgetown, and Hugh prepared to land at the Naval Office, hoping to find mail from home. His wound, stitched by Israel's skillful fingers, had closed and healed, leaving a red welt angling from his left eye to jawbone. More than once after the bandage had been removed, Israel and Jeremy had surprised him examining it in the steel mirror in his cabin. Like Israel, he would carry a scarred face home from the warm seas, and at times the thought stung him to bitterness. Wherever he went, the scar would mark him, as the pits of smallpox marked so many unfortunates. He had never been vain of his looks, had taken them as a matter of course, but buried within him and schooled by hard knocks and the ruthless years, he still carried the sensitiveness of the boy he once was. He would have to grow accustomed to staring eyes—harden himself to curious glances. Then a warmth flowed through him as he thought of the gray-haired woman who waited his return. Content, she'd love him always, scarred face or no.

He was getting into a white linen suit ornamented with large silver buttons, silver buckles at the knees of the breeches and on his shoes, when Jeremy appeared.

"A message from Governor Russell," announced the freckled mate, "just fetched by a skiff from the Naval Office."

Hugh took the sealed note and opened it.

"That was the Brentons' six-gun brig we saw when we came in," went on Jeremy. "Captain Scarlett will have news from home."

Hugh's face lighted, but because of the wound he smiled painfully from one side of his mouth. "News from home! 'Tis months since we've heard, Jeremy."

"Ay, near a year," said the mate, with a sigh. "My maid may have tired waiting."

"Not for you, Jeremy! She'd be a stupid maid who'd not wait for Jeremy Potts."

Jeremy left and Hugh opened the letter and read:

> We saw You come in and were Pleasured to learn you were Safe and Sound. Dame Russell and I hope you will Honor us with your Presence at Dinner at Government House tonight at eight o'clock.
>
>   Your humble and obedient

Gazing into his steel mirror, Hugh wound a white-lawn cravat about his brown neck. The face that looked back at him was high-cheekboned and lean, chiseled boldly as to nose and chin, and weathered by sun and wind. The eyes that stared back at him were the eyes of a man who had fought and suffered. Fine lines were beginning to radiate from their corners, and when he raised his brows, others traced his forehead. His mouth was generous, but it stiffened to a straight line as he considered the red scar that seared his left cheekbone.

"A pretty sight to bring to the Governor's table!" he muttered. "But Dame Russell is like a mother and will not pity me. Name of God, pity I'll not have! They can stare and smirk—I'm man enough to take that. But pity—"

In black periwig and white tropical linen, heavy with gold braid, the ruddy-faced Governor Russell, a man past middle life, with a pair of honest gray eyes, stood at the door of the white Government House to greet the returning privateersman.

"Welcome home, Hugh Jocelyn!" The grip of his extended hand tightened on Hugh's as he noticed the red scar on his guest's face. "You've—you've been in a sea fight! Tell me of it, here, before we join Dame Russell and the others."

Hugh gave his friend a brief account of the desperate battle in the cove. When he had finished, the Governor placed a hand on Hugh's shoulder. "'Tis unbelievable—how you fought them off! But—but don't play your luck too far. We could little endure losing you."

They entered a large reception room, and Hugh bowed over the matronly hand of the Governor's lady. As he straightened, he stared in amazement at a man and a girl who were watching him with broad smiles.

"Joe—Joe Brenton!" cried the delighted Hugh. "And Mistress Serena! Why—"

Joseph Brenton flung his arms about the big privateersman. "Hugh! Bless you! Hugh Jocelyn! I'm so pleasured to find you well and—" Brenton abruptly stopped, reddening to his wig.

Hugh's face, as well, filled with blood at his friend's embarrassment, and he turned to the girl waiting beside her cousin. "Mistress Serena! How dared you brave the war and sail to Barbadoes? The seas are fair dangerous!"

When he straightened from bowing over her hand, the brilliant eyes of the girl steadily met his, ignoring his wound as she smiled up at him. "Captain Jocelyn," she answered, "when bored, a woman may brave anything. I found Newport dull and would not let Joe sail alone."

There was another girl, Mistress Mary Minturn, a planter's daughter, with a simper and a wealth of blond hair, who stared with startled eyes at Hugh's scar as she was introduced, then allowed her languishing gaze to linger on his yellow hair and wide shoulders. A young man in scarlet uniform coat piped with blue, white waistcoat and breeches stepped forward.

"Captain Jocelyn, I believe you've already met Sir Wilfred Strait," said the Governor.

Hugh wondered what was coming. Was Strait about to expose his trick on the Vice-Admiral of the Leewards? Russell would wonder at his silence. His level gaze thrust into Strait's astonished eyes as he said, "Your servant, Captain! And how left you Governor Codrington? Well, I hope."

"Captain Jocelyn!" burst out the other. "But your wound?" Strait's eyes lingered on Jocelyn's scar. "You met the French? We had not heard!"

Governor Russell was studying Hugh with raised brows.

"Yes, we—met the French later," Hugh replied.

"They never attacked us," said Strait. "And we soon got help from Nevis and St. Kitts."

"Captain, that's a tale I must hear from your own lips," said the curious Governor. "You told me nothing when last here of all this; only of bringing in a prize there."

Hugh bowed. "You shall, your Excellency." He was laughing inwardly to learn that Codrington was still in the dark, but he would have to explain his silence to Governor Russell.

"Captain Strait, who is on his way to Trinidad," said Russell, "has told me of your capture of the French message and warning of Governor Codrington. You shouldn't be so modest, Captain Jocelyn. And your meeting with the French—I thought they were pirates who attacked you in the Virgins."

Hugh was thinking hard. "They were French pirates, Governor. We never met the French frigates." He shot an oblique glance at Strait.

Russell took the hint and Hugh turned to Serena, who had failed to conceal from Joe Brenton a startled look of pain as her eyes hovered for an instant on the red cicatrix on Hugh's face. He had never seen her so lovely as she stood, tall and erect, in her yellow lustring frock, with its virago sleeves, which bared her white throat and shoulders, setting off her wealth of dark hair. As she gave him news of Newport and of his family and friends, he sensed an undercurrent of suppressed interest, of warmth, in the girl whose eyes met his so candidly, and yet were so unfathomable. Never before had he felt warmth in Serena Brenton, and he wondered at the change.

The dinner table was heavy with silver trenchers piled with tropic fruits, yellow papaws, avocado pears, juicy mangoes, and aromatic guavas. Following the turtle soup were sweet, lacquered-skinned flying fish, baked dolphin, roasted doves and guinea hen, and chicken turtle baked in their shells, accompanied by vegetables of many kinds. Two blacks kept the glasses filled with malmsey and Canary, Chablis and Burgundy, from a captured French ship. Barbadoes was famous in the colonies for its silversmiths and cabinetmakers, and the great mahogany table and sideboards, with their shining silver, won the admiration of the Brentons.

While Hugh talked with the questioning Joe Brenton of his many cruises and meetings with the French, often, when he glanced across the table, he caught Serena's dark eyes studying him. True to form, Sir Wilfred Strait was speedily drinking himself into a voluble condition, toasting Mistress Minturn and Serena, whose eyes were constantly shifting from his flushed, immature face to that of the bronzed sailor across the table with the cutlass slash across his cheekbone.

At first, so deeply interested was Joe Brenton in Hugh's talk, that his cousin's abandonment of Sir Wilfred to the Barbadoes beauty on his other side passed unnoticed. Then, he studied her curiously. Serena was unusually elated. Challenge flashed from her black eyes as she raised her glass and said: "A toast to Captain Jocelyn! May he attain his heart's desire and soon return to Newport!"

His "heart's desire"! Hugh laughed. What had come over this strange girl? All the old reserve was gone. "'Tis most kind of you, Mistress Serena," he said.

Joe Brenton was full of wonder at the mood which was spurring his cousin on. There was a reckless abandon in her manner that he had never before seen.

"Have you no toast to offer Sir Wilfred?" demanded Dame Russell.

Hugh lifted his glass. "I give you Captain Strait, fearless soldier and judge of good food, good wine, and lovely women!"

Serena's dark eyes danced as they met Hugh's. "I note you did not say 'good women.' Has Captain Strait met none? Fie, Captain, 'tis most embarrassing!"

Strait had no reply and rose unsteadily to his feet. "I count that most kind of you, Captain Jocelyn," he chuckled. He smirked in turn at Mistress Minturn and Serena. "I give you the lovely ladies between whom I sit!"

"Like a thorn between two roses," added Hugh.

"But a thorn is dangerous," laughed Serena. "Now Captain Strait is scarce dangerous; are you, Captain? You'd harm no one!"

Strait gravely shook his head, then scowled. "None but the King's enemies!" he stoutly replied.

The eyes under Governor Russell's lifted brows found Hugh's and he dropped one eyelid.

Fixing him with her ogling blue stare, Mistress Minturn lisped across the table to Hugh, "It would pleasure us, Captain Jocelyn, if you told of this pirate fight when you took that cruel—"

She gasped and broke off short, flushing furiously as Jocelyn's face stiffened. Russell shook his head helplessly at his mortified wife. Then Hugh smiled across the table into Mistress Minturn's crimsoned face and said quietly: "I buried six Newport lads that day and came close to losing the sweetest sloop in the warm seas. The memory is too fresh and too painful. I crave your pardon but cannot speak of it."

There was a momentary hush, then Hugh found himself gazing into Serena Brenton's sympathetic eyes.

At length the dinner party moved out to the paved terrace, where there were a table and chairs. The air was heavy with the scent of jasmine and frangipani. Below them, in the distance, a gibbous moon painted a silver trail across the harbor, where lights glowed along the wharves. Joe was explaining to Hugh how Brenton business demanded that he come to Barbadoes on the heavily armed *Swordfish*, and that he could not dissuade Serena from joining him. Danger from pirates and French privateers, the discomforts of the brig's cabin, her family's objections, seemed only to add to her determination to see the warm seas. Joe carried messages written by Trelawney for Tom and Content, also letters from the Wantons and from the Englishman himself. The latter was worried over his brother, Lord John, whom he had heard from home was gaming and drinking heavily in the dissolute court set.

"And what did Stafford have to say, and my friends the Brinleys and Sanford, at my failure to return in two years?" Hugh asked.

Joe laughed heartily. "They fair filled the town with their talk. You had stolen Stafford's rightful share of the prize money and turned pirate. Sanford and Brinley wrote Dudley and the Deputy Governor at Boston urging your arrest in any English port. Carr Newbury and I had it out at the King's Head. He named you scoundrel and villain and I knocked him down."

Hugh's mouth stiffened. "So I'm rated pirate, am I, in my own home? Some day I'll sail in and jam the words of these fine gentry down their throats!"

Brenton raised a deprecatory hand. "Pay no heed to it, Hugh. Your friends are many; but you did break your contract with Stafford and, Quaker-like, he whines over his investment."

"Yes, I broke my agreement with that pinchpurse and would again, for I cannot lose months in a voyage home and back. The war may end in a year!"

"And you've made a fortune and a name," said Joe, patting Hugh's shoulder. "Lad, I'm happy for that!"

Hugh slowly lifted his glass of Canary and drank before he replied. "Yes, there'll be no more poverty and heartburning if I live and reach home with the sloop, but the Saint Domingue French are strong and the Jamaica English hard pressed. I'm sailing north, shortly, in their service, and that may be the last of the *Flying Fish*."

"No, no! I won't have you say that! We'll welcome you home to Newport some day."

After a time Serena joined the two men. "You have been talking with my cousin long enough, Captain Jocelyn. May a lone female, bored with a whittled captain's twaddle and the kittenish purring of a Barbadoes manslayer, listen to you?"

Hugh studied Serena's dancing eyes, surprised at her mood. He had never before that night seen her gay and effervescent. She seemed a different woman from the one whose reserve had always held him at a distance. There was an undertone of challenge in her manner which puzzled him. Then, instinctively, he turned the scarred side of his face from her as he answered with a bow, "It would pleasure us."

"What has Joe been telling you?" the girl demanded.

"He says that many Newport people are naming me pirate and demand I be hung," he laughed, as Joe left them, to join the Russells.

Serena drew herself up to her full height, and her black eyes flashed. "More are naming you a gallant privateersman who has greatly aided his country!" She spoke with such spirit and sincerity that Hugh was both surprised and touched. There was a personal note in her low-pitched voice, an indefinable tone new to Mistress Brenton.

"You are kind to say that," he replied. Again he turned his scarred cheek from her.

She drew a quick breath and, as if to prevent her words from reaching the ears of the others on the terrace, stood close to him. He was vividly aware of her nearness as he caught the faint fragrance of her hair. "I would say something to you that is very personal, Captain Jocelyn," she began. "It may displease you, but 'tis said in all friendliness."

"Whatever it is 'twill not displease me if said in all friendliness." He smiled down into her upturned face. "Friendliness in Mistress Serena Brenton has been a rarity to Hugh Jocelyn."

For a moment her eyes grew quizzical. Then, with a toss of her head, she smiled as she said, "How proud you were and easily stung to heed the uncivil carriage of a chit of a maid!"

"You forget," he objected, "that the chit of a maid, as you name her, was a Brenton and I but a fisherman and sailor."

"But your shoulders were wide and your courage already proven.

Yet your skin was overthin."

As she talked, standing close to him, away from the others, his eyes moved from where the jet hair rippled from her temples and low forehead, forming a widow's peak, to the white roundness of her throat. She was very lovely, this bewildering girl who had braved the dangers of a sea voyage to Barbadoes—very lovely—and baffling. "Yes, my skin always has been overthin," he agreed, and again conscious of his scarred cheekbone turned it from her.

"It is of that—what you have just done—I wish to speak," she suddenly said. "Why are you so self-conscious? Why, 'tis a badge of courage—a mark of honor! When I talk with you, I do not see your hurt or know it! 'Tis the man I talk with!"

Hugh felt the blood at the roots of his hair. She had shamed him. "Forgive me," he muttered. "I'll try to harden myself to it. Time will callous me."

Her eyes were flicked with pain as she impulsively flung back: "No, I will not forgive you! 'Tis disappointing to see a man of your worth so aware of his looks. 'Tis a womanish trait and unworthy of the man in you! What you have done is so much bigger than how you ever could look! Name of God, don't turn your face when I talk with you!"

Hugh thrilled to her words. "Are you sincere or making play with a defenseless man?" he weakly demanded. "Once you held me beneath the notice of a Brenton."

"You would not understand," she said. "But I wish to be your friend, Captain Jocelyn, and I feel 'tis such a pity to see you so bitter—so proud!" Then she laughed a tantalizing, low laugh, and there was a recklessness in her sloe-black eyes that keenly stirred the man who felt her nearness. Serena Brenton had suddenly turned siren, a woman with allure. "Captain Yellow Hair, the scourge of the French!" she derisively flung at him, with a flash of white teeth, "who fears to face a poor thornback maid but needs must turn his face! Fie!"

Hugh joined the exhilarated Serena in her laughter, then said with a low bow, "I pledge you, after this lessoning from so lovely a teacher, I shall try to forget it."

She suddenly sobered. "What I've said has been in all friendliness. We—we are friends, now, are we not? You've forgiven my moods and uncivil conduct of the past?"

"I have forgotten," said Hugh, "and count it most kind of you to offer your friendship."

"There speaks Trelawney and Joe Brenton's Hugh Jocelyn!" she cried, and taking a glass of Canary from the tray held by a black boy, she clinked it with Hugh's. "To our friendship!" she said, challenge and daring in her fathomless eyes. "Now let's be merry! Already that stupid cherub, Sir Wilfred, is making mad love there in the shadows of that hibiscus to the simpering Minturn. Sit you beside me, sir, on this settee and, like Will Shakespeare's Othello, thrill me with tales of the deeds of Captain Yellow Hair!"

"You mock me, Mistress Serena," laughed Hugh. "Am I as black as the Moor?"

"Scarce as black, but full as dangerous," she countered, as he sat beside her.

Across Hugh's brain flashed the brief suspicion that, after all, the girl who had so often before betwitted him, might even now be bubbling him. Under the mask of her seeming candor and friendliness she might secretly intend to draw him out to talk of himself—only, in the end, to fling his vanity in his face. But no, her eyes and voice had been too honest when she had chided him and offered her friendship. She was baffling and elusive but not shallow and insincere.

The party was drinking much wine, and Hugh wondered if this might be the explanation for her amazing frankness. But he sensed that it was not wine that had stripped the mask from the real Serena Brenton and revealed the truth of her. Furthermore, as he sat beside her on the moonlit terrace and talked, he became keenly conscious of the woman. He could feel the vibrant life in her. His senses responded to a physical magnetism which was insistent and disturbing. There was fire in the lovely Serena Brenton whose heart no man was said to have touched—fire which would be all-consuming when it once flamed.

Gradually, under her subtle questioning and lively interest in his career in the warm seas, she drew him to talk frankly about himself. The wall of reserve which had always stood between them crumbled before the magic of her charm and understanding.

"And your last fight?" Serena was saying, leaning toward the man at her side. "You say 'twas that pirate Picard whom you fought with Captain Paine off Newport? What a strange falling out!"

"Yes, it was strange it was to be Picard who should come so close to writing finis to the *Flying Fish* and burying us all in the Virgin Islands."

He heard the swift catch of her breath as she watched him with parted lips. "You mean—you mean it was as close as that—that you might all have been lost?"

Hugh nodded. "It was as close as that. With the sloop careened, we were caught on shore by three piraguas and over two hundred men while we had less than sixty. I had a strange premonition that day that it was to be finis for Hugh Jocelyn."

"Finis—for Hugh Jocelyn?" he heard her murmur. "But—but you fought—" she exclaimed, "fought when there was small hope, like the

Greeks at Thermopylae—and won!" In the moonlight her face was flushed and her eyes glowed. "You fought—and won!" she cried, and he watched her, amazed at her vehemence.

"When it looked grim for us," Hugh went on, "I even found myself saying aloud: 'Mistress Serena Brenton once said at Hammersmith that she craved to see men fight—fight when all hope was gone! Well, Mistress Serena, you should be here today!'"

The girl's eyes shone as they searched his face. She impulsively touched his hand. It was like a spark in priming powder. "Facing death on that lonely island," she exclaimed, "you—you thought of what a silly maid once said? You thought of me, when—when—" Her eyes misted and her sensitive lower lip quivered. To the man who watched her, gripped in an iron self-control, she seemed with difficulty to beat back a wave of emotion, then said huskily, "Thank you, Captain Jocelyn!"

For a space she gazed down at the sleeping harbor, her dusky head in silhouette. His eyes traced the line of her straight nose, the short upper lip, and the firm roundness of her chin. Her low-cut yellow frock bared a generous sweep of white shoulder, and her breast lifted as she breathed. It was a lovely picture she made in that half light. Her physical charm and appeal plagued him as food a starving man. Suddenly the consciousness of the gulf which separated them cooled his mood. He was mad! And she had offered him her friendship—the friendship of Mistress Brenton for Hugh Jocelyn, privateersman and foster son of a fisherman. That was, indeed, more than generous.

The evening climaxed in a round of merriment in which the mildly whittled Joe Brenton was the moving spirit, encouraged by Serena, in whom the wine seemed only to have aroused a spirited abandon. A spinet was brought to the terrace, and she delighted the company with old English songs sung in an untrained but rich contralto, while Hugh marveled at the swift change of her moods. The song which he was long to remember as he sailed the warm seas was Ben Jonson's verses "To Celia," "Drink to me only with thine eyes." Serena's gaze more than once lifted from the spinet to the big privateersman sitting on the settee in the shadows, and as she ended the song, she smiled at the man in white leaning toward her. For an instant he felt the beat of his heart. Then, with a shrug, he realized that it was the wine and the moon.

As he bade her good-night, her eyes held his with a look he could not fathom when she said, "Come home to Newport soon, Captain Hugh Jocelyn!" They did not again during the coming days recapture the mood of the poignant moments on the moonlit terrace of Government House.

Before his sloop slipped out of Carlyle Bay in search of the

French, Hugh entrusted Joe with letters for his family and friends, and said his farewell. But in Serena's eyes he found the old enigma as she wished him Godspeed.

At the Naval Office, before Hugh left, Governor Russell was extremely curious to hear the details of the affair at Antigua. The cautious Hugh corroborated Captain Strait's account of the capture of the French message with warning of the coming attack. But he stated that he never saw the French ships after leaving St. Johns. Adroitly avoiding Russell's cross-examination, patently prompted by the Governor's well-founded suspicion that all had not been told, Hugh maintained a strict silence as to Codrington's attempt to take half his prize money. Unless the avaricious Vice-Admiral of the Leewards some day showed his teeth and repudiated the clearance and certificate of character he had given him, Hugh had decided to forget the incident, for it was fraught with danger. To have revealed the truth of the matter to Russell and exposed Codrington would only have embarrassed his good friend and led to nothing. For Codrington was the King's man in the Leewards and beyond the challenge of a mere privateersman.

§79

A MONTH later the *Flying Fish* convoyed a French prize into Bridgetown. At the Naval Office Hugh found a letter from Trelawney. It read:

DEAR LAD:

All here are Well and Praying for your Return. I hope you saw Joe and Serena. We are fair fretting for Their return with News of you. Strange maid! She would go though her mother Raved. Bad news reached me but lately from Home. My brother, while Foxed, deeded his Barbadoes plantation to that rake-hell, Sir George Whitehead, to pay his losses at cards. So great was his Remorse when he realized what he had done that he Shot himself. With the Barbadoes property gone there is little left as the "Towers" is heavily Encumbered.

Sir George Whitehead is sending a lawyer, as agent, to record the Deed and take over the Property. For safety he sails in a Dutch ship touching at Bristol early in May and should arrive in Barbadoes in July. But there's Nothing to be done, Hugh, nothing. Without the Barbadoes property

John left me penniless. Do come Home soon, lad. We all need you. Content sends her prayers for you.

DICK

Hugh read and reread the letter. Dick, left without a penny by his wastrel brother! As he walked out of the Naval Office he muttered: "But there is something to be done! Christ's blood! There must be! Between Israel Brandy and Hugh Jocelyn there will be!"

Outside the office he met Governor Russell. "Hugh, I have a letter from London I wish to read you. It concerns a friend of yours and mine."

The two men repaired to an inner room and Russell read the letter aloud. It was from a mutual friend of his and Trelawney's and stated, as had the latter's letter, that Lord John Trelawney had shot himself after a debauch during which he had deeded his Barbadoes plantation, which was not entailed, to Sir George Whitehead, in payment of large losses at cards. A certain Gideon Rooke, a lawyer and Whitehead's agent, was to take the Dutch brig *Veda* from Bristol, early in May. The writer expressed his regret at the sad state of Lord Trelawney's affairs. It would be an empty baronetcy to which Dick Trelawney, now in New England, would succeed.

Russell looked at Hugh. "'Tis a shame, Captain, for Trelawney's property here is valuable. Now Dick will have little from that spendthrift brother of his."

Hugh scarcely heard the last words. He was thinking. Old Dick Trelawney, bless him, cut off without a penny! Here was something to be done! But what! Then he had an idea. "When the condemnation is settled, Governor, I'm sailing," he said.

"Why not stay a few days with us? You know how we enjoy your company. You have got Dame Russell to reading the poets till she quotes them on all occasions. Were she young, Hugh, I should be jealous."

"My best to Dame Russell, but I must be off, after the vendue. So long as there are prizes to be taken, I must sail. The war may soon be over."

"You have a pretty fortune already in our strong room."

"Remember, I own but half the sloop."

Back on the *Flying Fish*, Hugh called Israel and Jeremy for a conference. After reading the letter from Trelawney he said: "Well, what think you of that, Israel? Cheated Dick of his birthright in a drunken bout—signed away his plantation! Now Dick will not have a penny!"

"Um!" Israel's mouth twitched as he rubbed his bristly chin. "What comes to your mind, Captain?" he demanded, his small eyes twinkling.

"This Dutch brig was to sail early in May. She is due here soon, after touching at Surinam. We sail tonight."

"Sail where?"

"Where think you?"

Jeremy and Israel grinned into each other's faces. "But how do we get that paper from the slimy lawyer when we stop the brig?" demanded Potts. "There's still law in Barbadoes!"

Israel flung a pitying look at the freckled mate. "Jeremy, you be mate and leftenant and a handy man with a cutlass but, stab me, you talk like a bufflehead!"

"Give us your plan, Israel," said Hugh.

"I would sight her off Surinam, send a shot athwart her bow, heave her to, board her, and take that dogfish of a lawyer with his paper. That paper never reaches Barbadoes."

"And put our friend Governor Russell at his wit's end to keep us out of jail," laughed Hugh. " 'Twould be little less than piracy."

"What's your plan, then?"

"Well, it seems to me," said Hugh, "that we might chance to be cruising somewhere off Surinam seeking the French, and sighting a brig flying the Dutch colors, might suspect her of being a Frenchman misusing the Dutch flag. We stop her to learn the truth and find an English passenger who would prefer a quick run to Barbadoes with us than a long wait at Surinam."

"Ay, but what about the papers?"

Hugh laughed. "Leave the rest to me."

For a fortnight the *Flying Fish* patrolled the low coast of Surinam. Then one day the lookout in the crosstrees hailed the poop.

"Ho, the deck! Tops'ils of a big brig off the weather bow!"

Hugh raised his glasses. " 'Tis the Dutch flag, Israel, it may be our brig. Luff!" he ordered the men at the tiller. The sloop edged into the wind and headed for the distant sail.

Her big courses and topsails bellying, the brig drove down on the close-hauled sloop. As the *Flying Fish* carried the royal jack in her fore rigging and the white flag of New England at her peak, the Dutchman held to her course notwithstanding the suspicious action of the sloop. When the *Flying Fish* was within easy range, Israel fired a shot across her bow and the brig hove to. Hugh boarded her with two men in a light skiff he carried housed on the deck. As he threw his leg over the rail at the main chains, he was met by an irate Dutch master.

"Vat is dis, you do? Ve are Dutch brig *Veda* out of Amsterdam und Bristol! You are privateer! Vy you stop me?"

Hugh bowed. "Captain, the French have been flying the Dutch flag in these seas, as you know. A look at your papers is all I wish."

Hugh glanced about the deck at the gaping Dutch crew, then his eyes lit with satisfaction as they rested on a tall figure at the poop rail listening to the talk. Ah, Gideon Rooke! My man!

He accompanied the sputtering Dutch master to his cabin and went through the motions of examining the ship's papers, then apologized profusely for his interference with the voyage. As the Dutchman cooled off under the unusual politeness of a privateer captain, and he and Hugh were pledging the friendship of their respective countries in a glass of rum, the tall lawyer appeared.

"Your men tell me you're out of Barbadoes," he began. "I am Gideon Rooke, solicitor and agent of Sir John Whitehead, London, and bound for Barbadoes."

"Your servant, Mr. Rooke," said Hugh. "We are on our way to Barbadoes now."

The lawyer glanced at the Dutch master. "I could save much time if Captain Jocelyn would take a passenger."

"'Twould be a pleasure to favor you, Mr. Rooke. We'll land you in Bridgetown in two days."

"Yah! Dot ees de best for you," agreed the Dutch master. "Vid us you vill be t'ree veek before you see Barbadoes."

The lawyer's pale-blue eyes lit. "'Twill be a great help in the saving of time. My business in Barbadoes is urgent."

"And so is mine," replied Hugh. "We'll stow your chest in my skiff alongside and be off."

Rooke's chest was handed over the side into the skiff, where Hugh's sailors waited at the chains, and they pushed off. A sea was running and the lantern-jawed face of the London lawyer reflected his alarm as, occasionally, water slopped into the light skiff rowed by Hugh's men. Hove to, the sloop had drifted some distance from the brig, and the fearful eyes of the landsman scanned the rough sea with foreboding.

Hugh was studying the profile of the lawyer from the corner of his eye. The tight skin over the cheekbones and the thin, bloodless lips reminded him of the Quaker Stafford, who would take a quarter of the sloop's winnings when they reached Newport—for half the prize money would go to captain and crew, the remainder to the owners. He thought of the toil and danger his men had been through in the three years to win this money for Stafford.

Gideon Rooke could contain his fears no longer as a comber broke at the bow of the skiff and drenched the crew. "Name of God, Captain Jocelyn, shall we be drowned before we reach your sloop?" he gasped.

Hugh looked hard at the stroke oar as he replied, "Have no fear, Mr. Rooke; the boat seems to leak, I admit, but most of the water in her we've shipped over her gunwale."

"'Tis over my ankles already," whined the lawyer. "She's leaking badly."

The floor of the skiff was awash and the water making. The sloop now lay a hundred yards distant and her rails were lined with her crew watching the approaching skiff riding low from the weight of water she carried.

"A short stretch now and we're there," encouraged Hugh, bending over his feet and fumbling under the stern seat. "The sun has opened her seams and she seems to leak under us."

"But the water gains!" whined the lawyer. "She's settling, I tell you, Captain Jocelyn. We're sinking!"

"Can you swim?" asked Hugh of the shivering man beside him.

"Name of God, no! I'll be drowned! I'll be drowned!"

As they approached the sloop the skiff filled rapidly. "I fear we'll have to take to the water, Mr. Rooke," said Hugh, quietly. "Ho, the sloop!" he called. "Lower the longboat! We're sinking!"

"But my chest! Save my chest!" pleaded the lawyer, his arms about Hugh's shoulders as the boat shipped a sea.

"Are your papers in your chest? There's yet time to save them," demanded Hugh.

"No, no! My valuable papers are inside my shirt. Don't let me drown, Captain! Name of God, save me!" cried the terrified Rooke.

So that's where he carries the deed! "Have no fear, Mr. Rooke, I'll take care of you," comforted Hugh as the skiff settled deeper and shipped wave after wave.

As the longboat was lowered, the skiff wallowed to her gunwales and Hugh pushed away from her, holding the head of the frantic Rooke above water with an extended left arm. But, somehow, as the rescuing longboat approached, they both went under. Held in the vise of Hugh's left hand, the choking lawyer was again and again submerged until, exhausted and half-conscious from the water he had swallowed, he lay limp in Hugh's arm when the longboat reached them.

"Roll the water out of him and give him plenty of rum," Hugh ordered the waiting Israel and Jeremy when the skiff's crew reached the deck.

Brandy looked long and hard at the dripping master of the *Flying Fish* as the water ran from his clothes to the deck. "You sure pulled the plug in that skiff's bottom. But I feared she'd never fill. Where's the papers?" he whispered.

"Under his shirt. When the water's out of him, fill him with rum, put him in a bunk, and take his clothes to the galley to dry and—don't forget that shirt!"

Israel's face was split by a grimace. "Christ's blood, it takes smarter nor a London lawyer to bubble you, Hugh Jocelyn!"

"We owed it to Dick," said Hugh, quietly.

"Ay, we owed it to Trelawney."

Changing his clothes, Hugh went to the galley, where he found Israel alone. "Here it is, Captain." Brandy handed Hugh a wet document which Hugh carefully read, although blurred by water. It was the deed to the Barbadoes property of Lord John Trelawney, signed by a scrawled signature, with two witnesses.

Hugh held it over the burning wood on the galley grate and watched it steam, curl, and disappear in char. Then he inhaled a deep breath and said, as he watched the char disintegrate, "It was the least I could do for you, Dick, the very least!"

Hours later, when Rooke had recovered from his immersion and the rum Israel had industriously fed him, he clamored to see Hugh. "Captain Jocelyn, I've been robbed!" he whined. "My dry clothes are here with my shirt, but the valuable document I carried beneath it is gone."

Hugh scowled. "I'll call Gunner Brandy. He took charge of drying your clothes."

Israel appeared and Rooke demanded: "What did you with my shirt and the paper under it when you stripped me?"

Israel's jaw sagged. His small eyes widened in hurt surprise. "A paper? Under your shirt? Why, sir, you had no paper under your shirt and I would know who stripped it off you!"

"You lie!" screamed Rooke. "I carried a valuable deed under my shirt! I'll have you before the Governor at Bridgetown! I'll not be bubbled by a—"

"Belay, there!" Hugh's voice was brittle as ice. "You are a passenger on this sloop. Any more threats and I'll put you in irons."

Rooke silently nursed his wrath, suspiciously eying the two men standing beside the bunk he lay on. "Captain Jocelyn," he said at length, "I made this voyage for one purpose—to carry that deed here. Now it is gone!"

"You're sure that you saw no paper when you carried out his clothes to dry?" Hugh gravely asked Israel.

"There was none! Christ's blood, what would I be doin' hidin' his slimy paper?" protested the indignant boatswain.

"That's enough for me, then. Mr. Rooke, I've never known Bo's'n Brandy to tell an untruth. Your paper must have been lost in the water."

When the *Flying Fish* reached Barbadoes, the ungrateful passenger charged Hugh with taking the deed, and the two men appeared before Governor Russell for a hearing. After the Governor had heard the stories of both parties he said: "Mr. Rooke, no man on the sloop seems to have seen this deed you claim you carried next your body. It must have been left in your chest, which was lost."

But later, when Governor Russell talked with Hugh alone, he said: "Captain, 'tis a most mysterious disappearance. By a strange chance you, a friend of Dick Trelawney, stop a Dutch brig known to be carrying one Rooke, a London lawyer, who is in possession of a deed which would deprive said Trelawney of his inheritance in Barbadoes. Also, it falls out, oddly enough, to as skillful a seaman as Captain Hugh Jocelyn, that his skiff fills within sight of his sloop, thus half drowning his passenger, said Rooke. And, finally, while Rooke's clothes are drying and he half-conscious from water and rum, there disappears the deed he claims to have carried next his skin!"

Russell stopped, and in his gray eyes there was the suspicion of a twinkle. Hugh watched him with a face as cold and devoid of expression as stone. For a space the two friends looked hard into each other's eyes; then Russell went on: "Captain, I have always found you a man of your word. You say you know nothing of this deed. That is sufficient for me. But I should like to add that I envy Dick, now Lord Richard Trelawney, such a friend as you've proved yourself!"

Hugh made no answer. For an interval, the Governor gazed significantly into Hugh's cryptic face. Then he burst into laughter. "Hugh, Hugh Jocelyn," he said, shaking his head and clapping Hugh on the back, "name of God, you're a man to my taste!"

§80

IN FEBRUARY the Brentons carried home the last definite news of Hugh Jocelyn and the *Flying Fish* to reach Newport. After that it was nothing but rumor. On his next voyage, Captain Scarlett heard that Hugh was cruising off Hispaniola and the Windward Passage in the service of Jamaica. He also heard from the Brentons' agent, Elisha Sanford, that Hugh was gravely suspected of piracy, and that Governor Codrington, the Vice-Admiral of the Leeward Islands, had denounced him. But that was all. Months passed, and Content and Tom again walked with fear as they had two years before. From Governor Russell, Trelawney had learned of the safety of his inheritance, but had had no letter regarding it from Hugh. Gradually he, Joe Brenton, and the Wantons began to steel themselves for the news they feared would some day reach Newport.

Then one day, in December, 1697, over the Plymouth Path galloped the tidings that the Treaty of Ryswick had been signed. King William's War was ended. The war whoop of French and Indian raiding parties, bringing torch and tomahawk, torture and slow death along the New England frontiers, would be silenced, and the commerce of the little ports would again become safe from the attacks of privateers. On the Parade in Newport the news was announced with beat of drums and the firing of muskets and cannon. Rejoicing people filled the streets, for the long and bitter struggle between Canada and the English colonies was at an end.

Months passed, but the *Flying Fish* did not return. Joy had gone out of the life of Tom and Content, and of Lord Richard Trelawney, who would not leave Newport. The families of the crew were in mourning, for the war was long over; if Hugh and his men lived, the black hull of the sloop would long since have slid into Newport harbor.

One early spring day of 1698, Joe Brenton and Serena rode from the Brenton town house out to Hammersmith and down along the cliffs to the sea. Enjoying the salt tang of the mellow air, they followed the rocky and broken south shore through Rocky Farm. Passing Price's Neck and the Roaring Bull, slumbering off Cherry Neck, they left the Lily Pond and Spouting Rock and came out on the cliffs, with a view of the long Sachuest beach to the northeast.

"Hugh and I rode here the first time he came to Hammersmith," said Brenton. "I wonder if he'll ever see this lovely shore again."

Serena did not reply. Her dark eyes gazed fixedly at distant Sakonnet Point.

"'Tis a hard wrench for his friends," continued Brenton, "to be forced to lesson ourselves to the loss of him. There was such a richness to his nature. Trelawney says he never met such a fierce courage joined with such a quick mind and sensitive heart."

Still the girl was silent. Brenton glanced at her. Her eyes clung to the blue smear of the distant point. Then he said: "I fear he took that slash in his face overhard. He seemed sensitive about it in Barbadoes."

"Yes," she said, breaking her silence, "he took it overhard. He admitted it to me the night of the dinner, at Government House, and I told him it was beneath him to care."

"But he would care. He had a great pride."

"Yes, he was too proud and too bitter."

"Well, the war is long over and he not back, and I fear we must count him dead."

"Why?" The girl turned on her cousin fiercely. "He may have been captured and mayhap is now a prisoner! 'Tis only rumored he is dead. Why do you lose heart?"

"I am holding on with all the hope I can command. I've not really lost heart. Trelawney and I still hope."

She turned her horse. "Let us go back," she said in muffled tones.

They stopped their horses on the height above Brenton's Reef and gazed seaward.

Out of the haze in the far offing broke the top hamper of a sloop. "How I wish that sloop off there was the *Flying Fish*!" said Brenton. "'Twould be good to be the first to sight her—but that day may never come."

Impulsively the girl turned to her cousin. "I had the strangest dream last night. That was why I wished to come here today."

"What was the dream?"

Her candid gaze courageously clung to his. "I dreamed that Hugh Jocelyn was coming home. I saw his sloop heading in for the East Passage."

"You believe that much in dreams?"

"I was afraid not to come for fear it might come true."

"But if it did, Serena, 'twould mean little to you," he said provocatively.

"At Barbadoes we became friends," she said.

"I was glad of that. You were always oversharp, and fair insulted Hugh when he fetched Desire the parrot."

She did not answer and Brenton went on: "He was my friend and guest, and more than once you went out of your way to hurt him."

"Hurt him?" She turned abruptly on the speaker. "Surely he was man enough to take my betwitting. His shoulders could bear it. He was fair spoiled by his friends."

"'Twas not fair, though," persisted Brenton, "for he thought 'twas his humble birth and poverty and your Brenton blood and station that urged you to goad him."

She turned puzzled eyes on Brenton. "He thought I held myself above him?" she asked, slowly shaking her head. "He thought 'twas his birth and poverty?"

"Yes."

They were about to move on when Brenton again looked long at the distant sloop headed in for the Rhode Island shore. For an instant the sun touched her square topsail and threw her into relief.

"That's a big sloop out there," he said. "I wish I had the telescope."

"You don't mean you're in doubt—that you're wondering?" she asked.

He was shading his eyes with his hand, studying the moving craft. "There's something about her, Serena, something about the look of her, that fair startles me. She sails like—like—"

Serena's horse stood beside Brenton's and she reached and grasped her cousin's arm. "You mean—she looks like the *Flying Fish*?"

"I'll not stir from this point, Serena, until I know!" Brenton's eyes shone with excitement. "Let's dismount! 'Twill not be overlong before we know."

He swung her from her horse and noted the brightness of her eyes, and how tense she seemed.

For a space Brenton paced to-and-fro, casting occasional glances at the approaching craft, which was again veiled in haze. There was little talk between the two. A half-turn of the glass passed as they waited, then the masked sun broke through its curtain and flooded the misty sea. With dropped jaw Brenton gazed hard at the sloop caught in the light. "Name of God, Serena," he cried hoarsely, "'tis the *Flying Fish*! 'Tis Hugh! Hugh Jocelyn's alive!"

Serena gripped her cousin's arm, her anxious eyes on the sloop driving in for the bay. "You're sure? Oh—be sure!" she begged.

For a space Brenton studied the top hamper of the approaching craft. "'Tis she! 'Tis the *Flying Fish* or I'm a Frenchman! 'Tis her big mains'il and fine bows and her slinky way of moving through the water! Name of God, Hugh Jocelyn's come home!"

He cupped his hands as a rest for her foot, seated her in her saddle, then looked back. "She's heading for the West Passage! What's that for? She's not coming into the harbor!"

"His arrest has been ordered from Boston," said the girl. "He may not trust the Naval Office."

"I know!" cried the excited Joe. "I'll wager he's headed for Captain Paine's wharf, near the head of the island. I'm for Tom Stanton and Trelawney to sail over and greet him!"

Leaving Serena at the house, Joe Brenton rode to the King's Head and announced the arrival of the *Flying Fish* to an astonished audience. Then he picked up Trelawney, found Content and Tom Stanton at home, and the overjoyed party were soon on their way in the *Gull* bound for Tom Paine's wharf on Conanicut.

The news spread quickly through the port. Shortly the guns in King's Fort roared. Drawn by the sound of firing, men left shops and warehouses to hurry to the wharves. Up and down Thames Street and north over the Parade went the news: "The *Flying Fish* is home from the West Indy! Hugh Jocelyn has returned!"

But there was no black sloop at anchor in the harbor and men wondered if they had been duped. Then it was learned that she had stood up the West Passage. Captain Jocelyn was taking no chances. The war was long over and he was doubtless bringing home much prize money. Before putting his sloop under the guns of the fort he wished to learn how he would fare with the authorities. Jocelyn had a long head.

So went the talk along Thames Street.

From the door of the Butterfly a fat shape waddled to the end of the wharf to join the gossiping crowd. "God's blood," panted Betsy

Moon, tears standing on her ruddy cheeks, " 'twas a day like this when Israel come home short one leg and his face a mess! God bless him!"

At the sound of gunfire in the harbor a young matron in a spacious house on Spring Street had dispatched a black maid to learn the cause. The maid returned and announced, "Dey says, ma'am, 'tis de *Flyin' Fish* home f'om de Indy Sea!"

The blood slowly left the face of the young woman as her eyes widened in frightened unbelief. "What said you, the *Flying Fish*?" Her voice was thin and broken, and a hand fluttered at her throat. Then with a catch of the breath she seized the maid by the arms. "Say it again!"

"De *Flyin' Fish*!" repeated the black girl, wincing under the pain of the grip and staring into her mistress's stricken face with open-mouthed amazement. "Cap'n Jocelyn's back!"

"Captain Jocelyn—is—back?" murmured the stunned woman.

She turned away with a choked sob. "Name of God, Hugh Jocelyn is back!"

Slowly she crawled upstairs to her bedroom whispering: "Hugh's alive! God be praised! Hugh's alive! . . . Oh, why didn't I wait for him! Why did I let them persuade me! God have pity on me! God help me now!" And Lettice Newbury flung herself face down on her bed.

Standing on the starboard channels of the long black sloop anchored off Paine's wharf on the Conanicut shore, Hugh reached and gathered Content, at the rail of the *Gull* lying alongside, into his arms and kissed her radiant face. "Mother Content! Mother Content!" he murmured to the sobbing woman, while Trelawney and Joe Brenton watched.

The hood fell back from her white hair as her eyes feasted on the face of her boy. "Oh, my lad! My blessed lad! We thought you lost!"

Lifting her and swinging her over the rail into the arms of the chuckling Israel Brandy, who planted a resounding kiss on her cheek, Hugh swung Tom Stanton aboard. "Father Tom! Thank God, I'm home!"

Unable to speak, Stanton wiped his eyes on his sleeve while Brandy wrung his hand, and Hugh, one arm about his shoulder, soothed Content with the other. Then Trelawney reached him, and Brenton, and the Englishman's eyes were blurred with tears as he hugged the young man he had given up as lost. "Welcome home, lad! Welcome home!" was all he could say.

6. Home Is the Sailor

§81

THE EVENING was a busy one at the Stantons', as friends and neighbors dropped in to celebrate Hugh's return. After a talk with Tom Paine, Hugh had left the anchored *Flying Fish* and returned to Newport with his family and friends on the *Sea Gull*. Now presiding at a large wooden bowl of bumbo, made of rum, sugar, nutmeg, and water, Israel Brandy kept the wooden cups of his audience filled, as well as his own capacious stomach. Under the questioning of Stanton, Trelawney, the Wantons, and Benoni Tosh, the imagination of the master gunner rose to startling heights of artistry. Victory wrung from forlorn hopes—miraculous escapes—sea fights and tales of gunnery and cutlass play beyond the belief of man—rolled off Israel's rum-moistened tongue to the amazement of Hugh and the delight of their friends. Before the evening was over, in the master gunner's rum-spurred fancy, the *Flying Fish* had become a miracle of speed and a demon of fighting power, and its yellow-haired master a veritable scourge of the French in the warm seas.

"For all your tall tales, Israel," chuckled William Wanton, taking advantage of a pause while the gunner drained his cup, "I doubt if you met with as stout a fight as on the day when Picard's longboats boarded at Block Island and you slashed that Frenchman's head half off with your cutlass."

Sleeves rolled to the elbows of his great arms and a freshly filled cup in one hand, Israel shook a finger of the other in Wanton's grinning face. "Rot my bones, Captain William," he snorted in disgust, "you saw nought at Block Island to what we did on that Frenchman! You fancy you've seen that lad, there, lay on with cutlass and belt-ax? That day on the *St. Louis* your eyes'd stuck from your head like a pinched tautog's!"

Hugh raised a hand in protest. "Tell them of what Israel Brandy did that day."

"Ay, he did his part, I allow. You see, the *St. Louis* was a twenty-four-gun ship of war, too heavy for our ten; so we dodged her all afternoon like a dolphin dodges a ship's bow, till we had her fore and mizzen masts overside."

"Then you boarded her?" asked John Wanton.

"Ay, we went over her rail and found they still outnumbered us. It was all over her deck we fought. But Newport steel was too much for 'em!"

"Hugh tells me she was full of captured wine and brandy," said Wanton.

Israel grinned at Hugh. "She was—but shortly 'twas us who was full of it. We had tasted no wine in months, and our throats was fish-dry that day."

"That's what made such a stir, your taking a ship of war," said William. "The French put a price on Hugh's head, didn't they?"

"The mustees called him Captain Yaller Hair, and we was hunted from Cuba to the Grenadines. When we went ashore at Barbadoes, the people used to cheer us!" Brandy noisily drained his cup. "And that was proper, for we was savin' their trade."

"And they never caught you, you old eel!" laughed John Wanton.

"John, that sloop fair sailed circles round the French. And in course they had no gunner could shoot with Israel Brandy," said Israel, modestly.

"What was that trouble at Antigua, Hugh?" asked Trelawney. "Boston has it that you defied the Vice-Admiral of the Leeward Islands."

"Like all royal governors, except Russell of Barbadoes, who was my good friend, Codrington had come out to the islands to make his fortune, and carried an itching palm," explained Hugh. "When we took a rich prize, out of Bordeaux, loaded with wine and silk, and brought her into St. Johns, Antigua, for condemnation, he attempted to hold half our prize money, threatening to hang me as a pirate."

"To hang you?"

"No less! But I had foreseen trouble and, luckily, had taken a young Frenchman prisoner, who was most useful. Before the evening was over I had Governor Codrington swallowing his threats and he delivered the money."

"I don't understand, Hugh," replied Trelawney.

"I'll tell it you sometime, Dick," said Jocelyn, guardedly.

"Elisha Sanford wrote that you had been declared an outlaw by Codrington and had turned pirate," said William Wanton.

Hugh's face hardened. "Yes, I know. And I've reported to Joe Brenton that the letters I sent from Jamaica to Sanford to be carried home by Scarlett never reached Captain Scarlett."

Benoni Tosh snorted his anger. "And that, Hugh, I fling in Peleg Sanford's sour face tomorrow!"

"That's why we got no word from you in the last year and thought you dead or a prisoner," said William.

"That is why, for I sent letters to you all."

"Of course you know that Brinley has written Boston accusing you of piracy?"

"Yes. We spent the last of the war with the Jamaica fleet of guard ships and lost touch with Barbadoes. It was then Codrington and Sanford wrote accusing me. Scarlett had had no word from me and had heard rumors. But I have my commission and a certificate from Governor Beeston of Jamaica."

"The strange thing about it all, Hugh," said Trelawney, "is that Carr Newbury is supporting you. Tonight at the King's Head he insisted that your prize money had been got honestly."

Jocelyn turned wintry eyes on his friend. That afternoon, at Conanicut, Trelawney had told him of Lettice's marriage to Newbury but two months before. "How should he know?" Hugh roughly demanded. "He was scarce there!"

The remark was so abrupt and bitter that the Englishman wondered if it were stung pride or if, after all, Hugh had really cared for her.

"You have all needful papers to meet what Sanford and Brinley may charge you with?" demanded Benoni Tosh. "They will have your prize money seized if they can."

"Yes, I have the papers." Hugh's eyes hardened and the scar on his cheek filled with blood. "They'll have to find it first, Benoni. There's but one living man who knows where it's buried and that's Israel. And they have a ten-gun sloop to take before Sanford's itching fingers touch it."

Israel rolled his sleeves back from his huge arms and punctuated the air with his pipe as he roared: "No pimps from the Naval Office will lay slimy hands on that coin! 'Tis well stowed, now!"

"We want no trouble, Hugh," interposed Tosh. "Boston is hard after you and will have you arrested if they can. But we'll handle Judge of Admiralty Sanford, for he dare not try force. If your papers clear you, as you say, so will Governor Cranston and the Council, for I talked with him today. The old grudge Brinley bears you is behind it all."

The party broke up, and that night, after four years of roving, Hugh again slept on his pallet in the loft. As he sat on the stool which stood beside the low bed, his eyes wandered over familiar objects in the dim candlelight—the row of pegs along the massive oak beam of the frame of the house on which hung an old sea doublet and tattered shirts; side by side on the floor stood a pair of wooden-heeled shoes, as if waiting for his return; on a small slab table rested the hornbooks from which Trelawney had taught him his letters and the making of figures, and the first book he had ever owned, a battered copy of some of Shakespeare's plays, given him by the Englishman. The broken lance, with which he had speared his first swordfish, and a short cutlass leaned against the wall. Memories of his boyhood flooded his brain—a boyhood at once bitter and sweet, filled with aspiration and longing, with humiliation and unrest. And now he had come home to the white-haired woman and man who had taken him to their hearts and loved him as their own. He had returned with the fortune he had toiled and fought for, and the old age of those two below would be passed in peace and security.

So Lettice had married Newbury! It seemed incredible. All that fire and beauty wasted on a man whose first thought was money! He recalled their last meeting before she had been packed off to Boston by her family. How handsome she had looked when she savagely replied with her whip to her brother's insult! What a spirit! But on the rare occasions when they had both been in Newport before he sailed on his long cruise he had made no attempt to meet her—had treated her with silence. Why should she not forget Hugh Jocelyn lost in the warm seas! What had a roving privateersman to do with a Brinley! Yet the news of her recent marriage carried a sting he could not fathom. In vain he groped for an answer.

As for himself, there was work to be done when he had been cleared by Governor Cranston and had settled with Stafford. There was the farm on Conanicut he should buy, and the brig he should build for the trade with the Sugar Islands. For himself there was—his brows met as he slowly ran his fingers over his scarred cheek—well, time alone would discover what lay ahead for Hugh Jocelyn. With a sigh he blew out the light.

§82

THE return of the *Flying Fish* from the bourn of lost ships was for days the talk of the taverns. And the port was alive with gossip of the fortune Hugh Jocelyn had wrung from the French through the weight of his cutlass and the round shot from his demiculverins. Already, to the chagrin and against the protests of the new Judge of Admiralty, Peleg Sanford, Hugh's papers proving his legal title to the possession of the chests of gold and silver coin which lay buried on Tom Paine's farm had been passed on and approved by the new governor, Samuel Cranston, and his Council. Although Jahleel Brenton had brought from London the appointment of Sanford as judge of the new admiralty court, before retiring, Walter Clarke had refused to administer to him the oath of office. And Jahleel Brenton, in a desire for more efficient government in the colony, had advised Clarke's impeachment. Thus the struggle between the powerful Quaker element and those desiring a royal governor, or those who, like Brenton, simply advocated a more businesslike administration, grew bitter. And the arrival of Hugh Jocelyn, with large sums of prize money, gave the hostile Sanford and Francis Brinley their opportunity. Notwithstanding his commissions from the royal governors of the islands and the evidence of Hugh's papers, Brinley and Sanford openly accused him of piracy and demanded that Governor Cranston seize his property. But the people laughed while they looked at the harbor where the battle-scarred *Flying Fish* now lay at anchor, the black muzzles of her guns frowning from her open ports and her gun crews under Israel Brandy standing watch.

Said men in the street, "Sanford may whine for the Governor to strip Captain Jocelyn and his Newport lads of the gold they fought for and earned in four years in the warm seas, but who dares board that sloop? Not Sanford, nor Brinley—nor no king's officer!"

Hugh sent word to Stafford that he was ready for an accounting. With a carefully prepared statement of the sloop's four years' cruise, her winnings and expenses, and with certificates and vouchers from the Naval Offices where the prizes and cargoes were sold, he entered the Quaker's office in his warehouse on his wharf. Stafford was all smiles and affability as he extended a bony hand to the bronzed privateersman.

"Welcome home, Captain! We despaired of you more than once. But though you broke your agreement with us and put us in doubt of your intentions, we hear you brought home a handsome profit from the venture."

Hugh looked past the grimacing Quaker to a man who watched him from a chair at the far end of the room, and his face suddenly tightened. "I wish to talk with you privately, Mr. Stafford," he said, meeting the cool stare of the man in the chair with no sign of recognition.

"Ah—Captain Jocelyn—" Stafford coughed, patently embarrassed—"it is necessary to explain—that I—was only the agent—in supplying the funds for the purchase of a half-interest in the sloop."

Hugh gaped at the speaker in amazement. "That was not your money?" He turned to the man in the chair, who watched him through eyes that were too close set, and the truth dawned on him. He had fought and toiled four years to make this man the richer. "So you're the owner of that half-interest, are you?" he demanded of the leering Carr Newbury, who nodded his periwigged head.

"I'm the sole owner now, Captain Jocelyn," said Newbury. "I bought Richard Brinley's share when 'twas reported you were lost."

At the knowledge of the trick played on him by the pair of plotters who had bought into the sloop, Hugh was hot to take this cool Newbury by the throat and strangle him. But he beat back his anger. "So that's the way the land lies? I'm to account to Mr. Carr Newbury!"

"You are. And since you broke your covenant and failed to return in two years and, besides, are named pirate and buccaneer in Boston, I call it generous of me to lodge no complaint at the Naval Office and agree to an accounting."

"I am highly flattered that you reposed such confidence in me." Hot as he was at the situation, Hugh could not check a smile as he contemplated the husband of Lettice Brinley. How could she have been persuaded to marry him? What could have changed her so? "Well," he said, "of course you know that this money may be seized by Judge of Admiralty Sanford and your investment lost, Mr. Newbury?"

Newbury laughed. "I've stoutly maintained that you were no pirate, Captain. You have too much brains to make yourself a proscribed man and to sail into Newport without the proper papers. And I have no fear of Peleg Sanford. Let's to business!"

There seemed no way out. Hugh sat down with the two men and went over his figures. "After deducting all expenses and charges, the total winnings amount to thirty thousand pounds," said Hugh. "Your quarter share, Mr. Newbury, will amount to about seventy-five hundred pounds, a pretty profit on an investment of five hundred pounds."

"Ah!" Newbury expelled his breath with audible satisfaction. His eyes snapped. "I'm pleasured that you refused to come home and remained in the warm seas."

"Now," said Hugh, "there's the matter of your half share in the sloop. I'll not divide the ownership of such a gallant craft with a shilling hunter. I'll pay you exactly what was put into it, five hundred pounds."

Newbury reddened with rage, but the ice-blue eyes which bored into his made him pause. He choked back his anger and said, "Suppose I refuse to sell?"

"If you do, I'll take her out and scuttle her before I'll share her with you! Name of God, she's too sweet a craft for a smuggling Newbury!"

Again the latter went scarlet, but the bronzed sailor who so coolly insulted him could have broken him with his bare hands and Newbury was in no mood to be so mauled. "You are scarce choice with your language," he flung back.

"Why should I be choice with a trickster? I have yet a small score to settle with you!"

Stafford broke in with raised hands. "Gentlemen! Gentlemen! Let us proceed to business!"

So the figures were agreed on subject to a counting of the coin when it should be safe to remove it from where it lay hidden, and Hugh left.

He walked to his skiff, repeating: "To think that we fought to add to this man's moneybags! Had I known—had I known—I'd have found some way to bubble Mr. Carr Newbury! And I'll yet find it!"

One night Hugh sat in Trelawney's lodgings.

"How can I ever repay you, Hugh," said the Englishman, "for what you did for me! At great risk to your reputation and standing with Governor Russell, and to your fortune, you saved the Barbadoes property."

"Francis Russell well guessed what I had done, but he felt as I did—that your brother was swindled while foxed."

"Still, it was a great risk you took for friendship."

"For friendship?" exclaimed Hugh. "'Tis something far bigger and deeper than that! Whatever I am, you made me!"

The Englishman filled his own cup and Hugh's with malmsey brought home by the *Flying Fish*, "Here's to Captain Hugh Jocelyn! Much that I hoped for you has come true. You have your fortune and despite your enemies your worth is known in this port."

"Without your lessoning and care this could never have come to me, Dick. And here I am, with over eighteen thousand pounds and a sloop, if I can hold them from those who'd take them from me. What I want now is a home—a farm—where Tom and Content can spend the rest of their lives in comfort."

"Is that all of home you crave?"

"You mean Tom and Content and my friends are not enough?"

"Yes. With your nature, happiness would never be wholly yours unless shared with a woman."

For a time Hugh was silent. Then he said, "I've been wondering if she told you she was to wed."

"She thought you dead, Hugh. I did not see her for months. But since your return I've seen her, and a sadder or more wistful face a woman never wore."

Hugh frowned. "She was fair sweet and lovely, though willful as a colt." For an interval he examined his cup, then surprised Trelawney with, "Joe tells me his cousin has not wed, though many have asked her."

"She's a strange woman, Mistress Serena Brenton. Her family have long harried her for a confirmed thornback, but she flouts them."

"Likely she thinks these men not high enough of birth or fortune to aspire to a Brenton."

"You mistake her, Hugh. 'Tis no pride of birth with her."

"She's always been so distant with me—except at Barbadoes, when she seemed so changed. Mayhap 'tis her mother's pride in her."

Trelawney shook his head. "You're wrong. There's nothing of her mother in Serena Brenton."

"Nor in Desire. What a woman she's grown! She bade Joe fetch me to see her, and fair smothered me in the hug she gave me. Then she took my hand and told me she was to wed one of the Eastons, and asked my blessing. I told her that I took it hard at being thus jilted, and the child kissed me, vowing I should always be her dear friend."

Trelawney laughed. "I had fear, once, she would eat you alive some day."

"I was near losing my heart to her, she was that sweet and winning." After a pause, "Her sister did not so much as show herself and welcome me home."

"No doubt she was away," offered the Englishman.

As time passed, Trelawney was aware of a strange unrest and discontent in his friend and wondered at the cause. Hugh had come home with the fortune without which he had said life would be empty. And yet he was clearly unhappy. His allusion to Lettice had been disturbing to the solicitous Englishman. As for the girl herself, she was plainly distraught, and with Hugh's return might well become reckless. She was capable of anything. Nothing would check her—husband, family, or public opinion. In his present mood Hugh would meet her halfway. Trelawney shuddered at the thought.

That spring Hugh bought acreage from Tom Paine on Conanicut and planned his house commanding a view of Gould Island and the East Passage, with Newport in the distance. Shortly Content should have a roomy house and a garden as large as she wished, with a white servant and a black man to aid her. And Tom would own a fast sloop with which to fish at his pleasure, for he would fret without a boat.

Then, one morning, in obedience to the royal order, there was a beating of the drum on the Parade, and the bass voice of Benoni Tosh proclaimed that all suspected pirates were to be arrested, and warned all citizens not to harbor any such or receive their goods. The Brinleys, Sanford, and their party again clamored for Hugh's arrest, as having arrived after the peace with foreign gold and silver. But their demands fell on deaf ears. Governor Cranston and his Council were satisfied with Hugh's papers. Following this, letters went to Randolph and Dudley in Boston, and to the new Governor of New England, the Earl of Bellomont, in New York, accusing Hugh and others and denouncing Cranston.

One day, on boarding the sloop, Hugh was handed a letter by his mate, Jeremy Potts. He took the heavily sealed missive to his cabin and looked at the address. Lettice had written him.

She was overrash! Jeremy had told him the letter had been left by a black boy in a skiff. It was her slave, Aaron, who was known, and it was mad of her, for he might have been seen.

Hugh broke the seal and read:

> Oh, what Have I done to Myself? They told Me you were Lost. Hugh, Hugh, how can You forgive me? I must see you. If you would name the Day and Hour you would ride to Dexter's Lane I would be there. Now y^t You live I hate him. Name of God! Hugh Jocelyn, send me writing by Aaron who will return for it tomorrow, Where and When you will meet me. I'm in Torture. Forgive your
>
> LETTICE

Holding the letter in his hand, Hugh stared bleakly through a cabin port. "God help us!" he muttered. "She, a wedded woman! Should this happen and be known, her name would be bandied about Newport and I—how my enemies would rub their hands! God help us!"

When Aaron came in his skiff for the answer, Hugh gave him a note which read:

> You make me very Proud to know y^t the Years have not Washed away your Memory of me. But I will not have You take the Risk you mention. I will not have Your Name on the lips of the Gossips. Wait! I have not Forgot and shall yet find a Way.

He did not sign the note. He was dealing with a woman desperate with remorse who would, if need be, flout her husband and the town. He pitied her from the depths of his heart, but she was a married woman, and all the venom of Carr Newbury and the Brinleys would be loosed if they learned that he had secretly met Lettice. And yet, in his mood, he knew that he would meet her.

§83

ONE day, on Spring Street, Hugh saw a hooded figure picking her way over the rutted highway littered with rubbish swept from houses and muddy from recent rains. There was something familiar in the woman's back, muffled though it was in hood and blue camlet cape. She wore pattens to lift her red-heeled shoes from the mud and filth, and held her skirts high above shapely ankles encased in blue silk stockings.

As Hugh reached her, she turned her head, and he looked into the startled eyes of Serena Brenton. With a "Your servant, Mistress Serena!" he swept off his beaver hat.

"Captain Jocelyn!" Color tinted her cheeks as she gave him her hand in its silk mitt. "Welcome home, Captain Jocelyn! Your friends are overjoyed at your safe return!"

The girl's eyes were cryptic. Hugh instinctively turned his scarred cheek from her and she raised a disapproving finger. The blood drove into his face. "Your pardon! I forgot," he said. "You are kind, Mistress Serena. 'Tis good to be home."

She smiled. "'Tis good to have you home! Cousin Joe is a new man, and Mr. Trelawney—I mean Lord Trelawney—has fairly bloomed with happiness."

"'Tis kind of you to say so."

"Not kind, but true! When you came with Joe to wish Desire happiness, I was not in the house. You may not have known."

"No, I scarce thought you concerned with the return of the *Flying Fish*!"

Patently irritated, she flung back: "That is unworthy of you. You know 'tis untrue. Am I not your friend? Has not Joe told you how we watched her come in that day?"

"He but spoke of sighting us from Brenton's Point."

"I am indeed glad that you returned successful," said the girl, soberly, "and trust that you'll come soon with Cousin Joe to Hammersmith."

"But your mother?"

"My mother?"

"She likely holds me the pirate some make me out and would object to my coming."

Serena laughed, then her face was serious as her candid eyes met his, and he noticed with surprise a wistful twist to the firm mouth. "I hold you no pirate, Captain Jocelyn, as you know, and bid you come."

"'Tis most kind of you," Hugh answered, and with a "Your servant!" left her.

She had been as gracious, as friendly as on that night in Barbadoes. Surely Jahleel Brenton and her mother had not yet succeeded in poisoning her mind or she would not have mentioned coming to Hammersmith with Joe. But there was still that subtle reserve about her which, that night at Government House, in Barbadoes, she had dropped like a cloak when she spoke of his wound and talked of his life in the West Indies. Doubtless she was sorry for him—sorry for a man who was now forced to face life with a scarred face—sorry for the enemies he had made and their desperate attempts to have his hard-won fortune seized. Baffling though she was, there was something rare and fine in her—something which set her apart; for neither her mother nor her uncle could sway her. As Joe said, her mind and her soul were her own. As for her heart, no man had discovered it.

Hugh had not as yet seen Lettice. She had written him twice, and he had warned her that the coming of her boy, Aaron, to the sloop was too dangerous. Then there had been a long silence, while Hugh labored with his problem and his unrest. Most of his days he spent at Conanicut, overseeing the building of his house, barn, and wharf; and many of his nights he slept on the sloop, whose snug cabin contained his books and personal effects and boasted better reading light than he had at the Stantons'.

§84

IT was on a windless, moonlight night in June when Israel, Jeremy, and the crew had gone ashore that Hugh combed his yellow hair, cleaned his teeth with a soft wood stick dipped in salt and charcoal, glanced at his scarred face in his steel mirror, then, with a shrug, sat down to read. To the delight of Trelawney he had picked up a number of volumes of English drama, history, and philosophy in Barbadoes and Jamaica, and spent much time in reading from them. He laid aside a worn copy of Plutarch's *Lives* and opened a volume of the collected plays of Shakespeare and turned to *As You Like It*. It was of *As You Like It* they had talked that day on Dexter's Lane, and she had ridiculed Rosalind's patent disguise. The memory of her abandon started his blood, and he laughed as he recalled her calm exposure of round leg and her demand if he thought it would deceive any but a blind man. How direct and fearless and natural she was, and how reckless of the cost! And knowing her nature, he wondered at her silence, marveled at her following his recent advice. It was little like Lettice Brinley. It seemed that Lettice Newbury was more discreet. Poor Lettice! But she was wedded woman and only courted scandal or worse by writing him, and must have so decided. Yet, in his frame of mind, Hugh wondered if there were not something of fate in it—if some day she would not come to him with her love and he would take it. For he was lonely and unhappy and hungry for affection.

He idly turned the pages of the play and came upon the lines of

Rosalind: "Come, woo me, woo me; for now I am in a holiday humor and like enough to consent. Ah," Hugh repeated, "now, I am in a holiday humor and like enough to consent . . . whatever the cost."

He laid the volume down, lit his pipe, and drifted into reverie. "Now I am in holiday humor," he laughed bitterly. "I risked all and fought four years for fortune, and now—I am in holiday humor—for her." Should he write and meet her somewhere? And what would be the outcome? Surely only scandal and shame for her, for the Newburys held their heads high. And for him? The censure of friends and the satisfaction of his enemies. And yet his urge to hold her again in his arms was overpowering.

He glanced through a cabin port to the still harbor flooded with moonlight. Just what was he going to make of his life? He had come far at twenty-eight, had won fortune, and was going on, alone, adding to what he had, in shipping and trade. But for what? There was no one to share it with, no one to leave it to. And there was Lettice waiting with open arms. That would be life! Divorces were not difficult in the colonies. It could be done.

He was restless and embittered and his problem was baffling. He'd take the skiff and find company at the King's Head. Hugh emerged from the cabin hatch and stood on the poop scowling at the twinkling lights of the town. The anchored shipping showed no riding lights and their masts and spars were silhouetted against the luminous sky. He went to the rail and leaned against the cool brass tube of a falcon while he gazed at the houses on Thames and Spring streets, above which Arnold's windmill thrust two gaunt arms. What a confusion of love and hate, forthright honesty and sly greed, candor and duplicity, those moon-washed roofs sheltered. Yet he loved it, had fought for it, and it was his home. His home, unless they tried to take his fortune and drove him from the colony.

An oar splashed in the shadows off the sloop's quarter, and Hugh heard a low voice. "Hugh! Hugh Jocelyn!"

He went to the opposite rail. A skiff with a cloaked figure in the stern slid alongside. "Hugh, is that you?"

Every nerve in his body tightened as he peered down at the boat. "Ho, the skiff!" he answered. "Who is it?"

"Hugh, are you alone?"

There was no mistaking that rich voice. His blood was afire. "Yes!" he answered thickly. "You are mad, to come here! 'Tis too dangerous!"

There was a low laugh in reply. "Aaron adores me. 'Tis safe!"

"Move up to the chains," he said. " 'Twill be easier."

The skiff moved along the sloop's bilges, and from the chains Hugh reached and lifted the cloaked figure to the channels and swung her over the rail to the deck. He vaulted the rail. Eager arms tightening about his neck and soft lips crushed to his drove all hesitancy from him.

"Oh, my love!" she murmured. "It has been so long—so cruel long!"

They were in the cabin now, and her eyes shone through the slits in the velvet mask which covered her upper face. "Would you know me in this?"

"I'd know you by the fragrance and the sweetness of you! But why did you risk coming here?" he demanded, brushing the hood back from her heavy hair and removing the mask.

For answer, Lettice dropped her cloak, reached and drew his head down to her radiant face. "Because I was fair going mad, Hugh Jocelyn," she murmured. "I could endure it no longer, having you alive and not seeing you! Oh, crush me in your arms—hurt me!"

Her kiss was like the touch of flame. In a surge of passion he lifted her and held her lithe body against his. "I've been so hungry for this," he whispered. Then he suddenly remembered the scar on his cheek. He turned his face that she might see it in the dim candlelight. "You—you do not mind this hideous thing? I thought you'd shrink from it!"

She gave a little laugh. "Shrink from it? Why should I shrink from a wound? It but makes you dearer."

"I was in fear," he said, with relief.

She sat on his knees, and her fingers toyed with his yellow hair. "Tonight I've burned my bridges," she said. " 'Tis too late to repent! We are here, alone, with none to disturb us! Tonight you are mine, Captain Hugh Jocelyn!"

Hugh was trembling with the touch and allure of her. There was no turning back now. It was too late to save this headstrong girl from herself. "Tonight is ours!" he murmured, pushing aside her frock and kissing her throat and shoulder.

"Have no fear for me," she whispered. "Carr has gone to Narragansett to look at land. With him land comes first." She gave a mirthless laugh. "No one knows I'm away from the house, and Aaron would die for me. He's to return and take me back—before dawn."

Hugh smoothed back her rippling chestnut hair and held her burning face between his two hands, while her eyes grew dark as they shone into his. "It seemed a lifetime, Lettice; and how I've longed for you! You thought me dead?"

Her head on his shoulder, she said wistfully: "I gloried in your success and how I mourned you! Oh, how I mourned you in secret, Hugh! But at last I believed them. With you gone, I little cared what happened me."

"I know! I know! But what—will—become of us?"

With a low laugh, she kissed his eyes and mouth and neck. "Forget the future, sweetheart of mine! This night is our own!"

"Yes," he murmured, intoxicated with her fragrance. "Our own!"

They kissed long then she turned with a sigh and her eyes fell on the open volume on the drop table. "What were you reading?"

"Guess!"

She reached from where she sat on his knees, a round arm circling his neck, and picked up the open book. "*As You Like It!*" she cried. "And 'tis marked here! 'Come woo me, woo me, for I'm in a holiday humor and like enough to consent!' And you were thinking of me and Dexter's Lane when you marked these lines?"

"Thinking of you!" he whispered and, gathering her close, his exploring lips found her white throat.

She threw back her head and her languorous eyes smoldered into his. "And we are—in—"

"Holiday humor, Rosalind!"

"In holiday humor," she murmured.

The moon had long since dipped behind Conanicut when the masked and cloaked Lettice left the *Flying Fish* in the skiff. The man who watched from the rail was dizzy with memories of the hours spent with her. Nine years had passed since that day on Dexter's Lane. Nine years they had waited. What an intoxicating creature she was, that woman fading away into the shadows! The memories she had left held him giddy. The intensity of her passion had alarmed him. Visions of white underthings, jeweled garters flashing in the dim candlelight, danced through his brain. He felt again the warmth of her satin flesh and the cloud of her loosed hair in his face. Like the sweep of surf over a bar she had engulfed and overwhelmed him. He was drunk and bewildered, watching the skiff fade into the dusk—drunk with her loving.

And what was to come of it all? She could never stop with one meeting! Nor could he. In her ecstasy she had whispered that she did not fear death now, for she had lived—had shared life with Hugh Jocelyn.

As the east grayed, Hugh stripped and dove into the harbor. The water cooled the fever in his blood. A feeling of doubt, almost of regret, of fear for the future of the girl who had given so lavishly, would not down. Had he played the man that night? Yet to have sent her away would have been too monstrous—too heartbreaking. He could not have so humiliated her, and he could not have been so false to the passion she aroused in him.

Two days later, on Hugh's return to the sloop, Jeremy handed him a letter left by Aaron. It read:

They may Not take it from us now! We have Lived, Hugh Jocelyn! Mr. Trelawney will talk with you. He has something to tell. And I know You will understand.

LETTICE

Hugh read and reread the note. It sounded like a farewell. But why? What could have happened? Had her coming to the sloop been discovered? Sacrifice, renunciation were not in her headstrong nature. There had been no note of doubt or sadness in her talk that night. She had laughed him to scorn when he spoke of the great risk she ran. What was behind it all?

He realized that this affair with Lettice might lead to a scandal which would rock the town. Yet, in his present mood, with his enemies clamoring to have his hard-won fortune seized, he was reckless of the cost.

Was this to be the end? After the years a few mad hours—and then good-by, Lettice? He felt abandoned and cheated. Was life always to be like this? Could there be no happiness for Hugh Jocelyn? And yet he knew that with Lettice there could not be the happiness of which he had dreamed. Still, her appeal was very real. But why was she sending Trelawney to him? What could Dick convey that Lettice could not tell him in person? It was too mysterious and he'd seek out Trelawney at once for the solution.

The following night the two friends sat in the Englishman's lodgings on Coddington Street.

"Hugh, 'tis one of the hardest tasks ever set me—carrying her message," said Trelawney, his dark face reflecting the gravity of his thoughts. "She sent for me and told me that I was the sole person in Newport she could thus talk with—who would understand and who, she hoped, loved both her and you."

"Out with it, Dick! Name of God, what's happened?"

"To begin, strange as it may sound, she told me of going to the sloop."

"What? She told you that? She—she—"

"Hugh, I've never known a woman so outspoken and honest in my life. Some might call it a callous indifference to the niceties. But there's no prudish mincing of matters with her. She has no feminine reluctance to facing embarrassing truth."

"I know! I know! She startles one with her frankness. So she told you she had come to the sloop? She was certain of your friendship, Dick, to tell you that."

"She honored me with her confidence."

"Yes; 'tis like her."

"She said she could not endure seeing you again. She feared she might weaken. She could not bear to face a parting."

Stunned by the shock of the revelation, Hugh stopped pacing the floor and turned on his friend. "Name of God, man, out with it! Don't keep me waiting!"

"Hugh, she came to the sloop that night when fair desperate with the decision she had made."

"Decision?"

"Yes. Carr Newbury goes to Boston, perhaps to London, on business for his father. She is going with him."

"I—I don't understand. You mean that she's resolved to live on with Newbury?" Hugh felt suddenly cold and deserted as he struggled with the import of Trelawney's words.

"She doesn't know as to the future, but for the present she's resolved to leave Newport."

"Why?"

"Because she's a very gallant woman and a wise one. She insists that her father, Sanford, and others are set upon your ruin; that Lord Bellomont comes here, shortly, to inquire into the granting of commissions to pirates and the ignoring of the law by the colony. He swears he will hang someone high before he's through."

"What has that to do with us?"

"Everything. She says if she stays here, she could not keep from meeting you. That would lead only to your hurt, for your enemies have painted you black to Bellomont, and in Boston they name you pirate. She refuses to add to your danger, which, she says, is very real."

"'Tis strange to find one once so reckless now urging discretion," flung back Hugh, bitterly, as he fought with conflicting emotions.

"But you see she understands. She says she could scarce have brought herself to give you up if you had loved her."

"Loved her?"

"Yes, Hugh. She knows. She says if you had loved her you'd have flouted the town and taken her long before you sailed for the warm seas. But you never did. And she is right."

Faced with the stark truth Hugh was silent. At last he said, "So she's going away?"

"Yes. If you loved her, I'd not talk this way. But 'tis a fever of the blood, only. It would not last."

Hugh had no reply. Lettice had gallantly faced the sad reality of their intimacy while he had drugged himself with false hope. "Yes," he said, at last, "she has seen clearer than I."

IT was not without a bitter struggle that Hugh became reconciled to the renunciation of Lettice. He had moods when the urge to see her was almost overwhelming. He had even sent word begging her to see him if only for a last talk and a farewell, but, hard as it must have been, she had courageously clung to her resolve. Her inflexible will, which had formerly permitted no opposition to her slightest caprice, now served her in good stead to buttress her decision. So in the end he bowed to her wishes.

That summer, between trips to New York and Philadelphia with the armed *Flying Fish*, Hugh plunged into the completion of his buildings and the development of his farm on Conanicut. To Boston he took no cargoes, for his appearance there would have meant his arrest. But the sloop was built for speed and fighting ability, and her ten-ton battery, which Hugh refused to dismount, cut heavily into her carrying capacity. She was fighter rather than freighter.

With the arrival in New York of the new royal governor for New York, Massachusetts, and New Hampshire, the enemies of the Rhode Island charter had increased their efforts in appeals to Lord Bellomont, the Board of Trade in London, and the crown, discrediting Governor Cranston and the Rhode Island Assembly. Led by Francis Brinley and Peleg Sanford, newly appointed by the crown Judge of Admiralty, they repeated their demands that the colony be absorbed by Massachusetts under a royal governor. That would mean putting the two royalists once more in the saddle. Charges were openly brought that, since the peace had banned privateering, Rhode Island had become the resort of pirates with the connivance and to the secret enrichment of the authorities. But the doughty and astute Cranston insisted that while individuals may have broken the law, the Rhode Island government was innocent.

One late November night Joe Brenton and his friends sat in the King's Head. Having laid up the *Flying Fish* for the winter and having refused an offer to take an Ellery brig to the Sugar Islands on a joint venture, Hugh was still busy with his farm buildings at Conanicut and with watching the oak ribs of his new brig take shape around the forms in the Wanton yard.

"Rhode Island's in for it," said Brenton, emptying his glass of malmsey. "Lord Bellomont's been raving like a wild man in New York, naming half our merchants smugglers and friends of pirates.

He's picked up some of Tom Tew's men who've reached home from the Indian Ocean and swears he'll hang them all, then come to Rhode Island and hang most of us."

"Rhode Island's now nearer to losing her charter than she was under King James, when Brinley was Chief Justice," bemoaned Arnold.

"Bellomont is shortly coming to reside in Boston as royal governor, and Brinley, Randolph, and Dudley are bringing him here to put us to trial," said Brenton.

With a wintry face, Hugh, who was the most vitally interested of them all, sat in silence.

"The dangerous side of it is," said Trelawney, "there's much truth in Brinley's charges. We know that his unjust attack on Hugh is purely personal and vindictive, and also tied up with his quarrel with Governor Cranston and his Council, who cleared Hugh when he returned. But Bankes and Mayes were commissioned here and sailed with Tew to the Indian Ocean to turn pirates, and others have been since. And we've seen suspicious cargoes condemned and sold on the wharves to the handsome profit of certain merchants."

"True," added Sheffield, "Tom Tew lived here openly before his last cruise, when he was killed, as did Jones and Cutler; and some returned after Tew's death. The town's been full of Arabian sequins and Spanish doubloons as well as silk and calicoes from India."

"There's no doubt the law's been flouted by greedy merchants and shipowners," said Brenton, "but not by the Governor and Assistants to their private profit, as Brinley charges. However, Bellomont's coming to make an example of us, and with Brinley at his ear I fear for Hugh."

Hugh smiled dryly. "You need have no fear for me, Joe," he said. "Before I'll suffer Peleg Sanford's slimy hands to touch one silver shilling I've toiled years for and earned, I'll blow him and his Naval Office off the wharf and head the *Flying Fish* for the Indian Ocean!"

"And make yourself an outlaw, Hugh?" gasped Brenton.

"Yes, and make myself an outlaw!" coolly answered the privateersman as his friends searched his bleak face in astonishment.

"But—but you can't mean you'd defy the government?" demurred Sheffield. "They'd hang you, man!"

Hugh laughed bitterly. "Government? What kind of government had we when Brinley sat under Andros? They put me in the pillory as a boy for standing my ground. Now, with our charter gone and we a part of Massachusetts, with Brinley in the saddle again, if they attempt to ignore my papers and start a search to seize my prize money, I'll man the sloop with my old gun crews and give Newport a farewell they'll long remember."

His startled friends studied the lean face of the man in whose somber eyes lurked the glitter of ice.

"No, no, Hugh! We all stand with you," protested Brenton. "You'll do nothing reckless—you'll not—"

But Hugh calmly interrupted, "Dick, here, has news for you."

"What is it, Dick?" demanded Brenton.

The Englishman's eyes were dismal as he stared into his cup of Canary. Then he raised them to his friends' expectant faces. "I never told you," he began, "that I knew the Earl of Bellomont, Dick Coote he was in the old days at Cambridge and later, in London."

"Out with it!" exclaimed Brenton. "What was he like then, that we may judge him now? Is he a sleek and slippery courtier, playing the game of the crown ministers, his masters, or an honest but misguided servant of the king?"

"'Tis twenty years since I knew Dick Coote," said Trelawney. "He is of noble birth, an ancient Irish family, and not a Whig upstart."

"But what of the man himself?" asked Sheffield.

"Lord Bellomont, as I knew him, was an able and unscrupulous self-seeker under the mask of a lively and pleasing personality. He is a natural court politician."

"Energy and ability he seems to have," laughed Arnold, "by the speedy manner in which he has taken up Brinley's attack on our government. 'Tis rumored he has named us the most irregular and illegal in our administration that ever any English government was."

"He'll leave no stone unturned to ruin Rhode Island and arrest and hang Rhode Island men, once he's set his nimble brain to it," said Trelawney.

"And you speak from personal knowledge of the man?" asked Brenton, dubiously shaking his head over the colony's future.

"From too close association, once on a time," acidly replied the Englishman. "The man is as cold as sea water in January, and his palm has ever itched for gold. Friendship he knows not the meaning of." There was a faraway look in the Englishman's eyes.

"Then he'll make a dangerous enemy to the colony," grunted Brenton, puffing hard on his pipe, "and a dangerous one to Hugh. I fear for our charter and I fear for Hugh, for he was the last of the privateersmen home and will have to explain his absence so long after the peace."

"A dangerous because a shrewd and an unscrupulous one," said Trelawney. "He'd break his word to his advantage as he'd crush a straw between his fingers."

The square-shouldered figure of Tom Paine entered the room. He greeted the party and sat down next to Hugh. "There's bad news, Hugh, just in over the Plymouth Path."

"What's happened?"

"Captain William Kidd has been proscribed by the crown. Lord

Bellomont has ordered his arrest on his return to this coast. There's something fishy behind this!"

"Captain Kidd proscribed? Why?"

"They claim he committed acts of piracy in the Indian Ocean. He's been out four years with a royal commission, to hunt Long Ben Avery, Tew, Bankes, and Mayes, and the French East Indymen."

"What do you make of it, Captain Paine?" asked Joe Brenton.

Heavy lines radiated from Paine's squinting gray eyes as he rubbed his square chin. "Gentlemen," he said at last, "I've known Bill Kidd for twenty years as an able seaman and honest privateersman. With house and family in New York, he never turned pirate nor soiled the King's commission. There's something smoky about this act of the crown and Lord Bellomont. I wonder what's behind it!"

"In New York, last month," said Hugh, "I heard gossip that Lord Bellomont and Robert Livingston were backers of Kidd's venture. Also Kidd told the same to Israel and me in Barbadoes back in '93. 'Tis strange Bellomont would turn against his own man."

A sour look lay on Paine's pitted face. "Before Kidd sailed from New York with the *Adventure Galley*, in '94, he told his wife that Bellomont, Lord Chancellor Somers and other ministers of the crown had a heavy interest in the ship, that was fitted out in Plymouth but came to New York for a full crew."

Trelawney's sensitive mouth curled. His dark eyes glittered as they met Brenton's oblique look. "What do you make of it, Dick?" the latter asked.

"It sounds natural. 'Tis not the first time that Lord Bellomont has turned on his man."

Hugh leaned toward Paine. "Israel and I talked with Captain Kidd in Barbadoes, as you know. He had the look of an honest man and he was esteemed by the Governor and Council for his services against the pirates and the French privateers."

"So it seems that Lord Bellomont and the King's ministers obtain a royal commission for Kidd, back the venture with their money, and now, strangely, order his arrest," sneered Brenton. "But on what ground no one knows. Poor Kidd! There's small gratitude in high places."

Trelawney's face was somber with his thoughts. "Nor in Dick Coote, once he has no longer use for you. From the look of it, there's trouble brewing in London. My last letter states the Tories are pressing Somers and Shrewsbury hard. They're hot to oust them from the King's advisers. It may have been charged openly that the King's ministers have not been above turning a penny in private ventures like this of Bellomont's. And they now hasten to hide behind Kidd."

The weather-burned face of the old privateersman darkened with blood. "Rot me! If 'tis true and I was Bill Kidd, I'd show this pretty Lord Bellomont and his noble friends a merry chase to kitch me before I'd swing to save their skins!"

"Well spoken, Captain Tom!" cried Brenton. "And this is the man who comes to sit in judgment over us for our sins!"

"This is the man," said Trelawney. "And I warn you, the colony will find him a dangerous enemy." He turned to Hugh. "I'm so much in fear of what he may do to you, Hugh, that I'm almost persuaded to urge you to take your fortune and head the *Flying Fish* for the West Indies."

Hugh's eyes glittered. "Run like a frightened deer from danger before I see the nature of it? 'Twill take more than a lord to drive me away before I see how heavily gunned he is." Then he laughed. "Why, you're a lord, Dick, and harmless as a mouse!"

"Christ's blood, Hugh, stand your ground!" exploded Paine. "In '83 they were after me in Massachusetts Bay, swore my commission was forged; but I stood by and here I am. While we have our charter and Governor Cranston, we'll fight the lickspittles!"

Joe Brenton's dark face grew serious. "But, Captain, we may not long have our charter! Once we're absorbed by Massachusetts, Hugh would be at the mercy of Bellomont and Brinley."

"You forget that I already have Codrington's clearance," said Hugh.

"But you well know that Codrington has written Boston claiming that you turned pirate the last year of the war," said Joe.

"I can meet that," returned Hugh.

"With that as a club and the fact that you returned long after the peace with a fortune, they'll make out a case that Bellomont will jump at, coming as he will with blood in his yellow eyes for a victim of prominence. He'll give you no quarter!"

Paine's agate eyes flamed with anger. "Stand by, lad!" he snapped. "We'll see what happens to Kidd! Then if Brinley and Sanford want war, we'll give it them!"

Hugh's face stiffened with the wrath which stormed through him. "Yes," he bit off, "if Mr. Francis Brinley ever again crosses my bow, he'll pay for every long hour I stood in that pillory and for every lie he has uttered since!"

Grave with doubt and foreboding, Trelawney listened. He well knew the lengths to which an aroused Hugh Jocelyn, unjustly accused and convicted, was capable of going. He would not hesitate to defend with every black muzzle on the long sloop lying in the harbor the fortune he had torn from the war. Before he'd bow to the chicanery of colonial politicians suddenly returned to power, and turn over one gold Lyon dollar he'd carried from the warm seas, Hugh Jocelyn would fight his way out of Newport, an outlawed man.

But Hugh himself, nursing his anger, had no idea of being driven from Newport. He would fight—fight with every resource he possessed, fight for the fortune and the happiness he had dreamed of through the long, hard years. There was his farm on Conanicut and the brig on the stocks. There was Content and Tom and Trelawney and—and— He did not attempt even to formulate what lay vaguely deep in his mind—a dream, nebulous and unsubstantial. And yet, formless as it was, it lent a dynamic force to his resolve—to stand by and face what might come; then, if he lost, to give these scheming politicians of Newport such a lesson before he left that the name of Hugh Jocelyn would not soon be forgot.

§86

ONE late winter day when the Newport air carried spring in its mellow tang of the sea and the roads were clear of snow, Hugh rode up to Portsmouth to buy sheep and heifers and a yoke of young oxen for his Conanicut farm. The sturdy house which he had built near Tom Paine's, on the hill above the East Passage, with its great stone chimney and its barns, awaited occupants. And he intended to take possession shortly with Content and Tom, who was now the owner of a new fishing sloop. Dark as was the cloud that hung over his future, it had made no change in his plans. To the surprise and wonder of Newport, the man who was marked for slaughter betrayed no sign of nerves.

Closing the deal for the livestock, Hugh swung down a cart road used by farmers in drawing seaweed from Sachuest beach. Pounded hard by recent high tides, the beach gave excellent footing for a horse, and for a time Hugh sat filling his lungs with the sea-fragrant air and watching rafts of red-breasted mergansers, goldeneye and black duck, off shore. In the offing, above Cormorant Rock, herring gulls circled and dipped. The blue eyes of the man on the horse grew dreamy as they gazed out to the haze of the southern horizon. Two thousand miles away lay Barbadoes and the Windwards. For four years, at Bridgetown, Captain Hugh Jocelyn had dined at Government House, the honored friend of the Governor, and on leaving had carried the written gratitude of the officials for his services to the colony. At Newport, his home, there were those who called him retired pirate and would seize the fortune he had risked his life to wring from the French, and would gladly see him hung. At Newport, for which he had fought and would fight again, there were those who both envied and hated him. He was bitterly lonely and restless, and had resolved that if Bellomont did not try to send him to London for trial and so drive him from the colony when the brig was finished, he would take her himself to Barbadoes and then, if the cargo offered, to Bristol, England, that he might for a short space glimpse the great world.

Hugh reached the easterly end of the wide beach and had turned to canter back over the mile of surf-pounded sand when, in the distance, he saw a horseman. The two horses rapidly approached one another over the good going of the packed sand, hard as a road. Shortly the fluttering cape and side saddle betrayed the sex of the rider.

"A woman!" exclaimed Hugh. "Now who would seek this lonely beach in winter?"

On came the horsewoman, scarlet hood bobbing in the breeze behind her blown hair. Then, with a start, Hugh recognized her, and reining in his horse, doffed his beaver hat as the girl's mount slowed to a walk.

"Your servant, Mistress Serena!" he greeted, aware of a quick lift of his pulse, as he gazed at her vivid face framed by tumbled hair. Beneath the scarlet cape a blue riding habit of heavy serge clothed her graceful figure.

She stopped her horse near his, and a gloved hand brushed aside a black plume whipping across her eyes, as she exclaimed, "Why, Captain Jocelyn!"

"'Tis both a surprise and a pleasure!" he returned. "How came you on this lonely beach?"

A corner of her mouth curled, breaking a dimple in her cheek.

"Mayhap for the same reason as you," she laughed. "To be with my thoughts."

"I am back from Portsmouth, where I went to buy cattle for my farm on Conanicut."

"Cousin Joe has told me of it. Are you deserting the sea now that you have your heart's desire?"

He looked at her sharply. "Heart's desire? How mean you?" he asked, in a futile endeavor to penetrate the mystery of her dark eyes.

She smiled up at him. "Why, have you not now what you sailed to the West Indies in search of and risked your life for? Was that not your heart's desire?"

Hugh laughed. "I may not have it long if Brinley has his way. You forget, they only wait to prove me pirate and hang me. But the sea will ever hold me. 'Tis in my blood! I wished a farm for an anchorage, a home. Unless they make me a proscribed man, I hope to see Barbadoes again—in the new brig—and London."

"London—so far away and so brutal in the life of the court? Uncle Jahleel spoke much of it before his return as agent of the colony. He says, in London no man trusts another, much less a woman. 'Tis all surface and tinsel and heartlessness."

"I know, I know. Trelawney says so, too. But at the same time, 'tis the center of everything—of wit and learning as well as trade."

The black brows of the girl drew together as she turned her head and gazed out to where the gulls lazily circled and dipped around Cormorant Rock. "True we have little wit and learning here save in the talk of Dick Trelawney and Doctor Lodovic. You are well schooled, and doubtless feel the lack of it in us."

Hugh studied her lovely profile from the cloud of hair to the straight nose, half-parted lips, and firm chin. "But we have spirit and beauty here—and much pride," he boldly hazarded.

Lights flashed in her eyes as she turned on him. "How mean you—pride, Captain Jocelyn?"

He knew he had been overbold, but drove headlong on. "A haughty pride of birth and station, Mistress Serena. For a certainty we have sufficient of that in Newport."

"Captain Jocelyn," she said quietly, "you are pointing at me, but I am not offended by your straight speaking. I—I like your honesty. I know from Joe that in the past you have deemed me overproud and uncivil because of my Brenton name. But 'tis not so. That was not the cause. I—I—"

"Your pardon, Mistress Serena," Hugh hastened to say as she paused. "'Tis I who am uncivil now. I have long since forgotten the past."

"Then you believe me when I say that I have no pride of birth, only pride of loyalty—to myself?" she asked.

"I believe you," he said, "and crave your pardon. After your kindness and the offering of your friendship at Barbadoes it ill became me to mention pride."

"Then—then we may be honest friends, Captain Jocelyn, and have no more doubt of silly pride?"

"You do me great honor to name me friend here in Newport. You forget that some name me pirate and scoundrel."

"They speak from envy and hatred and the sure knowledge of your qualities, Captain Jocelyn—these little men who slander you and seek your trial."

"You are, indeed, my friend," he said.

"I think you no pirate," she said vehemently. "My Uncle Jahleel and my mother, as did I at first, listened to low stories from Barbadoes, writ by Sanford years ago. I later learned from Joe what prompted them and caused them to be bandied about Newport. As for these new charges, you forget I was the guest of the Russells at Barbadoes. Governor Russell swore by you."

"Then you do not believe them?" He watched her with twinkling eyes.

She laughed. "Believe Peleg Sanford and that popinjay, Richard Brinley? I'd as soon believe that night was day!"

"My thanks, Mistress Serena! That makes me very proud."

They rode on in silence toward the westerly end of the beach beyond which the cliff that lifted abruptly from the water had been split by a deep fissure as if by a giant's ax. As they rode, he glanced obliquely at the girl beside him, her scarlet hood, tilted from her face, accenting the intense blackness of her wind-tossed hair. And what meant she by pride of loyalty to herself?

They followed the cart track up behind Easton's Point to the first beach, where, at the fork of the road, she stopped her horse. "Captain Jocelyn," she said, "Lord Trelawney tells me you brought home many books from Barbadoes and Jamaica, some of the poet Dryden and of the dead Milton. I may not ask you to our house on Thames Street because of my mother. She's gone over to the Brinley and Sanford faction and deems you a man dangerous to virtuous maids and dames alike, and a fearsome pirate!" She threw back her head and laughed. "Did she know I rode with you this morning, 'twould give her the vapors and fair put her to bed, for she despairs of her thornback daughter."

Hugh's bronzed face reddened as she laughed up at him. And he thought he had never seen her lovelier than at this moment in that flash of white teeth and dancing eyes and wind-rippled hair.

"My mother and I have long disagreed," Serena continued, "and 'twould only set her more against you to ask you to the house. But I am fevered to read this Mr. Dryden of whom Dick Trelawney speaks. Could you lend it him so he could fetch it to me?"

"Only too gladly," replied Hugh. "But—but does this mean banishment? You often ride out here, you say. I have much business in Portsmouth this spring. Is it too bold in me to hope we might meet again?"

Her eyes smiled into his. "I ride every fine day up to the long beach," she said, "for the air and the view of the sea. If Captain Hugh Jocelyn chanced to be returning from business in Portsmouth some morning and also sought the long beach for a view of the sea, and we met—oh, surely, by chance—"

"'Twould pleasure Captain Jocelyn beyond all things!" Hugh impulsively broke in.

For a moment she searched his face as if to read his mind, then swung her horse, and with a wave of her hand, rode off.

He sat watching her until she disappeared up a fork of the cart road. Then he mused: "There's something rare and lovely about Mistress Serena Brenton. And all her old reserve seemed blown from her by the sea air. She was friendly and honest as a man about her mother's dislike of me. And she thinks me fit for her company and will meet me—meet me again on the long beach!"

A week later Trelawney found himself alone with Serena at the Brenton house on Thames Street. "Hugh sent these," he said, "but warned that you would find Dryden a pygmy after Shakespeare, whom you and I love. Here also are some of the Restoration dramatists he found in Jamaica—Wycherley, Shadwell, and Etherege. I find them thin, with occasional wit, but for the most part overcoarse and ribald, and harping ever on the one theme. I hear from London of new men being talked about—Congreve, Farquhar, and Vanbrugh—but doubt their genius. Take care to hide these from your mother's chaste eyes," he laughed.

Serena took the sheep-bound volumes which Trelawney handed her and, seating herself, hastily glanced through them while the Englishman contemplated the picture she made in her frock of yellow flowered taffeta, her dark head bent over the books. She suddenly turned and surprised his amused eyes.

"Why the smile, Lord Dick Trelawney?" she demanded.

"I was thinking," he answered, crossing his thin legs and nursing his chin with a hand, "what a change has come over Mistress Serena Brenton."

"Change? How mean you?" A slow color warmed her cheeks.

"Why, at last you seem to find in Hugh Jocelyn something of what Joe and I have always known and loved."

Serena's eyes stoutly met his as she replied: "You mean because I've been uncivil to him in the past?"

He nodded. "More than that. You have led him to believe you thought him unfit for your society."

"I've never thought that. It was—it was a far different reason."

"Well, 'tis pleasing when he's slandered by many, even by your mother and uncle, to find you his friend."

"You have loved him deeply since you took him as a boy to school him," said the girl.

"Since the day I first saw him in his skiff, with the sun in his yellow hair and on his brown back, I have loved him. He was so friendly and winning."

She slowly nodded. "Yes, he must have been."

"Stranger things have happened," Trelawney mused as he left. True, there was little on which to base the hope. And yet—it might fall out!

IT was summer, and Newport was alive with rumor. Already Brinley and Sanford had been to Boston conferring with the newly arrived Lord Bellomont and laying their plans with Dudley and Randolph for the destruction of the colony by the ultimate annulment of its charter. Under orders from the Lords of the Committee of Trade and Plantations, called the Board of Trade, and the crown itself, Bellomont was to proceed to Newport, examine the former governors, Easton and Clarke, and the deputy governor, Greene, who had commissioned Bankes and Mayes, as well as the new governor, Cranston, as to their activities during the war, the harboring of pirates in the colony, and the general maladministration of Rhode Island affairs, and to report forthwith. To further his designs against the colony, Bellomont had already commissioned the members of the new admiralty court to collect evidence against all those suspected of piracy. This meant that Hugh Jocelyn's commissions and clearances from the governors of the Sugar Islands would again be attacked. It also meant that he would be charged by adroit and relentless enemies with piracy and the illegal possession of prize money. And it would require all the resources of his keen brain to save his fortune and avoid immediate arrest and trial in Boston, where the implacable Bellomont would take measures to have him found guilty and sent a prisoner to London, where he would be subject to the tender mercies of a hard-pressed ministry seeking scapegoats in the colonies.

When Hugh appeared at the King's Head or on Thames Street, citizens despondent over the future of Rhode Island wagged their heads in wonder that a man certainly doomed if he stayed to face Bellomont should show so cool a front to the world. Captain Jocelyn was mad to stay and meet the venom of the Newport royalists. But Hugh calmly went his way, planning as if over his future there hung no shadow of a London dungeon or a hangman's rope.

Content and Tom grew steadily older under their burden of fear. With Israel it was different. His small eyes carried a vicious glitter when men spoke of the coming hearing. More than one had felt the weight of the master gunner's ponderous fist at a tavern when, emboldened by rum, he had jokingly called Brandy pirate. It was also the subject of comment in the taverns frequented by sailors that Brandy was often seen in close talk with some of his old gunners. It looked as if Captain Jocelyn was secretly enlisting his former crew, and the rumor drifted from tavern to tavern that the black sloop lying in the cove was being refitted for sea.

One night Captain Tom Paine sent for Hugh. Hugh's square, two-storied house, with its English overhang, stood back on the high shore above the East Passage but a short walk from Paine's residence. His farm had been part of the large holdings of the retired privateersman. As he approached Paine's house in the moonless night, Hugh suddenly stopped and gazed down past the wharf to the blurred bulk of a strange sloop anchored offshore. "What sloop is that?" he asked the lad who had brought the message.

"'Tis a stranger, sir. She slid in tonight after dark from the West Passage."

Hugh wondered what it meant. The strange sloop had waited until dark to round Conanicut Point from the West Passage, evidently to avoid being seen from Newport below. Why all this mystery?

Paine's door was opened by a servant and Hugh entered the great room, where two men sat before the dying supper fire. He looked past Tom Paine's grizzled head to the man who sat facing him, and his jaw dropped in his amazement.

"Name of God! Captain Kidd!"

Kidd rose and gave Hugh a calloused hand. "Captain Jocelyn, 'tis a wide reach of water from Barbadoes to Rhode Island and some years since we talked in Bridgetown. But you seem to remember me."

Hugh stared into the face of the outlawed seaman whose hand he gripped. Wanted by the crown as pirate, William Kidd had boldly sailed into Narragansett Bay and now stood in Tom Paine's house. What was behind it all?

"I remember you well, Captain," Hugh replied, seating himself and taking the pewter cup of spiced rum Paine handed him. "And I am sorry to hear of your misfortune. But I hardly thought to see you in Narragansett Bay."

In the dim light of the tallow dips Hugh noticed that Kidd had aged. His long hair, for he wore no wig, was heavily streaked with gray. Deep lines creased his forehead and furrowed his bronzed face from nose to mouth. His eyes were those of a man who had suffered and was under a heavy strain. Two heavy pistols, slung from his belt in holsters, and a cutlass bore mute witness to the fact that he was a wanted man. Hugh found himself wondering if he too, like Kidd, would find himself a wanted man.

"Hugh," said Paine, "there are few men in Newport I would trust in this matter, and you are one. Like Bill Kidd and me, you've sailed the warm seas and have proved your mettle on many a ship's deck. You're one of us and will understand. That is why I sent for you, and Captain Kidd agreed."

"You honor me with your confidence," said Hugh, wondering why this hunted man, back from the Indian Ocean, whom Lord Bellomont had ordered arrested on sight, was now risking capture by coming into Rhode Island water in the sloop anchored off Paine's wharf.

"Captain Kidd is telling you the story as he told it me. Then we'll put our heads together," said Paine.

Kidd drained his cup and Hugh noticed a blue-white scar marking his brown throat below the left ear. "After years in the West Indy and long service to the English colonies in two wars," Kidd began, "five years ago, in London, as I told you in Barbadoes, I agreed with Lord Bellomont to make a joint venture into the Indian Ocean. He was to obtain a royal commission, which he did, for the capture of Tom Tew, Long Ben Avery, and other known pirates. Added were the usual powers to take ships of the King's enemies."

"Yes, you spoke of this to Israel and me in Barbadoes in '93. Just who advanced the money for the ship and the outfitting of the venture?" asked Hugh.

"That I am coming to," said Kidd. "Lord Bellomont was the spokesman. But a number of the King's Whig ministers were finding the money—Lord Somers, the Chancellor, the Earl of Orford, First Lord of the Admiralty, Shrewsbury, and others."

"The King's ministers are up to their necks in it," remarked Paine.

"Up to their necks in it, Captain!" answered Kidd, gloomily. "Robert Livingston, of New York, and me paid one fifth the cost, the others the balance."

"So you bought and refitted the ship *Adventure Galley*, at Plymouth?" asked Paine.

"Yes, a thirty-four-gun ship of close three hundred ton. But my good men were pressed by the King's navy and I sailed for New York to ship a proper crew, but got but a scurvy lot."

"Go on," urged Paine of the man who seemed half dazed with his misfortune. "You reached the Indy Ocean and what fell out?"

"From the first I had trouble with my crew, a slimy lot of New York riffraff. Once they mutinied, but I cracked the skull of a gunner with a bucket and got them in hand. At last I took two ships of the Great Mogul." Kidd drew a hand across his eyes and sighed as if to blot out a painful memory. "I changed ships and sailed home in the *Quedah Merchant* with the prize goods and plate, which I left hid in the West Indy, for I heard news there of this stew in London. These ships I took carried French passes, making them lawful prizes."

"Then 'tis the East Indy Company that is behind all this?" said Hugh.

"Yes. It seems for some time the Tory Parliament have been fevered to get Somers and the Whig ministers removed and so clamored to the King. The East Indy people got wind of the fact 'twas Bellomont and his friends, the King's ministers, who backed this venture, and so added this to the fire in Parliament."

"Ah, I'm beginning to understand," said Hugh.

Kidd stared bleakly into the fire as he went on. "So, to save his face, Lord Somers makes me scapegoat, proclaiming me pirate."

"'Tis a foul mess of crown politics," snorted Paine. "Was I you, Bill Kidd, I'd sail for Hispaniola where the *Quedah Merchant* lies hid with your prize cargo and refuse to trust Bellomont. They'd have a merry chase catchin' Tom Paine."

"What has Bellomont done?" asked Hugh.

"I sent word to him in Boston that I was waiting to hear from him. He sent a sloop which I met off Block Island, offering me safe-conduct if I go to Boston."

"Don't go, Captain!"

"But he pledges me his word. He admits the French passes are good defense from all charges."

Paine vigorously shook his head, the smoke-gray eyes in his pock-marked face glittering. "Don't go to Boston! I like not the look of it. 'Tis but a trap."

"Captain," Hugh added, "you are mad to put yourself into Bellomont's power. He might take the French passes which are your defense. To save his face with Parliament, Somers will hang you!"

Kidd raised eyes filled with misery. "But my wife and family, in New York? What will become of them if I sail for the warm seas?"

"They'd rather see you a free man in the warm seas than hung as a pirate," Paine growled.

"But Lord Bellomont gives me safe-conduct here in his own hand," Kidd protested. He read aloud from the paper he held. "He says: 'Come to Boston and fit out to sail and fetch the other ship, the *Quedah Merchant*, which you have hidden with its prize cargo in the West Indies, and I make no manner of doubt to obtain the King's pardon. I assure you on my word and honor I will perform nicely what I have promised.'"

"God's blood," fumed Paine, "'tis the promise of a royal governor caught fair aback by a shift in the wind. I've seen a hundred such broken in my day!"

With vivid memory of Trelawney's picture of Bellomont's character, Hugh's anger rose. "Captain," he urged, "I have a friend in Newport who knew Bellomont well in England, and he says the man knows not the meaning of a promise. Don't trust him! He'll arrest you and send you to England for trial."

"But he has a large interest in the prize goods and hidden ship, worth thirty thousand pounds."

Paine impatiently rose and patrolled the room. "The great Lord Bellomont has his own and the necks of his friends to save, now. Like rats, they're fair in a trap and needs must escape, losing the cheese. All he wants is to get his hands on you and send you to London to swing, in order to make pretense of his innocence and that of Lord Somers and the others."

" 'Tis a trap, I tell you," insisted Hugh. "A mere bubble to lure you to Boston. Don't go!"

So they talked into the night, urging Kidd to sail for the warm seas and wait for events to shape themselves. Before Hugh left, Paine said, "Captain Kidd has buried two chests here, the contents to be held for his wife's use in case of need."

Hugh squeezed Kidd's hand in farewell. "Captain," he said, "sail for Hispaniola! Don't go to Boston!"

But within two weeks the news came over the Plymouth Path to Newport that Lord Bellomont had arrested Kidd when he arrived in Boston and was sending him to London for trial.

§88

WHILE NEWPORT was waiting for the coming of Bellomont, and Brinley and Sanford were busy plotting the ruin of the colony and the destruction of the privateersman whose face when he appeared on Thames Street or at the King's Head wore no evidence of solicitude for his future, Hugh's thoughts constantly turned to the girl at Hammersmith who, in those rides on Sachuest beach, had given him such surprising glimpses of the real Serena Brenton. Trelawney often brought him messages from her, but her mother's hostility barred Hugh from the Brenton home. And messages were poor solace to the man to whose imagination she had made so strong an appeal. Then, one day, with the return of some books of Hugh's, Trelawney brought him a note. It read:

DEAR CAPTAIN JOCELYN:
    Cousin Joe tells me You are Deep in Your farm work and are fitting the Brig for Barbadoes. Joe is most Anxious about the Hearing before the Royal Governor. But, knowing in what Regard Governor Russell held you I cannot Believe these Stories y^t You are to be sacrificed as an Example. It would Be too cruelly Unjust when you Have done so much for the colonies.

My thanks for the Milton and Ben Jonson. I would Like to talk of Them with you If you ever found Time to ride to Sachuest Beach this Summer. Lord Trelawney would carry me the Day you set and the Time of Morning.

Joe thinks you very Brave to stay and face the Hearing. But 'twould be Strange for Hugh Jocelyn to Avoid his enemies. Your friends pray for You.

Your most Obedient and Humble friend,

SERENA BRENTON

Hugh read and reread the note. She had written him! Serena had written him naming a meeting!

Trelawney carried Hugh's answer to Hammersmith. Captain Jocelyn would feel highly honored and happy to find himself on Second Beach on a certain morning in such charming company.

But that certain morning never arrived. The afternoon Hugh dispatched his note to Hammersmith by his friend a small sloop drove into the harbor before a half gale with the startling news that a pirate ship was in Martin's Vineyard Sound and had already taken a sloop and a brig bound to Newport from Boston. That night the beacon on Sandy Point, Block Island, blazoned the sky with its call for help to Point Judith, and the taverns of Newport were filled with excited citizens. The shipping was in danger and owners and merchants with cargoes at sea clamored for action by the authorities.

Leaving the *Flying Fish* at Long Wharf, where Israel with a crew of his old gunners, who had mysteriously appeared on Brandy's short notice, were removing the wooden tampions from her gun muzzles and storing powder and five- and nine-pound shot, Hugh hurried with William Wanton and Trelawney to the King's Head, where Governor Cranston was holding a conference with leading citizens. As he entered the smoke-filled room, men called to him from tables: "A health to Hugh Jocelyn! Thank God for the *Flyin' Fish*!"

Hugh returned the greetings of his friends and moved on between the tables. At some he was met with silent disapproval. Many smug Quakers still believed the fantastic tales of his profligacy in the warm seas, spread by the Brinley and Sanford faction. There were some who called him former pirate as they still called Tom Paine. And there were more who envied him the fortune which his cutlass had carved in four short years from the French. And, finally, there were the Brinleys and Sanfords, for reasons of their own bent upon the ruin of this upstart son of a fisherman who now owned a big sloop, a new brig, and a farm, and had brought a fortune home from the West Indies. These, the wide-shouldered Captain Jocelyn, elegant in blue broadcloth dressed with silver buttons, a lawn Steinkirk cravat wound about his brown neck, silver buckles at knees and on shoes, ignored as he approached the Governor's table. He had shouldered his way up among these merchants, shipowners, and gentry, and now, as ship and landowner and freeman of the colony, walked among them as an equal. In their extremity, the Governor and his Council had called upon Hugh Jocelyn, the man who was waiting to face Sanford's charges of piracy, to man his sloop, the only heavily armed craft in port, and attack the pirate threatening the coast. Worried shipowners were begging his aid, even some of the very men who had clamored for his arrest and trial. The irony of the situation etched a dry smile on Hugh's lean face. They were coming to him now, many who once held him unfit for their company. He coolly surveyed the anxious faces at the tables—faces fat and faces lean, of Quaker and Baptist and no creed, all frightened for the safety of their ships and cargoes.

Followed by William Wanton and Trelawney, he sat down at Joe Brenton's table near that of the Governor. The latter rose and asked for attention from the buzzing assembly, some of whom already showed their liquor.

"The Block Island beacon is burning," he said. "Our commerce is again in peril. A sloop in, late today, reports that a pirate ship in Vineyard Sound has already taken two coasting craft. There are Newport craft on the coast due here shortly. To save great losses and protect Block Island, we must act at once. Captain Paine will speak to us."

The new Governor Cranston, wise, tactful, yet stubborn, sat down, and Paine rose from a neighboring table. The narrowed eyes in the weather-burned, pitted face of the grizzled sailor slowly swept the room. There were those there who loved him and those who feared and hated him, calling him a former pirate; but all gave him a respectful silence as he spoke.

"A three-masted ship, heavy-gunned, breaks out a red flag off our shores," rasped Paine. "Rhode Islanders know what answer to make to that. Go out and fight 'em!" There was a roar of approval from the smoke-filled room. "Friends, there's no time to waste. But one craft lies in Newport tonight proper gunned, and fast and able enough to meet a twenty-gun ship—the *Flyin' Fish!*"

There were shouts of "Captain Jocelyn! Hugh Jocelyn and his *Flyin' Fish*! He'll take the pirate!"

Then, as men listened for Paine's next words, a shrill voice yelped from the rear of the room, "Takes a pirate to kitch a pirate!"

Anger drove through Hugh as he and his friends leaped to their feet. Tom Paine's face was blotched with wrath. "Fetch me that man!" he roared to those in the rear of the crowded room.

There was scuffling, angry voices, the thuds of blows, and the huge bulk of Benoni Tosh shouldered its way through the crowd dragging a struggling prisoner to a side door.

"Cuff him, Benoni! Shut his slimy mouth! 'Tis Eph Greene! Who let him in here?" came cries from the men at the tables watching the fracas. Reaching the door, Benoni aided the exit of the whimpering disturber with a last cuff and the lift of a heavy foot, and Greene sprawled in the dark outside.

Joe Brenton turned angrily to his friends. "I smell Richard Brinley behind this!"

Governor Cranston was standing with uplifted arms. "Men of Newport," he cried, "calm yourselves and listen to Captain Paine!"

Paine's stiff lips shaped a mirthless smile as he surveyed the excited assembly. "Send Captain Jocelyn with the *Flyin' Fish*, you say! For four years he harried the French from the Windward Passage to the Grenadines; but what said some of you who are here tonight when he sailed home last year? 'Jocelyn, the pirate!' you bawled. 'Seize his money and prize goods!'" Paine's fierce glance thrust into the black face of Sanford. "Did you board the *Flyin' Fish* with your men, King's Judge of Admiralty Sanford? Ay, you talked loud from the shore, but you knew what waited you if you set foot on that sloop—a cold swim in the harbor! You durst not board her! And you wait for the ear of Lord Bellomont to condemn the man you now beg to save your shipping, while you plot to put yourselves again in the saddle."

The room was in an uproar. Many cheered Paine's bitter attack on Sanford, but there were cooler heads that shook in disapproval. The round-faced Governor reached and pulled at Paine's sleeve. These were matters better left unsaid. Paine grunted an assent and went on:

"Now Newport asks Captain Jocelyn to fight for her. Hard as he's been used by some I see here tonight, he's ready to go. His powder and shot are stowed, but he needs more crew. At daylight we drum up for men. Spread the news!"

Paine sat down to noisy applause. The Governor rose and said, "Captain Hugh Jocelyn asks your attention."

Hugh rose, and his eyes coldly measured the expectant faces of both friends and enemies at the crowded tables. But friend or enemy, shipowner or merchant, tonight they needed him. On the straight shooting of his guns and the boldness of his seamanship rested the safety of many a sloop and brig owned by these men. Brinley and Sanford sat with Nat Coddington, the new Registrar of the Admiralty Court, and others, watching him narrowly. As he waited while shouts of "Health to Captain Jocelyn and the *Flyin' Fish*!" rocked the tavern, the picture of a boy standing in the pillory on the Parade flashed across his vision; then he saw a lad alone in the dusk on a wharf, battling for his life against hired assassins; following that a young swimmer fighting blindly through the fog for the Cuttyhunk beach. And a hot rage boiled in him. With an effort at control he began:

"If reports are true, 'twill be no easy matter to take this pirate. We shall be outgunned and outnumbered. But the *Flying Fish* has fought odds before!"

"That she has!" men shouted.

"A full crew of able lads we need, and Israel Brandy and Mate Jeremy Potts are hunting my old gunners tonight. We drum up for more men at daylight on the Parade, for there's no time to lose." Then suddenly all the pent wrath and resentment over the attempt of the Brinleys and Sanford to seize his prize money and crucify him before Bellomont stormed to the surface as Hugh's eyes met the hostile faces at Brinley's table. These men were expecting him to risk his sloop and his men's lives to save their precious property, and yet, on his return, would seek his ruin.

" 'Twas little more than a year past that I sailed into Newport after four years in the warm seas," he began. A hush fell on the room as men marked the bitterness in his voice and strained forward on their stools, their pewter cups unemptied and long-stemmed pipes neglected in their hands. "We had fought the King's enemies over a thousand miles of water, we Newport and Portsmouth men, and what we brought home we had risked our lives for, with fair chance of the rope or a French dungeon."

"Ay, 'tis God's truth!" answered a voice.

Then Hugh's bitter eyes locked with and held the sullen gaze of Peleg Sanford. "But despite your attempts to have our lawful prize money seized and your branding us as pirates, Mr. Peleg Sanford, my privateering commissions and credentials were found correct by Governor Cranston and the Council. Governors Russell of Barbadoes, Beeston of Jamaica, yes, and Codrington of Antigua, as well, whom you have quoted against me, gave me full clearance and even their written gratitude."

Cranston was tugging at Hugh's arm. "Have done with the past, Captain," he urged. "It serves no good purpose."

But the infuriated Hugh had that to say before the leading men of the port which had waited long for utterance and he shrugged off the Governor and continued, while Sanford and Brinley exchanged whispered comments with their friends and fidgeted on their stools as they cast oblique looks at the men around them.

"You, Judge Sanford," he went on, "published false reports from your precious brother in Barbadoes; and you, Mr. Brinley, and your noble son, helped scatter them to my damage. I have made no public statement of what I think of you. But here, now, before the men of Newport, I name you both liars and slanderers, for to injure me, you tattled what you knew was false, and you now wait to accuse me before Lord Bellomont!"

There was silence as men gasped at Hugh's deliberate insult to a king's officer. Then murmurs of approval rippled over the room.

"'Tis a lie!" exploded Sanford, rising and shaking his fist, his long face purple, as Hugh smiled at his helpless rage. "This man, here—"

But a sudden uproar drowned the protests of the unpopular Judge of Admiralty. Here was something to the taste of many in the room—the haughty Brinley and Sanford, who it was well known were seeking the colony's ruin, being pilloried in public. It was a rare treat, and they cried for more. But Governor Cranston insisted that Hugh sit down. Before he did he said quietly: "I have fought for Newport before. I shall fight again." Then he added with a wide smile, "Of course, I'll give a gentleman's satisfaction to doughty Leftenant-Colonel Sanford and to Mr. Brinley, on my return—if I do return."

Roars of raucous laughter greeted the offer. "Peleg Sanford fight Captain Jocelyn! Ho-ho, what a joke!" were hurled at the enraged Sanford and Brinley, who, with their friends, shortly left the tavern.

The delighted William Wanton flung his arm about Hugh's shoulder. "God's blood, Hugh, you told it them! I've waited long for this! Brinley feared to chirp a word with the crowd against him, and Sanford was fair wild!"

"Hugh," laughed Joe Brenton, "if you hadn't told them, I was all set to, and more! But 'tis as well. They would say I was foxed again!"

§89

AT daylight the drums rolled on the Parade. Many of Hugh's gun crews who had fought with him in the warm seas had already reported for duty and were busy on the sloop. Israel's secret visits to Portsmouth had borne fruit. The old crew of the *Flying Fish* except those at sea were rallying, to a man. Following the beating drums Hugh marched to the wharf with his volunteers, where Israel, Jeremy, and Tom Paine were checking the sloop's guns and gear. There Governor Cranston and a group of citizens shook Hugh's hand, wishing him Godspeed.

"Take no long chances, Hugh," begged Trelawney. "The pirate may be strong and not easily beaten. Here comes Joe, and he has someone with him."

Joe Brenton was working his horse through the crowd on the wharf, followed by Serena. He dismounted and swung his cousin from her sidesaddle. To the curious eyes of Trelawney and the others, her face was an enigma.

A thrill of pride and elation pulsed through Hugh as he greeted her. "'Tis a great honor, Mistress Serena, to have you ride from Hammersmith so early to see us off," he said, as Joe and the girl gave him their hands.

"Name of God! Great honor?" protested Brenton. "Think you you could keep Serena and me from wishing Godspeed to the *Flying Fish* however early she sailed?"

Serena laughed up into Hugh's face, "Captain Jocelyn is risking his life and sloop. 'Tis little enough that we lose a little sleep to bring him our best wishes."

"That gives me heart," he replied. "Now I know we shall take that pirate."

As they said good-by, Hugh felt that the hand that grasped his so firmly was indeed the hand of a friend.

Under jib, staysail, and topsail the *Flying Fish* moved out into the harbor to the salutes of muskets and cannon, shook out her big mainsail, rounded Goat Island, and beat down the East Passage for the sea. Driven by a lively south wind that afternoon, the fast sloop entered Vineyard Sound and shortly the watch in the crosstrees hailed the poop.

"Three-masted ship dead ahead!"

Through his glasses Hugh made out the topgallant sails of a vessel headed west. Evidently they had sighted the *Flying Fish* and were set for another capture. Hugh smiled grimly as he lifted his leather trumpet. "All hands stand by! Pass the word below!"

The deck of the sloop was suddenly alive with hurrying men.

"Gun crews stand by!" bawled the bass voice of Israel Brandy.

The *Flying Fish* drove on toward the enemy, her big mainsail, topsail, and jib bellying, gear creaking, a belt of foam boiling past her bilges as she heeled to the bite of her rudder.

Brandy's bare-backed gunners stood joking beside their pieces, their eyes bright with excitement as the wind whipped their long hair. In the bow Mate Jeremy Potts and Daniel Campanal were inspecting the musketmen, checking on cutlasses, hatchets, and boarding pikes. The seamen lounged at their stations, awaiting orders. On the poop the crews of the demiculverins and swivel guns watched Hugh standing beside the straining tillermen, talking with Brandy.

"They mistake us for another coaster, Israel. Can you judge of her guns yet?"

Israel lowered the telescope held to his eye. "She's heavy-gunned, as was said," he replied. "But she's pushin' half Vineyard Sound ahead of her square bow. She's slow, and I itches to put a broadside into her guts."

"How many guns?"

"I see eight, now; maybe more in her starboard battery. They be large demiculverins," said Israel, the glass again at his eye. "And her deck's full of people. Rot my bones, she's no less nor a pirate up from the warm seas!"

Hugh took the glass. "We'll give those big guns a wide berth and pound her from her quarter."

"Ay, we'll cut up her top hamper and cripple her as bluefish chop a school of mackerel."

Close hauled, the *Flying Fish* rapidly took the weather of the approaching ship. When a half-mile separated the speeding sloop from the ship, unable to follow the *Flying Fish* into the wind, a red flag was broken out from the stranger's main top.

"There she shows her true colors, lads," Hugh shouted. "She's no privateer! Remember, she's loaded with captured goods, which are ours for the taking!"

He was answered by shouts. "Prize goods! We'll soon have 'em, Captain! Lay us board and board with her!"

Far on the ship's weather beam, the nimble sloop jibed and drove down on her, the larboard gun crews working desperately with hand-spike and crow to train their pieces for a broadside as they passed the enemy's counter. At a hundred yards the *Flying Fish* sheered in, crossed the ship's square stern, on which was painted the name *Shark*, and puffs of orange smoke broke from her larboard ports as her guns roared. Hugh watched the havoc of the iron shot plunging through the pirate's bulwarks and rigging.

"Good, Israel!" he cried. "Keep the shots low!"

"Shark she is, is she?" growled Brandy. "She'll have no teeth to snap when we're done with her!"

The ship payed off quickly in an attempt to bring her starboard guns to bear on the sloop, but the driving *Flying Fish* sheered off to the bite of her rudder and the shots kicked white columns from the sea far off her beam. Tacking, the sloop again worked to windward of the clumsy ship. Israel was in his element, bellowing as he stumped back and forth, slapping the grinning gun crews on their bare backs. He shouted to Hugh standing beside the tillermen, "The rumbullions know now 'tis no coaster they put their teeth into but the liveliest sloop in the colonies!"

As a kingbird harries a hawk, time after time the nimble *Flying Fish* took the weather of the ship, drove down across her stern, raked her, and was off, while the *Shark*, unable to train her heavy guns on her enemy, was slowly pounded into a derelict, her sails and top hamper in ribbons and her decks strewn with dead, wounded and shattered gear.

"Christ's blood, there goes her mainmast!" bellowed Israel, as the *Flying Fish* crossed the ship's counter belching flame and smoke in another broadside, while the musketmen poured in a hail of lead.

The ship's mainmast swayed, sagged, then lurched overside, carrying a litter of rigging, and she lay helpless.

"Stand by to board!" shouted Hugh through his leather trumpet.

With musket, pike, and cutlass, Jeremy's men crowded the bow, while the *Flying Fish* came about and drove for the weather beam of the disabled ship. There was a roar of musket fire as grappling irons were flung, the sloop clamped on to her prey, and the yelling Jeremy Potts led his boarders over the ship's rail. The pirate's crew fought desperately as the wave of Newport men swept over her. But the long pounding by the sloop had turned her into a shambles.

Leaving his poop, Hugh joined Israel and his gun crews, who drove the beaten pirates down their afterhatch. But a group still remained on the shattered poop working desperately to swing a swivel to bear on the boarders, when Hugh and Israel reached it. They scrambled through the poop rail and charged as a swart-faced seaman, leaning against the whipstaff, leveled a pistol.

"Look out for the pistol!" warned Israel, hurling his hatchet at the pirate.

The pistol exploded, but the ax which bit into the pirate's shoulder spoiled his aim and Jeremy drove the point of his cutlass into the reeling man's chest. He slumped forward to the deck and the men at the swivel surrendered.

"Stand by with the prisoners and wounded on the ship, Jeremy," ordered Hugh, "while I check on the sloop!" He left Israel, Jeremy, and Chirurgeon Rodman to their work.

For a space Brandy stared curiously at the wounded pirate. He was short and swarthy, and as he lay twisting with pain, the light of recognition crept into Israel's eyes. "Stab my vitals, but it's you, is it?" He bent over and lifted a hand minus a forefinger. "Creach or I'm a mud shark!"

Jeremy joined him, and they carried the bleeding Creach into the cabin, where Chirurgeon Rodman was treating the wounded.

Later, as Hugh prepared to start for Newport with the *Flying Fish*, leaving Jeremy to bring in the battered ship under jury rig, Israel boarded the sloop and announced: "I have news for you. Who think you was the pirate who fired that pistol by the whipstaff and was master of this ship?"

"What mean you?"

"Christ's blood, 'twas no less nor Creach—John Creach—I let slip through my hands at the Break o' Day tavern!"

"You mean the sailor with the maimed hand?"

"No less."

But Israel failed to tell what had occurred in the ship's cabin before Creach died. That was to be a pleasant surprise for the captain of the *Flying Fish*.

The following day, under jury rig, the pirate ship *Shark* was worked into Newport harbor to the roar of cannon and the cheers of people on the wharves. Shorn of her top hamper, and with her gun ports and bulwarks battered by the demiculverins of the *Flying Fish*, the former menace to coastwise shipping was anchored to await condemnation by the prize court. It had been a profitable venture for Captain Jocelyn and his crew.

It was not long after his return from the taking of the *Shark* that, one morning, in response to a message from Hammersmith, Hugh was impatiently patrolling Sachuest beach. He had galloped the length of the white sands many times before he saw a rider angle down to the water and approach.

"How strange," she laughed, "that we both chance to be riding here this morning! Congratulations on your gallant taking of the pirate ship!"

Hugh's heart quickened as he watched her radiant face. "Mistress Serena," he said, "if you were to ride here every morning you'd never lack for company."

"But the Conanicut farm would suffer and the brig—I thought the brig was soon for Barbadoes?"

Hugh watched the breeze toying with a plume of black hair, then his face went bleak as he replied, "When they've done their worst with me there may be no brig—no—"

"Oh, don't say that!" she cried. "When you've done so much for the colony how could they be so unjust?"

"They're bent on destroying Rhode Island as a colony. And to aid their purpose, they aim to hold me up as a fit example of her seamen."

"Oh, I know, I know! Many fear what—what may happen. But if there's justice in the world—"

"Justice?" he laughed bitterly. "Of that I've seen little. What counts is a quick brain, a bold spirit, and a stout arm."

She smiled up at him. "That's what heartens me for your safety. You have them all."

He suddenly leaned from his saddle and asked impulsively, "Would it matter much to anyone if they had their way with Hugh Jocelyn?"

"Their way? How mean you?"

"Drove him from Newport?"

Her eyes widened. "Drove him from Newport? No one could drive him from Newport!" she cried. "They might arrest and try him, but drive him away—through fear? No!"

"You'd not have him submit to arrest and an unfair trial?"

"Captain Hugh Jocelyn would not submit to an unjust arrest!"

Her words spurred him to a new boldness. "Would it matter much to anyone if—he refused to be arrested and tried, and sailed—"

She courageously met his questioning eyes. "It would matter—oh, so much, to his friends," she answered in a low voice.

"And to no one else?"

For a space her gaze followed the dipping flight of a gull while he waited, then she turned with a disarming smile. "And to a poor thornback who haunts Sachuest beach when a certain—"

"Please—not that word!" he protested.

"Well, I am one—growing old, Mother warns me; and—"

"More lovely than ever!"

She colored, struggling with a sudden confusion. "Let us talk of the books you lent me! Think you not that Mr. Wycherley is but poor fare after the lavish riches of Mr. Shakespeare?"

Hugh smiled. He had small thought for the riches of Will Shakespeare or for poets in general when so near him on her horse sat so lovely a poem. "You did not care for the 'Plain Dealer' and the rest?" he asked.

"I found Wycherley, Shadwell, and Etherege lacking in all I most love in Shakespeare," she answered, as their horses walked side by side. "I prefer Marlowe, Ben Jonson, and the other Elizabethans to these moderns. Wycherley seems to have known no honest women—nor men either."

Hugh leaned toward her. "I would not give Ben Jonson's 'Drink to me only with thine eyes' for all the Restoration drama and Dryden's poetry!"

Her dark face lit. "Oh, they are lovely—those lines to Celia."

"They were lovely as you sang them that night in Barbadoes. They must have been lovely eyes to have so inspired him—eyes a man could drown in, like those I look into now, velvet black and—beyond reading." He stopped, amazed at his recklessness.

Her face masked her thoughts as her level gaze met his. "Please, let us talk of the poets, not of ourselves," she said.

He left her at the fork in the road, his blood singing. At last he sensed to the full what the poets meant. It was no mere fever of the blood, this thing called love, no allure of beauty and the senses, alone, but a magic conjured from a fusion of mind and heart and body.

But what had Hugh Jocelyn, over whom hovered a menacing future, to do with love? Out of pity she had been overkind to a man whose fortune was at stake—who was in great danger. Under the urging of Joe she was making amends for her incivility in the past.

Doubtless she had met him because she found his talk agreeable and informed, as she had Trelawney's. True, she had admitted, when pressed, that his going away would matter to her as well as to his other friends. But how could he tell that it might mean more? In naming her lovely, he had been rash and overbold. It had embarrassed her, yet she had shown no resentment at his daring. Still, it was scarce thinkable that so lovely a creature as Serena Brenton should care for a privateersman with a scarred face.

This love which at last had come to him made Hugh very humble and very blind.

§90

AT last a messenger in over the Plymouth Path brought the news of the coming of the royal governor on the following day. At a table in the King's Head the young governor, Cranston, sat with Easton, Walter Clarke, and the deputy governor, Greene, planning the defense of the colony. At another table Joe Brenton, Trelawney, and Hugh conversed in low tones. Joe nervously drummed with his fingers on the table as he talked. The face of the Englishman pictured the anxiety in his heart, for he knew Bellomont of old.

"Before he sailed for London from Boston," said Joe, "Uncle Jahleel wrote that Dudley was boasting that the crown would take our charter when Bellomont made his report, and that Hugh was already as good as a hanged man!"

Hugh's blue eyes glittered and the lines in his face set. "As good as a hanged man, am I? Well, if I'm as good as a hanged man, there are some in Newport now as good as dead men!"

"Name of God, Hugh, don't talk that way!" protested Brenton. "You've good friends here, who'll stand by to the end!"

"Had your uncle news of Captain Kidd?" asked Hugh.

"He's still in jail, in Boston, and goes soon to London."

"Put not your faith in royal governors," sneered Hugh. "Yesterday Peleg Sanford announced openly here in this room that he will prove my commissions and letters forged and will see me swing as a pirate!"

Trelawney's sensitive face saddened as he watched Hugh. Then the huge bulk of Benoni Tosh appeared at the door. He caught Hugh's eye and beckoned. Hugh left his friends and joined the Town Sergeant at a table.

"Hugh," began Tosh, on whose red face sat an unusual gravity, "the port is full of wild talk. Some of it frets me sore. I've seen you grow up from a boy and have ever been your friend."

"You have, Benoni."

The bulky Sergeant leaned across the table and said in a low voice, "There's talk that your old gun crews are back on the *Flyin' Fish* and that she's stored and provisioned."

Hugh's eyes thrust hard into his friend's anxious face. "What of it?" he demanded. "She has her clearance and manifests for a cargo to Charlestown."

"Hugh, the last two nights Israel Brandy has put aboard her sufficient powder and round shot to sink a fleet, and every lad now on this island who swung a cutlass with you in the warm seas is standin' by on her. Do you deny that?"

There was a twinkle in Hugh's eyes. "I neither deny nor affirm, Benoni! Now just what frets you to come to me?"

Tosh emptied at a gulp the pewter cup of ale in his hand. "Hugh, as Sergeant I'm on duty at Governor Cranston's house through this hearin'. 'Twill last days, and much may happen. They're goin' to falsely accuse you before Lord Bellomont. He hates us! He's comin' with blood in his eye. And he brings an escort and guard of regulars."

"I know all that! What of it?"

"He may order Governor Cranston to arrest you, though 'twould be against our charter. He may try to drag you to Boston for trial. I—I'm your friend. I don't like the smell of it. You're a fightin' man. You won't stand arrest. Israel, Jeremy, and your old crew will be there in the street, armed. They'd all die for you. Them devils of yours'll kill a hundred king's men before they'll see you taken. There'll be bloodshed, Hugh! I'm scared!"

Benoni wiped the sweat from his face with his sleeve.

"What next?" demanded Hugh, his eyes bleak with his bitter thoughts.

"Why—why, then you'll fight your way out of Newport and head the *Flyin' Fish*, God knows where, a proscribed man. A man wanted by the King and—and we'll never see you again!"

The flint in Hugh's face softened and his lip curled. "There's one thing you forgot, Benoni. When I go, if go I must, Newport will be lacking three of its citizens, Sanford, Brinley, and his noble son. But I rather think I'll take them with me as presents to the great Mogul or the Sultan of Zanzibar. There's Newbury, too, but he's lately married. I'll leave him."

"Name of God, have you lost your mind?"

Hugh coolly continued, "'Twill be of great service to Newport and the colony when it loses its charter to have no Brinley as Chief Justice nor Sanford as Judge of Admiralty."

Eyes bulging with amazement, Benoni sat open-mouthed.

"Christ's blood, Hugh Jocelyn," he gasped, " 'tis no matter for joking! You're in grave danger! But you wouldn't make yourself an outlaw?"

"If Lord Bellomont dances to Brinley's fiddling and orders my arrest, I'll make myself an outlaw, for in that case the law will be but a mockery."

Tosh nodded. "Yes, Hugh; that it will be! But put a brail on your wild ideas! Don't, man—don't start bloodshed in Newport! Don't do ought that will land you hangin' from a yardarm!"

Hugh gave the fearful Benoni his hand as they parted. "Benoni, I promise you I shall only defend my rights. But, Name of God, if they bring English soldiery here thinking to overawe us and they show their teeth, the lads who followed me four years in the warm seas will show them the worth of a well-swung cutlass!"

Hugh returned to his curious friends.

"What were you saying to Benoni that should make him look as if he saw ghosts?" asked Brenton.

"Pledging him my utmost endeavors to see that peace is maintained in Newport during the pleasant stay of the most noble, the Lord Bellomont," answered Hugh, with a dry smile.

"How does your uncle stand on this visit of Bellomont?" demanded Trelawney of Brenton.

Joe scowled. "He was betwixt the devil and the deep sea. He abhors the Quaker lack of education, laxity in government, and careless making and handling of our laws. He has demanded that they be printed, and advised the impeachment of Walter Clarke for refusing to swear in Sanford and Coddington. And he rejoices that, with Governor Cranston, Quaker control of the colony is over. But he is stoutly for the charter and against the schemes of Brinley, Sanford, and their party to have us swallowed by Massachusetts, as was Plymouth."

"Why is he still against me?" demanded Hugh.

" 'Tis a puzzle, Hugh. I have argued much with him over you, but he still thinks you a wild young man and a menace to the fair sex, though a daring and able privateersman," laughed Brenton, poking Hugh in the ribs.

Hugh thought of Serena. How could she well stand against her uncle's and her mother's prejudice? Still, it would matter little if they branded him as a pirate and drove him to the tropic seas. It would then be farewell to Serena Brenton.

At the narrows in Portsmouth, Richard Coote, Earl of Bellomont and Governor of New England and New York, accompanied by his staff and an escort of British regulars, was met by Governor Cranston and his Assistants with the Newport troop of horse. In the troop were Joe Brenton, Sheffield, and John Arnold, who stared in surprise at the man who left the ferry and mounted his horse with the aid of two attendants. That the royal governor was not a well man was evident. His slightly protruding, red-rimmed eyes were circled, and the pallor of his face heightened by his black campaign wig. He wore a gray beaver hat cocked on one side, a Watchet blue riding coat, and jack boots, and sat his horse stiffly, as if with discomfort.

Brenton muttered to the man riding beside him: "God save us! They say he suffers much from gout. We'll get no mercy from a sick man! I'm fair worried for Hugh Jocelyn."

The other looked significantly at Brenton. "From what I hear, Captain Jocelyn has taken good means to protect himself."

"Yes, but that would mean his leaving us and his ruin, so far as Newport is concerned, and I love him like a younger brother."

As the Governor and his escort rode down Broad Street and through the Parade, the people who had gathered to stare watched him pass in silence. Those who looked at the sallow-faced Earl had no heart for cheers. He had come with the heralded purpose of destroying the charter of Roger Williams and reducing the colony to a province of Massachusetts.

At the house of the Governor, on Thames Street, Cranston, Deputy Governor Greene, and the former governors, Easton and Clarke, received Bellomont and his party. In the street, outside, a crowd surrounded the English troopers lounging with their horses. Hostile eyes marked the scarlet uniforms piped with blue, the shining sabers, jack boots, and the brass-bound pistol butts protruding from the saddle holsters.

"'Twill take more than these pretty fellows to work Bellomont's will should he listen to Brinley and Peleg Sanford and try to seize Hugh Jocelyn for trial," whispered the little carpenter, Jerusa Sugars, to the grimy-faced blacksmith in leather apron and breeches beside him.

"Ay, glance down the street," said the other. "There wait three of the stoutest lads who ever split a Frenchman's skull with a cutlass. They were with Hugh in the warm seas."

Sugars looked past the gossiping crowd to where, at a distance, lounged three men in sailors' canvas drawers, wearing heavy cutlasses slung from baldrics. Their shirts were open, exposing bronzed chests; and their lean faces were tanned like leather, from years under a tropic sun. The carpenter nodded. "Sisson, the bo's'n, and the Hall brothers! Israel Brandy is doubtless somewhere about and plenty others. Name of God, they're all here! I fear Newport will see blood let if Lord Bellomont works his venom on Hugh."

"The *Flyin' Fish* is ready for sea," said the blacksmith.

"Ay, and her old crew standin' by," said Sugars, with a shake of the head. "But my heart grieves for Tom and Content. Hugh's the light of their eyes and now they bid fair to lose him and he but lately home with a fortune."

"There's more of 'em sittin' in that house!" exclaimed the blacksmith. "Yes, there's Brandy, on watch! I saw his mauled face at a window and the muzzle of a blunderbuss."

Aided by the whispered advice of Brinley and Sanford for two days, the irascible Lord Bellomont denounced and castigated the administrations of the present and former governors and bullied them with personal abuse. Then Captain Tom Paine was called.

"Captain Paine," rasped Bellomont, from behind the table where he sat with two secretaries, "Captain Kidd, now in jail in Boston, was at your house on Conanicut Island in June! What have you to say?"

Paine's features stiffened as he coolly met the accusing gaze of the Governor. "Your Excellency, do I stand indicted for the crime of having Captain Kidd at my house for a few hours? If he came, he came without warning and of his own free will."

Men anxiously watched Bellomont's mottled face as his pale eyes glared at the composed privateersman, arms folded across his barrel chest. "Captain Paine," he snapped, "I like not your deportment! You are under grave suspicion! Have a care that you answer civilly, yes or no, or you'll regret it!"

Paine coolly took the rebuff and eyed the eager faces of Sanford and Brinley seated behind Bellomont. His stiff features loosened in the wraith of a smile as he said, "Yes, my lord, in June Captain Kidd sailed into the bay and stopped at my house."

Bellomont shouted: "Knew you not he was a proscribed man? Why did you not arrest him?"

Again lights danced in Paine's eyes. "Arrest the pirate Kidd with his ten armed men on an armed sloop? I was alone with my farmer and am not fevered for an early death."

Bellomont's face soured as he contemplated the inscrutable features of the man facing him. Here was evidently a hard colonial nut to crack. He turned and whispered with Brinley, then said, "Why was he here, a proscribed man, in the colony of Rhode Island?"

"We had been shipmates years ago, in the warm seas, and he came for advice."

"What advice?" snarled the Earl.

Paine squinted into the caustic blue eyes raised to his. He took in a deep breath and shifted his arms on his chest before he answered, "He was in doubt of what to do, bein' writ to by your Excellency to come to Boston, with your promise of a safe-conduct and aid in his defense."

The heavy air of the room vibrated with suspense. Men gasped and sought each others' startled eyes. In his surprise and embarrassment, blotches of blood mottled Bellomont's sickly skin from his cravat to his black periwig. He angrily shook his right hand, distorted by gout, in the stone-hard face of the privateersman. "What say you?" he stormed. "'Tis a lie! I gave the pirate Kidd no safe-conduct!"

So still was the room that men could be heard breathing. Paine was overbold! He was going too far with the royal governor! He would sadly regret it! But the old privateersman's hard eyes stabbed Bellomont's without a flicker as he said, "I state but what he told me, your Excellency."

Francis Brinley leaned and whispered in the Governor's ear and the latter demanded, "What was your advice?"

"I told him that as there seemed many in high places interested in his venture to the Indy Sea he should move slow, that they might come to his rescue."

Bellomont's jaw dropped. Instead of the explosion of anger the listeners anticipated, the royal governor seemed stunned and speechless by the daring of Paine's reply. He hesitated, then snapped, "So you urged Kidd to ignore my letter delivered him at Block Island by my agent?"

"Sir, I did not! I said were I myself in such a pass, I would sail for the warm seas."

At the answer men audibly caught their breaths. Paine had crucified himself. His boldness had brought his ruin. But to their surprise, instead of an explosion of wrath, a sly sneer took shape on the Governor's unhealthy features. "Having yourself buccaneered in the warm seas, Captain," he said, with a curl of a thin lip, "you doubtless feel them safe for pirates and proscribed men."

There was the glint of sun on young ice in Paine's eyes as he said, "Safer than Boston, my lord!"

Murmurs marred the hush of the room. Was Tom Paine mad to so play with a royal governor?

Bellomont scowled. "How mean you?" he snarled.

"Kidd now lies in jail in Boston, waiting to be sent to London for trial!" came the reply, which sliced the air like the slash of a cutlass.

Again both Sanford and Brinley were at Bellomont's ear, but he impatiently waved them off. It was evident that he did not wish to pursue the matter. At length he said, "It is charged that Captain Kidd left gold and booty with you for safekeeping?"

"I saw no gold or booty," Paine truthfully answered. "He was ashore but a few hours and feared his sloop might be seen."

"You saw none?" sneered the Earl.

"No, my lord."

Bellomont motioned to Cranston and said, "Have Captain Paine's house searched at once for gold or booty and report tomorrow."

Sanford was at the Earl's shoulder whispering vehemently, but Bellomont shook his head as he nursed his chin in his hand. He winced as if in pain, then, after an interval, sighed, stretched, patted a yawn with his swollen hand, and asked the time of his secretary. Instead of the furious outburst of anger they had anticipated, to the amazement of those in the room the Governor was dismissing the wily privateersman. Without open statement Tom Paine had revealed that he was familiar with matters which Lord Bellomont could hardly have wished aired in Newport.

To the patent disappointment of Sanford and Brinley over the outcome of Paine's examination, the Governor abruptly announced, "We will adjourn until tomorrow when, Governor Cranston, you will produce this notorious buccaneer, Captain Jocelyn, whom you have coddled to your breast since he returned from the West Indies with his stolen gold after four years of flouting the law and the King's officers!"

Hugh's friends in the room stared bleakly into each other's eyes. His fate was sealed. Bellomont was clearly bent on his destruction. Already, without a hearing and a chance to defend himself, he had been convicted. Accepting the slander and false statements of Brinley and Sanford, the royal governor of New England would order Hugh arrested and taken to Boston for trial.

As the company filed out, Benoni, who as Town Sergeant had stood with his halberd behind the inquisitors during the session, walked to the window, and his anxious eyes searched the crowded street. Here and there the stalwart figures of those he sought towered above the gossiping men and women.

"They're there!" he muttered. "And they'll be there tomorrow—waitin'—all of 'em! When Bellomont orders Hugh's arrest and Governor Cranston refuses, as he will, he'll call on his redcoats! And then—Christ's blood! There'll come that bull roar of Israel's: 'Stand by to board! *Flyin Fish*, stand by!' And them lads'll rally round Hugh and cut them redcoats to fish bait as if on the deck of a Frenchman! Then they'll make for the sloop waitin' for 'em, with her shotted guns at her ports, and sail out of Newport for God knows where—proscribed men! What a pity! What a pity!"

That night at the King's Head Trelawney, Brenton, and Hugh sat with Tom Paine.

"You say he dropped you as a man drops a hot flip iron?" Brenton asked.

"Ay, I let him know I had knowledge of who was behind Kidd in his venture, and the news was as unwelcome as a mirror after smallpox. He feared to have it aired."

"That was a bold stroke, Captain, and a dangerous!"

"Yes, but it worked! Then he ordered my house searched for Kidd's gold. They're there now. Much luck to them!"

"He's condemned Hugh without a hearing," said Trelawney, his gray face drawn with anxiety. "We must plan for tomorrow! What do you advise?"

For a space Paine studied Hugh as he puffed on his pipe. Then he gravely shook his grizzled head. "Bellomont's primed full of poison! From what he said when he dismissed the hearing it's going hard with Hugh! He's swallowed their story. He wants a victim! I don't see how he can flout Hugh's papers and letters. Yet he can. He did that to Kidd. He's royal governor!" Paine turned suddenly on Hugh. "You ready for the worst? Your course set?"

"Ready!" said Hugh, quietly, while his friends watched his cryptic features.

They well knew what that interchange between the two privateersmen meant. It meant that Hugh Jocelyn would not be taken alive.

§91

THE following morning Thames Street was packed for a distance on either side of Governor Cranston's house. The previous night the news had spread through the taverns that Hugh Jocelyn was to be sacrificed to the enmity of the Brinleys and Sanford. Bellomont had called him buccaneer and lawbreaker at the hearing. He was a doomed man, already convicted. There had been but one topic of talk among the excited citizens—the ruin of Captain Jocelyn at the hands of his old enemies.

As Bellomont's military escort roughly rode back the curious crowd and made a passage for the entrance of the royal governor and his staff, Tom Stanton and Jerusa Sugars stood together, foreboding on their faces.

"They tell me the sloop was rowed last night from her berth at Long Wharf and now lies off the Wanton yard, out of range of the guns at King's Fort," whispered Sugars.

"Put a brail on your tongue, man!" muttered Stanton.

"I saw her," said a citizen at their elbow. "The brails are off her mains'il and her guns hauled to her ports. God help any who try to stop her!"

The embarrassed Stanton moved away, but everywhere in the crowd men were talking in low tones of the armed sloop ready to slip her hawser. Then the curious noticed that, gradually, bronzed sailors, big of limb and body, some with faces heavily scarred, were slowly closing on the troop of King's men seated on their horses before the Governor's house. At last, those who knew them by sight sensed the fact that the redcoats would shortly be surrounded by Jocelyn's old crew. But the laughing and gossiping went on between the men and women in the packed street, and the King's soldiers amused themselves with the ogling of Newport maids and the exchange of crude jests with the men.

Hugh appeared, shouldering his way through the crowded street, to be clapped on the back and greeted with: "Good luck, Hugh! Newport is with you!"

Jocelyn entered the house and stood in the doorway of the large fire room. From where he sat at a table at the end of the room between two secretaries, Bellomont raised his jaundiced eyes. Hugh advanced, stood before the royal governor, and bowed. The worried Benoni glanced through the window to the street.

"Captain Jocelyn," snapped Bellomont, "you returned last year from the West Indies with a fortune in money and goods. You are accused of obtaining much of this money illegally—of sundry acts of piracy—of that, later. Why, when you returned, did you refuse to report to the King's Judge of Admiralty but did present your commissions and papers to the Governor and Council?"

"Because, my lord," answered Hugh dryly, "on my return I found that Judge of Admiralty Sanford, not yet having taken oath before Governor Clarke, could not legally function, nor could Mr. Coddington as Register."

Bellomont reddened, coughed, and consulted a secretary and Sanford. Then he said: "It appears that you arrived in the spring, before oath was given them. In that, at least, you were within the law, which you've flouted in the West Indies."

Hugh folded his arms across his chest and waited.

"You have your commissions from Governor Easton here, and from Governors Russell and Beeston, properly issued and executed?"

"Yes, my lord, here are the commissions, the certificates and vouchers of the Naval Offices, and letters of thanks from Governor Russell and Governor Codrington."

Bellomont laughed sourly. "Letters of thanks for your services! Name of God! What services? Services to your itching palm? According to Vice-Admiral Codrington of Antigua, you plundered friend and foe the last year of the war!"

The scar on Hugh's face filled with blood. His fingers bit into the palms of his hands as he clamped down on his rising anger. A secretary and Sanford were busily examining the commissions Hugh had handed to the Earl.

Shortly Sanford burst out! "My lord, these letters and certificates are forgeries. I have the sworn statement of my brother in Barbadoes that Governor Russell never issued Jocelyn a commission nor gave him a letter."

The allegation was so preposterous that Hugh smiled. Bellomont turned on him savagely. "Before I'm through with you, you'll scarce have heart for a smile!"

Hugh nodded, then the thrust of his cold stare forced the protruding eyes of the royal governor to blink. "Governor Russell of Barbadoes was my personal friend," he said. "I dined with him often when in port. Most of my prizes were condemned there. I served him well and he was grateful. Elisha Sanford lies and he knows he lies if he swears that this commission and Governor Russell's letters are forgeries!"

A hush fell on the room. Hugh Jocelyn was only making his case the worse by his bold front.

"Let me see the commission and letter," said Bellomont. As he read, his eyes lit with surprise and his jaw dropped. "As I live, this is the hand of Francis Russell," he continued. "I heard from him lately and know his scratching with a quill as I know my own. The commission bears the great seal of the colony and seems in order."

Sanford's elongated face was purple with anger and confusion. "But, my lord," he protested, "I have the sworn statement of my brother that the signature is forged!"

Bellomont read Elisha Sanford's affidavit. "Your brother doubtless has good reason to suspect this man here," said the Earl, "but that name was writ by Francis Russell."

Sanford had no reply.

To the surprise of Hugh, Carr Newbury, but recently returned with his wife from Boston, rose. "My lord, may I speak?"

Bellomont nodded. "Have you proof to offer of this charge?"

"I would speak in support of Captain Jocelyn's honesty."

The men in the room sought each other's eyes. What was coming now? For Newbury's hostility to Jocelyn was well known.

"Proceed, Mr. Newbury."

"My lord, through an agent and unknown to Captain Jocelyn I ventured the purchase of shares in the sloop *Flying Fish*. On Captain Jocelyn's return he presented full reports of his cruises and prize monies, when he might have bubbled me, and paid in full my share. I believe him no pirate but an honest privateersman."

Sanford and Brinley glared at the speaker as he sat down. So the Brinleys and Newbury had fallen out? Hugh laughed inwardly at the situation. Fearing the loss of his seven thousand five hundred pounds, Newbury was supporting the man he hated.

There was loud whispering from the Brinley group and, shaking off his father's restraining hand, Richard rose. "My lord," he sputtered, "this man is no friend of Captain Jocelyn. He was paid seven thousand five hundred pounds of prize money which he fears he may lose! He bubbled me into selling my half-interest by spreading rumors that Jocelyn was dead or turned pirate, which I believe he did."

Bellomont's thin lips curled in a dry laugh, in which the room joined. "It would seem, Mr. Brinley, that your disbelief in this man comes rather belated."

A hum of approval greeted the Earl's sarcasm as he turned to Hugh. "So far as Barbadoes is concerned, your commissions and letters bear the signature of Governor Russell and seem in order. We'll now go into the charges of Vice-Admiral Codrington of Antigua. In letters to Boston he charges you with misconduct and grossly deceiving him at Antigua and with attacking and plundering vessels of friendly nations the last year of the war."

The room was hushed as men watched Jocelyn's face stiffen under his scar. Sanford and the Brinleys nodded with satisfaction. It looked bad for Hugh Jocelyn.

"Did Governor Codrington send proof of these charges?"

Bellomont's face purpled. "Do you deny or admit them?" he roared.

"My lord," replied Hugh, taking papers from his pocket, "the charges you cite are too vague and general. Under English law as a charged man I have the right to have them set forth in detail, with the proofs."

Bellomont's brows lifted in surprise. "Where studied you the law? This is no trial but an inquiry. Do you deny that you turned pirate?"

"I not only deny that but I maintain that you have no proofs of Governor Codrington's charges, and in reply to them I submit his own certificate giving me full clearance in the matter of the French ship *Bonneaventure*, thanking me for my services to him and Antigua, and vouching for my character."

The room hummed with whispered comment. Bellomont's face was mottled with blood. He took the papers, and pored over them with his two secretaries. Finishing the reading, he glared at Hugh. "These papers are dated in '96, before he discovered your true character and villainy! 'Tis in the last year of the war he charges you with piracy!"

"Does he send proofs of this rumored piracy in '97?" Jocelyn calmly asked. "I was not in the Leeward Islands but defending Jamaica. How does Governor Codrington know these things? How does Mr. Elisha Sanford know these things he swears to, when he was at that time in Barbadoes and the Governor of Barbadoes himself was ignorant of them, for after the war he received me in his house as a friend?"

The logic and icy calm of the charged man drove all self-restraint from the royal governor. His sickly features were mottled as he rose and shook a twisted hand in Jocelyn's face. "I believe you turned pirate the last year of the war! Honest prizes failed to glut your lust for gold, so you turned to plundering friendly ships to fill your money bags! You are charged with piracy in the year '97, the last year of the war! You offer nothing in refutation of those charges save Governor Russell's letter written in ignorance of your career a thousand miles away in Jamaica waters! Your previous character is attacked by loyal subjects of the King in Newport, Mr. Francis Brinley and Justice Sanford! I intend to make your case a warning to others and hold you for trial in Boston before an honest court!"

The room was thick with silence.

"I seem convicted, my lord, before I'm given chance to finish my defense." Hugh's voice was as hard as ice and as cold as he faced Bellomont. Men caught the glitter in his eyes and, knowing him, were frightened. Sweat poured from Benoni Tosh's alarmed face as he cast anxious eyes through a window at the crowd in the street, where the gun crews of the *Flying Fish* waited.

"You'll have your day in court, in Boston!" snarled the Earl. "Now, Governor Cranston," he ordered, "I demand that you place this man under arrest and hold him for delivery to me when I finish this inquiry."

The young Governor rose, trembling from anger and outraged pride. "My lord, we are a chartered colony and conduct our own affairs under our own laws. I cannot order the arrest of a man I know is innocent. 'Tis against our charter and all human conduct!"

For a space Bellomont's protruding eyes surveyed the man who had dared oppose his will. "A chartered colony, are you?" he cried. "Name of God! I'll soon make you something else! Of all the lawless, illiterate, and stiff-necked subjects of the King I have met, the people of this colony are the worst! You have connived at piracy and the carrying on of illegal trade and flouted English law! Now, as royal governor of New England and New York, I command you to arrest that man!"

It had come! Tosh moved to the window. In the fretting crowd massed in the street the veteran gun crews of the *Flying Fish*, their cutlasses slung from baldrics, had already closed in around the troopers. In a doorway, across the street, lounged two waiting men, their faces iron-hard with determination—Israel Brandy and Jeremy Potts. "Christ's blood!" gasped the Sergeant. "God help Newport! It's comin'!"

"Answer me, Governor Cranston," stormed Bellomont. "Will you arrest this man or shall I call my guard to—"

"Wait!" Jocelyn's voice whipped through the hush of the room like the snap of an ox goad. "I have here a letter from Governor Beeston which will prove that the Vice-Admiral of the Leewards was misinformed. Lord Bellomont, before you call your guard, I ask you to read it, for it will save—"

"Save what?" savagely demanded the Earl.

Hugh deliberately looked out the window to his waiting men before he replied. "Why, save your lordship some—some inconvenience—some—"

"What is it?" demanded Bellomont, taking the letter offered him. He pored over it with his secretaries, while Brinley and Sanford scowled their irritation at the delay in Jocelyn's arrest.

"You will note," said Hugh, "that Governor Beeston, of Jamaica, gives me his deepest thanks for my services during the past year and the letter is dated December, '97. During that year of '97, which was the last year of the war, Governor Beeston states that I was acting as a guard ship for Jamaica and fighting the French and the Tortuga pirates. I could scarce have been the pirate throughout '97 Governor Codrington names me and still have fought for Jamaica and Governor Beeston at the same time. The Vice-Admiral appears to have been badly mistaken."

Bellomont's face was stippled with purple blotches. He coughed loudly in an attempt to conceal his rage and embarrassment. He had met as adroit a brain as his own and he knew it. He had been set to send Jocelyn to Boston for trial; now the sole grounds for such action had crumbled under his feet. Hugh's argument was irrefutable. The Beeston letter cleared him of Codrington's false charges.

Ignoring the fidgeting Sanford who sought his ear, Bellomont said: "Governor Cranston, I withdraw my order. Captain Jocelyn, although I doubt not that much charged against you is true, in the face of Governor Beeston's letter and that of Governor Russell there appears, at present, nothing tangible on which to hold you."

Hugh bowed. Behind the table where the Town Sergeant stood with his halberd there rose a stentorian sigh of relief as Benoni wiped his dripping face on his sleeve. He glanced with a grin through the window to where Hugh's gunners ringed in the unaware troopers of Bellomont. In the room Jocelyn's friends silently gripped each other's hands. With bleak faces Brinley and Sanford sat nursing their defeat.

"My lord," said Hugh, "I have a matter into which I wish to go with Mr. Carr Newbury, Mr. Francis Brinley, and his son here."

The men in the room stiffened on their seats. Here was something they had not expected. What had Hugh Jocelyn kept from them which he was about to disclose? From the rear of the room Richard Brinley sneered audibly.

"Does it concern this proceeding, Captain?"

"It has to do with a felony, my lord, concerning which, as you are inquiring into the conduct of affairs of this colony, it appears you should be informed."

There was stirring of feet and whispering. A scowl lay on Francis Brinley's features. He glanced at his son, who avoided his eyes.

Bellomont nodded. "Proceed, Captain."

"My lord," said Hugh, "it is common knowledge in Newport that, on two separate occasions, when still a boy, I was attacked by strangers. First I was clubbed in the dark. Then, on a wharf, I was set on by an Indian and a slave. The slave was drowned, but the wounded Wampanoag was stabbed that night in the jail on Prison Street to seal his mouth."

"Who had reason to injure you?" demanded Bellomont, leaning forward with sudden interest.

"That I shall explain," answered Hugh. "But whatever their motive, someone in Newport was employing men to attempt to press or injure me. The war broke and after that they had small chance at me, for I was much at sea."

"But who would wish to have you injured and for what reason?" demanded Bellomont.

Hugh slowly swung and smiled significantly into Richard Brinley's leering face. Brinley's eyes slanted from the thrust of the privateersman's stare.

Francis Brinley sprang to his feet. "My lord, what purpose has all this talk? It leads to nothing."

"My lord," Hugh countered, "this talk leads straight to the men who, for years, sought to have me attacked or pressed. And they sit there!" Hugh pointed at Newbury, then at young Brinley, whose leer had suddenly faded. "That, by English law, is felony!"

Bellomont's hand found his chin. He scowled into the tense faces before him. "As I believe that this colony is the most irregular and illegal in its administration that ever any English colony was, and as I am ordered by the crown to look into and make report of matters in general in this lawless region, it appears proper to proceed with this inquiry. Continue, Captain Jocelyn."

There was an audible expulsion of breath through men's teeth.

"My friends and I learned from Landlord Turpin, of Providence," began Hugh, "that, previous to the attack on me on the wharf by the Indian and the black man, a sailor with a maimed right hand, in company with the Wampanoag and the slave, took a shallop bound down the bay. Following this attack the sailor was seen in the Butterfly tavern, in Newport, with a bag stuffed with silver and gold. Later, in the

Crown tavern in Boston, the same sailor offered money to two seamen to sail for Newport and attack me."

"How does this implicate the men you say wished you harm?" demanded Bellomont.

"I will pass over suspicion, my lord, and come to facts."

The air was electric with suspense. Men cleared their throats and stirred nervously on their stools. What was Hugh Jocelyn about to throw into Newbury's and Francis Brinley's faces?

Brinley's handsome features were alternately stippled with rage and pinched with apprehension as he studied the cool Jocelyn. Richard Brinley's eyes nervously darted to-and-fro as he gnawed a bloodless lip. Newbury sat, chin in hand, watching Hugh through half-closed eyes.

Jocelyn continued. "This sailor with the maimed hand was once in the power of my master gunner, Israel Brandy, after a brawl in a tavern. But he was taken to his sloop, which sailed that night, eluding the Town Sergeant. Since then he has not been heard from until this summer. You have heard that a pirate ship was on this coast last month? She was heavily gunned and had already done much damage to the shipping when I sailed with my sloop and took her."

Hugh pointed a finger at the elder Brinley. "And you, Mr. Francis Brinley, and you, Mr. Carr Newbury, may be interested to learn that the master of that pirate ship was none other than the sailor with the maimed hand, John Creach."

The room was in an uproar. Men stared dumfounded into each other's faces. Creach, the dead pirate, Newbury and Richard Brinley's man? It was unbelievable! How could Hugh Jocelyn prove this?

Benoni Tosh pounded on the floor with the butt of his halberd. "Order! Gentlemen! Order!" he boomed.

Bellomont sat quizzically studying Richard Brinley's face, etched with sudden alarm, as he whispered with his father. The room quieted and Francis Brinley indignantly protested:

"My lord, I object to this man coupling the names of my son and son-in-law with this pirate! What proof is there that Richard Brinley or Carr Newbury ever saw or knew this Creach?"

Bellomont's sallow countenance was an enigma as he watched Richard Brinley's frightened eyes, then shifted to the taut-faced Newbury. Tapping his chin with a finger as if trying to read Hugh's thoughts, for a space he studied the tall privateersman. At length he said: "Captain Jocelyn, you are accusing these men of plotting to injure you or have you pressed on a ship bound out of the colony. But no grand jury could indict on what you have yet offered. And you have not named a motive. Why should they wish you harm?"

"My lord, years ago Richard Brinley tried to run me down with his horse. I pulled him from his saddle and shook him and was lashed across the face. His father, then Justice Brinley of the Court of Quarter Sessions, had me arrested and tried. And, though I had but defended myself, I was sent to the pillory, where Carr Newbury rode to attack me though helpless. Richard Brinley never forgot my handling of him nor what I said in court at that time when Newbury supported his perjured testimony."

"But this seems hardly sufficient to lead them to injure you," objected Bellomont.

Hugh caught the hatred in Francis Brinley's smoldering eyes. The men in the room waited with held breaths to hear Lettice's name, for it was common knowledge that she had been the cause of Newbury's hostility to the privateersman. But Hugh disappointed them.

"On several occasions, my lord, we had high words, and once he was slashed across the face with a whip, but not by me. It was clear that Richard Brinley and Carr Newbury hated me." Hugh paused, then said quietly, "Afterward Newbury married Brinley's sister."

"Very well, proceed with your proof!" ordered Bellomont.

Hugh drew a folded sheet of paper from his pocket. Those in the room hunched forward, craning their necks. "My lord," he said, "this pirate, Creach, lay wounded in his cabin after we took his ship. Knowing he was about to die, he made this ante-mortem statement before three witnesses. With your leave I shall read it."

I, John Creach, mariner, late of Boston, in Presence of Death, Swears that Richard Brinley and Carr Newbury of Newport, give me Gold to maim, kill, or press on a ship bound for the warm seas, one Hugh Jocelyn, fisherman of Newport. I swears I had him set on Two Times. As I hopes for Mercy from my Maker this is True.

		his		
Signed,	X	Creach		
John				
		mark		

Witnesses:

John Rodman, *Chirurgeon*
Jeremy Potts, *Mate*
                 his
Israel   X   Brandy, *Master*
                      Gunner
              mark
All of Sloop *Flying Fish*

The room was electric with tension. Suppressed "Ah's!" filled the air. In disgust men scowled at the stunned Newbury and Richard Brinley, whose face was glazed with fear.

Governor Cranston beamed into Walter Clarke's wizened features. The mystery was solved.

Hugh handed the ante-mortem statement of Creach to Bellomont, who studied it curiously with his secretaries, while Francis Brinley and Peleg Sanford whispered, faces grave with apprehension. Finally, holding one hand in the other, as if in pain, the Earl cleared his throat and broke the silence. "Mr. Brinley," he said, "this is a grave matter. If this be a true confession, made in fear of death, and there appear the names of three witnesses who heard it and saw it signed, it would doubtless convince a grand jury." Bellomont hesitated. Richard Brinley sat with twitching lips, his panic-filled eyes on his father. "Mr. Richard Brinley, do you deny the truth of this statement and demand the production of the witnesses? Mr. Newbury, do you do likewise?"

Brinley was too agitated to reply. He licked his dry lips, his fluttering eyes avoiding Bellomont's stabbing gaze. But Newbury stood his ground. "I demand to see these witnesses!" he cried, sweat standing in beads on his face. "This confession is forged and false!"

"Captain Jocelyn," said the Earl, with a shrug, "I take it these witnesses stand ready to swear Creach made this confession in fear of death?"

"The witnesses wait outside, my lord."

"Bring them in."

Jeremy and Israel, still standing guard with the gun crews, were called with Rodman. Rodman and Jeremy were sworn and testified that Creach voluntarily made the confession in his cabin when dying from wounds, that Potts wrote it down, and that they both heard him swear to it and saw him make his mark after it was read to him. Then Israel Brandy stumped forward and faced Bellomont.

The latter's eyes fell from Israel's shaggy head with its scarred face to his big shoulders and the peg leg. "You are Israel Brandy, master gunner of the *Flying Fish*?"

"Ay, master gunner of the *Flyin' Fish*, ten guns, six swivels, and the best gunner in this port." Brandy glared around the room as if challenging a denial of his boast.

Bellomont's face clouded, then his thin lips curled as he turned and caught the eye of a secretary. "Did you see Creach make his mark after this statement was read him and was he then in fear of death?"

"In fear of death, my lord?" Brandy snorted. "Burn me! Could the slimy dogfish be else after Israel Brandy's ax and Mate Potts's cutlass sliced into him?"

Bellomont's hand covered his smile. His famous temper failed to function in the face of the peg-legged sailor's ingenuous answer. He glanced obliquely at his secretary, then said, "That will do, Gunner Brandy!"

But Carr Newbury was on his feet. "'Tis all perjured testimony, my lord!" he cried. "This paper is a forgery! I never saw this Creach! I bore no ill will toward Captain Jocelyn! These men have contrived this confession between them!"

"Enough of this, Mr. Newbury," replied Bellomont. "You shall have your day in court."

His face shot with anxiety, Newbury was silent. For a space Francis Brinley probed the telltale eyes of his son, then turned to Lord Bellomont. "I'm through, my lord!" he said bitterly. "I believed my son honest—and he lied to me! He's no longer son of mine!" In his anger he turned on Richard, "Get out of my sight!"

Men moved aside as young Brinley groped his way out of the room. Hugh's glittering eyes caught those of Cranston and Walter Clarke as he waited for Bellomont. The latter heaved a sigh; then to the amazement of the onlookers drew a flat silver box from a pocket, opened it, inserted thumb and forefinger, and held a pinch of brown powder to his nostrils, sniffed, then sneezed and touched his nose with a lace-edged handkerchief.

Cranston whispered to Clarke, "'Tis powdered tobacco, called snuff; a new London fashion!"

Bellomont turned to Hugh. "It would seem, Captain Jocelyn, that there has been a plot to injure you. Under English law that is felony. This appears now a matter for your grand jury, Governor Cranston."

"Yes, my lord! It will be gone into at once," answered Cranston.

But Hugh was not through. "My lord, my purpose in bringing this matter to your attention was solely to discover it to Mr. Francis Brinley. It seems that he has now seen the light," Hugh smiled into Sanford's sour face, "even if the truth has not yet dawned on the Judge of Admiralty. I make no accusation against Carr Newbury and Richard Brinley. The matter is dead. I have already forgotten them as one forgets the flies that sting you."

Bellomont's pale eyes were watching Hugh with frank approval.

"Spoke like a man of spirit, Captain Jocelyn!"

And so, for the day, as Lord Bellomont wrote in his journal which has survived, ended the "examination of persons and witnesses relating to the disorders and irregularities countenanced and practised by the government of the English Collony of Rhode Island and Providence Plantations in New England, in America."

A week later Bellomont returned to Boston, set on the destruction of Rhode Island as an independent colony under its charter. And in the end his energy and ability would probably have resulted in the revocation of the hard-won charter of Roger Williams and the merging of the little colony with Massachusetts had not Rhode Island, in her extremity, possessed a friend which had long been at its insidious work. The following year, in New York, the gout put an end to the career and to the endeavors of Lord Bellomont to destroy the Colony of Rhode Island and Providence Plantations.

§92

THAT night the news of the humiliation of Francis Brinley and the exposure of his son and Carr Newbury before Lord Bellomont spread through the taverns like fire through dry grass. Joe Brenton and Hugh's friends fed their joy over his acquittal and the disgrace of Brinley and Newbury with repeated cups of Canary. In their delight at the outcome of Hugh's examination, the irrepressible Wantons frequently burst into songs, the ribald nature of which would have crimsoned the faces of their young wives. Deep as was the anxiety of the officials and friends of the government over the hostility and patent disapproval of the royal governor, that night the tongues of most men were busy with Hugh's defense and the confession of the pirate Creach. At last the mystery of the attacks on Hugh Jocelyn had been solved, and feeling against Newbury and the Brinleys was strong.

For Hugh it was a happy moment. His record in the warm seas had baffled the designing Bellomont, and the accusations of Codrington and Sanford's brother dissolved into thin air. As they sat talking, Trelawney's hand found Hugh's arm. "He gave you far better treatment than I hoped for," said the Englishman. "Now the tongues of the slanderers will cease wagging."

"If they don't," said Hugh, "they'll have to answer to me for what they say. I'm through taking their abuse. Do you know, Dick, Bellomont looks like a man who suffers much. His hand is badly swollen with the gout and his face a sickly color."

There was pain in Trelawney's dark eyes. "He took what I loved from me. He deserves to suffer."

"Yes, though he was set at the opening to try me, he was too wise to go through with it. He coldly betrayed Kidd and will likely send him to London to his doom." Hugh added, "Some of those devils of gunners off the *Flying Fish* were put out at missing a fight. But that would have driven us all to sea."

"Speaking of London, Richard Brinley is on his way to Boston to take ship. Fearing that you would bring this matter before the next grand jury, his father has banished him to England and the Newburys are to remove to Boston where Carr will represent his father."

"Francis Brinley need not worry," said Hugh. "I am through with him."

"Let us talk of pleasant matters," said the Englishman. "I was told by a certain young woman who claims my admiration and affection that if I met a certain Captain Jocelyn tonight, I was to carry him her happiness and joy over the outcome of today's events."

Warmth flowed through Hugh at the mention of the girl who possessed his thoughts. "She sent no other message, Dick?"

"She did. She wondered if she rode day-after-tomorrow whether someone might also be riding on that selfsame beach."

Hugh's eyes shone with his pleasure. "Someone else of a certainty will. You will see her tomorrow that she may know?"

"I will," laughed the Englishman.

Two days later two riders met on Sachuest beach. Serena stopped her horse and flashed a radiant smile at the man whose blood was singing in his veins with the appeal of her fresh young beauty. Hugh thought he had never seen her so lovely. It was warm, and her lace love-hood was dropped back from the jet masses of her hair, her Kendall-green cape tossed over a shoulder.

"I give you joy in your victory!" she greeted. "Cousin Joe and I have been celebrating it."

"But I dare say your mother and your Uncle Jahleel when he learns of it in London will still hold me pirate."

"Is it necessary for us to fret about what they think?" she asked.

There was something in her eyes that sent the blood storming through his veins. "No," he said thickly.

They were riding side by side, and the salt breeze ruffled her hair. "Tell me," she said, looking straight before her, "now that Captain Jocelyn has been cleared by Lord Bellomont, will he change his mind and sail for Barbadoes and London?"

Hugh leaned toward her, striving to pierce the mystery of her dark gaze, but she did not look at him. "Why do you ask?"

She turned to him with a disarming smile. "Because his friends will miss him."

Lights danced in her black eyes, but Hugh dared not believe what he saw. "I said I was not sailing with the brig," he said. "But 'tis not too late to change my mind, unless—" He was vividly aware of her nearness, of the intensity of her gaze.

"Unless?" she repeated. Her eyes, avoiding his, looked steadfastly at the sea.

He burned his bridges. "Unless my going would mean as much to—to someone, as it would to me."

"What would your going mean to you?"

"It would mean loneliness and bitterness and yearning. It would mean absence from one I—"

He hesitated. A puff of air whipped her cape toward him. She reached for it, as he did, and their hands met and clung, clung like the hands of those drowning. A fierce joy pulsed through him. She gazed at him, the color suddenly drained from her face. She could not speak as she stared, lips parted.

He caught her bridle and stopped their horses, then leaned and drew her to him, his face in her tumbled hair. "Don't send me to Barbadoes!" he murmured. "I need you—so!"

She raised her glowing face as he held her with a trembling arm and their lips found each other. At length, through misted eyes, she smiled up at him. "Why, oh, why has it been so long?"

"So long?" he laughed softly in his elation. "The heart of Mistress Serena is hard to read. She always masked her thoughts in these black wells of eyes." He kissed each long-lashed eye in turn as if in punishment.

"She had to," murmured the girl. "Her thoughts were so wild and unseemly, and always of a fierce privateersman."

"She's been the only human in the world whose thoughts I feared."

"Had you known them, you scarce would have feared them. They were of you, and pleasant."

She sighed and, reaching, impulsively drew his face down to hers and kissed him. Then she pushed away and sat upright in the saddle, a feather of jet hair veiling her eyes. "What would my mother and uncle say could they see me now, captive of the bold Captain Hugh Jocelyn?"

"They would doubtless disown you."

"Would you own me, sir, if they did?"

He opened his arms and took her in. "I—love—you!"

"I've loved you for so long," she said, "and it seemed so hopeless! But come, let us walk. There's much to talk of. We travel too fast."

He swung her from her horse and walked beside her, his arm holding her close.

"You wonder, Hugh Jocelyn," she began, "why for years I was short and cold with you? 'Twas that pride of mine. I was furious that I loved you. For I could not share you with others. I had so much to give."

"You believed all the lies told of me?"

"At first, how could I help it? You were spoiled by women and your friends. 'Tis a wonder you've grown such a man!"

"For that," he said, sweeping her into his arms, "you pay dearly." And he kissed her hair and throat and mouth, and, taking fire, she recklessly responded.

The velvet nose of her horse nuzzled the back of Hugh's neck. Serena laughed up at him. "Like all the humans of her sex, the Duchess seems drawn to you!"

"I little dreamed Hugh Jocelyn could touch your heart."

She reached, drew down his head, pushed aside the yellow hair from the cicatrix on his cheek and touched it with her lips. Her dusky eyes glowed up at him as he held her. "The day they brought Joe from the sea fight and you stood in your tattered shirt beside the litter, your head bandaged, I knew not what it was then, but I later knew I fell in love with Hugh Jocelyn."

His eyes widened. "You loved me then?"

"Yes. I was too proud to confess it even to myself."

"And that is why you held me at such distance?"

"That is why. You little know women. 'Twas too deep and fine a thing to risk being trampled on." She threw wide her arms in a gesture of surrender. "The cold Serena Brenton is stripping bare her poor heart."

Hugh reverently lifted her two hands to his lips. "You spoke once of my having attained my heart's desire. My heart's desire is here, in my arms. I know now what the poets meant by love."

"I have known, oh, so long."

"Would Mistress Serena Brenton dare face the wrath of her mother and uncle and stoop to leave Hammersmith to live with a sailor on a humble Conanicut farm?"

"Mistress Serena Brenton would be the happiest woman alive if she were torn from her family by that selfsame sailor."

"Must the sailor wait? He is so starved for her and so lonely."

"The lady also is lonely."

"If he were to sail into Brenton's Cove some night next week, would he find her waiting on the shore with her chest?"

"He would."

And so it was arranged. In the following week in the full of the moon Hugh was to sail his small shallop into the cove, where she would be waiting with her clothes chest. From there they would sail to Jamestown, to the Magistrate, and then home. To attempt to reconcile Serena's mother to her marriage with Hugh would be time wasted. It would only result in driving the good dame to bed with the migraine and vapors over the disgrace to the family name.

Drunk with joy, Hugh placed Serena on her horse and watched her canter away.

§93

Only Tom, Content, Trelawney and Joe Brenton were told. Content was in a flutter of excitement. To Hugh Joe said, "I hold it an honor for a Brenton to have you as husband. As for Uncle Jahleel, in London, he'll cool off in time. He greatly respects your mettle and ability. Some day he'll respect your character, as do I."

Trelawney's delight shone in his thin face when Hugh brought the news. "My boy, my boy, my old heart is fair full tonight. I have so hoped for this."

"I know now, Dick, what it was the poets sang of," said Hugh. "'Tis something rare and wonderful, this love you hoped I'd know some day."

Trelawney placed both hands on Hugh's shoulders. "All my hopes have been realized. Dick Trelawney is a proud and happy man tonight. His work is done."

"I shall never be able to repay you, to prove the gratitude and affection I have for you, Dick. What little I am you have made me with your toil and thought over me. I shall never forget."

The September moon was washing the still harbor with silver as Hugh stood with Israel at Tom's old landing on the shore of the cove.

"Now what puts it into your head to sail the shallop over from Conanicut tonight? Stab me! 'Tis some woman business or I'm a Spaniard!"

"Israel, you're right, as usual!" chuckled Hugh. "But I could not well go without telling you. You've been a second father to me and made me a gunner and a seaman. I've loved you from the day we sailed down from Somerset in the sloop and you took me, a small boy, to your big heart."

"Stow that, lad! We've been mates, you and me, fished, privateered, swilled rum together, these many year. You're the sole chicken I ever had or wanted. I—I—well, stab my guts!" The old privateersman hesitated, choked down a gulp of rising emotion, and finished: "Hugh, I'm proud of my work! Burn me, I am!"

Hugh laid a hand on the wide shoulder of his friend. "I put into the cove to receive your blessing, Israel. Tonight Mistress Serena Brenton does me the honor to wed me."

"Stab my vitals!" The amazed Israel seized Hugh by the shoulders and peered hard into his face. "You speak truth? One o' them proud Brentons? Why, Jahleel has been against you! There be not one of 'em fit for my lad; but if you choose her, Israel's content."

"You will love her, Israel. I'm going now to pick her up at Brenton's Cove with her chest of clothes, stop at Jamestown where the Magistrate awaits, and take her to the farm."

"Slit my throat! Like the privateersman you are you slip into Brenton's Cove and steal her from under her mother's nose?"

"Yes. Her mother would go fair frenzical and take to her bed if told. So I sail with Mistress Serena to Jamestown and then home."

"Lad, I'm fair pleasured!" burst out Brandy, slapping Hugh's back. "'Tis high time you had a family started. Die I'll not till I trot a young Jocelyn on my knee and sea nurse him as I did his father! Stab me, I'll love her and them all, Hugh, as I have you!"

"God bless your bones, Israel Brandy!"

The hands of the two friends closed hard on each other.

As Hugh tacked across the harbor through the anchored shipping, his thoughts drifted back to the day when the *Gull* brought from Somerset a little lad of eight, his eyes wide with the strange sights of the port. Then he saw the lean figure of the forlorn Dick Trelawney sitting on the wharf the day they met, and a boy in the candlelight poring over a hornbook in the Englishman's lodging. Again he swam that half-mile against the Lascar and heard the shouts of the crowd. Lettice lashed him across the face while he laughed, and came to the pillory. The night on the sloop flashed across his memory like a falling star. Poor charming, reckless Lettice! Life had not been kind to her. He lived again that long swim from the pirate Bellamy, and fought the black man on the wharf. And then his thoughts turned to Seeth! Little had Hugh Jocelyn deserved such devotion!

In a panorama the years marched through his memory as the shallop worked through the anchored shipping on its way to Brenton's Cove. Hugh again fought through his first sea fight when he had gone sick with the fear of mutilation; then followed the two days' battle off Block Island. Next he saw the young Serena standing with her mother and sisters beside Joe's stretcher, and later, at Hammersmith, when she talked so strangely.

So his thoughts played with the past. His four years in the warm seas gave him little pause. Though they had made him rich, they seemed like a dream outside his life. But it was to Trelawney that his musing most often turned. Trelawney who had opened the riches of the mind to the hungry boy who aspired. It was to Dick that he owed whatever he was—wonderful, loyal, wise Dick Trelawney, God bless him! And now all the bitterness and discontent and restlessness had been washed away by the miracle of Serena Brenton's love. She was boldly trusting her life and happiness to the man many had maligned. She should never regret that trust, this girl who had kept her love sealed in her heart until he had found it.

The shallop reached the narrow mouth of Brenton's Cove, which was packed with shadow cast by the high shoulder of shore, for the moon was still low. Hugh let go the sheet of his spritsail and slid into the wall of murk. Farther in, on the Hammersmith side, there was a stretch of shelving shore used as a landing for small craft. It was here that Serena would be waiting with her clothes chest which Joe had taken care of. He peered into the blackness ahead as he slowly sculled the light craft alongshore. There, somewhere in the dense shadow, Serena waited—waited for Hugh Jocelyn. He could hardly believe it was not a dream—that it was true. He gave a low whistle and listened.

To his surprise, he heard the sound of voices. What had fallen out? Had she been discovered leaving the house and followed? Hugh groaned inwardly at the thought. What would she do? What could she do if they had come on her waiting with her chest? He could land and boldly claim her if she were there. But what a situation!

He pushed the shallop farther into the cove. Yes, men were talking in guarded tones somewhere on the shore ahead. But he heard no woman's voice. Serena was not there. They had forced her to return to the house. What an outcome to their cherished plans! After this her mother would have her watched. She would not be able to leave Hammersmith. What a trick fortune had played on them! He'd seize the bull by the horns and learn who these people were, lurking there in the blackness. If they were from Hammersmith and she had remained with them, he'd take her by force!

He pushed on, and at length the shallop slid into the shoal water of the landing. A rough voice called, "If you be from the Naval Office, you'd best turn back afore you're dumped in the cove with broken heads!"

Hugh's heart leaped. He had run into a party sneaking wine or silk ashore from a craft in the harbor, before reporting to the Naval Office. Some smug importer was cheating the customs, with a cart waiting on the road above to carry the stuff to his wharf.

"I'm from no Naval Office," he answered. "Strike a light and you'll learn who I am!"

"What do you here, then, at this hour?" came the sharp question.

"That's my business, friends!" rasped Hugh, leaving the shallop and moving toward the voice.

"'Tis ours as well!" At the same instant two men flung themselves upon Jocelyn, who laughed in their faces as he held them in his arms.

"Strike a light, you fools! I'm Captain Jocelyn!"

Steel struck sparks from flint. Tinder flared and lit Jocelyn's face as four men peered into it. "Name o' God, it's Captain Hugh! We thought you some of Sanford's men. What do you here?"

"I'm here on my own business—not yours. Leave me, and load your cart."

There was the suspicion of a chuckle. "Ay, that we will, Captain, and good luck to you!"

The men moved away. Hugh returned to the shallop and called: "Serena! 'Tis all right! I'm here with the shallop. Have no fear. They've gone."

From the shadows came the low answer: "I'm here, Hugh, with my chest. But they frightened me, those men!"

She groped her way to his arms and he held her tightly, kissing her again and again. "They were easing goods ashore from a craft in the harbor, to bubble the Collector. When I ran into them, I thought them people from Hammersmith sent by your mother. I feared you'd been followed and I had lost you!"

She gave a low laugh. "'Twould take more than smugglers to drive me from this blessed shore tonight."

He buried his face in her hair and whispered: "I can scarce believe 'tis you. Little I thought I should ever be stealing a Brenton maid."

"Little did this Brenton maid ever dream she'd allow herself so stolen!"

"'Tis too late now for you to change your mind," he laughed, stowing her chest aboard the boat. "We'll have the moon and the tide. There's no turning back."

For reply she stood on tiptoe and kissed him. "That is my answer, sir."

He lifted her, carried her through the shoal water to the small craft, and shoved off the bow. The light air filled the sail and the shallop headed out of the cove past the point for the East Passage. The sky was stippled with stars that winked a benediction, and the lifting moon lit their course with silver.

"'Tis a beautiful dream," she said, the fingers of a hand intertwined with one of his as they sat at the tiller. "I fear I'll waken and lose it. 'Tis all too wonderful and unreal. I, Serena Brenton, am sailing to my wedding with Captain Hugh Jocelyn!"

His arm tightened about her. "And I, Hugh Jocelyn, have cleared for the port of my heart's desire!"

Author's Note

In the last decade of the seventeenth century there were many words and phrases in common use which later disappeared from the idiom of the colonies. Through the years even geographic nomenclature and place names underwent changes.

In the old maps and records what we know as *Martha's Vineyard* is given as *Martin's Vineyard*. The island *No Man's Land* has had a recorded ownership for nearly three hundred years. In all probability it acquired its name from the Indian chief Tequenoman who was once the chief sachem of the Vineyard, for in the old maps and records it is spelled *Noman's Land*. On the map of Captain Cyprian Southack, made in 1707, the modern *Monemoy* is *Nanemoy*, and *Monomoy Point* is *Wreck Point*. Areas of the Nantucket Shoals are marked as dry at low tide. Captain Southack states that he crossed the Cape in a whale boat through a breach near Wellfleet. So, at that time, the tip of Cape Cod was an island. What was for years known as *Holme's Hole* is *Vineyard Haven*.

To mention but a very few of the colorful epithets and nouns in common use in the speech of the period there were:

Murderer, a blunderbuss shoulder gun or light swivel gun, loaded with chopped iron, nails and shot, which at short range was devastating in its effect.

Heart breaker, a coquettish curl worn in the neck.

In 1690 a man referred to his wife as his *second*, and to his female cousin as his *she cousin*.

A *thornback* was a girl who had reached the twenties when marriage seemed doubtful.

Prostitutes were called *quails*, *pheasants*, *mermaids*, *doxies*, *wagtails*; and a procuress was a *maquerelle*.

A slattern was a *drazel*; a rich widow, a *warm widow*; toadies and sycophants were *pickthanks*; a young profligate, a *rake-hell*; a ruffian, a *shagrag*; a toothpick, a *picktooth*.

The round oaths and expletives in use were picturesque and salty. But by the middle of the eighteenth century the idiom of the colonies had lost much of its quaintness and flavor.

The descriptions of the Great Swamp Fight by the Massachusetts historians ignore Treat's attack with his Mohican allies on the rear wall of the stockade. In his letter to Governor Leverett, Joseph Dudley does make the statement that the wall was scaled, but he fails to say by whom. The Reverend Hubbard and Hutchinson declare that the Mohicans gave little aid, even firing into the air when the attack was made.

Later, Palfrey and Channing follow the early historians in stating that the Indians proved untrustworthy. But the fact that the Mohicans were bitter enemies of the Narragansetts and that there was much loot in the stockade would cast grave doubt on the truth of this statement.

Conclusive proof, however, that the Mohicans were of great aid to Major Treat and his men is found in the *Connecticut War Journal*, kept by the authorities at Hartford. This journal states that the families of Uncas, the chief sachem of the Mohicans, and of his son, Owaneco, who led the Indians under Major Treat, were at this time at Hartford and at the close of the war the Mohicans were given presents by the Governor and Council in appreciation of their services at the Great Swamp Fight. Throughout the war Treat and Major Talcott used the Mohicans as scouts and, unlike the Massachusetts Bay troops, were never ambushed.

It was the policy of the Massachusetts Theocracy to ignore Connecticut. Little Rhode Island with its freedom of worship was held in supreme contempt. It is not surprising that the early Massachusetts historians gave no credit to Treat and his Mohicans for the victory of the Great Swamp Fight.

G. M.